D0498837

18
F.

Praise for Peter F. Hamilton

The Dreaming Void

"Dozens of scenarios, a surprisingly well-delineated cast of thousands, plotting enough to delight the most Machiavellian of readers and, this time out, a far leaner and more purposeful product: a real spellbinder from a master storyteller." —*Kirkus Reviews* (starred review)

"Peter F. Hamilton [is the] owner of the most powerful imagination in science fiction, the author of immense, complex far-future sagas. . . . *The Dreaming Void* is his best yet."

—Ken Follett, *New York Times* bestselling author of
The Pillars of the Earth

"This is a book that arguably nobody else in Brit SF could have even attempted. Epic, multi-stranded, full of wonders." —*SFX*

"A gripping planetary epic." —*Romantic Times Book Reviews*

"In the tradition of grand-scale SF sagas . . . densely plotted and intensely thought-provoking." —*Publishers Weekly*

"Truly epic adventure." —*Booklist*

"A massive and intricate opening salvo . . . Hamilton pushes the technology to and beyond the limits we are accustomed to." —*Analog*

The Temporal Void

"Packed with great storytelling . . . just about everything a reader could hope for in the middle book of a trilogy." —*SFF World*

"Hamilton is the clear heir to Heinlein in my view. Large-scale space opera told through a shifting and interlinked cast of people from various walks of life, [his writing is] amazing storytelling."

—Mark Andreessen, founder of Netscape

"A great, sprawling, ripping yarn reminiscent of Golden Age Science Fiction."

—SF Crowsnest

"A gripping story, with the fates of two universes at stake."   —SF Site

"Fusing elements of hard SF with adventure fantasy tropes, Hamilton has singlehandedly raised the bar for grand-scale speculative storytelling."

—*Publishers Weekly*

The Evolutionary Void

"The author's mastery of the art of the 'big story' earns him a place among the leading authors of dynastic SF. A strong addition to any SF collection."

—*Library Journal*

"With intimate storytelling threads woven through a grand tapestry of epic adventure, the tale will . . . captivate returning fans who can dive right in."

—*Publishers Weekly*

"Peter F. Hamilton is one of the best space opera writers around today."

—*Analog*

Pandora's Star

"Should be high on everyone's reading list . . . You won't be able to put it down."

—Nancy Pearl, National Public Radio

"An imaginative and stunning tale of the perfect future threatened . . . a book of epic proportions not unlike Frank Herbert's *Dune* or Isaac Asimov's Foundation trilogy."

—SFRevu

Judas Unchained

"Richly satisfying . . . wonderfully imagined . . . Hamilton adroitly leaps from the struggles of one engaging, quirky character to another."
—*Publishers Weekly* (starred review)

"Hamilton tackles SF the way George R. R. Martin is tackling fantasy. . . . There's a sense of wonder here that's truly unchained."
—SF Reviews

"[Hamilton] manages to update an old form for the new century of readers with brio, élan and brilliance. . . . [His] style is un-showy but powerful, transparent and forceful."
—Scifi

"You're in for quite a ride."
—*Santa Fe New Mexican*

"Hamilton has assembled [the book] with great care into a big picture that doesn't resolve or reveal all its secrets until the last . . . while paying tribute to decades' worth of SF from the pulps to the Singularity . . . with a mixture of fondness, perception, and irreverent wit."
—*Locus*

"[This SF dynastic thriller] ably balances a large and varied cast of human and nonhuman characters with a complex plot filled with personal drama, political intrigue, and nonstop action. . . . Recommended."
—*Library Journal*

"No one does widescreen space opera quite like Peter F. Hamilton"
—Richard K. Morgan, author of *Altered Carbon*

"Sweeping in scope and emotional range . . . carried me with rapt attention to the end."
—*San Antonio Express-News*

Misspent Youth

"[A] genuinely superb novel by any standards . . . not to be missed."
—*Starburst*

THE MANDEL FILES

Volume 1

MINDSTAR RISING

A QUANTUM MURDER

THE MANDEL FILES

Volume 1

MINDSTAR RISING

A QUANTUM MURDER

PETER F. HAMILTON

BALLANTINE BOOKS   NEW YORK

The Mandel Files volume 1 is a work of fiction. Names, characters, places, and incidents are the products of the author's imagination or are used fictitiously. Any resemblance to actual events, locales, or persons, living or dead, is entirely coincidental.

A Del Rey Trade Paperback Original

Mindstar Rising copyright © 1993 by Peter F. Hamilton
A Quantum Murder copyright © 1994 by Peter F. Hamilton
"Greg Mandel: A Retrospective View of His Future" copyright
© 2011 by Peter F. Hamilton

All rights reserved.

Published in the United States by Del Rey, an imprint of
The Random House Publishing Group, a division of
Random House, Inc., New York.

DEL REY is a registered trademark and the Del Rey
colophon is a trademark of Random House, Inc.

The novels *Mindstar Rising* and *A Quantum Murder* were originally published separately in the United Kingdom by Pan Macmillan, an imprint of The Macmillan Group, a division of Macmillan Publishers Limited, in 1993 and 1994 respectively and in the United States by Tor Books, a division of Macmillan Publishers, New York, in 1996 and 1997 respectively.

ISBN 978-0-345-52635-9
eBook ISBN 978-0-345-52823-0

Printed in the United States of America

www.delreybooks.com

2 4 6 8 9 7 5 3 1

GREG MANDEL

A Retrospective View of His Future

One of the things I always find myself saying about science fiction, especially mine, is that it's not predictive. I'm best known for my space operas, which take place in the far future. The technology I invent for them is advanced and sophisticated, "indistinguishable from magic," as Arthur C. Clarke was fond of saying. From a personal point of view, far-future SF is quite safe for me to write. If that sounds paradoxical, consider this: I'm (probably) not going to be around in six hundred years' time for people to grin at and say, "Well, you got that bit wrong."

However, before I started writing far-future epics there was Greg Mandel. I began writing *Mindstar Rising* back in 1989, although it didn't get published until 1993. I set it in forty years' time, which back then I didn't really consider as qualifying for the near-future label. It was safe enough. Twenty years on, I'm having considerable second thoughts about that.

Of course, I have the ultimate SF writer's "get-out" clause: that Greg's future is an alternate to the one we're racing toward. The events that shaped Greg's world are definitely starting to diverge from current global political, economic, and technological events. For a start, our technology is definitely gaining ground on anything Greg had. Back then I was quite pleased to come up with the cybofax gadget for him. After all, this was the eighties, everyone had Filofaxes, an electronic version was a reasonable extrapolation. Throw in a telephone function (mobiles in those days were the size of a paperback), and it would be a very plausible consumer item for someone to be carrying around in 2030. I now own an iPhone, which probably has more functionality than I ever envisaged for the cybofax. That's due to the get-out clause; Greg's world suffered a warming and a credit crash earlier and more severe than ours has, and corporate techno-logical development slowed down. His world also had Gracious Services, a kind of hacker training community, while we have Anonymous and all their friends, a much looser collective. There were also airships, which sadly no amount of wishful thinking by enthusiasts will ever resurrect for commercial transport.

So there are similarities, a few overlaps, but no predictions come true. Shame about that, but what I was doing with the Greg books was explore ideas, generalities rather than specifics. On that score I think I've done okay. The trilogy remains set in a credible version of society in twenty years' time. I don't think I could have asked for more from my first novels.

Mind you, the kind of parallels—alternate history, or over-fanciful speculation, or not pragmatic enough—I'll be drawing in another intro-duction in another twenty years' time really should be quite interesting.

—PETER F. HAMILTON

RUTLAND, UK

2011

MINDSTAR RISING

1

Meteorites fell through the night sky like a gentle sleet of icefire, their sharp scintillations slashing ebony overload streaks across the image Greg Mandel's photon amp was feeding into his optic nerves.

He was hanging below a Westland ghost wing, five hundred metres above the Purser's Hills, due west of Kettering. Spiralling down. Wind strummed the membrane, producing near-subliminal bass harmonics.

Ground zero was a small crofter's cottage; walls of badly laid raw stone swamped with some olive-green creeper, big scarlet flowers. It had a thatched roof, reeds rotting and congealing, caked in tidemark ripples of blue-green fungal growths. A two-metre-square solar-cell strip had been pinned on top.

Greg landed a hundred metres downslope from the cottage, propeller spinning furiously to kill his forward speed. He stopped inside three metres. The Westland was one of the best military microlights ever built – lightweight, highly manoeuvrable, silent, with a low radar-visibility profile. Greg had flown them on fifteen missions in Turkey, and their reliability had been one hundred per cent. All British Army covert tactical squads had been equipped with them. He'd hate to use anything else. They'd gone out of production when the People's Socialism Party came to power, twelve years previously. A victim of the demilitarization realignment programme, the Credit Crash, the Warming, nationalization, industrial collapse. This one was fifteen years old, and still functioned like a dream.

A time display flashed in the bottom right corner of the photon amp image, spectral yellow digits: 21:17:08. Greg twisted the Westland's retraction catch, and the translucent wing folded with a graceful rustle. He anchored it with a skewer harpoon. There'd be no danger of it blowing away now. The hills suffered frequent twister-gusts, and this was March, England's rainy season: squalls abounded. Gabriel hadn't cautioned him about the wing in her briefing: but Greg always followed routine, engrained by sergeant majors, and way too much experience.

He studied the terrain, the amp image grey and blue, smoky. There were no surprises; the Earth-resource satellite pictures Royan had pirated for him were three months old, but nothing had changed. The area was isolated, grazing land, marginally viable. Nobody spent money on barns and roads up here. It was perfect for someone who wanted to drop out of sight, a nonentity wasteland.

Greg heard a bell tinkling from the direction of the cottage, high-pitched and faint. He keyed the amp to infrared, and upped the magnification. A big rosy blob resolved into a goat with a broad collar dangling a bell below its neck.

He began to walk towards the cottage. The meteorites had gone, sweeping away to the east. Not proper shooting stars after all, then. Some space station's waste dump; or an old rocket stage, dragged down from its previously stable discard-orbit by Earth's hot expanded atmosphere.

'At twenty-one nineteen GMT the dog will start its run towards you,' Gabriel had said when she briefed him. 'You will see it first when it comes around the end of the wall on the left of the cottage.'

Greg looked at the wall; the ablative decay which ruled the rest of the croft had encroached here as well, reducing it to a low moss-covered ridge ringing a small muddy yard.

A yellow blink: 21:19:00.

The dog was a Rottweiler, heavily modified for police riot-assault duty, which was expensive. A crofter with a herd of twenty-five llamas couldn't afford one, and certainly had no right owning one. Its front teeth had been replaced by mono-lattice silicon fangs, eight centimetres long; the jaw had been reprofiled to a blunt hammerhead to accommodate them; both eyes were implants, retinas beefed up for night sight. One aspect Gabriel hadn't mentioned was the *speed* of the bloody thing.

Greg brought his Walther eight-shot up, the sighting laser glaring like a rigid lightning bolt in the photon amp's image. He got off two fast shots, maser pulses that drilled the Rottweiler's brain. The steely legs collapsed, sending it tumbling, momentum skidding it across the nettle-clumped grass. In death it snarled at him, jaws open, eyes wide, crying blood.

He walked past, uncaring. The Walther's condensers whined away on the threshold of audibility, recharging.

'At twenty-one twenty and thirteen seconds GMT, the cottage door will open. Edwards will look both ways before coming out. He will be carrying a pump-action shot-gun – only three cartridges, though.'

Greg flattened himself against the cottage wall, feeling the leathery creeper leaves compress against his back. The scarlet flowers had a scent similar to honeysuckle, strong sugar.

21:20:13.

The weather-bleached wooden door creaked.

Greg's espersense perceived Edwards hovering indecisively on the step, his mind a weak ruby glow, thought currents flowing slowly, concern and suspicion rising.

'He'll turn right, away from you.'

Edwards boot squelched in the mud of the yard, two steps. The shot-gun was held out in front, his finger pressed lightly on the trigger.

Greg came away from the wall, flicking the Walther to longburn, lining it up. Edwards was a bulky figure dressed in filthy denim trousers and a laddered chunky-knit sweater; neck craning forwards, peering through the moonlit gloom. He'd aimed the shot-gun at the ramshackle stone shed at the bottom of the yard.

The goat bleated, tugging at its leash.

Edwards was somehow aware of the presence behind him. His back stiffened, mind betraying a hot burst of alarm and fear to Greg's espersense. He tightened his grip on the shotgun, ready to spin round and blast away wildly.

'Drop it,' Greg said softly.

Edwards sighed, his shoulders relaxing. He bent to put the shot-gun down, resting its barrel on a stone, saving it from the mud. A man who knew weapons.

'OK, you can turn now.'

His face was thin, bearded, hazel eyes yellowed. He looked at Greg, taking in the matt-black combat leathers, slim metallic-silver band bisecting his face, unwavering Walther. Edwards knew he was going to die, but the terrified acceptance was flecked with puzzlement. 'Why?' he asked.

'Absolution.'

He didn't get it, they never did. His death was a duty, ordered by guilt.

Greg had learnt all about duty from the Army, relying on his squad mates, their equal dependence on him. It was a bond closer than family, overriding everything – laws, conventions, morals. Civvies like Edwards never understood. When all other human values had gone, shattered by violence, there was still duty. The implicit trust of life. And Greg had failed Royan. Miserably.

Greg fired. Edwards' mouth gaped as the maser beam struck his temple, his eyes rolling up as he fell forwards. He splashed into the thin layer of mud. Dead before he hit.

Greg holstered the Walther, breath hissing out between clenched teeth. He walked back down the hill to the Westland without giving the body another glance. Behind him, the goat's bell began to clang.

*

He refused to think about the kill while the Westland cruised over the countryside, his mind an extension of the guido, iced silicon, confirming landmarks, telling his body when to shift balance. It would've been too easy to brood in the ghost wing's isolated segment of the universe, guilt and depression inevitable.

Rutland Water was in front of him, a Y-shaped reservoir six and a half kilometres long nestling in the snug dark valleys of the county's turbulent rolling landscape. A pale oyster flame of jejune moonlight shone across the surface. Greg came in over the broad grass-slope dam at the western end. He kept low, skimming the water. Straight ahead was the floating village; thirty-odd log rafts, each supporting a plain wooden cabin, like something out of a Western frontier settlement. They were lashed together by a spiderweb of cables, forming a loose circle around the old limnological tower, a thick concrete shaft built before the reservoir was filled.

He angled towards the biggest cabin, compensating for the light gusts with automatic skill. At five metres out he flared the wing sharply. Surging air plucked at his combat leathers; his feet touched the coarse overlapping planks which made up the roof, legs running, carrying him up towards the apex as the propeller blurred. He stopped with a metre to spare. The tan, scrumpy-like odour of drying water-fruit permeated the air, reassuring in its familiarity.

The Westland's membrane folded.

'Greg?'

He watched Nicole's bald head rise above the gable end. 'Here.' He shrugged out of the harness.

She came up the ladder on to the roof, a black ex-Navy marine-adept dressed in a functional mauve diving bikini. He couldn't remember her ever wearing anything else. Even in the moonlight her water-resilient skin glistened from head to toe; she looked tubby, but not overweight, her shape dictated by an all-over insulating layer of subcutaneous fat, protecting her from the cold of deep water.

'How did it go?'

'All sorted, no messing,' he replied curtly.

Nicole nodded.

Two more marine-adepts swarmed briskly up the ladder and took charge of the Westland. Greg appreciated that, no fuss, no chatter. Most of the floating village's marine-adepts were ex-Navy, they understood.

They'd colonized the reservoir around the time Greg moved into his chalet on the shore, seeding and harvesting their gene-tailored water-fruit. Their only concession to the convulsions of the PSP years was to store Greg's military gear for him, and, very occasionally, provide sanctuary for an activist on the run from the People's Constables.

'I'll be back tomorrow,' Greg told Nicole as he climbed into his ancient rowing boat. When the neurohormone hangover had gone, when the memory of Edwards had faded, when he felt human again.

She untied the pannier and tossed it into the boat after him. 'Sure, Greg. Take care.'

*

Back on land he headed for the pub to forget the kill. The Army had taught him how to handle that as well. How to suspend human feelings in combat, to refuse the blame for all the deaths, the pain, suffering, horror. Greg had never woken screaming like others in the regiment had.

He knew what he needed, the release which came from drink and women, gluttoning out, sluicing away the memory of Edwards in a wash of basement-level normality.

He had a good feeling as he walked into the Wheatsheaf at Edith Weston; esper intuition or old-fashioned instinct, it didn't matter which, the result was the same. Static-charged antici-pation. He opened the taproom door grinning.

The Wheatsheaf's landlord, Angus, had come up trumps; his new barmaid was a tall, strapping lass, twenty years old with a heart-shaped face, wearing her thick red hair combed back from her forehead. She was dressed in a long navy-blue skirt and purple cap-sleeve T-shirt. A deep scoop neck showed off the heavily freckled slope of her large breasts to perfection.

Eleanor Broady. Greg stored the name as she pulled him a pint of Ruddles County, topping it with a shot of Angus's home-made whisky. It lasted longer that way, he couldn't afford to knock back pints all night.

Greg sat back and admired her in the guttering light of the oil lamps. The Wheatsheaf was a run of the mill rural pub, which reverted true to the nineteen-hundreds ideal with the demise of the big brewery conglomerates. Flash trash fittings melting away surprisingly fast once mains electricity ended and beer had to be hand-drawn from kegs again. Either relaxing or monumentally dull according to individual sensibilities. Greg liked it. There were no demands on him in the Wheatsheaf.

He was wedged in between a group of local farm workers and some of the lads from the timber mill, billeted in the village's old RAF base. The resident pair of warden dodgers were doing their nightly round, hawking a clutch of dripping rainbow trout they'd lifted from the reservoir.

Eleanor was a prize draw for male attention. Slightly timid from first-night nerves, but coping with the banter well enough.

Greg weighed up her personality, figuring how to make his play. Confidence gave him a warm buzz. He was seventeen years older, but with the edge his espersense gave him that shouldn't be a problem. What amused her, topics to steer clear of, he could see them a mile off. She'd believe they were soul twins before the night was out.

Her father came in at eleven thirty. The conversation chopped off dead. He was in dungarees, a big stained crucifix stitched crudely on the front. People stared; kibbutzniks didn't come into pubs, not ever.

Eleanor paled behind the bar, but stood her ground. Her father walked over to her, ignoring everybody, flickering yellow light catching the planes of his gaunt, angular face.

'You'll come home with me,' he said quietly, determined. 'We'll make no fuss.'

Eleanor shook her head, mute.

'Now.'

Angus came up beside her. 'The lady doesn't want to go.' His voice was weary but calm. No pub argument was beyond Angus; he knew them all, how to deal with each. Disposal expert.

'You belong with us,' said her father. 'You share our bread. We taught you better.'

'Listen—' Angus began, sweet reason.

'No. She comes with me. Or perhaps you will recompense us for her schooling? Grade four in animal husbandry, she is. Did she not tell you? Can you afford that?'

'I worked for it,' Eleanor said. 'Every day I worked for it. Never ending.'

Greg sensed how near to tears she was. Part of him was fascinated with the scene, it was surreal, or maybe Shakespearian, Victorian. Logic and lust urged him up.

Angus saw him closing on the bar and winced.

Greg gave him a wan reassuring smile – no violence, promise.

His imagination pictured his gland, a slippery black lens of muscle nestled at the centre of his brain, flexing rhythmically, squirting out milky liquid. Actually, it was nothing like that, but the psychosis was mild enough, harmless. Some Mindstar Brigade veterans had much weirder hallucinations.

The neurohormones started to percolate through his synapses, altering and enhancing their natural functions. His perception of the taproom began to alter, the physical abandoning him, leaving only people. They were their thoughts, tightly woven streamers of ideas, memories, emotions, interacting, fusing and budding. Coldly beautiful.

'Go home,' he told Eleanor's father.

The man was a furnace of anger and righteousness. Indignation blooming at the non-believer's impudence. 'This is not your concern,' he told Greg.

'Nor is she yours, not any more,' Greg replied. 'No longer your little girl. She makes her own choices now.'

'God's girl!'

It would've been so easy to thump the arrogant bastard. A deluge of mayhem strobed through Greg's mind, the whole unarmed combat manual on some crazy mnemonic recall, immensely tempting. He concentrated hard on the intransigent mind before him, domination really wasn't his suit, too difficult and painful.

'Go *home*.' He pushed the order, clenching his jaw at the effort.

The man's thoughts shrank from his meddling insistence, cohesion broken. Faith-suppressed reactions, the animal urge to lash out, fists pounding, feet kicking, boiled dangerously close to the surface.

Greg thrust them back into the subconscious, knowing his nails would be biting into his palms at the exertion.

The father flung a last imploring glance to a daughter who was genuinely loved in a remote, filtered manner. Rejection triggered the final humiliation, and he fled, his soul keening, eternal hatred sworn. Greg sensed his own face reflected in the agitated thoughts, distorted to demonic preconceptions. Then he was gone.

The taproom slowly rematerialized. The gland's neurohormones were punishing his brain. He steadied himself on the bar.

There were knowing grins which he fended off with a sheepish smile. Forced. A low grumble of conversation returned, cut with snickers. An entire generation's legend born, this night would live for ever.

Eleanor was trembling in reaction, Angus's arm around her shoulder, strictly paternal. She insisted she was all right, wanted to carry on, please.

Greg was shown her wide sunny smile for the first time, an endearing combination of gratitude and shyness. He didn't have to buy another drink all night.

*

'Kibbutzes always seemed a bit of a contradiction in terms to me,' Greg said. 'Christian Marxists. A religious philosophy of

9

dignified individuality, twinned with state oppression. Not your obvious partnership.' He and Eleanor were walking down the dirt track to his chalet in Berrybut Spinney, a couple of kilometres along the shore from Edith Weston. The old time-share estate's nightly bonfire glimmered through the black trees ahead, shooting firefly sparks high into the cloudless night. A midnight zephyr was rucking the surface of Rutland Water, wavelets lapping on the mud shallows. He could hear the smothered-waterfall sound from the discharge pipes as the reservoir was filled by the pumping stations on the Welland and Nene, siphoning off the March floodwater. The water level had been low this Christmas, parched farmland placing a massive demand for irrigation. Thousands of square metres of grass and weeds around the shore that'd grown up behind the water's summer retreat were slowly drowning under its return. As the rotting vegetation fermented it gave off a gas which smelt of rancid eggs and cow shit. It lasted for six weeks each year.

'Not much of either in a kibbutz,' Eleanor said, 'just work. God, it was squalid, medieval. We were treated like people-machines, everything had to be done by hand. Their idea of advanced machinery was the plough which the shire horses pulled. God's will. Like hell!'

Greg nodded sympathetically, he'd seen the inside of a kibbutz. She was chattering now, a little nervous. The restrictive doctrine that'd dominated her childhood had stunted the usual pattern of social behaviour, leaving her slightly unsure, and slightly turned on by new-found freedom.

Greg felt himself getting high on expectation. He was growing impatient to reach the chalet, and bed with that fantastic-looking body. Edwards' face was already indistinct, monochrome, falling away. Even the neurohormone hangover had evaporated.

The tall ash and oak trees of Berrybut Spinney had died years ago, unable to survive the Warming. They'd been turned into gigantic gazebos for the cobaea vines Greg and the other estate residents had planted around their broad buttress roots, dangling huge cascades of purple and white trumpet-flowers from stark skeletal boughs.

He'd spent long hours renovating the estate for the first three years after he moved in, putting in new plants – angel trumpets, figs, ficus, palms, lilies, silk oaks, cedars, even a small orange grove at the rear: a hurried harlequin quilt thrown over the brown fungal rot of decay. The first two years after the temperature peaked were the worst. Grass survived, of course, and some evergreen trees, but the sudden year-round heat wiped out entire ecological systems right across the country. Arable land suffered the least; farms, and the new kibbutzes, adapted readily enough, switching to new varieties of crops and livestock. But that still left vast tracts of native countryside and forests and city parks and village greens looking like battlefields scoured by some apocalyptic chemical weapon.

Repairs were uncoordinated, a patchwork of gross contrasts. It made travelling interesting, though.

Greg and Eleanor emerged from the spinney into a rectangular clearing which sloped down to the water. The dying bonfire illuminated a semicircle of twenty small chalets, and a big stone building at the crest.

'You live here?' Eleanor asked, in a very neutral tone.

'Yes,' he agreed cautiously. The chalets had been built by an ambitious time-share company in conjunction with a golf course running along the back of the spinney, and a grandiose clubhouse/hotel perched between the two. But the whole enterprise was suddenly bumped out of business thanks to the PSP's one-home law. The chalets were commandeered, the golf course returned to arable land, and the hotel transformed into thirty accommodation modules.

Greg always thought the country had been bloody lucky the PSP never got round to a one-room law. The situation had become pretty drastic as the oceans started to rise. The polar melt plateaued eventually, but not before it displaced two million people in England alone.

'I never asked,' she said. 'What is it you do?'

He chuckled. 'Greg Mandel's Investigative Services, at your service.'

'Investigative services? You mean, like a private detective? Angus told me you had a gland.'

'That's right. Of course it was nothing formal in the PSP decade. I didn't go legit until after the Second Restoration.'

'Why not?'

'Public ordinance number five seven five nine, oblique stroke nine two. By order of the President: no person implanted with a psi-enhancement gland may utilize their psi ability for financial gain. Not that many people could afford a private eye anyway. Not with Leopold Armstrong's nineteenth-century ideology screwing up the economy. Bastard. I was also disbarred from working in any State enterprise, and social security was a joke, the PSP apparatchiks had taken it over, head to toe, by the time I was demobbed. Tell you, they didn't like servicemen, and Mindstar veterans were an absolute no-go zone. The Party was running scared of us. As well they might.'

'How did you manage?'

'I had my Army pension for a couple of years after demob.' He shrugged. 'The PSP cancelled that soon enough. Fifth Austerity Act, if I recall rightly. I got by. Rutland's always had an agriculture-based economy. There's plenty of casual work to pick up on the farms, and the citrus groves were a boon; that and a few cash-only cases each year, it was enough.'

Her face was solemn. 'I never even saw any money until I was thirteen.'

He put his arm round her shoulder, giving a little reassuring shake. 'All over now.'

She smiled with haunted eyes, wanting to believe. His arm remained.

'Here we are,' he said, 'number six,' and blipped the lock.

The chalet's design paid fleeting homage to the ideal of some ancient Alpine hunting lodge, an overhanging roof all along the front creating a tiny veranda-cum-porch. But its structure lacked genuine Alpine ruggedness: prefab sections which looked like stout red-bark logs from the outside were now rotting badly, the windows had warped under the relentless assault of the new climate's heat and humidity, there was no air-conditioning, and the slates moulted at an alarming rate in high winds. The sole source of electricity was a solar-cell strip which Greg had pasted to the roof. However, the main frame was sound; four by four hardwood timber, properly seasoned. He could never understand why that should be, perhaps the building inspectors had chosen that day to put in an appearance.

The biolum strip came on revealing a lounge area with a sturdy oak-top bar separating it from a minute kitchen alcove at the rear. Its built-in furniture was compact, all light pine. Wearing thin, Greg acknowledged, following Eleanor's questing gaze. Entropy digging its claws in.

The corners of her lips tugged up. 'Nice. At Egleton, there'd be five of us sharing a room this size. You live here alone?'

'Yeah. The British Legion found it for me. Good people, volunteers. At least they cared, did what they could. And it's all paid for, even if it is falling down around me.'

'They were bad times, weren't they, Greg? I never really saw much of it. But there were the rumours, even in a kibbutz.'

'We rode it out, though. This country always does, somehow. That's our strength, in the genes, no matter how far down we fall, we're never out.'

'And you don't mind?'

'Mind what?'

'Me. I was in a kibbutz, that made me a card carrier.'

His arms went round her, hands resting lightly on her buttocks. Faces centimetres apart. Her nose was petite and pointed. 'Only by default. Nobody chooses their parents, and I'd say you un-chose yours pretty convincingly tonight.' His nose touched hers, rubbing gently.

She grinned, shy again.

The bedroom was on his right, behind a sliding door. A tiny pine-panelled room which was nearly filled by a huge double bed, there was a half-metre gap between the mattress and the walk.

Eleanor flicked him a quick appraising look, and her grin became slyer, lips twitching. Greg leant forward and kissed her.

He cheated with her, just as he'd done with all the others. His espersense was alert for exactly the right moment. It came a minute into the kiss; his hands found the hem of her T-shirt and he was pulling it off over her head, muffling her giggles. The long skirt and silky panties followed quickly.

Her figure was just as spectacular as his imagination had painted it for him. Eleanor's years at the kibbutz had toughened her, more so than most of the girls he had. He found that erotic; her flat, slightly muscular belly, wide hips, broad, powerful shoulders, all loaded with athletic promise.

Greg's own clothes came off in a fast heated tussle, and they moved on to the bed.

It lasted for an age, building slow. With his eyes he watched the blue and black shadows flow across her smooth damp skin as she stretched and twisted below his hands. With his mind he sensed cold shooting stars igniting along the glistening trail left by the tip of his tongue, then fire along her nerves into her brain, adding to the glow of arousal. He saw what excited her, the words she wanted to hear; then exploited the discoveries, whispering secret fantasies into her ear, guiding her into the permutations she'd never dared ask from a partner before.

After the initial astonishment of making love to someone who not only shared her desires but actually relished them, Eleanor shook loose any lingering restraint. Greg laughed in delight as she let her enthusiasm run riot, and told her how she could repay him.

When he asked, she rose up in the way he loved, poised above him, light from the slumbering bonfire licking at her flesh, deepening her mystique. His hands finally found her breasts. She grinned, seeing his weakness, and played on it, drawing out the poignancy before she twined her legs around him, and pulled herself down. Her mind became almost dazzlingly bright as she used him to bring herself to orgasm, all coherency overwhelmed by animal instinct.

Greg let go of Edwards and duty and guilt, and concentrated solely on inflaming Eleanor still further.

2

Julia Evans sat at the dresser in her bedroom while the maid brushed daytime knots out of her long chestnut hair. It had to be done every night; she hadn't allowed her hair to be cut for years, and now it hung almost down to her waist. Her best feature, everyone said, striking.

She studied her face in the mirror, plump cheeked and bland, wearing a slightly sorrowful expression. It wasn't an ugly face, by any means. But at seventeen some allure really ought to be evolving.

Access Vanity#Twelve, she told her bioware processor implant silently. At least she had had a sense of humour when she began this memory sequence.

A mirage of her own face, six months younger, unfurled behind her eyes. She compared it to the one in the mirror. There was some change. A burning-off of puppy fat, her cheeks were rounder then. Fractionally.

There had been a time, a couple of months back, when she'd considered *plastique*, but eventually shied away. Having herself altered to match some channel-starlet ideal would be the ultimate admission of defeat. As long as there was still some development there was hope. Perhaps she was being impatient. But how wonderful it would be to make the boys ogle lustily.

Commit Vanity#Twenty-five. The mirror image, with all its melancholia.

'Thank you, Adela,' she said.

The maid nodded primly, and made one final stroke with the brush before departing, Julia watched her go in the mirror, some deep instinct objecting to ordering people around like cattle. But it was an instinct which was nearly dead, the Swiss boarding school had seen to that. Besides, Adela wasn't one of the grudging ones. At twenty-two years of age she was close enough in years for Julia to feel comfortable with her; and she was certainly loyal enough – to the extent of sharing Wilholm Manor's considerable quantity of below-stairs gossip.

Julia shrugged out of her robe and flopped down on the big circular bed, stretching luxuriously on the apricot silk sheets. The room was huge, so much empty space, and all her own. So very different to the little stone burrow she'd lived in for the first ten years of her life at the First Salvation Church warren. Space was undoubtedly the best part of being rich.

The bedroom was a celebration of opulent decadence, with its satin rose ceiling, thick pile carpet, walk-through wardrobes, a marbled bathroom. It was a feminine room; a *boudoir*, foreign and exotic.

She'd spent a fortnight with an increasingly harried interior designer selecting exactly the style she wanted. A distant memory of an old memox video-cartridge, a costume romance of handsome dukes and willowy heroines in a more genteel age.

Her grandfather had come in when the bedroom was finished, his eyes rolling with bemused tolerance. 'Well, as long as *you're* happy with it, Juliet.'

He hadn't paid many visits after that. Not that she minded him. But it was delicious to be left alone, privacy still seemed a bit of a novelty. Her security hardline bodyguards accompanied her everywhere outside the mansion; not nudging her shoulder, they were too professional for that, but always close, always watching. And once inside Wilholm's 'ware-saturated perimeter nothing went unseen.

Some part of Julia's nature rebelled against being a cosseted princess, treated like some immensely precious and delicate work of art. Yes, she was valuable, but not fragile. However, there were subtle ways to defy the surveillance, to indulge herself without suffering the silent censure of the hardliners' ever-vigilant eyes, keeping some little core of personality secret to herself.

Open Channel to Manor Security Core. The 'ware came on line, a colourless menu of surveillance circuits and defence gear streaming into her mind, all of it listed as restricted. She fed her executive code in, and every restriction was lifted.

Access Surveillance Camera: West Wing, First–Floor Corridor. Route Image Into Bedroom Three.

She rolled over and rested her chin in her hands, legs waving idly. A picture formed on the theatre-sized wall-mounted flat-screen opposite the bed. It showed the corridor outside, a slightly fuzzy resolution. Adrian was walking down the thick strip of navy-blue carpeting, dressed in a long burgundy towelling robe. Barefoot, she noted, and no pyjama trousers either.

Peeping Tom, her mind chided. Her cheeks were suddenly very warm against her palms, but Pandora's box was open now.

Adrian stopped outside one of the bedroom doors, and looked furtively both ways along the corridor before opening the door without knocking.

For one glorious instant Julia allowed herself to believe it was her bedroom he'd entered, even twisting round to look. But of course her door was closed.

Access Surveillance Camera: West Wing, Guest Suite Seven.

Katerina's room, bathed in a musky green light. Now here was something very interesting. By day it was Adrian who took charge of their little group; Julia and Katerina listened to him, laughed at his jokes, followed him when he wanted to go swimming, or horse riding, or playing tennis. But here in private the roles were reversed, Adrian did as Kats told him.

Julia studied her girl friend as best as the irritatingly grainy image allowed. Kats had lost some of her youthful daytime frivolity, becoming imperious, a confidence verging on arrogance.

Open Memory File, Code: AmourKats.

So she could retain all the impressions she saw on the big screen, and then retrieve them at any time for future consideration. AmourKats was going to be an objective study in seduction.

Kats was kneeling on her bed as Adrian came in, dressed in a provocative taupe-coloured silk camisole top and a short waist slip, blonde hair bubbling down around her shoulders. A real-life sex kitten. She told Adrian to take his robe off.

It was more like an order, Julia thought. Her heart leapt at the prospect of seeing Adrian naked at last, jealous and excited. Seeing him in his swimming trunks all afternoon had been a real treat.

Adrian was nineteen years old, ruggedly handsome, and possessed of a truly heavenly physique, each muscle perfectly proportioned, nothing like the ugly excess of a body-builder, just naturally lean. **Mesomorph**, her implant dictionary subsection told her.

The towelling robe formed a dark puddle around Adrian's feet.

Julia slowly turned on to her side, looking away from the flatscreen; shame finally overpowering greed.

Exit Surveillance Camera.

Adrian had been so nice to her, treating her no differently than he did Kats during the day as the three of them roamed Wilholm's vast grounds. She'd really hoped the attraction was mutual this time. She never seemed to be able to attract, much less hold, a boy as desirable as Adrian.

The memory of Primate Marcus, leader of the First Salvation Church, floated out of that little dark core of anguish to haunt her once more. He'd favoured her mother for several months when Julia had been eight. The patronage had enabled her to walk like a queen through the desert commune's airy underground tunnels, the happiest time of her young life. Daughter of the Primate's chosen one.

Primate Marcus was an obese fifty-year-old, wrapped in a huge toga to hide his slovenly frame. With her eyes closed she saw the big round head with its full grey beard leaning down towards her. Fat fingers adorned with gold rings tickled her ribs, and she shrieked her joy. The air had been thick and sweet from his marijuana. 'One day soon, I'll fill you with Jesuslove,' his slurred voice rumbled.

She had laughed then. Shuddered now.

But then, she thought miserably, that was always the way when it came to men – boys. She just never seemed to have any luck. So far they had fallen into two categories; the first she hadn't even believed existed until afterwards. More handsome than Adrian, wittier than a channel comedian, with the culture and manners of a Royal. But most of them had no real money – executive assistants, flavour-of-the-month artists, impoverished aristocracy, men who could make deals to retire on if they just had backing. They haunted the fringes of society, sharks who homed in on her name, her money like fresh meat, which in a way she was. She had been too young, too stupidly blind with the whirlwind of holiday romance. And in bed his immaculate body had made her scream out in glory. Only afterwards did she find out she was simply part of his grand scheme.

She had fled from one extreme to the other. Back to her exclusive Swiss school, and into Joel's arms, a boarder at the boys' school down the road. He was the same age as her, the sensitive type, mild-mannered, caring, just perfect for a true first love, she knew he would never exploit her. And in bed he was an utter disaster; she would lie in his twitchy embrace and remember how sensational sex could be. Thankfully it had fizzled out soon enough, her leaving her school, him returning to France, neither making much effort to keep in touch.

The soul-bruising knocks and disappointments had set up a barrier, a psychological flinch. And the boys seemed aware of her mistrust, finding it difficult to breach. Anyone who could was too smooth, those that couldn't would be like Joel. What she wanted more than anything was one good-looking boy who didn't know who she was to look at her and think: yeah!

Then Kats had come to stay at Wilholm, injecting some

much-needed laughter to the long procession of warm, wet, boring days; and she'd brought Adrian with her. Adrian: who fitted the bill as though he had been born for her, mature, athletic, no doubt very experienced in bed, fun, intelligent, not at all arrogant. And when he had smiled and said hello there had been no barrier, no hesitancy at all. It would've been utterly sensational, if Kats hadn't enchanted him first.

Julia shivered slightly at the involuntary recollection of Primate Marcus and the cult. She'd been ten when the upheaval came, the big Texan, known later as Uncle Horace, had arrived to take her away. Over the sea to a near-mythical Europe and a grandfather she'd never even known she had. Lady Fauntleroy, the other commune kids had teased before she went, bowing, curtseying. She'd giggled with them, playing along, secretly terrified of leaving the gently curving sandstone passages with their broad light-wells and the eternal magnificent desert above. Her mother had stayed with the cult, her father had accompanied her.

The bioware processors helped Julia suppress the name, the whole concept of *father*, pushing him below conscious examination, a fast, clean exorcism. He brought too much pain. Childhood ignorance was a blissful existence, she reflected.

Europe and Philip Evans, her grandfather; and the astonishing revelation of Event Horizon. A company to rival a *kombinate* in size, heroically battling the British PSP, which surely made Grandpa a saint. Socialism was the ultimate Antichrist.

Her grandfather had sent her to the school in Switzerland, where starchy tutors had crammed her with company law, management procedures, finance; twittery *grande dames* teaching her all the social graces, etiquette and deportment, refining her. She'd dropped her American accent, adopting a crystal-cut English Sloane inflection to lend a touch of class. A proper Lady. Then on her sixteenth birthday she'd left the school and spent a month in Event Horizon's ultra-exclusive Austrian clinic.

She was given five bioware implants, nodes of ferredoxin protein meshed with her synaptic clefts: three memory-cell clusters, two data processors; a whole subsidiary brain to cope with the vast dataflows generated by Event Horizon. The parallel mentality didn't make her a genius, but it did make her analytical, objective. A conflation of logic and human inspiration, she was capable of looking at a problem from every conceivable angle until she produced a solution. An irrational computer.

'It's the only way, Juliet,' Philip had told her. 'I'm losing track of the company, it's slipping away from me. All I ever get to see in cubes are the summaries of summaries, a shallow overview. That's not enough. Inertia and waste are building up. Inevitably, I suppose. Department heads just don't have the drive. It's a job to them, not a life. Maybe these nodes will enable you to control it properly.'

Julia let desire war with her conscience. How did you captivate a boy like Adrian?

Access Surveillance Camera: West Wing, Guest Suite Seven.

A laughing Kats was straddling Adrian, playing with him, her hands caressing, tongue working slowly down his chest. He was spreadeagled across the mattress, clutching the brass bedposts with a strength which came close to bending them, face warped in agony and ecstasy, pleading with her.

Commit AmourKats.

Julia had never done anything like this, not leading, not making all the moves. She wasn't sure she would have the nerve. Kats seemed so totally uninhibited. Shameless. Was that the key? Could boys home in on abandon? Kats sat back on Adrian's abdomen, then crossed her arms and gripped the hem of the camisole. She peeled it languidly over her head, shaking her hair out. Julia felt a sharp spasm of envy at seeing her friend's well-developed body. That was one reason why Kats had Adrian, she acknowledged bitterly, they looked like godlings together. At least she had longer legs than Kats. Skinny, though; nothing like as shapely, two beanpoles really.

Exit Surveillance Camera.

Her mental yell was contaminated with anger and disgust. Peeking on the lovers had seemed like a piece of harmless fun.

Certainly using the security cameras to spy on the manor's servants had been pretty enlightening. But this wasn't the gentle romantic love-making she'd been expecting. Nothing near.

Pandora's box. And only a fool ever opens it.

Anger vanished to be replaced with sadness. Alone again, more than ever now she knew the truth.

Boys were just about the only subject she never discussed with her grandfather. It never seemed fair somehow. He'd taken over every other parental duty, a solid pillar of comfort, support, and love. She couldn't burden him with more. Not now. *Certainly* not now.

Part of the reason for her being at Wilholm was so she could be his secretary. Philip Evans needed a secretary like he needed another overdraft, but the idea was to give her executive experience and acquaint her with Event Horizon minutiae, preparing her to take it over. A terrifying, yet at the same time exhilarating prospect.

Then this morning at breakfast he'd taken her into his confidence, looking even more haggard than usual. 'Someone is running a spoiler operation against Event Horizon,' he'd said. 'Contaminating thirty-seven per cent of our memox crystals in the furnaces.'

'Has Walshaw found out who was behind it?' she'd asked, assuming she was being told after the security chief had closed down the operation. It was the way their discussions of the company usually went. Her grandfather would explain a recent problem, and they'd go over the solution, detail by detail, until she understood why it'd been handled that particular way. Remote hands-on training, he'd joked.

'Walshaw doesn't know about this,' Philip Evans had answered grimly. 'Nobody knows apart from me. I noticed our cash reserves had fallen pretty drastically in the last quarterly financial summaries. Forty-eight million Eurofrancs down, Juliet, that's fifty-seven million New Sterling for Christ's sake. Our entire reserve is only nine hundred million Eurofrancs. So I started checking. The money is being used to cover a deficit from the microgee crystal furnaces up at Zanthus. Standard accounting procedure; the loss was passed on to the finance division to make good for our loan-repayment schedule. They're just doing their job. The responsibility lies with the microgee division, and they've done bugger all about it.'

She'd frowned, bewildered. 'But surely someone in the microgee division should've spotted it? Thirty-seven per cent! What about the security monitors?'

'Nothing. They didn't trip. According to the data squirt from Zanthus, that thirty-seven per cent is coming out of the furnace as just so much rubbish, riddled with impurities. They've written it off as a normal operational loss. And that is pure bollocks. The furnaces weren't performing that badly at start-up, and we're way down the learning curve now. A worst-case scenario should see a five per cent loss. I checked with the Boeing Marietta consortium which builds the furnaces, no one else is suffering that kind of reject rate. Most of 'em have losses below two per cent.'

The full realization struck her then. 'We can't trust security?'

'God knows, Juliet. I'm praying that some smartarse hotrod has found a method of cracking the monitor's access codes, however unlikely that is. The alternative is bad.'

'What are you going to do?'

'Sit and think. They've been gnawing away at us for eight bloody months, a few more days won't kill us. But we're taking a quarter of a million Eurofranc loss per day, it's got to stop, and stop dead. I have to know the people I put on it are reliable.'

They couldn't afford major losses, Julia knew. Philip Evans's post-Second Restoration expansion plans were stretching the company's resources to breaking point. Microgee products were the most profitable of all Event Horizon's gear, but the space station modules tied up vast sums of capital; even with the Sanger spaceplanes, reaching orbit was still phenomenally expensive. They needed the income from the memox crystals to keep up the payments to the company's financial backing consortium.

The fact that he'd admitted the problem to her and her alone had brought a wonderful sensation of contentment. They'd always been close, but this made the bond unbreakable. She was the only person he could really trust in the whole world. And that was just a little bit scary.

She'd promised faithfully to run an analysis of the security monitor programs through her nodes for him, to see if the codes could be cracked, or maybe subverted. But she'd delayed it while she went horse riding with Adrian and Kats, then again as the three of them went swimming, and now subverting the manor's security circuits.

Guilt added itself to the shame she was already feeling from spying on the lovers. She'd been appallingly selfish, allowing a juvenile infatuation to distract her. Betraying Grandpa's trust.

Access High Steal.

Sight, sound, and sensation fell away, isolating her at the centre of a null void. Numbers filled her mind, nothing like a cube display, no coloured numerals; this was elemental maths, raw digits. The processor nodes obediently slotted them into a logic matrix, a three-dimensional lattice with data packages on top, filtering through a dizzy topography of interactive channels that correlated and cross-indexed. Hopefully the answer should pop out of the bottom.

She thought for a moment, defining the parameters of the matrix channels, allowing ideas to form, merge. Any ideas, however wild. Some fruiting, some withering. Irrational. Assume the monitors are unbreakable: how would I go about concealing the loss? An inverted problem, outside normal computer logic, its factors too random. Her processor nodes loaded the results into the channel structures.

The columns of numbers started to flow. She began to inject tracer programs, adding modifications as she went, probing for weak points.

Some deep level of her brain admitted that the metaphysical matrix frightened her, an eerie sense of trepidation at its inhuman nature. She feared herself, what she'd become. Was that why people kept their distance? Could they tell she was different somehow? An instinctive phobia.

She cursed the bioware.

*

Philip Evans's scowling face filled her bedside phone screen. 'Juliet?' The scowl faded. 'For God's sake, girl, it's past midnight.'

He looked so terribly fragile, she thought, worse than ever. She kept her roguish smile firmly in place – school discipline, thank heavens. 'So what are you doing up, then?'

'You bloody well know what I'm doing, girl.'

'Yah, me too. Listen, I think I've managed to clear security over the monitor programs.'

He leaned in towards the screen, eyes questing. 'How?'

'Well, the top rankers anyway,' she conceded. 'We make eighteen different products up at Zanthus, and each of the microgee production modules squirts its data to the control centre in the dormitory. Now the control-centre 'ware processes the data before it enters the company data net so that the relevant divisions only get the data they need – maintenance requirements to procurement, consumables to logistics, and performance figures to finance. But the security monitoring is actually done up at Zanthus, with the raw data. And that's where the monitor programs have been circumvented, they haven't been altered at all.'

'Circumvented how?'

'By destreaming the data squirts from the microgee modules, lumping them all together. The monitors are programmed to trip when production losses rise above fourteen per cent, anything below that is considered a maintenance problem. At the moment the total loss of our combined orbital production is thirteen point two per cent, so no alarm.'

Julia watched her grandpa run a hand across his brow. 'Juliet, you're an angel.'

She said nothing, grinning stupidly into the screen, feeling just great.

'I mean it,' he said.

Embarrassed in the best possible way, she shrugged. 'Just a question of programming, all that expensive education you gave me. Anybody else could've done it. What will you do now?'

'Do you know who authorized the destreaming?'

'No, sorry. It began nine months ago, listed as part of one of our famous simplification/economy drives.'

'Can you find out?'

'Tricky. However, I checked with personnel, and none of the Zanthus managers have left in the last year, so whoever the culprit is, they're still with us. Three options. I can try and worm my way into Zanthus's 'ware and see if they left any traces, like which terminal it was loaded from, whose access card was used, that kind of thing. Or I could go up to Zanthus and freeze their records.'

No way, Juliet,' he said tenderly. 'Sorry.'

'Thought so. The last resort would be to use our executive code to dump Zanthus's entire data core into the security division's storage facility, and run through the records there. The trouble with that is that everyone would know it's been done.'

'And the culprit would do a bunk,' he concluded for her. 'Yes. So that leaves us with breaking into Zanthus. Bloody wonderful, cracking my own 'ware. So tell me why this absolves the top rankers?'

'It doesn't remove them from suspicion altogether, it just means they aren't the prime suspects any more, now we know the monitor codes weren't compromised. Whether security personnel are involved or not depends on how good the original vetting system is. Certainly someone intimate with our data-handling procedures is guilty.'

'That doesn't surprise me. There's always rotten apples, Juliet, remember that. All you can ever do is hope to exclude them from achieving top-rank positions.'

'What will you do now?'

The hand massaged his brow again. 'Tell Walshaw, for a start. If we can't trust him then we may as well pack up today. After that I'll bring in an independent, get him to check this mess out for me – security, Zanthus management, the memox-furnace operators, the whole bloody lot of them.'

'What sort of independent?'

He grinned. 'Work that out for yourself, Juliet. Management exercise.'

'How many guesses?' she shot back, delighted. He was always challenging her like this. Testing.

'Three.'

'Cruel.'

'Good night, Juliet. Sweet dreams.'

'Love you, Grandee.'

He kissed two fingers, transferring it to the screen. Her fingers pressed urgently against his, the touch of cold glass, hard. His face faded to slate grey.

Julia pulled the sheet over herself, turning off the brass swan wall-lights. She hugged her chest in the warm darkness; elated, far too alert for sleep to claim her.

Access Surveillance Camera: West Wing, Guest Suite Seven.

3

Eleanor had been living with Greg for exactly two weeks to the day when the Rolls-Royce crunched slowly down the dirt track into the Berrybut time-share estate.

It was two o'clock in the afternoon, and the sky was a cloudless turquoise desert. Eleanor and Greg shifted towels, cushions, and drinks out on to the chalet's tiny patio to take advantage of the unseasonable break in the weather. March was usually a regular procession of hot hard downfalls accompanying a punishing humidity. Greg could remember his parents reminiscing about flurries of snow and hail, but his own childhood memories were of miserable damp days stretching into May. Fortunately, typhoons hadn't progressed north of Gibraltar yet. Give it ten years, said the doomsayer meteorologists.

Eleanor stripped down to scarlet polka-dot bikini briefs, a present from Greg when he found she couldn't swim, promising to teach her. He rubbed screening oil over her bare back. Pleasantly erotic, although the heat stopped them from carrying it any further. They settled down to spy on the birds wading along the softly steaming mudflats at the foot of the sloping clearing. Most months saw some new exotic species arriving at the reservoir, fleeing the chaos storms raging ever more violently around the equatorial zones. The year had already seen several spoonbills and purple herons, even a cattle egret had put in a couple of appearances.

Greg lay on the towel, eyes drooping, letting the sun's warmth soak his limbs, slowly banishing the stiffness with a sensuousness that no massage could possibly match. Eleanor stretched out beside him on her belly, and loaded a memox of Tolkien's *Lord of the Rings* into her cybofax. Every now and then she'd take a sip of orange from a glass filled with crushed ice, and scan the shoreline for any additions.

Usually the girls he went with would drift away after a couple of days, maybe a week, unable to cope with his mood changes. But this time there hadn't been any; he had nothing to get depressed about, her body kept the blues at bay. And her humour, too, he admitted to himself. She rarely found fault. Probably a relic of her claustrophobic kibbutz upbringing, you *had* to learn tolerance there.

He wasn't quite sure who was corrupting who. She was sensual and enthusiastic in bed, they screwed like rutty teenagers on speed each night. And he hadn't bothered to see any of his old mates since she moved in, not that he was pushing them out of his life. But her company seemed to be just as satisfying. It would be nice to think – dream really – that he could cut himself loose from the pain and obligations that came out of the past.

The rest of the country was in an electric state of flux, one he could see stabilizing in a year or two. He had wondered on odd occasions if he could manage the transition, too. Start to make a permanent home, stick to ordinary cases, earn regular money. There was just so much of the past which would have to be laid to rest first.

Whistles and shouts floated down from the back of the chalet row, the estate kids' twenty-four-hour football game in full swing. Up towards Edith Weston, bright, colourful sails of windsurfers whizzed about energetically. The county canoe team was out in force, enthusiastically working themselves into a collective heat stroke as their podgy coach screamed abuse at them through a bullhorn. Hireboats full of amateur fishermen and their expensive tackle drifted idly in the breeze.

Greg hadn't quite nodded off when he heard the car

approaching. Eleanor raised herself on to her elbows, and pushed her sunglasses up, frowning.

'Now that is unreal,' she murmured.

Greg agreed. The car was old, a nineteen-fifties vintage Silver Shadow, its classic, fabulously stylish lines inspiring instant envy. The kind of fanatical devotion invested in both its design and assembly were long-faded memories now, a lost heritage.

Astonishingly, it still used the original combustion engine with a recombiner cell grafted on, allowing it to burn petrol. Two pressure spheres stored its exhaust gas below the chassis, ready for converting back into liquid hydrocarbon when the cell was plugged into a power source. The system was ludicrously expensive.

He watched in bemused silence as it drew up outside the chalet, shaming his two-door electric Fiat Austin Duo. Out of the corner of his eye he could see his neighbours staring in silence at the majestic apparition. Even the football game had stopped.

Given the car, the driver came as no surprise; he was decked out in a stiff grey-brown chauffeur's uniform, complete with peaked cap.

He didn't bother with the front door, walking round Greg's vegetable patch to the patio, scattering scrawny chickens in his wake. The way he walked gave him the authority. Easy powerful strides, backed up by wide powerful shoulders and a deep chest. He was young, mid-twenties, confident and alert.

He looked round curiously as he approached. Greg sympathized, the little estate had begun to resemble a sort of upmarket hippie commune. Shambolic.

Eleanor wrapped a towel around her breasts, knotting it at the side. Greg climbed to his feet, wearily.

The chauffeur gave Eleanor a courteous little half-bow, eyes lingering. He caught himself and turned self-consciously to Greg. 'Mr Mandel?'

'Yes.'

'My employer would like to interview you for a job.'

'I have a phone.'

'He would like to do it in person, and today.'

'What sort of job?'

'I have no idea.' The chauffeur reached inside his jacket and pulled out an envelope. 'This is for your time.' It was two thousand pounds New Sterling, in brand-new fifties.

Greg handed it down to Eleanor, who riffled the crisp plastic notes, staring incredulously.

'Who is your employer?' he asked the chauffeur.

'He wishes to introduce himself.'

Greg shrugged, not that impatient for details. People with money had learnt to become circumspect in advertising the fact. Furtiveness was a national habit now, not even the Second Restoration had changed that. The PSP's local committees had become well versed at diverting private resources to benefit the community. And they'd made some pretty individualistic inter- pretations on what constituted 'community'.

Greg tried to get a feel from his intuition. Nothing, it was playing coy. And then there was the money. Two thousand just for an interview. Crazy. Eleanor was waiting, her wide eyes slightly troubled. He glanced down at the frayed edges of his sawn-off jeans. 'Have I got time to change first?'

*

The Rolls-Royce's dinosaur mechanics made even less noise than an electric car, sublime engineering. There was a glass screen between Greg and the chauffeur, frosty roses etched around the edges. It stayed up for the whole drive, leaving questions still- born. He sank into the generous leather cushioning of the rear seat and watched the world go by through sombre smoked windows. Chilly air-conditioning made him glad of the light suit he was wearing.

They drove through Edith Weston and on to the A1, head- ing south. The big car's wheelbase bridged the minor roads completely. Over a decade of neglect by the PSP had allowed grass and speedwells to spread out from the kerbs, spongy moss formed a continuous emerald strip where the white lines used to be. It was only thanks to farm traffic and bicycles that the roads had been kept open at all during the depth of the dark years.

Horses and cyclists pulled on to the verge to let them pass, curious faces gaping at the outlandish relic. The impulse to give a royal wave was virtually irresistible.

There was some traffic on the dual-carriageway A1 – horse-drawn drays, electric cars, and small methane-fuelled vans. The Rolls-Royce outpaced them effortlessly, its suspension gliding evenly over the deep ruts of crumbling tarmac.

The northbound side of the Wetland bridge had collapsed, leaving behind a row of crumbling concrete pillars leaning at a precarious angle out of the fast-moving muddy water, pregnant from five weeks of heavy rains. The bridge had been swept away four years ago in the annual flooding which had long since scoured the valley clean of all its villages and forms. During the dry season the river shrank back to its usual level, exposing a livid gash of grey-blue clay speckled with bricks and shattered roofing timbers, the seam of a serpentine swamp stretching from the fringe of the Fens basin right back to Barrowden.

The chauffeur turned off the A1 at Wansford, heading west, inland, away from the bleak salt marshes which festered across the floor of the Nene valley below the bridge.

Greg hated the waste, President Armstrong's legacy. It was all so unnecessary, levees were amongst the oldest types of civil engineering.

The Rolls turned off on to a dirt track. It looked like an ordinary farm path across the fields of baby sugar cane, leading to a small wood of Spanish oaks about three-quarters of a kilometre away. There wasn't even a gate, simply a wide cattle grid and a weatherbeaten sign warning would-be trespassers of dire consequences.

The chauffeur stopped before the grid, and flicked a switch on the dash before driving on. There was nothing between the metal strips, no weeds, puddles, only a drowning blackness.

They drove through an opening in the trees, under a big stone arch with wrought-iron gates, kept in excellent condition. Stone griffins looked down at the Rolls with lichen-pocked eyes.

There was a long gravel drive beyond the gates, leading up to a magnificent early eighteenth-century manor house. Silver windows flashed fractured sunbeams. A tangle of pink and yellow roses boiled over the stonework, tendrils lapping the second-storey windowsills.

Five dove-grey geodesic globes lurked amongst the forest of tall chimneystacks. Very heavy-duty satellite antennas.

The Rolls pulled to a smooth halt level with the grey stone portico. 'Wilholm Manor,' the chauffeur announced gravel-voiced as he opened the door.

A couple of gardeners were tending the regimented flowerbeds along the edge of the gravel, stopping to watch as Greg stepped out.

Something was moving in the thick shrubbery at the foot of the lawn, dark, indistinct, bigger than a dog, slipping through the flower-laden plumbago clumps with serpentine grace. Spooky. Greg reached out with his espersense, detecting a single thread of thought, diamond hard. He placed it straight away, an identification loaded with associated memories he'd prefer to forgo. He was focused on a gene-tailored sentinel panther. It padded along its patrol pattern with robotic precision, bioware archsenses alert for any transgressors.

He sucked in his breath, stomach muscles clenched. The Jihad legions had used similar animals in Turkey, a quantum leap upwards from modified Rottweilers. He'd seen a sentinel take out a fully armoured squaddie after the animal had been blown half to bits, jaws cutting clean through the boy's combat suit. They were fucking lethal. The manor's elegant façade suddenly seemed dimmer; fogbound.

He was shown through the double doors into the hall by an old man in a butler's tailcoat. The interior was as immaculate as he'd expected. Large dark oil landscapes hung on the walls; the antique furniture was delicate to the point of effete, chandeliers like miniature galaxies illuminated a vaulting ceiling: a décor

34

which blended perfectly with the building. But it was all new, superimposed on the ancient shell by a stage dresser with an unlimited budget. The paint was glossy bright, the green and gold wallpaper fresh, the carpets unworn.

Greg hadn't known this kind of opulence existed in England any more. Yes, his usual clients were well off. But at most that meant a detached house with maybe three or four bedrooms; or some overseas-financed condominium apartment loaded with pieces of family heritage saved from the magpie acquisition fever of tax-office apparatchiks.

Given normal circumstances the local PSP committee would've turned the manor into accommodation modules for about forty families who'd then work the surrounding land in some sort of communal farm arrangement, either a co-op or a fully fledged kibbutz. Wilholm's renovation was recent, post-Second Restoration.

The butler led Greg up a broad, curving stair to the landing, and he caught a glimpse of the formal gardens at the back. Bushes clipped into animal shapes sentried wide paths. A statue of Venus in the middle of the lily pond sent a white plume of water shooting high into the air. Spherical rainbows shimmered inside the cloud of descending spray.

The inevitable swimming pool was a large oval affair, a good twenty metres long. A tall tower of diving boards stood guard over the deep end, and there was a convoluted slide zigzagging along one side. A couple of big inflatable balls were floating on the surface. Three teenagers cavorted about in the clear water; two girls, one boy.

They seemed out of place, interlopers, their lively shrieks and splashes discordant with the funereal solemnity that hung through the rest of the manor.

He was shown into Wilholm's oak-panelled study; and the day finally began to pull together into some sort of sense. Philip Evans was waiting for him.

There had been this girl, Greg couldn't remember her name now, but the two of them had got rapturously drunk watching the coronation together. The triumph of the Second Restoration remained for ever buried in that alcoholic netherland, but he distinctly remembered Philip Evans sitting in the abbey's congregation. The cameras couldn't keep off him. A small man in his mid-seventies, stiff-backed, using a stick to assist his slow walk, but managing to smile brightly none the less.

Philip Evans was the PSP's *bête noire*; their Whitehall media department set him up as a hate figure, a campaign of vilification which left Orwell's Emmanuel Goldstein standing. It'd backfired on them badly. Evans became a romantic pirate to the rest of the country. A living legend.

Event Horizon's cybernetic factories floated with blissful impunity in international waters, churning out millions of counterfeit gear systems each year. Molecular-perfect Korean flatscreens, French memox-crystal players, Brazilian cybo-faxes, a long, long list of the consumer goodies which R&D-starved State factories couldn't match, and PSP economic policy prohibited importing.

His fleet of Stealth transports made nightly flights over England, distributing their wares to a country-wide network of spivs like demonic Santas. They proved unstoppable. One of the PSP's first acts on reaching office had been to disband most of the RAF.

The black-market gear hurt the economy badly, undermining indigenous industries, turning more people to the spivs. A nasty downward spiral, picking up speed.

Evans had changed for the worse in the intervening two years since the coronation. The flesh sagged on his face, becoming pasty-white, highlighting dark panda circles around his eyes. His hair had nearly gone; the few wisps remaining were a pale silver. And not even the baggy sleeves of his silk dressing-gown could disguise how disturbingly thin his arms were.

He was sitting at the head of a long oak table. Two holo cubes flanked him, multi-coloured reflections from their swirling graphics rippling like S-bend rainbows off the highly polished wood.

Greg sniffed the cool dry air; there was a tart smell in the study, peppery. Philip Evans was badly ill.

The ageing billionaire dismissed his butler with an impatient flick of his hand. 'Come in, Mandel. Can't see you properly from here, boy, my bastard eyes are going along with the rest of me.'

There was another man in the study, standing staring out of the window, hands clasped behind his back. He didn't look round.

Walking down the length of the table Greg saw that Evans was only whole above the waist. His legs and hips had been swallowed by the seamless cylindrical base of a pearl-white powerchair, torso fusing into an elastic chrome collar. It was a mobile life-support unit, analogue bioware organs sustaining the faltering body. But the mind was still fully active, burning hot and bright.

Greg shook his hand. It was like holding a glove filled with hot water.

'What do they call you, boy? Greg, isn't it?' The accent was pure Lincolnshire, blunt, as much an attitude as a speech pattern.

'Yes, sir.'

'Well, I'm Philip, Greg. Now sit down, it ricks my neck craning up at you.'

Greg sat, one chair down from Evans.

'This is my security chief, Morgan Walshaw.'

The man turned, looking at Greg. He was in his late fifties, with close-cropped grey hair; wearing a blue office suit, plain fuchsia tie. Shoulders squared. Definitely ex-military. The recognition was instantaneous. A mirror.

Eyeing each other up like prize fighters, Greg thought. Stupid.

'Mr Walshaw doesn't approve of my asking you here,' Evans explained.

'I don't disapprove,' Walshaw said quickly. 'I just consider this an internal affair; sorry, nothing personal.'

Greg looked to Evans, politeness software loaded and running. Showing respect. 'May I ask why you chose me in particular for a job? Random selection is, frankly, unbelievable.'

'Haven't decided whether you are going to do a job for me, yet, boy. You'll have to prove you're what I'm looking for first. I believe you cleared up a problem for Simon White last year? Delicate, a real ball-crusher. That right?'

'I know Mr White, yes.'

'All right, don't go all starchy on me. I do business with Simon, he recommended you. Said you only work for the top man, keep your mouth shut afterwards. Right?'

'That's correct,' Greg said. 'Naturally I offer confidentiality. But in taking on corporate cases I do so only for the board or chairman. Office politics are a complication I can do without.'

'You mean I couldn't hire you?' Walshaw asked.

'Only if the chairman approved.'

'You're ex-Army?' the security chief persisted. 'Mindstar?'

'Yes.'

'So it was the Army which gave you your gland,' Evans said. 'How come you didn't sign on with a *kombinate* security division after you were demobbed, or even turn tekmerc?'

'I had other things to do, sir.'

'You could've earned a fortune.'

'Not really,' Greg said. 'The idea that gland psychics are some kind of superbreed is pure tabloid. If you want someone who can see through brick walls then I'm not your man. Glands are not an exact science. I tested out psi-positive with top marks on esp, so the Army volunteered me for an implant thinking I would develop a sixth sense that could pinpoint enemy locations, index their weapons and ammunition stocks. But the workings of the mind don't follow a straight logical course. I was one of the disappointments, along with several hundred others. People like me were one of the major factors in the decision to abandon the Mindstar programme, and that was long before the PSP obliterated the defence budget.'

'So what can you do?' Evans asked.

'Basically, I can tell if you're lying. It's a kind of super empathy, or intuition, a little mix of the two. Not much call for that on the battlefield. Bullets rarely lie.'

'Don't run yourself down, boy. Sounds like you've got the kind of thing I'm looking for. So tell me, did I enjoy my breakfast orange?'

Greg saw the gland, glistening ebony, pumping. Physically, it was a horrendously complex patchwork of neurosecretory cells; the original matrix had taken the American DARPA office over a decade to develop. An endocrine node implanted in the cortex, raiding the bloodstream for chemicals and disgorging a witches' brew of neurohormones in return.

The answer was intuitive: 'You didn't have orange for breakfast.'

Morgan Walshaw blinked, interest awakened.

Evans grunted gruff approval. 'The last quarter profits from my orbital memox-crystal furnaces have been bad. True or false?'

'They've been awful.'

'You ain't bloody kidding, boy.' The chair backed out from the table, and trundled over to a window. Gazing mournfully across the splendid lawns, the billionaire said, 'This job isn't for my benefit. I suppose you know I'm dying?'

'I guessed it was pretty serious.'

'Lymph disorder, boy, aggravated by using the old devil deal hormone to keep my skin thick and my hair growing. So much for vanity, serves me right. This *thing* I've got, very rare, so they tell me. After all, it would never do for me to die of something common.' He snorted contemptuously at his own bitterness. 'Everything will go to my granddaughter, Julia. She's the one out there in the pool; the brunette. The lovely one.'

'What about her parents? Don't they stand to inherit?'

'Ha! Call 'em parents? Because like buggery I do. If I hadn't paid off her mother she'd still be in that Midwest cult commune, smoking pot and screwing its leaders for Jesus. And that son of mine is incapable of taking on Event Horizon. Couldn't anyway, even if he wanted. Legally incompetent.

'Best detox clinics in the world have tried to straighten his kinks. Too late. He's been on syntho so long – and I'm talking decades – the dependence is unbreakable. You cold-turkey his body and the lights go out. They shoved him through the whole routine – counselling, group analysis, deprivation motivation, work therapy – it amounted to one great big zero. The only time he even knows there's an outside world is when he's tripping.' The anger rose again. 'It's fucking humiliating. I was prepared for some rebellion, a bit of antagonism between us. That's the way it always is between father and son. But him! We had nothing, no love, not even hate. It was like everything I was achieving didn't even register with him. He walked out the door on his twentieth birthday, and that was it, not another word for twenty-five years. The only reason I found out I had a grand-daughter was because that freako cult he wound up with tried to leach me for donations.

'That's why I've got to safeguard the company. For her. I'm not going to last for much longer, and she doesn't have the experience to take it on right away.'

'But surely you'll be leaving Event Horizon in the hands of trustees?' Greg asked. 'People you know can manage it properly.'

'Damn right.' There was a fierce spark of elation in Philip Evans's mind. 'Event Horizon has the potential to become a global leader in gear manufacture. While other, landbound, English companies rotted under the PSP's intervention I bought in new cyber-production equipment for my factory ships, kept my overseas research people well funded. Now I'm moving it all back home, consolidating. The company's growth potential is phenomenal; it'll create jobs, foreign exchange, build and sustain a national supply industry, stop the sink back into an agrarian economy. We can match those bloody German kombinates, and the best the Pacific Rim Market can offer – new economic superpower, my arse. I'll show 'em England isn't dead yet.'

'Sounds good. So why do you need me?'

Evans scowled. 'Sorry, I run on. Old man's disease. By the time you accumulate the resources to accomplish something worthwhile, time's up.

'The problem, boy, is my orbital operation up at Zanthus. Someone is running a spoiler against the company. They've turned the operators of my microgee furnaces up at Zanthus, thirty-seven per cent of my memox crystals are being deliberately ruined. That adds up to seven million Eurofrancs a month.'

Greg let out an involuntary whistle. He hadn't known Event Horizon was that big.

'Yeah, right,' Philip Evans said. 'I can't sustain that kind of loss for much longer. Lucky I caught it when I did—' and there was a hint of pride at the accomplishment. Still on the ball, still the *man*. 'The organizer circumvented some pretty elaborate security safeguards too. Means whoever they are they're smart and organized.'

'They're clever all right,' Walshaw conceded. He pulled out a black wood chair opposite Greg and sat down.

'And even the security division is under suspicion,' Evans said. 'Including Morgan here, which is why he's so pissed off with me.'

Greg sneaked a glance at Walshaw, meeting impenetrable urbanity. The man had not – nor ever would – sell out. Greg knew him, the type, his motivation; he'd no grand visions of his own, the perfect lieutenant. And in Event Horizon and Philip Evans he'd found an ideal liege. The old billionaire must've understood that too.

Walshaw nodded an extremely reluctant acknowledgement. 'The nature of the circumvention does imply a degree of internal complicity, certainly knowledge of the security monitor procedures was compromised.'

'He means the buggers are on the take, that's what,' Evans grumbled. 'And I want you to root 'em out for me, boy. You're about the nearest thing to independent in this brain-wrecked world. Trustworthy, as far as we can satisfy ourselves. So then: four hundred New Sterling a day, and all the expenses you can spend. How does that sound?'

'Do I have to sign the contract in blood?'

'Just don't screw me about, boy. I've spent close on twenty years fighting that shit President Armstrong and his leftie storm-troops, now he's gone I'm not going to lose by default. Event

41

Horizon is going to be my memorial. The trailblazer of England's industrial Renaissance.'

Greg felt a twinge of admiration for the old man, he was dying yet he was still making plans, dreaming. Not many could do that. 'Where do you want me to start?' he asked.

'You and I will go down to Stanstead,' Morgan Walshaw said. 'Assuming I'm trustworthy.'

'Don't be so bloody sarcastic,' Evans barked.

'Stanstead is Event Horizon's main air-freight terminal in England,' Walshaw explained, quietly amused. 'All our flights out to Listoel originate there.'

'Listoel?' Greg asked.

'That's the anchorage for my cyber-factory ships out in the Atlantic,' Philip Evans said. 'A lot of Event Horizon's domestic gear is still built out there, and it's where my spaceline, Dragon-flight, is based. Anyone going up to Zanthus starts at Listoel.'

'Calling in the management personnel and memox-furnace operators who are currently on leave won't be regarded as particularly unusual,' Walshaw said. 'Once they arrive, you can use your gland ability to determine which of them have been turned. After that, you and a small security team will go up to Zanthus and pull whoever circumvented the security monitors, along with the guilty furnace operators working up there. We'll fly up replacements from the batch you've vetted.'

'You want me to go up to Zanthus?' Greg asked. There was a sensation in his gut, as if he'd just knocked back a few brandies in rapid-fire succession.

'That's right, boy. Why, that a problem?'

'No.' Greg grinned. 'No problem at all.'

'It's not a bloody holiday,' Evans snapped. 'You get your arse up there, and you stop them, Greg. Hard and fast. I've got to have something concrete to show my backing consortium. They're due for the figures in another six weeks. I've got to have something positive for them, they'll understand a spoiler, God knows enough of the *kombinates* are trying to throttle each other rather than do an honest day's work. What they won't stand for is me dallying about whingeing instead of stomping on it.' Philip Evans subsided, resting on the powerchair's tall back. 'That just leaves this evening.'

'What's happening this evening?' Greg asked.

'I'm throwing a small dinner party – some close friends and associates, one or two glams, plus Julia's house guests. There's a couple of people I want you to screen for me. I've invited Dr Ranasfari. He's leading one of Event Horizon's research teams, a genuine genius. I've got him working on a project I consider absolutely crucial to my plans for the company's future. So you handle with care.' Evans stopped, looking as uncomfortable as Greg had yet seen him. For a moment he thought it was the illness. But the old man's mind was flush with an emotion verging on guilt. Walshaw had turned away, uninterested. Diplomatic.

'The second . . .' Philip Evans nodded vaguely at the window. 'That lad out there . . . Adrian, I think his name is. Julia seems quite taken with him. Leastways, she doesn't talk of hardly anything else. Don't get me wrong, I don't object to him, not if he makes her happy. Nothing I want more than to see her smiling, she's my world. It's just that I don't want her hurt. Now, I know you can't expect eternal commitment, not at that age, and he seems pleasant enough. But make sure she's not just another tick in his stud diary. Life's going to be tough enough for her, being my heir, she surely doesn't deserve bad-news boyfriends as well.'

4

There was a dinner jacket waiting for Greg in the guest suite after he'd finished bathing. It fitted perfectly. He put it on, feeling foolish, then went out to find his host. At least he had remembered how to do up his bow tie.

The lights throughout the majority of Wilholm's rooms were old-fashioned electric bulbs, drawing their power from solar panels clipped over the splendid Collyweston slates. He had to admit that biolums' pink-white glow wouldn't have done the classical décor justice. Evans had obviously gone to a lot of trouble recreating the old building's original glory.

The ageing billionaire chortled at the sight of Greg as he waited for his powerchair on the east wing's landing, flushed and fingering his starched collar. 'Almost respectable-looking, boy.' The powerchair stopped in front of him. Evans cocked his head, taking stock. 'I hope you know which knives to use. I can hardly pass you off as my aide if you start savaging your avocado with a soup spoon, now can I?'

Greg wasn't sure if the old man was mocking him or the marvellously doltish niceties of table etiquette, so religiously adhered to by England's upper-middle classes – what was left of them. Probably both.

'I was an officer,' Greg countered. Not that he'd graduated from Sandhurst, nothing so formal. It was what the Army had called a necessity promotion, all the Mindstar candidates were captains – some obscure intelligence division commission. A week of learning how to accept salutes, and three months' solid slog of data interpretation and correlation exercises.

'Course you were, m'boy; and a gentleman too, no doubt.'

'Well, I always took my socks off before, if that's what you mean,' Greg said.

Evans laughed approvingly. 'Wish I had you on my permanent staff. So many bloody woofter yes-men—'

The chair took off towards the main stairs at a fast walking pace. The old man looked much improved since the afternoon. Greg wondered how he'd pay for that later.

The three teenagers were heading for the stairs from the manor's west wing. Evans waited at the top for them. The taller girl bent over and gave his cheek a soft kiss, studying his face carefully. There was genuine concern written on her features.

'Now, you're not going to stay up late,' she said primly. It wasn't a question.

'No.' Evans was trying hard to make it come out grumpy, but fell miserably short. Her presence resembled a fission reaction, kindling a fierce glow of pride in his mind. 'Greg, this is Julia, that wayward grandchild I've been telling you about.'

Julia Evans nodded politely, but didn't offer her hand. Apparently her grandfather's employees didn't rate anything more than fleeting acknowledgement. In silent retaliation Greg tagged her as a standard-issue spoilt brat.

Actually, he acknowledged she was quite a nice-looking girl. Tall and slender, with a modest bust, and her fine, unfashionably long hair arranged in an attractive wavy style that complemented a pleasant oval face. She wore a slim plain silver tiara on her brow, and a small gold St Christopher dangling from a chain round her neck. He thought her choice of a strapless royal purple silk dress was sagacious; she had the kind of confident poise necessary to carry it well, and not many her age could claim the same.

The boys would look twice, sure enough. Because she was sparky in that way that all teenage girls were sparky. It was just that she hadn't developed any striking characteristics to lift her out of the ordinary. And right now that was her major problem. She was a satellite deep into an eclipse. Her primary, the girl she stood beside, was an absolutely dazzling seraph.

Her name was Katerina Cawthorp, introduced as Julia's friend from their Swiss boarding school. A true golden girl, with richly tanned satin-smooth skin, and a thick mane of honey-blonde hair which cascaded over wide, strong shoulders. Her figure was an ensemble of superbly moulded curves, accentuated by a dress of some glittering bronze fabric which hugged tight. A deliciously low-cut front displayed a great deal of firm shapely cleavage, while a high tight hem did the same for long elegant legs. Her face was foxy; bee-stung lips, pert nose, and clear Nordic-blue eyes which regarded Greg with faint condescension. He'd been staring.

Katerina must have been used to it. That sly almost-smile let the whole world know that butter would most definitely melt in her mouth.

Julia wheeled her grandfather's chair on to a small platform which ran down a set of rails at the side of the stairs.

'That father of yours, is he coming down?' Evans asked her sourly.

'Now don't you two start quarrelling tonight.'

'Probably skulking in his room getting stoned.'

She slapped his wrist, quite sharply. 'Behave. This is a party.'

Evans grunted irritably, and the platform began to slide down. Julia kept up with it, skipping lightly.

Naturally, Katerina's descent was far more dignified. She glided effortlessly, an old-style film-star making her grand entrance at a blockbuster première.

It left Greg free to talk to the boy, Adrian Marler; he didn't have to ask anything, Adrian turned out to be one of nature's gushers. He launched into conversation by telling Greg how he'd just begun to study medicine at Cambridge, hoped to make the rugby team as a winger, complained about the New Conservative government's pitifully inadequate student grant, confided that his family was comfortably off but nowhere near as rich as the Evans dynasty.

Adrian was six foot tall with surf-king muscles, short curly blond hair, chiselled cheekbones, and a roguish grin that would send young – and not so young – female hearts racing; he was also intelligent, humorous, and respectful. Greg felt a flash of envious dislike for a kind of adolescence he'd never had, dismissing it quickly.

'So how did you meet Julia?' he enquired.

'Katey introduced us,' Adrian said. 'Hey listen, no way was I going to turn down the chance to crash out at this palace for a few days, meet the great Philip Evans. Then there's gourmet food, as much booze as you want, clean sheets every day, valet service.' He leaned over and gave Greg a significant between-us-men look, before murmuring, 'And our rooms are fortuitously close together.'

'She seems a nice girl,' Greg ventured.

Adrian's eyes tracked the slow-moving, foil-wrapped backside in front of them with radar precision. 'You have no idea how truly you speak.' His mind was awhirl with hot elation.

'Are we talking about Julia or Katerina?'

Adrian broke off his admiring stare with obvious reluctance. 'Katey, of course. I mean, Julia's decent enough, despite her old man being a complete arsehole. But she couldn't possibly match up to Katey, nobody could.' He dropped his voice, taking Greg into his confidence. 'If I had the money, I'd marry Katey straight off. I know it sounds stupid, considering her age. But her parents just don't care about her. It's a scandal; if they were poor the social services would've taken her into care. But they're rich, they sit in their Austrian tax haven and treat her as a style accessory. To their set it's fashionable to have a child, the more precocious the better. That's probably why she and Julia are such closeheads. Near-identical backgrounds; both of them ignored from an early age.'

Greg suddenly experienced a pang of sympathy, prompted by his intuition. Adrian was a regular lad, one of the boys, likeable.

He deserved better than Katerina. Although he didn't know it, his infatuation was doomed to a terminal crash landing. His rugged good looks and lack of hard cash marked him down as a passing fancy. Naïvety preventing him from realizing that the teeny-vamp sex goddess whose footsteps he worshipped was going to chew him up then spit him out the second a tastier morsel caught her wandering, lascivious eye.

Still, at least it meant Greg could start the evening by giving Evans one piece of news which he wanted to hear. Though whether it was good news was debatable. To Greg's mind, Julia would be hard pushed to find a better prospect for prince consort.

Philip Evans received his guests in the manor's drawing room. Its arching windows looked out on to the immaculately mown lawns where peacocks strutted round the horticultural menagerie along the paths. Maids in black and white French-style uniforms circulated with silver trays of tall champagne glasses and fattening cheesy snacks. A string quartet played a soft melody in the background. Greg felt as if he'd time-warped into some Mayfair club, circa nineteen-thirty.

The men were all dressed in immaculately tailored dinner jackets, while the women wore long gowns of subdued colours and modest cut. It made Katerina stand out from the crowd; not that she needed sartorial assistance for that. A stunning case of overkill.

Greg saw that despite his blunt Lincolnshire-boy attitude Philip Evans made a good host. He slipped into the role easily. A lifetime immersed in PR had taught him how.

Julia stuck by his side; officially the hostess, being the senior lady of the family. The guests treated her with a formal respect not usually directed at teenagers. They must know she was the protégée, Greg realized. She accepted her due without a hint of pretension.

Greg hovered behind the pair of them, maintaining a lifeless professional smile as he was introduced as Philip Evans's new personal secretary. The old billionaire had assembled an impressive collection of top rankers for his party – a couple of New Conservative cabinet ministers, and the deputy prime minister; five ambassadors; financiers; a sprinkling of the aristocracy; and some flash showbiz types, presumably for Julia's benefit.

Lady Adelaide and Lord Justin Windsor, Princess Beatrice's children, were also mingling with the guests, two tight knots of people swirling gently round them the whole time. Greg had managed to exchange a few words with Lady Adelaide; she was in her early twenties, and as politely informal as only Royalty could be given the circumstances. He gave way to the press of social mountaineers well pleased; Eleanor would love hearing the details.

As he left, he saw Katerina moving with the tenacity of an icebreaker through the people around Lord Justin. She wriggled round an elderly matron with gymnastic agility to deliver herself in front of him, blue eyes hot with sultry promise. For one moment, watching Lord Justin's quickly hidden guilty smile, Greg allowed his cynicism to get the better of him. Could the young royal be the reason Philip Evans was unhappy about Adrian? Lord Justin was only five years older than Julia; a union between them was the kind of note an ultra-English traditionalist like Philip Evans would adore going out on. He eventually decided the thought was unworthy. Philip Evans might be devious, but he wasn't grubby.

The new arrivals seemed endless. Greg wanted to undo his iron collar, he wasn't used to it. But all he could do was smile at the blur of faces, sticking to form. The guests weren't a night-stalker crowd, he realized grimly, not the ones who cruised the shebeens searching for pickups and left-handed action. This was class, the real and the posed. Their conversation revolved around currency fluctuations, investment potential, and the latest Fernando production at the National Theatre. Nobody here would be looking for a quiet moment to slip upstairs with someone else's escort. Greg steeled himself for hours of excruciating boredom.

There was one guest for whom Julia abandoned all her

decorum, rushing up and flinging her arms round an over-loud American. 'Uncle Horace, you came!' She smiled happily as he patted her back, collecting an over-generous kiss. The man was in his late fifties, red-faced and fleshy, his smile seemingly permanent.

The name enabled Greg to place him: Horace Jepson, the channel magnate. He was the president of Globecast, a satellite broadcasting company which had multiple channel franchises in nearly every country in the world; screening everything from trash soaps and rock videos to wildlife documentaries and twenty-four-hour news coverage. The PSP had refused Globecast a licence while they were in power, although the company's Pan-Europe channels could always be picked up by Event Horizon's black-market flatscreens, complete with a dedicated English-language soundband. The PSP raged about imperialist electronic piracy; Globecast calmly referred to it as footprint overspill, and kept on beaming it down. Greg had never watched anything else in the PSP decade.

Horace Jepson gave Philip Evans a hearty greeting, while Julia clung to his side. Then she steered him adroitly away from a cluster of the celebrities who'd begun to eye him greedily, introducing him to one of the New Conservative ministers instead.

It was an interesting manoeuvre: if those manic self-advancing celebrities had sunk their varnished claws into Jepson he would've had little chance of escaping all evening. So Julia Evans wasn't quite the airhead he'd so swiftly written her off as, after all. In fact, her thoughts seemed extraordinarily well focused, fast-flowing. He couldn't ever remember encountering a mind quite like hers before.

She returned and took her grandfather's hand. They shared a sly private smile.

It was a rapport which was quickly broken when Philip Evans spotted a couple making their way towards him and muttered, 'Oh crap,' under his breath. Julia glanced up anxiously, and gave her grandfather's hand a quick, reassuring squeeze.

He studied the advancing couple with interest to see what had aroused the sudden concern and antipathy in both Julia and Philip. They were a handsome pair. She was in her mid-twenties, draped in at least half a million pounds' worth of diamond jewellery, and wearing a loose lavender gown which showed almost as much cleavage and thigh as Katerina. The man, Greg guessed, was forty; he had a dark Mediterranean complexion, and obviously worked hard to keep himself fit. Each strand of his thick raven-black hair was locked into place.

Greg's espersense sent a cold, distinctly prickly sensation dancing along his spine as they approached. Beneath those perfect shells something disquietingly unpleasant lurked.

'Philip. Wonderful party,' the man said, his accent faintly continental. 'Thanks so much for the invite.'

Philip returned the smile, although Greg knew him well enough by now to see how laboured it was without resorting to his espersense.

'Kendric, glad you could come,' he said. 'I'd like you to meet my new secretary. Greg, this is Kendric di Girolamo, my good friend and business colleague.'

Kendric smiled with reptilian snobbery. 'Ah, the English. Always so eager to do down the foreign devil. Actually, Greg, I am Philip's financial partner. Without me Event Horizon would be a fifth-rate clothing sweat-shop on some squalid North Sea trawler.'

'Don't flatter yourself,' Evans said in a tight flat voice. 'I can find twenty money men bobbing about any time I look into a sewer.'

'You see,' Kendric appealed to Greg, 'a socialist at heart. He has the true Red's loathing of bankers.'

The knuckles on Julia's hand were blanched as she gripped her grandfather's shoulder, holding back the tiger.

The sight of someone as ill as Evans being deliberately provoked was infuriating. Greg allowed the neurohormones to flood out from the gland and focused his mind on ice – hard, sharp, helium cold. A slim blade of this, needle-sharp tip resting lightly on Kendric's brow, directly above his nose. 'Don't let's spoil the party atmosphere,' he said gently.

Kendric appeared momentarily annoyed by a mere pawn interrupting his grand game.

Greg thrust his eidolon knife forwards. Penetration, root pattern of frost blossoming, congealing the brain to a blue-black rock of iron.

It felt so right, so easy. The power was there, fuelled by that kilowatt pulse of anger.

Kendric blinked in alarmed confusion, swaying as if caught by a sudden squall. The hauteur which had been swirling triumphantly across his thoughts flash-evaporated. His knees nearly buckled, he took an unsteady step backwards before he regained his balance.

Greg's own unexpected flame withered, sucked back to whatever secret recess it originated from. Its departure left a copper taste filming his suddenly arid throat. He turned to the woman. 'I don't believe we've been introduced.'

'My wife, Hermione,' Kendric said warily; and she held her gloved hand out, the jewels of her rings sparkling brightly.

Her eyes swept Greg up and down with adulterous interest. She seemed mildly disappointed when all he did was shake her long-fingered hand.

He found himself comparing her to Eleanor. Only a few years separated them, and put in a dress like that Eleanor would be equally awesome. Except Eleanor would laugh herself silly at the notion of *haute couture*, and she'd never be able to mix at this kind of party – Ashamed, he jammed that progression of thoughts to a rapid halt.

'Married, Mr Mandel?' Hermione enquired. Her voice was the audio equivalent of Katerina's dress, husky and full of forbidden promise. Now why did he keep associating those two?

'No.'

'Pity. Married men are so much more fun.'

Temptation had never beckoned so strongly before. She was

one hell of a woman, but there was something bloody creepy scratching away behind that beautiful façade.

'We will talk later,' Kendric said to Philip in a toneless voice. 'Scotland needs to be finalized. Yes?'

'Yes,' Philip conceded.

Satisfied with this minor victory he moved on to give Julia a light kiss. Hermione followed suit, then wafted away with a final airy, '*Ciao.*' But not before she winked at Greg.

Julia stood rigidly still for the embrace. Greg's espersense informed him she was squirming inside. She had good reason, there was a burst of unclean excitement in Hermione's mind as their cheeks touched.

'Who the hell are they?' Greg asked as soon as they were out of earshot.

Julia was kneeling anxiously by her grandfather's power-chair. The old man had sagged physically. His mind was grey.

She looked up at Greg with shrewdly questioning eyes. 'Thank you for making Kendric back off,' she said.

He detected her thoughts flying at lightspeed, never losing coherence. Odd. Unique, in fact.

'You have a gland,' she said after a few seconds.

Philip's low chuckle was malicious. 'Too late, Juliet, you've had your three.'

'Oh, you,' she poked him with a finger in mock-exasperation. But there was an underlying current of annoyance.

'Di Girolamo is moneyed European aristocracy,' he explained. 'And he's right about us having financial ties; although being my partner is a complete load of balls. Did you ever buy any of my gear when the PSP was in power?'

'Yeah. A flatscreen, and a microwave too, I think. Who didn't?'

'And how did you pay for 'em?'

'Fish mainly, some vegetables.'

'OK, The point is this: at the local level it was all done by barter. There was no hard cash involved. I would fly the gear in, and my spivs would distribute it, sometimes through the black market, sometimes through the Party Allocation Bureau. So far a normal company production/delivery set-up, right? But none of your fruit and veg is any use to me, I can't pay the bankers with ten tonnes of oranges. So that's where Kendric and his team of spivs comes in; he makes sure I get paid in hard currency. His spivs take the barter goods and exchange them for gold or silver or diamonds, some sort of precious commodity acceptable internationally – New Sterling was no good, it was a restricted currency under the PSP. They lift them out of the country, and Kendric converts them into Eurofrancs for me. It was a huge operation at the end, nearly two hundred thousand people; which is partly why the PSP never shut us down, you'd need a hundred new prisons to cope. Since the Second Restoration I've been busy turning my spivs into a legitimate commercial retail network – they're entitled to it, the loyalty they showed me. But now New Sterling has been opened, there's no need for Kendric's people any more, not in this country.'

'Kendric also used to make himself a tidy profit while he was arranging the exchange,' Julia put in coldly.

'I would've thought you could have arranged the exchange by yourself without any trouble,' Greg said.

'Nothing is ever simple, Greg,' Philip replied. 'Kendric's management of the exchange was part of my original arrangement with my backing consortium. I needed a hell of a lot of cash to fund Listoel, and I didn't have the necessary contacts with the broker cartels back in those days, not for something that dodgy. Kendric did. His family finance house is old and respectable, well established in the money market. And he offered me the lowest rates, a point below the usual interest charges in fact. We got on quite well back then, despite his faults he is an excellent money man. The trouble is, he's been getting a mite uppity of late, thinks he should have a say in running Event Horizon. Involve the consortium with the managerial decision process. Bollocks. I'm not having a hundred vice-presidents sticking their bloody oars in.'

'So why are you still tied in with him? You're legitimate now.'

'Scotland,' Julia said bitterly.

''Fraid so,' Philip confirmed. 'The PSP is still in power north of the border so my arrangement with Kendric is still operating up there. Our respective spivs are virtually one group now, they've worked together for so long. It'd be very difficult to disentangle the two, not worth the effort and expense, especially as the Scottish card carriers aren't going to last another twenty months.

'And of course the di Girolamo house has an eight per cent stake in Event Horizon's backing consortium. And guess who their representative on the board is.'

'I still don't get it,' Greg complained. 'Why should a legitimate banker offer an illegal operation like yours a low rate in the first place? At the very least he should've asked for the standard commercial rate. And there are enough solid ventures in the Pacific Rim Market without having to go out on a limb here.'

'It's the way he is, boy,' Philip said quietly. 'He doesn't actually need to get involved in anything at all. The family trust provides him with more money than he could ever possibly spend. But he's sharp. He sees what happens to others of his kind – they party; they ski, power glide, race cars and boats, take nine-month yachting holidays; they get loaded or stoned every night; and at age thirty-five the police are pulling them out of the marina. Half of the time it's suicide, the rest it's burnout. So instead of pursuing cheap thrills, Kendric gets his buzz by going right out on the edge. He plays the masterclass game, backing smugglers like me, leveraged buyouts, corrupting politicians, software piracy, design piracy – I bought the Sony flatscreen templates Event Horizon uses from him. It's money versus money. His ingenuity and determination are taxed to the extreme, but he can't actually get hurt. I might not like him personally, but I admit he's been mighty useful. And he's exploited that position to grab his family house a big interest in Event Horizon. Clever. I like to think I'd have done the same.'

'I'll get rid of him,' Julia whispered fiercely. Her tawny eyes were burning holes in Kendric's back as he chatted up a brace of glossy starlets.

Philip patted her hand tenderly. 'You be very careful around him, Juliet. He eats little girls like you for breakfast, both ways.'

Greg could sense her raw hostility, barely held in check by her grandfather's cautionary tones.

He sat next to Dr Ranasfari for the meal, an exercise in tedium; the man seemed to be a sense of humour-free zone. Ranasfari's doctorate was in solid-state physics, and his conversation was mostly of a professional nature; it all flew way over Greg's head. Although, curiously enough, Ranasfari loosened up most when he was talking to the ever-jovial Horace Jepson.

In the event, dogged perseverance finally enabled Greg to check him out as clean. He couldn't believe Ranasfari even knew what duplicitous meant. The Doctor had a very rarefied personality, perfectly content within the confines of his own synthetic universe. A genuine specimen of a head-in-the-clouds professor. Whatever project Philip Evans had him working on it was completely safe.

5

Wilholm's library was a long, airy room on the ground floor, its arched ceiling painted with quasi-religious murals in rich, dark reds, greens, blues, and browns. Below this unchristian pantheon, glass-fronted shelves ran the length of the walls, illuminated from within by tiny biolum strips; there were matching marble fireplaces at each end of the room, an oriel window giving a view out across the rear lawns. Three tables spaced down the centre had genuine nineteenth-century reading-lamps at each seat. The air-conditioning was set to keep it degrees cooler than the rest of the manor. It was the room Julia preferred to work in: bringing Event Horizon data into her bedroom always seemed intrusive somehow. There had to be some distinction between private and working life, especially as she had so little of the former.

She sat in a plain admiral's chair behind a polished rosewood table, wearing a hyacinth cardigan over a peach chambray button-through dress, watching interviews on a big wall-mounted flatscreen. The image was coming over the company datanet from Stanstead.

Morgan Walshaw had commandeered a whole floor in the company's airport administration block, using it to keep the furnace operators in isolation while they were processed.

He and Greg were doing the interviews in a modern office with a window wall overlooking the giant new freight hangar which Event Horizon used. Both of them sitting behind a chrome and glass desk, Morgan Walshaw in his usual suit; Greg in a red and white striped shirt with braiding down the placket, a black and white mosaic tie.

It was a tedious way to spend the day, but she persevered. A penance for her earlier misdemeanour, that and a refuge, occupying her mind so that memories of Adrian couldn't encroach in that sneakily persistent way they did whenever she had a spare moment. He'd left this morning, together with Kats, the pair of them driving off on his Vickers bike, holographic flame transfers sparkling along the chrome gear-mounting. Julia had watched them go, kicking up a cloud of dust and gravel as they zoomed off down the drive, hard rock blaring from the speakers. It looked like a lot of fun.

Now monotony and responsibility had closed in on her again. Alone in a room with a thousand leather-bound books, not one of which she would ever read. Neither would Grandpa, come to that. They were just part of the ritual of being rich. Put into warehouse storage abroad while the PSP ruled, and brought back here for glass-shelf storage. The tangibility of money. Stupid.

Greg and Morgan Walshaw were stretching in their swivel chairs as they waited for the next furnace operator to come in. Julia poured herself another cup of tea from the silver service on the table, and munched a Cadbury's orange cream from the plate of biscuits. She'd never really paid much attention to Event Horizon's security division before, it was an alien sub-culture with its own language and etiquette and violence. Too much like an elaborate lethal game, freelance tekmercs and company operatives playing against each other at the expense of their employers. One of her bodyguards, Steven, had told her that once you were in security you never came out.

She'd secretly hoped to see a bit of action, a few sparks fly, in addition to learning more about the investigation procedures Morgan Walshaw used. But the interviews Greg had been running seemed to be fairly straightforward: – Name – Sorry to interrupt your furlough, but it is urgent – We're reviewing the contamination losses of memox crystals – Do you have any idea why it should be so high? – Have you ever been approached by anyone who wanted you to act against the company? Seven or eight questions then he'd say OK and Morgan Walshaw would dismiss them. So far they hadn't uncovered anyone involved with the spoiler operation.

The impression Julia got from the screen was remoteness. Greg never smiled, never frowned, his tone was scrupulously impartial, he hardly appeared to be aware of the interviewees. She wondered what she'd feel if she was sitting there in the office with him. A tingling in her head as his espersense teased apart her emotions for examination? Her grandfather had said be couldn't read individual thoughts. Julia wasn't sure, he seemed so judgemental.

Julia sipped her tea as the next furnace operator came in. The woman was the fifteenth to be interviewed, a forty-three-year-old called Angie Kirkpatrick, wearing a khaki sports shirt and Cambridge-blue tracksuit trousers; medium height, fit-looking, self-assured – but then all of them were.

Angie Kirkpatrick sat on the other side of the desk from Greg and Morgan Walshaw, her expression of polite expectation carefully composed. Julia knew something was wrong straight away. Kirkpatrick probably wasn't aware of it, she had nothing to compare her interview to. But Julia could see Greg was sitting straighter, more attentive. Morgan Walshaw had picked up on Greg's state, too. Julia studied Kirkpatrick closely, still unable to see any evidence of culpability.

'We're investigating the high contamination level of memox crystals coming out of Zanthus,' Greg said. 'But then you guessed that, didn't you?'

'The contamination has been quite high,' Angie said.

'Wrong answer,' said Greg. 'How long have you been working the spoiler?'

'What?'

'The whole eight months?'

'I don't know—'

'Seven months?'

'Listen!'

'Six?'

'Hey, you can't just—'

'Five?'

'Start accusing me—'

Greg leaned back in his chair and smiled. Julia was very glad she wasn't receiving that smile, it was predatory.

'Five months,' said Greg, a simple statement of fact.

'This ... What is this?' Angie demanded. She was looking straight at Morgan Walshaw.

'It's word association,' Greg said. 'I say a word, and I watch to see how your mind reacts. Is there stress and guilt, or is there merely innocent confusion? It doesn't matter what your verbal answer is, your thoughts don't lie.'

Julia almost felt a pang of sympathy for the woman. Betrayed by her own soul. Greg's ability was eerie, silent, unfelt, and devastatingly accurate. A whole heritage of fear was built around people who could divine thoughts. Quite rightly, surely everyone was entitled to some core of privacy. She pulled her cardigan tighter over her shoulders.

'Stress and guilt, that's what peaked at five months,' Greg said.

'You've got a gland,' Angie said. Her defiance had gone.

'That's right.'

She flushed hard. 'I ... I hadn't got any choice. They knew. Things. About me. Christ, I don't know how they found out.'

'Just give us the details,' said Walshaw, sounding bored, or perhaps weary.

'What'll happen?' Angie asked.

To you? We probably won't prosecute, if you're being truthful about them blackmailing you. But you won't ever work in orbit again, not for anyone, we'll make quite sure of that.'

'I didn't have any choice!'

'You could've come to us, we could've set a counter trap.'

'I don't know. There's no difference between you, any of you. People like me, well, it's not fair.'

'Never is,' Walshaw muttered.

Watching Angie hunching in on herself, Julia realized the woman had already submitted, the fight had gone out of her. She was going to do exactly what Walshaw told her to. What an awesome reputation psychics had, that even their presence could sap the will like that. No wonder the PSP had been so troubled about the animosity of the Mindstar Brigade veterans.

'How did they turn you?' Greg asked.

Angie flinched when he spoke. 'Are you still looking into my mind?'

'Yes.'

She nodded reluctantly. 'OK. I was doing some uppers. Zanthus, it gets to you, you know? Four months in a dormitory can, everyone crammed together at night, recycled piss to wash with, can't taste your food. It just gets to you. It's no High Frontier dream, only sounds that way from down here. Anyway, it gets to the stage where you've really got to force yourself to turn up at Stanstead at the end of your furlough. I've got two daughters, see, they're beautiful kids, really – smart, happy. I take care of them when I'm on furlough, my ex has them when I'm up there. I hate the idea of him having them at all, but some choice, right? So seven years of this shit is too much; my eldest, she's fifteen, she's got a boyfriend, she's got exams this year. I should be there. Saying goodbye, it hurts like hell. So six months ago I've got to take something to ease the pain.'

'What about your pre-flight medical?' Walshaw asked. 'You must've known the drugs would show up.'

'Maybe I wanted it to,' Angie said. 'Deep down. You know how strict Event Horizon is about narcotics abuse. Give Philip Evans that, he wants us healthy. Others have been caught, they got transferred, they were given therapy, kept their pay grade. We get a good medical cover deal, you know? But they found me before the furlough ended.'

'Names?' Greg asked.

'Kurt Schimel. But he didn't talk with a German accent.'

'That's all?'

'No, there were a couple more with him, a man and a woman. No names.' She began to describe them.

Access Company Personnel File: Kirkpatrick, Angie. Zanthus Micro-gee Furnace Operator.

Julia stopped listening: Angie's file was unfolding in her mind. A data profile of names, dates, figures, promotions, training grades, personal biography, medical reports, biannual security reviews, her ex-husband. Her daughters were called Jennifer and Diana, there were even pictures. Ordinary, she was so ordinary. That was what struck Julia most. It was a big disappointment, she'd wanted to understand the woman, her motivations. Knowing the enemy. But now she didn't know whether to hate the she-demon who'd tried to wreck everything her grandfather had built, or pity the pathetic woman who'd screwed her own life beyond redemption.

'They offered to flush my blood system clean,' she was saying. 'There'd be no trace of the drugs left when I went for the medical. They also smoothed out my bank account so the balance wouldn't show all those cash purchases when security ran its six-month review. And I'd only have to fox the crystal furnace 'ware for a year; their money would've been enough to let me get *out* afterwards. Just me and the girls, go and live quietly somewhere. God, you don't know what kind of deal that was to me.'

'I do,' Greg said.

Angie shuddered, hugging her arms across her chest.

Greg was staring into space above her head. 'You said fox the furnace 'ware. I get some interesting implications from that. Would you elaborate on that for me, please.'

Julia returned her attention to the interview. She would never have picked up on that detail. What kind of an impression had Greg seen? She wanted to ask him: What do minds look like? Didn't think she'd ever have the courage.

'Nothing much to it,' Angie said. 'Schimel gave me a program to load into the furnace's 'ware, it adjusts the quality inspection sensor records.'

'The memox crystals weren't actually contaminated, then,' Greg said thoughtfully.

'No. That wouldn't have worked. The security monitors would trip if more than thirty-seven per cent came out bad, see? No way could we ever be allowed to go over the magic figure, that'd blow the whole gaff, right. Reconfiguring the injector mechanism each time you wanted to ruin a batch wasn't on, you'd never get a fine enough control over the output. It's not like flicking on a switch, you know. It takes time to make the blend perfect again, and the time varies. Some of those furnaces are a bitch to run. Then you've got the genuine duff batches to consider. What Schimel's program did was start with the genuine percentage of failures then forge the rest.'

Julia sat bolt upright, her tea forgotten. Frustration manifested as a surge of hot blood. She wanted to take Angie by the throat and shake the stupid tart till she rattled. Forty-eight million Eurofrancs' worth of perfectly good memox crystals deliberately dumped into the atmosphere to burn up. It was an appalling thought. Event Horizon's cash reserve reduced to incendiary molecules in the ionosphere.

Walshaw was giving her an entomologist's stare, deciding exactly how worthless she was. And it took a lot to get the coldly civil security chief riled.

Greg was shaking his head in bemusement. 'You mean you just chuck away good crystals?'

'Yes,' she whispered dully.

Walshaw opened his cybofax. 'I want the names of all the other furnace operators you know that are involved.'

'Do I have to?' she asked. 'I mean you'll find them anyway, won't you?'

'Don't piss me off any further,' Walshaw said in a tired voice. 'Names.'

Julia heard a metallic scrape behind her, and turned in the chair. The manor staff were supposed to leave her alone when she was in here. But it was her father, Dillan, who was opening the library door.

She watched the wrecked man move dazedly into the room, hating herself for the pain she felt at the sight of him. He was wearing jeans and a bright yellow sweatshirt, with elasticated plimsolls on his feet. At least he'd remembered to shave, or someone had reminded him. There were a couple of male nurses on permanent call at the manor, for when he got difficult, and when he had nightmares. He wasn't much trouble, not physically, spending most of his days in a small brick-walled garden that backed on to the kitchen wing. There was a bench by the fishpond for him when the weather was fine, and a Victorian summerhouse for when it rained. He would read poetry for hours, or tend to the densely packed flower borders, throw crumbs to the goldfish.

And that was it, she thought, holding her face into that well-practised expressionless mask. All he was capable of, reading and weeding. The nurses gave him three shots of syntho a day.

If we were poor, she thought, they'd lock us all away as crazy, the whole Evans family, all three of us, three generations. A dying man with grandiose aspirations for the future, a syntho addict, and a girl with an extra brain who can't make friends with anybody. We probably deserve it.

Dillan Evans smiled as he caught sight of his daughter. 'Julie, there you are.'

She rose smoothly from the admiral's chair, switching off the flatscreen and its images of treachery. Her father walked towards her, taking his time over each step. He was trying to hide a bunch of flowers behind his back.

She couldn't despise him, all she ever felt was a kind of bewilderment mingling with heartbreaking shame. For all his total syntho dependency, she was his one focal point on the outside world, his last grip on reality. He'd come with her to Europe, not caring about the location, not even caring about having to live in the same house as his father again, just so long as he was with her. Even the First Salvation Church had been glad to get him off their hands, and they recruited new bodies with the fervour of medieval navies.

'For you,' Dillan Evans said, and produced the flowers. They were fist-sized carnations – mauve, scarlet, and salmon pink.

Julia smelt them carefully, enjoying the fresh scent. Then she kissed him gently on the cheek. 'Thank you, Daddy. I'll put them in a vase on the table, here look, so I can see them while I'm working.'

'Oh, Julie, you shouldn't be working, not you, not when it's a bright sunny day. Don't get yourself tangled up in the old bastard's schemes. They'll leach the life out of you. Dry dusty creatures, they are. There's no life in what he pursues, Julie. Only suffering.'

'Hush,' she said, and took his hand. 'Have you had lunch yet?'

Dillan Evans blinked, concentrating hard. 'I don't remember. Oh, God, Julie, I don't remember.' His eyes began to water.

'It's all right,' she said quickly. 'It's all right, Daddy, really it is. I'm going to have my lunch in a little while. You can sit with me.'

'I can?' His smile returned.

'Yah, I'd like you to.' She held the flowers up. 'Did you grow these?'

'Yes. Yes I did, up from tiny seeds. Like you, Julie, I grew you, too. My very own snowflower. The one stem of beauty in the frozen wilderness of my life.'

She put her arm in his, and steered him towards the library door.

'I was looking for your friend,' Dillan Evans said. 'The pretty one. I had some flowers for her as well.' He began to look around, his face tragic.

'Katerina?'

'Was that her name? She had hair that shone so bright in the sun. I showed her round my garden. And we talked and talked. There's so few do that. Did you know she can charm butterflies on to her finger?'

Julia winced at the thought of Kats talking to her father. Had Adrian been there as well?

She closed the library door behind her, blocking out the worries of the present. But only so she could suffer in a different way, she thought bleakly. Typical.

'Like an angel,' her father said in a wistful tone. 'Radiant and golden.'

6

Greg had never been in an airship before. In fact the last time he'd been airborne in anything other than the ghost wing was in the Northern European Alliance's retreat from Turkey. The experience had left him with unsavoury memories of air travel.

As with all retreats it was chaos bordering on utter shambles. Only the RAF emerged with any credit, commandeering anything with wings that didn't flap in one last ballbusting effort to get the squaddies out before the fall of eternal night. Greg wound up jammed between two bloodsoaked medevac cases in a severely overloaded Antonov-74M, watching pinpoint nova flares floating serenely through the air in a desperate bid to lure the Jihad legion's Kukri missiles from the jet exhausts.

There was a universe of difference. The *Alabama Spirit* was a *Lakehurst*-class ship on the Atlantic run; a leviathan, first-class passengers had individual cabins, three lounges, their own dining room, a casino, and twenty-four-hour steward service.

He'd taken a Dornier tilt-fan shuttle up from Stanstead the previous evening, after he'd finished interviewing the furnace operators and the Zanthus managers. It had been dark when they embarked above the English channel, all he'd seen through the Dormer's cabin window was an oval of darkness blotting out the wisps of pale moonlit cloud. The airship's outer skin was one giant solar collector, providing electricity for the internal systems. Hydrogen-burning MHD generators powered a pair of large fans at the rear. He was looking forward to reaching Listoel in daylight and seeing the *Alabama Spirit* unmasked.

Morgan Walshaw had sent six security personnel along with him. Five hardliners, Bruce Parwez, Evan Hains, Jerry Masefield, Isabel Curtis, and Glen Ditchett to handle the arrests, they'd all had duty tours up at Zanthus before, knew how to handle themselves in free-fall. He'd checked them out, satisfied with what he'd found, tough, well-trained professionals. The staff lieutenant was Victor Tyo, a twenty-five-year-old Eurasian, who looked so fresh-faced he could've passed himself off as a teenager without much trouble. It was his third field assignment, first in an executive capacity, and he was determined to make it a success.

Greg watched the approach to Listoel from the gondola's Pullman observation lounge, right up at the prow. Two kilometres below the lounge's curving transparent walls the deep blue Atlantic rollers stretched away to merge with the sky at some indefinable distance. The ride was unbelievably smooth.

'Have you ever been up to Zanthus before?' he asked Victor Tyo.

'Yes, I went up last year. The company launched a new microgee module, a vaccine lab. I helped interface our security monitor programs with its supervisor gear. It's my familiarity with the monitor programs which got me assigned to the case. Part of my brief is to upgrade them.'

'That and the fact you've been cleared yourself. I'm supposed to vet the security staff out at Listoel and Zanthus, too. Until then, they're on the suspect list along with the furnace operators and managers.'

Victor Tyo shifted uncomfortably. 'That's some pretty powerful voodoo you've got there. Did you actually read my mind to clear me?'

'Relax, I can't read minds direct. I sense moods readily enough, but that's not quite good enough. For instance I can see guilt, but most people have something to be guilty about. Petty criminals are the worst for that – the bloke fiddling his lunch expenses, accepting payola. Simply because they are so petty it gnaws at them, becoming a dominant obsession.'

Victor's mind began to unwind, relieved he wasn't an open book for Greg to flick through at leisure. 'Do I have much guilt?'

'More like anxiety,' Greg reassured him. 'That's perfectly normal, pre-mission nerves. You must lead a commendably sin-less life.' He turned back to the window; the ocean below was turning green.

Most of the *Alabama Spirit*'s first-class passenger complement had been drifting into the Pullman lounge for the last few minutes. A flock of stewards descended, offering complimentary drinks to the adults, and explaining the docking procedure to the excitable children.

The sickly green tint of the water was darkening, reminding Greg of over-cooked pea soup. Even the foam of the white horses was a putrid emerald colour.

Listoel was straight ahead, a stationary flotilla of some forty-odd cyber-factory ships safely outside territorial waters, where hard-core ideological rhetoric wasn't worth hard-copying, and there were no politicians demanding kickbacks. They were big, mostly converted oil tankers by the look of them, forming a cluster twenty kilometres across, with the spaceplane runway at their centre, a concrete strip three and a half kilometres long. Approach strobes bobbed in the water, firing a convergent series of red and white pulses at the end of the concrete. Four large barges, supporting cathedral-sized hangars, were docked to the other end. Another thirteen floated near by. Greg spotted five with the Event Horizon logo, a blue concave triangle sliced with a jet-black flying V, painted on their superstructure.

Each of the cyber-factory ships was venting a torrent of coffee-coloured water from pipes at its stern. They were the outflows of the thermal-exchange generators. Every ship dangled an intake pipe right down to the ocean bed, where the water was ice cold and thick with sediment nutrients. The generators' working fluid was heated to a vapour by the ocean's warm surface water, passed through turbines, then chilled and condensed by the water from the bottom. The system would function with a temperature difference over fifteen degrees, although the efficiency increased proportionally as the difference rose.

The nutrient-rich water between the cyber-factory ships churned with activity; nearly a hundred breeder and harvester ships followed each other in endless circular progression. Fish were hatched, they gorged themselves on the rich bloom of algae, they were killed; the complete cycle of life embedded between two rusting hulls. Pirate miners were docked with some of the cyber-factories, distinguishable from ordinary cargo ships by the spiderwork crane gantries which lowered their remote grabs on to the ocean bed to collect the abundant ore nodules lying there.

Riding high above the anchorage was a squadron of tethered blimps, reminding Greg of pictures of London during World War II. He stood up at the front of the gondola in the midst of a silently fascinated crowd of children and their equally intrigued parents, watching a long probe telescoping out of the *Alabama Spirit*'s tapering nose. The increasingly frantic whine of the small directional thrust fans was penetrating the gondola as they manoeuvred the bulbous probe tip into the docking collar mounted on the rear of the stationary blimp.

They were close enough now for Greg to make out the blimp's slender monolattice tether cables. A clear flexible pipe ran up one of them, refracting rainbow shimmers along its entire length. Hydrogen electrolysed from seawater by the thermal-exchange generators would be pumped up it, refilling the *Alabama Spirit*'s MHD gas cells.

The probe shuddered into the collar, which closed about it with a loud clang, reverberating through the *Alabama Spirit*'s fuselage struts. Greg had seen those struts when he embarked, arranged in a geodesic grid, no wider than his little finger. The fibres were one of the superstrength monolattice composites extruded in microgee modules up at Zanthus or one of the other orbital industry parks. It was only after those kind of materials had been introduced that airships became a viable proposition once again.

Greg and Victor Tyo took a lift up to the *Alabama Spirit*'s flight deck, a recessed circle in the middle of the upper fuselage. The other five members of the security team were waiting for them, along with a cluster of Event Horizon personnel who were beginning their three-month duty tour at Listoel.

A handling crew were loading a matt-black environment-stasis capsule into the cargo hold of the tilt-fan standing in the centre of the flight deck. Greg could see radiation-warning emblems all over the cylinder. He knew it contained a Merlin, a small multi-sensor space probe riding a nuclear ion-drive unit, designed to prospect the asteroids. Philip Evans had been launching them at a rate of one a month for the last three years. Greg had listened to him explaining the programme at his dinner party, clearly in his element, with an audience which hung on every word.

'Investing in the future,' the old billionaire had said over after-dinner brandy. 'I'll never see a penny back from them, but young Juliet here will. I envy her generation, you know. We're poised on the brink of great times. Our technology base is finally sophisticated enough to begin the real exploitation of space. My generation missed out on that; we were hopelessly stalled by the crises at the turn of the century – the Energy Crunch, the Credit Crash, the Warming, the disaster of the PSP. They all put paid to anything but the immediate. But now things are stabilizing again, we can plan further ahead than next week, set long-range goals, the ones with real payoffs. Unlimited raw materials and energy, they're both out there waiting for her. Just think what can be achieved with such treasure. The wealth it'll create, spreading down to benefit even the humblest. Fantastic times.'

Philip Evans's corporate strategy had Event Horizon flourishing into one of the leaders in deep-space industry. And the Merlins were an important part of his preliminary preparations; prospecting the Apollo Amor asteroids for him, a class of rocks well inside the main belt and the most easily accessible from Earth. The Merlins sent back a steady stream of securely coded information on their mineral and ore content.

When the consortium of German, American, and Japanese aerospace companies finally rolled their scramjet-powered space-plane out, launch costs would take a quantum leap downwards. The single-stage launcher would open up a whole panoply of previously uneconomical operations. One of which was asteroid missions.

And with its carefully accumulated knowledge of extraterrestrial resources Event Horizon would be in the vanguard of the mining projects, so Philip Evans said. In a prime position to feed refined chemicals back to the constellations of microgee material-processing modules projected to spring up in Earth orbit.

Greg had been aware of an undercurrent of dry humour in the old man's mind as he expanded his dream, as though he was having some giant joke on his guests. But the Merlin was real enough. It was just that the whole enterprise seemed whimsical, or at best premature. There had been rumours about the space-plane, now eleven years behind schedule; some said scramjet technology just couldn't be made to work, and even if it could the cost savings would be minimal.

Greg's status earned him a seat at the front of the tilt-fan's cramped cabin, looking over the pilot's shoulder. She lifted them straight up for fifty metres then rotated the fans to horizontal and banked sharply to starboard.

He'd been right. In the light of day the *Alabama Spirit* was spectacular. A huge jet-black ellipse framed by the dreaming sky, like a hole sliced direct into intergalactic night. It was four hundred metres long, eighty deep, sixty broad. Two contra-rotating fans were spinning slowly on the tail, keeping its nose pressed firmly into the refuelling blimp.

Their descent in the tilt-fan was a long spiralling glide. Even here, where energy shortage was a totally redundant phrase, the pilot was reluctant to burn fuel. She must've been a European, Greg thought, obsessive conservation was drilled into EC citizens from birth.

They flattened out at the bottom of the glide and lined up on one of the big cyber-factory ships, swinging over the bow and pitching nose-up as the fans returned to the vertical. Greg read the name *Oscot* painted on the rusting bow in big white lettering.

The Dornier settled amidships with minimum fuss, its landing struts absorbing any jolts.

Greg tapped the pilot's shoulder. 'Smooth ride. Thanks.'

She gave him a blank look.

He shrugged and climbed out.

Sean Francis, *Oscot*'s manager, nominally captain, was waiting at the foot of the airstairs. He was tall and lean, dressed in a khaki shirt and shorts, with canvas-top sneakers, broad sunglasses covering his eyes.

Greg dredged his name up from Morgan Walshaw's briefing file. Thirty-two years old, joined Event Horizon straight out of university, some sort of engineering administration degree, fully cleared for company confidential material up to grade eleven, risen fast, unblemished reputation for competence.

He reminded Greg of Victor Tyo; the resemblance wasn't physical, but both of them had that same hard knot of urgency, polite and determined.

The security team spilled out of the tilt-fan to stand behind Greg, waiting impassively. Sean Francis looked at them with a growing frown.

'My office was told you're here to check on our spaceflight operations, yes?' Sean Francis said. 'I'm afraid I don't understand, the Sangers are a mature system. I rather doubt their flight procedures can be improved after all this time.'

Greg produced the card Walshaw had provided, which Francis promptly waved away. 'It's not your identity I'm questioning,' he said, 'merely your purpose. OK?'

'This is not the place,' Greg said quietly. 'Now would you please verify my card.'

Francis held out his cybofax, and Greg showed his card to the key. There was an almost subliminal flash of ruby light as the two swapped polarized photons.

He took his time checking the authorization before nodding sadly. 'I see. Perhaps my office would be a more suitable venue. Yes?'

The seven of them started down the length of the deck towards the superstructure, drawing curious glances from *Oscot*'s crew.

Instinct made Greg look up towards the south-west. There was a black dot expanding rapidly out of the featureless sky, losing height fast. It was a returning Sanger orbiter, curving in a long shallow arc, pitched up to profile its sable-black heatshield belly. Greg tracked its descent, working out that it would reach zero altitude right at the end of the floating runway. He held his breath.

The orbiter straightened out three hundred metres from the runway, wings levelling. It smacked down on the concrete, blue-white plumes of smoke spurting up from the undercarriage. Small rockets fired in the nose, slowing its speed.

'What if it missed?' Greg asked. The orbiters didn't have a jet engine, they couldn't go around.

'They don't,' Sean Francis said.

7

'It's impressive,' Morgan Walshaw admitted. 'One of the biggest tekmerc deals for quite some time. We estimate thirty to thirty-five of them were assembled to turn our memox-crystal furnace operators. As far as we can tell, they started last June, and they were still recruiting until November. That kind of involvement would take *kombinate*-level resources.' There was a grudging note in his voice that implied respect, or even admiration.

Julia didn't like that, the security chief was supposed to be guarding her and Grandpa, not paying compliments to their enemies. It was that bloody dividing line between the legal and illegal again, too thin, far too thin.

'So it's impressive,' Philip Evans grunted. 'So is your division's budget, Morgan. Question is: what are you doing about it?' He was sitting at the head of the table in the study with Julia and Morgan Walshaw on either side, facing each other.

Julia would've liked to voice her own criticism, but didn't quite have the nerve. Morgan Walshaw was a forbidding figure, he'd always been stern around her, as if she didn't match up to his expectations.

'My priority at the moment is to halt the spoiler,' Walshaw said. 'Thanks to Greg Mandel we've rounded up all the guilty furnace operators who were on their furlough. Unfortunately none of the Zanthus management personnel he interviewed were responsible for circumventing the security monitors, we have to conclude the culprit is up there now. Mandel should be able to find him without any trouble.'

'Told you that boy was just what we needed,' Philip Evans said.

Walshaw remained unperturbed by the implied criticism, his composure mechanical. 'Yes. We shall have to give serious consideration to employing gland psychics in security after this. The tekmercs seem to be making good use of them.'

Julia pulled a face. Her grandfather caught it and squeezed her hand softly.

'Certainly, I believe the tekmerc team who ran the spoiler used them quite extensively on this occasion,' Walshaw went on. 'We've been running some deep analysis on our furnace operators, and there is overwhelming evidence that the tekmerc team assembled a comprehensive profile on every one of them. Bank accounts, medical records, past employers' personnel files, they were all sampled by the team's hotrods. I think we'd be correct in assuming that the likely candidates were also scanned by a psychic to see if they would be susceptible in the final instance. It's very significant that not one of the furnace operators they approached ever came to us.'

'How many did they turn?' Philip Evans asked,

'So far, we've nabbed fourteen, out of a total of eighty-three on furlough. Greg Mandel and Victor Tyo are due up at Zanthus tonight. Probability suggests there are between four and six furnace operators currently in orbit who've been turned. We've done our best to make sure no news of the round-up has leaked. Not that they can run, but there is the prospect of sabotage to consider. Out of the fourteen we've already got, two had consented to kamikaze if they were cornered up at Zanthus.'

'Bloody hell!' Philip shouted. 'What kind of people do we employ? That's damn near twenty per cent of them willing to sell us out at the drop of a hat!'

'It's over now, Grandee,' Julia said in a small voice. 'Please.' She bowed her head so he wouldn't see how upset she was. It'd been a good morning for him, he'd eaten well, and he wasn't swearing like he usually did, even his colour was almost normal. But now she could see the pink spots burning on his cheeks, showing just how badly worked up he was, which wouldn't do his heart any good.

There were some days when she wanted it all to be over, this pain-drenched clinging to life. And that wish only brought more guilt. Psychics would be able to see that clearly. Perhaps Walshaw would hold off using them until afterwards. She ought to have a word with him about that.

When she looked up the security chief was staring candidly out of the window.

'All right, Juliet,' her grandfather said in a calmer voice. 'I'll be good.'

She gave him a tentative smile.

'I don't believe the crystal-furnace operatives are representative of Event Horizon personnel as a whole, nor any of the other Zanthus workers for that matter,' Walshaw said. 'Theirs is an extraordinarily high-stress situation. There is an average of three fatalities a year, a significant chance of radiation poisoning, and the psychological pressures from living in such a closed environment are way above normal. Those factors came out time and again from all the interviewees.'

'Yeah, OK,' Philip Evans said grumpily. 'I'm a no-good mill owner, exploiting his downtrodden workers. What else is new? You got any good news for me?'

'Greg Mandel should've pulled the last of the furnace operators by this time tomorrow. We'll be sending up the replacements on an afternoon flight, so from tomorrow evening the spoiler will be over. Plus, the memox crystals tagged as contaminated last week haven't been dumped yet. That's nearly two million Eurofrancs we'll recover.'

'Jesus, chucking away perfectly good crystals like a crap dump. That's a bugger, that is.' He gave Julia a forlorn smile.

Walshaw shrugged. 'Only way to do it.'

'What about the people who organized this?' Julia asked. Walshaw hadn't said anything about them, as if they didn't matter. He lived for the game, not the players, she felt sure of it.

'Difficult,' he said.

'Why?' She made it come out flat and cold, and never mind if he disapproved.

'This is what we call a finale deal. It's all cut-offs, understand? The tekmercs who made the moves, turned our people, they'd be assembled by an old pro, someone with a reputation. This leader, he's the only point of contact between the team and the backers, the ones who want Event Horizon spoiled. Now first we'd have to find one of the tekmercs. OK, maybe we could do that; they've all gone to ground right now, but a deal this size is going to leave traces, and we've got some pretty accurate descriptions. Once we get a tekmerc we extract the team leader's name.'

'How?' she blurted, cursing herself instantly. This was why she'd never probed security before. The secret horror, and fascination. Right down at the bottom of all the smart moves were people who deliberately inflicted pain on each other, who chose to do that.

'Not as bad as you might imagine,' Morgan Walshaw said placidly. 'Not these days. There are drugs, sense overload techniques, gland psychics. Greg Mandel would just read out a list of names to the tekmerc, and see which chimed a mental bell. But even if we obtain the name, it still doesn't do us any good. That team leader, he'll already have vanished off the face of the Earth. Finale, remember? He won't put this deal together for anything less than a platinum handshake. New identity, a *plastique* reworking from head to toe – hell, even a complete sex change, it's been known. You see, it's not only us he's hiding from now. His ex-employers, they know he's the only link back to them, and that I'm going to be hunting him. They want him zapped.'

'So why would he do the job in the first place?' Julia asked.

Morgan Walshaw smiled gently. 'Kudos. A finale is the top of the tree, Julia. If you've come far enough to be asked, you're good enough to survive. No tekmerc ever turns down a finale.

Take this one; for the rest of time, he's going to be the one who burnt Event Horizon for forty-eight million Eurofrancs. He beat me, he beat your grandfather. And even if I catch him, or they catch him, nobody's ever going to know. His reputation has made it clean.'

'Bugger of a world, isn't it, Juliet?'

She turned to her grandfather, surprised by his level questing stare.

'You approve,' she accused.

'No, Juliet, I don't approve. I regard tekmercs as pure vermin, dangerous and perennial. Doesn't matter how many you stomp on, there's always more. All I hope is that you've learned something from this sorry little episode. Don't ever lower your guard, Juliet, not for an instant.'

She dropped her eyes to the table. 'You will try, won't you?' she asked Walshaw.

'Yes, Julia, I'll try.'

'Me too.' She pressed her lips together in a thin determined line.

'You'll do nothing, girl,' Philip said.

'They nearly ruined us, Grandpa! Everything you've built. We've got to know who. I've got to know who. If I'm going to stand any chance, I need the name.'

'Doesn't mean you go gallivanting about chasing will-o'-the-wisps.'

'I'll do whatever I can,' Julia said with stubborn dignity. She subsided into a sulk, certain that Walshaw would be silently censuring her outburst. Well, *let* him, she thought. Anger was an improvement on boredom. If only she didn't feel so apprehensive with it.

8

The laser grid scanned slowly down Greg's body, a net of fine blue light that flowed round curves and filled hollows. He was quietly thankful he kept in trim: this kind of clinical catechism was humbling enough, suppose he'd got a beer gut?

He'd spent an hour in the Dragonflight crew centre, out on one of the spaceplane barges. An annexe of the payload facility room, composite-walled cells filled with gear-module stacks, most of them medical. The medical staff had been anxious to test him for exceptional susceptibility to motion sickness; space-adaptation syndrome, they called it.

'If you do suffer, we have drugs that can suppress it for a couple of days,' the doctor in charge had said. 'But no more than a week.'

'I'll be up there a day at the most,' Greg told him. He was confident enough about that. The interviews at Stanstead had gone well. After Angie Kirkpatrick had cracked it'd been a simple matter of cross-referencing names.

The laser grid sank to his feet, then shut off. Greg stepped out of the tailor booth, and a smiling Bruce Parwez handed him his clothes. A long-faced man with bright black eyes. Dark hair cut close, just beginning to recede from the temples. His broad-shoul-dered build was a give-away, marking him down as a hardliner.

'Your flightsuit will be ready this afternoon,' the technician behind the booth's console said, not even looking up.

Greg thanked him and left, glad to be free of the ordeal.

Sean Francis was waiting for them outside. 'The medics have given you a green light,' he said. 'But I don't think we've ever sent up anyone with so little free-fall training before.' Francis had been markedly relieved when Greg had cleared his ship's modest security team, taking it upon himself to see him through his pre-flight procedures. He had been grateful for the assistance, but found the man irritating after a while. He supposed it was culture clash. In age they were contemporaries. But after that, there was nothing. Francis was a dedicated straight arrow, high-achiever. It made Greg pause for what might've been.

'I've got several hundred hours' microlight flight time,' Greg said.

'That'll have to do then, yes?'

'We'll take care of you,' Bruce Parwez said. 'Just move slowly and you'll be all right.'

'You had many tours up at Zanthus?' Greg asked.

'I've logged sixteen months now.'

'Is there ever much trouble up there?'

'Tempers get a bit frayed. Bound to happen in those conditions. Mostly we just separate people and keep them apart until they cool off. There's no real violence, which is just as well. We're only allowed stunsticks, no projectile or beam weapons, they'd punch clean through the can's skin.'

They walked along a corridor made of the same off-white composite as the crew centre, bright biolums glaring, rectangular cable channels along both walls. Then they were out into a sealed glass-fronted gallery running the length of the hangar's high bay, half-way up the wall.

Greg looked down at the Sanger booster stage being flight-prepped below. It was a sleek twin-fin delta-wing craft, eighty-four metres long with a forty-one-metre wingspan. The fuselage skin was a metalloceramic composite, an all-over blue-grey except for the big scarlet dragon escutcheons on the wings. Power came from a pair of hydrogen-fuelled turbo-expander-ramjets which accelerated it up to Mach six for staging. Greg had only seen the spaceplane on the channels before; up close it was a monster, an amalgamation of streamlined beauty and naked energy. Fantastic.

'How many Sangers does Dragonflight operate?' Greg enquired as the three of them moved down the gallery to see the orbiter stage being prepped in its big clean room behind the high bay.

'Four booster stages, and seven orbiters,' Francis said. 'And they're working at full stretch right now. The old man has ordered another booster and two more orbiters from MBB, they ought to arrive before the end of the year. Which will be a big help. Strictly speaking, we can't afford to take an orbiter out of the commercial schedules for a Merlin launch, although I appreciate his reasoning behind the exploration programme. I just regard it as somewhat quixotic, that's all. Still, it's his money, yes?'

The orbiter, which rode the booster piggyback until staging, was a smaller, blunter version of its big brother; thirty-five metres long, rocket-powered, and capable of lifting four and a half tonnes into orbit, along with ten passengers.

Clean-room technicians dressed in baggy white smocks were riding mobile platforms round the open upper-fuselage doors. The Merlin had been removed from its environment-stasis capsule overnight, now it was being lowered millimetre by millimetre into the orbiter's payload bay.

The probe was surprisingly compact; cylindrical, a metre and a half wide, four long. Its front quarter housed the sensor clusters, their extendable booms retracted for launch; two communication dishes were folded back alongside, like membranous golden wings. The propulsion section was made up of three subdivisions; a large cadmium tank, the isotope power source, shielded by a thick carbon shell, and six ion thrusters at the rear. It was all wrapped in a crinkly silver-white thermal protection blanket.

Greg let his gland start its secretion again, beginning to get a feedback from the technicians' emotional clamour. It was the first time he'd ever encountered the space industry. These people were devoted. It went far beyond job satisfaction. They shared an enormous sense of pride, it was bloody close to being a religious kick.

The Merlin had finally settled on its cradle inside the orbiter's payload bay. As the overhead hoist withdrew, the mobile platforms converged, allowing the huddles of white-suited technicians to begin the interface procedure. The pallet which would deploy the spacecraft in orbit was primed, attachment struts clamped to load points, power and datalink umbilicals plugged in. Monitor consoles were hive-cores of intense activity.

Greg nodded down at the little robot probe and its posse of devotees. 'What happens next?'

'We mate the orbiter to the top of the booster. After that the barge will dock with the airstrip. Your launch window opens at half-past eight, lasting six minutes.'

The payload bay doors hinged shut, bringing Greg one step closer to Zanthus. And it still didn't seem real.

*

From *Oscot*'s deck the western horizon was a pastel-pink wash flecked with gold; the east a gash into infinity, not black, but dark, insubstantial, defying resolution, a chasm you could fall down for ever. Greg watched the crescent of darkness expanding as the Atlantic rolled deeper into the penumbra; occlusion slipping over the sky, giving birth to the stars. There was no air movement at all, dusk bringing its own brand of stasis. The world holding its breath as it slid across the gap between its two states.

Greg was wearing a baggy coverall over his new flightsuit. The coppery coloured garment fitted him *perfectly*, a one-piece of some glossy silk-smooth fabric, knees and elbows heavily padded. It had a multitude of pockets, all with velcro tags; small gear modules adhered to velcro strips on his chest – atmosphere pressure/composition sensor, medical monitor, Geiger counter, communicator set. He'd even been given a new company cybofax, capable of interfacing with Zanthus's 'ware, which was in the big pocket at the side of his leg. There was also a lightweight helmet, which he felt too self-conscious to put on before getting into the Sanger.

The first real stirrings of excitement rose as he led the security team towards the waiting tilt-fan at the prow, the realization that he was actually going into space finally gripping. *Oscot*'s deck was a bustle of tautly controlled activity. The ever-present grumble of the thermal generators' coolant water was being complemented by the lighter braying of mobile service units. Five Lockheed YC-55 Prowlers were already on the deck. They were ex-Canadian Air Force stealth troop/cargo transports. Their shape was a cousin of the original B2 bomber, a stumpy, swept bat-wing, with an ellipsoid lifting-body fuselage; the entire surface had a radar-nullifying matt-black coating. There were no roundels, not even serial numbers. True smugglers' craft. Greg watched as the sixth rose silently up out of its day-time sanctuary, an old oil tank converted into a split-level hangar. The big elevator platform halted at deck level with dull metallic clangs which rumbled away into the gloaming. The stealth transporters seemed to draw a thick veil of cloying shadow around themselves, eerily other-worldly.

Sean Francis caught Greg staring. 'Neat machines. Yes?'

'I didn't know you still used them,' Greg said.

'Sure. Their avionics are a bit outdated now, but they're more than adequate to infiltrate Scottish airspace. That's our main target, their PSP is pretty shaky right now. It'll only take a small push and they'll fall.'

Greg watched large pallets of domestic gear systems being loaded through the Prowlers' rear cargo doors. 'You build all that stuff here?'

'Yes. It's a pretty broad range – crystal players, home terminals, microwaves, fridges, bootleg memox albums – that kind of thing. Our sister ship, *Parnell*, churns out more of the same, along with a whole host of specialist chemicals for our microgee modules up at Zanthus.'

'So Event Horizon only has the two cyber-factory ships left out here now?' Greg asked.

'That's right. There used to be nine of us out here a couple of years back, but the rest have left now. They're docked in the Wash outside Peterborough. Their cyber-systems are being stripped out and reinstalled in factories on land. All part of the Event Horizon legitimization policy. They were all gear factories, except for *Kenton* and *Costellow*, those two used to specialize in producing the actual cyber-systems themselves. Real top of the range stuff; all our own designs, too. The old man kept research teams going ashore in Austria, they provided us with the templates; good enough to match any of the Pacific Rim gear. Bloody clever that.'

'Oh?'

'Don't you see? Philip Evans has built up a capability to expand the company at an exponential rate. The cyber-systems are *that* sophisticated. All he needs is raw material, and financial backing. The factories will multiply like amoebas, yes?'

'You sound like you're happy with Event Horizon.'

'Christ, I mean totally. Philip Evans is a genius. Event Horizon has so much potential, you know? A real crest-rider. And I've done my penance out here, ten years' bloody hard graft. When *Oscot* docks I'm going to be in line for a divisional manager's slot.'

*

The integrated Sanger was sitting at the end of the runway, white vapour steaming gently out of vent points on both orbiter and booster, glowing pink in the fast-fading light. Greg's intuition made itself felt as he walked down the gantry arm towards the orbiter's hatch. It wasn't much, a ghost's beckoning finger, distracting rather than alarming.

For a moment he was worried that it might be the orbiter. That'd happened before, a Mi-24 Hind G in Turkey which was going to take him and his squad on a snatch mission behind the legion lines, he'd balked as he was climbing in. It was a mindscent, the chopper smelt wrong. The Russian pilot had bitched like hell until a maintenance sergeant had noticed the gearbox temperature sensor was out. When they broke the unit open, it turned out the main transmission bearings were running so hot they'd melted the sensor.

But this touch of uncertainty was different, there was no intimation of physical danger. He knew that feeling, clear and strong, experiencing it time and again in Turkey.

He hesitated, getting an enquiring glance from Sean Francis.

'We've only had eight fatalities in twelve years of operations,' the *Oscot*'s captain said helpfully.

'It's not the spaceplane,' Greg answered. Precisely how much his intuition was gland-derived was debatable, but when he did get a hunch this strong it usually squared out in the end. Even before he'd received the gland, Greg had believed in intuition. Every squaddie did to some degree, right back to Caesar's footsoldiers. And now he had the stubborn rationale of neuro-hormones to back the belief, giving it near-total credibility.

The rest of the security team were watching him. He gave them a weak grin and began walking again.

The orbiter's circular hatch was a metre wide, with a complicated-looking locking system around the rim. Bright orange rescue instructions were painted on to the fuselage all around it. Greg shrugged out of his coverall and put his helmet on before he was helped through by the launch crew.

It was cramped inside, but he was expecting that, low ceiling, slightly curving walls, two biolum strips turned down to a glimmer. Another circular hatch in the centre of the rear bulk-head opened into the docking airlock.

'You the first-timer?' asked the pilot. He was twisted round in his seat, a retinal interface disk stuck over one eye, like a silver monocle. The name patch on his flightsuit said Jeff Graham.

'Yes,' Greg said as he sat in the seat directly behind the pilot. Puffy cushioning slithered under his buttocks like thick jelly.

'OK, only one thing to remember. That's your vomit lolly.' Jeff Graham pointed to a flexible ribbed tube clipped to the forward bulkhead in front of Greg. Its nozzle was a couple of centimetres wide, a detachable plastic cylinder with REPLACE AFTER USE embossed in black. 'You even feel a wet burp coming on, then you suck on that. Got it? The pump comes on automatically.'

'Thank you.'

The rest of the security team were strapping themselves in; they were the only ones in the cabin. Greg fastened his own straps.

Jeff Graham returned his attention to the horseshoe-shaped flight console. The hatch swung shut, making insect-clicking noises as the seal engaged.

'Is there a countdown?' Greg asked Isabel Curtis who was sitting across the aisle.

She gave him a brief acknowledging smile. A wiry, attractive thirty-year-old woman with bobbed blonde hair. He could make out the mottled pink flesh of an old scar, beginning below her right ear and disappearing under the collar of her blue flightsuit, 'No. You want to hear flight control, it's channel four. Give you some idea.'

Greg peered down at his communicator set, fathoming its unfamiliar controls, and switched it to channel four. The voices murmuring in the headset were professionally bland, reassuringly so.

He followed the procedure: gantry-arm retracting, the switch to internal power, umbilicals disconnecting, fuel-pressure building, APU ignition. Half-remembered phrases from current-affairs programmes.

The take-off run was a steady climb of acceleration, turbo-expander ramjets felt rather than heard, an uncomfortable juddering in his sternum. The build through the Mach numbers, night sky devoid of reference points, floor tilted up at an easy angle.

'Go for staging,' flight control said.

The orbiter rockets lit with a low roar, vibration blurred

Greg's vision. There was a hint of white light around the edges of the windscreen. Acceleration jumped up, pushing him further down into the cushioning. The stars grew brighter, sharper.

*

The Merlin was deployed a hundred and thirty minutes after take-off, on the second orbit. The Sanger was five-hundred-and-fifty kilometres above Mexico. Greg had spent the whole time staring out of the windscreen, mesmerized by the globe below, the dazzle of daylit oceans, sprinkle of light from Europe's night-time cities, green and brown land that seemed to be in pristine condition, the muddy stain in the sea which marred every coastline. There were none of the physical symptoms he'd been told to look out for, just the strangeness of arms that waved about like seaweed; a whirling sensation, like a fairground ride, if he turned his head too fast.

A small screen on Jeff Graham's console showed the Sanger's payload doors hinging open. The little probe nosed out of its cradle, umbilical lines winding back on to their spools, loose ends flapping about. It seemed to hover above the Sanger as its communication dishes unfolded.

'We stick with it until Cambridge finishes the systems check,' Jeff Graham told his passengers. 'Never know, we might wind up taking it back.'

But the babbling background voices confirmed the Merlin's integrity somewhere over the Mediterranean, and Jeff Graham fired the orbital manoeuvring rockets, raising the Sanger's orbit. The last Greg saw of the Merlin was a dwindling grey outline over pale moonwashed water.

*

They caught up with Zanthus over Fiji, an orbit ten kilometres lower, closing fast. The terminator was a brilliant blue and white crescent six-hundred kilometres below, expanding rapidly as they raced towards the dawn.

Zanthus rose out of the penumbra into direct sunlight. Greg

saw a globular cluster of diamonds materialize out of nowhere. Occasional silent lightning flares stabbed out from it as the sun bounced off flat silvered surfaces.

'That's something, isn't it?' Jeff Graham asked.

'No messing,' Greg said hoarsely. It was the biggest of the eight space-industry parks in Earth orbit.

The sun lifted above the Pacific, shining straight into the Sanger's cabin. Electrochromic filters cut in, turning down the glare.

Greg watched in silent respect as the Sanger slowly slid underneath Zanthus. Jeff Graham began to fire the Sanger's orbital manoeuvring rockets, raising altitude, their trajectory a slow arc up to the space industry park which would end in synchronized orbits.

Zanthus began to resolve, individual light-points growing, assuming definite silhouettes. The largest was the dormitory, right at the heart. Ten cans, habitation cylinders fifty metres long, eight wide, locked together at one end of a five-hundred-metre boom; at the other end a vast array of solar panels tracked the sun. The whole arrangement was gravity-gradient stabilized, the cans pointing permanently Earthwards.

Floating around the dormitory were the microgee modules, one hundred and fifty-six materials-processing factories arranged in five concentric spheres. The formation was a loose one, a shoal of strange geometric insects guarding their metallic queen. There was no standardization to the modules; they ranged from small boxy vapour-deposition mesh-moulds brought up by the Sangers up to the fifty-metre-long, two-hundred-tonne cylinders launched by Energia-5. All of them flaunted a collection of solar panels, thermal-dump radiators, and communication dishes, and some had large collector mirrors, silver flowers faithfully following the sun. Red and green navigation lights twinkled from every surface. Abstruse company logos bloomed across thermal blankets, as if a fastidious graffiti artist had been let loose; Greg hadn't known so many different companies used Zanthus.

Three assembly platforms hung on the outer edge of the

cluster, rectangles of cross truss-beams, with geostationary antenna farms taking shape below long spidery robot-arms. Greg saw the Globecast logo on the side of one gossamer dish.

Personnel commuters, manipulator pods, and cargo tugs wove around the modules, slow-gliding three-dimensional streams that curled and twisted round each other, white and orange strobes pulsing, marking out their progress. There were spaceplanes moving in the traffic flows, rendezvousing with the five servicing docks, big triple-keel structures that acted as fuel depots, maintenance stations, and cargo-storage centres. The spaceplanes unloaded their pods of raw materials, receiving the finished products from the microgee modules in exchange. Greg counted nine Sangers attached to one dock, staggered by how much their cargos would be worth. Philip Evans had mentioned how much Zanthus's daily output came to, but the figures hadn't registered at the time, silly money.

Greg watched Zanthus expand around them as Jeff Graham eased the Sanger into one of the traffic lines. An errant image of his gland discharging milky fluids. Neurohormones chased around his brain, and he deliberately focused inwards, on himself, letting his mind wander where it would. It was a different state from the one he used to tease apart the strands of other people's emotions. Introspective. He was isolated from the security team's thoughts, alone and strangely serene.

If that peak of intuition he'd experienced hadn't concerned the Sanger, then, he reasoned, Zanthus itself must be the cause. He reached right down to the bottom of his mind, and found the sense of wrongness again. It was too small, too flimsy to represent any danger, but it remained. Obstinate, and ultimately unyielding.

Frustrated, he let it go. Something wrong, but not life-threatening. The situation irked him. He knew he must be overlooking something, some part of the spoiler that wasn't what it seemed. Yet the operation was so clear-cut.

As if shamed by its failure, his gland dried up.

The Sanger was creeping up to the dormitory, its big cans

dominating the view through the windscreen. Event Horizon used three of them for its hundred-and-twenty-strong workforce, a third of Zanthus's total population.

Greg saw a Swearingen commuter back away from one of the Event Horizon cans, a windowless cylinder with spherical tanks strapped around both ends. Tiny stabs of white fire flickered from its thruster clusters.

Jeff Graham rolled the Sanger with a drumfire burst from the RCS thrusters. A huge Event Horizon logo slid past the windscreen; the peak of the flying V was missing, patched over with a rough square of hoary thermal foam. The RCS was firing almost continually. A screen on the flight console showed an image of the payload bay, with the airlock tube extended. A matching tube jutted out of the dormitory can, the two barely half a metre apart.

Contact was a small tremble, the whirring of electrohydrostatic actuators clamping the two airlock tubes together.

Jerry Masefield released his belt, and drifted up out of his seat, using the ceiling handholds to crawl down to the rear bulkhead. Greg pressed his belt's release, and cautiously pushed down with his palms. Victor Tyo and Isabel Curtis watched closely. He grinned at them and grasped one of the ceiling handholds. His legs developed a momentum all of their own, pulling his torso along until he was lying flat against the ceiling.

Stomach muscles were the key, Greg decided, keep the body straight and rely on his arms to pull him about. He hauled himself towards the rear bulkhead, remembering to take inertia into account as he stopped.

There was a ripple of applause. The rest of the team were swimming out of their seats. Jerry Masefield had opened the airlock hatch and disappeared inside. Greg swung slowly round the rim and followed him into the can.

*

Greg couldn't quite figure out the section of the dormitory can he'd emerged into, a tunnel with a hexagonal cross-section, three and a half metres wide, bright biolum strips every five metres, hoops protruding everywhere. Logically, it ought to have been a connecting corridor, except it was full of people. They lingered near the walls, aligned with their feet towards him, a foot or hand hooked casually round the hoops, all of them wearing flightsuits and helmets. A large proportion were eating; their food resembled pizza sandwiches, the same pale spongy dough, tacky fillings. No crumbs, Greg realized, and no need for plates and cutlery. Twenty metres away, four exercise bikes were fixed to the walls, riders pedalling away furiously. There was a sign opposite the airlock, an old London Underground station strip: Piccadilly Circus.

It was the noise that got to him first. Conversations were shouted, air-conditioning was a steady buzz, cybofax alarm bleepers were going off continuously, the PA kept up a steady stream of directions. Then there was the air – warm, damp and stale. He began to appreciate Angie Kirkpatrick's point of view.

The dormitory commander, Lewis Pelham, and Event Horizon's Zanthus security captain, Don Howarth, were waiting for him. Lewis Pelham didn't attempt to shake hands, holding on firmly to one of the hoops as the rest of the security team boiled out of the airlock. 'My orders are to afford you full cooperation,' he said.

He had that same flat professionalism as Victor Tyo and Sean Francis, Greg noted. Did Philip Evans have a clone vat churning them out? 'Somewhere private,' he suggested, raising his voice above the din.

Pelham smiled, big lips peeling back, a round face. 'Sure.'

'It's shift change,' Howarth said. 'Not like this all the time, don't worry.' His face was fluid-filled, too, a ruddy complexion.

They slapped the hoops, moving off up the tunnel, skimming along effortlessly. Greg climbed after them doggedly, one hoop at a time. A few cheers and jeers pursuing his progress.

'Five days,' Howarth said, 'and you'll be outflying a hummingbird.' He was waiting by an open hatch. 'Through here.'

It was a toroidal compartment, wrapped round the central

tunnel. A space station as Greg understood it, consoles with flatscreens and cubes flashing graphics and data columns, bulky machinery bolted on to the walls, lockers with transparent doors. Five beds were staggered round what Greg thought of as the floor, assuming the entrance hatch was in the ceiling. Lewis Pelham had orientated himself the same way as Greg, holding the edge of a bed to maintain his position. The security team followed suit as they came in.

'This is the sick bay,' Pelham said. 'Nobody in today. Will it do?'

'Do you have a brig?' Greg asked.

Pelham and Howarth exchanged a glance. 'We can clear the suit-storage cabin if it's really urgent,' said the security captain.

'Good enough.' His gland began its secretions. 'Close the hatch, Bruce,' he said.

Bruce Parwez elevated himself, and spun the lock handle.

Lewis Pelham regarded Greg without humour.

Greg closed his eyes as the compartment became insubstantial. Minds crept out of the shadow veils bordering his perception, a swarm of pale translucent pearls, compositional emotions woven tautly into penumbra nuclei. He focused on the two strangers before him. 'Now, to start with, do either of you know anything about the excessive memox-crystal contamination?'

9

Julia flung herself at the problem as she took her horse Tobias on their morning ride. There was a strong sense of urgency pushing her to find a solution now, almost one of despair. Greg Mandel had located the person who'd circumvented the security monitors, and the five guilty memox-furnace operators up at Zanthus. The replacement operators were flying up today, their Sanger bringing the security team and the prisoners down. It would be over soon, congratulations all round, and a small security office left intact to track down one of the tekmercs. A vague hope, even less of finding the team leader and through him the backers.

Julia didn't even bother to open her eyes in the saddle. Tobias knew their route, down the edge of the manor's rear garden, past the spinney at the end of the trout lake, and into the meadows beyond. The horse's lumbering rhythm was soothing, rocking her gently back and forth on his back.

Normally she enjoyed Wilholm's grounds. The landscape crew hadn't been given much time after the communal farmers moved out, but they'd managed to recreate quite a reasonable approximation of a traditional English country-house garden. The flat lawns were clipped low, showing broad cricket-pitch stripes, young staked trees poked up at regular intervals, moated with colourful begonia borders. There was a citrus grove in the old walled orchard where apples and pears used to grow. Long winding rose-covered walks. Ancient-seeming statues.

Even her grandfather had been impressed. 'The plants aren't the same, of course,' he'd told her on their first inspection. He'd been in fine form that day, she remembered, genial and outgoing. It was a day or two after they'd moved in, a small treasured hiatus before the illness really took hold. He never spoke to anyone else as he did to her, never opened himself. 'You wouldn't find any of these in Victorian gardens, not outside the conservatories. That was the zenith of the art, Juliet. But it's a damn good copy for all that, I can almost believe I'm back in my youth. I wish you'd seen England as it was, girl. We all said we hated it, the wet and the cold. Pure bollocks. You could no more hate the country than you could your own mother. Weather made Englishmen.'

The way he painted the land before the Warming had made her envious of his memories. Try as she might she just couldn't visualize Wilholm under a metre of snow.

But he seemed reasonably content with the facsimile. And he always had the roses and honeysuckle, immortal.

Now she ignored both varieties of the fragrant flowering plants while whirlpools of data rotated lazily in the open-ended logic matrix her augmented mind had assembled.

It was a simulacrum of Event Horizon's Zanthus operations, a vast web of data channels incorporating every activity, programmed to review the entire previous twelve months, the first three giving her a baseline for comparison. Byte packages slid smoothly along the matrix channels, interacting at the nodes, dividing, recombining.

The convoluted phantasm reminded her of a brass clock she'd seen in London once, sitting on a pedestal in the window of a Fulham Road antique shop. A real clock in a glass dome, every working part visible. She'd stood for ten minutes watching the little cogs clicking round, superbly balanced ratchet arms rocking fluidly, fascinated by the delicate intricacy. Then the minute hand had reached the hour, and it began to make twanging sounds, like a broken spring uncoiling; cogs on the outside of the mechanism shot out on telescoping axles gyrating wildly. The whole thing had looked like it was exploding. Julia had clapped her hands and laughed delightedly as it folded itself back together, ready for the quarter-hour strike. There was that same elegance and effortless precision in the matrix function.

She needed the knowledge it would produce. The fact that someone could wound Event Horizon so badly had frightened her more than she liked to acknowledge. It went deeper than mere corporate damage; what little control she had over her life was being manipulated, cut away. Her future was being decided right now by how well other people could defend her and Grandpa from unseen enemies. Fighting shadows.

It was the claustrophobic sense of not being able to do anything which was the worst. If she just *knew*.

The simulacrum was intended to give her some part in the struggle, to make the reliance less than absolute. She was going to start at the beginning, the furnaces, then work right back through the company, cross-reference every connection, examine every link, however tenuous. Somewhere, in all that hellishly convoluted maze of data, there would be anomalies, a mistake, a clue to the origin of the spoiler. Nobody was perfect enough to cover their tracks entirely. She'd find it. Data was her medium, a universe where she reigned. Processing power cost nothing, there was only time challenging her now.

New channels began to branch from the bottom of the matrix; how the microgee products were used, sales, maintenance, personnel, finance arrangements, tie-ins with other companies. The Zanthus matrix became the tip of a rapidly growing pyramid.

Queries began to surface.

A memox-furnace operator who'd left suddenly around the time the spoiler started. Julia plugged into Event Horizon's datanet, squirting a tracer program into the company's data cores. The woman had been four months pregnant, skipped her contraceptive in orbit. Doctors were worried about the baby's bone structure, it'd spent two months developing in free fall.

Faulty ionizer grids in the memox furnaces three months ago

had slowed production. But the batch had affected other companies as well, Boeing Marietta had paid compensation.

There was a small but regular fluctuation in monolattice filament output, starting nine months ago. A three per cent shortfall every month, and always in one batch. According to production records the filament extrusion ratio was incorrect, each time.

Julia cross-referenced it with the memox data. It fitted like a jigsaw. Whenever the monolattice filament output dipped, the memox crystal output rose to compensate, maintaining total production losses at a level thirteen point two per cent.

She'd found it. Though what the hell it was, she hadn't got a clue.

End HighSteal#Two. Her processor nodes sucked the data mirage back into nothingness. There was a brief impression of free fall, dropping back into the world of primary sensations. The clammy late March heat, blouse sticking to her back, tight sweaty Levis, smell of horse breath, birds trilling, red pressure on her eyelids.

Julia blinked, focusing slowly. A cloud of midges were orbiting the brim of her tatty boater.

She was in what she called the crater field. Two acres of small steep-sided hummocks and hollows, like the earth had been bombed or something. Buttercups smothered the rich emerald-coloured grass all across the slopes.

A twitch on Tobias's reins, and he plodded towards the derelict tea plantation.

The communal farmers had tried to grow it on a PSP grant. Tea was fetching a good price after the Sri Lankan famine reduced the global harvest by a third, and England's new climate provided near-ideal conditions for cultivation. But these were gene-tailored trees, and some nameless State lab had screwed up the DNA modification. The shoots were fast-growing all right, but the leaves ruptured into bulbous cherry blisters before they were ripe enough for picking. The plantation had gone the way of most PSP initiatives, abandoned and left to rot.

Julia dismounted, letting Tobias nuzzle round in the clover.

The shire horse was becoming unfortunately flatulent in his old age. Poor dear.

He was another legacy of the communal farm, too old for plough work any more. The labourers had left him behind for Philip Evans to knacker, a trifling expense for a multi-billionaire.

Julia had found him alone in the stables as she explored Wilholm the day they moved in. She'd fallen for the great shaggy animal at first sight. He was woefully thin, his coat caked in mud, covered in sores from the plough harness. And he'd looked at her so mournfully, as if he knew what the future held. That had been the last time anyone at Wilholm, including Grandpa, had dared to mention the knackers. She refused to ride anything else, and ignored the snickers and winks of the staff when they saw her on the back of the huge plodding beast.

'You'll have to lose that sentiment of yours, girl,' Philip Evans had scolded. 'Can't run Event Horizon on sentiment.'

Except she knew damn well he would have done the same thing.

The tea trees had been laid out in unerringly straight rows. Nearly a third of them had died, but the remainder, left un-tended, had spread wildly, swamping the gaps, rising up to merge overhead.

Julia left Tobias behind, walking a little way down one of the long tunnels of black branches. Her trainers crushed the crisp dead leaves littering the ground, making sharp popping sounds. For one moment she almost believed they heralded the long lost autumn, an end to England's eternal Indian summer, when frost would fall and pull down white-fringed leaves. She missed the snow. It had been such a long time since a flake had fallen on her outstretched palm. In Switzerland even the Alps had occasionally been denuded of their sparkling white caps.

She sat with her back to the smooth bole of one of the living trees. The temperature had dropped appreciably in the orange-hued shade. She fanned her face with the boater and pulled out her cybofax.

When Greg's face formed on the little screen it didn't match her memory of him. Free fall had swollen his cheeks, his eyes seemed enlarged, but even through the slightly distorted features he looked dispirited. Something she would never have imagined. She'd been a little bit afraid of him the other night. Physically he wasn't exceptionally big, the same height as Adrian, but there'd been an impression of strength; the way he moved, clean and unhurried, knowing nothing would be in his way. And he'd never smiled, not meaning it anyway. Like he was only play-acting civilized. He'd seemed a very cold fish, hard. Which, on reflection, was an interesting kind of challenge. What would make him take notice of someone, respond with kindness? And if he did, how safe that person would feel with such a guardian angel.

'Miss Evans,' he said, expectant.

Julia wedged the cybofax into a fork on the gnarled branch in front of her, and put her boater back on. 'Julia, please.'

'Julia. What can I do for you?'

'I called about the spoiler operation.'

'You can tell your grandfather I've got all the guilty furnace operators under custody, and the person who destreamed the microgee module squirts.'

Tell Grandpa, indeed. Like she was some sort of second-rate office messenger. 'Oh, yah. Is Norman Knowles under sedation yet? Mr Tyo's report said he put up quite a struggle.'

'How the bloody hell did you know that?'

'My executive code gives me access to all the security division communications.' She regretted saying it instantly, flinching inwardly at how pompous she must've sounded.

'Oh. Well anyway, Knowles isn't going to be any more trouble. It's finished now, we're due down in another six hours.'

'It isn't finished, Greg.'

He frowned, inviting explanation.

She began to reel off her research findings, praying he wouldn't think she was talking down to him. The girls at school always said she talked as though she was delivering a lecture. But he listened intently, not interrupting like most people.

'You discovered this yourself?' he asked when she'd finished, and there was definitely a tone of respect in his voice.

'Yah. The data was all there, it's just a question of running the right search program.' Julia knew her cheeks would be red, but didn't care.

'How much is the monolattice filament worth?' he asked.

'That's what doesn't make sense,' she admitted. 'The total loss is only nine hundred thousand Eurofrancs.'

'And that bothers you?'

'Yah! It's ridiculous. Why go to all that trouble? The memox spoiler works perfectly, there's no need to add the monolattice filament to it.'

Greg didn't exactly smile, but she could sense his tension easing. 'Tell you,' he said, 'I knew something about this spoiler operation was funny. You believe in intuition?' The question was sharp, as though the answer really mattered to him.

Julia forgot the tea plantation, the bark pressing into her back, muggy air. She felt real good talking to him like this, treated as an equal, not the patronized boss's granddaughter, not a scatty teenage rich girl. Right now she was a real person, for the first time in a long time. Maybe the moment would stretch and stretch.

Commit GregTime. To sip and savour whenever she felt down.

'I had to keep working on the Zanthus data,' she said carefully. 'Like it wouldn't let me go.'

He nodded, satisfied with her response. 'It's up here. I can feel it, no messing.'

Which sounded pretty strange. Was that what he'd meant by intuition? 'What's up there?'

'The twist. We're overlooking something, Julia.' He paused, eyes closed, an impression of effort. 'What was the monolattice filament intended for, anything important? Are you going to get clobbered with penalty clauses for non-delivery?'

Julia used the nodes to plug into the company datanet, remonstrating with herself, it was an obvious question. She traced the monolattice-filament contracts, running a quick analysis. 'Not that I can find,' she said. 'But I'll have the lawyer's office double check to be on the safe side.'

'Right. In the mean time, I'll start interviewing the monolattice-filament module people.' He let out a long breath, rubbing his nose. 'Lord, how many of them are there?'

'Seven. We don't make much monolattice filament.'

'That's something. You'd better call Morgan Walshaw; bring him up to date, and have him round up those on their furlough. I'll have to vet them once I get down.'

'Right.'

'That was a terrific piece of work, Julia. Exactly the sort of proof I needed.'

Julia watched his image intently. His camouflage of emotional detachment had slipped fractionally, he was keen now, animated. He looked much nicer this way, she decided. 'What proof?'

'That the spoiler doesn't conform.'

'But how does knowing it's odd help? That just makes it more confusing to me.'

He winked. 'Have faith. Now I know, I'll keep looking. And I can look in the weirdest places.'

'Where?' she demanded eagerly.

'Right in my own heart. Now you'll have to excuse me, I've got to get Victor Tyo organized.'

'Right, sure.' Granting him a favour.

End GregTime.

His image winked out, what might have been a smile tantalizing her. She reached out and plucked the cybofax from the tree. Grinning stupidly, feeling wonderful.

One of Wilholm's sentinel panthers was looking at her five metres away, violet saucer eyes unblinking. She clicked her fingers and it padded over. Warm damp breath fell on her cheek.

'Good girl.' She stroked it behind pointed flattened ears. It yawned lazily at the affection, pink tongue licking its double row of shark-heritage teeth. Tobias snorted disapproval, shaking his thick neck, then went back to foraging the grass.

Right in his own heart?

10

Alexius McNamara dropped through the sick bay's hatch, dressed in the sky-blue flightsuit which all the microgee module workers wore. His jowls overflowed his helmet strap, fingers resembled sausages. It was the last week of his shift.

'Grab him,' Greg said simply. He'd soon learnt to speak in a half shout, sound didn't carry far in free fall.

Victor Tyo and Isabel Curtis were already anchored to the chamber's walls on either side of the hatch. They clamped him between them with the efficiency of a tag-wrestling team, his legs and arms immobilized. Don Howarth jabbed a shockrod into his neck.

Greg had recognized the mental genotype as soon as he appeared: fissures of lassitude, leprous self-loathing. One of the kamikazes. He wasn't taking chances with them any more. His interview with Norman Knowles, one of the five managers, had finished badly. Greg had sensed Knowles was the one who'd circumvented the security monitors at the same time as Knowles worked out he had a gland. Unfortunately, Greg hadn't sensed Knowles was one of the kamikazes in time. Jerry Masefield had taken the brunt of the attack before he had been subdued. There was something uniquely disquieting about small globules of blood spraying about in free fall.

'Fuck you!' McNamara shouted.

The shockrod dug deeper. Don Howarth was a man worried for his position and pension. McNamara snarled.

Greg pushed off the wall, and stopped himself ten centimetres from him. They were inverted, and Greg sensed how that irritated the man. The Zanthus crew put a lot of stock in orientating themselves to a universal visual horizon.

'Spit at me, and I'll shove that shockrod up your arse, no messing,' Greg said calmly.

McNamara gave a start, thought about it, and swallowed.

'That's right. They sent me up here because I have a gland.'

Frightened eyes peered at Greg from within wells of flaccid flesh.

'You've been screwing around with the monolattice-filament extruder 'ware, McNamara. Writing off perfectly good fibres. How long have you been doing it?'

'Hey, psycho freak, your gland gives you cancer, know that? You'll die rotting.'

'Don't,' said Greg. 'The whole nine months? Eight? Seven?' He sighed. 'Seven it is.'

'Bastard.'

'How did they get a lever on you?'

'Eat shit and die, boy-lover.'

'We have this sweep going between us, you see. A fiver each, so you can understand we're anxious to know. With a lot it's sex. Drugs are quite popular. Then there's the gee-gees. Some are just cracking apart, can't take the stress. But I think you're a straight money man, McNamara. Greed, that's your bang, isn't it? Pure greed.' Greg could smell breath heavy with herb seasoning. 'Did they tell you why?'

'What?' McNamara was clenching his muscles rigid, trembling, his face hot.

'Why they only wanted that three per cent taken out? Why not go for the jackpot like the memox furnaces?'

There was nothing in his mind, no indication that he knew an answer, even the reference to the memox furnaces had surprised him. The tekmerc team had been good, Greg acknowledged, textbook. The furnace operators didn't know who'd circumvented the security monitors, McNamara hadn't known about the furnace operators. Tight thinking all the way down the line.

He stopped his gland secretion, and turned wearily to Bruce Parwez. 'OK, I'm through with him. Stash him in the suit cabin.'

'Right.' He began to truss McNamara with nylon restrainer bands, arms, ankles, knees. The seething man was eventually hauled out of the sick bay by Isabel Curtis and Lewis Pelham.

'It must be getting crowded in that cabin, five furnace operators, now two from the filament modules,' Greg said to Victor Tyo.

'Tough.'

'Yeah. How many more?'

'McNamara was the last. Unless you want to work through the other microgee products.'

'Christ, don't. Morgan Walshaw or Julia Evans would've been in contact if any other products were involved with the spoil.'

'Yes, the last word I got from Walshaw was that he'd got up a team to analyse the output of every module.' Victor fought against a smile. 'I don't think he was too happy that Julia Evans had found another security breach.'

Greg wedged his foot under one of the beds. His first impulse was to sit down, but the position made his stomach muscles ache. Everything about free fall was unnatural. There was a fish bowl on the wall beside the bed, a sealed metre-wide globe with a complicated-looking water filter grafted on to one side. Ten guppies were swimming slowly round. Even they were all keeping their bellies towards the wall, though the angle made it look as if they were standing on their broad rainbow tails.

'What was bothering him?' Greg asked. 'That it was another breach, or that Julia Evans found it?'

'Both, I think.'

'What's wrong with Julia?'

'Nothing. I met her once, nice kid.' Victor popped a mint out of a tube with his thumb, snagging the spinning white disk in midair with his tongue. 'Except we're all a bit worried about her grandfather. She's sort of young to be taking over a company like this. There are eighty thousand of us, you know. Most have dependants. That's a lot of responsibility for a teenage girl.'

'Yet she's quicker off the mark than the whole of the security division.'

Victor smiled boyishly. His face seemed almost unaffected by free fall. 'There is that.'

The sick bay suddenly rang as if it'd been hit by a hammer. Greg winced, he knew that was something he'd never get used to. The thermal stabilization went on for fifteen minutes every time the dormitory crossed the terminator, the can's metal skin expanding or contracting, protesting the adjustments with loud groans and shrieks.

'Shall I tell the pilot we're still OK for our original departure time?' Victor asked.

'Yes. We'll get the first flight off anyway, and make sure McNamara is included. He's not the type I want up here a moment longer than necessary. You and I will go down in the second flight.'

'McNamara's that bad?'

'Total nutcase, no messing.'

'Right, I'll assign all our hardliners to go down on that flight, five of them, five of us; Knowles can go down with them as well. We can borrow a couple of hardliners from Howarth to come with us.'

'How long can we delay the second flight?'

'You're the boss; as long as you want. Physically the Sanger can stay up here for thirty-six hours, but it'd be cheaper to send it down and wait for another.'

'Plan for that, then. If anyone objects, tell them to contact Walshaw. And if he wants to know what the deal is, tell him to call me.'

'Do you think there are some more tekmerc plants up here?'

'Unlikely.'

'Why are we staying, then?'

'To find out why the monolattice-filament output was being tampered with.' Greg wasn't too keen on having to explain his instinct to Victor. The security lieutenant was a programmer, confined to the physical universe where everything was precisely arrayed and answers were logical, black and white. Perhaps he was being unfair. But empathy was the tangible half of his gland-enhanced psi ability. Intuition, on the other hand, was a track leading down the black-ice slope to the hinterlands of magic, witchery. The province of prophets and demons.

Julia Evans was young enough to be impressionable. Victor, he suspected, would be a mite sceptical.

'I thought the tekmercs were holding the filament extruders in reserve,' Victor said. 'Then after we pulled the furnace operators, they just bring them into line.'

'No. The tekmercs would know we'd check the other microgee modules eventually. And you've toughened up the security monitors yourself; there won't be a recurrence. There's no way they could ever hope to pull the same stunt twice in a row. They're too professional for that.'

'Right.' Victor thumbed his communication set, and began talking to the Sanger pilot docked to the can.

The guppies were chasing tiny grains of food which the filter unit was pumping into their globe. Greg rubbed his eyes, yawning, a faint throbbing of a neurohormone hangover making itself felt at the back of his head. The last decent sleep he'd had was on the *Alabama Spirit*. Two – no, three nights ago. But the idea of sleep was foreign, he knew his body well enough to tell when he needed to bunk down. Ever since they'd arrived at Zanthus he'd been on the verge, time stretched up here, knocking biorhythms along with the rest of normality. It was his mind that needed to wind down, a whole stack of accumulated Zanthus-time memories pressing in on him.

Voices percolated through the sick-bay hatch, interspaced by a salvo of plangent creaks from the can shell. Piccadilly Circus was filling up, the shifts changing over again.

Greg realized his gland was active again, though he couldn't remember a conscious decision to use it. The secretions brought on an unaccustomed dreamy sensation; it felt good, warmth and confidence washing through him, lifting the depression Alexius McNamara had left behind. The answer was close now, a surety.

He heard a protracted clanging as one of the Swearingen commuters docked with the can, hums and whines took over. Another wave of voices broke, the high, restless kind people used when they'd just come off work.

The answer clicked.

11

Julia raced out of the bathroom just as Adela was about to pick up her cybofax. 'I'll get it,' she called over the shrill bleeping. She tightened the belt on her robe and threw away the big yellow towel she'd been drying her hair with. Adela shrugged, and began to close the curtains. Torrential rain was beating against the thick windows.

Julia dropped on to the bed and picked up the cybofax. Greg's face appeared on the screen. She flushed scarlet. 'Give me a moment, Adela, please.'

Adela picked the towel off the carpet, giving her a meaningful look before closing the bathroom door behind her.

'Are we secure?' Greg asked.

Julia pushed back some of her hair, it was all rat tails. Why did he have to call when she looked like this? 'Yah.'

'Great. I know what the twist is.'

Julia stared at him numbly. 'And you called me first?'

'Yeah. You see, I need it confirming before I go to Walshaw or your grandfather. So I thought you could do some research for me.'

'Me?'

'You uncovered the monolattice filament discrepancy. It's as much your discovery as mine. I thought you'd want to see it through.'

'I do,' she said quickly.

Commit GregTime#Two.

'Right then,' Greg said. 'It's a Luxemburg-registered company that has to be checked out. Can you do that for me?'

'Of course. But, Greg, what's the twist?'

He smiled, and she noticed how drawn he looked.

'I think the memox crystals are being shipped down to Earth.'

'Oh,' was all she said, because the jolt sent her thoughts racing. 'Greg, the Sanger flights are well documented. Their cargo manifests are finalized weeks in advance. It'd be awfully difficult to sneak anything on board, certainly on a regular basis.' She didn't like puncturing his idea like that, he seemed so keen about it.

But Greg's smile just broadened. 'Forty-eight million Euro-francs, Julia. When I took the case, we thought the crystals were being contaminated, dumped. But they're not contaminated, are they? They're perfect. For forty-eight million, it's worth trying to bring them down, even if you couldn't get away with it. Tell you, I'd try. If it's possible, those tekmercs will've done it; maybe they've found a psychic who can teleport the stuff back to Earth for them.'

'Teleport?' she squawked in alarm.

'Old Mindstar joke, sorry.'

'Ah.' The goosebumps on Julia's forearms began to settle.

'The thing is, to find the flights the crystals went down on, Event Horizon would have to run a computer search through past spaceplane flights up to Zanthus. Say, over the period of a couple of months.'

'God, Greg, do you know how many spaceplane flights rendezvous with Zanthus in one day, let alone a month?'

'Today there were twenty-three. That's where my problem lies. I'm convinced it's happening, but getting Morgan Walshaw to mount an investigation on that scale, with just my intangible hearsay to go on, would be difficult. That's even if the spacelines would co-operate and open their data cores to you, which is doubtful, and assuming the tekmercs haven't wiped the records anyway.'

'So what's this company you want me to check out?'

'The weak link. There's always one.'

'I know,' she whispered fervently.

'Yes? Well, anyway, memox crystals, good or bad, are taken from the furnace modules to the servicing docks. From there, they're either loaded into a Dragonflight Sanger, or included in a waste-dump stack, depending on how the batch was coded. Ample scope there for hanky-panky.'

Access High Steal#Two.

She fired off a tracer program as soon as the simulacrum materialized. 'It's a contractor!' she shouted excitedly.

'Right. Event Horizon doesn't own any inter-orbit craft. There are three specialist transport companies based up at Zanthus to serve the manufacturers. You pay High Shunt to move your cargo around, and to perform your waste dumps.'

'It's got to be them.'

'No messing. Now if you'd just care to prove it for me.' He was grinning at her.

She beamed right back, it was like they had some sort of affinity bond or something. And she'd been the one he'd come straight to. Not Morgan Walshaw, not Grandpa. Her. 'Coming up,' she said.

It wasn't even difficult. Event Horizon's commercial intelligence division compiled a survey of every company they did business with. Large or small, each of them was scrutinized before the contract was finalized.

Julia's executive code plugged her right in. High Shunt's daedal aspects expanded in her mind, a comprehensive listing of its history, management structure, performance, assets, personnel. It was a respectable company, formed eight years ago, good safety record, developing as Zanthus grew.

List Ownership.

A stream of banks, pension schemes, trust funds, and individuals flooded through her, giving percentages and acquisition dates. One of them leaped out at her as if it was haloed in flashing red neon. Thirty-two per cent of High Shunt was owned by the di Girolamo family house.

'Gotcha, Kendric,' she whispered.

12

Stanstead airport was subtly depressing. New developments were erupting like shiny volcanic cancers in the middle of abandoned jet-age structures, vibrant young challengers. But the chances for inspiration which new materials and energy technologies provided, the opportunities to learn from the past and build a commercial enterprise which complemented the local environment, had all been lost; the steel and composite structures worshipped scale, not Gaia. They had neither grace nor art, simply history repeating itself. Stanstead had originally been built on the promise of the postwar dream, only to find itself betrayed like the rest of the country.

Greg looked down on the architectural shambles from an office on the top floor of Event Horizon's glass-cube administration block, and wondered how many times that cycle would turn down the centuries. Hopes and aspirations of each new age lost under the weight of human frailties and plain bloody-mindedness.

The airport's ancient hangars were dilapidated monstrosities, corrugated panels flapping dangerously as they awaited the reclamation crews. Next to them were six modern cargo terminals made from pearl-white composite; a constant flow of Dornier tilt-fans came and went from the pads outside. Black oval airships drifted high overhead.

He could see an old An-225 Mriya at the end of the barely

serviceable runway. The Sanger orbiter he'd returned in yesterday had been hoisted on top by a couple of big cranes. The configuration was undergoing a final inspection before flying back to Listoel.

He heard Philip Evans's querulous voice behind him, and closed the grey-silver louvre blinds which ran along the window wall, shutting out the sight of the tilt-fans hovering outside. The glass was sound-deadened, blocking the incessant high-frequency whine of their turbines.

Only Morgan Walshaw and Victor Tyo were in the office, sitting in hotel lobby silicon-composite chairs at a big oval conference table. There was a large flatscreen on the wall at the head of the table, showing Julia and Philip Evans in the study at Wilholm. Julia's hair was tied back severely, and she was wearing a double-breasted purple suit-jacket over a cream blouse. Going for an executive image. It didn't quite come off; her face, despite its current solemnity, was far too young. People would underestimate her because of that, he knew. He had.

But it was Philip who worried him. The old man looked just awful; a heavy woollen shawl wrapped round his thin frail shoulders, eyes that were yellow and glazed. His deterioration even over the five short days since the dinner party was quite obvious. He seemed to be having a great deal of trouble following the proceedings, his attention intermittent.

Julia shared Greg's opinion, judging by her expression. Her pretty oval face was pale and drawn, crestfallen. It looked as though she hadn't slept for days, her big tawny eyes were red-rimmed, never leaving her grandfather. He wondered if he'd asked too much from her, especially at this time.

'It was Kendric di Girolamo who organized the spoiler operation,' Greg said. 'The evidence which Julia has unearthed for us puts it beyond doubt.'

The corners of her lips lifted in acknowledgement.

'My girl,' Philip rumbled.

'We had two problems arise out of what we discovered,' said Greg, 'which when taken together cancel each other out. We already knew that with his control of High Shunt, Kendric could divert the memox crystals from the waste dump. But that left us with the question of how he could get hold of a Sanger to bring them back down to Earth. At five hundred million Eurofrancs each, it's too expensive for him to buy one, besides we'd know if the di Girolamo family house owned a spaceplane. And to hire one from a legitimate spaceline he would've had to list the cargo manifest, both for the operator and the spaceport authority. It would've been impossible for him to explain where the memox crystals originated from. Oh, he might've been able to do it once, or even twice. But not on a regular basis. The space industry is close knit, it knows itself. If he was bringing down three flights of memox crystals a month, the pilots and payload handlers would've started to ask questions.

'Then we have the second problem: why did he bother with the monolattice filament when he'd already corrupted the memox-furnace operators? Julia found the answer to that.'

'After I found High Shunt was owned by the di Girolamo house, I took a closer look at all the other companies working up at Zanthus,' she said, reading from her cube. Her voice was like a construct, level and droning. 'The clincher was a company called Siebruk Orbital. It's the smallest one up at Zanthus, consisting of a single standard microgee module staffed by two technicians. They're listed as a research team investigating new vacuum-fabrication techniques.'

'So?' Philip asked.

'*Fabrication* techniques,' Greg said. 'I think they're turning the monolattice filament into small re-entry capsules inside that module. Then they fill them with memox crystals and hand them back to High Shunt for a waste dump, retro-burning them so they fall into the atmosphere.'

'Siebruk Orbital belongs to Kendric?'

'Siebruk Orbital is registered in Zurich, which gives total anonymity for the owner,' said Julia. 'But the Sanger which launched the module was a Lufthansa charter. It was put up ten months ago, which, incidentally, fits the timing perfectly.

Payment for the flight came from Siebruk Orbital's company account at the Credit Corato bank in Italy. All perfectly legal and above board. However, the di Girolamo family finance house has a thirty-five per cent stake in Credit Corato. It's supposition, of course.'

'Has to be,' Philip said softly. He was looking at something off screen, wistful.

Victor Tyo activated the terminal on the table in front of him, the cubes lit. 'After Greg came to me with this, I ordered a review of data from our Earth Resources platforms, specifically the oceans under Zanthus's orbital track. There are three designated areas for waste dumps, all over water in case burn-up isn't complete. Two over the Pacific, one over the Atlantic.' An image formed in one of the cubes, a white dot on a blue background. The dot began to move, trailing a white line behind it. After a minute the centre of the image was a near-solid blob of white. 'What you're seeing is a movement record built up over the last two months of a ship in the Atlantic, two hundred kilometres east of the waste dump area. As you can see, it stays within a patch of ocean about fifty kilometres in diameter. We did a computer simulation of a non-lifting-body profiled descent trajectory, two hundred kilometres is well within the established criteria. I believe the ship is Mr di Girolamo's recovery vessel.' The cube display changed, showing an overhead view of a ship at sea. 'This was taken at first light this morning with a platform's high-definition photon amp.' The angle of the cube image shifted in increments until the ship appeared to be leaning over at forty-five degrees. The name *Weslin* was visible on the side.

'According to Lloyd's data core, *Weslin* is owned by MDL Maritime,' Julia said. 'MDL Maritime is another Zurich-registered company. Credit Corato handles its account.'

'Bingo,' Morgan Walshaw said quietly.

Philip's eyes found the camera, looking down at Greg. Confusion distorted his enervated features. 'Why?' he asked. 'Kendric di Girolamo has a large legitimate financial interest in

Event Horizon through his family finance house. He was hurting himself with the spoiler.'

'The spoiler made him forty-eight million Eurofrancs; and as to Event Horizon's suffering, he wouldn't lose a thing, not in the long run,' Greg said. 'You see, he wasn't looking to make a killing from the crystals directly, they were a means. With Event Horizon's declining profits on top of your health situation he would have gained enough leverage with the other members of the backing consortium to have himself appointed to the board of trustees you've arranged to run Event Horizon until Julia comes of age.'

'It's a reasonable enough request,' Julia put in reluctantly. 'The consortium are entitled to a representative. I doubt we could keep their nominee off. Not legally.'

Philip nodded slowly. 'The consortium has mentioned it . . . Someone . . . to oversee their interests.' His voice sounded terribly weak. Julia was looking at him, almost in pain with what she saw. His head turned from the camera again. Greg thought he was looking out of the study window. 'Then what?' he whispered.

'This is just theory, you understand, based on what you told me about Kendric trying to muscle in on the management side of Event Horizon. But after Kendric landed his boardroom seat I'd say that he simply planned to close down the spoiler, bringing Event Horizon's accounts back to their usual profit level. He'd disguise the link of course, make it an issue; shuffle personnel, target resources at the furnace maintenance division, but that kind of high-profile result would guarantee him the chairmanship. Now, because Event Horizon is a family company, he can never own it. But as chairman he could oversee a massive asset-stripping raid, presumably by his own front companies. That sort of money he is most definitely interested in. Julia and the consortium would be left with nothing.'

Julia had listened raptly the night before, after she'd pulled the information about Siebruk Orbital for him. 'So simple,' she'd said, when he'd finished explaining. 'I had all the pieces before you and I didn't put them together. If you hadn't had your suspicions that the memox crystals were being brought down, we would never have uncovered Kendric's involvement.'

It was his intuition, of course. A foresight equal to everyone else's hindsight. He hadn't told her that. Let her go on thinking he was a magician. Event Horizon might have a few more jobs coming up, and they paid bloody well.

'I see,' said Philip. 'Either way, Kendric wins. How typical.'

'What are we going to do about di Girolamo?' Victor asked.

'The options are regrettably limited,' said Walshaw. 'Our respective Scottish operations are almost fully integrated. We can hardly untangle them now, certainly not with the Scottish PSP so close to falling. A replacement for Kendric would be hard to find.'

Julia cleared her throat. 'The ship in the Atlantic.'

'Yes,' Walshaw said. 'I can arrange a hardliner assault. We might even retrieve some more of our memox crystals.'

'See to it,' said Philip. 'You've done some good work for me here, Greg, I won't forget. You too, boy.'

Victor ducked his head.

Julia took her grandfather's hand, steadying the shaking fingers. 'That's enough, Grandee.'

'I'll get back to you later,' Walshaw said.

Julia gave him a vaguely remorseful nod before the image blanked out.

Greg spent another ten minutes filling in details for Walshaw before saying goodbye. He'd been away from Eleanor for too long.

'There's a permanent job for you at Event Horizon if you want it,' the Security Chief said as Greg reached the door.

'Thanks, but no thanks,' Greg said. He didn't even have to think about it. Office hours, suit, tie, the same people day after day. He had wanted something regular, but not regimented. 'I'm not ready for that yet.'

The nineteen-fifties Rolls-Royce was waiting for him on

Stanstead's buckling grey concrete as he came out of the administration block, chauffeur already opening the door.

*

Philip Evans died two days later. His funeral was the biggest civic event to be held in Peterborough for two generations. The Prime Minister and two senior royals were in respectful attendance.

His will named Julia Hazel Snowflower Evans as his sole beneficiary.

13

Julia watched the crackling life of the night-time city through the Rolls-Royce's tinted windows, impatient for the ride to be over, the drama she'd conceived to unfold. She could almost believe they were driving through some German metropolis. Peterborough's New Eastfield district possessed the same frantic pace and power, the strut that came from being number one.

Its buildings were post-Warming, laid out in a precise geometrical array, like Manhattan before the Anarchy March. They were foreign-funded, a thorn in the side of the PSP, physical evidence the Party couldn't fulfil its promises. All of them followed the same palaeo-Spanish theme, six-storey, marble or cut stone, with long balconies that sported a profusion of greenery and flowers. Smart-uniformed doormen stood outside the gingery smoked-glass lobbies.

Wealth was everywhere, in clothes, jewellery, salon beauty; in the absence of bicycles and graffiti.

The road was clogged with traffic: gas-electric hybrid BMWs and Mercs cruised up and down, their headlights and tail-lights two contrasting severed ribbons of light. The folksy tables of pavement cafés were spread out under brightly striped awnings, alternating with arched entrances into small arcades of exclusive shops. Brightly lit windows full of designer-label clothes and esoteric gear silhouetted the fast-moving pedestrians, painting their faces in cool neon tones. Soft warm rain had fallen earlier in the evening, its residual sheen reflecting gaudy biolum ads in long wavering flames from walls and paving slabs.

But the prosperity was only a few blocks across. A ghetto of the rich. She remembered Grandpa saying that New Eastfield was a seed, that in a proper economy this kind of life style would spread out like a microbe culture, consuming and changing its surrounding neighbourhoods, right out to the city boundaries. He'd wanted the New Conservatives to build cores like it in every English city, showcases for a top-led society, the acceptable face of capitalism.

Good old Grandpa. An eternal optimist. But there were a *lot* of people enjoying the balmy evening street life.

'Are you sure Bil will be there?' Katerina asked.

Julia turned away from the window, back to the subdued oyster shade inside the car. Her friend was wearing a skintight black tube dress; a slash down the front was loosely laced up, showing the deep cleft between her breasts. Brazen, but Julia was forced to admit she looked wonderful. Her hair was a fluffy gold cloud.

'He was invited,' Julia said tonelessly. Bil Yi Somanzer: the hottest, meanest rock and roller in the history of the world, ever. Even Kats would look ordinary around his groupies. She smiled in the shadows; Kats had only agreed to come after she'd promised her Bil would be there.

'Well, Julie, dear, anyone can *invite* him. Having him turn up is different.'

'He'll be there. Stars and the media, they need each other. Feed off each other. And media doesn't come any bigger than Uncle Horace.'

Kats wasn't convinced, fuchsia lips screwing up petulantly, but Adrian nudged her quiet. He was wearing a white jacket, black bow tie, a red rose tucked into his buttonhole. Stunningly handsome. And he'd silenced Kats from spouting off inanely because he knew she was still supposed to be shaken over Grandpa's death. Her feelings mattered to him.

The Rolls dipped down into the giant Castlewood condominium's underground garage. Horace Jepson had his own private park on the second level. Thick metal doors swung open as the chauffeur showed his card to the lock.

Steven Welbourn and Rachel Griffith, Julia's two bodyguards, hurried out of the trail car as the little convoy came to a halt. Both of them were wearing formal evening dress, Steven in a dinner jacket, Rachel in a long navy-blue gown. Their alert faces scanned the stark, brightly lit concrete cave. They needn't have bothered, two of Horace's own security staff were waiting for them.

There was a distinct air of farce about the entire scene. But Julia was careful not to show disapproval. Steven and Rachel were just doing their job, and she got on quite well with them. Steven had been with her for years, almost since she came to Europe, a twenty-seven-year-old with sandy hair that she teased him was already thinning. He was sympathetic about her circumstances, and his discretion had been demonstrated time and again, considering the schoolgirl truancies which he could have told her grandfather about. Rachel had been with her for about a year; a twenty-two-year-old with neat close-cut mousy hair; she came across as a mix of big sister and maiden aunt. Courteous, but an absolute stickler for security protocol, always checking the toilet cubicle first, which could get embarrassing. Of course, one day she might be very glad of them. Besides, any complaints would find their way back to Morgan Walshaw. And then there'd be another bloody lecture.

The five of them squeezed into the penthouse lift. Kats and Adrian didn't notice the press, lost in a private world of furtive smirks and hungry looks. Julia gritted her teeth.

The lift opened straight into the vestibule of Horace Jepson's suite. Music and conversation hit them as the doors slid apart.

On her previous visits, the centre of the penthouse had been divided up into various function areas by hand-painted Japanese silk screens depicting scenes from mythological battles, *samurai* and improbable creatures. Now the screens had all been folded back against the walls leaving one big open space. Coloured jelly-blobs of hologram light swam through the air, wobbling in time to a loud acid-thrash version of 'Brown Sugar'. Bodies packed the black-tiled dance floor, a rainbow riot of frantic movement; older sweating men with younger energetic girls. More people lined the vestibule walls under the umbrella of fern fronds; drinking, chattering excitedly. She recognized a lot of faces from the channels.

Trust Uncle Horace. There was nothing refined about this party, it was deliberate Dionysian overload without a refuge, forcing you to enjoy. She wondered if he'd have a topless model bursting out of a cake at some point. More than likely.

Horace Jepson broke free of the crowd, shooing away a girl who had the glossy vibrancy and dazzling pout of a Playmate. He was smiling warmly at Julia. A genuine smile, she thought. Then it flickered slightly as he took her in, as though she'd come in the wrong sort of dress, or something. But she'd chosen a five-thousand-pound Dermani gown, pale pink silk with a mermaid-tail skirt; nothing like as tarty as the rest of the girls she could see, so that couldn't be it.

His smile had mellowed by the time he reached her. He took both her hands and gave her a demure peck on the cheek.

It was almost saddening. He used to give her big bear hugs and a huge slobbery kiss. Funny, she'd always hated them at the time. Now they were a part of an old familiar world, lost and gone for good.

'I was afraid you weren't going to come,' he said.

'Try keeping me from a party.'

'That's my gal. Say, look, I'm real sorry about Phil. One of the best, you know?'

Behavioural Response: Sorrow.

She'd loaded the program in the processor node to remind her, keyed by any mention of Grandpa. For her to giggle at his name, at people's earnest sympathy, would never do.

'Thank you. Do something for me, Uncle Horace?'

'Sure, honey.'

'Don't treat me like glass. I won't break. And it only makes it worse.'

'Right.' He grinned at Katerina and Adrian. 'Come on in, you guys. We're just getting warmed up. Plenty of action here tonight.'

Julia thought his glance hovered around Kats' cleavage. Then he was looking over her shoulder at Steven and Rachel, a faintly puzzled expression on his face as Kats dragged Adrian past him into the throng.

'No escort, Julia?'

''Fraid not.'

'Hell gal, why didn't you let me know? Cindy could've fixed something up for you. That girl's got a list of boys bigger than a census bureau.'

'Maybe next time.'

'Damn, Clifford won't be over before the weekend. He would've done, just fine. You met Cliff before? My boy? From my first marriage.'

'You've mentioned him,' she said drily. Had the two of them walking down the aisle in his mind.

'Oh well, let me introduce you to a few people. Hey, maybe I can have one dance. Make an old man happy.'

'I think your friend would scratch my eyes out first,' she nodded at the Playmate girl.

'Ouch, Julia. There's a lot of Philip in you,' he said admiringly.

She quashed the laugh while it was still in her gullet.

Sorrow.

'Good. Because I'd like to do some business with you.'

Horace Jepson suddenly became wary. 'Most of Globecast's contracts with Event Horizon are pretty much cut and dried.'

'Well, not formal business. More a favour.'

'Go on.'

'There's a programme I might want broadcasting. It's important to me, Uncle Horace.'

'What sort of programme?' he asked cautiously.

124

'A planet-wide exposé. Every current-affairs channel Globe-cast owns.'

Now his face really fell. 'Julia, honey, do you know the kind of legal angles on this? I mean, if you're really hot on rubbishing someone, then hearsay ain't no use.'

'I've got the proof. All we need.'

'Damn, but I wish you didn't grow up so fast.'

*

Kendric di Girolamo was at the party, and Hermione. Julia didn't know when they'd arrived. Kendric was his usual oily suave self, dancing with a girl who made the Playmate look like a hag.

Their eyes met and held. She gave him a cool, level gaze. Quietly satisfied at the startled light in his eyes. Quickly hidden.

He knew full well she couldn't stand the sight of him; expected a girlish glare, a tossed head, flouncing off in a huff. Instead he got a dispassionate assessment from a multi-billionairess. Small wonder he was surprised. Hopefully concerned.

Squirm, she wished him silently. Her eyes moved on sedately, showing him how little he mattered. Fighting the impulse to whoop for joy. It'd begun.

*

Horace Jepson had hired a five-piece rock band for the evening, the Fifth Horseman, their axemen tooled up with reasonable copies of Fenders. They were dressed in torn T-shirts, studded leathers, and thigh-length boots. Clean, though, Julia noticed. But they were a tight outfit for all their synthetic attitude, the rhythm pumping out of their Gorilla stacks hot and fast. The singer had a Ziggy Stardust stripe across his face, 3D paint opening into middle-distance.

*

She danced with Bil Yi Somanzer to a number that could've been 'Five Years'. Uncle Horace had introduced them, interest in her name and wealth finally penetrating the mega-star's syntho stupor. Basking in the jealousy which lashed out in tangible waves from the other girls. His skin was smooth and shiny from *plastique*, his voice slurred. He groped her backside and asked if she fancied a quick trip to one of the bedrooms. The band finished their stuff, and they parted. His reputation upheld.

*

Seeing Kats standing on a table trying to Bunter down a long glass of champagne to the boisterous cheers of an admiring audience of young blades. The hologram blobs congregated around her legs in a silent red and green swarm, floating up inside her skirt. Adrian hovering on the sidelines, tolerant, fixed smile.

*

Talking to a young French finance manager who was helping Uncle Horace to expand Globecast into Europe. He was nervous about her, stammering, telling her about the investment ratios of various gilt stocks, and the new junk-bond markets opening in South America. She turned down his invitation to dance. Boring.

*

Kendric offering a gentlemanly hand to Kats as she climbed down off the table, face flushed. He handed her a drink. Hermione joined them, palpably excited. Laser fans swept across the trio, sparkling off jewels, teeth, lips, fluorescing Kats' cloud of hair into an electric-pink halo.

*

A dance with Adrian. Doing his duty. A smoochy number, so he'd have to hold her close. Swaying rhythmically with the feel of his hard body pressed against hers, his hands on her back.
'You dance well,' she told him.
'Oh, yeah, thanks.' Distracted.
She shivered beneath his hands.

*

Kendric and Kats dancing. She was hanging on to every word he uttered, both laughing ebulliently, plainly delighted with each other's company. Her body flowed with the music, lost to the beat, wild and sensual.

*

Half a dance with Uncle Horace. His face red and puffing as he gave up, leading her over to the seafood buffet. Picking out their food together, Horace with something to say about every dish, urging her to sample. His own plate piled high. Divine crabs.

*

A cocktail that took the bartender an elaborate three minutes to prepare. Only it tasted like orange juice that someone had spilled vinegar into. She flashed him a smile saying how wonderful it was, and poured it into the punch bowl when no one was looking, green ice-swan sculpture and all.

*

Kendric and Kats nearly alone on the dance floor. Doing the lambada. Adoration in her eyes.

*

She chatted to the Playmate girl, whose name was Cindy, and was actually a data-compression expert. So much for first impressions. Cindy was raucous and worldly wise, and had lots of funny stories about men in general. A life lived in the fast lane, with no regrets. She hung on to every word, Cindy gave her a window on the kind of world she so rarely glimpsed.

*

Cindy was well into a completely unbelievable recital of her recent Spanish holiday when both of them became aware of the shouting. The Fifth Horseman ground to a halt in a dissonant metallic skirl.

Adrian, Kendric, and Kats stood in the middle of the dance

floor, two against one. Kats stood beside Kendric, breathing heavily, sweat-darkened tassel ends of her hair sticking to her shoulders. Hologram blobs orbited the trio slowly.

'Enough!' Adrian yelled.

Kendric raised a warning finger. 'Go home, little boy, you're making a fool of yourself.'

'I'll go all right, you people make me want to puke. And you're coming with me.' He tried to grab Katerina, but she dodged nimbly behind Kendric.

'No way,' she shrilled. 'I'm having some real fun. First time in bloody ages, too.'

Julia knew Kats well enough to see how she was loving the scene, milking it. The centre of attention. All the glitzy people she worshipped were focusing on her, asking who she was, a girl so desirable she was worth fighting over in public.

Kendric grinned. 'That seems pretty plain, little boy. Go play somewhere else.'

'Come on,' Adrian entreated. His fists were clenched, face beaming hatred at his rival.

Kendric's arm snaked protectively round Katerina, his hand squeezing her breast. 'I do so detest these revolting peasants. Why don't you and I go somewhere quieter? My yacht is anchored in the marina.'

Katerina's face was flushed with triumph. She tossed her head. 'Sounds good. Better than anything Mr Ten Centimetres here ever offered me.'

Kendric roared with laughter. There were snickers from the guests. Adrian paled, staring at Katerina in complete and abject incomprehension.

There was a voice inside Julia's skull pleading at her to rush over and throw her arms round Adrian. He was too honest, too decent for this to be happening to him.

Somehow she managed to keep her feet in place, clinging magnetically to the black tiles.

Kendric and Katerina turned as one. Walking away. Adrian

stared at their departing backs, his hands had fallen limply to his side.

'Katey,' he called after her.

She let out a playful squeal as Kendric pinched her rump, giggling. Never looking round.

'Katey!'

Julia closed damp eyes.

The music boomed again.

*

Julia waited for five days after the party before she sat in the chair at the head of the study table and called Kendric. The arrangements with Globecast had taken a while to finalize, but Uncle Horace had come through in the end, God bless him. And then there was her nerve to screw up.

When the phone's flatscreen activated, Kendric was sitting on the aft deck of his yacht, the marina forming a bright enticing backdrop, slightly out of focus. The sight of him stiffened her own resolution. He was wearing a lemon-yellow silk shirt, open at the neck, looking supremely relaxed, impenetrably black glasses covering his eyes, just the right amount of stubble shading his chin, emphasizing masculinity. It was a calculated pose, she thought, intended to demonstrate the ease with which he moved through life, his authority and influence. The epitome of an international wheeler-dealer.

It was working, too, the effect seeping out through the screen to abrade her own confidence. She gripped the armrests on her chair against the impulse to smooth down her hair. Wishing she'd taken some time to straighten out her own appearance. Her blouse was nothing special, a hundred-and-fifty-pound Malkham, she'd already worn it a couple of times before. She should've worn a Chanel suit.

'Hermione was only saying the other day we don't see enough of you, Julia,' Kendric said. 'It's such a pity. We're having a party here on the *Mirriam* tomorrow night, nothing formal. Why don't

129

you come along? A lovely young girl like you ought to involve herself socially. Katerina tells me you don't have many friends. That makes me so sad.'

Julia didn't trust herself to speak for a moment. That little cow Kats had told him that! How he and that dyke Hermione must've laughed. God, what else had she told them?

'I'm afraid I'm a very busy person nowadays, Mr di Girolamo. I'm in industry, you see, not finance. It means I have to work for a living.'

'Julia, please. What is all this Mr di Girolamo? I am Kendric, your friend, your grandfather's friend.'

'Bullshit. Grandpa tolerated you. I won't. Don't think I don't know what you're after.'

'After, Julia?'

'Ranasfari's project. That's what it was all about, right?'

He smiled a wounded smile. 'So much of your late grand-father you have inherited. You are a straight talker. I respect that, Julia. It is a rare commodity. Pleasing in this world of deceit. So in return I too will be a straight talker. You have to tolerate me, or at least my family house. It's in our contract. Unbreakable.' The smile hardened. 'A profitable arrangement all round.'

'I've had my financial division draw up a buyout agreement, your house will be well compensated.'

'And you expected our house to agree to this? Julia, you are more naïve than I thought. Multi-billion Eurofranc contracts are not torn up because of schoolgirl temper tantrums.'

'You are the house's representative in the consortium. Your family will accept your judgement in this matter.'

'And my judgement is no.'

'You won't like the alternative.'

'Threats, Julia? Has it come to this? And with what will you threaten me?'

'A scandal.' She was disappointed by how hollow it sounded. A whole complex of doubts was rising. She'd banked so much on forcing Kendric to accept the buyout. Never even considered he would refuse. There was no way now she could mitigate failure.

Kendric chortled delightedly. 'A scandal. In this world? In this day and age? Scandal is dependent on perspective, Julia. You smuggle three and a half million Eurofrancs' worth of gear into Scotland every night. Isn't that a scandal? Everyone knows I am a lovable rogue. Certainly your dear grandfather did. After all, Event Horizon bought all those templates from me.'

'The memox-crystal spoiler.'

'Ah yes, I heard your orbiting furnaces were producing a depressing amount of contaminated crystals. How unfortunate for you.'

'The rest of the consortium would be very upset to hear that you planned to steal Event Horizon's assets, don't you think? It might be difficult for the di Girolamo house to find partners after that.'

'Fantasy,' he said. But there was no smile any more.

She let go of the armrests and placed her hands on the table, pleased by how steady they were. 'The onus is on proof, of course. Even if I could prove your involvement, the family would simply disown you, claim they weren't involved, which they possibly weren't. The house could survive your fall. What the house would not tolerate is for you to drag them down with you.'

'An admirable summary,' he mocked. 'So where is this alleged proof?'

She played the terminal keys, squirting data over to the yacht's gear cubes. 'First understand I am not bluffing. See this? It's Globecast's Pan-Europe channel schedule for next Tuesday; the *Investigator Chronicle* documentary is going to be given over to you, Kendric. I'm going to make you a star. All the data my security people turned up on your crystal-spoiler operation was passed on to the programme's researchers. We even found them a re-entry capsule to show, it was bobbing about amongst *Weslin*'s wreckage. You know about those capsules, Kendric, they're the sort Siebruk Orbital assembled up at Zanthus.'

'No, Julia, I do not know.'

'Wrong.' She called up her ace from the terminal's memory core. 'Take a good look, Kendric. That's a transfer order for eight million Eurofrancs to be paid into the account of the newly formed Siebruk Orbital company from your family house, eleven months ago. And, Kendric, it's your authority code on the order. You own Siebruk Orbital. And the di Girolamo house funded it.' She requested the terminal to show the second transfer order. 'Then five months later you went and repaid the money, without any interest. Money you recovered from selling the memox crystals. My money, Kendric. Did they know? Did you tell them you were borrowing family money to finance your own schemes?'

He was hunched over his terminal cube, studying the two transfer orders without a trace of humour left. 'Where did you get these?' he demanded. A crow's feet wrinkle indented the skin on either side of his mouth as his lips compressed.

'The Credit Corato bank, of course.'

'Impossible. They are forgeries.'

Julia felt the tension drain out of her. She leant back into the chair and grinned wickedly at the screen. 'No forging involved. Accessing the bank's records is the president's prerogative. So is waiving client confidentiality, though I don't intend to make it a habit.'

'President?' Shock raised his voice an octave.

'I bought it. Well, fifty-three per cent, anyway. Quite a good investment actually, according to my accountants. I'm the di Girolamo finance house's new partner. How does that grab you?'

'Bitch,' he breathed.

'Careful, Kendric. I might just lower my offer. Schoolgirl temperament, you see.'

'You bought the bank?' He sounded incredulous.

'Yah.'

'You bought the bank just to make me authorize the buyout?'

'Yah.'

He looked from the cube to the phone screen and back again, bewildered. 'How much did all this cost you?'

'Plenty, but it was worth it.'

'I don't believe this. Do you hate me that much?'

'What do you think, Kendric?' she asked, her voice dangerously shaky.

'I think you are impulsive, dear Julia. If you go on frittering Event Horizon away like this there will be nothing left in a few years. What would your grandfather think of that?'

Behavioural Response: Sorrow.

But she didn't need the reminder, not any more. 'He shared my opinion of you,' she murmured.

'Indeed? And if I don't authorize your buyout offer?'

She shrugged. 'The *Chronicle* people get a copy of the transfer orders. They'll go ahead and broadcast then. Without them, the programme would be one big libel case.'

Kendric squared his shoulders, clearing his throat, salvaging what dignity he could. 'Very well, Julia. If that's the way you want it.'

*

His capitulation left her feeling omnipotent. As soon as his image vanished she called Adrian. It was a formality. She knew she was on a winning streak.

Get a grip on yourself, girl, she told herself sternly, you must look barmy with this grin plastered across your face. People would cross the street to avoid you. But the grin remained.

Then Adrian appeared on the screen, and all the wonder blew away in a blast of trepidation, chilling her heart. He'd lost his verve, the chirpy smile and devilish glint were gone. Brokenhearted. Just how hung up on Kats had he been?

'Hello, Julia, nice to see you.' The words said it, but not the voice, that was funereal. Had she called too soon?

'Sorry to bother you, Adrian. I can call back if it's not convenient.'

'No, please, I'm deep into cell composition right now. God, it's dull.'

'Oh, well, that's something. At least I'm more interesting than an amoeba.'

He looked blank for a second, then smiled sheepishly. 'That did come out wrong, didn't it?'

'Not to worry. Look, I wouldn't have called, but I need this truly enormous favour, and I don't know who else to turn to.'

'What?' There was a flicker of interest.

'Well, there's this publishing company which is throwing a big book-launch party next weekend. And I've got to go, it's a social obligation. Event Horizon won the contract to supply them with memoxes, you see. Only the embarrassing thing is, I haven't got anyone to go with. The business keeps me so busy right now, I don't get to meet people my age.'

He scratched the back of his neck, staring at the floor, looking very unhappy. 'I dunno, Julia—'

'I've got to find someone, Adrian. People will think I'm funny if I just keep turning up to these events by myself all the time. It'll only be for the weekend. I could have the car pick you up, you wouldn't miss any lectures.'

'Oh, I see.' A grin plucked at his mouth. 'Well, we can't have people thinking that, now can we? I'd be honoured.'

They sorted out details, and she signed off glowing. Yes. He'd said yes! *Honoured.*

14

Greg had settled comfortably into his morning regimen when the phone shrilled. He was straddling the wooden bench in the lounge, back flat against the chalet wall, lifting the bar smoothly, letting it fall, push again. The exercise was mindless, easing him into a near dream-state. Push. Relax. Nothing to it. He'd rigged the pulley up to a pump which filled the chalet's rafter tank. Twenty minutes each morning was enough to top it up. It supplied the toilet and shower in the bathroom. The jacuzzi didn't work any more, there weren't enough solar cells on the roof to heat that much water. He didn't mind, showers with Eleanor were more than enough compensation.

She'd blossomed beautifully over the last six weeks, independence giving her a seasoned self-assurance. There was very little left of the timid, uncertain girl he'd seduced that night in the Wheatsheaf. Easy youthful enthusiasms had given way to measured assessments. Eleanor voiced her own opinions now instead of quiescently accepting other people's, and she no longer watched over her shoulder, fearful of past shadows. If her father ever showed up again, he would be in for the shock of his life. Greg almost wished he would come.

The real foundation of their relationship was the level of trust, which was total. That was unique to Greg. He'd never escaped the habit of letting his espersense sniff out the faults and insecurities of anyone in his presence. It was a behavioural reflex, one of the psychologists assigned to the Mindstar Brigade had told him, establishing your superiority over everyone to your own satisfaction. Don't worry about it, we'd all do it if we could.

With Eleanor it wasn't necessary. He knew her too well.

The phone jarred his mind away from introspection. He ignored it. Push. Relax. Perhaps the caller would give up. Push, slop of water overhead. Relax. His belly was like steel now, flat and hard; legs solid, arms powerful. He'd never been fitter, not even as a squaddie. It made him feel good, confident, capable of tackling anything.

The phone kept on shrilling. There was a dump facility in the terminal for messages, but the caller wasn't using it. Push. Relax. Someone must want him urgently.

He let the bar fall and walked over to the new Event Horizon terminal. The chalet was all kitted out with Event Horizon gear now. And he'd left a whole lot more in the delivery van, there simply hadn't been room for all the stuff that Julia had sent. Eleanor had had a ball picking out what they could use.

The fee money had been good as well. He'd paid off the outstanding instalments on the Duo, then went to town refurbishing the chalet – new carpets, curtains, restoring the furniture; stripped the roof down and replaced the tiles; tacked on a second solar panel to power the new air-conditioner. There hadn't quite been enough cash to replace the shaky walls, but the money ordinary cases brought in should see to that before the end of the year. He'd already worked on a couple since the memox skim, both corporate, sniffing out dodgy personnel.

The phonescreen swirled and Philip Evans's face appeared. 'Hello, Greg. I need your help again, boy. Someone is trying to kill me.'

Greg suppressed a smile. Ten years in the business, and nobody had ever phoned in a cliché before. 'Bodyguard services aren't really my field, sir, wouldn't your own security . . .' He trailed off and stared at the screen, stared and stared. Small muscles at the back of his knees began to twitch, threatening to topple him.

When he looked back on it, he blamed his exercise-induced lethargy for putting his mind on a ten-second delay to reality, that and intuition. It wasn't just the voice and image which convinced him, any animation synthesizer could mimic Philip to perfection. But this *was* Philip Evans, grinning away at the other end of the connection. Both the natural and neuro-hormone-boosted faculties squatting in his brain forced him to accept it at a fundamental level.

The black-clad funeral procession wending its way through Peterborough's rain-slicked streets occluded his vision.

'You're dead,' he told the image.

'Gone but not forgotten.'

That malicious chuckle. Perfect. *Him.*

'Sorry to give you a shock, m'boy, but I'd never have called unless it was absolutely vital. Can you come out to Wilholm? I really can't discuss too much over the phone. I'm sure you appreciate that.'

The tone mocked.

Greg's skittish nerves began to flutter down towards some kind of equilibrium. Shock numbness, probably. 'I . . . I think I can manage that. When?'

'Soon as possible, Greg, please.'

The image wasn't perfect, he realized. This was a Philip Evans he hadn't seen before, flesh firmer, skin-colour salubrious. Stronger. Younger by about a decade.

'OK. Are you in any danger right now?' At some aloof level, he marvelled at his own reaction. Treating it as just another prosaic problem. Spoke volumes for Army training.

'Not from anything physical. The manor is well protected.'

Physical. So what was a ghost afraid of anyway, being exorcized? Should he stop off to buy a clove of garlic, a crucifix, a grimoire? 'I'm on my way.'

He pulled on his one decent suit, barking a shin on that idiotically oversized bed in the scramble to shove his feet into a pair of black leather shoes. Thought about taking the Walther, and decided against.

The Duo bounced along the estate's gravel track and lurched on to the road. He set off towards Wilholm Manor coaxing a full fifty-five kilometres per hour from the engine, rocking slowly in the seat. The Duo had thick balloon-type tyres, made out of a hard-wearing silicon rubber. They were designed to cope with the country's shambolic road surfaces without being torn to ribbons. A typical PSP fix, he thought, adapting the cars to cope with their failure to maintain the roads.

There was a white watchman pillar standing outside Wilholm's odd cattle grid. He wound the side window down, and showed his card to it.

'Your visit has been authorized, Mr Mandel,' a construct voice said. 'Please do not deviate from the road. Thank you.'

The manor's spread of ornate flora was in full bloom, a spectacular moiré patchwork of sharp primary colours. Big jets of water were spurting across the parched lawns. He could see the two gardeners working away amongst the rose beds. They leant on their hoes to watch him walk up to the front doors. However did that idle pair manage to keep the grounds in such a trim condition?

The butler opened the door. Morgan Walshaw stood behind him, his face drawn. A quick check of his mind showed Greg he was labouring under a prodigious quantity of anxiety.

'Mandel.' Morgan Walshaw greeted him with a curt nod. 'This way.' A stiff finger beckoned. Greg followed him up the big curving staircase. The butler shut the doors silently behind them as they ascended.

'What the fuck is going on?' he asked the security chief in a low tone. 'Did he fake his death, or what?'

Walshaw's face twisted into a grimace. 'Explanations in a moment, just ride it out, OK?'

They arrived at the study and Walshaw opened the door, giving Greg a semi-apologetic shrug as they went in.

The interior was almost the same as it had been on his last visit. Big table running down the middle, stone fireplace, dark panelling, warm sunlight streaming through small lead-lined panes of glass, dust motes sparkling in the beams.

In the middle of the table was a circular black column: seamless, a metre tall, seventy-five centimetres wide. It rested on a narrow plinth which radiated bundles of fibre-optic cables like wheel spokes. They fell over the edge of the table and snaked *en masse* across the Persian carpet to a compact bank of communication consoles standing by the wall.

Julia was seated at the head of the table where her grandfather used to sit, wearing a rusty-orange coloured cotton summer dress, with a slim red leather band around her brow holding back her long hair. One of the two gear cubes in front of her was showing tiny editions of himself and Walshaw walking up the stairs together; the other had his Duo driving up to the manor.

Her mind was beautifully composed. Greg recognized the state; the kind of tranquillity which follows a severe emotional jolt.

His skin crawled with rigor, an animal caution awoken. There was something deeply unsettling about walking into the study.

Her tawny eyes never left him.

He looked at the column, ghoulish images creeping into his mind. Frankenstein, zombies, the undead, brains in glass tanks . . .

'Thank you for coming,' said Philip Evans's voice, all around, directionless.

Greg's eyes remained fixed on the column. 'Stop fucking about, where are you?'

'Good question. Unfortunately philosophy was never my strong point. I've thrown off my mortal coil sure enough; but my mind has been saved. You're looking right at me, boy. It's a neural-network bioware core. A real special one, custom grown, you might say. The lab team spliced my sequencing RNA into the ferredoxin nodes, replicating my neuronic structure. Then when I was dying they used a neuro-coupling to translocate my memories. Not a copy, not some clever Turing personality-responses program, but my actual thought processes. Axon stimulators literally squeezed me out of my skull and into the NN core. Continuity was unbroken, my faculties are intact – enhanced if anything. Memory retrieval is instantaneous, there's none of that scratching around forgetting people's names and faces. I have access to all Event Horizon's data too. Locating that memox-crystal skim took me four days when I was flesh and blood. It wouldn't take me ten seconds now. And there's no pain, Greg. I'm free of it. Not just death illness, but all those aches which mount up over the years, the ones you learn to ignore, only you never can of course. They've gone.'

Greg pulled out one of the solid wooden chairs and sat heavily. 'Jesus Christ.' The column must be solid bioware. He tried to work out how much that would cost. Fifteen, twenty million? Bioware was horrifically expensive. Immortality for billionaires. He wasn't sure whether he was fascinated or utterly disgusted. The concept didn't sink in readily.

'I can create the image of myself in a cube again, if that would be easier for you to talk to, boy.'

Greg shuddered. 'No, thank you.'

Morgan Walshaw sat next to him, resting his hands on the table, face blank.

'Why am I here?' Greg asked stoically.

'Because we have a problem,' said Julia. 'Someone is trying to wreck Event Horizon's future.'

He received the distinct impression she was enjoying his discomfiture.

'You see, Greg,' she said, 'Dr Ranasfari has succeeded in developing a viable room-temperature giga-conductor for us.'

Greg looked at her sharply. 'You're kidding!'

He remembered some Royal Engineering Corps officers he'd been stationed with once had talked about the stuff. A panacea, they'd called it. The answer to the energy shortage, to carbon dioxide pollution. Every university and *kombinate* in the world had its own research team working on giga-conductors before the Credit Crash. Then there were innumerable mega-budget military programmes; a giga-conductor would have produced a whole new generation of weapons.

'Told you he was a genius, boy. Edison of the age. Dedicated, too; it took him over a decade of solid grind to crack.'

'Quiet, please, Grandpa. It's a tremendous breakthrough, Greg, its energy storage density is phenomenal. It will replace every other form of power-storage system in existence; gear, cars, ships, planes, airships, spaceplanes, they'll all use it. And it's cheap, clean, and relatively easy to produce. Our whole way of life will be altered, it's a revolution equal to the introduction of the steam engine.'

'And Event Horizon holds the patent,' Philip chuckled savagely. 'We're going to wipe the floor with the opposition. A Custer and the Indians massacre. I'll make damn sure of that when I introduce the stuff on the market.'

Greg took another look at the mass of fibre-optic cables leading out of the plinth, trying to work out the NN core's bit rate. 'You're still running Event Horizon,' he said. All Philip Evans's talk about arranging for trustees he had confidence in, and the flash of cunning at the time, came flooding back to him.

'Damn right I am, boy. There are no trustees, never were, the nominees are all Zurich fronts. Event Horizon is my life. No individual in the world can run a company better than me. I'm talking fifty years' worth of accumulated experience. There's no substitute for that. It's the efficiency of dictatorship. A group of trustees would be worse than useless, lawyers and airhead accountants; they'd never push the giga-conductor with the kind of vigour necessary to effect a complete domination of the market. Discussion groups, reports, delays for consultation. What a load of crap. Event Horizon run by a committee would shrivel up and die an ignominious death. This is the perfect solution.

'Before now, when a family company grew too big for one person to pay attention to every detail it used to stall. It was

141

inevitable. Responsibilities had to be delegated, the initial individual-led drive was diluted. But the NN core solves even that. I can devote myself one hundred per cent to each problem, no matter the size; co-ordinate every policy; supervise every division. No *kombinate* will be able to match a company run along these lines.'

'You were doing pretty well before,' Julia said acidly. 'One ordinary person, and an ill one at that. With the right people in key posts Event Horizon will prosper. All that's needed is direction, a firmness of purpose, the big decisions made quickly and implemented without delay.'

'And you can do that, Juliet, can you?'

'Yah.'

'Rubbish. You don't have anything like the experience.'

She was angry now, straight-backed rigid, gripping the arms of her seat. 'I do.'

'Node implants don't give you experience, girl, just theory. All that money you spent getting rid of Kendric, pure bloody folly.'

Greg flicked a glance at Julia, intrigued. Her cheeks were burning red, embarrassed rather than angered. Implanted nodes had been banned in England by the PSP, for the usual heinous crime of élitism. The New Conservatives had yet to repeal the Act. But at least he could finally explain away her remarkably smooth thought currents, and that marvellous ability to fish obscure data out of memory cores.

'It's like chess,' Philip Evans explained gently. 'You know how each piece should move, but you don't know the rules, the strategy. You'll learn, Juliet, really you will. It just takes time. And I'm here to bridge the gap for you.'

'But the NN core is untried,' she said, fighting to keep her voice level. 'How do we know all your memories translocated? Suppose these miraculous thought processes of yours are incorrect? And you're basing judgements about the company's entire future on them.'

Finally Greg understood her terror. She was afraid of losing everything; that wonderful edifice which was Event Horizon collapsing to rubble because it was balanced on a single assumption. And she had no way of checking the NN core's integrity. No control.

'If I could bring us back to our current problem,' said Morgan Walshaw. 'Unless something is done to solve it we may lose the core anyway.'

'You told me someone tried to kill you,' Greg said.

'Damn right, boy. Yesterday evening the NN core's inputs were blitzed, saturated with override-priority data squirts. Every channel simultaneously; ground links and satellite circuits. It was clever, the attacker was attempting to force me out of the NN core with the sheer quantity of input. With all the data being given a priority code the core-function management program would have to assign it storage space, eventually displacing my memories. I would've been erased, for God's sake! That's attempted murder in my book.'

'So what went wrong?'

'I'm not a rational, neatly mathematical program. I fought back, began wiping their data as it came in, changed the priority codes, shut down the Event Horizon datanet – and you wouldn't believe how much that's going to cost us. They bloody nearly succeeded, though. If I'd been a Turing personality-responses program it would've been all over.'

Greg was fast getting out of his depth. He remembered questioning a legion cleric his squad had captured in Turkey, a fanatical fundamentalist, so devout he didn't even acknowledge the infidel's existence: his associative-word trick had been useless. The sense of displacement was familiar. He tried to sort out some sort of priority list in his mind.

'Have you safeguarded yourself from that attack method being employed again?'

'Yes. It's a question of code encryption, I've altered my acceptance filters so that only half of my input circuits will accept priority squirts. Of course, there's nothing to stop them from thinking up new methods.'

'So the problem is now centred around tracking down the source of the attack, right?'

'And eliminating it,' said Walshaw.

Greg opened his eyes. 'Your department.'

Walshaw gave him a brief nod.

'So where did the data squirt originate from?' Greg asked.

Walshaw ran his hand through what was left of his hair. 'We've no leads on that, I'm afraid. There were at least eight separate hotrods who hacked into the Event Horizon datanet, probably more, but with the shutdown we lost a lot of data. The blitz was well organized. All eight violators used multiple cut-outs to prevent us from tracing them.'

'I'm surprised they got in so easily.'

'Entry is no problem,' said Philip Evans. 'It's when you try to get our main account to transfer a million Eurofrancs to your Zurich bank or peek into research-team memory files that you run into trouble. Nobody has ever had a requirement to fend off this type of infiltration before. Its own crudity was what made it so successful.'

'Crude?'

'Well, relatively.'

'I'm trying to eliminate possibilities,' Greg said. 'It wasn't a blanket attack, was it? What I mean is, it was purposefully directed at you. They knew you were here?'

'Yes. I would say it's got to be one of those bastard *kombinates*. They've discovered Ranasfari cracked the giga-conductor, and they're badly worried. Anyone with a gram of sense can see the upheaval it's going to cause. Trouble is, they can't destroy it, there's no turning the clock back. Instead they've settled for the next best thing, which is yours truly. Without me Event Horizon won't be nearly as successful in marketing the stuff. They'd only have Julia and the non-existent trustees to deal with.'

'So that rules out joyburners,' Greg said. 'They don't work in packs, anyway. How well guarded is the knowledge of your continued existence?'

'Only twelve people in the world knew,' said Morgan Walshaw. 'Thirteen counting yourself. That's myself, Julia, Ranasfari, and the team which grew the NN core.'

'Just nine of them?' Greg asked incredulously.

'There's nothing complicated about the process,' said Philip. 'We've had neuro-coupling for eight years now, and the RNA splice is a standard procedure. It's only the cost of this much bioware which prevents it from becoming widespread.'

'OK, next question. Would the hotrod team which launched the blitz have to be told you were here, or could they find out by analysing the data flow through Event Horizon's network?'

'They'd know the NN core was an important part of the network from observing the data flow, but that's all. Unless they were specifically told what the NN core was, the best they could guess is that it was an ordinary bioware number-cruncher loaded with a Turing personality-responses program.'

'In other words, they know about you.'

'Looks that way, boy.'

'With only twelve people knowing about the core, I can pin down that mole for you, no messing,' Greg said. 'So where is the other leak liable to have come from?'

'Ministry of Defence, I hope,' said Walshaw.

'Most likely,' Philip Evans admitted. 'Morgan here kept a tight security cordon around the giga-conductor project, but we had to co-operate with the MOD. It was on a confidential basis, of course, but leaks are inevitable on a project this big. You just have to balance the risk against the payoff.'

'Two separate leaks,' Morgan said. 'It's an appalling lapse. One I could accept, but compromising the NN core and the giga-conductor as well, that hurts.'

Greg paused, worried about what Walshaw had said, his intuition producing that annoying tingle again. Two separate, simultaneous, high-level leaks was stretching coincidence a long way. 'Did you ever find out how Kendric's tekmerc team acquired their data on Zanthus's security monitor parameters in the first place? They must have had copies to work out that destreaming manoeuvre.'

Walshaw frowned, glancing at the black column. 'We are still tracking down the actual tekmercs. They've taken a lot of trouble to cover their tracks.'

'So nobody I found passed the data over?'

'No.'

'Could it have been a hotrod burn which pulled the data?'

Julia cleared her throat, giving Walshaw an enquiring look. The security chief nodded reluctantly.

'To get at the monitor programs you would have to either burn straight into the security division's data core or copy the programs direct from Zanthus's 'ware,' she said. 'Zanthus would probably be the easiest option, but you would need to be up there to do it.'

'If it was a hotrod burn,' Greg mused.

'Bloody hell, boy; you're not telling me we've still got a Judas in the company?'

'There is no such thing as coincidence,' Greg said soberly. 'Two leaks on the two greatest ultra-hush projects Event Horizon is running, plus a loose end over the security monitor programs. Make up your own mind.'

'I said that it had to be someone familiar with our security data procedures,' Julia said.

'So you did, Juliet, so you did.'

Walshaw shook his head in dismay, lips drawn taut. 'This means we're going to have to open the field of enquiry to include the whole security division headquarters staff, two hundred and eighty personnel.' He cocked an eyebrow at Greg. 'Exactly how many interviews can you handle?'

'Tell you, not that many, not in the timescale we'd need. Remember, if this mole exists, he'll know we're gunning for him now, he'll be watching for us. At the first sign of any security operation geared to pinpointing him he'll vanish – if he hasn't already. My advice is work from the other end, that way we can keep the operation at a manageable level; track down the blitz hotrods and the people who paid them, and then we'll find out if there is a mole in your senior staff.'

'You just said there was!' Philip sounded irritated.

'Covering my options.'

'Bloody hell.'

'If it is just one person, then it's going to be a very senior staff member,' Walshaw said. 'The security around the NN core was rock solid, damn it.'

'A staff member or an executive assistant,' Greg said. 'Someone who had access to financial records, and saw how much money was being spent on an ultra-hush bioware project.'

Walshaw took a stiff breath. 'Possible,' he said.

Greg's espersense registered exactly how much the admission cost him. 'OK, back to the hotrods,' he said. 'Is the Ministry of Defence the only outside institution you've informed about the giga-conductor?'

'Yah,' said Julia. 'Bringing them in was an integral part of Grandpa's campaign.'

'Oldest dodge in the book,' Philip said. 'Offer the military a worthwhile new technology, and they fund its development from shaky prototype right the way through to fully functional operational status; then you tack civil applications on the back at minimum cost. The production-facility pump has already been primed by good old taxpayers' cash.'

'They leapt at it,' Julia confirmed. 'The country's entire defence forces have to be rebuilt after the PSP virtually dismantled them. And we can provide them with a new generation of high-energy global-range weapons. Concepts even the Germans and Americans haven't got yet.'

'The whole world is going to be hammering on our door,' Philip Evans said gleefully. 'The fees from licence production will rake in a couple of billion Eurofrancs each year alone, minimum; then there's our own profits. Think of how Event Horizon will grow with that kind of annual investment in its infrastructure.'

"The Ministry of Defence will conduct their own inquiry, of course,' said Morgan Walshaw. 'See if any of their personnel were the source of the leak. And if they were, who the data was channelled to. We've told them that the blitz was aimed at the lightware crunchers we use in the giga-conductor project. There's no need for them to know about the NN core.'

'Bloody right, boy. Something like this would bring the fruitcakes pouring out of the woodwork. Everyone and his grand-mother would want to be loaded into an NN core.'

'Somebody outside Event Horizon already knows, though, Grandpa.'

'Don't remind me, girl. At least they've not made it public, for whatever reason. Probably afraid of losing whatever advantage they've got over the other *kombinates*. That'll be something for you to watch for, Juliet, if they do get me. Whichever bastard is the first to put the pressure on you for a low licensing-fee, they're the ones.'

'Don't talk like that,' she said, quietly insistent. 'Nobody's going to get you.'

'Are your security programmers trying to backtrack the hot-rods behind the blitz?' Greg asked Walshaw.

'Yes, although I don't hold out much hope of success. The hacker community is a hard one to crack, our best chance is if a rumour escapes. Someone bragging, stoned or drunk.'

'I'll see what I can do, I have a contact in that area.'

'Who?' asked Philip.

'Tell you, you pay me for results, and that's what you'll get. But your money doesn't entitle you to know my sources. Without confidentiality I'd never be able to hang on to them.'

'Oh, pardon me.' Philip shovelled on the sarcasm, thick and dripping.

'Sounds like a reporter,' Julia muttered tartly.

'I'm reassembling the team which built the NN core for you to interview,' Walshaw told Greg. 'We disbanded them after Mr Evans was successfully translocated. Shouldn't take more than a day or two. They're all still employed by us.'

'Right then, in the mean time I'll get started on Ranasfari's research team,' Greg said briskly. 'Oh, by the way, Julia?'

She looked up, half smiling, expectant.

'Who've you told that your Grandpa's still intact?'

'No one!' It emerged as an indignant squawk. Her mind flamed like a solar flare from high-energy outrage. No guilt, no subterfuge.

'How dare you!'

'Sorry, just checking that . . .'

'He's my grandpa!'

'Juliet, shush. Greg's doing exactly what I asked him here for.'

She shut up, but spiked Greg with an evil glare.

He swivelled round to look enquiringly at Walshaw.

'I have never told anybody that Philip Evans's memories are intact, nor that Event Horizon has perfected a giga-conductor,' the security chief said formally. True.

'Aren't you going to ask me, boy?'

Julia was suddenly very alert, giving Greg an intent stare, her mind coloured by a strange mix of curiosity and trepidation.

The hairs along the back of Greg's neck pricked up. He concentrated. Right at the edge of perception was a faint nebulous glow. Details were non-existent. Half-life? Half-death? Not a mind as he knew minds. And yet, and yet . . .

'No,' he said eventually.

'Ah well, worth a try.' The disembodied voice was utterly devoid of emotional content.

The study window showed green grass and blue sky. Reality. Greg focused on that. A flock of dark birds flew by. Infinitely reassuring in their normality. 'We've got four lines of investigation,' he summarized. 'The hotrod pack which launched the blitz, the team which built the NN core, Ranasfari's giga-conductor research team, and a possible executive-level mole; that's a lot of ground for me to cover. I'm going to need money, not to mention help. There's a colleague I'd like to bring in, spread the load a little.'

Walshaw produced a card from his pocket, embossed with the company's triangle and flying V emblem. 'This will give you unlimited access to any Event Horizon facility, it also provides you a credit line direct to the company's central account. Please try not to spend more than half a million.'

The little oblong of active plastic sat in Greg's palm, innocuous. Half a million. Eurofrancs or New Sterling? He didn't ask. These people were *serious*.

'Who's your colleague?' Julia asked, her face lifted with interest.

'Another psychic; a Mindstar veteran like myself.'

'What's his speciality?'

'Her. Her speciality. She can see into the future.'

She didn't call him a liar to his face, but his espersense told him it was a close-run thing.

15

Julia closed the study door behind her, looking round in sudden desperation. She couldn't let Greg go without at least trying to explain. Damn Grandpa for blabbing like that. When he was alive in the flesh he would never have said anything to hurt her.

He was walking down the stairs, head just visible bobbing above the railing.

'Greg! Wait.'

He turned round, paused. She ran along the landing, ankle-length skirt flapping round her legs.

Standing in front of him, her resolution wavered. What did he actually think of her? There'd never been any thank-you card for the van of gear she'd sent to his home. But would someone like Greg even think about thank-you cards? Damn that bloody Swiss snob school. It'd distorted her perspective on real life. As if anyone else ever bothered about *Debrett's Etiquette* in this day and age, let alone treated it as a bible.

He was watching her with quizzical respect. But was it *bought* respect? Oh hell. She searched his face for a hint of sympathy, any sign of that brilliant moment when they seemed to think as one. 'They didn't alter me, you know.' There, she'd gone and said it, betrayed her insecurities. Would he laugh?

'What didn't?' Greg asked.

She blinked, that wasn't the response she'd been expecting.

'The bioware nodes. People think they turn you into some

kind of mental freak. But it's just like having an encyclopedia on permanent call, that's all. I'm a total whiz at general-knowledge questions.' She flashed a bright entreating smile.

'Of all the people in the world, I'm the least likely to be prejudiced against you.'

'Oh ... yah,' she knew her cheeks would be reddening. God, how stupid. She was making a complete fool of herself. Why couldn't conversation flow from her lips? Kats never had the slightest trouble talking to men, no matter what she said they'd smile and agree. 'What's it like? I wanted a gland. But Grandpa said no.'

'I'm glad he did,' Greg said gently. 'The price is far too high. Take my case. I have to steel myself against people, build a high wall to shut them out. Every mind is awash with fears and intolerance and fright, all the human failings. We school ourselves to hide them from showing in our voices and expressions, but to me it's an open book. I'd drown in it if I let my guard down. And there's the pain, too. Actual physical pain from the neurohormones, it can cripple me if I don't keep a firm control over the secretion levels.'

Commit GregTime#Three. Nobody else was ever this honest with her about themselves. It must mean he felt something, even if it was only a variant of parental concern. 'Why don't you have it taken out, if it's that bad?'

'I'm a psi-junkie, Julia. I couldn't give up the gland any more than you could give up eyes. Once it's in, you're hooked. But if I was living my life again I'd run a million miles rather than have a gland.'

She nodded with earnest sympathy. 'I didn't realize. I thought one might help me run Event Horizon, show me who was disloyal. I took the assessment tests and came out esp positive. Grandpa was furious.'

'You'd be spreading yourself too thin. Run with what you've got, Julia. Event Horizon is going to demand every scrap of your attention. You can always hire specialists like me to combat specific problems.'

'But how do I know who to trust?' she whispered insistently.

His fingers found her chin, tilting her head up. 'That's everybody's problem, Julia, not just yours. It's an unending question. People change, someone who you could entrust with the crown jewels one day will sell out for a pound the next. You want my advice? Put your faith in Morgan Walshaw. Strange as it may sound, people like that need someone to work for. So long as you don't evolve into some kind of irresponsible playgirl he'll remain loyal.'

She pulled a face. 'Morgan? God!'

'Just remember, loyalty doesn't mean slavish obedience. If he disagrees with you on some issue he won't be doing it simply to spite you. Ask him to explain his reasons, and *listen* to the answer.'

'You're worse than Grandpa,' she moaned.

'Life's a bitch, then you die. No messing.' He grinned, and started down the stairs again.

She walked in silence with him until they reached the hall. The air was cooler in the big vaulting chamber, its black and white marble tiles drawing away April's dry heat.

'Greg . . . there's something else.'

'Hey, what am I, your confessor?'

'No, this is about the blitz.' She knew he'd changed, hardening somehow. It was like she'd spoken a codeword, switching his mind from levity to total attention.

She started to tell him about Kendric, the buyout, her threat; speaking rationally, without rancour. And doing it that way made her mortified by how petty she sounded. What was it Kendric had said? Schoolgirl temper-tantrum.

'I couldn't let him go unpunished,' she said. 'He set out to destroy everything Grandpa spent fifty years of his life building, not to mention my future.'

Greg looked troubled, staring at one of the Turner landscapes without seeing it.

'Do you think I was right?' she asked nervously.

'Yeah, probably. I'd have done the same, I think.'

'So the blitz might have been Kendric's vendetta against Grandpa and me? Nothing to do with the giga-conductor.'

'Could be. But I think it's reasonable to assume Kendric is involved up to his neck; he's certainly my first choice. This possible mole implicates him directly.'

'You keep calling him "possible".'

'Yeah. It's almost too easy to write everything off on to one masterspy. But the evidence is pretty strong. Who knows? And now I think about it, this whole giga-conductor thing adds a new dimension to the memox-spoiler operation. Kendric was more than likely after the patent the whole while, that was the asset he really wanted to strip.'

'That's what I thought. But I couldn't tell you at the time. Sorry.'

'No problem. I didn't need to know. Tell me, exactly when did Dr Ranasfari crack the giga-conductor?'

'Tenth of November.' She didn't have to query the nodes, the date was ingrained. The last time she'd seen Grandpa really happy.

He sat slowly on an old monk's bench, thinking hard. She hovered, agitated. Wanting to know what he was mulling over, unwilling to interrupt. The hall's silence amplified every sound as she fidgeted.

'Half-way through the memox spoiler,' Greg mused. 'So it had already been working for a few months. The thing is, if the mole, or whoever, had already breached the security cordon around Ranasfari, then it's odds on that it was Kendric, or Kendric got word of it. Pirate data traffic is his speciality, after all. Tell me, would he have known in advance that Ranasfari was going to crack the giga-conductor? What I mean is, was the breakthrough sudden?'

'Not really. Ranasfari has been working on the project for a decade, he was confident of a positive result for almost a year beforehand. Then he produced a cryogenic giga-conductor last May. A room-temperature version was only a matter of time after that; a lightware cruncher problem, solving the chemical make-up, rather than any revelation in fundamental physics.'

'Yeah, I figured something along those lines. You see, ten years is a hell of a long time to keep something hushed up. If the mole informed Kendric about the cryogenic prototype, then he would have had time to organize the memox crystal spoiler. The dates certainly fit.'

'But you don't think so?'

'Not sure.'

'Why?'

'If Kendric knew about the giga-conductor, why did he authorize your buyout of the di Girolamo house?'

'I told you, I blackmailed him.'

'A couple of billion Eurofrancs each year, that's what your grandfather said the giga-conductor royalty licence would bring in, is that right?'

'Yah, in fact it's a conservative estimate.'

'So answer me this: with an eight per cent stake in Event Horizon, which you could never legally make him give up, why should Kendric worry about his family house being dragged through the mud? In fact, you would've looked pretty bloody silly if he hadn't knuckled under; exposing one of your own financial backers as a shark, then still having to cut them in on a share of your giga-conductor profits.'

The nodes turned the problem into neat packages of equations for her. Greg and the hall slipped away as she pushed them through a logic matrix. They began to develop a life of their own, the channels unable to confine them, twisting out of alignment. The instability began to absorb more and more of the nodes' processing power. She scrambled to maintain cohesion, loosening the parameters, adding additional channels. But her mind originated nothing ingenious enough to halt the imminent collapse. She observed helplessly as the channels wound in on themselves, constricting in ever-tighter curves, sealing the data packages in closed loops.

The bioware-generated edifice crumpled beyond salvation. Her imagination invested the scene with sound. From a vast distance she could hear a cathedral of glass slowly toppling over.

'Kendric couldn't have known about the giga-conductor,' she said finally.

'You reckon?'

'Yah. No. Not really. It's a paradox, you see, he must've known, yet he couldn't have.'

'That's the way I see it.' He seemed ridiculously cheerful. 'Know what we're going to do about it, Julia?'

'What?'

'Put Kendric at the top of the suspect list, then forget about him. Concentrate on tracking down the source of the leaks. When I've done that I'll see where they lead. Then we might begin to understand the game he's playing.'

She wasn't certain any more. Problems should be logical, solutions readily available. The pride she'd possessed in her own ability was dented: the nodes had always been a bulwark in her defence against other people, elevating her soul. No matter appearances and social awkwardness, she knew she was superior. Now this. Unable to provide her with an answer for the first time. And it was an answer which was utterly critical.

But Greg didn't seem unduly bothered, which gave her a certain degree of confidence. The guilt that this might have been all her fault was dissipating. What more had she been expecting from him?

He rose from the black-polished bench. 'Couple of days, week at the most, and it'll all be over, no messing. You can look back and laugh.'

'Thank you, Greg.'

'You haven't seen the bill yet. Walk me to the car? I might get lost otherwise; normally when I'm in buildings this size there are hordes of other people queuing to catch their trains.'

She laughed. A joke. He was joking with her. Then her father came into the hall, and the sudden bud of joy was crushed as though it'd never been.

Dillan Evans was wearing jeans and a baggy brown sweater which was fraying at the end of the sleeves. He was walking with a drunkard's hesitancy, taking care that his feet only trod on the black tiles.

'Hello, Daddy,' Julia said quietly.

He nodded absently at her, and looked Greg up and down with bleary eyes.

Julia felt like weeping. It was bad enough witnessing her father's state in private, having it exposed like this only exacerbated the pain.

She watched in dismay as he straightened up ponderously. 'Bit old for her, aren't you?' he said to Greg.

'Daddy, don't, please,' her voice had become high, strained. She caught Greg's eye, a tiny motion of her head telling him to say nothing. Please. He inclined his head discreetly, thank God.

Dillan grunted roughly. 'Out of the way, don't embarrass us, keep out of sight, keep your mouth shut, never know what might come out. Want me to shut up, Julie? Is that it? Want your father to keep his dirty mouth closed. Afraid of what the old fool will say? I'm only looking after your welfare. I've got a right to meet my little girl's men friends.'

'Greg is not a boyfriend, Daddy. He's someone who works for us.'

'Work, eh?' A crafty expression twisted his vacant face. 'Been up to see the old bastard, have you?'

'What?' Julia blurted, alarmed.

'The old bastard. Up there in the study.'

'Grandpa's dead, Daddy. You watched the funeral on the channel,' she enunciated with slow deliberation, as though she was explaining a particularly difficult fact to a small child.

'Oh, Julie, Julie. How you hate me, a disgrace, a failure as a father. Beneath contempt. Written off. Well I'm an Evans, too, don't forget. A mighty Evans. I see things, I listen to what's going on. I know.' He started up the stairs, clinging tightly to the banister rail. His foot slipped, nearly sending him tumbling. He looked round at her mute face staring up at him. 'I could have

157

done it. If he'd given me the chance, I could've run the company. Bastard never gave me the chance. He did this to me, his own son! Not you, though, Julie; everybody loves you. He does, I do. Everybody does.' The words spluttered into incoherence. He glanced round nervously, suddenly confused as to where he was, what he'd been saying. His hand pulled hard at the banister, starting himself off on the climb again. He began muttering fractured words as he went.

Julia buried her face in her hands. After a while she felt Greg's arm round her shoulder. Misery compounded as she found she was quivering silently.

'Sorry,' she mumbled, lowering her hands to wipe at her eyes. Absolutely refusing to cry. Then the implications of what her father had said penetrated. 'Oh, God, do you think he was the one?'

'Not deliberately, if that's what you mean,' said Greg. 'Maybe he let something slip. But it wouldn't do any good asking him. I doubt he'd remember. And I couldn't tell whether or not he was telling the truth.'

She considered that, if Greg couldn't make sense of her father with his ability – 'His mind has gone, hasn't it? I mean, really gone, destroyed.'

'Julia.' He held her firmly, a hand on each shoulder. 'Isn't it about time you booked him into a clinic?'

'He's my father,' she insisted plaintively. 'He needs me.'

'He's hurting you, Julia. Far too much. You can't hide that from me, remember? A clinic will care for him properly. You can visit. Hell, you can afford to build a clinic. Put it in a house like this one, he won't even realize the difference.'

She studied something away to the side of his head, swallowing hard. 'Maybe,' she whispered.

'You should get out,' he expanded blithely, changing tone, breaking the mood. 'A girl like you ought to be beating off the boys with a stick. Stay up till the wee hours at disreputable parties. That sort of thing. Do you the world of good. Wilholm is grand to look at, but it isn't exactly jumping and jiving, now is it?'

'No,' she smiled meekly. 'I'm going away next weekend, actually. A book launch.'

'A what?'

'A book launch. It's a big PR event, lasts for two days, truly swish. Naturally the Evans heir was invited.'

'Good. It's a start. Now, what about a boy?'

'I know someone,' she said defensively. And the thought lit that idyllic warming core of delight.

They walked out into the furnace heat of a cloudless day. The sun's glare yellowed half of the sky.

'Goodbye, Greg, and thanks again.' She stood very close as he blipped the Duo's lock. Would he kiss her?

He tugged the Duo's door open and smiled affectionately, like a doting uncle. 'Any time.'

Oh well.

She waved at the car until the curve of the drive took it from view.

End GregTime#Three.

She'd have to edit her father out, though.

16

Scorching April sunlight metamorphosed the A1 into a bubbling ribbon of tar, for once reversing the rampant greenery's encroachment. Nettles and grass were sucked below the surface by sluggish eddies, consumed and fossilized within the black brimstone.

The Duo moved along the northbound carriageway with one continuous ripping sound. Greg drove automatically, trying to make sense of the case. He hadn't admitted it to Julia, but Kendric di Girolamo had him badly worried. A paradox, she'd said. And she was right. Intuition convinced him Kendric was involved with the blitz attack somewhere along the line, no faint tickle either. But why had the man allowed her to buy him out? Maybe Gabriel would know.

He drove straight through Edith Weston, on to Manton, and turned right, freewheeling down the hill towards Oakham, saving the batteries. A dense strip of rhododendron bushes planted along the side of the railway line running parallel to the road was in full bloom, tissue-thin scarlet flowers throwing off a pink haze as they basked in the rich sunlight. Greg barely registered them; he was worried by the idea of a high-placed mole hidden somewhere among Event Horizon's staff. The last thing he needed was an opposition that was being fed his own progress reports. Maybe it would be best not to keep Walshaw a hundred per cent up to date. More subterfuge, more complexity.

Dillan Evans disturbed him, as well. Not so much his state, but the fact that he could piece together his father's particular bid for immortality from the snippets of conversation he'd picked up around the manor. If Dillan Evans could, anyone could. That definitely meant interviewing all of Wilholm's staff. Another neurohormone hangover to anticipate. Or had Dillan Evans realized because he knew exactly how avaricious and egotistic his father was? That, given that the bioware's capability existed, he would inevitably spend a fortune bringing it to fruition and constructing an NN core. Either way, it left Dillan as a real monster of a loose end. No messing.

Greg had been surprised how bravely Julia handled her father. Her mind's peppy sparkle had dimmed severely in his presence, but her outward composure had been beautifully maintained. He admired that kind of dignity.

He even felt a degree of pity for Dillan. It would've been so easy to condemn him, but he couldn't find the scorn. He deserved compassion more than anything; a lost ruined man, cowering in the double shadow of his parent and child.

His sorry state made Julia all the more remarkable – or perhaps not, the best roses grew out of manure heaps. And despite being the end product of a decidedly screwed-up family, she shone like the sun. Embarrassingly so in his presence.

Sighing resignedly at the memory, he drove into Oakham, reducing speed as the cycle traffic built up around him. When Greg was a teenager it'd been a sleepy rural market town, home to nine thousand people. Then the Warming melted the Antarctic ice, and Oakham received a spate of refugees from the drowned Fens. Its population rose to well over the fifteen thousand mark, and all without a single new house being authorized by the PSP county committee. The town became a microcosm of English life, compressed, confined, and frantically scrabbling to adapt to the environmental and social revolutions of the new century.

Greg slowed to a crawl by the library at the end of the High Street. People were dismounting from their bicycles, wheeling them forward into the dense crowd ahead. The High Street was packed with market stalls, but there was just enough space left for the Duo between them and the waist-high piles of slowly degenerating kelpboard boxes which swamped the pavement. Greg grated into the gap with a broadside of horn blasts, and followed a shepherd driving his small flock of rotund beasts, gene-tailored for meat heaviness. The Duo's wheels squelched softly on the carpet of grey-brown turds they laid on the pitted tarmac.

The buildings on this side of the street were mostly old estate agents and building societies. They'd all closed down in the Credit Crash, and the PSP had requisitioned the empty premises under the one-home law, converting them into accommodation modules. Even now there was little improvement in the housing pressure; council and government were locked in a squabble over funds for a new estate on the southern edge of the town. Entire families had crammed into the makeshift facilities behind the shops' broad plate-glass windows, the oldest relatives sitting amongst the bleached displays like flesh-sculpture buddhas watching the world go by.

Not all of the old retail businesses had gone under: there was still a hotel, a couple of butchers, a recently de-nationalized bank, and a century-old family gear business that had survived; but most of the town's trade had been usurped by the thriving High Street market. The stalls were crude wooden trestle affairs, keeping the sun at bay with awnings of heavy cloth, patterned in brightly coloured stripes or loud checks. Animals bleated mournfully in their pens, birds squawked inside cramped wicker cages. Pyramid mounds of fruit were stacked high, every colour of the rainbow. Ranks of skinned rabbits hung from poles, stall owners languidly flicking leafy switches at them to keep the flies off. There were clothing stalls, cobblers, tinkers, gear repairers, distillers with an astonishing array of liqueurs, carpenters, potters, the whole repertoire of manual crafts clamouring for attention.

Three hundred metres and ten minutes later Greg cleared the

market and turned right into Church Street, parking outside a little bakery shop.

On the other side of the road was a head-high stone wall, rapidly disappearing under an avalanche of dark waxy-leafed ivy. There was a raised garden behind it, enclosed by buildings on two sides and a chapel on the third. He went through the open wooden gate and took the steps two at a time.

The garden and buildings used to be part of the Oakham School campus, but private education hadn't lasted six months after the PSP came to power, swept away in the card carriers' Equalization crusade. And after that the refugees had hit town demanding somewhere to live. The campus was requisitioned as fast as the shops, playing fields given over to allotments.

The school's Round House was a plain circular building sitting on the south side of the raised garden, three storeys high, and built from pale Stamford brick. Its door was closed and locked. Greg stood in front of it, motionless, waiting. It was a game he and Gabriel played. After half a minute he admitted defeat once again and turned to the small touchpanel set into the brick. He started pecking out the six-digit code for room seventeen.

'Come on up,' Gabriel's voice chimed out of the intercom before he'd finished. The lock buzzed like an enraged hornet.

Gabriel Thompson had been a major in the Mindstar Brigade, possessed of the most reliable precognition faculty ever recorded. She was thirty-nine; only two years older than Greg, but judging from physical appearance alone he would've said it was closer to twenty. Her fair hair had already faded to a maidenly pearl-white, flab was accumulating all over her body. She wore a fawn-coloured woollen cardigan and tweed skirt, making her broad and shapeless, a half-hearted attempt to disguise her physical deterioration.

It pained him to see her this way, a prematurely middle-aged spinster. Especially as his mind insisted on remembering her as that neat, efficient young officer in Turkey. A fine-looking woman in her day, idolized like an elder sister.

He was given a moody stare as he entered her room on the second floor; it was one of thirty in the Round House, originally intended to sleep two girl boarders. As a permanent bedsit it was terribly cramped.

'Typical,' she said. 'Only ever visit when you want something.' Badly applied dabs of make-up made her face shine in the golden afternoon sunlight filtering through the net curtain.

'Not true. Oh, Eleanor says hello.'

'I doubt it.' Gabriel began pouring tea from a silver pot into two bone china cups, all neatly laid out ready.

Rock music from one of the other rooms thumped out a soft bass rhythm in the background, echoing down the stairwell.

'So what have you come for this time?' she asked.

'Philip Evans.'

'He's dead.' She paused for a moment, then her eyes widened in surprise. 'Christ!'

All she needed was a word, a phrase; extrapolating the future from there. Events closest to her came across strongest. There would be no point in him asking her what was going to happen to someone on the other side of the world, she wouldn't be able to see them.

She'd described the probabilities to him once, explaining her limits after he'd asked her for some impossible piece of intelligence information when they were fighting the Jihad legion.

I'm standing at the mouth of a very large river, she'd said, at the moment when the future becomes the present; and I'm looking across the land where the water originated, seeing the first fork, and beyond that the tributaries branching away, and then the tributaries' tributaries, splitting, multiplying, ad infinitum. The far horizon gives birth to a trillion rills, all converging to the mouth, each one the source of a possible destiny. They are the Tau lines, future history. On their way towards me they clash and merge, building in strength, in probability, eradicating the wilder fringes of feasibility as they approach confluence, until they reach the mouth: the point of irrevocable certainty.

She could send her mind floating back along those streams,

questing, probing for what would come. The prospect terrified her, he knew. She'd hidden that from the Army, but of course he'd seen it at once. The knowledge cost him; as the one person whose empathy allowed him to see the true extent of that dread he felt protective towards her. He was her involuntary confessor, obligated.

Way ahead of her, at the furthest extremity of each of those streams, where the flow was little more than a trickle in the dust, her death waited for her. She refused to let her mind roam far into any of the possible futures; but even that self-imposed proscription meant she lived with the mortal fear of the streams drying up, one by one, the drought inching towards her; a reality so blatant she'd never be able to shield her eldritch sight against it.

Greg thought of himself sitting in a plane as it began its long fall out of the sky; standing paralysed by fear in the middle of the road as some huge lorry bore down, brakes squealing, unable to stop in time. She had to live with the prospect of seeing that eventuality raising its head every minute of every day. Knowing that it was inevitably going to happen.

So he forgave her for going to seed. His espersense was a heavy cross. He would never have the strength to carry hers.

'Exactly,' he said. 'Philip Evans made it back from the grave. Can you see who's behind the blitz on his NN core?'

'Hmm.' Her mind betrayed how intrigued she was. 'I'll have a look.' She cut a slice of almond cake and began munching, staring up at the ceiling, eyes unfocused.

He sipped his tea, trying to identify the herbs. Rosemary, possibly. The market stalls weren't particularly choosy what they ground up.

'Not a thing,' Gabriel said.

He didn't show any disappointment. (Was there some alternative-universe Greg Mandel currently raging at her failure?) The answer did exist. Down one of those Tau lines was a future where he and Gabriel teamed up and successfully tracked down whoever had attacked Philip Evans. But for the moment the distance was too great. She wouldn't stretch herself that far, not even for friendship's sake.

'Will you help?' he asked.

She looked dreadfully unhappy.

'No big visions,' he reassured her. 'Just cross out probabilities for me, eliminate suspects and dead ends. That kind of thing. I've got to interview Event Horizon's giga-conductor team tomorrow, that's over two hundred people. Then I'll probably wind up having to go through the security division's head-quarters staff for the mole. My espersense can't last out that long. Twenty's my limit. And that hurts bad enough.'

'All right,' she whispered.

He held up the card Morgan Walshaw had given him. Gabriel stared at it, mesmerized. He could sense the trepidation mounting in her mind. She wanted to soar into the future and find out what it meant. The larger, ever-present dread held her back.

'Afterwards,' he said, 'succeed or fail, I'm going to pay for your operation. That's your fee, Gabriel, that gland is coming out.'

She looked at him incredulously, her mind spilling out hope. Her eyes watered. 'I can't,' she moaned.

'Bullshit,' he said softly. 'I'm the one who can't, I can keep my demons at bay. You can't. You think I'm blind to what the gland has done to you? You're getting out, Gabriel, no more living under the pendulum.'

Tears began to roll down her cheeks, smearing the makeup. She twisted round to avoid his eyes, looking out of the window.

He put his hands on the nape of her neck, feeling the solid knots of muscle, massaging gently. 'I hate seeing you like this. You don't live; you crawl from day to day. It's a miserable existence. Too timid to walk under the open sky in case a lightning bolt hits you. It's got to stop, Gabriel. No messing.'

'You bastard, Mandel. I'd be nothing without the gland, nothing.'

Outside, the sun shone down on the school's old chapel on

the other side of the garden, its pale stone gleaming like burnished yellow topaz.

'You'd be human.'

'Bastard. Prize bastard.'

'Truthful bastard.'

He turned her to face him. She was suddenly busy with a
lace handkerchief, wiping away tears, making an even worse
hash of the make-up.

'Tomorrow,' he said. 'We'll start with the Event Horizon
Astronautics Institute, OK?'

She looked confused for a moment, then gathered her
thoughts, entering into that familiar trance for a few seconds.
'Yes, that's a good start.'

'Right, then. I'll pick you up at nine o'clock.'

'Fine.' She sniffed hard, then blew into the handkerchief.

Greg leant forward and kissed her brow.

17

A pair of dolphins spiralled around Eleanor, silver bubbles streaming out from their flashing tails, wrapping her at the centre of an ephemeral DNA helix. Playful scamps. She'd come to love the freedom of the water over the last few weeks. Down here, surrounded by quiet pastel light, tranquillity reigned; life's ordinary worries simply didn't exist below the surface. Sometimes she spent hours swimming along the bottom of Rutland Water; one small part of her mind checking the long rows of water-fruit rooted in the silt, while her memories and imagination roamed free. Daydreaming really, but this gentle universe understood and forgave.

The marine-adepts had warned her about the state. 'Blue lost', they called it. But she couldn't believe it was that dangerous. Besides, the reservoir was finite, not like the oceans they talked of, where some of their kind never returned. Swimming away to the edge of the world.

She helped tend their crops three or four days each week; with inflation the way it was, the water-fruit money came in useful. And she could spend the time thinking about life, the world, and Greg, weaving the strands in fanciful convolutions; so that when she left the water behind her mind was spring fresh and eager for the sights, sounds, and sensations of land again. Mental batteries recharged. The world outside that ever-damned kibbutz was too big to endure in one unbroken passage.

She felt a dolphin snout poking her legs, upsetting her balance. It was Rusty, the big old male. She knew him pretty well by now, though some of the others were hard to distinguish. Rusty had a regular ridge of scar tissue running from just behind his eyes down to his dorsal fin. The marine-adepts never talked about it, so she never asked. But something had been grafted on to him at one time. She didn't like to think what.

They'd brought eight dolphins with them to the reservoir to help harvest their water-fruit. The dolphins' long, powerful snouts could snip clean through a water-fruit's ropy root. All of them were ex-Navy fish, their biochemistry subtly adjusted, enabling them to live comfortably in fresh water as well as salt. Greg said that was so they could be sent on missions up rivers. But whatever Rusty had been made to do back then hadn't affected his personality; he could be a mischievous devil when he wanted to be.

Like now.

She suddenly found herself flipped upside-down, whirl currents from his thrashing tail tumbling her further. The remains of Middle Hambleton spun past her eyes. Shady rectangular outlines of razed buildings rising from the dark grey-green alluvial muck. One day she was determined she'd explore those sad ruins properly.

She stretched her arms out, slowing herself, then bent her legs, altering her centre of gravity, righting herself. A shadow passed over her, Rusty streaking away, beyond retribution. She let herself float upwards.

At the back of her mind she was marvelling at her own enjoyment. She, a girl who couldn't even swim six weeks ago, even though the kibbutz at Egleton was right beside the reservoir. The marine-adepts had thought that hilarious.

For the first few weeks after she'd moved into Greg's chalet she'd had a sense of being divorced from selected sections of his life. Apart from the Edith Weston villagers everyone he knew was ex-military; the marine-adepts, Gabriel, that mysterious bunch of people in Peterborough he'd referred to obliquely a couple of times, even the dolphins. They were a hard-shelled clique, one that'd formed out of shared combat experiences. She could never possibly be admitted to that. And the marine-adepts were naturally reticent around other people; it wasn't quite a racial thing, but they did look unusual until you were used to them. The only time they left the reservoir was to drive their water-fruit crop to Oakham's railway station.

Breaking through their mistrust had been hard going. The turning point had come when Nicole had finally taken over her swimming lessons, more out of exasperation than kindness, she'd thought at the time. But a bond had formed once she realized how keen Eleanor was, and the rest of the floating village's residents had gradually come to accept her. A triumph she considered equal to walking out on the kibbutz in the first place.

She could never hope to match the marine-adepts in the water. They had webbed feet which enabled them to move through the water with a grace rivalling the dolphins, and their boosted haemoglobin allowed them to stay submerged for up to a quarter of an hour at a time. But with flippers and a bioware mirror-lung recycling her breath she was quite capable of helping them in the laborious nurturing of the water-fruit. Planting the kernels deep in the silt, watching out for fungal decay in the young shoots, clearing away tendrils of the reservoir's ubiquitous fibrous weed which could choke the mushy pumpkin-like globes. The marine-adepts had staked out eight separate fields in the reservoir, and earned quite a decent living from them.

Her only real failure among Greg's friends had been Gabriel Thompson. The woman was so stuck-up and short-tempered Eleanor had wound up simply ignoring her. She suspected Gabriel had a jealousy problem. Always mothering Greg.

She broke surface five hundred metres off shore, about a kilometre away from the Berrybut time-share estate. The sun was low in the sky, and she could see flames rising from the estate's bonfire.

Rusty's chitter tore the air ten metres behind her. She slapped the water three times and he vanished again. Some Navy dolphins had been fitted with bioware processor nodes to make them totally obedient to human orders. But Nicole said the Navy had left Rusty's brain alone. The marine-adepts used a hand-signal language to talk with the reservoir dolphins. Eleanor had mastered most of it, and Rusty nearly always did as she asked. That little edge of irrepressible uncertainty in his behaviour was what made him such fun.

She felt the change in water pressure as he rose underneath her, then she was straddling him, clutching desperately at his dorsal fin as he began to surge forwards. Homeward-bound fishermen in their white hireboats stared with open-mouthed astonishment as she sped past, slicing out an arc of creamy foam in her wake.

Rusty let her off fifteen metres from the shore, where the bottom started to shelve. A flock of panicky flamingos took flight, pumping wings creaking the air above her. She gave her steed an affectionate slap and waded ashore, arms aching from hanging on against the buffeting water.

The familiar claimed her as she walked up the slope to chalet six. Meat roasting on the bonfire, pork by the smell of it. Dusty whirlwind of the football game, rampaging along the side of the spinney. Swapping easy greetings with the few adults milling about. Dogs underfoot, Labradors, who made the best rabbiters. A couple of wolf-whistles following her progress. She smiled at that. Something else she wouldn't have been able to cope with before.

She wore a one-piece costume whenever she went into the water now. The polka-dot bikini which Greg had bought her was far too skimpy for any serious diving – typical lecherous male. Not that she wanted to change him. Night time with Greg was one continuous orgy, hot, strenuous, sweaty, and tremendously exciting; another fruit forbidden to her at the kibbutz.

The Duo was parked in its usual spot. She was looking forward to hearing what he'd been called away to, the message he'd left on the terminal had been oddly brief.

She shrugged out of the mirror-lung, and plugged its nutrient coupling into the support gear on the veranda.

Greg was inside, dressed in an old purple sweatshirt and shorts, fooling around with the kitchen gear. Whatever he was cooking smelt good.

'My saviour.' She gave him a radiant smile. 'After your message I wasn't sure if you'd be back, and I haven't got the energy left to cook.'

He slurped a spoonful of the sauce he was simmering. '*Béarnaise*, it's nice, try some.' He held up the spoon.

She took a sip as his other arm slipped around her waist, hand coming to rest on her buttock. 'You're right, not bad.' For a moment she thought he was going to dump the meal and urge her into the bedroom. He always got turned on by the sight of her in a wet swimming costume. And there was plenty of time before she was due behind the bar at the Wheatsheaf. But then she looked closely at his face, and wrinkled her nose up. 'God, you look awful.'

'Thank you.'

'Sorry . . . but, what have you been up to?'

'Do me one favour,' he implored.

'What?'

'Just don't tell me I look like I've seen a ghost.'

*

'I don't like it,' Eleanor murmured.

It was long past midnight, the time for honest talk. They were lying on top of the big bed, the duvet crumpled up somewhere on the floor. The heat from making love beneath it would have been intolerable. As it was, they'd left the window full open, curtains wide to let the balmy night air flow around their bodies.

A quarter-moon was riding high in the sky, bathing the room with a spectral phosphorescence. She stretched out on her side beside him, her hands pillowing her head.

'Why not?' There was a certain tenseness in his voice.

'Just don't,' she said.

'Female intuition?'

'Something like that.'

He wet the tip of his forefinger and began to trace a line from her shoulder to the flare of her hips, innocently curious. 'I'm supposed to be the one with the hyper-senses.'

'You want logic? OK. It's too big. You're a one-man band, they're warring armies. They're out to kill each other, Greg. That security man, Walshaw, said as much. This giga-conductor stuff, it pushes the stakes too high. You don't know who the other side is, you don't know who to watch out for. There are an awful lot of *kombinates* who will suffer because of the giga-conductor. Any one of them could decide they don't want you interfering.'

'Firstly, I share Julia's conviction that Kendric di Girolamo is involved somewhere, the mole is his plant. So at least I know one direction of attack which I should be guarding myself from. And secondly, I'm not convinced that it is the giga-conductor which is the root cause of the blitz. Erasing Philip Evans's memories wouldn't halt its introduction, not with the Ministry of Defence pushing it. He's important, but not that important, no matter what he likes to think. I suppose it's partially conceit. By maintaining that Event Horizon can't do without him, he's justifying the expense of the NN core. I'm not so sure. Julia has inherited his drive, more if anything; and she's bright, she learns fast. She's just very young, that's all. No crime. The company won't fail with her in charge.'

'A personal vendetta extended to wiping a Turing personality program? Come on, nobody's that obsessive.'

'Don't you believe it. Philip Evans trod hard on a *lot* of toes to build up Event Horizon. In any case . . .'

'What?' She looked at him intently, seeing the confusion on his moonlit face.

'Philip Evans's memories aren't just a simple Turing program, there's more to it. He's not alive, I'll grant you that. But neither is he wholly dead. I saw something with my espersense.'

Eleanor stroked his abdominal muscles lightly, fingers dancing as she considered what he'd said. She never quite knew how to interpret his psi ability, it all sounded so vague and mystical, like tarot cards and reading tea leaves. Yet he did have the talent, no denying that. Her father's horror and fright still returned to her occasionally.

'All right,' she said, 'if it is di Girolamo, or someone else, looking for vengeance, they are even less likely to appreciate you coming between them and the Evans family.'

'All I shall be doing is interviewing Event Horizon personnel to find their mole, and seeing if my own contacts know anything about the blitz. There's no danger in that.' He took her hand and brought it up to his lips, kissing her knuckles. 'Look, this is what I've been wanting to break into for years. It's a regular case, just interviews and data correlation, and it pays regular money. I'm not going to touch the hardline side.'

'What do you mean, break into? I thought this is what you did.'

'Part time,' he said. 'But this is the second time in a few months that Event Horizon has called me in to sort out their problems. No amount of advertising and PR work can generate that kind of reputation. This could be what I need to make the switch. I could maybe put myself on a business footing, get an office, a secretary, some assistants – hell, pay taxes too. I think I'd like that.'

She moved closer, resting against him, feeling hot sweaty skin pressing into her belly. It was a funny mood he was in; indecisive, which wasn't like him at all. 'I don't want to change you, Greg.'

He grinned and patted her backside lightly. 'Too late, you already have. Don't you want me to have a regular job?'

'I'd like that, yes. But I don't want you getting hurt trying to build some kind of impossible reputation.'

'Tell you, there's no worry on that score, I'll be perfectly safe, Gabriel's coming with me.'

'I see.' It would have to be Gabriel he took along. Eleanor reckoned her psi ability was completely tabloid. But if she started protesting now he'd think she was just being childishly petulant. And she could hardly see the two of them running off together,

Gabriel had to be at least ten years older than Greg. Whatever bond they had between them was locked safely in the past.

'I'm only being practical,' he said. 'Gabriel can spot trouble long before it starts. And whilst we're on the subject of practical, you might care to look at the chalet walls some time. We're providing a home for more insects than you'll find at a natural history museum.'

'Money,' she said in disgust. 'It always boils down to money.'

'The way the world's built. Nothing to do with me.'

She rested her head on his chest, listening to his heartbeat. 'I know. I wasn't angry at you.'

'There's something else wrong, too,' he said. 'I simply cannot believe a mole, no matter how highly placed, could breach a security cordon which Morgan Walshaw set up; certainly not a security cordon around something as ultra-hush as the giga-conductor. The stuff is Event Horizon's entire future. You haven't met him, but take it from me, he's as good as they come. Reliable, smart, experienced, he just doesn't make elementary mistakes. If it had been breached at any time in the last ten years, he'd know.'

Eleanor thought he was saying it mechanically, as though he was trying to convince himself with repetition. 'So the mole isn't an executive, he's on the inside of the cordon.'

He shifted his shoulders, restless. 'Doubtful, Walshaw would arrange to have every one of Ranasfari's research team vetted and constantly reviewed. And if the mole was on the inside, how come he knew of Philip Evans's NN core?'

'Oh, yes. Hey, what about a psychic? Surely someone with a gland could peer in on both the giga-conductor laboratory and the clinic where they spliced the NN core together?'

'Unlikely, although I admit it's possible. There aren't many of us, not even worldwide. And the premier-grades, the ones whose esp is powerful enough to reach into Event Horizon's research facilities from a distance, you can count them on one hand. Not that they're used for anything so mundane as trawling in any case. It's like this; to bring in a premier-grade psychic you have to know there's something worthwhile for them to peek. Almost a catch twenty-two scenario. Normally, premier-grades are brought in to acquire specific items, like a formula or template. And as Event Horizon has already patented the giga-conductor that would seem to preclude their involvement. If a *kombinate* had acquired the giga-conductor's molecular structure they would've slapped down the patent before Event Horizon. The blitz would never have happened.'

'A prescient like Gabriel, then. One of them looked into the future and saw Event Horizon churning out the giga-conductor, and sold the information to a *kombinate*.'

'Gabriel is the best prescient there is, and she didn't know, not even with her own future interwoven with the giga-conductor.'

Eleanor nearly said that it could'ye been a prescient who wasn't so totally neurotic as Gabriel, but held her peace. Greg could get quite unreasonably defensive when it came to the silly woman. It was the military clique thing again. She knew she would never be able to appreciate the kind of combat traumas which they had been through together in Turkey.

'So what are you trying to say?' she asked.

'Just that it doesn't ring straight. Blitzing the core out of spite isn't *kombinate* behaviour.'

'It was a vendetta, then.'

He let out a long wistful sigh, frowning. 'Wish I knew.'

'Poor Greg.'

She snuggled closer, brushing her breasts provocatively against his torso as she slid on top of him. Greg had a thing about big breasts, which she exploited ruthlessly when they were having sex. He glanced down owlishly, frown fading.

'I was thinking,' he said. 'Why don't you come with me when I visit my contacts? There's one in Peterborough I'll probably visit.'

She tried not to show any surprise. Nicole had dropped the occasional hint that he'd taken an active part in the events leading up to the Second Restoration, and she'd guessed that was tied up somewhere with his old Army mates in Peterborough. But he'd never offered to introduce them before.

'I'd like that.' Short pause. 'Will Gabriel be coming?'

'Er, no. The contact I'm thinking of doesn't like too many visitors. We can go the day after tomorrow; I fixed up to take Gabriel to Duxford in the morning, interview Ranasfari's people. Shouldn't take long.'

'Right.' She thought it was about time to lighten the atmosphere, take him away from intrigue and human failings. She tapped a hard fingernail on his sternum. 'Now what about this Julia? She sounds a bit of a handful to me.'

'She is. You'll never guess what she wanted me to do.'

'What?' She couldn't help the note of bright curiosity which bubbled into her voice.

'I'll show you.'

18

The crude placards lined the M11 for kilometres either side of Cambridge. Large kelpboard squares, sprayed with fluoro-pink lettering that dribbled like a window's condensation. They flapped beneath sturdy sun-blistered road signs, themselves so old the few legible names had distances in miles.

CAKE AND EAT IT NOW!

'What's the matter with them?' Gabriel exclaimed irritably as the Duo passed Little Shelford. 'Do they want those bloody card carriers back in power?'

KRILL DON'T HAVE BOLLOCKS
THEY JUST TASTE LIKE THEM

'You are deep into student country,' Greg told her, amused by her reaction. 'What did you expect? They just don't like governments, full stop. Any sort of government. Never have, never will. They think demonstrating political awareness is exciting. You should encourage questing young minds.'

DIGNITY NOT ECONOMIC THEORY

The Duo's cooler was going full blast, grinding out uncomfortable gusts of frigid air. Gabriel's grunt was lost in the noise of the fans.

'They can't have it both ways,' she said. 'Two years ago there wasn't any food at all. Inflation is the price you pay for a free-market economy. Wages rise to cope, it's cyclic.'

'But do student grants rise as well?'

'Christ, whose side are you on? If they're so bloody aware they should know freedom isn't perfect. If they'd tried protesting when Armstrong was running the country they would've become non-people before you could say community responsibility.'

'So put up your own banners, tell them, not me.'

The motorway was in surprisingly good condition. Dead sycamores with peeling bark and bleached wood rose out of the scrub tangle at the edge of the hard shoulder. Greg toed the brake as they approached a large densely packed patch of scarlet flowers shining with livid intensity under the Sahara-bright sun. He thought they were poppies at first, except they were too big. A single palm-sized petal, waxy; thousands of them waving in the breeze.

'Someone agrees with you,' he said drily, inclining his head.

Two young men in sombreros and dirty jeans were ripping down one of the kelpboard placards. Their bicycles lay on the fringe of the flamingo flower carpet. He spotted badges with the deep-blue crown of the New Conservative party emblem pinned on their T-shirts.

Gabriel nodded with tight approval at this vandalism of graffiti. Greg returned to the tarmac ahead. Crazy world.

He turned off the nearly deserted road at junction ten, on to the A505. There was a new brightly painted green and gold sign at the side of the sliproad.

DUXFORD
Event Horizon Astronautics Institute

Freshly torn scraps of kelpboard littered the grass below it, flapping like broken butterflies in the hot dry breeze.

The Astronautics Institute was an all-new construction that'd sprung up out of the ruins of the Imperial War Museum. Armstrong's extremist followers had gleefully set about eradicating the museum's exhibitions and aircraft collection after they'd come to power, calling it a war pornography monument. The cabinet declared that Duxford was to become the National Resource Reclamation Centre, intended as the prestigious mainstay of the PSP's self-sufficiency policy. They said it would dismantle the war machines scrapped under their demilitarization programme and turn them into useful raw material for industry.

Greg remembered the hundreds of APVs and Challenger IV tanks parked in the Chunnel marshalling yards after he got back from Turkey. All earmarked for Duxford and ignominy.

But all Duxford had ever achieved was to smash up the beautifully restored aircraft displays, and the first few train-loads of redundant Army vehicles. The promised smelters had never materialized, and the dole-labour conscripts had rioted. For eight years the abandoned hammer-mangled wrecks on the runway had snowed rust flakes on to the concrete, oil and hydraulic fluid seeping through the cracks, poisoning the soil. Then after the PSP fell, Philip Evans chose the site to be the foundation of his dream.

The Astronautics Institute had been visible as a gleaming blister on the horizon ever since the Duo passed junction eleven outside Cambridge. After that Greg found himself constantly readjusting his perspective to accommodate the size of the thing. It was *huge*.

He'd spent a few minutes the previous evening reviewing the data which he'd been given at Wilholm. But it'd completely failed to prepare him for what he was seeing now.

The main building was a five-storey ring of offices, research labs, and engineering shops, eight hundred metres in diameter, presenting a blank wall of green-silvered glass to the outside world. The area it enclosed had been capped by a solar-collector roof, giving the staff a voluminous hangar-like assembly hall for space hardware.

Construction crews were still finishing it off; two motionless cranes stood on opposite sides, piles of scaffolding littered the raw packed limestone surround, ranks of silent contractor vehicles were drawn up across the parking yards. Standard transit containers full of Event Horizon's own cybernetics were stacked outside the assembly hall's sliding doors, waiting to be installed. A saucer-shaped McDonnell Douglas helistat hovered overhead, its five rotors generating an aggressive down-draught as it struggled to maintain its position against the light north-easterly wind. A container was being winched down out of its belly hold, swaying like a pendulum in the gusts. Two more helistats waited high overhead.

Greg could see machinery and gear being moved from their temporary accommodation in patched-up Museum buildings into the Institute. With the bulk of the structure complete, Event Horizon's research, design, and management teams were starting to take up permanent residence.

A rag-tag army of scrap merchants had been let loose on the old airport, piling vans and horse-drawn carts high with the twisted shards of metal which were still strewn across the runway and taxi lanes. One of the merchants had modified an old street-cleaning lorry to sweep up the thick stratum of rust, and a dense cloud of orange dust foamed up from its bald tyres as it thundered up and down the concrete strip.

Philip Evans had built his mindchild with an eye to the future. Its proximity to the University colleges had proved subversively addictive, offering finance and top-range research facilities to budget-starved faculties. A move which put the cream of the country's intellect at his disposal.

Physically, the Institute was a totally self-contained complex, taking the concept of centralization right to its extreme. It could design and fabricate mission hardware ranging from torque-neutralizing screwdrivers for orbital riggers right up to the refineries which would latch on to asteroids and leach out the ores, minerals, and metals. Independent and efficient. And with the money the giga-conductor royalties would bring in, Greg realized, quite capable of achieving the space-activist dream: exploiting the solar system's wealth.

It also housed the team which had cracked the giga-conductor. Philip Evans had brought Dr Ranasfari back to England after the Second Restoration, wanting to keep a tight rein on his company's resident genius. Setting him up at the Astronautics Institute had been Morgan Walshaw's idea.

With so many recently assembled research and design groups scattered throughout the old museum buildings while they waited for their new facilities to be completed, the place was in a constant state of flux. Ranasfari's team could establish themselves in an office and laboratory unit at the centre and remain unnoticed amongst the flustered crowd. The lost in plain view concept had worked for two years.

'No wonder Evans was so upset when the memox spoiler began to affect Event Horizon's profit margin,' Greg said as they drew close to the Institute's gates. 'How much did this lunatic conceit cost him, for Christ's sake?' The data squirted from Philip Evans's NN core into his cybofax concerning the Institute had only given him generalities, PR gloss. No hard financial facts.

Gabriel answered with a shrug. He sensed a cold trickle of intimidation damping her thought currents.

The Institute was circled by a mushroom ring of ten geodesic spheres housing the satellite uplinks. On the eastern side was a peculiar horn-shaped antenna, unprotected from the elements. It had a temporary look to it. People were walking among the dove-grey Portacabins at its base, ant size. The damn thing must've been thirty metres high. Scale here was something else again.

Greg had a shrewd idea that that was the source of Gabriel's dismay. She'd grasped the Institute at once. With him, the ego-ablating effect was taking time, a slow dawning of his own utter insignificance.

A four-metre chain fence topped by razor-wire marked out the perimeter. There was a smaller fence inside, fine granite chippings between the two. A guard-dog run, or at least some form of hunt animal.

The entrance road was split into five channels, each with a pole barrier. Greg chose number one. The Duo had to pass over ratchet spikes before they got to the red-and-white striped barrier.

'What does he keep in here?' Gabriel muttered. 'Crown jewels?'

'Oh no, something far more valuable than that. Knowledge.'

A company bus drew up in lane two, full of sanitized young technical types, all of them wearing pale shirts and neat ties. Greg showed his new card to the white watchman pillar, and the barrier raised itself obediently.

'But can we get out so easily?' Gabriel asked.

'Your department.'

There were three parking yards. He found a space in the first, in the shadow of a big JCB. Gabriel climbed out, twisting her pearls self-consciously. The air was stifling, so Greg slung his leather jacket over his shoulder.

'We don't belong here,' Gabriel declared. She'd turned a complete circle, taking in the strange conflation of creaky old buildings, chaotically jumbled wreckage, and new mega-structure with a childlike expression of awe. 'You and I. It's not our world.' Her mind state verged on depression.

'Don't be such a Luddite,' he said.

She gave him a soft, pitying smile. 'You don't understand. This place, it has destiny. I can feel it, portent after portent, the weight of them pressing down, suffocating. Future history, eager to be enacted, glories waiting to be born.'

Her words triggered his own instinct, a feedback reinforcing misgivings. Another reason Gabriel lived alone, even he had to take her in small doses. What she saw, rambled about, there was no escape from knowing it was all true. Suppose she was to hint the approach of his own death?

There was a work crew laying the last stretch of paving slabs between the yard and the main building. A clump of bedraggled and confused daffodils were sprouting in one of the concrete troughs beside the entrance.

'Ready?' he asked just before they went in. 'Shouldn't take long.'

'You're telling me this?'

He grinned at the old reliably cranky Gabriel and waved the magic card at the door pillar.

*

Ten minutes later Greg was standing beside the front rank of seats in a deserted ten-tier press gallery, looking out into the Institute's Merlin mission control. It was the final humbling, he was a small bewildered child permitted a privileged glimpse of adults playing some marvellously intricate game, understanding nothing.

On the other side of the tinted glass, concentric semicircles of consoles faced big wall-mounted flatscreens showing pictures of alien worlds. Young shirtsleeved controllers sat behind them, studying cubes full of undulating graphics, muttering instructions into throat mikes. The central display was a map of the inner solar system, a snarl of coloured vector lines showing the disposition of the Merlin fleet.

The scene should've been generating a flood of urgency and excitement. Greg hadn't forgotten the emotion of the Sanger crew out at Listoel. Instead he received an impression of tension, his espersense confirming the mass anxiety.

Nervous knots of the controllers were forming at random amid the gear consoles, talking in low, concerned tones, breaking up to reform with different members, human Brownian motion.

'Bit of a flap on at the moment, I'm afraid,' said Martin Wallace. He was an Institute security officer who'd been summoned in a hurry by the authority vested in Greg's card. A stocky Afro-Caribbean in his late thirties, uncomfortable with

Greg and Gabriel's appearance and what it implied. 'Trouble in orbit. One of the Merlins has packed up for no apparent reason. The flight management teams are shitting bricks,' he stopped and flinched. 'Sorry, ma'am.'

Gabriel bit back a smile.

Greg peered through the glass, recognizing one of the figures in conference around the flight chief's desk, 'How long before we can see Dr Ranasfari?' he asked as he rapped his knuckles on the thick glass.

'Shouldn't be long.' Wallace stood at attention, upset by Greg's breach of etiquette.

Greg rapped again, harder.

Irked faces turned to look. Greg beckoned to Sean Francis. The young executive started, then nodded and headed for the door to the press gallery, brushing off protests from the cluster of senior controllers he was in deep conversation with.

'This is as good a place as any,' Greg said. 'We'll do our interviews here. You see that we're not disturbed.'

'Right.' Wallace backed out, not exactly bowing, but coming close.

'Macho,' Gabriel drawled. 'Any orders for me, Captain?'

'Yeah, now you mention it, Major, start skipping through the giga-conductor team. All the possible interviews I could have with them, see which of them, if any, leaked the information.'

Her good humour darkened. 'Don't want much, do you?'

'I'm not asking you to stretch. Just find what you can. I'll be satisfied with anything, even a string of negatives.'

'All right.'

Sean Francis bustled in. Completely unchanged, still pleasant, firm, capable, eager. Annoying.

'What brings you here?' he asked after Greg introduced him to Gabriel.

'I'm investigating the hackers' assault on Event Horizon's data network.'

'Really? You believe someone here is involved, yes?'

'Could be. What are you doing here? I thought you were bound for greater things. Julia told me you'd made the management board.'

Greg's first-name terms with his boss didn't escape Sean Francis's notice; a sharp spike of interest rose in his mind at the mention of her name. Outwardly, his positive cheeriness expanded. 'Ah, but this *is* greater things. Miss Evans appointed me as an independent management examiner after *Oscot* anchored in the Wash for decommissioning. I travel round company installations and report back directly to the trustees. This way I build up a working knowledge of Event Horizon second to none. Means I'm going to be on line for a top-rank management position in a couple of years, yes? Opportunities like that only happen once in a lifetime. I grasped it. And, well, here I am.'

'Doing?'

'Troubleshooting. Miss Evans has given the Merlin project a high priority rating. I'm here to hustle them along.'

'So what's the problem?' Greg asked. His gland began the neurohormone infusion. Sean's mind swam into a sharper focus.

'Merlin malfunction. Number eighteen, it's the first series-four model. Lot of high hopes riding on it. But the bitch is stalled in Earth orbit, three and a half thousand kilometres up. Absolutely dead in the water. Disaster time. We're talking reputations on the line here.'

'Ranasfari's?' Gabriel asked sharply.

Francis cocked his head to one side to look at her. 'Why do you ask?'

'Humour us, Sean,' Greg said, and showed him his new Event Horizon card.

The sight didn't flummox him quite like it had Wallace, but his mind tightened appreciatively. 'So? I'm impressed. This attack on the datanet is being taken seriously, yes?'

'The Trustees attach a certain importance to it,' Greg said. 'Now, what about Ranasfari?'

'Do you know what he's been working on?' Sean Francis asked cautiously.

'Room-temperature giga-conductor,'

'Fine, OK, had to be sure. You understand? Can't just shout my mouth off, yes?'

'We understand,' said Gabriel.

Francis caught the undertone of irony. 'The series-four Merlin is fitted with giga-conductor power cells. Thing is, Event Horizon has put in a bid to fit the RAF's Matador AGM-404 exospheric interceptors with the same marque of cells. If it is the giga-conductor which has screwed up then we're really up the old creek, yes?'

'And is it?' Greg asked.

'Too soon to say. They're still running the fault analysis.' Sean Francis's mind betrayed a lot of apprehension. Greg wrote it off as the pressure. Failure this soon after his promotion would send him tumbling right back down to the obscurity he'd clawed his way up from.

'Why do you need giga-conductor power cells on a nuclear-powered spaceprobe?' Greg asked.

'The isotopes only power the thrusters during the flight phase, lifting the Merlin out of Earth orbit and boosting it along its interception trajectory. Once it's matched velocities with its target asteroid they're jettisoned along with the shielding, which reduces the total mass to just over a tonne. Manoeuvring becomes a lot simpler and faster without all that surplus mass to shift around. The giga-conductor cells charge off the solar panels and provide power to the thrusters for the final approach phase, as well as moving the Merlin around the surface after rendezvous. Some of these Apollo Amor rocks are quite large, we need forty or fifty sample points to build up an accurate picture of the ore composition.'

Greg could see the little group of flight controllers round the chief's desk craning their necks in his direction, impatience registering in their surface thoughts.

'You'd better be getting back,' he told Sean Francis. 'Glad to see you're getting ahead. One last thing: did you know Philip Evans is still alive?'

From an academic viewpoint Francis's reaction was a fascinating emotional evolution. His initial stare was pure disgust; from there Greg's espersense read him progressing through disbelief and into contempt, then back into worry, and finishing up plain confused.

'I saw the body,' he said eventually.

'Right, well, thanks for your time.'

'I hope you're not going to be so tasteless with Miss Evans. She was very close to her grandfather.'

'Of course not. I'll tell you why I had to ask you that, one day,' he said, projecting as much *bonhomie* as he could muster, which simply served to deepen Francis's confusion.

He flicked an uncertain glance at Gabriel, and departed, a much puzzled man.

'Congratulations,' Gabriel said archly. 'You've just ruined his entire day. He can't concentrate on anything, he's so mixed up by that last crack of yours.'

'Tough. Life at the top isn't all roses. The sooner he learns, the better off he'll be.'

'Do you have to be so bloody rude to everyone?'

'We don't have the time to piss about. Whether that arriviste likes me or not isn't something I'll lose any sleep over. I'm doing my job the only way I know how.' He caught the antagonism rising in her. 'Besides,' he said resignedly, 'it's Philip Evans who's tweaked me.'

'Philip Evans?'

'Yeah. That NN core of his is fucking weird, unsettling. For a start I can't stop wondering if I'd translocate my thoughts if I was given the opportunity; I mean, it's a sort of immortality, isn't it?'

'And suppose some smart hacker breaks in, every dark secret you ever had will be wide open to them. Blockbuster stuff, if they publish it.'

'Yeah, you're right. Forget it. What did you see in Mr Dyna-mism Francis's future?'

'Nothing much, a lot of frenetic activity here for the next few days, several consultations with young Julia Evans about the Merlin. In fact he seems to have taken rather a shine to our Miss Evans.'

'Sean Francis?' Greg couldn't keep the reproach from showing in his voice. Cursed himself silently. 'But he's years older than her.'

Gabriel's grin was wicked. 'He's three years younger than you. And she doesn't regard you as out of reach, now does she?'

Years of experience prevented him from showing the slightest ire. 'The girl's got a silly crush, that's all. I can handle that. But Sean Francis, marrying the boss's granddaughter, well, that's . . .'

'Shocking? But Julia isn't the heir any more, she *is* the boss now.' Gabriel put her hand over her heart, sighing fulsomely. 'I think its romantic, myself.'

'Does he? No, don't answer that, I don't want to know.'

'Julia's really got you in a tizz, hasn't she?'

'Can we get back to the case, please?'

She chuckled. 'Certainly, Gregory. You can forget about Sean Francis, he really is a clean-cut square, his only failing is his ambition. He looks at every problem to see how he can benefit from it.'

'That's no crime.'

There was a knock on the door, Martin Wallace poked his head round. 'Dr Ranasfari's here.'

'Show him in,' Greg said, and mouthed *Kid gloves* to Gabriel, suddenly wishing he'd thought to warn her in advance.

Dr Ranasfari was in a foul mood. He looked like he hadn't slept for days. His eyes were red-rimmed, his hair was hanging limply, small flakes of dandruff dusted his collar. Creases criss-crossed his white shirt. There was no tie. Even the Institute's regulation security tag was missing.

His mind reflected his physical appearance; dull, shot through with frissons of agitation. The prospect that his creation had failed, coupled with the blitz against his patron, had come as a severe shock, Greg guessed. Jolting the secure academic world through which he moved. And now he had to answer impertinent questions. He wore hostility like a hedgehog coat.

'I'll be as quick as I can,' Greg said. 'I'm sure you have to get back to the Merlin.'

No response.

'Have you ever told anyone about Philip Evans's NN core?'

'Certainly not.'

'What about the giga-conductor?'

'No.' Ranasfari sounded uninterested.

'Unintentionally perhaps, a slip of the tongue? One mistake would be all it'd take. People place a lot of weight on your words.'

'Please, Mr Mandel. Ask your questions, reassure yourself. But don't attempt to ingratiate yourself. I fully appreciate the emphasis Philip Evans places on your investigation, I have already discussed it with him. That is why I agreed to see you. Your conclusions from a minimum data source during your earlier instance of employment indicate your professional competence. Although, I personally suspect a degree of intuition was involved on your part.'

'It was.'

'Interesting. Is that part of your psi-enhancement?'

'It seems to be, although it's very much a secondary facet. Now, a loose word?'

'No. I don't make that sort of mistake.'

'You of all people must appreciate the logic that there has been a serious leak within Event Horizon. Knowing about both the giga-conductor and the core logically makes you a suspect. However, now I'm satisfied you are not the origin of any leak' – Ranasfari smiled thinly – 'that leaves the team which grew the core, and your own giga-conductor researchers.'

The physicist's thin lips compressed dolefully. 'I realize this. It . . . is difficult to accept that one of my people is responsible. I hope you are not asking me to point an accusatory finger?'

'No. But I'd appreciate any other leads from your department. For instance, the lightware cruncher you used to design the original cryogenic giga-conductor with, could that have been hacked?'

'No, it is isolated from the Event Horizon datanet.'

Greg paused for a moment, waiting for any ideas to surface from his subconscious. He was aware of a background ache behind his temple. Options were converging at an alarming rate, he had a growing sense of conviction that the assistants weren't going to be the leak origin. Perhaps he'd picked the assumption off Gabriel. She was sitting on the bottom tier of seats, eyes closed, lost among the Tau multiplicities.

'Exactly how serious is this Merlin failure?' Greg asked, intuition prompting.

'Unless the cause can be determined precisely then it will be a major set-back to both programmes,' Ranasfari answered.

'Both?'

'Yes, the Merlin prospecting missions, and the commercial production of the giga-conductor.'

'When did the Merlin actually fail?'

Ranasfari picked up on the flash of excitement in his voice. 'I think I see what you are driving at. Yes. The Merlin failed yesterday morning, eight twenty-four, to be precise.'

'After the blitz.'

'Correct; approximately ten hours. Do you believe the two events are connected?'

Greg was certain of the connection. But there was a fragment of bedlam jarring what would otherwise have been an immaculate fusion of disjointed thoughts. The implication that it wasn't an obvious union. Yet it seemed straightforward. He almost let out a groan; this was as bad as the memox spoiler.

'The attack against Philip Evans could've been a blind,' Greg ventured. 'Remember the blitz was perpetrated against the whole Event Horizon network; one of the hackers could easily have tampered with the Merlin control programs while it was going on.'

'But why the delay?'

'An attempt at disassociating the events? No, wait a minute, how much altitude could the Merlin add in ten hours? Would it make recovery more difficult?'

'Altitude increase over ten hours would be approximately one thousand five hundred kilometres; you have to remember that at the start of the flight the Merlin masses four times as much as it will when it rendezvouses with its target asteroid. That means a low initial acceleration. But certainly that additional fifteen hundred kilometres would add considerably to the cost of recovery. Its current three-and-a-half-thousand-kilometre orbit is way above the Sanger ceiling. An inter-orbit tug would have to be chartered specially, which is a totally uneconomic prospect. Physical recovery was well down our option list. In fact, given normal circumstances, it wouldn't be considered unless a second Merlin suffered a similar failure. There are a great many conceivable reasons for the shutdown; the giga-conductor cell is not the only new component in series-four models. Few components are common to every Merlin, its development is a continual process of evolution. And, of course, the giga-conductor cells performed perfectly in the space environment simulation tests, they were most extensive.'

'But in the mean time a question mark hangs over introducing the giga-conductor cell.'

'Yes, unfortunately. A Ministry of Defence team from Boscombe Down has already arrived to review our fault-analysis data.'

'What has happened to the Merlin? Is it a total breakdown?' Greg asked.

'It looks like it. The propulsion system has shut down, and the communication tink has been severed. It won't even respond to signals directed at its omni-directional antenna.'

'Could its state have occurred by transmitting a rogue set of instructions, ordering it to shut down?'

'Indeed,' Ranasfari agreed. 'Providing you had the correct codes.'

'Which, presumably, are stored here in the Institute's memory cores.'

'Yes.'

'And are they isolated from the Event Horizon datanet?'

'No.'

'So the attack could be an attempt to discredit Event Horizon's giga-conductor, which at the very least would delay military funding of your production lines, giving your rivals an opportunity to make up lost ground.'

'That is certainly a theoretical possibility.' The shadowy overtones of worry were lifting from Dr Ranasfari's mind. 'I congratulate you, Mr Mandel.'

Greg felt a weight of relief lifting. 'I'd like to be kept informed of your progress on analysing the Merlin failure.'

'Certainly.'

'And if you can't find anything concrete may I suggest chartering an inter-orbit tug to recover it.'

'I doubt the expense would be authorized.'

'Mission planning will cost nothing. And if I don't come up with any positive leads I'll press Philip Evans to cough up the money.'

'I'm sure someone as persuasive as yourself will have no trouble. Good day, Mr Mandel.' Dr Ranasfari exited with what might have been the ghost of a smile on his mouth.

Gabriel gave him a slow laconic clap, the sound echoing hollowly in the empty gallery. Her eyes were still closed. 'I am impressed. That was one of the slickest pieces of seduction I've seen for many a year. Poor Eleanor couldn't have stood a chance.'

Greg ignored the crack. 'Simple logic. You want wholehearted co-operation, get them on your side. And empathy does have its uses. Like charm, some of us have it.'

He slouched on the journalist's seats next to her, letting the foam below the black imitation leather mould itself to his buttocks, and stretched his legs out. Beyond the glass, dismay seemed to be tightening its grip.

'How goes it with Ranasfari's team?'

'Total washout.' Her eyes fluttered open. 'If you interviewed every one of them all you'd find is a couple who've got a nice racket flogging off Event Horizon equipment and five syntho-heads. You were right, Morgan Walshaw knows how to handle security.'

'Has to be either the Ministry of Defence, or a mole, then.'

'Shaping up that way,' she agreed. 'So what now?'

'Elimination. My intuition says the Merlin failure and the blitz are related in some way. At the moment the only way I can reconcile the two is if the attack on Philip Evans was intended to divert his attention while the Merlin was hashed up to discredit the giga-conductor.'

'That's pretty tenuous, Greg. A few giga-conductor cells which may or may not have failed aren't going to bring the whole enterprise to a grinding halt. The breakdown could've been some kind of freak overspill from the attack on the NN core. That would be a connection of sorts.'

'No, the Merlin breakdown wasn't an accident.'

Gabriel didn't respond. At least she never questioned his intuition.

'Can you see the result of the failure analysis?' he asked.

'Sorry. Too far in the future from where we are.'

'Well, not to worry, we'll find out in due course. It might all turn out to be empty hypothesis, Lord knows psi intuition isn't stone-scripted. But I'd put a great deal of money on that connection. I'll decide for sure after we've interviewed the NN core team. Walshaw should have reeled them in by the day after tomorrow. By the way, what can you see of Ranasfari?'

'Oh, God.' She let out a long contemptuous breath. 'Definitely a contender for the world's most boring human being. He just doesn't have any interests outside his professional work. I'm sure it can't be healthy.'

'Leaves him open to blackmail?'

'I shouldn't think so. What could you possibly corrupt him with? In any case, he doesn't do anything remotely incriminating for the next few days, make that a week. And you've already cleared him.'

'True.' He pushed all the suspicions emanating from intuition out of his mind, cancelling the gland secretions, trying to sketch in a wholly logical course on the resultant virgin whiteness. 'I want to take you to Wilholm and meet Philip Evans sometime.'

'What for this time?'

'Two things. Give the staff the once-over to see if they knew about the NN core. And see if there's going to be another attack on him. If there is, it would mean I'm wrong about the opposition aiming at the giga-conductor. We'd be back to vengeance, Kendric di Girolamo, and the mole.'

'Makes sense. When?'

'Tomorrow afternoon. I'm busy in the morning.'

'So you are.'

He couldn't tell whether her carefully neutral tone was disguising anger or amusement. Her mind gave the impression of total indifference. A balance of the two, perhaps?

'Will Julia be at Wilholm in the afternoon?' he asked.

A broad smile spread across Gabriel's chubby face. 'You know, I do believe she will.'

19

Ninety per cent of England's road network had been abandoned in the PSP decade; the energy crunch put paid to most private travel, and the incendiary sun steadily deliquesced the tarmac to a worthless residue. A pre-Warming style maintenance programme was out of the question, economically unfeasible, environmentally unsound. Motorways and critical link roads were kept open, but the rest was left to waste away. People who could afford cars bought them configured to cope with the rough terrain. The A47 was one of the roads the PSP was forced to refurbish; it was an essential transport artery between Peterborough and the A1, and the PSP desperately needed the goods which the city manufactured. It meant that the A47's traffic levels were high, and most of the vehicles commercial. Driving down it was a new experience for Eleanor; she began to realize how different England's city life had become from the pastoral existence of the countryside and smaller market towns. It was almost as though the country was developing a split personality. Of course, the gulf was more pronounced here than anywhere else.

Peterborough struck her as a tripartite Babylon, the old, the new, and the waterbound condemned by adverse circumstances to live with each other, rival siblings cooped up in the same house. It sat on the shore of the gigantic salt quagmire which used to be the most fertile soil basin in all of Europe. The

Lincolnshire Fens were originally marshes, drained over centuries to provide a rich black loam which could grow any crop imaginable. They were perfectly flat, like Holland; on clear days you could see for forty or fifty kilometres over them, so some of Oakham's refugees had told her. The trouble was, the Fens' average height above sea level was two metres; in some places, like the Isle of Ely, they were actually below sea level. When the Antarctic ice melted they never stood a chance.

Peterborough absorbed nearly two-thirds of the population displaced by the rising water; the city had no choice, it was hemmed in between the new sludge to the east and a shabby band of tent towns on the high ground to the west. None of the refugees was going to move; they had lost their homes, they had found a functioning urban administration, and they were through with running, so they sat and waited for government to get off its arse and do something. The three attempts the PSP mounted to disperse them ended in riots. So the Party was left with no choice. They poured money into permanent accommodation projects, as well as allowing in foreign investment to ease the load on the Treasury, and as a result it became one of the most prosperous cities in England. Huge housing estates mushroomed to serve vast industrial precincts, a crazy mismatch of developments sprawling venomously over the green belt. A deepwater port was built above the drowned cathedral; dredgers reopened the Nene, gouging out a new laser-straight channel directly into the Wash.

Trade links, determination, and money, lots of money; that was the giddy synergy brew. Peterborough became England's Hong Kong, a unique city state of refugees determined to carve themselves a new life. High on that special energy which crackles around Fresh Start frontiers. Everybody was on the up and up, on the make, on the take. If you couldn't find it in Peterborough, it didn't exist. A philosophy completely out of phase with the rest of the country's lethargy. The PSP city hall apparatchiks just couldn't move fast enough to keep track of the construction chaos that boiled out from the suburbs. Half of the economy was underground, Eurofrancs only; smuggling was rife; spivs bought themselves penthouses in New Eastfield. A resurgent Gomorrah, her father had called it.

Eleanor followed a big methane-powered articulated lorry down the gentle slope towards the bloated Ferry Meadows estuary, née Park, the Duo's suspension thrumming smoothly on the tough thermo-cured cellulose surface. The A47 turned left at the bottom of the slope, running along the top of a small embankment above the filthy, swirling water. After the lorry rumbled round the bend, she could see a string of ten barges moored across the mile-wide estuary between the base of the embankment and Orton Winstow. Artificial islands of rock and concrete were rising beside each of them.

She watched a crane swinging its load of rock from a barge across to the centre of an island, dropping it with a low rumbling sound. A cloud of dust billowed up. When it cleared, she could see a gang of men swarming over the pile, rolling rocks down on to flat-topped carts so they could be packed behind the encircling wall of concrete.

The idea for an eddy-turbine barrage had been started back when the PSP was in power. They were generators that looked like propeller blades, mounted in narrow nacelles and tethered between the islands where the current spun them as it ebbed and flowed.

Peterborough's post-Warming industrial base had been founded on light engineering and gear production, easily served by the city's electricity allocation from the National Commerce Grid, and supplemented by solar panels. But the explosion of manufacturing had begun to attract heavier industries, pushing the power demand close to breaking point. Then after the Second Restoration the newly legitimized Event Horizon arrived. With its wholly modern industries, Peterborough was the obvious choice to supply the cyber-factories with components once Philip Evans brought them ashore. The already vigorous city went into overdrive. But its expanded fortunes brought it up against infra-structure capacity limits. The eddy-turbine barrage was intended to relieve the now chronic energy shortage, one of a dozen projects rushed into construction to cope with the excessive demands Event Horizon was placing.

The traffic was snarled up in front of the Duo. Eleanor slowed, and saw a bus in front of the lorry had stopped to let out its passengers. They were all men in rough working clothes, carrying or wearing hard hats. They joined a group of about seventy waiting on the embankment below the road, level with the line of barges. There was a small jetty at the bottom of the embankment. A boat had just cast off, ferrying some of the men out to the islands. She could see a clump of men who'd been left behind on the jetty arguing hotly with a pair of foremen.

'They'll be lucky,' Greg murmured as the Duo drove past the crowd milling aimlessly on the embankment.

'Why?'

'Tell you, the eddy-turbine barrage is a council project, right. Unless you're on the city council labour register, there's no way you'll get to work on it.'

'Well, why don't they sign on with the council, then?' she asked.

'A lot of people on the dole right now are ex-apparatchiks. And the New Conservative Inquisitors have got their hands full purging the administration staff of any that got left behind after the PSP fell. The government is nervy about them; what with inflation and the housing shortage, a few well-placed PSP leftovers could cause serious grief. So the last thing the council wants is to take them back, especially not on a project as important as this one.'

'Why don't you apply to join the Inquisitors?' she teased. 'That'd be a regular job.'

Greg grinned. 'They couldn't afford me.' He pointed ahead. 'This is the turn. We'll park in Bretton and walk the rest of the way.'

She took a left through the old Milton Park golf club entrance. The Duo powered along the rough cinder tracks lined by hemispherical apartment blocks that'd sprung up to replace the greens, uses, and bunkers. The three-storey buildings were self-contained Finnish prefabs, a burnished pewter for easy thermal control. Fast-growing maeosopsis trees dominated the estate, their long branches curved over the tracks, affording a decent amount of shade. There were small allotments ringing each of the silvery hemispheres, laid out with uniform precision.

'Tidy,' she remarked, approvingly. 'They've got a different attitude here.'

'You're not being fair. Think what this'll be like in twenty years' time. Just the same as Berrybut.'

'It might, then again it might not. These people are more in tune with the future, they believe in it.'

They drove by a clump of mango trees in full fruit. She saw children playing around the trunks, seemingly immune to the ripe temptation dangling above their heads. 'Whatever happened to scrumping?'

'Do you want to move?' Greg asked.

'No.' She grinned. 'You couldn't live here.'

They left the rustic eloquence of the Milton estate behind and slowed, slotting into the chain of vans and rickcarts trundling through the grid maze of the Park Farm industrial precinct. It was made up of bleakly functional sugar-cube factory units with coal-black solar-collector roofs. Nearly half of them sported the Event Horizon triangle and flying V emblem, she saw, most of the rest were overseas companies, some *kombinate* logos. The foreign factories were anathema to the PSP, economic imperialism, but they had to let them in to pay off the massive investment loans which the Tokyo and Zurich finance cartels had made in Peterborough's new housing.

'Do you mean you would move if it wasn't for me?' Greg asked.

'Don't be silly.' She was still grinning. He looked like he had bitten something sickly.

'You don't have to come with me to see Royan, you know,' he said. 'It isn't exactly a picnic at the best of times. It'll only take me an hour or so.'

'Oh, no,' she said loudly. 'You don't get out of it that easily, Greg Mandel. Do you realize I know practically nothing about the time between you leaving the Army and meeting me? This is the first glimpse you've ever allowed me into this section of your life.'

'You only had to ask.'

She shot him a quick glance. 'If you'd wanted me to know, you would've told me. And now you're starting to. I'm not sure what it means, but I'm bloody pleased.'

'He takes some getting used to,' Greg offered. She recognized the tone, regret for the impulse decision to invite her. Just how bad could his friend be?

'You said he was hurt?'

'Very badly. Completely disabled, and burnt. It's not pretty.'

'I won't embarrass you, Greg.'

'I didn't imagine you would; rather, the reverse. My past is not totally savoury.'

'Women?'

'No!'

'There were,' she corrected demurely. 'That sort of knowledge isn't exactly hereditary.'

He gave her a weak smile and gave up. Happier, though, she thought. However badly disfigured this Royan turned out to be, she was determined Greg would never be disappointed he'd introduced them.

The narrow streets and iron-red bricks of Bretton were registering through the windscreen. She parked in an old school yard, next to an impressive New Conservative council banner proclaiming its incipient refurbishment as the community's cultural centre. The classrooms were all boarded up, and someone had driven surveyor's stakes through the playground.

She got out and looked at him expectantly. He was wearing Levis and his leather jacket over an olive-green T-shirt. She'd dressed in a shapeless navy-blue sweatshirt and black jeans; nondescript, as he'd told her. Now she was beginning to realize why; Bretton was a backwater, untouched by the vitality which roared through the rest of the city. The houses she could see all had heavy wooden shutters over the windows, and solid metal security doors.

Greg blipped the Duo's lock.

They were quickly surrounded by about fifteen kids, none of them in their teens yet. Silent, eyes shining bright out of grubby faces.

'Car watch, fella?' piped a prepubescent voice.

'Highway robbery,' Greg protested.

The ritual was a relief in an obscure fashion, putting her back on solid ground. Bretton was still plugged into the rest of the city, during the day, at least.

'Five pounds,' the lad said.

'I think we'll park in the next street,' Greg retorted.

'Four.'

'It's very dirty,' Eleanor pointed out.

The kids put their heads together.

She exchanged an amused glance with Greg.

'Three,' declared the summit. 'And we wash it, too.'

'Half now?'

'Two now,' said the highly affronted ringleader.

He and Greg showed cards, both of them pictures of woe.

'Wonder what Walshaw will make of a three-pound transport expense item?' Greg mused whimsically as the kids moved in on the Duo, two racing away for water and sponges.

She let him guide her into the centre of Bretton, pleased he was with her. The place looked rough. She would never have gone into it by herself.

The main street was roofed over by an erratic collage of plastic sheeting, solar cells, corrugated iron, even thatch; all supported by an equally bizarre collection of trusses like telegraph poles and rusting chunks of electricity pylons. It was a twilight world where relief from the sun's heat was tempered by the clouds of arid dust any motion kicked up. The stalls snaking along the pavements lacked the cramped clutter of Oakham's disarray, here the shops were coming back into use. There was a greater emphasis on material goods. Food was appearing in packages again. But no tins yet, she noticed.

They grazed the stalls for stuff Greg said Royan would want. Junk, Eleanor thought. He picked out circuit boards, electric motors, inexplicable mechanical gizmos that were parts of bigger machines, antique watches, the wind-up sort. Three plastic carrier-bags full, which came to thirty pounds. There was no logic behind it. He seemed delighted when he found a Sanyo VCR. It was lying among Mickey Mouse phones and kettles on a stall which was half lobster-tanks, half broken gear. He haggled the owner down to a tenner and departed well pleased.

She began to wonder about Royan again. Strange gifts.

They walked out of Bretton and into the Mucklands Wood estate; and Eleanor decided that Bretton wasn't so bad after all, not compared to this. The fifteen high-rise blocks which had risen out of the dead forest were council-run low-cost housing. They represented the least successful aspect of the city's expansion programme. A throw-back to the worst of the nineteen-sixties style of instant slums.

They were twenty storeys high, identical in every respect right down to the cheap low-efficiency slate-grey solar-cells clinging to every square centimetre of surface. Heat shimmer twisted the blocks' harsh geometry, blurring edges; it was as though nature was trying to distort the inhuman ugliness which their desolate lines delineated. The ground between them was a wasteland. Less than half of the estate's intended employment workshops had been built, and those that the council had completed were abandoned, either burnt out or gutted. The Trinities gang symbol was scrawled everywhere, brash and sharp, a closed fist gripping a thorn cross, blood dripping. She'd heard of the Trinities, even in the kibbutz. Anti-PSP in a big way.

Mucklands Wood could've been deserted. Nothing moved; worse, there was no sound: there should've been something coming from those hundreds of grimed windows, music or shouting. Their footsteps crunched loudly on the badly rucked limestone path.

She stuck close to Greg's side, eyes darting about nervously. 'Is this part of your past?' she asked.

'Briefly. I taught some of the people who live here.'

'I never knew you were a teacher.'

'Tell you, not your sort of teaching, school and such. I trained them in streetcraft.'

'Streetcraft?'

'Techniques to break police ranks, ambush their snatch squads, how to counter the assault dogs. That kind of thing. It's a reversal of the counter-insurgency courses the Army gave me.'

'Oh.' You wanted to know, she told herself. Her eyes dropped to the crushed yellow stone fragments of the path.

'Stay calm,' Greg said quietly.

She glanced at him, puzzled. His eyes had that distant look. He was using his gland.

Then the Trinities boy stepped out from his hiding place behind a crumbling employment workshop wall, he did it fast and smooth, simply *there*. And it was all she could do not to yelp in surprise. He fitted her image of an urban predator perfectly, almost a stereotype. Asian, somewhere in his mid-twenties, with hair cropped close, wearing a filthy denim jacket with the arms torn off, slashed T-shirt, and tight leather trousers. Two bowie knives and a compact stun puncher were clipped on to his belt. There was some sort of gear plug in his left ear. A taut strap running round his neck held his throat mike. The Trinities emblem was painted on his jacket.

He leered at her, and she knew he could read her fright. 'What the fuck are you arseholes? Hazard junkies?'

There were more Trinities spreading out of the ruins behind her and Greg, dressed in a grab bag of camouflage jackets, jeans, and T-shirts. Faces hard, carrying weapons ranging from knives up to things whose function she couldn't guess. They fanned out, forming a tight blockade.

'Cool it, mate,' Greg said levelly and put a bag down, holding out his right hand, very slowly.

The youth's sneer faded when he saw the Trinities card Greg was holding. 'Where you get that?'

'Same place as you.'

'No shit?' He pulled out his own card and showed it to the one in Greg's open palm. Confusion twisted his features as his card acknowledged Greg's authenticity. 'I don't know your face.'

'I don't know yours,' Greg said.

'Don't smartarse me!' he shouted.

'Greg's one of us, Des,' a throaty female voice said from behind Eleanor. Out of the corner of her eye she saw a small figure with spiky mauve hair, wearing tourniquet-tight leopard-skin jeans and a sleeveless black singlet. The girl's age was indefinable; thin-faced, she could've been anywhere between fifteen and thirty. She was cradling a big gauss-pulse carbine casually across one arm. Bandolier straps crossed her flat chest, loaded with red-tipped slugs. Additional power magazines were clipped to her belt. Her face was one big smirk.

'Shut the fuck up, Suzi,' shouted the boy confronting them. 'Hear me? You could drive a fucking tank through that mouth of yours. This is my turf, I'm the Man here. These bastards could be Party.'

Eleanor held on to Greg's forearm with her free hand, pinching. Suppose the card wasn't good enough?

Greg grinned faintly. 'Hi, Suzi.'

The mauve-haired girl gave him an impish thumbs up.

Des's face darkened. 'You know these?' his forefinger jabbed at Greg.

'Sure,' said Suzi. 'Greg's been Trinity from way back. Taught me all kindsa things.' Her eyes met Eleanor. 'Good, too, isn't he?'

Eleanor kept her face perfectly blank, emotions frozen, just as they'd been for all those years in the kibbutz. 'Depends on the material he's got to work with, dear.' Not the greatest come-back in the world, but pretty bloody good, considering. Even Greg seemed vaguely surprised; approving, too, she suspected. Suzi started laughing.

'So why the big reunion?' Des asked.

'I'm here to see Son,' said Greg.

'Christ, Des, let the man through.'

'Last fucking warning, Suzi, I'll rip you good if you don't shove it.'

'Just ask Father,' Greg said. 'He'll tell you my credit is good.'

'Yeah? So what about her?' Des pointed at Eleanor. 'I don't see no card.'

'She's with me.'

'No shit?'

'Des, the man has our card, that makes him one of us.'

The new voice was deep, it didn't seem loud, but it carried to everyone. Authoritative, Eleanor decided. The Trinities were suddenly still and attentive. There was a hint of irritation in the voice, which she was very grateful wasn't directed at her.

When she looked round she saw a tall black man picking his way over the cracked concrete footings of a stillborn employment workshop. She thought he looked about the same age as Greg, moved the same way too, dangerous grace. Most of his two-metre frame was muscle. He was wearing combat fatigues, clean, with knife-edge creases, a blue beret sporting a single silver star; she recognized it as an old-style British Army regimental insignia. Greg's memory cores at the chalet were full of military trivia like that.

'Shit, yeah, Father. But—' Des began.

'But *nothing*! Man with a card is one of us, always. We don't all dress like crap. You got that?'

Des's head lolled about like a moody nodding doll. 'Sure, OK, Father. I just didn't want to take no chances, y'know?'

The tension had evaporated from the other Trinities. Some of them grinned publicly at Des's squirming, led by Suzi.

'I know, boy. Now, is it going to happen again?'

'No, sir.'

'I don't hear you so good.' The big man's eyes flashed round the circle of Trinities.

'No, sir!' they yelled gleefully.

206

'Dismissed,' he barked. Suzy flipped Greg a jaunty wave as the troop filtered away over the barren artificial moonscape.

Greg and the black man were bearhugging each other.

Muscles slackened all over Eleanor's body in one convulsive shiver, she hadn't been aware how tightly wired she'd become. So many weapons, and not even Greg could've protected them if that animal Des had got it into his mind to shoot. Mucklands Wood was like nothing she'd heard of before, undiluted anarchy. The cold flush pricking her skin wouldn't abate now until she was back in the safe sanity of the Duo, heading out.

Greg and his friend released each other, both smiling broadly.

'Man, you've been AWOL a long time.'

'That's the way it goes.' Greg shrugged. 'I can't afford to be seen with the likes of you nowadays, I'm a respectable professional now, legitimate.'

'Legitimate, shit. Soft, that's what.'

'Yeah. Teddy, meet Eleanor. Mate of mine.'

Teddy's smile got wider as he swept her with an appraising gaze, then he pulled his beret off in a gesture of hopeless gallantry. 'Christ, officers always did steal the best of everything.' He offered his hand, and drew her knuckles to his lips. The ultimate stamp of approval. It cleared the air marvellously.

'Bit jumpy, aren't they?' Greg said as the three of them walked towards the nearest tower.

'Yeah, sorry about that,' Teddy growled. 'We had us a chunk of extra-parliamentary action against some Party hacks two days back. Couple of my troops got hit. They're just keeping alert. Can't blame 'em for that.'

'You expecting some retaliation?' Greg asked.

Teddy shrugged. 'Dunno. The war isn't nearly over, Greg. There are tens of thousands of card carriers out there. Smart, well organized, and tough with it. They'll do it to us all over again if we let 'em.'

'Are the Blackshirts making any serious moves?'

'No bullshitting, Greg, they are screwing this city. Almost as bad as we did. Trouble most nights, police are stretched to the limit. Inquisitors can't seem to get on top of 'em. Blackshirts have got Walton sewn up tight and hard, nobody in, nobody out unless they say so. We sit and eyeball each other over the A15; and I keep pissing myself over what they're cooking up in there. Son watches what he can, of course, but even he's got limits. What I'd like is some Spiral-armed Mi-24s, go in and beach-head the place, flush the bastards out. Just like the good old days.'

'This isn't the good old days, Teddy. We got rid of them, and they aren't coming back. The Blackshirts are just a bunch of zombies, don't know they're dead yet.'

'I know how to tell 'em.'

'How many of them are in there now?'

'Maybe two hundred regular Blackshirts, five if they called in the hardliners they've got scattered about the county. But it's the rest who give me sleepless nights. Half of 'em still work in city chambers. If they get their act together they could cause a lotta pain. This inflation is stirring people up, man, lotsa grumbling about the New Conservatives. And you bet they've got it all planned out, fucking Party always loved plans. I can't fight that, Greg. That ain't physical, man. Physical I can handle. I gotta leave 'em to the New Conservative inquisitors. More fucking bureaucrats. I tell you, it plain drives me nuts.'

'People won't fall for the PSP twice,' Eleanor said. 'They're not that daft.'

Teddy smiled softly down at her. 'Gal, I sure as shit hope you're right. Cos it ain't just here, every town in the country is the same. Party ain't got the power no more, but that don't mean they don't want it again. Bad. But whichever way it tilts we're ready for 'em, AKs loaded and Bibles to hand. You bet.'

'So how is Goldfinch, anyway?' Greg asked.

Teddy rolled his eyes, sighing in despair. 'Crazy as ever. Man, you should hear his sermons now. He's overloading on the vengeance routine, hot for it he is, and slick with it. Keeps the kids in line but good, they know they're fighting for what's right.

Time just floats on by when he's in that pulpit. Even been getting civvies from Mucklands coming, too. You want to see him?'

'I'll pass. It's Royan I'm here for.'

'Thought so. See you're loaded up with his rubbish.'

Two Trinities stood guard at the doors into the tower. They saluted smartly as Teddy walked by, never even giving Eleanor the eye. The hall belied the appearance of the building's external decay, clean and tidy, if somewhat spartan.

She thought she saw Greg wink at a tiny camera lens peeking out of the top of the doorframe.

'I won't come up,' said Teddy. 'Your rap's probably big hush anyway.'

'Not from you,' Greg said.

'Thanks, man. Anything you need the Trinities for?'

'It isn't shaping up that way. But if it does.'

'We're here, Greg, always here. Ain't got no place else to go. You come in and say goodbye before you go.'

'Right.'

Teddy gave Eleanor another fast smile and disappeared into the old warden's flat. She got a blink of maps and screens on the wall, heavy-duty communication gear on boxy desks, and an enormous colour print of Marilyn Monroe.

The lift doors opened, and Eleanor leant heavily on the rear wall. She let out a hefty relieved breath, and gave Greg a hard stare. 'Perhaps you were right about me not coming,' she said.

'Hey, I apologize about Des, I didn't know that was going to happen.' He punched for the top floor, and the lift began to hum upwards.

'Maybe you didn't, but I should've. This estate, it saps hope, breeds people like that.'

'You're wrong there. Mucklands Wood is one of the safest places to live in Peterborough.'

She snorted disbelief.

'Straight up. Providing you're a resident. The Trinities don't tolerate theft and violence against their own.'

'Vigilantes.'

'Call them what you like. Just don't forget those troops are the ones who stood against the PSP's Constables when the violence was at its worst.'

'I'm sorry, Greg. I didn't mean to knock them, I see how deep your involvement goes. And I am glad I came. When my nerves calm down I'll be able to express it better.'

'Tell you, you did all right out there. Lot of people would've run.'

'Me too, if I'd thought it would've done any good. Was Teddy being serious about the PSP still being active in Walton?'

'Sure.'

'Well, why doesn't the government do something?'

'Like what? We're living under a judicial system now. The rule of law is paramount. Being a member of a political party isn't an offence in this new, fair England. Being in the Trinities, doing what they do, now that is a crime.'

She shook her head in wonder. 'It's all so wrong. Stupid.'

'Yeah. I know.'

20

The lift halted with knee-bending suddenness, and chimed metallically as the door slid open. The corridor outside was narrow, its walls unpainted breeze blocks; a greening biolum strip ran down the length of the ceiling. Greg and Eleanor walked down to the end, and he knocked on the familiar panelboard door of 206. There was a brief flicker of guilt; he hadn't visited for weeks. Now he'd come because he wanted something.

Qoi opened the door. A thirteen-year-old Chinese girl dressed in a blue silk Mao suit with red and gold fantasy serpents embroidered on her sleeves. She bowed deeply. 'He is expecting you,' she said in a voice pitched as high as birdsong.

206 was a dole family's accommodation module, three rooms and a cupboard-sized hall. It was on the corner of the tower, which gave it two windows. Being a bachelor, Royan wasn't entitled to it; but as he wasn't listed on the council's occupancy register they were unlikely to insist he vacate it.

The door to Royan's room slid open and a gush of hot humid air, rich with the smell of humus, spilled out. The interior was a bastard offspring of a botanical garden and an experimental CAD-CAM shop.

Thirty blue-white Solaris spots shone down on four rows of red clay troughs which grew clumps of orchids, fuchsias, cyclamen, African violets, gloxinias, and jasmine; tall standard hyacinths towered over them, giving off a thick cloying perfume.

A little wheeled robot scuttled along the alleys between the troughs. It was a patchwork of miscellaneous components, something a surrealist sculptor might've built in a fit of hallucinogenic dementia. A droopy flexible hose which ended in a copper watering-can spout hung out of one side, sprinkling milky water over the sphagnum moss that frothed across the surface of the troughs' loam.

One wall was covered from floor to ceiling in TV screens, not modern flatscreens but the antique glass vacuum-tubes of the last century. They'd been taken out of their casings and stacked edge to edge, like bricks, in a metal frame. Some were showing channel programmes, some relayed images from cameras dotted around the tower, others had reams of green script unfurling in a constant cascade from top to bottom.

An aluminium tripod stood in the middle of the floor, its camera silently tracking Greg as he ducked round the hanging baskets full of busy Lizzies and fleshy trailing nasturtiums. Twin fibre-optic cables fell from the back of the camera, snaking across the abraded brown lino to Royan's nineteen-sixties vintage dentist's chair; they terminated in the black modem balls filling his eye-sockets.

Greg sensed the gag-reflex of Eleanor's mind as she fought to control her revulsion and shock, barely managing to contain a phobic groan.

He forced himself to grin and nod at Royan's bloated, T-shirted torso. Royan didn't have any legs; and his arms ended just below the elbows, their stumps capped with grey plastic cups which sprouted fibre-optic cables, plugging him into various 'ware cabinets about the room.

All the screens went blank. Then words began to form, metre-high letters, phosphor green, strangely fragmented by the reticulation of black rims.

HELLO, GREG. WHO'S THE LADY?

Royan was fifteen that night six years ago, Greg's last street fight. Set up as a march on Peterborough's council hall protesting about the latest protein rationing. The Trinities were infiltrating the crowd, thirsting for aggro. It was a big crowd, ugly. The Party called out the People's Constables.

People's Constables: a replacement for Special Constables. Greg could just remember them from his youth; weekend policemen, who used to dress up in their smart dark uniforms and make an enthusiastic cock-up of directing traffic at the Rutland county fair.

People's Constables were in a different league. A different fucking universe, as far as Greg was concerned. Recruited from the ranks of extreme-left shock-troops and black-flag warriors who'd kicked police and beat up press photographers at rallies and marches, it was the biggest case of role-reversal since Dracula turned vegan. The People's Constables came under the direct authority of local PSP committees, employed to smash heads whenever people complained about the latest drop in living standards. Basic Party militia.

Their favourite weapon was a bullwhip, with a lash of mono-lattice carbon. They were taught to go for the legs first.

Royan, flush with the élan of youth, was in the crowd's front rank. He was caught in the first charge. The crowd retreated leaving their downed behind. People's Constables clustered like angry wasps about each of the inert bodies, slashing with hot fury.

It was the Trinities who retaliated, prepared by Teddy and him, driving the Constables back with a berserker bombardment of molotovs, lighting the night sky with a lethal fallout of fireballs.

Greg had dragged Royan out of the flames, far, far too late. He often wondered if he'd have done the boy a bigger favour by going for a beer instead.

'This is Eleanor,' Greg said.

HI ELEANOR. YOU ARE VERY PRETTY.

'Go ahead,' Greg told her. 'Just speak normally, he can hear.'

Royan's ears were the only sensory input he had, lying in hospital, his sole means of clinging to sanity. It was a month before he was given an optical modem, and another fortnight before he got his forearm axon splice. The axon splice gave him the ability to communicate, the nerve impulses intended for his amputated hand feeding a computer input. Whenever he visited, Greg thought of ghostly transparent hands typing a keyboard in some incorporeal alien dimension.

Eleanor cleared her throat self-consciously. 'Hello, Royan. Glad to meet you.'

I LIKE YOU. YOU DIDN'T YELL, OR ANYTHING.

'Hands off,' Greg warned. 'She's mine.'

LUCKY. LUCKY. LUCKY. GREG IS VERY LUCKY.

'I know. Brought some junk for you.'

EVERY LITTLE HELPS.

He directed Eleanor to tip out her bag of redundant gear on to a big flat-top workbench. Royan had fixed up two obsolete General Electric car-factory Waldo arms beside the bench, their spot-welding tips replaced with multi-segment talon-like grippers. Greg could never understand how the floor took the weight of the brutes.

They telescoped out with juddering clumsy motions and began sorting through the pile. He put the Sanyo VCR down next to the scuffed glass bubble which held Royan's micro-assembly rig.

JACKPOT. LOTS OF GOOD BITS IN THAT. THANKS TO BOTH OF YOU.

It never mattered what he brought, Royan would eventually find a way to use it. Patiently tinkering with nominally incompatible modules until they could be fused together and incorporated into his cybernetic grotto.

Another of the pot-pourri robots rolled up to Greg and Eleanor, a Pyrex jug full of steaming coffee balanced on its roof.

HELP YOURSELVES.

Greg sipped gingerly as the waldos whirred away industriously behind him. The coffee was excellent, as always. Royan fiddled it out of the inventory computer of a plush New Eastfield delicatessen, directing its delivery van to a Trinities safe house in Bretton. Eleanor's eyes widened in appreciation as she tasted the brew.

'Job for you,' Greg said.

PARTY INVOLVED?

'Don't think so. But the person who's hired me hates them more than you do.'

IMPOSSIBLE. WHO IS IT?

'Tell you in a minute. First part of your help is answering questions for me. I need to know the kind of information floating round the circuit at the moment. Will you do that?'

SHOOT.

'Have you heard about the blitz against the Event Horizon datanet?'

CHUCKLE CHUCKLE. THE CIRCUIT HAS BEEN BUZZING WITH NOTHING ELSE FOR THE LAST THREE DAYS. BIGGEST DEAL SINCE MINISTRY OF PUBLIC ORDER MAINFRAME WAS CRASHED.

'Who set it up?'

NO IDEA. BIG PUZZLE. RECRUITING NOT DONE THROUGH THE CIRCUIT. ODD ODD ODD.

'Could the hotrod pack have been foreigners?'

NO. CIRCUIT KNEW ABOUT IT TOO SOON. HINTS DROPPED. NO NAMES THOUGH. UNUSUAL. IF I'D TAKEN PART I'D WANT PEOPLE TO KNOW MY HANDLE. THAT KIND OF BURN PUSHES THE GOING RATE UP, MAYBE EVEN DOUBLES IT. SILENCE WOULD HAVE TO BE BOUGHT. LOTS OF MONEY INVOLVED.

'So how would I go about recruiting without using the circuit?'

GOOD QUESTION. TEKMERC WHO HAS WORKED WITH SOLO HOTRODS BEFORE. SHRUG. THEY'D HAVE TO HAVE GOOD CONTACTS.

The little robot that'd been watering the troughs ran across the floor to a tap on a wall and eased itself underneath. Water poured into its tank. Greg watched the operation over the rim of his cup. 'Tell me about Philip Evans.'

HE WAS THE OWNER OF EVENT HORIZON. DIED A MONTH BACK. RICH. RICH. RICH.

'That's it?'

NO. THERE'S WHOLE MEMORY CORES LOADED WITH BIOGRAPHICAL DATA. YOU WANT A PRINT OUT?

'No thanks. What I meant was, is there anything current?'

OPPOSITION MPS PROTESTED ABOUT COST OF HIS FUNERAL. THAT'S THE LAST ENTRY.

'OK, I've got a big hush for you. Philip Evans's memories have been stored.'

AH HA.

'Tell me how you'd go about doing that.'

BEST WAY WOULD BE IN A BIOWARE NEURAL NETWORK. FERREDOXIN HAS THE POTENTIAL. YOU'D HAVE TO SPLICE EVANS'S SEQUENCING RNA INTO THE NODES. DUPLICATE HIS BRAIN STRUCTURE, THEN SQUIRT HIS MEMORIES INTO THE CORE WITH A NEURO-COUPLING. THE COST WOULD BE UTTERLY LOONY. BUT I SUPPOSE PHILIP EVANS COULD AFFORD IT. AFTER ALL, THAT'S ONE WAY OF TAKING IT WITH YOU. RIGHT?

'Right.' Greg thought for a moment. 'So all you'd have to know to deduce the nature of Evans's core was that his memories had been translocated, nothing else?'

YES. IT'S BEEN RAPPED ABOUT FOR YEARS. HAMBURG UNIVERSITY LOADED A TURING PERSONALITY INTO THEIR BIOWARE CRUNCHER A FEW YEARS BACK; ITS RESPONSES REALLY WERE INDISTINGUISHABLE FROM A HUMAN'S. ALL IT LACKED WERE BACKGROUND MEMORIES. I RAPPED WITH IT ONCE. CREEPY CREEPY CREEPY.

'If you knew of a bioware core which housed some kind of sophisticated personality responses program, how would you set about disabling it?'

MACRO DATA SQUIRT. FORCE THE PERSONALITY PROGRAM OUT OF THE CORE.

'Did you think of that yourself, or was it something you picked off the circuit?'

ALL MINE, CROSS HEART. IT'S OBVIOUS SOLUTION.

'Does that mean it wasn't a personal attack against Evans?' Eleanor asked. Intense interest had resulted in her coffee going cold. She'd either forgotten, or had accommodated, Royan's state, acting perfectly naturally. There weren't many who could do that.

Royan would've noticed, too; he was an acute observer within his small kingdom. For some obscure reason Greg was delighted.

He wanted them to be friends, to approve of each other. It meant a lot to him, although he couldn't say exactly why. The bloody quacks would have lots of psychobabble about resolving the past, no doubt.

He poured himself another coffee. 'It's a possibility,' he admitted. 'Any hacker observing the Event Horizon datanet would know a lot of management decisions were originating from that one core. Whether or not they knew it was Philip Evans himself, I'm not sure.'

IF IT WASN'T FOR VENGEANCE, THEN IT WAS PROBABLY CONNECTED WITH EVENT HORIZON'S GIGA-CONDUCTOR. AM I RIGHT, OR WHAT?

'You're right.' Greg wasn't surprised; Royan kept himself well plugged in to the circuit, trading data whenever it was to his advantage. 'Philip Evans believes the blitz was an attempt at a spoiler; reducing Event Horizon's ability to market the giga-conductor by removing his managerial experience. So how did you find out about the giga-conductor?'

EVENT HORIZON HAVE A GIGA-CONDUCTOR DEVELOPMENT CONTRACT WITH THE MINISTRY OF DEFENCE.

'My God,' said Eleanor. 'Does everyone know about the country's military secrets?'

NOT NECESSARILY. BUT THE GIGA-CONDUCTOR IS SUCH A BIG DEAL IT'S IMPOSSIBLE TO KEEP IT UNDER WRAPS. WEAPONS APPLICATION PROJECT DETAILS HAVE BEEN LOADED INTO THE MINISTRY OF DEFENCE MAINFRAME. THAT MAKES THEM AVAILABLE TO PEOPLE LIKE ME, AND THERE ARE A LOT OF PEOPLE LIKE ME. CHUCKLE CHUCKLE. WELL NOT QUITE.

Greg considered that; Event Horizon's giga-conductor wasn't half as secret as Morgan Walshaw had believed, yet the Ministry of Defence had only been brought in after the patent was filed. He still couldn't believe a *kombinate* would bother with a spoiler like the blitz, not after the chance of filing their own patent had been lost.

'When did you find out about the giga-conductor?'

THIRD WEEK IN DECEMBER. MINISTRY OF DEFENCE BEGAN A NEW ULTRA-SECURE FILE AT THE START OF THE MONTH, I WAS INTERESTED. TOOK A COUPLE OF DAYS TO BURN.

He used the teaspoon to lift the skin off his coffee, running the dates through his mind. If he assumed another hotrod had burnt open the Ministry file around the same time as Royan, then the blitz could well be a *kombinate* operation. But how had they discovered the NN core existed? He was back to the question of the mole's existence again. 'Could you pull data from Event Horizon's security division memory cores without tripping any alarms?'

IF YOU ASKED ME TO, I MIGHT CHANCE IT. BUT I'D HATE TO HAVE TO TRY. WHAT DID YOU WANT PULLED?

'The Zanthus microgee-furnace production-monitor programs.'

WOW! WEIRD WEIRD WEIRD. ANY MEMORY CORE CAN BE BURNT OPEN, BUT SOME ARE MORE DIFFICULT THAN OTHERS. EVENT HORIZON IS MOST EQUAL OF ALL.

'Do you know anyone else who could do it?'

THERE ARE ABOUT FOUR OR FIVE OF US WHO COULD WRITE MELT PROGRAMS GOOD ENOUGH. BUT IF YOU WENT TO THE CIRCUIT WITH THAT REQUEST IT WOULD COST YOU TWENTY THOUSAND NEW STERLING, MINIMUM.

Greg grunted, the answer was about what he expected. Kendric could afford that, no messing, but would he have bothered to asset-strip Event Horizon if he hadn't known about the gigaconductor? There were still too many unknowns. 'Does anyone on the circuit know how the blitz ties in with the Merlin failure?'

WHAT MERLIN FAILURE?

'That answers that,' he muttered in an undertone. He gave Royan a quick outline of the spaceprobe's breakdown. 'Intuition tells me they're connected. But I can't see how. I'm just not convinced about the validity of the blitz. What could it hope to achieve?'

DUNNO. THE AMOUNT OF EFFORT EXPENDED MOUNTING THE BLITZ IS COMPLETELY OUT OF PROPORTION TO THE DAMAGE IT WOULD CAUSE. EVENT HORIZON LOST A LOT OF DATA IN THE RESULTANT DATANET SHUT-DOWN, BUT NOTHING CRITICAL. THAT IMPLIES VENGEANCE.

The green letters with their subliminal flicker jolted him. He shook his head at his own slowness. The blitz had exactly the kind of protective layers as the memox-crystal spoiler, each one a cover for the one underneath, and progressively more complex, more subtle. Kendric di Girolamo's method of operation. A bright sensation of satisfaction rose up; identical patterns, and intuition now both focused on Julia's nemesis. That coincidence was far too much to ignore. Except . . . Kendric was smart, he wouldn't use the same pattern twice. Unless that was what he wanted people to think.

Greg sipped the last of his coffee reflectively; there were limits to paranoia. Go with your intuition, he told himself, at least you know you trust that.

SO WHAT DO YOU RECKON, HOLMES?

'Insufficient data. You want to do me a huge favour?'

FIND OUT WHO WAS IN ON THE BLITZ?

'Got it in one.'

GRIN. SILENCE IS GOLDEN AT THE MOMENT, SO IT'LL MEAN HACKING HOTRODS. ACCESSING THEIR MEMORY CORES TO SEE IF THERE'S ANY REFERENCE TO THE BURN. AND IT'LL HAVE TO BE THE SOLO HOTRODS. THAT COTERIE WEREN'T VIRGINS. OOPS. PARDON MY FRENCH, ELEANOR.

She looked straight at the camera, brushing loose strands of titian hair from her face, and gave him a warm smile.

'If that's too big a deal for you, I can bring some help in from Event Horizon's security division,' Greg said solemnly.

HOW SOON DO YOU WANT THE ANSWER, SMARTARSE?

Greg saluted the camera with his empty coffee mug. 'Soon as possible, if not before.'

Royan's mouth parted a slit, revealing bucked teeth yellowed by the pulped vegetable mush Qoi fed him. His version of a smile. THE HUNT IS ON.

A whole load of apprehension lifted from Greg. Nobody hunted better than Royan, nor had more practice. And he took it seriously, deadly serious. Royan had monitor programs stashed in every major public data core in the country;' sleepers watching for key words and names. Out of the four hundred and seventy

219

People's Constables on duty the night of the riot there were less than two hundred left alive. The boy had been hunting them out ever since he plugged his axon splice into a gear terminal; seeking out their home addresses, tracking them through promotions, transfers, redundancies. Greg and the rest of the Trinities were told where to find them, what they looked like now, at what point in their daily routine they were most vulnerable.

Greg had personally taken out sixteen for him.

'Thanks,' Greg said.

SNEAKY PRESENT FOR YOU, GREG. YOU MIGHT HAVE A USE FOR IT. GIVE ME YOUR CARD.

One of the waldos stretched out across the work top, claw opening. He fumbled in his Levis pocket and fished out the Event Horizon card. The tarnished silver metal closed about it, and the arm retracted, rotating on its vertical axis, then slid out again, pushing the card into a slot on one of the gear consoles banked up behind the flat-top bench.

HEY, GREG, DO YOU KNOW HOW MUCH CREDIT THIS BUGGER CAN TRANSFER, QUESTION MARK, TRIPLE EXCLAMATION MARK.

'Yeah, so go careful.'

TRUST TRUST TRUST. WHERE'S IT ALL GONE? PUT YOUR RIGHT HAND ON THE BLUE SQUARE.

He leant across the bench as a square lit up on a gear module, and did as he'd been told, pressing with his fingertips. Nothing visible happened.

I'VE BEEN WRITING THIS FOR THE TRINITIES. THOUGHT THEY MIGHT BE ABLE TO USE IT TO GAIN UNLAWFUL ENTRY.

The card popped out of the slot like a slice of toast. Greg snagged it neatly.

THUMBPRINT WILL ACTIVATE CREDIT AND ID CONFIRMATION AS USUAL, LITTLE-FINGER PRINT WILL ACTIVATE DATA-CRASH CANCER. ITS SQUIRT SHOULD BOLLOCKS UP GEAR LOCKS, AND TAKE OUT ENTIRE MEMORY CORES.

Greg looked at the card. Out of the two of them it was rapidly becoming the more useful.

YOU'LL BOTH COME BACK TO VISIT ME, WON'T YOU?

The screens blanked out, then, PLEASE, appeared in bright scarlet letters, fuzzy round the edges.

'Yes,' Eleanor said quickly, and looked at Greg for confirmation.

'Yes,' he echoed.

I'D LIKE THAT, said the letters, reverting to green.

One of the waldos slid out in front of Eleanor and opened its claw with the panache of a conjuror producing the coin that'd just been swallowed. There was a Trinities card resting in the mechanical palm. FOR YOU, MY NEW PRETTY LADY FRIEND. THE TROOPS OUTSIDE WON'T GIVE YOU ANY HASSLE IF YOU SHOW THEM THIS. SO YOU DON'T HAVE TO WAIT FOR HIM TO BRING YOU.

'You do know him well, don't you?' Eleanor said coyly, her eyes danced with amusement.

The camera whined as the lens twisted round, zooming in for a close up on Eleanor's face. She held her poise without flinching.

WE CAN HAVE A GOSSIP. IT'S BEEN YEARS SINCE I HAD A REALLY GOOD GOSSIP ABOUT SOMEONE BEHIND THEIR BACK. IT'LL BE FUN. THE STORIES I CAN TELL YOU ABOUT HIM.

'You've got a date.'

'Hey,' Greg protested.

YEAH. SNEER. YOU GOT A COMPLAINT?

He held his hands up. 'I'll be back, too.'

GOOD. MISS YOU. GREG. BAD.

'Promise,' he mouthed to the camera.

Qoi materialized silently at their side and showed them out.

21

Julia took the broad stairs of Wilholm Manor two at a time, her burst of speed nearly skidding her feet from under her when she reached the hall's polished marble tiles. She pushed up the heavy iron latch on the front door. Rachel came out of the old butler's pantry, looking miffed; it should have been Steven on duty, but he'd called in sick. The disapproving expression fell from her face to be replaced by her usual natural diligence.

Julia enjoyed the momentary lapse. So Rachel was human after all. Wonder who was in there with her?

She pushed the big oak door open and went outside. It was raining lightly, drops falling vertically from a high, almost nebulous cloud sheet. The air seemed solid with humidity. She stood under the portico, heart pumping strongly.

You in a hurry, girl?

Julia clamped down on her racing thoughts as the silent voice whispered into her brain, resenting the way her grandfather was interpreting her actions. He'd loaded a personality package, coded OtherEyes, into one of her processor nodes, digesting her body's senses in real-time, feeding the formatted sensations back to his NN core.

I'd go crazy otherwise, he'd pleaded. *Camera images are no substitute, flat and insipid; I'm human, damn it, I need human touch and smell, heat and cold. Not all the time, just the occasional reminder. Keep in touch with the real world.*

So she'd acquiesced; and still wasn't sure if it was such a good idea. She'd carefully reviewed the processor node's basic management program, making sure its neural-interface flow was strictly one way. Acceptance only. None of her thoughts could seep in for him to examine. Not bloody likely. But despite the precautions, it meant having Grandpa chuntering away inside her mind the whole time OtherEyes was loaded. There were advantages – his insights could be illuminating – but he did *moan* so.

From her position she could see a pair of forlorn-looking wheelbarrows that'd been abandoned down at the far end of the garden, piled high with weeds. She didn't blame the gardeners for taking a break from the heat and damp. She was already perspiring under her white cotton summer dress. Her skin itched.

Too bloody hot it is, Juliet.

Show me your April, she asked, on some fey impulse.

For an instant the trees lost their leaves, their branches becoming thick black crockery cracks superimposed on a band of sombre grey landscape. There were no flowers in the garden, though the shrubs were covered in a crop of glossy scarlet berries. Steam shifted to clammy mist, cold water droplets clinging to branches and grass. Icy air cut through her thin dress. Small bedraggled birds pecked for worms in the slushy gravel. A remote style of beauty, lonely.

The strange apparition withered. She was rubbing her bare arms against the lingering impression of chill.

Now those were the days, her grandfather said happily.

I suppose.

But she wouldn't want it to happen very often, say every five years.

The Duo rolled out of the warm drizzle, and pulled up close to the portico. There was someone sitting in the passenger seat. Julia smiled a welcome.

Isn't he a bit old, Juliet?

Her smile locked.

Greg is a nice man, Grandpa. He doesn't patronize me like everyone else. You've no idea what a relief that is.

223

She was going to have to go back over the processor node's inputs; he was learning far too much of her private self, that aspect of personality which should remain secret. Her own body language was playing traitor.

Greg got out of the Duo, scurrying quickly round the rear of the car for the shelter of the portico. He shook out the collar of his leather jacket, nodded at Rachel. He wasn't bothering with suits any more, Julia noted. Levis and T-shirts were more agreeable on him, anyway; he'd never looked quite right in a suit, caged. It was great to think he felt familiar enough around her to relax, let her see his real self. Most people were so guarded with her.

'Hello, Greg. Was it something important?' Or did you come just to see me? Unlikely, but . . .

Lovesick. Your knees have gone all watery, Juliet. Mental laughter.

Grandpa, if you don't stop that right now I'll cancel the link. First and final warning, OK?

No bloody sense of humour, that's your trouble, m'girl.

Greg was looking at her strangely, head slightly cocked as though he was concentrating on a faint voice. 'Could be,' he said pleasantly. 'Brought someone to see you and your grandfather.'

The woman getting out of the Duo's passenger seat, with some difficulty, was about fifty, Julia thought as she sized her up. Dressed in a pleated maroon skirt and a flower-print blouse under a woollen jacket, a double string of pearls around her neck. Her fading fair hair had been given a light perm. Julia didn't quite know what to make of her. She certainly couldn't be Greg's girlfriend. Surely? Perhaps his aunt.

Now there's a candidate for a healthy diet if ever saw one.

It took a great deal of willpower not to clench her fists. And what must Greg be seeing in her mind?

Shut! Up! Julia shouted into the node.

'This is Gabriel Thompson,' Greg was saying. 'My Mindstar colleague.'

Julia forgot all about the exasperating intrusion in her mind, suddenly excited and fearful in a way she couldn't explain. She opened her mouth.

'Yes, I can,' said Gabriel.

Julia gaped, elated, then suspicious. Recovering her composure. 'You must know that is the first thing everyone is going to ask you by now,' she countered.

'True.' And there was a burst of humour in the woman's deep-set leathery eyes. Gone almost before it registered.

She looks so sad, Julia thought. Haunted.

If her ability is real, then she will be able to see her own death approaching. How would you feel about that, Juliet?

'There must be an easy way of proving you can see the future,' Julia persisted as the three of them walked up the stairs toward the study. Rachel had gone back to the butler's pantry, satisfied Greg and Gabriel posed no threat.

'I can give you a short-term localized prediction, but you must remember that you possess the ability to alter that future. Nothing is a certainty. For instance, I could tell you what I see you eating for dinner tonight; but it would be singularly pointless as you could order the cook to prepare something else just to prove the prediction wrong.'

'So make it something I won't alter.' She glanced at Greg to see if he approved of her badgering. He must've understood how intrigued people would be.

Eighth time you've looked at him.

Wipe OtherEyes.

The abrupt silence was like an empty hole, torn out. She felt a fragment of guilt, this was Grandpa she was punishing. But he shouldn't abuse the privilege, he *had* to learn that.

Gabriel's eyes had that distant focus, just like Greg. As though the gland lifted them out of this universe for a while.

'This afternoon, four o'clock, you'll get a call from your precision cybernetics division in London. The manager will submit the last quarter returns; and he'll keep emphasizing the efficiency figures, they're up by five per cent.'

'All right,' Julia said enthusiastically. Four o'clock, an hour and a half, she could wait that long. Typical of regional managers to fish for compliments.

'Unless you call him first and ask for the report,' Gabriel pointed out.

'I won't. I think I believe anyway. You'd never be so bold if you weren't certain.'

Greg and Gabriel both seemed content with her answer. She showed them into the study, walking straight to her seat at the head of the table.

'Look, Grandpa, Greg's come to visit us, and he's brought a friend.'

Julia noticed Gabriel's reticence as she sat down. The woman's gaze never left the black column on the table as she perched on the front edge of the wooden seat. If she really could see the future how could anything shock her?

Julia listened to her grandfather saying hello in a civil tone, giving away nothing. Then Greg started to report on his progress to date. Her eyes wandered while he was speaking and she saw Gabriel was using the gland again.

'Bugger,' Philip Evans exclaimed when Greg had finished. 'That fucking Ministry of Defence, more bloody trouble than it's worth. I never knew it leaked that badly. The whole hacker circuit, you say?'

''Fraid so, they all know you've cracked the giga-conductor, and been awarded development contracts.'

'So it could be any of the *kombinates*,' Julia said. 'You've no leads.'

'A lot of negatives, which is cutting down the field considerably. At the moment my personal suspicion is Kendric di Girolamo and a highly placed mole. Place as much emphasis on that as you wish.'

'Vengeance.' Philip Evans sounded sceptical. 'If he's that twisted why not try to assassinate Juliet here? Got to be cheaper than buying eight hotrod hackers, and their silence. She's well protected, but no security is proof against a professional hardliner tekmerc, not when he's striking out of the blue.'

She shrank a little inside, compressed by steely arctic fingers.

It's only theory, she told herself, don't let it bother you. But there was no need for him to say it quite so bluntly.

'I don't know,' said Greg. 'I still don't understand why Kendric allowed Julia to buy him out. Even if he didn't know about the giga-conductor when he started the memox-spoiler operation, he certainly did by the time she confronted him.'

'I see what you mean,' Julia said. 'We filed the patent on November the fifteenth, and informed the Ministry of Defence on the seventeenth. Even assuming Kendric doesn't have a mole feeding him data, he ought to have known it existed by the end of the year at the latest, like your contact did; which would've given him months to work out the implications before I hit him with the buyout. He should've held on for all he was worth, risked family displeasure over Siebruk Orbital. For those stakes they would've forgiven him anything. In fact, now he has withdrawn the di Girolamo house, they're going to be furious with him when I go public with the giga-conductor and they realize what they've lost out on.' The idea of Kendric giving up bothered her deeply. Kendric was smart and crafty. That bastard would have something in reserve. She knew he would.

Gabriel stirred, blinking rapidly. 'Wilholm's staff are clear,' she announced.

'From what?' Julia asked.

'From knowing your grandfather is stored in this NN core. They hadn't put it together like your father.'

Julia knew her cheeks were reddening at the reminder, and didn't care, not any more. 'How do you know?'

'I scanned the possible futures where Greg interviews each of them this afternoon, he wouldn't find any culpability. Oh, except that your gardeners are flogging ten per cent of Wilholm's vegetables on the village market.'

'Little buggers,' Philip squawked.

'Oh shush, Grandpa, I know all about that.'

'How come?'

'I'm mistress of the manor, remember? It's my job to know.'

She turned back to Gabriel. 'I thought you said nothing about the future was certain?'

'Not in the future, no,' said Gabriel. 'But if the staff had known about the NN core and passed on the data, that would mean they'd pieced the knowledge together in the past, it's already happened, an immutable fact.'

'Yah ... right.' It sounded kind of screwy, but the nodes confirmed the logic. Providing you believed in precognition in the first place.

'That just leaves Dillan, then,' Philip said, and Julia knew that tone of voice well enough. They were heading for another blazing row once Greg and Gabriel left. She wondered if Gabriel had seen it already. The woman's alleged ability was disturbing. It might be a good idea to be out on Tobias at four o'clock.

'Not quite,' Greg pointed out. 'We still have the whole NN core team to interview tomorrow, as well as the security division headquarters staff.'

'I know all the NN core team, they're good people, boy. No worries on that score. It'll be Dillan, or someone in security, or even this mole of yours, you'll see.'

'The NN core team still have to be checked off,' Greg said, polite but unyielding. 'Process of elimination; old procedure, but it can't be improved on.'

'Don't interfere with the experts, Grandpa. Isn't that what you always say?'

'Juliet, you're impossible!' Even with his construct voice he managed to convey affection.

A truce. She pulled a face at the NN core.

'What about you, Gabriel?' Philip asked. 'Can't you see the results of these interviews Greg is going to hold?'

'Sorry. That's tomorrow morning, and several kilometres away. Can't stretch that far.'

'Well, what about if Greg was to interview Dillan? Today, here?'

Gabriel stiffened. 'Your son has no idea whether or not he told anybody. He is only aware of your translocation on odd occasions,' she said reproachfully. The implication for responsibility hovered almost tangibly in the air.

Julia realized that Gabriel was more redoubtable than her appearance suggested. Like Greg, the gland gave her total access to a soul's weakness. Did Grandpa have a soul? That old-style-April chill closed around her.

Primate Marcus was preaching to her again, hand on Bible, scorning hubris and human greed. Temptations that would result in your ultimate downfall. Sweet Jesus had shown people the way by rejecting both.

And Grandpa certainly hadn't abandoned anything.

'What about the NN core?' Greg asked.

'Yes,' said Gabriel. 'Though it could go either way.'

'What's that supposed to mean, m'dear?' Philip Evans asked.

'As I explained to Julia, the future is never definite,' Gabriel said. 'There are a multitude of alternate possibilities. The best indicator of certainty is when a lot of those futures hold a common theme. You understand? It's like gambling. If two-thirds of the possible futures which I see have it raining tomorrow, then it will most likely rain. But it isn't an absolute. The further into the future, the more hazy my predictions.'

'So what's going to go both ways?' Julia asked raptly.

'A second attack on your grandfather's NN core. I'd say there was a sixty per cent probability it will happen.'

'Does this attack succeed?' Philip asked.

'Not if you take simple preventive measures,' Gabriel said. 'Forewarned is forearmed. Do you believe me?'

'Damn right I do, m'dear. What sort of attack, a data-squirt blitz like last time?'

Gabriel paused, frowning. Ice-maiden formidable. Julia had the impression a lot of it was theatre, like a gypsy's crystal ball. Overawing the superstitious peasants.

'A Trojan program. It's indexed as an ordinary factory-quota update, but once inside your filters it multiplies like a hot rabbit, expanding to take up all the available memory capacity.'

'When?'

'If it happens, it'll be some time on Tuesday morning. Of course, the nearer we get to the event the more specific I can get; and I can also give you more accurate odds.'

'I want to know every change, m'dear. No matter what time of the day or night, you get in contact with me whenever those odds shift.'

'Can't you tell us who sends the Trojan?' Julia asked plaintively.

'I'm sorry. Wherever the origin of the attack is, it's not close to Wilholm.'

Julia sat back and sighed wanly.

'Whoever they are, they seem determined,' Greg said thoughtfully.

'It has to be a personal vendetta,' Julia said. 'That means Kendric's behind it, and the mole exists, doesn't it?'

'Possibly,' Greg said. He seemed strangely reluctant to commit himself. But she knew. It was Kendric. She'd always known. There was almost a feeling of contentment accompanying the conviction.

'I'd like you to get some of your security programmers hooked into the Event Horizon datanet,' Greg said. 'See if they can backtrack the hotrods if this second attack does happen.'

'Good idea, boy. I'll get Walshaw on it.'

Greg and Gabriel rose. He gave Julia an encouraging smile. 'Don't worry, it's just a question of waiting to see which lead takes us to the organizer. After tomorrow's interviews our options should be clear enough to start making some headway.'

She couldn't draw as much comfort from his words as she would've liked. The promises were too vague. But at least he was trying to help her, some part of him cared.

The two of them departed, leaving her alone in the study with the feverishly active memories of a dead man, and the hot rain swatting the window.

22

Half-past two in the morning found Greg lying on his back, hands behind his head, staring up at the blackness which hid the bedroom ceiling. He could hear the reservoir's wavelets swishing on the shore outside.

The deer had come to drink under cover of the night, venturing out of the new persimmon plantation at the back of Berrybut spinney. His fading espersense perceived their minds as small cool globes of violet light, timid and alert. Eleanor had been entranced with them for the first couple of weeks after she'd moved in, waiting up each night to see them slip furtively out of the trees.

The afternoon rain had lowered the temperature appreciably, but sleep was impossible. Intuition was running riot inside his cranium, even though he'd ended the gland's secretions. Swirling random thoughts clumped together, producing an image. It didn't matter how many times he told himself to forget it, the image just kept reforming. The same one, over and over.

Eleanor let out a soft hum, and wriggled slightly. He hoped he featured in that dream.

No good. He wasn't going to sleep.

Greg went through the usual mincing motions as he slid gingerly out of bed, making far more noise than if he'd just done it properly. Eleanor sighed again. He pulled the duvet up round her bare shoulders, then put on his towelling robe and went into the lounge.

Through the chalet's front windows he could see the moonlight painting the checkerboard pattern of Hambleton peninsula's meadows and orange groves in mezzotint contrasts. Silent and serene. Strange how remote it seemed from the kind of global-class corporate battles fought only a few kilometres away in Peterborough. He sometimes wondered if a day would come when he wouldn't be able to leave, giving up on the external world and all its conflicts. And who would really be hurt if he did let go? Certainly not Eleanor.

Greg closed his eyes, but instead of Rutland Water's landscape there was only the taunting image.

Not this time, then.

He disconnected the Event Horizon terminal's voice input, opting for the silence of the touchpad keyboard so Eleanor wouldn't be woken. That done, he began to set up a link to Gracious Services.

Even Royan wasn't clear on where the circuit's name originated, but under its auspices England's hackers would pull data from any 'ware memory core on the planet – for a price.

Greg logged into Leicester University's mainframe and entered a cut-off program that'd disengage the instant anyone tried to backtrack his call. Royan had written it for him years ago. He couldn't afford to be anything but ultra-circumspect dealing with Gracious Services. He didn't want any of its members uncovering his own identity and selling the information in turn – the ultimate irony. The average hacker had a moral code which made an alley tomcat a paragon of virtue by comparison. After confirming the cut-off's validity he routed the link through another cut-off in the Ministry of Agriculture on to the Dessotbank in Switzerland, crediting it with a straight ten thousand pounds New Sterling direct from Event Horizon's central account.

After that it was just a question of establishing two more cut-offs, one in Bristol city council's finance mainframe, then on through the CAA flight control in Farnborough, and dialling the magic number.

Gracious Services had a nonsense number, there was no

phone on the end of it. But every English Telecom exchange computer in the country had been infiltrated with a catchment program that would slot the caller directly into the circuit.

Never, not once, in all the years they were in power, did the PSP manage to tap the Gracious Services circuit, nor expunge the catchment program from Telecom's exchange computers. They tapped individual phones, and caught people using Gracious Services that way, but that was all. Rumour had it the card carriers used the circuit themselves on occasion.

The terminal's flatscreen snowstormed for a second then printed:

> WELCOME TO GRACIOUS SERVICES.
> WE AIM TO PLEASE.
> DATA FOUND, OR MONEY RETURNED.
> NO ACCESS TOO BIG OR TOO SMALL.
> JUST REMEMBER OUR CARDINAL RULE: DO NOT ASK
> FOR CREDIT!!!
> PLEASE ENTER YOUR HANDLE.

Greg typed THUNDERCHILD, his old Army callsign.

GOOD MORNING THUNDERCHILD: YOUR UMPIRE IS WILDACE. WHAT SERVICE DO YOU REQUIRE?

PHYSICAL LOCATION OF INDIVIDUAL.

OK THUNDERCHILD, I'VE GOT SEVEN HOTRODS RARING TO BURN FOR YOU. IS THIS GOING TO BE A GLOBAL SEARCH?

I BELIEVE THE INDIVIDUAL TO BE IN EUROPE. QUITE POSSIBLY IN ENGLAND.

THIS IS THE WAY IT IS, THUNDERCHILD. A EUROPE-WIDE SEARCH WILL COST YOU FOUR THOUSAND FIVE HUNDRED NEW STERLING. IF WE GET A NEGATIVE RESULT, THAT MEANS YOUR TARGET ISNT IN EUROPE, IT'LL ONLY COST YOU TWO THOUSAND. IF YOU WANT US TO RUN A GLOBAL SEARCH IT WILL COST YOU SEVEN THOUSAND. OK?

RUN A EUROPEAN SEARCH FOR ME, WILDACE.

YOU GOT IT. I HOLD THE MONEY. I DECIDE HOW IT'S SPLIT.

SOUNDS GOOD.

DEPOSIT FOUR THOUSAND FIVE HUNDRED POUNDS NEW STERLING
INTO TIZZAMUND BANK, ZURICH, ACCOUNT NUMBER WRU2384ASE.

Greg entered Wildace's number, authorizing the transfer from
his Dessotbank account.

OK THUNDERCHILD, YOUR CREDIT IS GOLDEN. WHO IS THE TARGET?

The image coalesced in his brain, rock solid, grinning arro-
gantly; and he typed: KENDRIC DI GIROLAMO.

Greg's imagination painted the picture for him; seven people
scattered across England, dark anonymous figures hunched over
their customized terminals, mumbling into throat mikes, touch-
typing, watching data flash through cubes. It was a race, the first
one who satisfied Wildace they had the correct answer would get
the money, less Wildace's commission. Reputations were made
on the circuit. It took twenty or thirty runs, successful runs,
before anyone could even think about going solo.

Royan had trained himself on the Gracious Services circuit.
He could've gone solo, running data snatches against *kombinates*
for the tekmercs. But, of course, he had a different set of
priorities.

Greg sat back, wondering if he had time for a drink. He didn't
have a clue how long the run was going to take. He didn't use
the circuit often; the last time had been almost a year previously,
tracing a money sink set up by Simon White's accountant.

Whatever he asked for, Gracious Services invariably produced
an answer. Their only failure to date had been confirming
whether or not Leopold Armstrong had died the day the PSP
was overthrown. They weren't alone. New Conservative inquisitors had drawn a blank. Even the combined ranks of the
Mindstar Brigade vets had been stumped. Most people thought
he was dead, including the surviving top-rank apparatchiks.
Possibly trying to create a martyr, Greg thought, two years was
an impossibly long time to remain hidden if he was alive.

There had been very little of Downing Street left after the

electron-compression warhead had detonated. The explosion created a deep glass-walled crater one hundred metres across, flattening every building for five hundred metres beyond its rim. Hundreds of silver rivulets scarred its slopes, molten metal which had solidified as it trickled downwards. The only human remnants were individual carbon molecules, mingling with the oily black pall clotting the air overhead.

Some said the warhead was American, others Chinese. Both had denied involvement. But it had to be one of the two superpowers, they were the only nations who had mastered the technology.

Neither had seemed a likely candidate to Greg. There had been talk in Turkey of the Northern European Alliance buying some electron-compression warheads from the Americans. The weapon that would turn the tide, was the squaddies' camp rumour. It could've been deployed to take out entire airfields or tank battalions, megatonnage blasts without the radiation and fallout of fission weapons. Rich man's nuke.

Nothing had ever come of it. So Greg reckoned that if the Americans wouldn't hand them over to the Alliance, they were even more unlikely to give one to the urban predator gang which claimed to have smuggled it into Downing Street. Certainly the New Conservative inquisitors never bothered to find out.

Greg had made his small contribution to the search for Armstrong, but for once not even his intuition could say whether the President had survived, he had no belief one way or the other. He just wished Armstrong dead dead dead; burning in Dante's hell for ever more.

He gazed out of the chalet lounge's window while the unbidden reflections drifted past, bringing the associated emotions back with them, the elation and the suffering. Flames and laughter.

Seventeen minutes after Gracious Services began the search, his terminal's flatscreen came alive again.

GOT HIM FOR YOU, THUNDERCHILD. KENDRIC DI GIROLAMO
CURRENTLY ON BOARD HIS YACHT *MIRRIAM*, DOCKED AT
PETERBOROUGH'S NEW EASTFIELD MARINA, BERTH TWENTY-SEVEN.

THANK YOU, WILDACE, Greg typed.

NO PROBLEM. HOTROD HANDLED BLUEPRINCE BURNED HIM FOR
YOU. SAYS IF YOU WANT ANOTHER RUN HE'LL BE HAPPY TO OBLIGE,
FEE NEGOTIABLE.

I'LL REMEMBER.

PLEASURE TO DO BUSINESS WITH YOU, THUNDERCHILD. WILDACE
SIGNING OFF.

So Kendric was in Peterborough, was he? Close to the action.
How convenient.

Greg made one final call, then headed back to the bedroom.

23

The sheer number of Event Horizon facilities springing up in Peterborough after the Second Restoration, coupled with Wilholm's proximity, meant that the company had to establish a large finance division in the city. Julia used it as her *de facto* head office, so it was only natural that Morgan Walshaw should use it for his security division's command centre as well. It was a temporary arrangement while both divisions waited for their respective custom-built headquarters to be completed. The building they had moved into for the interregnum was the old Thomas Cook office block, situated at the top of a small bluff overlooking the Ferry Meadows estuary, on the western side of the town. In doing so they'd ousted the PSP Minorities Enhancement Council staff who had occupied it ever since currency restrictions put an end to the glories of package holidays.

After Event Horizon had taken over, the company engineers immediately set about building a concrete embankment along the bluff to halt the erosion which was eating towards the foundations. At the base of it they planted three small lagoons of gene-tailored coral to house a set of tidal turbines which powered the finance division's gear. Seeing a building which wasn't plastered with the glossy black squares of solar-cells came as something of a novelty.

The security office inside, which Greg and Gabriel had been loaned for interviewing the NN core team, was a cramped cell of a room with a metal table and three plastic chairs. It looked out towards Longthorpe, where gulls strutted about on the partially exposed mudflats.

Emily Chapman left the office without looking round, her rigid back conveying stark disapproval. She had every right to be upset, Greg acknowledged. He was actually doing the interviews with the NN core team. He'd thought it politic; Gabriel had dropped into one of her best prickly sulks at having to examine his possible interviews with over two hundred and fifty of the security staff in the building, and told him to take a share of the load himself, for a change. But she could've timed it better, though.

The trouble was, Philip Evans had been right; the NN core team were all grade-A people – keen, loyal, honest, hard working, churned out by Event Horizon's blandification programme. They hadn't taken kindly to his accusations.

'Shit creek, and no messing.' He could feel a neurohormone headache coming on. Thank God there had only been nine of them to question.

'Don't swear,' Gabriel snapped primly.

'I've got a right. None of them leaked the information about the NN core. How are you doing with the security personnel?'

'You wouldn't find anything.'

'What? None of them have any shameful secrets?'

'They might well have, but if so they can certainly hide it from you.'

His unwinding espersense caught her gelid mind tone. Egg-shell walking time. 'Bugger, you know what that means.'

'Dillan Evans.'

'Yeah, unless we can produce this mole pronto. And I'm now having serious doubts he ever existed. Christ, how am I going to tell Philip? Maybe I'll tell Julia first, she's pretty protective when it comes to her father. Can't say I blame Dillan, though, the man is totally fucked. Not rational.'

'Saved by the bell.'

'What?' His cybofax bleeped. 'Oh.'

The call was a data squirt, a scramble code he knew by heart. Royan. His spirits lifted as the decrypted message rolled down the cybofax's little screen. Royan had found one of the hotrods involved in the blitz: Ade O'Donal, operating from Leicester under the handle Tentimes. Greg snapped the cybofax shut with a flourish; at last he could take some positive action, get out of dead company architecture and pull in hard information. When he glanced up Gabriel was already standing by the door, expectant. 'Coming?' she asked.

*

Greg drove past the ranks of company buses in the car park and out on to the A47.

Getting under way didn't noticeably alter Gabriel's disposition. 'Fascinating,' she said. 'The lovely Eleanor, a fully-fledged Trinity urban predator. The mind boggles.'

'I wish you'd make an effort. That girl's never said a single bad word about you. And God knows she's entitled.'

'Greg, you can't just abandon all your old mates in her favour, however besotted you are with her gymnast legs and top-heavy chest.'

He pulled his anger down to a tight incendiary ball. Anger never did any good, not against Gabriel. But it was fucking tempting to let fly once in a while. Not this time, though. He needed her. And she knew it. 'Eleanor gets on perfectly well with the marine-adepts, and Royan has taken a shine to her.'

'That was the first time you'd been to see Royan for two months. You know how much that boy worships you.'

Fell into that one, he told himself. Just as she'd intended, guiding his conversation down the Tau line she'd selected.

Greg gunned the Duo along the A47 above the flooded remains of Ailsworth. Her words had kindled not so much guilt as a sense of melancholy.

Arguing with her when she was being this waspish was impossible. Whatever he said in his defence she'd have a parry honed and ready, the best of all possible answers. Besides, truthfully, he had neglected Royan. Eleanor made it easy to forget. Life and the future, rather than Royan, a shackle to an emetic past. He just wished Gabriel didn't use a sledgehammer to ram home the point.

He was aware of her studying his face intently. She gave a tart nod and leant back into the seat cushioning.

*

The last section of road leading into Leicester cut through a banana plantation. Methane-fuelled tractors chugged between the rows of big glossy-leafed plants, hauling vast quantities of still-green fruit in their cage trailers. Cutter teams moved ahead of the tractors, machetes flashing in the sun.

Incorporated in the city boundary sign was the prominent declaration: PSP Free Zone.

'Oh yeah?' said Gabriel.

Greg let the snipe ride, though he conceded she had a point. Leicester council had earned a reputation for sycophancy during Armstrong's presidency; it was one of the last to acknowledge the Party's perdition.

That obedience was the root of its downfall; a numbing historical repetition, those showing the most loyalty receiving the least. With such devotion assured, the PSP had no need to pump in bribe money. Leicester had declined as Peterborough had risen. Now the city's New Conservative-dominated council was striving hard to obliterate the image of the past in an attempt to attract hard-industry investment.

'Give them a chance,' Greg said. 'It's only been two years.'

'Once a Trot, always a Trot.'

'Exactly where would you be happy living?' he asked in exasperation.

'Mars, I expect. Turn left here.'

'I know.'

He turned off the Uppingham Road and nudged into the near-solid file of bicycle traffic along Spencefield Lane. The big old trees whose branches had once turned the road into a leafy

240

tunnel were long dead. New sequoias had been planted to replace them. They were grand trees, but Greg couldn't help wondering whether they were a wise choice if the residents were aiming for permanency; give them a couple of centuries and the sequoias would be skyscraper high.

The original trees had been trimmed into near-identical pillars six metres high, supporting giant cross-beams over the road. Each arch was swathed in a different coloured climbing rose. The sun shone through the petals, creating a blazing sequence of coronal crescents. It was like driving under a solid rainbow.

Greg slowed the Duo to a walking pace as they passed the entrance to an old school. Cars were clustered along the verge ahead, sporty Renaults, several Mercs, one old Toyota GX4. Image cars.

'Shouldn't there be sailboards strapped on top of them?' Gabriel said under her breath.

Greg concentrated on house numbers, praying she'd snap out of it before long. Of course, he could always ask her when her mood was due to end. He clamped down on a grin. 'That's the address.'

The house was hidden behind a head-high brick wall that had a hurricane fence on top, a thick row of evergreen firs hid most of the building from the road. The gate was a sturdy metal-reinforced chainlink, painted white. Cameras were perched on each side, their casings weather-dulled.

'He's having a party,' Gabriel said, with facetious humour disguising the tingle of nerves Greg knew would be there.

'How nice. A big one?'

'For him. It's enough to provide us with cover, anyway.'

Greg parked the Duo beyond the last of the guests' cars. 'Front or back?'

'Front, of course. Your card is good for it.'

He felt a burn of anticipation warming his skin, heightening senses. Black liver-flesh of the gland throbbing enthusiastically.

They strolled back to the gate, unhurried, unconcerned. Greg showed his Event Horizon card to the post, using his little finger

241

for activation. The gate's electric bolt thudded, and the servos swung it back.

It remained open behind them, its control circuitry bleached clean. He sent a mental note of thanks to Royan.

The mossy gravel drive crunched under their feet. O'Donal's house was a large one, three storeys of dull russet brick with inset stone windows, the slates on the mansard roof a peculiar olive-green. Nobody had bothered with the front garden for years, the grass was tangled and overgrown, and dead cherry trees were still standing. Some sort of stone ornament, a birdbath or a sundial, poked up through a tumble of cornflowers. A brand-new scarlet BMW convertible was parked in front of the triple garage.

'The man that answers the door is a minder, he'll make trouble if you let him,' Gabriel said. 'Take him out straight away.'

'Right.' He rang the bell. Music and laughter wafted over the roof.

Greg saw him coming through the smoked glass pane set into the grimy hardwood door, an obscure blotch of brown motion, swelling to cloud the whole rectangle.

The door was pulled open.

'Hello, sorry we're late.'

The man behind the door was street muscle in a suit; early twenties, tall, stringy, dark hair, broad forehead crinkling into a frown.

Greg stepped forward neatly, one foot on the mat the other coming up, further and further. Fast. It was victory through surprise. A smiling man and a portly spinster eager to party just didn't register as a threat. Not until the carbon-mesh-reinforced toe of Greg's desert boot smashed into his kneecap.

His mouth opened to suck in air, eyes wide with shock. He was toppling forwards, leg giving way, and bending to clutch desperately at his shattered knee.

Greg brought his fist straight up, catching the minder's chin as he was on his way down. The force of the blow snapped his head back, lifting him off his feet, back arching, arms and legs flung wide.

He crashed back on to the shiny blue ceramic tiling, skull making a nasty cracking sound, a thin stream of pea-green vomit sloshing from his slack mouth.

Greg took in the dark hall behind him with a quick glance, espersense wide for alarmed minds. Big tasteless urns holding willowy arrangements of dried pampas grass making the most impression. But the hall was empty. Nobody had witnessed their arrival.

'Jesus, Greg.' Gabriel was kneeling beside the prone minder, feeling for a pulse.

Greg opened the cloakroom door. 'In here.' There was a wicker dog-basket on the floor, jackets were piled high on a washbasin; it smelt of urine and detergent. 'Come on!'

Gabriel shot him a filthy look, but took hold of the minder's left arm as Greg grabbed the right. They pulled him across the tiles.

'If he was going to die you'd have told me not to hit so hard.'

'You know bloody well it doesn't work like that,' Gabriel said. 'There are a million ways you could've dealt with him.'

'Well, is he going to be all right or not?'

'I don't bloody know, some futures have him dying.'

Greg shoved the dog basket out of the way and left the minder with his head propped up against the toilet bowl. Gabriel rolled up one of the jackets and slipped it behind the minder's head. He was still breathing.

'How many futures?' Greg asked.

'Some.'

Greg recognized the defensive tone, and relaxed. The minder would survive.

'There's a rear belt-holster,' Gabriel said reluctantly.

Greg knelt down and felt underneath the minder. Sure enough, he was carrying a Mulekick, a flattened ellipsoid in grey plastic, small enough to fit snugly into Greg's palm, with a single sensitive circle positioned for the thumb and a metal tip that discharged an electric shock strong enough to stun a victim senseless.

'We'll need it later,' Gabriel said cryptically.

Greg dropped it into his jacket pocket and followed her back out into the hall.

The house would've given any half-way competent interior designer nightmares. To Greg it looked as though it'd been decorated by someone watching a home-shopping catalogue channel and picking out all the furniture and fittings which had the brightest colours. There was no attempt to blend styles.

The lounge had two three-piece suites, one upholstered in overstuffed white leather, the other done in a bold lemon and purple zigzag print. A harlequin array of biolum spheres hung from the ceiling on long brass chains, imitating a planetarium's solar system display. Dark African shields hung on the wall, along with spears, tomahawks, broadswords, and longbows. The weapons were interspersed with antique rock-concert posters, mostly from Leicester's De Montfort hall – Bowie, Be Bop Deluxe, Blue Oyster Cult, David Hunter, The Stranglers, one for The Who at Granby Hall in 1974. If they were real, and they looked it, they must've cost a fortune.

The party was in full swing on the other side of the lounge's sliding patio doors. Thirty or so people were clustered around the back garden's baby swimming-pool. Led Zeppelin was blasting out of tombstone-sized Samsung speakers.

A petite blonde girl in a lime-green one-piece swimsuit shoved the patio door open. Robert Plant's fearsome vocals slammed into Greg's eardrums. She came in dripping water all over the deep white pile carpet. He caught a whiff of bittersweet air. Quite a few of the partygoers round the pool were puffing away on fat Purple Rain reefers.

'Hi,' the blonde said when she saw Greg and Gabriel. 'We're out of champagne again.'

'Can I help?' Greg asked.

'S'all right, I know where it is.' She looked at Gabriel. 'You want a suit for the pool?'

'No thank you.'

'We'll get something to drink first,' Greg said. 'Have a rap with Ade. Is he out there?'

'Sure,' said the blonde. 'Over there by the grill, in the lubes stupid hat. Hey, can you cook?'

'Sure.'

'Try and get him to let you do the steaks, OK? He's half pissed already, we're gonna be eating coal if it's left to him.'

'You got it. How do you want yours?'

She pulled long wet strands of hair from her face, uncovering a dense constellation of freckles. Hazel eyes sparkled at him. 'Juicy,' she purred.

'Already done.'

She peeked surreptitiously at the people outside. 'Catch you later,' she promised. There was a corrupting wiggle in her walk as she headed for the kitchen.

'Would you like me to wait?' Gabriel enquired, oozing salaciousness.

'We have to stay in character.'

'Nice for some. Let's get this over with.'

'How do you want to play it?'

Gabriel stared thoughtfully out at the party. 'Sucker him in here, first. Then arm-twist him into taking us to his gear cache. We'll apply the real pressure there.'

'Is that here in the house?'

'Yes. In the basement. Quite a set-up. Our Tentimes is an ambitious lad.'

They went out through the patio door into heat, noise, and a smell of charring meat. None of the guests paid them any attention, they were all concentrating on the pool.

Somebody had rigged a pole across the water. Two naked girls were sitting astride it, facing each other; one was white with sunburnt shoulders, the second was Indian. They were whacking each other with big orange pillows. The crowd roared its approval as the white girl began to slip. She fell in slow motion, abandoning the pillow and gripping frantically at the pole, sliding inexorably towards the horizontal. A flurry of blows from the Indian girl speeding her progress, aided and abetted by wild shouts of encouragement from the side of the pool. At the last minute she let go of the pole and grabbed the Indian girl. They both shrieked as they hit the water. The white flowerbloom of spray closed over them sending up a plume which soaked some of the spectators.

Groans and cheers went up. The girls surfaced giggling and spluttering. Furious little knots of partygoers formed, passing money back and forth.

'Jenna next,' someone called.

'And Carrie.'

'Two to one on Carrie.'

'Bollocks, evens.'

'I'll take that.'

The two new girls began to edge towards each other along the pole.

Ade O'Donal stood on the cracked ochre flagstones at the shallow end of the pool, white chef's hat drooping miserably, a wooden spatula in his hand. According to Royan's data squirt he was twenty-four, but his sandy hair was already in retreat, both cheeks were sinking, becoming gaunt, his skin was pasty white, reddening from too much sun. He wore an oversized azure cotton shirt speckled by sooty oil spots from the barbecue, and his loud fruit-pattern Bermuda shorts told Greg who had chosen the house's furniture.

O'Donal grinned gormlessly round the faces of his friends as the girls poised ready. Then his eyes met Greg's and froze.

The wooden spatula slashed downwards. 'Go,' O'Donal shouted. The girls began pummelling at each other, the blows from their saturated pillows sending out clouds of sparkling droplets. Partygoers began cheering again. The blonde in the lemon swimming suit was walking round the pool filling glasses, a magnum clasped in each hand.

The Indian girl clambered out of the pool, cinnamon skin glistening, and shook her long black dreadlocks. She pressed up against O'Donal, her high conical breasts leaving damp imprints on his shirt as she kissed him. He handed her his glass, which she tossed down in one smooth gulp.

O'Donal pushed her away and walked round the pool towards Greg and Gabriel.

They retreated into the lounge. O'Donal followed.

'Are you with someone?' he asked; his voice was firm, ready to deal sternly with gatecrashers.

'We're here to see you, Ade,' Greg said.

'This is a private party, pal. Guests only.'

'Private party. Big house. Lots of expensive friends. You're coming up in the world, Tentimes,' Gabriel said.

O'Donal's jaw muscles hardened. He slid the patio door shut, muting the music and catcalls. Greg sensed the cold apprehension rising in his mind. O'Donal's eyes kept straying to the door leading to the hall.

'Sorry, Tentimes,' Greg said. 'Your hard case couldn't make it. It's just you and us.'

'Will you quit with that handle,' O'Donal hissed edgily. 'These people don't know who I am.'

'What do they think you are?'

'Programmer on a commission to Hansworth Logic.' He brightened. 'Hey, I never expected you to show in person, y'know. I mean, I don't mind you coming, no way. I just didn't think it was the way you worked. So what is it, you want me to run another burn?'

'You're sweating, Tentimes,' said Gabriel. 'This is all new to you, isn't it? The high life, money, girls?'

'We'd never have guessed,' Greg said, looking pointedly round the lounge.

'Hey, look, what the fuck is this?' O'Donal demanded. 'And what have you done to Brune?'

'Don't know, didn't stop to check,' said Greg. 'What does it matter? Ace hotrod like you can afford plenty more like him.'

O'Donal's apprehension now blossomed into outright worry. A little muscle spasm rippled across his bony shoulders.

The pillow fight outside had degenerated into a wrestling match. One girl ripped the bikini top off the other. The spectators whooped approval.

O'Donal licked his lips. 'Hey, come on, who are you people?'

'We're from Event Horizon,' said Greg.

O'Donal's already pale face blanched still further. 'Oh, shit.' He took a half step backwards, ready to turn and bolt, then stopped at the sight of the Walther eightshot in Greg's hand.

'You're not used to this, are you, Tentimes?' Gabriel asked with silky insistence. 'A solo hotrod, your combat is all mental. Well, this time the feedback is physical. You want my advice? Play ball. Don't annoy us. There are another seven who took part in the blitz. We'll just work down the list until we get some co-operation.'

'I didn't have any choice!'

'Tell us about it,' Greg suggested. 'Downstairs.'

'Down? Where?'

'Your terminals,' Gabriel said.

'Shit, how . . .' O'Donal clamped his mouth shut as Greg flicked the Walther's nozzle towards the door.

Out in the hall O'Donal stopped and sniffed the air, then his eyes found the smear of viscous liquid on the tiles. A small pulse of anger coloured his thoughts. 'Through here,' he said, pointing dully at a recessed door.

'You open it,' Gabriel ordered. 'Seeing as how it's keyed to your palmprint. I'd hate my colleague to receive that thousand-volt charge.'

O'Donal swallowed hard, almost a gulp. As he turned to the door Greg slapped the back of his head, knocking his face against the flaking varnish. The cook's hat fell off.

'Shit!' There was real fear in O'Donal's voice and mind. He looked at them to plead, a bead of blood seeping out of his left nostril. 'I wasn't gonna. Honest, shit. I wouldn't have. Shit, you've gotta believe me!'

'Sure,' Gabriel crooned.

Behind the hall door were fifteen steps leading down to

another door made of bronze-coloured metal. It slid open at O'Donal's voice command.

'Impressive,' Gabriel murmured.

The basement had been built as a wine cellar; the scars where the racks had been ripped out were still visible on the rough brick walls. A metal air-conditioning duct which had ensured the bottles were kept at a perfectly maintained temperature ran along the ceiling.

The basement was a hotrod's crypt now, smelling faintly of acetone. There were five terminals sitting on a low pine table, all different makes, each hardwired with customized augmentation modules. Hundreds of memox crystals were stacked neatly on narrow oak shelving. Four big cubes clung to the wall facing the table, two on either side of a long flatscreen which was lit up like a football stadium scoreboard. The Gracious Services circuit, detailing burns in progress, hackers on line, requests, available umpires. Greg searched, and sure enough saw Wildace's name.

'Expensive, too,' Greg said. 'According to the circuit you've only been solo for six months. Means you've been scoring pretty good, Tentimes. How do you do it?'

'What . . . what are you going to do to me?'

Greg shoved the Mulekick against the matt-black surface of the Hitachi terminal on the table. There was a flat crack as the power tubes discharged. A zillion precious delicate junctions were smelted into worthless cinders. The smell of scorched plastic filled the air.

O'Donal yelped as though he'd received the jolt. 'Oh, *shit-fire*, do you know how much that *cost* me?' He stared aghast at the ruined Hitachi.

'Don't know, don't care,' Greg said indifferently. 'Now, where's the money coming from?'

'They give me targets, pay good.'

'They?'

'They, him, her, shit I don't know. We've never met.'

'Got a name, a handle?'

'Wolf.'

'How does Wolf get in touch, through the circuit?'

O'Donal shook his head, eyes blinking rapidly. 'No, that's the sting, man. Wolf calls over the phone. Direct! God, you've no idea how bad that trip was the first time. I mean, that's the whole point of the circuit, right? It protects us as individuals, no hassle, no danger. You pay your dues, and you're covered. It's worked that way for twenty goddamn years. Then Wolf comes along and blows it right out of the water. Why me, I mean what did I do?'

'When did Wolf first contact you?' Greg asked patiently.

''Bout ten months ago.'

'But not through the circuit?'

O'Donal glanced from Greg to Gabriel, face screwing up from anger and, strangely, outrage. 'It was in a pub! I was having a drink with some mates and the fucking phone goes behind the bar, asking for me by name. Wolf knew who I was, where I was, knew about my burns. That is like the most heavy-duty shit a hotrod can get, y'know.'

Greg whistled, intrigued in spite of himself. It'd take good organization to spring a net like that; money and expertise. And for what? A team of tame hotrods. Who would want that? And more to the point, why? 'How does Wolf get in touch now?'

'Call box. I have to check in every three days. Dial a number, just like you do for Gracious Services. If there's a burn in the offing I get run around town for an hour until Wolf's happy I'm not pulling a backtrack.'

Gabriel was sitting in the black leather high-back chair behind the table, tenting her fingers and staring up at the pewter-coloured duct, lost in thought. 'The method of recruiting interests me,' she said. 'This Wolf definitely knew you were an active hacker?'

O'Donal nodded sullenly. 'The bastard read out a whole list of my burns.'

'How complete a list?'

'Dunno.' He caught the look Greg gave him. 'Yeah, all right. I didn't spot any missing.'

'Going back for how long?' she asked.

'Couple of years, ever since I plugged into the circuit.'

'Have you ever had a criminal record?'

'What? No.'

'Don't lie,' Greg said. The guilt had glinted in his mind.

'I'm not,' O'Donal insisted hotly. 'No record.' He flushed hard, not looking at Gabriel. 'Got pulled once, mind. Pigs said she was underage. Shit, I mean no way, not that size, melon city.'

'When was this?' Gabriel asked keenly.

'Six, seven years back.'

'The police, did they search your home?'

'For sure, tore it apart, bastards. They had to drop the charges after that.' He sniggered at the memory. 'My mates went and visited her for me. Straightened her out but good. She didn't want to talk to no one after that, least of all the pigs.'

'Were you into gear then?'

'Yeah, a bit. Nothing serious though, not then.'

'And where were you living?'

'Steve Biko tower.'

Gabriel smiled acute satisfaction. 'Your turn,' she said to Greg, as if it was some kind of channel quiz show.

'I'd like a list of all the burns you've done for Wolf,' he said.

O'Donal scowled sourly, but began typing on the Mizzi terminal.

'Carefully,' Gabriel warned. 'Make sure the code is the right one. We don't want any mistakes like a call for help, or anything equally tiresome. And believe me, I'll know if it isn't the right one.'

The truth finally dawned. 'Shit. You two, you're psychic, right?'

'Got it in one,' Greg said. 'How else did you think we found you?'

O'Donal's subconscious discharged a heavy rancorous stream of revulsion and dread, contaminating his conscious thoughts.

Greg showed his cybofax to the Mizzi, and O'Donal squirted the list of his burns over.

'How much do you get paid for a burn?' Greg asked.

'Depends, normally around five grand.'

'And for the Event Horizon burn?'

'That was a real big deal, I got fifteen for that.'

'No messing. So which half were you in on?'

'I don't follow you, man. What halves?'

'The attack was twofold, remember? The priority data-squirt blitz against the core, and the shutdown instructions beamed up to the Merlin. Which were you in on?'

'I don't know nothing about no Merlin shutdown. All Wolf told me to do was hack into the Event Horizon datanet and fire off a squirt at some bioware cruncher core. Man, you've never seen anything like that blitz memox, custom job.' He lifted a glittering black sphere the size of a tennis ball from the table, multi-faceted like an insect eye. 'The multiplex compression in this lover is absolute genius. Hell, I can't even retro the bytes. Sure wish I could. I'd love to be able to write my own like this someday.'

'Did this Wolf tell you what the core was?' Greg asked.

'Sure, it's some kind of fancy Turing personality responses program they've whizzed up to manage the company.'

'Have you ever thought of backtracking the money transfers from Wolf? Find out who he is? Hit back, perhaps.'

'Yeah. Big zero.'

'How come?'

'I ain't up to that, man,' O'Donal muttered quietly.

'Not up to much, are you, Tentimes?' Greg plucked one of the memox crystals from the shelves, reading the handwritten label. 'This a core-code melt virus?'

'Yeah.'

'Wolf supplied it, right? How many of them come from Wolf?'

'Some, 'bout half. I write my own, too, man!' O'Donal was stuffed with righteous indignation. 'I see what you're getting at, I'm no cyborg, man. I've got my own scene outside that arsehole. I'd have made solo without Wolf. I would!'

'Give me your bank account number, the one your Event Horizon burn money was paid into.'

O'Donal clutched at his hair with both hands, pulling hard. 'Shit, no way man, I've got everything stashed in there. I only burnt your fucking company once.'

Greg jammed the Mulekick down on O'Donal's Akai terminal. Blue-white static tapeworms writhed across the heat-dump fins, snapping and popping like arid matchwood.

'All right!' O'Donal shouted. 'Jesus.' He looked down hopelessly at the tiny wisp of smoke rising from the back of the Akai.

The restraint of fear was wearing thin, anger was predominating again. Greg knew he'd have to do something about that. Soon.

O'Donal's fingers trembled softly as he squirted the information from the Mizzi to Greg's cybofax. 'Hey, listen, you ain't going to like *do* anything to me, are you? I co-operated man, really I did. You know it all now. God's honest truth, every last byte.'

'That's right,' Greg said, and straightarmed O'Donal with the Mulekick, punching the electrode deep into his small flaccid beer gut.

O'Donal's cheeks inflated, eyes bulging. Alcohol-toxic breath rushed out of him, and he curled up, collapsing backwards on to the terminals. Memox crystals went glissading over the cold brick floor.

'Did you enjoy that?' Gabriel asked.

'No. Come on, time for us to make our exit.'

Greg sneaked a peek through the lounge door on the way out. The pool was filling up; people fully clothed, people half-clothed, naked people; empty magnums and sodden burger baps were bobbing about among them. A cloud of thick blue-black smoke was mushrooming up from the barbecue grill, the steaks and sausages were burning fiercely. Led Zep was crashing out 'Whole Lotta Love'. Hell of a party.

Greg tugged the Duo away from the kerb in a tight U-turn, ignoring the shrill clamour of incensed bicycle bells, and headed back towards Oakham.

Gabriel hunched down in the passenger seat and devoured the information O'Donal had squirted into his cybofax.

'Make any sense to you?' Greg asked.

'Nothing obvious leaps out. The targets are companies and finance houses. Most of the time Wolf wanted logic bombs crashed into their data cores; though there are some data snatches too, mainly high-tech research.'

'Doesn't tell us much. I'll squirt it over to Morgan Walshaw, get his economic intelligence team to run an analysis on it, see who benefits most.'

'But you've got a pretty good guess. I know you. You're almost happy about finding this list.'

'Yeah. What odds will you give me that our friend Kendric di Girolamo comes up top of the beneficiaries?'

'You really have got it in for him, haven't you?'

'Yep, logic and instinct both. All I need is proof, and darling Julia's avenging angel will take it from there.'

'I'm not so sure,' Gabriel said. 'That entrapment gig this Wolf character snared O'Donal with, it's very long-term. Find a gear-crazy kid who's growing up in exactly the right sort of environment that'll turn him to hotrodding, then tap his phone for seven years just to get the evidence to nail him with. Why? I mean what's he doing for Wolf that he wouldn't have done ordinarily on the Gracious Services circuit?'

'Let's see. How many burns are on that list?'

'Thirty-two, including the one against Event Horizon.'

Greg slowed the Duo and turned on to the B6047 heading for Tilton. It was a terrible road, so overgrown in places that the tarmac had vanished under grass and thistles. He steered into the ruts left by the farm wagons to get some decent traction, hoping nothing was coming the other way.

'Thirty-two is one hell of a lot of burns for a ten-month period,' he said. 'And Wolf has a team of at least eight hackers running these burns for him. Gracious Services is normally pretty independent, but even their umpires might begin to wonder what was going down. They're smart, if there is a pattern to the burns they'd spot it. Wolf isn't the type to leave his flank exposed like that.'

'Hence the need for privacy. Yes, I can buy that. Well, we'll just have to see what Walshaw's people come up with. By the way, what did you want O'Donal's account number for?'

'Wolf chose O'Donal because he isn't a true hotrod, not yet. He's a greenhouse product, force-grown; given viruses on a plate instead of developing his own talent to write them. That way he can't stray from Wolf's carefully ordained path. O'Donal doesn't have the ability to backtrack the credit transfers, but Royan sure as hell does.'

'That still doesn't explain away the police complicity in O'Donal's entrapment.'

'Kendric has more than enough money to bribe a squad or two of underpaid bobbies.'

Gabriel groaned in dismay. 'Christ, and Eleanor thinks I'm neurotic.'

24

Julia closed the heavy panelled door behind her, stepping into the understated elegance of the Princess of Wales suite. The room made her uncomfortably aware of just how uncouth her own bedroom was. Here, she was surrounded by temperate shades and smooth curves, the brocade-covered furniture seemed to flow into the walls. Several antique pieces were dotted around, and instead of clashing with the modern setting they complemented it to perfection. Part of their appeal was in their placing, she'd decided. She was continually afraid she'd bump into one of the little Pope chairs and ruin the whole effect. She'd never be able to put it back in the exact spot.

Several huge bouquets of fresh flowers filled the air with their perfume. She breathed down the scent and headed for the bathroom. The evening had been an utter delight so far, she was determined not to lose the theme now.

'See you in a couple of months,' was her grandfather's parting shot as she'd left Wilholm. He was paring down the sarcasm now, but couldn't resist one last dig.

She'd brought eight suitcases with her to the Marlston Hotel for the book launch. Actually, it was the gala relaunch of the Alaka publishing company. They'd decided to promote their new catalogue in grand style, no expense spared. A three-day junket for celebrities, financiers, aristocrats, and the media, even some of their authors were there. Three days, and more importantly, three nights.

Julia hadn't been quite sure what level the event was going to be pitched at, so she'd made some meticulous preparations. The first night dinner-dance had turned out to be a formal occasion; so, after much deliberation, and consulting Adela, she'd chosen a twelve-thousand-pound Salito gown. It was midnight black, because it was hard to look bad in black; scarlet and gold moiré patterns skipped across the fabric at every movement; the back was low, and the skintight front uplifting. For once she'd abandoned her St Christopher and worn a single diamond choker. Her hair had taken Adela and the hotel's in-house crimper three-quarters of an hour to arrange; they'd made it seem slightly ruffled, as though it wasn't styled at all. The most difficult thing to do with hair the length of hers.

And it'd worked a dream. A miracle. Walking slowly down the stairs to the reception with Adrian on her arm she'd felt like a queen on her way to her coronation. Every head in the hall had turned to watch her progress, seven channel cameras had focused on her.

Serene, the nodes had yelled into her mind; grinning or giving a thumbs-up like some crass ingénue would've wrecked everything. But she'd kept her composure, and Adrian had walked tall beside her.

Alaka's chairman had hurried to the bottom of the stairs to receive his guest of honour. The band had struck up, and she'd been offered champagne by a liveried waiter. All on camera.

She grinned oafishly at her reflection in the bathroom mirror, dignity gone, clapping her hands in celebration. The Salito split down its invisible seam and she wriggled out of it, kicking off her shoes. Choker and panties joined them on the mossy purple carpet.

Two minutes. The time since Adrian had said goodnight. A soft kiss that had lasted far longer than politeness dictated. His room was two doors down the corridor.

He'd stayed with her all evening, turning down offers to dance with anyone else. And there'd been a lot of good-looking girls who'd asked him. Most of them were the daughters of the rich and famous that Alaka had invited. Julia had enjoyed their company, girls her own age who weren't so self-conscious and hung up about money as most people. There had even been a couple of them she wouldn't mind meeting again, potential friends.

Yes, it had been the best evening for quite some time.

Three minutes. Naked, she looked at herself in the full-length mirror. Not totally displeased. Her figure was lanky, but elfin rather than skinny. Her breasts were nicely rounded, even if she didn't have Kats' milk-beast size, and they didn't sag at all. Reasonably broad feminine-looking hips, too. And an all-over tan that'd taken two days on her balcony to perfect.

An uncomfortable sensation of emptiness was plaguing her stomach. What had Adrian seen when he looked at her? Her figure or her money and name? She couldn't forget that Bil Yi Somanzer hadn't even noticed her before Uncle Horace told him who she was.

Four minutes. Her bedtime lingerie was laid out ready. Adela hadn't been consulted in that department, not at all. Julia had bullied herself into making the decision. Kats wouldn't have had any second thoughts.

She drew a deep breath and pulled on the French knickers; they were sheer silk, a pale peach colour, inset with lace. Her robe was white silk, ankle length. The combination was simple, sensual.

Impact was the most important thing. Overwhelm him, get him off balance and push. She studied the mirror critically, then retied the belt. It still wasn't right. Five more goes and the front of the robe was open to her navel, showing a long V of deeply tanned skin, and a more than generous slice of breast.

Seven minutes. Julia went back out into the bedroom, dimming the biplums to a faint rose-tinted glow.

Rachel was on duty outside. When they'd arrived, Julia had told her that Adrian was to be allowed in At Any Time. Rachel's face had never flickered, the woman must be a cyborg.

258

How long to wait? That was the real twister. Give him say twenty minutes – no, fifteen ought to be enough. All he had to do was take off his dinner jacket.

Nine minutes. She stood by the bed. An antique four-poster. So romantic.

If he wasn't here after fifteen minutes then she'd damn well go to his room. If she could find the nerve. What if his door was locked? What if he said no? What if one of those little vixens from the party was with him?

God, don't even think about it.

Ten minutes.

There was a light rap on the door.

'Come in,' she said, furious at the sudden quaver afflicting her voice. She almost let out a whimper of relief when she saw it was Adrian. He was wrapped in his burgundy towelling robe. Bare feet, no pyjamas.

She blipped the lock. Sealing him in.

'Julia!' There was a note of surprised admiration in his voice; and desire lighting his eyes as he drank down the sight of her.

She couldn't stand it any more, and ran at him. Swept up in strong warm arms. Spinning round and round. Both of them laughing jubilantly.

25

On Saturday morning Greg parked the Duo in a side street just outside New Eastfield, and handed over a fiver to the local teeny-bopper extortionists before walking out into the plush precinct's tranquil boulevards. He'd used the Event Horizon card to splash out on new light-grey slacks, blue canvas sneakers, and a jade-green pure wool Stewart sweater. His usual jeans and T-shirt would've aggrieved the private police squad which New Eastfield's residents employed.

One major contributory factor to Peterborough's post-Warming prosperity had been its burgeoning maritime links. The Nene allowed cargo ships to sail right into the heart of the city. They docked at a new port and warehouse complex which had sprung up in the place of the old shopping precinct and Queensgate mall.

In addition to the commercial shipping, an armada of nearly seven thousand small boats had set out from the Norfolk Broads as the Antarctic ice melted, converging on the city. They'd anchored around the island suburb of Stanground; their moorings evolving into a hugely complicated maze of jetties built out of timber scavenged from the roofs and floors of deluged buildings out in the Fens. The boats at the centre were trapped there now, ten years' worth of rubbish clogging the water around them, embedding them in an artificial bog. He'd heard that around ten thousand people lived in the sprawling boat-town.

The actual figure was uncertain, Stanground's inherent chaos made council hall governance nigh on impossible. An aspect which the residents took full advantage of. The narrow twisting channels were Peterborough's main haven for smugglers, pumping hard currency Eurofrancs into the city's economy.

Finally, there was an impressive squadron of pleasure craft. The potential of the city's industrial vigour, coupled with the kind of seedy spice endemic to monstrous overcrowding, proved a powerful attraction to Europe's shipborne rich. People who ran their mini-empires of financial trusts and venture projects from floating gin palaces. They were a flock in eternal migration, never in one port long enough to qualify for the taxman's attention.

They had their own marina in New Eastfield, north of the Nene's main course. The quays were concrete, substantial, immaculately clean. Every requirement was catered for, from stores supplying five-star food and maritime gear to a not-so-small dry dock capable of providing complete refits.

Greg hit the marina itself around eleven; a whole community of clubs, sports complexes, shops, restaurants, and pubs along the waterfront, open to permit holders only. Royan had loaded his ID into the membership computer. The promenade was a kilometre long, built from huge granite cubes. Five quays stabbed out into the deep harbour that'd been dredged for the yachts of the mega-rich.

A gauzy layer of cumulus cloud diffused the sun into a sourceless light overhead. The humidity this close to the Fens basin approached steam-bath levels.

He found Angelica's, a single-storey flat-roofed emporium opposite the centre quay where the *Mirriam* was berthed. It was a food hall selling wholesale quantities of *nouveau* delicacies he didn't even know how to pronounce.

Greg walked down the cul-de-sac side alley and found the delivery bay's metal roller-door at the rear. Beside it, embedded in the bricks, was a series of metal rungs. He started to climb.

The uniformity of the solar-collector roof was broken by two satellite-dish weather domes and three big conditioning stacks, their fans spinning silently. Dead centre was a box structure of slatted wooden panels which housed Angelica's water tanks. Greg crouched down and scuttled over to it. One of the slat panels was hanging loose. He pulled it aside and slipped in.

The panel opened into a narrow gap between two big water tanks, one and a half metres wide, three long. There wasn't enough headroom to stand up, and he had to hunch down with his hands brushing the floor. What space there was had nearly been used up.

At the far end, various photon-amp lenses were poking through the slats, their cables feeding a jumble of compact gear modules. Weird little halos of coloured light cloaked five miniature flatscreens which flickered with the image of the good ship *Mirriam*, half covered with red digital read-outs.

Right in front of the entrance panel was a pile of drink cans and food wrappers. Greg nearly put his foot in an adult-sized potty that had been connected in to Angelica's plumbing by a ribbed flexible pipe. There was only one smell: ripe human.

Between the rubbish and the gear was a thin yellow sponge mattress. Suzi was lying on it, wearing blue shorts, soaked a shade darker by sweat. Her mauve spikes had drooped in the torrid heat.

She peered at him out of the gloom. 'Christ, 'bout time you showed. See what we've been suffering for you.'

'All in a good cause.' He stepped over the potty and squirmed on to the mattress beside her. One of the gear modules poked sharply into his back.

'Cosy,' Suzi smirked spryly. 'You wanna do it? There's enough room if you ain't into anything too kinky.'

Greg was suddenly very aware of her tough little body pressing against him. 'We'd die of heat exhaustion.'

'Yeah, tits the size that new girl of yours was stacked with, can't say I blame you.'

Greg nearly started to protest, but thought better of it. 'I hope you're not handling the observation all by yourself. This heat is bad for you. Seriously.'

A growl rumbled up from the back of her throat. 'Shit no. It's four-hour shifts only up here. The rest of the squad is spotted round the marina, some of them signed on with the company that's got the franchise to keep the promenade clean. And there are another two in hire cars for tailing Kendric's Jag when he goes runabout. We've been drawing up a habits and behaviour profile. Just like you taught us, right? *Know* the man, get to understand him. No hassle in that, talk's pretty loose around here. One of us made barman at a pub the crews use, nothing they like better than slagging off their owners.'

'Sounds good so far. What have you got for me?'

Suzi wriggled a hand free and pointed at the screens. This Kendric, he's a fucking Martian. Not of this earth, y'know? The lives these yacht people lead. Un-be-lievable! Tell you something, though, no way is he a card carrier. I mean, the PSP's local chairpricks, they had it all, right? Eternal junket time. But they haven't got nothing compared to this geezer. The money he's got. He wouldn't last five minutes if they ever got back in power.'

'Ah.' He'd wondered about the peak of vexation in her mind. 'No, Kendric's not Party. But my guess is that he's involved in a spoiler against Event Horizon. And with the economy all shaky with inflation right now, Event Horizon taking a tumble would be serious bad news. The only people who'll benefit are the PSP relics in legitimate opposition. That good enough for you?'

'What's the spoiler?'

'Ministry of Defence. Ultra-hush.'

'Figures,' she agreed without much enthusiasm. 'Son told us Kendric was plugged into big-league corporate operations.'

Greg studied the various images on the five screens. *Mirriam* was the biggest yacht in the marina. Sixty-five metres long, gleaming silver-white, with jet-black ports. Crewmen stripped to the waist were visible, washing down the wide afterdeck. 'Is Kendric on board right now?'

'Yeah, as always. Believe me, nothing at all happens in this marina before noon. They're all too busy sleeping off last night's orgies. Right now, it's business time for Kendric. He holds a couple of conference sessions in the mid-deck lounge each day. There's a whole bunch of squarearse lawyer types who turn up each morning to see him. Don't know what they rap about in the cabin, *Mirriam*'s ports are screened, but anything they say out on the deck we've got on a memox cartridge for you.' Her eyebrows puckered up. 'Isn't that Julia Evans girl in charge of Event Horizon now?'

'Yeah. She owns it.'

'No shit? Heard Kendric on about her . . .' Suzi began typing on a keyboard. 'Remember the file code,' she muttered, and consulted a cybofax. 'Here we go.'

One of the small screens changed to a scene on the *Mirriam*'s broad afterdeck. Greg squinted down at it. Kendric was sitting on one of the plastic recliners, dressed in an open-neck shirt and tailored shorts, drinking from a tall cut-crystal glass. The man with him was in a suit, his collar undone, tie hanging loose. He looked to be in his late forties, a flat bulldog face with red skin.

'Here,' said Suzi. She handed Greg an earpiece.

'. . . missing out badly,' the man in the suit was saying, in a faint Scottish brogue. 'Our Party is damn near down, Kendric, it cannot last long. Terrible thing, food's short, there's no gear, no methane for the farms. People are going to the spivs like never before. There's a hell of a turnover in silver right now. If you could just have a wee word with young Julia Evans, come to an arrangement wi' her till the Party goes down. I can ship it out by the tonne.'

'Impossible,' Kendric said flatly. His face was dangerously hard. 'That frigid bitch and I have severed all our business contacts. There will be no resumption.'

''Tis a lot o' money, Kendric.'

'Ride it out. I'm closing some deals that will make the black currency market utterly trivial. And I certainly shall not forget your forbearance.'

The man in the suit shook his head sadly, and took a drink from his glass.

The image froze. 'Didn't mean much at the time,' said Suzi. She pecked at the keyboard again.

This time it was evening. A gauzy layer of cumulus cloud glowed copper above the *Mirriam*. There was a crowd of about fifteen people drinking on the afterdeck, the women in low-cut cocktail dresses; men in suits or blazers. Laughter, clamorous conversation, and the chink of glasses filled the earpiece.

Kendric was standing at the stern with two other men. One tall and slim with thinning blond hair, the second a handsome African in brightly coloured northern tribal robes.

'You have got to provide the house with alternative investments, Kendric,' said the blond-haired man. 'And fast.'

'I've acquired some options in a Pacific Rim portfolio,' the African said earnestly. 'They'll give you a sixteen to seventeen per cent return, guaranteed minimum.'

'No,' Kendric said.

'You won't find anything better. Not short term.'

'I'm sorry. I know how hard you worked to put them together. But no.'

'You should've hung on, Kendric,' said the blond man. 'We could've squared it with the family over Siebruk.'

Kendric's handsome features darkened. 'That deranged little shit, Evans. Buying a fucking bank! I've never heard of anything so . . . so—' He clutched at the polished brass taffrail. 'God damn that bitch!'

The blond man turned to look out over the marina.

'Look,' said the African. 'The family is going to insist on an equivalent viability from the money released by pulling out of the Event Horizon backing consortium.'

Kendric didn't respond.

'The family—' began the blond man.

'Put them off,' Kendric snapped. He caught himself, and rested a companionable hand on the blond man's shoulder. 'Six months, Clancy. If I haven't come through by then, I'll step down from the family board anyway. OK?'

Greg considered the faces on the screen. The two financiers' obvious concern. Kendric's driving anger. And intuition was totally spurious. A cornered animal had no choice in the way it reacted. 'Have you got a record of all the visitors?' he asked.

Suzi tapped the sensor array with possessive pride. 'No sweat. Day or night, anyone on or off gets tagged. We've got infrared and low level, for night work. Not that we need them, that baby is lit up like a football pitch after dark. And we've got an antenna rigged to intercept *Mirriam*'s local calls. But there's nothing we can do about her satellite uplinks. Trouble is, the local calls have all been the big zero so far, social gabbing and ordering booze, that kind of crap.'

Greg grunted and wiped some of the sweat off his forehead. 'Good. If I know who he's been seeing, I might be able to get a clearer idea of exactly what he's planning.'

'You figuring on doing an extra-parliamentary number against him?'

'Insufficient data.'

She bent back and dragged a koolcan of orange from the heap at her feet. 'I'd like in if it happens.' She twisted the tab ninety degrees.

Greg watched frost forming over the can with something akin to lust. 'No promises. As I said, this is big league. Black-hat spooks with viral wasps and funny midnight accidents.'

Suzi pulled the tab and gulped down the icy stream of bubbling orange, burping loudly. 'Figures.'

'So what happens in the afternoon?'

'She – Hermione, right? – goes shopping, maybe does lunch with a load of airhead cows just like her. Evening, they party; sometimes on one of the other yachts, mostly on theirs, 'bout twenty-five came to it last night. Then after midnight they take off for the Blue Ball. That's a casino in New Eastfield. Hottest spot in town, people say. We tailed them for you, but no fucking way could we get past the bouncers. They pack up around three or four and come straight back. Spoke to a couple of the casino's waitresses, though. They reckoned Kendric and Hermione usually pick up a girl at the Blue Ball, bring her back to *Mirriam* to provide themselves with some fun. These waitresses, a friend of theirs let herself get talked into going along with them once. Bad scene, Greg, no sadism, but she was really put through her paces. Kendric and Hermione screwed her brains out. Then she got kicked off the next morning. Apparently, they all do. One-nighters; fuck and forget.'

'What about the crew?'

Suzi grinned knowingly. 'Just in case you're thinking of visiting, right? There's nine real crew, sailor types, including the captain. On top of that you've got seven assorted staff, cooks, maids, and such. Then there's six bodyguards, mean-looking bastards. Oh, here,' she leaned over him, tiny pointed breasts squashing against his cheek, damp and salty. He detected a glint of amusement in her mind. She scrabbled amongst the gear modules and came back with a memox crystal. 'This has got all the visitors' faces and times they turned up. We managed to get names for a few of them.'

One of the flatscreens switched to the *Mirriam*'s blueprints. 'There are always at least four people left on board,' Suzi said, pointing at it. 'We think we've got their cabins assigned, but you can never be sure.'

Names had been superimposed over the various cabins.

'Great. Where did you get the specs from?' Greg asked.

'Son snatched them. *Mirriam*'s hull was built in Finland, but she was fitted out up in Tyneside. Apparently the English are still unbeatable when it comes to quality handicrafts.'

Greg squirted the memox crystal data into his cybofax, and began skipping through the faces. The images were good, high definition, most seemed to be staring straight into the lens. Morgan Walshaw should be able to assemble profiles on them.

'Oh yeah,' Suzy muttered. 'They've got themselves a perma-nent doxy on board, too. She don't do much; too fucking stoned the whole time by the look of her. That Kendric, *ménage à quatre* every night, some stud, huh?'

Greg flipped through the index until he came to the girl; she'd been given a number, but no name. Her face appeared on the cybofax's little screen.

'That's some looker,' Suzi said, craning over his shoulder. 'Wouldn't mind her for myself.'

'Has she been on board the whole time?'

'Yeah, since we've been watching, anyway. Why, you know her?'

'Yes. Her name is Katerina Cawthorp.'

*

SO WHY I***FYRNST . . . +! IS JULIR'SSSS FRIEND SHCKED UUUUP WITH KENDRIC DI GIROLAMO???

'I don't know the specifics,' Greg said, his voice raised, strained.

Royan was jittering about in his dentist's chair, shoulders jerking in an erratic pumping rhythm. Royan was having one of his bad days, and when Greg considered just how shitty even Royan's good days must be. . . .

CONNNNECTED?

'There is no such thing as coincidence.'

WAS I HE%%%%LPING YOU WITH 10TIIIIMES>>?

The catheter bag which dangled below the chair on a chrome coathook was filling with an oily bilious liquid.

'Big help. He was a blackmail victim, not a proper hotrod. Someone has been feeding him sophisticated viruses to use on burns.'

THINK HE WAS ODDDDDD. TOOOO QUICK TO GOOOO SOLO. NOT EN***£' SHITTTT END END END. NOT ENOUGH CIRCIT SKORES TO HISSS HANDEL. HURTSSS GREEG. REALLLY HURTS MEEEEE.

And how could he answer that? He smiled broadly, feeling a prize turd. 'Hey, you made a friend in Eleanor. She's planning on coming back.'

BEAUTY AN>>>>## BEAAST. HORRRIBLENASTY FILTH!!!£ MEMEMEMEME. YOU SCREW BABIESBABIES MAKKK""" MAKE BABIES TOOOGETHER . . . IIIIIIIII WANNT WANT SHITFILLTH.

£%::))   GOOOOOOO AWWWWAY GGRE&

Greg couldn't move. Revolted and horrified. He wanted to get out, out and never come back. Break free. The Trinities, the Constables, Blackshirts, this tower, this room, Royan; they were all facets of his ingrained guilt, soul-devouring.

DON'TTTTTT CRY.

He rubbed knuckles into his eyes, vision blurring.

QUUIK<<<< WHYCOME???

Qoi appeared in the kitchen door, concern marring her fragile, sensitive features. She flashed Greg a look he couldn't begin to interpret.

WHY

'I needed you to run a finance backtrack for me. I think it's the missing link, the one that'll tie Kendric to the hotrods.'

The screens exploded into an incoherent image-mash: channel shows, himself seen through Royan's eye camera, sticky tears smearing his cheeks, mad computer graphics, starchy-neat data tables dissolving into tight vortices of green and blue alpha-numerics. One of the little trash robots trundled across the floor, gears grinding harshly, and bumped into a plant trough. It backed off, and hit the trough again, and again. Bewitched with a mindless insect sentience.

Qoi was at Royan's side, pinching his nose with one hand, trying to push a feed bottle's nipple into his mouth. He flung his head from side to side, a desperate thrumming sound rose in his throat.

DATA DATA DAT — — — — — — — LEAVE IT IT IT""

A multitude of red and green LEDs lit up on one of Royan's cranky gear consoles. Greg retrieved the memory O'Donal had given him from his cybofax, and showed it to the console. Squirting.

The screens were showing a giant still picture of Trafalgar Square. Greg recognized it instantly. A euphoric classic. The day the PSP fell; beamed out live by every channel in the world. The crowd singing God Save the King, orange flames rising from a hundred PSP banners, ten thousand Union Jacks waving in joyful celebration, a residue of smoke from Downing Street boiling through the air. The scene was swelling, individual pixels becoming golf-ball sized, a nonsense mosaic.

Royan sounded as though he was choking. Qoi had got the nipple into his mouth, he was sucking frantically; treacly globs of mashed apple running down his chin, dribbling on to an already badly stained T-shirt.

Behind Greg the robot suddenly stopped its mad battering. There must've been something in the apple. Royan was visibly wilting.

'You go now, please,' Qoi said, bowing from the waist.

The lunatic kaleidoscope shrank as the screens began to wink out one by one.

Qoi's small expressive eyes were filled with a sorrow that had no right inhabiting someone her age. 'Nothing more you can do.'

26

A flock of black storks were flapping lazily overhead as Greg walked up the *Mirriam*'s gangplank. The bodyguard teleported out of nowhere to block his path, a hand holding both railings. He was wearing a red and green striped rugby shirt and coffee-coloured shorts. 'You looking for something?' he asked in strongly accented English.

'Yes, Mr di Girolamo.'

'He's not expecting you.'

Greg couldn't see the bodyguard's eyes, they were hidden behind wrapround Ferranti sunglasses. His neck was thickly muscled, displaying a vast network of protruding veins. Whatever steroids he was taking, they were playing hell with his blood pressure.

'Just tell him Greg Mandel is here to see him.' He held up the Event Horizon card.

The bodyguard thought it over then called over his shoulder. Another bodyguard appeared at the top of the gangplank; a black bear of a man, over two metres tall, shoulders in proportion, sweat glinting on his broad forehead. The two of them exchanged a brief murmur, then the first stabbed a meaty forefinger at Greg. 'You. Don't move.' He disappeared below deck, leaving his replacement to fold his arms and look Greg up and down contemptuously.

Greg ignored the attempted intimidation. If Kendric was

relying on people like this to protect him from a professional snatch posse then he was in deep trouble. They looked tough, and probably knew their combat routine, but put them up against a tekmerc hardliner team and they wouldn't last the opening second.

Muddy water lapped quietly against the yacht's hull.

Greg had deliberately waited until midday to give Kendric a chance to recover from his partying at the Blue Ball.

'You've cracked,' Suzi had barked when he told her he was going on board.

'Tell you, I have to get near Kendric,' he said.

'Why, for Christ's sake?'

'Ask him questions, see how he reacts.'

'Crazy.' She crossed herself, eyes rolling. But she helped organize the back-up, positioning the Trinities around the marina. Greg couldn't find any fault in her method, Suzi had been one who listened.

Knowing the squad was providing covering fire gave him a degree of confidence walking into the lion's den. The orders Suzi had were simple enough: on no account was he to be taken into the yacht itself.

'OK, you can come up.' The first bodyguard had returned. The set of his jaw radiated severe disapproval.

Mirriam was sixty-five metres of sheer beauty. Whatever his other faults, Kendric certainly knew the difference between refined style and pretentious glitz. *Mirriam* was conceived as a shrine to the former. Her polished wooden decks gleamed with a rosy sheen under the desert-bright sun. Every immaculate brass fixture was mirror bright. The low-friction white paint was painful on the eyes.

Greg was led round to the afterdeck. It had integral couches with puffy leather upholstery forming an island in the centre, several recliners dotted about. There was a clutch of chrome gym equipment on the starboard side, just outside the lounge-cabin doors.

Katerina was lying prone on the bench press, using its leg lift, a big LCD counter notching up each pull. She was dressed in tight black neoprene sprinter shorts, green stretch-leggings, and the top of a loose mauve T-shirt that'd been slashed in half, its ragged hem barely covering her large breasts. Her mane of blonde hair was held back with a broad white elastic towelling band. She was perspiring heavily, drawing breath through her nostrils, an expression of grim concentration on her perfect chiselled features.

'I do know you,' she said through clenched teeth. The weight she was lifting was almost as much as he used in his own regimen. 'You were at Julie's house.'

'That's me,' Greg said. 'Nice party, wasn't it?'

'You can go now, Mark. Kendric will be out in a minute.'

The bodyguard looked like he wanted to protest, but didn't quite know how. Greg flashed him a sunny smile, receiving a dark scowl for his trouble.

Despite the Ferranti glasses, Greg could tell the man's eyes were on Katerina as he shuffled off forward. It was understandable, given the circumstances. His own gaze kept switching between her fantastic legs and her abdomen, hypnotized by the hard cords of muscle flexing below her smooth tanned skin. Ever hopeful her little scrap of T-shirt would ride up just that fraction higher.

'Ninety-seven, ninety-eight, ninety-nine, finish,' she gasped.

'Is it worth it?'

Her head dropped back to rest on the bench's thin padding. 'Kendric likes me to be fit,' she said, her voice was high, childlike and remote. 'He says that anyone blessed with a body as good as mine has a duty to keep it in tip-top shape. He wouldn't enjoy me so much otherwise.'

'And what Kendric says and enjoys is important, is it?'

Her eyes closed. 'Yes. Very. They do things to me, you see, such wonderful things. If I can't please them in turn, they might stop. I couldn't stand that.'

The passive sing-song lilt she used to recite her doctrine gave him a chill. He folded his espersense around her.

Katerina's mind was strange; unruffled, as though she'd been popping tranquillizers. There was little mental activity, she was taking only the minimum notice of her surroundings; it was almost a hibernatory state. But there was no sign of any post-trauma withdrawal, nor any of the jagged rents of chemical-induced damage he had been expecting. Greg went deeper.

Beneath the sluggish currents of her surface thoughts there was a treasured core of memory, a glowing centre of delicious anticipation and joy. But for all its bright glory, it was a contaminant, tainting every thought.

'What wonderful things?' he asked softly.

Katerina's face became dreamy. 'They love me,' she said.

'How do they love you?'

'Sometimes gently. Sometimes so fiercely they make me cry. It doesn't matter which. It always ends wonderfully.'

Greg felt his skin going slick with cold sweat. 'How long has this been going on, Katerina?'

'Ever since I came here. Time doesn't really bother me now, I'm too happy. Adrian tried, of course, tried so hard, but it never came with him, not properly. I'm so lucky they took me away from him, I might never have known otherwise.'

'When did they take you away?'

She looked out vacantly across the marina, her mind nearly losing the thread of thought. 'At the party, Uncle Horace's party, Bil Yi was there, that's what Julie promised. So I went. Only they were there too. He was funny and kind, it was exciting.' She turned back to look at Greg. An angel's face vandalized by tears. 'He's so strong. And I'm afraid.'

Kendric di Girolamo slid open the cabin-lounge door and stepped on to the aft-deck. Hermione followed a pace behind.

'Mr Mandel,' he took Greg's hand in a limp grip. 'So nice of you to call. I trust Katerina has been entertaining you satisfactorily.' He was wearing a navy-blue blazer with bright brass buttons and a spotted silk handkerchief peeping out of his breast pocket, a dark green cravat filling the top of his open white shirt. White

274

flannel trousers and dark blue sneakers completed the nautical image.

Hermione bestowed a gracious smile. A musky breath of orchid perfume stole around Greg, caressing, starting off that certain tingle. The weeks hadn't dimmed the memory of her beauty. Skin deep, he warned himself, camouflage. She was dressed in a cerise off-the-shoulder gypsy top and blue knee-length skirt. He was reminded of a bird of prey waiting to pounce, mesmerically deadly.

Katerina rose from the padded bench, bare feet slapping on the wooden deck as she came to stand close beside Kendric. 'I've done my routine,' she said, looking up adoringly at his face. 'All of it, everything you said.'

Greg turned away from her desperate search for Kendric's approval. Studying the New Eastfield skyline.

Kendric gently wiped her tears with his forefinger, an act which resulted in an almost electric jolt firing through Katerina's mind. His touch was awakening her. An incredibly warped version of Sleeping Beauty and Prince Charming.

'Well done, my dear. I shall attend you in a little while. I have to have a few words with this gentleman first.'

The desolation on her face was heartwrenching.

'Come along, darling,' Hermione said. 'It's just silly man's talk. We'll go and get you ready. You're all smelly after that exercise. A nice shower is just what you need.' She took Katerina's hand and led her back into the cabin.

Katerina looked back at Kendric, eyes round, imploring. 'Hurry.'

Kendric blew her a kiss.

The door closed. Through the blackened glass Greg could just make out Katerina pulling off her mauve T-shirt. Hermione's arm slipped possessively round the girl's narrow waist, leading her deeper into the *Mirriam*.

'Such an exquisite young girl,' Kendric said, watching Greg's face with narrowed eyes. 'I have always admired your English roses. After one has broken through that cool reserve, their adventurousness knows no bounds.' There was a fragment of disappointment registering in his mind at Greg's refusal to show the slightest execration.

'I'm afraid I can't stop long, Mr di Girolamo,' Greg said. 'My friends would worry about what'd happened to me.'

'No,' Kendric said, his thoughts were steely.

'I'm sorry?'

'No. You're not staying at all, Mandel. Katerina let you on board. My mistake; you should not have been allowed within a million kilometres of the *Mirriam*.'

'But I was wondering if you could help me.'

'I enquired about you after our first encounter. I know what you are. A gland psychic. A Mindstar veteran. You were not going to ask me anything, you were going to uncover. Event Horizon's truthfinder general, sent to pry by your whore-daughter mistress.'

Greg held his dismay in check. 'Any answers you give would be entirely voluntary. I can't read people's thoughts.'

'So you claim, and other people fervently hope. It is a particular human weakness you pry on, Mandel; we want, need, to believe we are secure against you. But I have a vast repository of confidential commercial information in my brain. I choose not to believe the word of a repulsive grotesquery, a failed laboratory experiment.'

Greg let the neurohormones discharge into his brain, desperately searching round with his intuition. There was guilt here, a strong scent; Kendric and Julia were tied together, hating each other, feeding off each other. With a shock he knew she was as guilty as Kendric. Both of them wilfully stimulating the other's black obsession, a perverted symbiosis.

He was jerked out of his meditative analysis by hands like a pair of vices clamping round his upper arms. The bodyguards were standing on either side of him.

'Mark, Toby, throw him off,' Kendric said.

'I'm going,' Greg told them. He sensed rather than saw Mark's smirk.

'Too right,' the bodyguard said.

Greg contracted his espersense, neglecting the other minds arrayed around the *Mirriam*, focusing on Kendric alone. 'Wolf,' he shouted.

There was no reaction. No guilt, fright, consternation, panic. The name hadn't registered. Instead, a band of mild puzzlement tapered through Kendric's mind. It was followed by a rising tide of wry satisfaction when he realized how shaken Greg was by the negative.

Toby and Mark frogmarched him off the aft-deck and down the side of the superstructure, Kendric's laughter chasing him all the way.

He was dropped abruptly at the top of the gangplank, stumbling. Something with the force of a runaway train slammed into his backside. He tried to curl up into the trusty old paratroop landing crouch, but it didn't seem to work very well. He saw a fast, confusing snapshot sequence of yachts and water and sky at impossible angles, each black interstice punctuated by a new burst of pain that mercifully shut off almost as soon as it registered, leaving a patch of numbness. The bioware node spliced into his cortex which regulated his gland was also programmed to blank out nervous impulses above a predetermined pain level. Mindstar had included the limiter as an experiment to try and alleviate shock in combat injury cases, but the Army had never brought it into widespread use, there was too much danger of squaddies ignoring the damage they'd received and making it worse.

The unyielding concrete of the quay arrested his helter-skelter momentum with a sickeningly loud slap. His brain seemed to be floating at the centre of a closed insensate universe. There was harsh laughter from afar followed by running feet. Hands grasped him, hauling him upright.

'Shit. You OK? Can you walk?'

Tactile sensation eased back, the cortical node reopening enough nerve channels for him to regain control over his limbs. Bruises throbbed sharply across his legs, arms, and back. His left leg was shaking. Both hands smarted from wide slashes of grazed skin, filming over with blood. Tunnel vision showed his suede desert boots at some vast distance. He couldn't breathe through his nose, it was full of warm sticky liquid.

'Come on, lean on us.' That was Suzi.

Greg did so, gratefully.

'You want those pillocks taken out?' There was a note of hope colouring her voice.

'No.' He shook his head. Big mistake. The world reeled alarmingly, acid bile rose, scouring his throat.

'Green south, green south, stand down. We're bringing Thunderchild in. Gold west, cover please.'

There was a small Cambridge-blue three-wheel sweeper-float ahead of him now, its front roller brushes retracted, inclined at forty-five degrees, looking like rusty felt mandibles. The name GUS'S SANITIZING was written down the side in bold yellow letters.

Greg was urged on to the narrow seat in the Perspex-bubble cab, and Des climbed in behind the wheel while Suzy rode shotgun on the footplate. The two Trinities were both wearing jaunty red shirts and matching trousers, complemented with Gus's company caps, burger-bar uniforms.

Des swooped the float into a hard turn, and set off back down the quay at a good five kilometres per hour, squirting a thick spray of bubbly detergent in their wake. He fumbled with the dash switches and cut the rain of cleanliness, cursing hotly.

'I've got to go back,' Greg said, pinching his nose between thumb and forefinger.

'Fuck that,' Des said. 'We've blown cover hauling you out. I've gotta get my squad safeguarded. Standard procedure; you should know that, Mr Military Hotshot. This operation is now over.'

'What the hell do you want to go back for?' Suzi asked.

'I have to see something.'

They shot out on to the promenade, and Des tilted the

joystick sharp left. Pedestrians hopped out of the way, hurling abuse.

'Listen,' Des said. 'You wanna go back, that's fucking fine by me. I'll stop right now and you can walk. But you're on your own. We've been burning our arses off for you, and I don't see anything to show for it.'

'OK, drop me here.'

'Shit.' Suzi and Des exchanged anxious befuddled glances. 'You can't,' said Suzi. 'Come on, Greg, you can't hardly walk. We'll bring you back in a couple of days, when it's cooler.'

'It has to be now.'

'The photon amps are still in place, how about we take you back to Angelica's? You can watch from there.'

Greg probed his nose tenderly, it didn't feel broken, and it'd stopped bleeding. 'Not that sort of watching, not visual. I want to use my espersense on them.'

'Jesus,' Des spat. 'You Mindstar?'

'Yeah.'

'Bloody hell,' Suzi muttered. 'I knew there was something about you. Father never said nowt.'

Greg said nothing, he had always held back from mentioning it to the Trinities. People developed funny attitudes to psychics, kids especially. Let them just think he was lucky, outfits like that put a lot in superstition.

'Jesus,' Des said. 'Fucking Mindstar active in Peterborough. Think on it. Party always pissed itself over you people. Look, just what is going down on that yacht?'

'If I knew for sure I wouldn't have to go back.'

'Shit, just how close do you have to get?'

They compromised. Des drove into the maze of service alleys behind the promenade shops, and swapped clothes with Greg. Then he went off to organize the squad's withdrawal, leaving Suzi to drive Greg. There'd be no more retrieval posses if Toby and Mike came after them; but the snipers would remain in place until Greg had finished.

Suzi drove back out on to the promenade and deployed the brushes before moving up the quay next to the *Miriam*'s mooring. Seagull crap dissolved into creamy puddles, frizzy bristles whisking it away into the float's tanks.

'Stop here,' Greg told her once they were opposite Kendric's yacht.

She climbed out of the little cab. 'Don't be too long,' she implored, and lifted the engine cowling.

Greg relaxed, sinking back into the thin cushioning of the bench, and instructed the cortical node to shut out the sharp throbs of pain his nerves were reporting loyally.

The gland: stressed, taut like a marathon runner's calf on the home straight. A sluice of neurohormones bubbled out amongst his axons.

He wanted a sensory extension that went way beyond his usual short-range emotion perception. To find it he retreated inward, ignoring his blood heat, heartbeats, breathing. The state waited for him right down at the bottom of the mental well, a fragile central pool. Gaseous shapes meandered below its surface. He slipped softly below the interface.

Greg perceived shadows, treacherous grey cobwebs congealing into misleading forms, aching empty gaps of grainy mist. The vision was silent, neither hot nor cold. Through it all, minds shone like diamond-point mirages, a flat cyclonic swirl of fireflies with himself at the tranquil storm-eye. He concentrated, seeking the opaque distortion of *Mirriam*, the familiar signature of one mind.

The water resolved as a sheet of black ice, a dead zone; he drifted across it, stretching out close to his absolute limit. *Mirriam*'s hull rose above him, a cliff of insubstantial gauze. Passing through.

The three figures were cloudy alien protrusions into his lonely universe; their shape fuzzy, a pseudo-locus rippling around a solid kernel. Kendric and Hermione slid fluidly over and round Katerina, the three together a tightly knit serpentine coil.

Katerina was a soul in torment, hating herself for what she

was doing, unable to refuse. She closed out the degradations Hermione performed, warm with the conviction her reward would come.

Greg observed her arousal growing as Kendric pleasured himself with her, his mind leaking distorted pictures of Julia. Fissures of intense rapture multiplied through her mind, interlacing, spreading to conquer, reducing her to animal abandon. Orgasm brought a blazing concussion of frenzied ecstasy, a neural nova.

Instinct and dusty memory fused within Greg's tarnished cranium, and at last he knew what Kendric had done to her.

The intangible universe twisted, spectral images elongating and spiralling down to a tightly wound vanishing point. The marina's sights and sounds boiled up around him, solid and loud.

'Let's go home,' he said weakly. Sustaining such a vast psi-effusion was severely debilitating. Gravity seemed to have quadrupled.

''Bout time,' Suzi grumbled, slamming down the cowling and locking the catches with a vicious twist. 'You look like shit, you know?'

'Thank you.' The sky overhead was jaundiced, its turbidity fluctuating in time to his heartbeat.

'That gland must really take it out of you.' Her foot pressed down on the accelerator pad.

'It does.'

'Thought so, you were thrashing about like you were having a nightmare. Get what you want?'

'Yes.'

'Hey, your nose has started bleeding again.'

'It'll stop in a minute.'

27

'Of course Kendric wouldn't know Wolf's name,' Eleanor snapped irritably. 'He's the man at the top, the one with the cleanest hands in town. He buys people who buy people who buy Wolf. That's why there was no response to the name, there'll be a whole chain of tekmercs between him and the cutting edge of the operation to get rid of Philip Evans. It's like that precaution you use in gear, what do you call it? And keep still.'

'Cut-offs.' Greg's voice had a throaty rasp to it.

She'd got his hands spread out on the chalet's kitchen bar, spraying his knuckles with Colman's dermal seal. From her own past experience she knew it stung, but it was the best on the market. The treacly salve fizzed over his grazes, quickly solidifying into a flexible powder-blue membrane which would enhance tissue repair, moulting after a couple of days.

Eleanor concentrated on keeping her hand steady as she moved the can back and forth, getting an even deposit. Her shoulders ached, and her back was cramped from hunching over him for three-quarters of an hour. She was getting tired, and her temperament showed it.

The lion roar of the Triumph bike trailing the Duo into the Berrybut estate had triggered some kind of premonition in her. She'd come running from the shore as Des helped Greg out of the Duo. There seemed to be blood all over him, his Stewart sweater was torn, he couldn't walk without leaning on Des.

She'd felt resentful as Suzi and Des carried him into the chalet: an invasion of her personal space. The chalet was symbolic with all that was good in life right now. They were violating that, harbingers of pain and violence. She knew she'd always associate them with disruption now, no matter how much Greg praised them.

They'd seen Greg on to the lounge sofa and departed on the Triumph, Suzi, surprisingly, as awkward as she was. Who would have thought the girl possessed that much sensitivity?

Eleanor had been thankful for her animal husbandry courses, it let her deal with his injuries without the vapours, keeping a rigid leash on her nausea. She'd frozen his nose and clotted the burst blood vessels inside, painted numb-all on his swollen left eye, immobilized his left ankle in a thick sock of quik-set medical polymer, and generally cleaned him up. The clothes would have to go, though; she'd throw them on the bonfire tonight.

'You're right,' he said. 'Tell you, I thought I'd got it all sussed. I thought Kendric would light up like a Christmas tree when I mentioned Wolf. It was the proof I'd need to convince Morgan Walshaw. And I've got to convince him somehow. Kendric is absolutely jungle crazed about Julia.'

'I know,' she said. 'I reviewed the surveillance memox the Trinities made.'

'That's not the half of it. Kendric really is—' He broke off, letting out a long painful breath. 'That's why I went on board. I'm worried about Julia, what he'll do. Stupid of me. Breaking all the rules about personal involvement. So you wind up with me looking like this. Sorry. Not a nice sight for you.'

She'd never heard him sound so dejected. She leant over the bar and touched her lips to his face. 'I couldn't live with the kind of man who felt nothing for her. You wouldn't be human.'

'That's been said before.'

'Not by me.' She began spraying again. 'Besides, this is nothing; superficial apart from the ankle, and that'll be all right in a week.'

'Good. Anyway, my visit wasn't a complete disaster. You remember Katerina Cawthorp?'

Eleanor paused, flipping through her mental files. 'Friend of Julia's?'

'Got it. Well, right now she's living with Kendric and Hermione.'

'And Hermione?'

That brought a weak grin to his lips. 'Yeah. That's how Kendric must've found out about Philip Evans's NN core. He would be bound to question Katerina about every aspect of her relationship with Julia, and that includes her time at Wilholm. She told him about the NN core. There is no mole, never has been.'

'So how did Kendric get hold of the Zanthus security monitor programs?'

'A topnotch solo hotrod burnt into Walshaw's cores. Kendric could afford it.'

She finished spraying on the dermal seal, and inspected his hand. 'But what about the buyout?'

'Yeah,' he admitted. 'I still don't understand that. But the blitz was definitely a vengeance act. Katerina proves that; she's the link, the common factor. God, Eleanor, you wouldn't believe what he's done to that poor kid. Tell you, she's a virtual cyborg, no messing.' He flexed his fingers gingerly, watching the dermal-seal stretch over his knuckles.

'Has he drugged her?' she asked.

'Sort of. That's something else we'll have to sort out when this is finished. Christ, as if we didn't have enough to do identifying Wolf and the remaining hotrods.'

'You know, if you wanted to flush some compromising evidence out of Kendric's brain you should've asked him how much the blitz had cost him. Then you'd have seen the guilt, clear-cut and irrefutable. I'll have to bind that forefinger.'

'Bugger. Next time I'll take you along. Someone who can think straight.'

Her heart fell. 'Oh, Greg, you're not thinking of going back there are you? Wasn't this enough?'

'No, I'm not marching up to confront Kendric again; I've learned my lesson. From now on the macho routine is all down to Morgan Walshaw and his hardliners. Hopefully, all I have to do is wait for Royan to backtrack Wolf's payments to O'Donal, find out who the hell he is. Then we can start establishing how Wolf is plugged in with Kendric. The proof's there, somewhere, like you said, another intermediary between Wolf and Kendric, maybe two. But I'm *convinced* it's him at the end of the trail. Does that sound paranoid to you?'

'No, I believe your intuition works; and like you say, having Katerina on his yacht explains how he knew about the NN core.' She consulted the Event Horizon terminal. The first-aid kit's diagnostic was plugged into it, the cube showing a white-shadow schematic of Greg's body. His pain points glowed a mild amber; she'd treated all of them. He was relaxed now, growing drowsy from the general tranquilliźer she'd given him earlier. She held open his right eyelid, shining the pencil light directly on the pupil, then away, watching the dilation. The terminal said it was within acceptable limits. 'Have you been overdoing the gland?'

'Used it a bit, nothing much.'

She thought he sounded defensive. Not that she could even begin to give a qualified opinion on neurohormone abuse. Just a feeling, though; he appeared enervated, more than the cuts and sprains could account for. Why did men always try and disguise their weaknesses? 'I think you might be slightly concussed. A hospital check-up wouldn't hurt.'

'No need to bother them. I'll spend tomorrow resting.'

'Promise?'

'All that's scheduled is a trip to Wilholm Manor to check out Gabriel's prediction of a second attack against the NN core.'

She peeled the diagnostic pick-up from the nape of his neck where it was interfacing with his cortical node and coiled up the fibre-optic lead. The compact unit slotted neatly into the moulded foam of the first-aid kit; a well-worn aluminium case, Army green with a big red cross painted on. Surplus to requirements, Greg had told her. There was a comprehensive range of dressings and medicine inside, all top quality. She'd thought he was a hypochondriac when she first saw it.

'That's all right then,' she said, 'providing your new billionaire girlfriend doesn't excite you too much.'

'Please! Give me a break.'

'Oh, I almost forgot. Dr Ranasfari called this morning, charming man, left a message for you.' She licked her lips at the memory. 'He made a pass at me.'

'Shit.'

'Greg!'

'Sorry. You're kidding. Ranasfari? He made a pass at you? Never.'

'He did. Men have been known to.'

'Impossible, my dear. Ranasfari doesn't like people, any people. We're not rationally precise data packages.'

'Don't be so bitchy, or are you just jealous?'

'Neither, simply observant. So what did the good doctor want to tell me?'

'There was definitely an outlaw instruction beamed up to the Merlin, shutting it down. Seven seconds are missing from the uplink's log, an hour before the shutdown. He said it was a very sophisticated interruption. They probably wouldn't have spotted it if you hadn't told them to search for it. They're reviewing the Institute's 'ware memory cores to see if someone snatched the Merlin codes. But so far they haven't found any trace of a breach. He says whoever did it must be the best hotrod in existence, covering their tracks like that. The Institute 'ware has premier-grade data-guardian programs, the security programmers thought they were unbreakable.' Greg was staring at her, confusion and disbelief tugging at his face. Lost. 'Something wrong?'

'Ranasfari can't have said that. It doesn't fit.'

Seeing him like this, exhausted, wounded, and cripplingly despondent, she felt an overwhelming surge of affection for him. The case had been taxing him; punished by the gland, driven by his own ruthless brand of determination, beaten up by Kendric's bastards. Maxed out. All she wanted to do was help, ease the burden. If only he didn't have this stupid code of his, always giving a hundred per cent. It was too much of him.

'Well, Ranasfari did say it. And it's time you were in bed, Greg Mandel.'

'No, no, you don't understand. The blitz was a vengeance attack.'

'Yes, you said. You proved Kendric ordered it.'

'Yeah, well, sort of.'

'The Merlin,' she said, beginning to understand.

'If the Merlin was deliberately sabotaged,' he said, 'then the blitz was part of a *kombinate* spoiler operation.'

'You are concussed. There's nothing to say the Merlin shut-down couldn't be vengeance, too. Kendric wanting to wipe Philip Evans, and damage Event Horizon at the same time by undermining confidence in the giga-conductor cells. Hit Julia from both sides at once. After all, we know he's already used a top-grade hotrod against Event Horizon to pull the security monitors. He probably used the same hotrod to shut down the Merlin.'

'Oh, yeah, right.'

It was obvious he wasn't convinced. She began to speak with slow deliberation, voicing her thoughts almost as they formed. 'The motive for launching the blitz depends on whether Kendric knew of Philip Evans's NN core. If he did, it was him out for vengeance; if not, it was a *kombinate* spoiler. Right?'

'That's about the size of it.'

'Good. So, how bright is Katerina?'

'What?'

'Don't you see? It all hangs on her, whether or not she knew about the NN core. And from what you've told me about her before she met Kendric, she sounds like the all-time champion bimbo. Could she have worked out what was going down at Wilholm?'

His eyes closed, face pained. 'Dunno. She had a good educa-tion.'

'Means nothing. Who would know if she's got enough brains?'

'Julia, I suppose. Certainly poor old Adrian. I knew it would happen, that she'd dump him. Should've warned him, given him the benefit. He wouldn't have listened.'

Eleanor ignored his ramblings. Knowing the sense of excitement derived from solving human intricacies. Finally appreciating how Greg could become so wrapped up in his cases. There was a certain addictive quality to unravelling the carefully crafted deceits of other people, it was a form of conquest, outsmarting them. 'Then you'll just have to ask Julia. But not today, I think.'

28

Wilholm's lawn sprinklers were working at full strength, their long white plumes adding a faint coppery tang to the dry pollen-clogged air. Julia ran down the garden path, giggling wildly, trying to dodge the spray shooting out of the rotating nozzles. The cotton of her emerald-green dress was already damp. She glanced over her shoulder and saw Adrian had almost caught up. A shriek, a last triumphant burst of speed from her legs, and she reached the gravel drive ahead of him.

OtherEyes Access Request.

Adrian yelled behind her, cursing, and she turned, cracking up at the sight of him caught full square in one of the foamy jets. He slopped on to the gravel trailing dark footprints.

'I'm bloody drenched,' he wailed, laughing with her.

He was too; T-shirt and tennis shorts clinging to his skin. She draped her arms round his neck, kissing him exuberantly. 'My very own Mr Wet T-shirt.' The giggles set in again, unstoppable.

OtherEyes Priority Access Request.

His hands found her rump, squeezing with interest. 'Do we have enough time before he gets here?' His breath was hot in her ear. He'd begun to nuzzle her neck, aiming for that place he'd found which was exceptionally ticklish.

She let out a heartfelt sigh, squirming in his arms as his tongue licked below her ear. 'Not this morning. Busy.'

'Afternoon?'

She nodded eagerly. Adrian was insatiable. Wonderfully, fabulously insatiable.

Alaka had been disappointed by the non-appearance of their star guest at most of the functions after Friday night. But she didn't give a flying fig about that. This was love.

And Adrian felt the same about her, so enraptured he'd come back to Wilholm with her on Sunday night.

'I'm afraid to let you out of my sight,' he'd said. 'I can hardly believe a girl like you would even look at someone like me.'

So she did her best to convince him, realizing his every wicked fantasy on her big apricot silk bed, and in the jacuzzi, the shower, dresser chair, deep-pile rug. And Adrian could be very wicked indeed.

Her grandfather hadn't said anything about Adrian coming to stay, not a peep. She hoped that meant he'd finally accepted her as an equal. Part of his kindness before, she knew now, had been the type a teacher shows a gifted pupil. That she could be groomed to manage Event Horizon was his driving concern. She forgave him that. Right now she could forgive anybody anything,

OtherEyes Access Request: Please Juliet.

'All afternoon,' Adrian growled insistently.

'Absolutely.' He was going back to the college in the evening, which would give them a solid six hours to practise yet more of that rapturous sex. Then there was next weekend to look forward to. Thank the Lord Cambridge wasn't far away. Although she would've travelled to Tasmania for him.

Julia heard the sound of tyres on the drive, and began to disentangle herself. Suddenly wondering what the hell she must look like; hair tangled, front of her dress damp from where she'd pressed against Adrian, cheeks flushed, and grinning like a madwoman. Greg would hardly need his empathy to see what she'd been getting up to.

Adrian kept hold of her hand as the little Duo pulled up in front of the portico. The car's arrival frightened Wilholm's flock of snow-white doves into flight above her.

Open Channel to NN Core. Load OtherEyes, Limiter#Three. Sight and hearing only, so her grandfather wouldn't be able to sense her racing heart, nor experience Adrian's adventurous hands.

Thank you so very much, Philip Evans said. *So sorry to trouble you. In case it's of the remotest interest, we think the Trojan program which Gabriel predicted has been loaded into the Event Horizon datanet. There was a highly sophisticated code melt in our Doncaster silicon-fibre plant 'ware two minutes ago; they are scheduled to squirt their production data to me in another five minutes.*

Julia suddenly hated the real world for intruding on her private happiness, it seemed to delight in conspiring to reduce her time with Adrian – Greg's visit, unseen hackers. Why couldn't they leave her alone? Petty grubbing manipulators, all of them, pissing in the wind. They weren't going to alter society, nor bankrupt Event Horizon, nor make the Sun revolve around the Earth, turn water into wine. The sum total of their activities was so near to zero as to be derisory. People were so bloody stupid, and insensitive; animals that'd learnt how to wear clothes.

Her arm tightened instinctively around Adrian. He didn't know how much of a comfort he was.

Don't be so sarcastic, Grandpa, it's very unbecoming. Have Walshaw's security programmers managed to backtrack?

Not yet.

Total surprise.

Give them some credit, Juliet, that melt was hard to spot.

If they'd written a decent guardian program in the first place there wouldn't have been a melt through.

Her grandfather answered with a reproachful silence. Surprising what could be read from emptiness.

Greg climbed out of the Duo. Julia let out an involuntary gasp. His left eye was swollen and black, heavily bruised; a moulded white surgical dressing covered his nose; his hands seemed to be all blue dermal membrane; he was limping.

Christ!

'What happened?!' she demanded anxiously.

He smiled heavily. 'I had a little chat with your friend, Kendric di Girolamo.'

'My God! He did this to you?'

'His bodyguards.'

'Oh, Greg. You shouldn't even be out of bed. Come along with you, out of this hot sun.'

Greg shrugged. 'Not as bad as it looks.' His eyes were fixed on Adrian. Accusing, Julia thought, certainly not indifferent. My God, could he be jealous?

Adrian stirred uncomfortably under the stare, gripping her hand that little bit tighter.

'Adrian, isn't it?' Greg asked.

'Yes, sir.'

They reminded her of two stags, scraping hoofs before they locked antlers. Disturbing to think she might be the cause, but then again it didn't exactly hurt her ego.

Greg's cut lips quirked slightly, breaking the spell. 'The name's Greg. Nice to see you again.'

Adrian relaxed a little at her side.

She gave him a huge sunny smile. 'This conference won't take long, darling. Would you see to Tobias, I've been neglecting him shockingly.'

'Sure thing.' He pecked her cheek and gave Greg a quick curious glance before heading off towards the stables.

Another thing about him, he understood the way Event Horizon business dominated her life, and made allowance, never making unreasonable demands. There weren't many who'd do that. He was going to make a smashing doctor with that kind of sympathy.

'Nice lad,' Greg offered as they reached the shade of the portico. There was sweat on his forehead.

She slipped her arm into his, steadying his walk; glad to have someone trustworthy to confide in. 'Nice? Greg, he's gorgeous. And you should see him with his shirt off. Totally hunky!'

'Lucky Adrian.'

Doncaster is squirting, now!

Julia nearly groaned aloud. How could she have forgotten about Grandpa? He would've heard every word. That bloody OtherEyes was going to have to be rewritten again.

Greg was looking at her speculatively. A blush was rising up her cheeks.

*

Morgan Walshaw was waiting for them in the study. He did a double take at Greg's injuries, frowning, then signalled them to sit.

Julia pulled out her chair at the head of the table. The dark polished surface in front of her was cluttered with gear modules and cubes. Morgan Walshaw was devouring information from three cubes fed by an elaborate-looking customized terminal. Next to her grandfather's NN core was a Commodore bioware number cruncher, a maroon hexagonal block fifty centimetres across and twelve high. A thick bundle of fibre-optic cables linked it to the study's communication consoles. Her grandfather called it junior; he'd unplugged his NN core from Event Horizon's datanet, plugging in the Commodore as a replacement. It'd been loaded with a Turing personality responses program; and he'd spent the last three days reformatting it to shuffle Event Horizon's data squirts in a routine fashion.

'Will you look at that.' Her grandfather's gruff voice rumbled around the study.

The biggest cube on the table was displaying a schematic of the Commodore's databuses, a nightmare Mobius topology of fine turquoise lines binding together a miniature globular cluster of sparkling jade stars.

A cadaverous pink stain had begun to wash through the image, spreading down the lines and branching at every star, tainting everything in its path.

'Christ, the bugger's expansion rate is phenomenal. About fifth power,' the directionless voice exclaimed.

The cube showed an unhealthy homogenous pink blob.

'Six seconds from reception to total domination. Incredible.

293

Whoever they are, they're serious. I would never have been able to stop it if it'd got into the NN core. That's all down to Gabriel. Where is she, Greg?'

'Her psi-function takes a lot out of her. She's at home recuperating.'

'Well, try and get her back here. I want to thank her personally.'

If Greg was aware of the irony he didn't show it. 'I'll tell her.'

'So. Kendric had you roughed up, did he, boy?'

'My fault. I confronted him.'

'Why?' Julia asked.

'Taking a short cut. I wanted to establish that Kendric was the one who paid Wolf.'

'Well, of course he is,' she exclaimed.

Greg shook his head gingerly. 'No. That's the problem. Kendric isn't directly behind the blitz. Not that I could prove, anyway. My intuition says he's involved in some way, though.'

'Well, there you are then,' she said.

'I wanted something a little more concrete.'

'What for?'

She saw Greg and Walshaw exchange an edgy glance. It was so bloody annoying. Why couldn't they speak in front of her?

'Concrete proof for concrete action,' Walshaw said quietly.

'Oh.' She put her hands flat on the table, studying the nails intently.

'It wasn't a complete waste of time,' Greg said. 'I think I can prove Kendric does know about the NN core.'

'Ah!' Philip said triumphantly.

Julia suddenly realized Greg was staring right at her.

'Katerina Cawthorp is living with Kendric on his yacht,' Greg said.

'Still?' Julia blurted.

'You knew about it?'

'I knew she'd gone off with him, I was there when it happened. I thought Kendric was another of her one-night stands. Kats is like that, you see. Bit of a bed-hopper.'

294

'What I'd like to know is whether or not she's bright enough to work out that your grandfather was planning to translocate his memories into the NN core,' Greg said. 'She was here for a few days. The opportunity exists.'

'A week.' Julia stared pensively at the leather-bound books on the wall shelving, not bothering to cut in the processor node. Remembering all those years she and Kats had spent together at school. Only time's perspective gave them a totally different slant, like an old play whose plot she'd forgotten. They'd seemed like great days while they were happening, insufferably tedious now. 'Kats never paid any attention to classes, too busy with boys,' she said slowly, reluctant to condemn. 'But no, she's not stupid. It's just that I find it hard to believe Kats would bother listening to idle business chatter, let alone interpret it.'

'She wouldn't have to interpret it, Kendric would do that for himself,' Greg said.

'I'm sure I never mentioned the NN core project in front of her. I wouldn't have, there'd be no point, science and finance simply don't fit into her world view. And Grandpa and I certainly never discussed it at meals.'

'She may have overheard it being mentioned. There's a certain thrill in eavesdropping on the conversations of someone as powerful as your grandfather. Even if she couldn't make sense of it at the time she might remember what was said.'

'True enough,' said Walshaw. 'Though the Kendric connection is still circumstantial.'

'Don't be obtuse, Morgan,' Julia said. After all Greg had gone through he didn't deserve disparaging observations. 'Of course Kendric's guilty, he reeks of it.'

'I wasn't disagreeing,' the security chief said mildly. 'It is the degree of Kendric's involvement which seems to be unresolved.'

'Not the exact degree, no,' Greg said. 'But he's in deep, no messing. And I think we can rule out a mole now we know about Katerina.' He glanced at Walshaw for confirmation.

'Yes.'

'OK, that just leaves the question of why Kendric allowed Julia to buy him out. I still don't understand that, and it bothers me. We know he's in trouble with the family over the money he withdrew from Event Horizon's backing consortium, and he's working on some deals to try and fill the gap, provide the house with an equal return. That's got to be the key, these deals of his. And they're tied up with you somewhere.' He shot Julia a fast glance.

She knew he meant his intuition again. It gave her a creepy feeling, the way his suspicions about the spoiler had turned out to be true. Now Kendric was making unknown deals.

'Raw materials?' Walshaw suggested. 'Is he buying up the options on the compounds that go into the giga-conductor?'

'No,' said Philip. 'There aren't any really rare minerals involved in any case. And I've made quite sure we have a safeguarded stockpile of the chemicals we use. That's an elementary precaution, I did that even before we filed the patent.'

Greg rubbed the dressing on his nose with a forefinger. 'Tell you, my own impression is that Kendric has made some sort of alliance.'

'With who?' Julia asked.

He gave her a wan smile. 'Don't know. Someone, some organization, who would benefit from having your grandfather wiped. Kendric is an influence peddler, you see. Once he established that Philip Evans's memories were stored in the NN core, he could barter the information in exchange for an investment opportunity that'd give the family house money a return equal to the Event Horizon backing consortium. Get someone else to do his dirty work for him, and make a profit at the same time. That's his style.'

'A *kombinate*?'

'No, I never believed it was a *kombinate* behind the blitz, a month-long delay in introducing the giga-conductor would be a nonsense when you consider their cyber-factories would have to be totally rebuilt to produce the stuff.'

'What, then?'

'Sorry, I can't tell you. That's just the feeling I get out of all this.' He shrugged. 'Kendric definitely has some sort of scheme in mind, the buyout is proof of that, as well as his hatred for you.'

'Mutual,' Julia said automatically.

'I know.'

And the way he said it made her glance at him, he'd sounded disapproving.

'What about this Wolf bloke?' Philip said. 'He's had two goes at me now. Seems to me, you ought to be concentrating on him, boy.'

'I was coming to that. My contact has backtracked O'Donal's payments; he squirted Wolf's identity to me this morning.'

'May we know the name?' Walshaw asked.

'Charles Ellis. Currently residing at the Castlewood condominium, New Eastfield, Peterborough.'

She couldn't help the little start of interest. 'I know that place. Uncle Horace lives there, it's not far from the marina. That proves Ellis is connected to Kendric, doesn't it?'

'Not necessarily. It's a perfectly logical place for someone that rich to gravitate to. Although I admit it's pushing coincidence a long way.'

'Rich?' Walshaw enquired. 'What is he, a tekmerc?'

'Apparently not,' said Greg. 'According to my contact Ellis is a data fence. He normally goes under the handle Medeor. Wolf is a totally new venture for him.'

'What do you propose as your next step?' Walshaw asked. His grey eyes had narrowed, contemplating Greg with reserved, vaguely threatening preoccupation.

'Pay Charles Ellis a visit. He's the last link, the connection between the team of hotrods who ran the blitz and whoever paid for it.'

'Seeing as how you're so close I'd like to send one of my operatives along with you,' Walshaw said. 'I know you prefer to work independently, and I respect that. But the stakes are mounting.'

'I wasn't going to object,' Greg said. 'Just make sure he's briefed not to interrupt.'

'He won't.'

'One more thing, have you had any luck with the analysis of Tentimes' burns?' Greg asked.

'If you mean is there a single beneficiary, then the answer is no.' Walshaw paused, looking concerned. 'But seven manufacturing companies have gone under because of O'Donal; and some of the financials are on a sticky wicket, although they'll never admit a thing. And now we know what to look for, the researchers have spotted several similar victims outside O'Donal's list. It looks like all eight of Wolf's hotrods are very active; they've caused a lot of damage in the last year. It prompts the question why?'

'Yes,' said Philip. 'If that kind of disturbance is being repeated by others like him I'd hate to think of the long-term consequences.'

'Perhaps that's Wolf's goal,' Greg said. 'Trying to sabotage Event Horizon's long-term prospects.'

'I don't mean just us, boy. I've run my own analysis on the burns and their fallout. They're totally indiscriminate. If that sort of thing isn't halted soon it'll add at least another couple of points to inflation, and that's already running too high as it is. A further rise would blow the Chancellor's budget to pieces.'

'You mean even Kendric would suffer?'

'Everybody suffers,' Walshaw said bluntly.

'Could it be another government? If England's industrial output goes down, who'd step in to make up the shortfall?'

'Just about everybody,' Philip concluded miserably. 'Bloody Pacific Rim would be the biggest beneficiaries, of course.'

Julia saw the connection without having to kick in her processor nodes. 'A finance house,' she said firmly. Both men looked at her. 'A finance house would benefit from a change of interest rates, if they knew for sure it would happen.'

'That's right, they would. Good girl, Juliet.'

'The di Girolamo house?' Walshaw mused.

'Why worry?' she said brightly. 'Greg can do his word-association thing with Ellis to find out the details. You'll have it all solved for us by tonight, Greg, won't you?'

Greg sat back in his chair, a tired smile playing over his battered face. 'How much do you want to bet on that?'

29

Greg kept a cautionary eye on Julia as she walked out to the car with him. There was a confidence about her which had been absent before; she'd always had poise, but it'd been stilted and formal. This was a natural grace. No doubt Adrian had a lot to do with it. The kind of stability he offered putting her at ease with other people.

Adrian hadn't changed all her habits, though. He thought her emerald broderie anglaise dress was something Maid Marion would've been perfectly at home in; it had puffball cap sleeves, a lace-up bodice and a skirt hem riding several centimetres above her knees. Nice legs. The girl's clothes sense was the weirdest, nobody else her age wore anything remotely similar. But, of course, she wasn't like anybody else her own age. Just wanted to be.

She lifted the front door's iron latch for him, eager to please. Sparrows, goldfinches, and a couple of hoopoes squabbled underneath the sprinklers' cascade, pecking at the grass for worms that'd risen in the artificial rain. The direct sunlight set off an uncomfortable itch on Greg's face and hands.

'Hop in,' he said, as he blipped the Duo doors, 'I've got something to say to you.'

Her face lit up with mischief. 'Greg, really! And Adrian so close by.'

He sensed that ghostly extraneous thought current leave her

mind with lightning swiftness. Her own thoughts were a fast-paced mixture of excitement and contentment. Julia was one happy girl. He flicked the jammer on, screening the Duo's interior from the manor's security surveillance sensors. 'Julia.'

Her expression dropped at his tone. 'What?'

'Katerina.'

'Oh, her. What about her?'

'I'm going to be very nice to you, and I'm not going to put you over my knee and give you a damn good wallop. Although God knows you deserve it, or worse, after what you've done.'

'What?' She was spluttering, hauteur and outrage gathering within her mind.

'Your grandfather was quite right about you. You're a sciolistic; you know the moves, but not the governing laws.'

'I don't know what you mean.'

'Oh, you worked it out very nicely on a surface level, I'll grant you that. What you failed to appreciate were the undercurrents.'

'Stop talking in euphemisms, it's bloody annoying.'

'I've seen inside Kendric's mind,' Greg said. 'He dreams of you, Julia.'

'He does?' She was suddenly very uncertain.

'He hates you, and fears you. He wants to destroy you. No. He's obsessed with destroying you. Not merely Event Horizon, but you personally, physically. He wants you beneath him, Julia, spread-eagled and screaming. He's sick in a way you'll never know.'

'I do know,' she insisted quietly.

'No, not really; you still haven't twigged, have you? Loathing is an abstract to you, a word whose meaning you've looked up in a dictionary. Kendric is its physical embodiment, lethal, and scatological to boot. You will never understand the sheer intensity of his revenge psychosis. It's a monstrous personality dysfunction.

'Tell you, Kendric sets up targets to knock down, fixates on them, devoting himself singlemindedly to their downfall. For the kind of left-hand business he's involved with it's a commendable trait. He'd been pretty successful, too; built up a good reputation for reliability, top man in the field. He'd never really known failure. Then I come along, hired by your grandfather, and we thwart him in what was probably his most ambitious scheme ever: asset-stripping Event Horizon. His first true débâcle. Then you followed it up by humiliating him with blackmail. Anyone flying that high is going to be hurt bad by the fall. Small wonder you dominate his thoughts; any normal person would be bitter, but with a wacko like that it was probably the push over the edge. You misjudged him completely, and now Katerina is suffering because of that.'

'She went with him,' Julia said defiantly. 'It was her choice.'

'Of course it was, but you engineered it. You and your oh-so-logical nodes, meticulously sketching out all the conceivable scenarios the players could be combined in. You've got Kendric, rich, handsome, an expert in seduction, kinky wife who doesn't object to him playing the field. Katerina, in your eyes naïve, also sex-mad and your close friend, who just happens to have in tow a very desirable stud who you've had your eye on for some time. And finally the poor old stud himself, Adrian, who Katerina had almost tired of anyway.

'You invited Katerina and Adrian to Horace Jepson's party, a real fiesta rave atmosphere complete with the world's greatest rock star. Katerina could no more refuse that than a bee can ignore pollen. And you chose it because that party was the perfect melting pot. Kendric walks in, sees you, the lonely little rich girl with probably her only real friend in the world, who by lucky chance is a real stunner and just as randy as he is. Well, he jumps at it, doesn't he? And he succeeds easily, because he's got the same sex appeal as Adrian, loaded with a suavity Adrian couldn't begin to match, and filthy rich with it. Katerina simply leaps at him.

'Kendric thinks he's scored a double bonus, depriving you of a friend and confidante, and at your age friends like that are terrifically important, plus he gets himself and Hermione a nice chunk of fresh meat to fun around with. You, in the mean time, get rid of Katerina, in whose company any girl will look like one of Cinderella's sisters, and get to console a devastated Adrian, who gratefully repays you with the only currency he's got.'

There was a long moment of excruciating silence.

'Kats did, you know.' Julia was sitting perfectly still, gazing unseeingly straight down the drive. 'School, parties, clubs; nobody even knew I existed. Not with her there. Her bust, her legs, God, even her voice is total audio-sex.' She sniffed, blinking furiously, neck still rigid. 'Do you know why I grew my hair so long? Do you? Because boys like a girl with long hair. Somebody told me that when I was eleven, and I've never had it cut since. I thought it would give me a chance, because there's nothing else to attract them. But of course her hair's long too, and shiny blonde.' Julia turned to look straight at him, unrepentant, hot determination shining bright in her mind. 'All I've got is my brains. And if brains is the only way I can grab hold of a boy, then by *God* that's how I'll grab one. And there's nobody, not you, not Grandpa, nobody, who is going to tell me different!'

Greg could see how much pain and loneliness was bottled up behind those stubborn eyes. That was something about her he'd misunderstood, assuming it was brattish cattiness which had provided the motivation behind her conniving. The spoilt rich kid who didn't get the treat she wanted, planning silent revenge on those who'd denied her.

'Oh, Julia, Julia, what are we going to do with you? If you'd sat down and tried to come up with a more harmful own goal you couldn't have found anything worse than giving Katerina to Kendric.'

'I realize that now,' she said miserably. 'But how was I to know anyone walking round Wilholm could work out what Grandpa intended, or that Kats would be so willing to tell Kendric.'

He winced inwardly. 'She doesn't have a lot of choice.'

'There's something you didn't mention, isn't there? About Kats. I never expected her to stay with Kendric for more than a day or two; not with Hermione insisting on her share. My God, you just can't get any more hetero than Kats. That's why I never felt any remorse, you see. As if one more man would make any difference to her. She said she had her first boy at thirteen. Thirteen! I just wanted their fling to last long enough to disillusion Adrian. But sticking it out like this is way out of character for Kats.'

The sprinklers began to die down outside the Duo, leaving the whole front garden glistening under a glacé patina. Tall chrysanthemum stems bowed under the weight of the crystalline droplets which mottled their big bulbous flowers.

'Have you ever heard of something called phyltre?' Greg asked.

She came as near to embarrassment as he'd ever seen her. 'I remember someone mentioning the name once. Some sort of drug?' she said distantly.

'It's not quite a drug. Phyltre is a symbiotic bacterium which lives in the blood stream, similar biotechnology principle as the gland. Strictly speaking it's a physiologically benign parasite. The most expensive narcotic ever created, a logical extrapolation from the old Ecstasy drug. It boosts orgasmic pleasure tenfold, a genuine designer high.'

'Oh.' Julia was studying her nails with minute attention.

'Pavlov would understand what Kendric has done to her. It's the nastiest form of conditioning I've ever come across. If, and only if, she does exactly what he tells her to then he takes her to bed and gives her that super-orgasm for a reward. She doesn't know it can happen with anybody.

'I imagine one of the first things he made her do was recount every conversation she'd had with you for the last few months, looking for something to use against you. He really lucked out discovering your grandfather's NN core plans.'

Julia was silent for a minute, then said, 'Thanks for not saying any of this in front of Grandpa.'

He glared at her, feeling his hands ache as his blood rose.

'Now what?' she cried.

'There's just nothing that gets through to you, is there? I tell

304

you that there's a maniac out there who wants your blood; that you're responsible for your best friend being raped twice a day for over a fortnight, that her mind's being systematically destroyed, and all you say is thanks for not telling a swarm of electrons floating round in a mutated vegetable. You fucking ice-bitch!'

'Well, for Christ's sake what do you want from me!' she screamed back. 'I know all about bloody Kendric. I know more than anybody. I knew he was behind this right from the beginning. But all you cleverdick hardliners did was charge off after moles and hotrods. Nobody ever listens to a word I say, I'm just a nothing. I'm a signature on the bottom of papers. A performing seal. Well I'm not. I'll bloody well show all of you. Nobody's going to treat me like a joke after this. I'm going to kill that bastard di Girolamo for what he's done to me and Grandpa. And you, *gland freak*, you're going to get the proof for me, like you've been paid for. That's all you are, a paid freako let out of the zoo. And if you want to stay out of your cage, freako, you'll do what I bloody well tell you!'

Greg slapped her. Not hard, his hand was still sore. But Julia stared at him for one frozen horrified second, then burst into tears.

Greg raised his eyes heavenwards, cursing his own blundering stupidity. He saw the gardeners walking past the Duo, their wellingtons squelching through the puddles on the lawn. They glanced over at the car, its hot muffled voices, grey misted windows, seeing a figure hunched up in the front seat, face in hands, rocking back and forth. One turned to the other and barked a remark, there was a burst of lusty laughter, and they walked on. The shallow imprints left by their footprints slowly filled with muddy water behind them.

'Greg? I didn't mean it.'

'I know. I'm sorry I slapped you.'

'Didn't hurt.'

Her cheeks were smeared with silver snail's trails of tears, nature's aphrodisiac. She looked terribly fragile and appealing.

The ivory tower princess fallen to earth with a bump, lost and frightened in the world she'd only ever glimpsed from afar. Greg wanted to put his arms round her and give her a big comforting hug. Resistance came hard.

A big teardrop formed on the bottom of her chin. 'Greg, he doesn't want me,' she said in a tiny voice.

'Julia—'

'No really.' Red-rimmed eyes blinked in anguish. 'He's already had me.'

She was suddenly in his arms, pressed against him, shivering uncontrollably. He hugged her, stroking her spine to give what reassurance he could. Praying he'd misheard, knowing he hadn't.

'I was fifteen,' she said.

'Shush. It's over.'

'No, I want to say it.'

He studied her face, seeing the need; his espersense slid behind the hot skin and damp eyes. She really was terrified of Kendric. Funny, he'd never noticed that before, but she'd always toughed out any mention of his name. 'Then tell me.'

'It was my fifteenth birthday party. I'd never been happier, the PSP had just fallen, Grandpa's illness hadn't developed, and me and all my friends were dressed up in such wonderful dresses. Kendric came with a present for me, perfume, all gift wrapped. Uncle Kendric. He and Grandpa hadn't fallen out then, you see. He gave me the perfume, and said that was only half of the present. He told me his nieces and nephews were all going to go cruising on the *Mirriam* for a fortnight, a di Girolamo family outing, and would I like to come. I *pleaded* with Grandpa to let me go. Grandpa never can say no to me. And then when I went on board there was only Kendric, no relatives, no family cruise. He was waiting for me. My present. I was too young, too stupidly blind with romance to realize. He was so handsome, the older man, rich, and cultured, and charming. God was he charming. You can't know what a man like that is capable of doing to the mind of a silly fifteen-year-old. The whole thing was like a channel drama made by the best director in the world, alone together on a yacht, surrounded by sea, shorelines, and golden sunsets. I loved every second of it. Believed every word he said. He hadn't married Hermione then. I thought I was the one. I was going to marry him. I was going to have his babies for him. I didn't believe God could create a monster like Kendric. Not on this world, the Good Earth.'

She finished with a limp twitch of her lips. Greg carefully brushed some tangled wisps of hair from her face.

'God,' she choked. 'You must think I'm bloody worthless.'

'I think you're quite beautiful, actually.'

Punished eyes widened in surprise.

'Yes,' he said. 'I never got in touch after you sent all that gear to the chalet, I didn't trust myself.'

'With me?'

He gave a slight nod.

'Oh.' She wiped the back of her hand across her face, spreading her tears around. Greg smiled, and pulled a paper hanky from the glove compartment.

They drew apart a little. But the spark of intimacy remained. It would always be there, he knew, carried to the grave.

He cleared his throat, resentful that some analytical part of his brain never switched off, not even through this. 'Julia, did you tell Kendric about the giga-conductor?'

She wiped the last tear away and crumpled the hanky. 'No. All this happened a year before Grandpa told me about Ranasfari and the giga-conductor research project; Ranasfari wasn't even close to a cryogenic giga-conductor then. Kendric didn't have any ulterior motive for seducing me. I was just fun, a notch on his bedpost. He enjoys it, the game he plays in his mind, me and all the other dumb little girls are no different to his business deals. The lies and clever words corrupt us, then we belong to him, worship him. He gets as much satisfaction from our beguilement as he does from the sex. He's a power junkie.'

He looked away, trying to lose the terrible image of Julia, a younger, smaller, more delicate Julia, lying below Kendric.

'You will get the proof, won't you, Greg?' she asked urgently.

'I'm so scared of him. I've not told anybody that before, but he frightens me.'

'I'll provide the proof Morgan Walshaw insists on, no messing.' He kneaded his temple with thumb and forefinger. 'There's a couple of things I want you to do for me.'

She regarded him with comic seriousness. 'Anything.'

'Firstly, go back into the house and have a word with Walshaw. I want your personal protection stepped up. You're not the only one Kendric frightens; before yesterday I hadn't realized exactly how warped that man is. He is quite capable of having you killed. Especially now he realizes that his games are over. It's gloves-off time, I'm afraid, Julia.'

'Right.'

'Secondly: Katerina. I'm going to put a stop to that.'

'I don't understand.'

'Snatch her from the *Mirriam*, and then shove her through detoxification treatment. But that's going to cost.'

'Money doesn't bother me.'

'Right. I suppose it'll have to be in America or the Caribbean. I haven't looked into it, hell, I don't even know if you can detoxify a phyltre user. If not, then it'll be a good research project for Event Horizon to undertake.'

Julia nodded in relief. 'I promise, Greg. Whatever it takes. Event Horizon has a clinic in Austria, they can do anything there.'

Greg didn't share her glibness about that, but at least she was genuinely intent on making amends. 'Fine. I'll snatch her back tonight.'

'Tonight?'

'Yes. I don't want to leave her on the *Mirriam* a minute longer than necessary, I'd develop nightmares. I'll bring her to Event Horizon's finance division offices. Your people can take her from there.'

'I'll come.'

'No, Julia.'

'Yes. The finance division is just as secure as Wilholm. And I want to see her. After all, I'm the one who put her there, and I've had a taste of what she's been through.'

He nearly started to say no again, but there wasn't a logical argument against her going. Besides, he could see Julia wasn't going to be moved. Philip Evans wasn't the only one she could wrap around her little finger. 'All right, but you get Walshaw to make the travel arrangements, and turn up around midnight prepared for a long wait.'

'Do you want the company security hardliners to help you?'

'No. I'm not familiar with their capabilities. I do know all about the people I'm going to be using.'

'What people? Tekmercs?' she asked with frank curiosity.

'Tell you sometime.'

She gave him a timid smile. 'That's a date.'

Greg turned the jammer off, and Julia opened her door.

'Julia.'

She froze with her legs out of the car.

'Don't try so hard, girl. You're not exactly a frump, you know.'

Her smile widened, becoming coquettish. 'And Adrian isn't just a lump of muscle, either. He's very bright, and kind. And I like him a lot.'

'Then I'm happy for you. See you later.'

He didn't rate a wave this time; she simply stood watching him drive off, looking small and sad. He folded the rear-view mirror's image up and tucked it away in a corner of his mind. The last thing he needed now was any more guilt rattling round inside his skull.

30

Greg drove into Peterborough under a sky which the sun had transformed into a bitter saffron hemisphere raked with the occasional static pillar of cloud. He turned up the windscreen's opacity, muting its eye-smarting intensity. There was a taut thread of pain running through his cortex, the neurohormones' legacy.

It wasn't helped by wondering how he was going to square what he was doing with his promise to Eleanor. And then there was tonight's snatch looming large. Another unforeseen. Events were ganging up on him, dictating his actions.

The conspiracy was unnerving, tenaciously eroding any sensation of control over his life. He was a squaddie back in Turkey, utterly dependent on the wisdom of hidden enigmatic generals and the throw of God's dice. Never again, he'd sworn. Easy to say.

He blended the Duo into the arterial flux of traffic flowing through Peterborough's outlying suburbs; a dawn to dusk convoy hauling the city's lifeblood of goods from the industrial sectors to the port and the railway marshalling yard.

Hendaly Street was the same as all the rest in New Eastfield, a long straight gorge of white buildings with grand arched entrances, wide balconies, dark windows, and ranks of flags fluttering on high. Pagoda trees thrust up out of the pavements in the centre of brick tubs; people sat on the benches round them, pensioners soaking up the sun, youngsters with VR bands plugged into gamer decks. Eleanor would enjoy living here.

He had to stamp hard on the brake as the red light came on ahead of the Duo. Its meaning had almost been lost down the years. Working traffic lights, by God!

The frontage of the Castlewood condominium was eighty metres long, standing back from the other buildings along the street, and screened with a discreet row of tall Caucasian elms. The entrance was below ground level, served by a private loop of road with card-activated barriers at each end.

Greg parked a hundred metres further down the street and showed his card to the meter, punching in for six hours.

'Six hours?' a voice queried. 'I wish I had an expense account like that.'

Greg turned, and smiled. 'Victor. You're looking good.'

Victor Tyo's babyfaced good looks smiled back. 'Riding high, thanks to you. I was promoted up to captain after our Zanthus excursion, got assigned to the command division down by the estuary. I guess Walshaw must approve of me.'

'You're my contact today?'

'Yes. Again. I was at the office when the call came in.' He tipped a nod at the Castlewood. 'We've had it under observation for twenty-five minutes now.'

'We?'

'The rest of my squad. They're covering all possible exits. We wouldn't want our man to filter out without us knowing. I've already checked with the concierge, Ellis is at home right now. A human concierge, by the way, this place is definitely for premier-rankers. I couldn't afford to rent the broom cupboard in there.'

Walshaw hadn't actually mentioned anything about a squad, but Greg could appreciate his reasoning. Ellis wasn't the end of the line, but he was near. His confidence rose a fraction. Backup wouldn't come amiss, not if they were as on the ball as young Victor.

'Will this be a long operation?' he was asking. 'Some of the observation positions are improvised, temporary.'

'It shouldn't take more than an hour, two at the outside.'

'Fine. Did you fall down some stairs?'

Greg's hand went to the stiff white mould over his nose. 'Not exactly. A run-in with a friend of Mr Ellis.'

'I see. Do you want a weapon before we go in?'

'Are you carrying?'

'Yes. A Lucas laser pistol.'

'That ought to be enough. You keep it.' Greg began to walk towards the Castlewood's nearest barrier.

'Fine.' Victor showed a card to the gate beside the barrier. 'Concierge's pass,' he explained.

Greg lifted an appreciative eyebrow. And only a twenty-minute head start. Morgan Walshaw ought to start worrying for his job. 'Will it open the apartment doors as well?'

Victor did his best not to appear smug. 'Of course.'

The Castlewood was built in a U-shape. The two wings had a conservatory-style glass roof slung between them, curving down to form a transparent wall at the open end. The glass was tinted amber, cooling the sunlight which shone down on a bowling green, tennis courts, an Olympic-sized swimming pool, and a separate diving pool. Four tiers of balconies made a giant amphitheatre of the enclosure. Their long strips of silvered sliding doors staring down on the athletically inclined with blank impersonality.

Charles Ellis owned a penthouse apartment on the fourth storey, at the tip of the east wing. One of the most expensive in the condominium. Victor stood outside the door, glancing at Greg for permission.

He held his hand up for the young security captain to wait, and probed with his espersense. There was only one mind inside, a muddled knot of everyday worries and conflicts. Not expecting trouble.

'He's alone,' Greg said. 'To the right as we go in.' He pointed through the wall.

'Fine,' Victor acknowledged respectfully. He showed the concierge card to the lock. There was a soft click.

The apartment was five large rooms laid out in parallel, with a hall running along the back of them. Surprisingly, the décor was old-fashioned throughout. Uninspiring, sober prints and dingy Victorian furnishings, all black wood and thick legs draped in cream-coloured lace. The internal doors were heavy varnished hardwood, with brass hinges and handles, opening into rooms with dark dressers and tables. Chairs were gilt-edged, upholstered in plain shiny powder-blue fabric, marble-top tables with bronze legs.

The lounge where they found Charles Ellis had six glass-fronted teak wall cabinets exhibiting hundreds of beautifully detailed porcelain figurines. There was a profusion of styles, with animals predominating; whoever owned them was obviously a dedicated collector. Rich, too, though Greg was no real judge, but money had its own special tell-tale radiance. And it haunted those shelves. He could feel the love and craftsmanship which had been expended in the fashioning of each exquisite piece.

Ellis was a small man in his early fifties, barely over one and a quarter metres tall. His body and limbs didn't quite seem to match, his torso was barrel-shaped, going to fat, but his legs and arms were long and thin, spindly. He had a narrow head, with tight-stretched skin, thin bloodless lips, and a prominent brow overhanging nicotine-yellow eyes. Lank oily hair brushed his collar, leaving a sprinkling of dandruff. He hadn't shaved for a few days, his stubble patchy and grey.

His unbalanced frame was wrapped in a paisley smoking jacket with a quilted green collar. He was sitting in a high-backed Buckingham chair watching a news channel on a big Philips flatscreen, thick velvet drapes hung on either side of it, like theatre curtains. The flatscreen was showing a rooftop view of some desert city, indefinably African; its streets were awash with refugee trains, twisters of black smoke rising from shattered temple domes. A chrome-silver fighter flashed overhead, discharging a barrage of area-denial submunitions; tiny parachutes mushroomed in mid-air, lowering the shoal of AP shrapnel mines gently on to the beleaguered city.

Charles Ellis turned his head towards Greg and Victor, disturbed by the draught as they opened the lounge door. His facial muscles twitched, pulling the skin even tighter over his jaw-bone.

The flatscreen darkened as he rose from the chair, curtains swishing across it; he had to push hard with his bandy arms to lift himself. 'How did you get in?' he asked.

'Door was open,' Greg said.

'You're lying. What do you want?'

'Data.'

His expression was thunderstruck. 'How did you know? Nobody knows I deal in data.'

Greg gave him a lopsided apologetic smile. 'Somebody does. Cover him.'

Ellis swayed backwards as Victor produced his Lucas pistol. 'No violence, no violence.' It was almost a mantra.

Greg walked across the room and looked down on the Castlewood's dark blue diving pool. The lounge was on the corner of the building, two sides of it were glass. The balcony ran all the way round, one-third of it under the condominium's weather-resistant covering.

'Whoever you are, you're an idiot,' Ellis said. 'You have absolutely no conception of what you've gone and walked into. The kind of people I associate with can tread you back into the mire that gave you birth.'

Greg smiled right back at him, baring his teeth. 'I know. That's why we came, for your top-rank friends.'

Whatever Ellis was going to say died on his tongue.

'Wolf,' Greg said. Naked alarm rocked Charles Ellis's already fraught mind. 'Medeor.' It produced the same response. 'Tentimes.'

'Never heard of them.'

'Wrong. I'm psychic, you see.'

Ellis's face hardened, forestalling the onrush of fear and suspicion kindling behind his eyes.

'In fact, you are Wolf, aren't you?'

True, the mind before him blurted helplessly.

'Thank you,' said Greg.

Ellis looked at him with revulsion and hatred.

'Do you know what these are?' Greg asked Victor casually. He rested a hand on one of the three grey football-sized globes that were sitting on a leather-topped Edwardian writing desk. A Hitachi terminal was plugged into each of them with flat rainbow ribbons of optical cable. 'They're Cray hologram memories. You can store half of the British library in one of these.'

Greg tapped the Hitachi's power stud. LCDs flipped to black across its pale-brown surface, forming a standard alphanumeric keyboard. The cube lit with the Crays' data storage management menu. 'You'll note that they're kept in isolation, not plugged into the English Telecom grid. So nobody can hack in. After all, bytes are money, especially when you know how to market them as well as Medeor here.'

'What are you going to do?' Ellis's voice was a grizzled rasp coming from the back of his throat.

'Whatever I have to.' Greg read the menu codes and accessed the first Cray. 'Sixty-two per cent capacity used up,' he observed. 'That's one fuck of a lot of data. Now I could go through a whole list of names I'm interested in and see which your mind flinches at, but that would be very time consuming. So I'm just going to ask you to tell me instead. Who paid you to organize the blitz on the Event Horizon datanet?'

Ellis shook his skeletal head, jaw clenched shut. 'No.'

Greg showed his card to the Hitachi's photon key, using his little finger to activate it. The percentage figure began to unwind at an impressive speed as Royan's data-crash cancer exploded inside the Cray. He hadn't been totally sure it would work on lightware. Admitting now he should've had more faith. The percentage numerals vanished from the cube, sucked away down some electronic black hole. The cube placidly reverted to showing the menu.

'No!' Ellis howled, an unpleasant high-pitched wheezing sound. He ignored Victor's unwavering Lucas pistol to stumble frantically across the lounge to the antique writing desk, looking down in consternation at the cube display. 'Oh my *God*! Do you know what you have done?' His hands came up to claw at Greg, stopping impotently in midair. His face was contorted with fury. 'There were seven million personnel files in there, everybody of the remotest interest in the country. Seven million of them! Irreplaceable. God curse you, gland freak.'

'Kendric di Girolamo,' Greg said calmly.

Stark horror leapt into his mind at the name.

It was very strange; a circle of bright orange flame suddenly burst from Ellis's head to crown him with a blazing halo. For one fleeting moment his mind inveighed utter incomprehension, wild eyes beseeching Greg for an answer. Then the flickering mind was gone, extinguished in an overwhelming gale of pain. The corpse was frozen upright, steaming blood spewing fitfully out of its nose and ears. Its corona evaporated, there was no more hair to burn; the skull blackened, crisping. He heard the iron snap of bone cracking open from thermal stress.

Realization penetrated Greg's numbed thoughts as the reedy legs began to buckle, pitching the body towards him.

'Down!' he screamed. And he was dancing with the corpse, slewing its momentum to keep it between himself and the silvered balcony door as he flung himself on to the fringed Wilton rug. They crashed on to the worn navy-blue weave together. There was a drawn-out sound of glass smashing as Victor tumbled to the floor behind him.

Greg was flat on his back, the throat-grating stench of singed hair and charred flesh filling his nostrils. A wiry hand twitched on his thigh, not his. Ellis's dense curved weight pressed into his abdomen.

'Jesus,' Victor bawled. 'Jesus, Jesus.'

'Shut up. Keep still.'

The air heaved, alive with raucous energy; creaking and groaning as it battled to stabilize itself. A pile of paper forms took flight from the Edwardian desk, rustling eerily as they fluttered about the invisible streamers of boiling ions. The end of the discharge came with an audible crack which jumped the carpet fibres to rigid attention, dousing them in a phosphorescent wash of St Elmo's fire.

Greg sent his espersense whirling, perceiving the star sparks of minds swilling through the concrete beehive maze of the Castlewood. Seeing the galvanized ember of victory fleeing.

'OK, they've gone,' he croaked through the backlash of neurohormone pain. Even that sliver of sound seemed distant.

Victor was kneeling beside him, a rictus grimace on his face, rolling Ellis's body off. The back of the skull had cleaved open, a fried jelly offal spilling out.

Victor wrenched aside and vomited; coughing, dry retching, and sobbing for an age. When his convulsions finished he was on all fours, his hair hanging in tassels down his forehead, skin sallow and filmed with cold sweat. 'Jesus, what did that to him?'

Greg looked at the wall opposite the balcony door; it was criss-crossed by narrow black scorch marks. Glass fragments from the cabinets were heaped on the carpet, figurines glowed a faint cherry pink on smouldering shelves. 'Maser,' he said. 'Probably a Raytheon or a Minolta, something packing enough power to penetrate the silvering on the glass.'

'Bloody hell. What now?'

Greg wriggled his legs from under the small of Ellis's back, and propped himself up on his elbows, gulping down air. Looking anywhere but at the ruined flesh at his feet. The world was a mirage, wavering nauseously. 'Cover up. Call your squad, this apartment has got to be scrubbed clean, there must be nothing left to prove we ever visited. You'll have to take the body out tonight – cleaning truck, something like that. And get these Crays to Walshaw. Lord knows how long it'll take to go through their contents, though.'

'No police?'

'No police. We need the Crays' data. Besides, I'd hate to try and explain what we were doing here. Let Ellis become another unperson, nobody's going to ask questions.'

'Oh. Yes.' Victor was dazed, moving and thinking with a Saturday night drunk's shellshocked apathy.

'Call your squad now.'

'Right.' He tugged his cybofax out of an inner pocket. 'Your nose is bleeding.'

Greg dabbed at the flow with some of Ellis's tissues while Victor yammered out increasingly urgent instructions. Flies were beginning to feed on the open skull. Greg pulled a white lace tablecloth over Ellis, and collapsed into one of the low chairs, exhausted.

'On their way,' said Victor. 'You want to flit, find a doctor or something?'

'No. I think I'll just sit here for a minute. Oh, and be sure to have this place swept for bugs.' His nose had stopped bleeding.

Victor hovered anxiously, head swivelling round the apartment, missing the body each time. 'Bloody hell, what a cock-up.'

'Not your fault. But it proves one thing.'

'What's that?'

Greg gave him a battle-weary smile. 'I'm close.'

'Yeah, but Greg . . . What have you got left now?'

'A name. Confirmation.'

'That di Girolamo character you mentioned?'

'Yep. It was beautiful the way Ellis's mind funked out. You should've seen it.'

'If you say so. This is all way above my head. Surveillance and back up, Walshaw says. You sit there and take it easy for a while. I'll see to the clean-up.'

'Sure.' Greg drew his cybofax out of his leather jacket's inside pocket, taking care not to make any sudden motions. His brain sloshed from ear to ear each time his head moved.

He flipped the cybofax open, and keyed the phone function with difficulty. His fingers were stiff, devoid of feeling.

The cybofax bleeped for an incoming call. Unsurprised, he let it through. *Knowing.*

Gabriel's face appeared on the little screen. 'No,' she said, with ominous resolution.

'I'm sorry, but you have to. There's no one else.'

'No, Gregory.'

'Look at me, a proper look. Right now I couldn't even sense a tiger's brain if it was biting me. Tell you, I've got to have psi coverage to get that girl out. You'll be saving lives, Gabriel. The Trinities will bloodbath the *Mirriam* without perfect intelligence information – where Katerina is, where the crew are, and what they're tooled up with.'

'You're a bastard, Mandel.'

'No messing. See you at the briefing.'

After that, it was the difficult call. Eleanor.

31

True to prediction, one of the yachts docked at the same quay as the *Mirriam* was hosting a party. A brassy, high-wattage rave; hysterical guests spilling out on to the quay itself, dancing, drawing syntho, swilling down champagne. Perfect cover. By two o'clock in the morning it still hadn't peaked.

At five minutes past two Greg walked down the quay with Suzi, the pair of them holding hands and laughing without a care in the world. He wore a dinner jacket that felt as though it was made of canvas, and reeked of starch. Suzi had slipped into a 1920s gold lamé dress, low cut with near-invisible straps, a blonde bob wig covering her gelled-down spikes. With her size and figure she looked impossibly young – fourteen, fifteen, something like that. He reckoned that as a couple they fitted the scene perfectly. Anyone would think it was fathers and daughters night. Thank heavens for café society, immutable in a fluid world.

They infiltrated the party fringes, anthropoid chameleons.

Big Amstrad projectors were mounted on the yacht, firing holographic fireworks into the night. Upturned faces were painted in spicy shades of scarlet and green by carnation bursts of ephemeral meteorites.

Suzi lingered to watch a girl dressed in a sequin bikini and dyed ostrich feathers limbo her way under a boat-hook held by two semi-paralytic Hoorays.

Greg checked his watch and tugged Suzi's arm with gentle insistence, steering her into the wrap of darkness at the end of the quay. Three minutes before they had to be in position. The snatch had to be performed with exact timing; one mistake, one delay, a hesitation, and they'd be heading down the wrong Tau line and all Gabriel's planning would come to naught. He'd tried to emphasize that to the Trinities, drilling it in.

The limbo girl failed to make it, overbalancing and winding up flat on her back. The flesh of her overripe body quivered with helpless laughter. One of the Hoorays poured champagne into her mouth straight from the magnum. She lapped at the foamy spray spilling down her cheeks, her mind light-years away.

Greg and Suzi tottered away from the revellers. Nobody was paying them a second glance.

'Lady Gee was right,' Suzi said from the corner of her mouth. He could sense how tight her small body was wired, rigid with restless tension.

The Trinities had been, to say the least, sceptical when Gabriel began outlining the evening's events. Their agnosticism had been whipped in staggered increments as the prophecies unfurled with uncanny precision – the party, which crewmen would leave the *Mirriam* for the evening, the exact time Kendric and Hermione left for the Blue Ball, the fact that Katerina had been left behind.

Other couples had drifted into the seclusion of the quay beyond the party, exploiting the penumbra of privacy provided by covered gangplanks. Greg kept his eyes firmly on the *Mirriam* ahead; Suzi peeped unashamedly, chortling occasionally.

Mirriam looked deserted, lit only by the intermittent spectral backwash from the Amstrads. Yet Gabriel had said there were seven people on board, two of Kendric's bodyguards, four sailors, and Katerina. She'd even reeled off their locations.

Greg wished he could use his espersense to confirm, but that was a definite no-no. The anaemia which the neurohormones had inflicted on the rest of his body had lifted during the afternoon and physically he was shaping up, but another secretion would cripple his brain.

They reached the *Mirriam*'s gangplank and folded into the midnight shadows it exuded. He checked his watch again.

'How about we go for total realism?' Suzi whispered with a giggle in her voice as she twined her hands round his neck.

'Twelve seconds,' he answered. The gangplank was one long pressure pad according to Gabriel.

'Oh, Daddy, give it to me good,' she yodelled.

He could feel her shaking with laughter and a crazy burn of exhilaration.

Right on time a voice said, 'Hey, sorry folks, but you're gonna have to move along.'

Greg was facing the quay so he couldn't see the speaker, but he recognized Toby's baritone rumble. Besides, Gabriel said it would be him. He carried on smooching with Suzi.

There was a faint vibration as Toby walked down the gangplank.

'I said—'

Suzi's Armscor stunshot spat a dart of electric-blue flame. Greg heard a startled grunt and turned just in time to catch Toby before he hit the gangplank. Asking himself why the hell he bothered.

Suzi was racing up the gangplank. Greg followed dragging Toby. The bodyguard's breathing was ragged, slitted whites of his eyes showing in the fallout from the silent twinkling lightstorm overhead.

As always Greg experienced the conviction of operating under divine protection. With Gabriel's guidance he'd become omnipotent.

Suzi ducked into the darker oval of an open hatch, fumbling her photon amp into place as she went.

Greg pulled his own photon amp out of the dinner jacket's pocket. That reassuringly familiar pinching as the band annealed to his skin. *Mirriam* resolved into cold hard reality around him, nebulous leaden shadows stabilizing into sharply defined blue and grey outlines.

02:12:29, flashed the yellow digits.

'At two hours, twelve minutes and thirty-five seconds GMT the crewman will exit the cabin-lounge door on to the after-deck,' Gabriel had said, her voice raised above the Trinities' scoffing.

Greg dumped Toby on the glossy polished decking and ran for the afterdeck, black leather shoes squeaking.

02:12:35.

'At twelve minutes and forty-one seconds GMT he'll move into your line of sight.'

02:12:38.

Greg stopped and assumed a marksman stance with his Armscor. Lining it up one metre wide of the corner of the superstructure.

02:12:41.

The crewman obviously knew something was amiss; he came round the corner of the superstructure fast, crouched low.

The photon amp showed a monster crab scuttling right at him, metre length of pipe instead of claw. He fired.

'The crewman's name is Nicky.'

Metallic clangour as the crab's erratic momentum skated him into the railing, pipe skittering away anarchically. 'Bye, Nicky,' Greg whispered.

'Radar cancelled,' Suzi's voice squawked in his earpiece. 'God, this place is exactly like Lady Gee described it. Wild!'

Greg finished up at the stern, scanning the glum water of the marina and its flotsam carpet of decaying seaweed. Oily ripples slapped lazily at *Mirriam*'s hull.

'On the taffrail you'll find a control box with six weather-proofed buttons. Press the second from the left.'

The box was there. Rigid forefinger pressing. A stifled drone of a motor lowering the diving platform ladder.

The inflatable dinghy surged out of the gloaming, four figures hunched down, muffled engine cutting a hazy wake through the seaweed. It turned a finely judged arc and rode its bow wave to a halt at the foot of the ladder. The first three figures swarmed up the ladder, dressed in combat leathers and helmets. Des and two of his troop, Lynne and Roddy.

They ignored Greg and crossed the deck to the half-open cabin-lounge door. Des slid it right back and the three of them rushed in.

Greg leant over the taffrail to see Gabriel puffing her way up the ladder. She was wearing a balaclava and a heavy night-camouflage flak jacket, restricting her movements; it was the largest the Trinities had in stock. He put his hand down and diplomatically helped her over the railing.

She tugged the balaclava off, wiping the back of her hand across her perspiring forehead. 'We're too old for this Greg, you and I, believe me. If you weren't such a bloody ignorant stubborn bugger.' A resigned smile lifted her lips. Shaking her head. 'Crazy.'

Greg smiled fondly. 'Tell you, I have a horrible feeling you may be right.'

'That's my boy.' A sudden frown wrinkled her plump features. 'Damn.' She thumbed the comm set in her breast pocket. 'Lynne, it's not that hatch, go to the next one ... that's right. The crewman is standing behind the cowling.'

'Come on,' Greg said. 'Time for you and I to rescue the damsel.'

'You know, Teddy's done a good job with those kids,' Gabriel admitted grudgingly as they moved into the lounge.

Greg negotiated the unfamiliar obstacles and found the central companionway. A tube of impenetrably black air, which even the photon amp had difficulty discerning.

'Are we all right for some light?' he asked.

'Yes. One moment.'

Greg heard her shut the lounge door, then the biolum strip came on. He peeled the photon amp off. Suzi slithered down a narrow set of stairs from the bridge.

'Mega,' she breathed, pulling off her wig and ruffing up her mauve spikes. "You got it spot on, Lady Gee. All of it. Where you said, when you said. It's fucking incredible.'

'Thank you, my dear.'

The three of them headed for the lower deck. Thick vermilion carpet absorbed their footfalls down the stairs. One of the crewmen was lying on the bottom step, his limbs shivering spastically from the stunshot charge. Des was waiting for them outside the master bedroom's door, helmet off, grinning broadly, his hair a dark sweaty mat.

'All right!' he whooped blithely. 'We breezed it, no problem. You ever need a job, Gran, you come'n see me, OK?'

'You're too kind,' Gabriel said.

Des missed the mounting testiness, but Suzi winked at Greg, rolling her eyes for his denseness. Lynne and Roddy clattered up the stairs from the crew quarters below.

'Shall we get on with it?' Gabriel said, hurriedly forestalling the compliment Lynne had opened her mouth to begin. She took an infuser tube out of her flak jacket and handed it to Suzi. 'You'll need this.'

Suzi turned it over, mildly curious. 'What for?'

'She's a big girl.'

Des and Roddy exchanged a glance.

'Is she armed?' Lynne enquired.

'No.'

Greg knew that mood well enough, Gabriel at her most obdurate. There'd be no budging her now.

He opened the bedroom door. There was a subdued pink light inside.

'Hoo boy.' Suzi groaned in pawky dismay. Des and Roddy piled in behind her for a look,

Katerina was sprawled across a huge circular water-bed, wearing an Arabian harem slave costume; strips of diaphanous lemon chiffon held together with thin gold chains. It was a size too small, strained by the curves of her breasts and hips. The chiffon was so flimsy they could see her large areolas through it, dark purple-brown circles with aroused nipples.

Katerina batted drowsy eyelids at the five faces staring down at her. 'I'm ready,' was all she said.

Roddy let out a low admiring whistle. 'Makes it all kind've worthwhile, doesn't it?'

Des sniggered.

'For God's sake find something to wrap her in,' Greg said. Annoyed at their abrupt lapse of discipline. Hardly surprised, though. The porno-starlet stage setting sapped any sense of urgency. He let out a hiss of breath, silently cursing Gabriel for not warning him. 'Suzi, help me get her up.'

Katerina looked up with innocent bewilderment as they each took an arm and tugged her into a sitting position. 'I remember you,' she said to Greg. 'Will you make it happen, too?'

'Not tonight.'

'But this is the paradise place. The hurt and the wonder always happens here.'

'Bollocks, what's she on?' asked Suzi.

'Phyltre. Stuff's blowing her brain apart.'

Katerina turned her head to focus on Suzi. 'Can you make it happen?'

'No way, girl. Come on, let's get you out of here.'

Something in Suzi's inflexible tone must've finally penetrated Katerina's befuddled brain. 'I don't want to leave, not here, not the wonder. Not ever.'

Suzi brought up the infuser in a no-nonsense manner.

Katerina's bare foot lashed out, catching Suzi full in the stomach. She went down with a silent *oof*, curling around herself and fighting for breath. Greg was suddenly left holding a screaming, scratching, biting, kicking she-demon. Gabriel was right, Katerina was big, and strong, and utterly deranged. Tapering lavender nails slashed at his eyes, a knee thudded into his pelvic bone, a tornado of golden hair filled the air. He felt soft flesh, hard flesh. Hampered by not wanting to hurt her. An inhibition rapidly dissolving.

Des made a grab for Katerina's shoulders, succeeding only in ripping her mock slave-costume. All three of them tumbled to the floor in a frenziedly bucking heap. Then Lynne waded in, trying to pin Katerina's arms down. Roddy managed to grab hold of one leg. Finally a wheezing Suzi slammed the infuser on Katerina's neck with unnecessary force. For one horrendous moment Greg thought it wasn't going to have any effect, but a look of outright surprise shot across Katerina's enraged face and she subsided into a limp bundle shrouded in wispy scraps of lemon fog.

'Goddamn ... ungrateful ... bitch,' Suzi spat between shudders. Her face was chalk-white. Greg thought she was going to kick the unconscious body. Probably wouldn't have stopped her.

'She doesn't know what she's doing,' he offered in apology. 'Hey, you all right?'

Her hands were still clasped tight around her abdomen. 'Yeah. Bitch.'

Roddy wrapped a towelling robe around Katerina, and Des carried her out in a fireman's lift.

Gabriel stood to one side as they filed out of the master bedroom. 'Told you so,' she said.

*

The seven of them rode the dinghy back to Event Horizon's finance division offices, stealing quietly across the Nene's scummy water, making good headway against the outgoing tide. City noises thrummed around them; sirens, horns, the trill of gas-powered traffic, peals of jukebox music from riverside pubs. The sough of the dinghy's electric outboard was lost without trace.

Des dodged the big freighters anchored in the middle of the river outside the port. They were waiting for the early morning tide to provide the draught they needed to take them down the channel to the Wash. Rust-streaked metal giants, sprinkled with tiny navigation lights, their bows a check pattern of hoarfrost where their liquefied gas tanks nestled against the hull. Greg could hear a steady *plop plop plop* as chunks of the mushy rime fell into the water.

Once the freighters were left behind it was a straight ride up the Nene to the Ferry Meadows estuary. The Trinities loosened up, schoolboys returning from a day outing. Their hive-buzz chatter percolated about the inflatable – *Mirriam* crewmen I have zapped.

Des even had a beacon to aim at. Philip Evans had chosen to celebrate his company's triumphant return to solid land with a thirty-five-metre-high sign perched on top of Event Horizon's finance division offices. Its core was a macramé plait of colourful neon tubes orbited by stylized holographic doodles – expanding geometric graphics, cartoon characters, origami birds, and, at Christmas time, a traditional Santa replete with sledge and reindeer. Monumentally vulgar, but mesmerizing at the same time.

The deep-throated gurgling of the tidal turbines grew steadily louder as they drew near the little quay jutting out from the steep concrete embankment below the ugly cuboid building.

Victor Tyo was waiting for them, huddled in a parka against the fresh pre-dawn air rising off the estuary. He offered a gentlemanly hand to Gabriel, then grappled a semiconscious Katerina ashore. She groaned as her bare feet touched the cold concrete.

'Why are her hands tied?' Victor asked reasonably, as Greg stepped ashore and took some of the weight.

'Coz there wasn't enough rope for her fucking neck,' Suzi growled out of the dark.

Victor peered down at the inflatable dinghy with its oblique cargo of well-armed hardliners and an underage girl in a revealing gold party frock. 'Bloody hell.'

Des gunned the throttle and the little craft surged out into the darkness. 'See ya, Greg,' Suzi called. 'And take care of Lady Gee, she's outta this world.'

*

Walshaw and Julia were waiting in a big corner office on the third floor. Rachel Griffith stood outside. It was a monastically simple room; the walls and ceiling were painted a uniform white, contrasting against the all-black fittings. Greg knew it was Walshaw's office without having to be told. An extension of his personality. Comfortable, efficient, and uncluttered. The furniture was unembellished, two chairs in front of a broad desk, a settee against the wall. Honey-yellow louvre blinds shut out a view of what Greg's sense of direction told him would be the estuary. The air was warm and slightly damp; stale, the way it got after people had been breathing it for several hours.

Walshaw was sitting behind the desk when they walked in. Greg was surprised to see the surface covered in little balls of scrunched-up paper.

Julia was rising from the settee, knuckles screwing sleep out of her eyes. She was wearing a V-necked lilac dress with a pleated skirt. A tangerine woollen cobweb shawl was drawn around her shoulders.

She allowed herself a rueful grin. 'Midnight, he says. It's gone three.'

Then Victor Tyo and one of his squad members carried Katerina in between them. She'd begun to hum tunelessly.

Julia stared at her old schoolfriend, humour and toughness leaching from her face. Whatever zombie incarnation she'd been girding herself for, it wasn't a match for the mental-husk reality provided.

Katerina was lowered on to the settee, utterly uninterested in her environment.

Julia sent Greg a silent desperate plea that this was some awful nightmare, not real.

Walshaw frowned disapprovingly at the grubby rope wrapped round Katerina's wrists. Greg pointed to the fresh scratches on his face.

'See if you can find some padded cuffs,' Walsaw told Victor. 'And tell Dr Taylor to stand by. She'll probably need sedating.'

Victor nodded crisply and departed, happy to be out of the office.

Julia sank down on to the settee, peering timidly at the

beautiful empty shell slumped quiescently beside her. 'Kats? Kats, it's me, Julia. Julie. Can you hear me, Kats? Please, Kats. Please.'

Katerina's lost eyes swam round. 'Julie,' she sighed inanely. 'Julie. Never thought it would be you. They bring so many others for me, but never you. It's late, isn't it? I can feel it. It's always late when they come for me. We'll be good, won't we, Julie? You and I, when he watches? If we're good then I can go to him afterwards.'

'Yah,' Julia stammered. Her eyes had begun to brim with tears. 'Yah, Kats, we'll be good. The best. Promise.' She pulled her shawl off and tucked it clumsily around her friend's trembling shoulders. 'I'd like you to leave us alone now,' she said without looking round.

Greg had known some officers who could speak like that. Commanding instant obedience. Rank had nothing to do with it, their voice plugged directly into the nervous system.

As he left the office he saw Julia tenderly smoothing back Katerina's dishevelled tresses.

The corridor was narrow with a high ceiling, built from composite panels which cut up the original open-plan floor into a compartmented maze. A pink-tinged biolum strip ran overhead, its unremitting luminescence showing up the threadbare rut running down the centre of the chestnut carpet squares.

Walshaw closed the door behind him. Rachel moved down towards the lift, giving them a degree of privacy.

'I've been doing some checking this afternoon,' Walshaw said. 'There's a clinic on Granada which claims it can cure phyltre addiction.'

'Successfully?' Greg asked.

'Forty per cent of the patients recover. I was wondering. Miss Thompson, isn't it?'

Gabriel was resting with her back flat on the wall, head tilted back, eyes closed, her breathing shallow. Greg recognized the state, he'd seen it in the mirror often enough. That relentless enervation which siphoned the vitality out of every cell.

'Morgan, to someone of your age and ex-rank I'm Gabriel,

OK? But no, I can't tell if it works with Katerina. That's too far into the future.'

'I don't think Julia will give up,' Greg said. 'Not now.'

'No, I don't suppose she will,' Walshaw agreed.

'You know Kendric di Girolamo is going to have to be eliminated, don't you?' Greg said.

Walshaw reached up languidly and began massaging his neck. 'Eventually, yes.'

'No. Not eventually. You've seen what he's done to that girl; and that was just for *fun*. The guy's an absolute loon. Tell you, I've seen inside his mind. Homicidal psychopath isn't the half of it. Julia needs head-of-state-level protection while he's on the loose, no messing.'

'Julia has been badgering me to do the same thing. She is even more intent than you, if anything.'

'Hardly surprising, after what she went through with Kendric. Paedophile shit.'

Walshaw turned his head very slowly until he was staring directly at Greg. 'What?'

'Kendric and Julia; he seduced her. You didn't know?'

'She hates Kendric.'

'Not always,' Greg said. He couldn't ever remember seeing Walshaw so thrown before, not even the blitz and the possibility of a leak in the giga-conductor project had upset him this much. Another of Julia's secret admirers.

'So that's what is behind this sudden urge for blood,' Walshaw said tightly.

'It's not just a wronged girl's *lex talionis*. Kendric is dangerous, believe me.'

'I do.' For a second the security chief looked heartbroken. Greg was suddenly glad he didn't have the use of his gland at that moment, there were some secrets people were entitled to keep. He guessed Julia had become a surrogate daughter to Walshaw over the years. That strange character flaw of his, the need to have someone to provide him with a purpose in life.

'Kendric can't be eliminated right now, dangerous though he

undoubtedly is,' Walshaw said. 'Your episode with Charles Ellis at the Castlewood condominium confirms there is someone else involved, the organizer of the blitz. Kendric couldn't have arranged for the sniper at Ellis's penthouse, because he didn't know Wolf. Which makes Kendric our last link with the organizer. And we have to find out who that is.'

'But Wolf knew Kendric,' Greg said. 'Weird.'

'Not really,' said Gabriel. 'The organizer is their link, a one-way databus who passes on all Kendric's intelligence to Wolf. But there's no return flow, Wolf has nothing Kendric needs to know. And Kendric would've told the organizer that you'd confronted him, that you knew about Wolf. So the organizer fixed for the sniper. Morgan here is right, Greg. We can't get rid of Kendric, he's your only hard lead left. In fact he ought to watch out, the organizer must realize that, too.'

'Shit,' Greg muttered in frustration. 'Kendric won't take us to the organizer, not now. He's too smart. They'll never contact each other again.'

Gabriel opened her eyes. 'Snatch him,' she said flatly. 'That's your only option. Snatch Kendric. Interrogate him. Snuff him.'

'Risky,' said Walshaw. 'A quick clean kill is one thing, snatches have a tendency to get messy no matter how good the hardliners you use. Lots of questions asked.'

'My precognition would make sure there's no mess.'

'I'll authorize it,' Julia said firmly.

Greg hadn't seen her emerge from Walshaw's office. But now she stood in the corridor, head held high, in complete control of herself, as if the bomb-blast of Katerina had never happened. No longer the ivory-tower habitué but very much the Princess Regent. Some small part of him mourned the passing of the timid, sweet girl he'd first met on a sunny March day. Innocence was the most appealing of human traits.

Morgan Walshaw shifted uneasily as Julia's chillingly bright gaze turned on him, demanding. 'If that's what it takes to sort this out, then that's what'll happen,' she said. 'It's bad enough having Kendric coming at me like this, but unknown enemies as well, that's totally out. I'm not having it. And the snatch is the way to unmask them. That bastard Kendric has been banking that we won't fight him on his own level. Well, his credit has just run out.'

'Julia—' Walshaw said.

'No arguments, just *do* it!'

Greg could see how much effort it took Walshaw to retain control, no espersense needed for that.

'It isn't up to me, Miss Evans.'

Julia realized she might've overstepped the limit. 'I'm sorry, Morgan. It's Kats, you see, she keeps asking for him. Doesn't say anything else. Bastard. I think she'll have to be sedated.'

'OK.' He raised a cybofax and muttered into it. 'Doctor's on her way.'

'Who then?' Julia asked. 'Who is it up to?'

Walshaw looked at Greg. 'That's you, Greg. If it's to be done, it's to be done properly. Would you interrogate him?'

Greg had seen it coming, ever since Gabriel blurted the idea of a snatch. It'd given him a few seconds to chew the proposition. He spread his palms wide. 'Preparations wouldn't hurt. Mind you, I'd be physically incapable of interrogating anyone for a couple of days anyway. That might give us enough time to analyse the Crays' data. See if we can't find some leads in them. Ellis should've left one.'

He noticed Julia's face had gone blank, focusing inwards. Must be using her nodes, running their arguments through analysis, battling the pros and cons against each other, trying to reach the conclusions ahead of them. In a way it was a power similar to Gabriel's.

'We're going through the Crays now,' said Walshaw. 'Although I don't know what the hell you did to one of them, it crashed one of our lightware crunchers when we plugged it in, bloody thing is so much rubbish now. The other two Crays are clean, although it'll take time to make sure there aren't any concealed wipe instructions buried in them.'

'What have you got so far?' Greg asked.

'Ellis had quite an extraordinary accumulation of data, everything from minutely detailed personal dossiers through to industrial templates. Trivia and ultra-hush all jumbled together. It's going to take some sifting, even with the light-ware crunchers hooked in.'

'What did you mean, Ellis should've left a lead?' Julia asked.

'Standard practice,' Greg explained. 'If you're plugging into those kind of deals you cover your back. Benign blackmail, to make sure your partners don't get any funny ideas afterwards. There'll be a record of all the burns he arranged as Wolf; money, clients, the names of his hotrod team; data he bought and sold as Medeor, names, companies. Every damning byte. And it'll be somewhere where it can be found after he's dead. In the Crays, the Hitachi terminal's memory core, his cybofax, public data core on a time delay, hell, even an envelope left with a lawyer.'

'Nothing else?' Julia asked.

'Pardon?'

'You don't think there's anything else important in the Crays?'

For some reason her slightly querulous attitude made him aware of how immensely tired he was. He was travelling on buzz energy, had been for hours, and it was running out fast now they'd got Katerina back.

'I wouldn't know, I expect they're a goldmine of illegal circuit activity.'

'That's all?' Julia was leaning forward, studying his face intently. He had the uncomfortable impression he was being judged. Crime unknown. And, frankly, he didn't give a shit.

'All I can think of, yeah.'

Dr Taylor stepped out of the lift, accompanied by Victor who was carrying her case. She was a young woman wearing a plain cerise trouser suit, her dark hair French pleated. She had a quick word with Morgan Walshaw and went into his office. Julia started to follow, but the security chief laid a light restraining hand on her arm. For a moment she looked like she'd rebel, then nodded meekly. Victor closed the door softly after he'd gone through.

'Thank you for bringing Kats back to me, Greg,' Julia said, abruptly all humble contrition.

Greg gave up trying to find motives for her oscillating moods. She was on an emotional rollercoaster; depressed by Katerina, frightened by Kendric, trusting in him, Gabriel, and Walshaw to deliver her from evil. Poor kid.

'It hurts so much just seeing her,' Julia said. 'Serves me right, I suppose.' She reached round her neck with both hands and unhooked a slim gold chain. 'For you. From me. And you don't even have to give me a kiss for it.' She favoured him with a sly weary smile.

It was a St Christopher pendant, solid gold.

'Well, put it on then,' Julia said.

He mimicked a grin, feeling itchy under Gabriel's heartily bemused eye, and fastened it round his own neck. The little disk was warm on his skin as it slithered down beneath the open neck of his crisp dress shirt.

'To keep the demons at bay,' Julia said. 'Even though you're not a believer.'

*

Greg pulled out of the finance division's nearly deserted car park, turning the Duo west on to the artificial lava surface of the A47. There was a single car in front of them. It wasn't quite dawn. The gross Event Horizon sign splashed the surrounding land with a guttering medley of coloured light.

'I feel sorry for that girl, you know,' Gabriel said. She was looking out of the window at the clumps of hermes oak scrub along the side of the road. Beyond the bushes was a near-vertical drop to the ruffled waters of the estuary. In the distance were the dark shapes of the hydro-turbine islands, moonglazed foam rumbling round them.

'Katerina! Who wouldn't?' Greg said.

'No, Katerina is pure survivor breed. I meant Julia; she has no real family, few friends her own age. And you're on the borderline yourself, now, despite her token of esteem.'

'How do you figure that?'

'If Ellis hasn't left anything in the Crays, or whatever, about Kendric or the organizer, how do you think she'll feel about you? You've managed to be right all the way so far. She trusts you because of that. Implicitly. Screw up now and it'll all end in tears.'

'Not a chance. I know Ellis's type down to his last chromosome. A hyper-worrier. He's a little-man intermediary who's lucked into a real super-rank underclass operation; elated and terrified all at once. He'll have taken precautions. That means a way of pointing his finger from beyond the grave.'

'Oh, yeah?'

'Yep. Ellis's major problem was that he never got round to telling his paymasters he was insured.' Greg slowed as the car in front turned off on to the sliproad for the bridge ahead, then accelerated again as the cutting walls rose on either side.

Gabriel said: 'I still don't think Ellis would take such—'

The front nearside tyre blew out.

The Duo veered violently to the left, straight towards the near-vertical slope of the cutting. Greg saw sturdy grey-white saplings, impaled in the headlight beams, lurching towards him. The steering-wheel twisted, wrenching at his hands, nearly breaking his grip. He jerked it back as hard as he could, with little or no effect. The Duo's three remaining tyres fought for traction on the coarse cellulose surface. It was slewing sideways, screeching hard. A flamboyant fan of orange sparks unfolded across the offside window. That alpine-steep incline was sliding across the windscreen, rushing up on the side of the Duo. Horribly close. They'd spun nearly full circle and Greg could feel the tilt beginning as the car began to turn turtle. Then there was a boneshaker impact, a damp thud, and they were disorientatingly, motionless. Silence crashed down.

Soon broken.

'Shitfire,' Gabriel yelped. She was staring wild-eyed out of the windscreen, drawing breath in juddering gulps. 'I didn't know!'

She whipped round to look at him, frantic, frightened, entreating. Which was something he'd never ever seen in her before. And that alarmed him more than the blow-out.

'I didn't know, Greg! There was nothing. Nothing, fuck it! Do you understand?'

'Calm down.'

'Nothing!'

'So what! You're tired, and I'm knackered. It's only a bloody tyre gone pop, small wonder you didn't see it. Non-event.' Even as he spoke he could feel some submerged memory struggling for recognition. Something about the tyre-performance guarantee. Puncture proof? That bonded silicon rubber was tough stuff.

Thankfully, Gabriel subsided into a feverish silence; eyelids tightly shuttered, mind roaming ahead. Did she suffer visions of her gland pumping furiously? He'd never asked.

Greg concentrated on his hands, still clenching the wheel, white-knuckled. They wouldn't let go.

What appeared to be a eucalyptus branch was lying across the windscreen. Its purple and grey leaves shone dully in the waning rouge emissions from the office block's sign.

Looking out of his side window he could see the bridge nearly directly overhead. They'd only just missed crashing into the concrete support wall.

'Greg—' Gabriel said in a low frightened moan.

Upright shapes were moving purposefully through the dusky shadows outside the sharp cone of light thrown by the Duo's one remaining headlight.

Greg stared disbelievingly at them for one terrible drawn-out second. 'Out!' he shouted. His door opened easily enough and he was diving out, racing for the back of the Duo. A mini-avalanche of loose earth and gravel had digested the rear of the car. His hands flapped across his dinner jacket, hitting every pocket. Panicking. Trying to remember where the fuck he'd left the Armscor stunshot.

There were three of them approaching; two men, one woman.

Walking down the middle of the road with a glacial panache, cool and unhurried. A confidence that'd tilted over into sublime arrogance.

The Armscor had gone, swept away by the tide of pitiful sloppiness he was screwing his life with. Given it to Victor? Suzi? Left it in Walshaw's office?

He stuck his head above the Duo's roof, ducking down quickly. The ambush team was closing in remorselessly, empty silhouettes against that idiotic phallic sign and its happy floating Disney projections. They were still carefully avoiding the head-light beam.

Gabriel's door was jammed up against the earth of the cutting; her frantic shoving couldn't budge it more than halfway open. The gap wasn't nearly large enough for her bulk.

One of the men levelled a slender long-barrelled rifle at her. Greg squirrelled away his profile: leather trousers tucked into calf-high lace-up boots, last-century camouflage jacket, blind plastic band of a photon amp clinging to his face, designer stubble, small pony tail.

'Mine,' the man said.

A narrow streak of liquid green flame spewing from the end of the rifle, and Gabriel was jerking about epileptically.

Greg turned and ran for the slope of crumbling earth, clawing at the dense treacherous scrub lassoing his legs, keeping low. The eucalyptus saplings were neatly pruned, a bulbous flare of foliage on top and bare slim boles, providing a meagre cover. He grabbed hold of them in a steady swinging rhythm, hauling himself upwards, feet scrabbling for purchase. The embankment seemed to stretch out for ever.

It was an animal flight. Blind instinct, equating the sliproad at the top of the embankment with the grail of sanctuary. Pathetic, some minute core of sanity mocked.

'There,' came the triumphant shout from below.

The shot caught him three metres short of the summit, where the saplings and scrub had given way to a bald mat of grass which bordered the sliproad. The pain seared down his nerves like a lava flow. He saw his arms windmilling insanely, fingers extended like albino starfish.

As he fell there was just one question looping through his brain. Why hadn't Gabriel known?

32

Greg woke to find he couldn't move. His toes and fingers were tingling, not so much pins and needles as pokers and knives; the aftermath of a stunshot charge. Arms and legs ached dully. Guts knotted tight, rumbling ominously. A livid collection of aggravated bruises and scrapes.

His cortical node prevented the worst peaks of neural fire from stabbing into his brain, but the cumulative effect was atrocious.

He opened his eyes, seeing greyness distorted by octagonal splash patterns. His whole body was quivering now, drumming against whatever hard surface he was lying on. The tingling bloomed into a sandpaper rasp which the cortical node hurriedly muted.

Consciousness seemed like nothing but constant suffering. He instructed the node to disengage his nerves altogether. Sensation fell away, leaving him alone in grey nothingness. He closed his eyes and slept.

At the second awakening his thoughts were clearer. He'd stopped bucking, still on his back and unable to move. Genuine tactile sensation had replaced the tingling. The surface he was lying on was vibrating faintly. Heavy machinery, somewhere not too far away. A stifled monotonous hum backed the supposition.

He opened his eyes again, focusing slowly.

Gabriel was lying beside him, shuddering, in the throes of stunshot backlash. Her mouth gaped, drooling beads of saliva.

Greg tried to reach out to her, found his hands were immobilized under his back. There was a rigid bracelet about each wrist, bolted to the floor; it was the same for his ankles.

Bloody uncomfortable.

They were in a small empty compartment, metal walls, metal floor, metal ceiling. Painted grey. The only light was coming through a grille in the door.

Greg blinked at that door, haunted by its familiarity. It was rectangular with curved corners, fastened by bulky latches. The last time he'd seen that particular arrangement was on board the *Mirriam*. 'Oh, shit.' And under way too, by the sound of it.

Thinking logically, they'd have to be heading down the Nene. Or up? No, the river wasn't deep enough to take the *Mirriam* west of Peterborough. The Wash and the open sea, then.

Next question: Why?

Not just to dump them overboard. There were far simpler ways to dispose of bodies. Besides Kendric had gone to a great deal of trouble snatching them alive.

Nothing pleasant, hundred per cent cert.

'Greg?' Gabriel's voice was tiny, fearful. 'Greg, it's gone.'

'What has?' His own voice wasn't much better. 'No, wait, think before you speak. Remember they'll probably be listening.'

'Bugger that. My precognition won't work. I don't know what's going to happen to us.'

'You really gave your gland a workout snatching Katerina, remember? We all have to throttle back occasionally, nature never intended our brains to take the psi strain.'

'Shut up and listen, arsehole. There is absolutely nothing. I can't see a second into the future. I don't even know what you're going to say!' He could hear the fright bubbling through her voice. She was holding back a long, terrified scream.

Hear it, but not sense it.

The corrosive throb of overdriven synapses had faded, he must've been out for several hours. He'd recuperated enough to use the gland again. It began to discharge a murky cloud of neurohormones. But that secret gate into the psi universe remained firmly shut. He couldn't even perceive the glow of Gabriel's mind, not fifty centimetres from his own. Impossible. His skin crawled, goose bumps rising at the black sense of deprivation. Mortal again. After fifteen years it was hard.

'Me too,' Greg said. 'Not a peep.'

The breath came out of her in a woosh. She let her head rest on the decking, staring into a private purgatory. 'What have they done to us, Greg?'

'They haven't done anything to us. You were using precognition right up until the Duo crashed. We didn't eat anything dodgy, we certainly weren't infused with anything.'

'What then?'

'Must be something which affects psi directly.'

'What?' she shouted.

'I don't fucking know. Ask Kendric, he's the one into pilfering new discoveries before they even make it out of the laboratory.'

Gabriel closed rheumy eyes in anguish. 'Funny, I always thought I didn't want to see the end coming. Now I'm sure it is coming I'd like to see it. Not knowing is too much like cold turkey.'

'Silly girl. You just want to see which of our escape plans works the best.'

'Escape plans,' she snorted in a resigned amusement which nudged disapprobation. 'Sure, Greg. Sure.' After a while she asked, 'What do you think they want us for?'

'Information. They want to know what we've discovered of their operation, how much of that we've told Walshaw. Once they know that they'll see what they can salvage. Hopefully that isn't going to be much, we've done a pretty good job up to now.'

'Great. That makes me feel one hell of a lot better.' She lapsed into sullen silence.

*

Greg guessed they'd been lying in the blank metal cell for a couple of hours before the hatch swung open.

It was Mark who drew the latches, accompanied by two more

of Kendric's bodyguards. A biolum came on above them. After hours of dusk, the glare sent Greg's tear ducts into frantic action.

'Still on your backs?' Mark gloated. 'I thought I'd be pulling you off each other by now. Or aren't you up to that? Maybe fancy something different, animals and the like? I heard you gland freaks are kind've warped.'

Gabriel glared at him silently, realizing just how nasty things could turn if she started antagonizing him.

Mark bent down and released Greg's legs with a complex-looking mechanical key.

Greg was jerked roughly to his feet. Every ache and pain suddenly doubled in intensity. His legs nearly collapsed as a wave of nausea hit him. He saw the front of his dress shirt was stained by a long ribbon of dried blood; his nose had been bleeding again while he'd been unconscious.

One of the bodyguards supported him as he stumbled out into the corridor. It didn't possess anything like the ostentation of the upper decks. Pipes ran along the walls, red letters were stencilled across small hatches. The engine noise was more pronounced.

Another three bodyguards were waiting for him outside. Including Toby, who glowered with unconcealed menace.

'Christ,' Greg croaked. 'I must scare you lot shitless.'

'Gonna have you, white boy,' Toby whispered dangerously. 'Gonna take you a-fucking-part.'

'Not yet, Toby,' Mark said, pushing a shaky Gabriel ahead of him. 'When the Man has finished with him.'

Greg was marched up and out on to the afterdeck. The sun was nearly full overhead. Well over six hours since they'd been snatched from the Duo. Would Walshaw have noticed? He'd told the security chief he would help to analyse the data in the Crays, but he hadn't given a specific time. Of course, Eleanor would be frantic, but would she ring Walshaw? And even if she did there was nothing to make him look here.

At least he'd been right about 'here'. The *Mirriam* was sailing sedately down the Nene.

The course the Nene took for the first thirty kilometres east of Peterborough was a new one. The PSP's delay in authorizing construction of the city's port meant that the old river course had been lost at the start of the Warming, disappearing beneath the water and silt which laid siege to the city boundaries. A couple of years later, when the wharves' foundations were being laid, the dredgers cut a straight line from the port right out to the old estuary at Tydd Gote.

Mirriam was following a huge container freighter out towards the Wash. There was another freighter trailing a couple of kilometres behind. They were the only things moving in a very confined universe. All Greg could see was river, sky, and high gene-tailored coral levees, covered in tall stringy reeds.

The tide was full, just beginning to turn, showing a thin line of chocolate mud below the bottom of the reeds.

Mirriam seemed to be losing ground on the freighter in front. Greg glanced over the taffrail to see four crewmen inflating two odd-looking craft on the edge of the diving platform. They were blunt-nosed dinghies with a couple of simple benches strung between the triplex tubing that formed the sides. A loose surplus of leathery fabric ran round the outside. It was only after a big fan, caged in a protective mesh, hinged up to the vertical at the rear of one of the dinghies that Greg realized they were actually hovercraft.

Gabriel nudged him and he turned to see Kendric approaching. *Mirriam*'s owner was wearing olive-green track-suit trousers and a light waterproof jacket. Hermione was at his side, as always; dressed in natty designer equivalents of her husband's attire. But it was the woman keeping a short distance behind who held Greg's attention.

She was in her late twenties with a second chin just beginning to develop; her dumpy face was framed by straight jet-black hair, cut in a fringe along her eyebrows, falling to her shoulders at the sides. Her skin was dark and leathery, heavily wrinkled from excessive sun exposure.

He was convinced that she was the woman he'd seen at the

ambush. He could still see her slightly bulky frame in that trio walking calmly down the road.

Kendric's gaze swept across Greg and Gabriel, utterly unperturbed. A cattleman checking his stock.

'Put them in with Rod and Laurrie,' Kendric said to Mark. 'You and Toby come with us.'

'Yes, sir,' Mark replied.

'Postponed,' Toby muttered in Greg's ear. 'That's all.'

'Right, get them down there,' Mark was saying.

Kendric and Hermione began to descend the ladder to the diving platform. The crewmen were holding the fully rigged hovercraft steady in *Mirriam*'s wake.

'You'll have to take our cuffs off,' Greg pointed out.

'Maybe we'll just throw you down,' said Toby.

'Take 'em off,' Mark said. 'And you two, don't think about jumping.'

Greg just managed the climb down the ladder, frightened his weak, trembling hands were going to lose their grip. He flopped down in the bottom of a hovercraft, exhausted and horribly woozy.

Gabriel sat on a bench next to him, breathing heavily. One of the crewmen cuffed them both again.

'Are you all right?' Gabriel asked, her face anxious.

'Yeah.'

He heard the fan start up, an incessant droning whine. There was a surge of motion, then the deck tilted up as they climbed the levee wall. The dizziness returned.

When they were down the other side, he struggled into a sitting position against the tough plastic of the gunwale, trying to take an interest in the journey. The sour-faced woman was perched on the rear bench, her waterproof zippered up against the occasional scythe of spray. Her hair was blowing about in the slipstream.

One of the *Mirriam*'s crewmen was up front, steering from behind a little Perspex windshield. A bodyguard was sitting behind him, giving Greg and Gabriel the occasional impersonal glance. At least Toby wasn't on board. He managed to get his eyes above the gunwale.

It'd taken centuries to drain the original fenland marches and turn them into farmland; generations had laboured to liberate the rich black loam from the water, rewarded with the most fertile soil in Europe. The polar melt drowned them in eighteen months. The Fens basin wasn't a sea, it was mud, tens of metres thick with a tackiness gradient that varied from a few centimetres of weed-clogged salt water on the surface down to near-solid treacle.

An ex-Fenman living in Oakham had once told Greg that it was possible to tell the age of a Fens house by looking at its doorstep. The older it was the more the loam would've dried out and contracted beneath it, leaving the doorstep high and dry. Really ancient cottages had a gap below the bottom of the stone and the ground.

Greg couldn't see any doorsteps; on the few lonely farmhouses still visible he was hard pushed even to see the doors. Twelve years of sluggish tidal suction had chewed out their foundations, pulling them down into the absorptive alluvial quagmire. Some of the sturdier buildings had managed to retain their shape, upper floors rising out of the brown-glass surface over which the hovercraft were racing. But the majority had subsided into tiny flattened islands, with juncus rushes growing out of the shattered bricks and skeletal timbers. Ragged felt hems of blue-green algae encircled all of them.

The hovercraft took a gently meandering course, avoiding the solid protrusions and swollen semi-submerged branches of dead copses in wide curves. Greg and Gabriel were following Kendric's craft, slicing through the fine spray its passage whipped up. Behind them, the horizon was marked by a fine green line. The Nene levee. Which meant they were heading approximately south. It didn't make any sense to Greg. There was nothing ahead of them.

Nobody lived in the basin. Crabs and gastropods thrived in the nutrient-rich sludge. But no one could earn a living from catching them. An ordinary fishing boat would stick fast in the mud. Conceivably a very light sail-powered catamaran or trimaran might be able to move about. And the idea of deploying nets or pots was laughable. In fact, hovercraft were just about the only vehicles which could be used successfully on the Fens basin.

From being the most fertile tract of land in Europe the Fens had reverted into a zone of barren desolation rivalling the Sicilian desert for inhospitableness. The sheer sameness of the quagmire was numbing Greg, bleeding away any last reserves of hope and defiance into the stifling atmosphere. Endless kilometres flowed past, compounding the sense of isolation. Gabriel had hunched up in her seat, defeated.

His attention drifted. Analysing his predicament was suddenly futile, tiresome in the heat and moisture. His thoughts began to freefall, wondering what Eleanor was doing right now. And please don't let Kendric think she was important.

'Greg.'

The urgency in Gabriel's voice made him look round quickly. A town was rising out of the horizon's uncompromising interface between brown and blue. It was like a mirage, its base lost in the black and silver ripples of shimmering inflamed air. Kendric's hovercraft was powering straight for it, leading them in.

'Hey.'

The bodyguard sitting behind the pilot turned, boredom reigning. 'What?'

'Where are we?' Greg asked.

'Wisbech. Why, does it make a difference?'

He should've known. Wisbech was the harbinger. The self-declared Capital of the Fens was the first instance of wholesale evacuation in England. At the start of the Warming, excessive rains and record tides had sent the Nene cascading over its banks. And in those days the river ran straight through the centre of the town.

Greg had remained glued to the flatscreen for a week while pontoons of news channel cameras chugged through the flooded streets. He remembered the pictures of drowned orchards ringing the town, the sodden refugees slumped apathetically in Royal Marine assault boats, clutching pathetically small bundles of possessions. It was something out of the Third World, not England. The novelty of such scenes had paled rapidly in the months, and then years, which followed, as town after town succumbed to the water.

Wisbech only looked whole from a distance, close-up it was in a sorry state. The outskirts had collapsed completely, leaving a broad inverted moat of rubble, protecting the town's heart from the larger vagaries of the swelling mud tides.

Both hovercraft slowed, manoeuvring cautiously around hummocks coated in vigorous growths of reeds. The narrow channels between them were choked with algae, so thick in some places it resembled a green clay. It was stirred up by the hovercraft's downdraught, freeing pockets of rancid gas. Gabriel and the crewmen coughed and swore, clamping their hands over their faces, Greg couldn't smell a thing; his throat began to dry, though.

Five metal streetlamps marked one channel for them, miraculously remaining upright after all these years. The conical algal encrustations around them were actually solidifying, turning them into cartoon desert islands. From the height of the poles left above the surface Greg guessed that the street must've been about one and a half metres below the hovercraft.

Further in, the mounds became more regular, the channels echoing the street pattern they covered. Sections of walls had survived here, triangular, cracked, and leaning at crooked angles. The brickwork was obscured by a viscid pebble-dash of gull droppings. An eerie desynchronized harmonic from the electric fans was bouncing back off them, amplifying their natural soft purr to a vociferous clattering reverberation.

Overhead, hundreds of gulls twisted in devious helices, calling shrilly, the high-decibel feedback from the entire flock a brazen fortissimo rolling across the ruins. Greg realized it was impossible to creep up on Wisbech.

They swept out of the mounds and into a suburb that was still standing; two-storey houses bordering a light industrial estate. The mud came half-way up the ground-floor windows. There was no glass left in them. Second-storey windows were shattered, crystalline shark teeth sticking out of mouldering frames. Walls bulged, roofs sagged alarmingly, shedding tiles like autumn leaves. Gutters were wadded with grass and bindweed.

Moving on.

The Nene's old course was a serpentine semiliquid desert, three hundred and fifty metres wide, flat and featureless. All the embankment buildings had been pulverized by the febrile floodwater, their debris sucked away by the inexorable vortices generated by the clash between currents of salt water and fresh water. Since then the eternal mud had oozed back, a great leveller.

Wisbech used to have a bustling port, the river lined by ugly warehouses and towering cranes. Greg had no way of telling where the iron titans had once stood.

Both hovercraft picked up speed on the flat. The heat pressed down, magnified by still, heavy air. Even the gulls abandoned the chase.

Greg received a pernicious impression of waiting *depth*. He was eager to reach the other side.

Their destination was becoming apparent straight ahead, on the other side of the old river course. The most prominent building there was. An old brick mill tower, slightly tapering, stained almost completely black with age.

Greg didn't understand how it could've possibly survived until they arrived at its base, riding noisily across the buckled corrugated roof of a petrol station which was elevated half a metre above the mud. The tower had been built on the summit of a raised stony mound. While chaos and ruin had boiled all around, it had remained aloof and untouched.

Tufts of tough bermuda grass grew around its base; there was a good two metres of hard-packed earth between the bricks and the mud. The blades in front of the door were trampled down.

Kendric's hovercraft beached itself on the left of the door, Greg's drew up on the right. The pilot kept going until the bow was bumping the filthy brick, then killed the lift.

The tower door opened and a man came out. He was fortyish, dressed in a fawn sweatshirt and olive-green Wranglers; his shoes were black leather, polished to a sergeant major's shine. A brown belt holster held a Browning 9mm automatic.

Kendric and Hermione alighted from their hovercraft. Greg was hauled to his feet beside Gabriel. The man from the tower took in the fresh crimson splash down his shirt, the way he kept swaying from side to side.

'You were told: intact,' he said to Kendric. There was no deference shown. Kendric seemed to be among equals at last.

'He can walk, he can talk,' Kendric retorted indifferently, and marched off into the tower.

'Un-cuff them,' said the man, 'and get them upstairs. He's waiting.'

The crewmen began deflating the hovercraft. Mark unlocked the cuffs and waved them into the tower.

Resignation had settled in long ago. Greg stepped across the door, shuffling like one of the undead, shamed and impotent.

The basement was bare, brick walls and concrete floor, a smack of dampness in the air, but not as much as there should've been. He spotted a bright conditioning duct disappearing into the rude wooden plank ceiling. A deflated hovercraft of the same kind they'd arrived in sat in the middle of the floor. There was a cast-iron staircase opposite the door.

'Up,' said Mark.

Shiny black shoes were already vanishing through the hole in the ceiling.

The first floor was also one big room, appreciably drier, used for storing crates of food. There were quite a few Harrods hampers stacked beside a small grey metal desk.

The second floor was a living room, carpeted in a thick steel-blue soft pile. Its furniture was modern, matching timber-framed leather chairs and settee, a low ceramic coffee-table, and rose-teak executive desk with a recessed Olivetti terminal. Cupboards and a glass-fronted drinks cabinet were fixed to the wall, purpose built, they fitted the shallow incline perfectly. Light shone through a single frosted glass window half-way up the wall. The brickwork had been left uncovered, scrubbed clean.

The dumpy woman who'd accompanied Greg on the hover-craft was waiting at the top of the stairs. Which was impossible, because she was following him up. Had to be twins.

But that revelation was blown straight out of his mind by the next person he saw. Kendric was talking earnestly to Leopold Armstrong. And Greg knew he'd finally met the person who'd organized the blitz on Philip Evans's core.

England's ex-president was fifty-seven, but still trim and fit; his meaty face had a few more lines than Greg remembered, his mop of neatly cut silver hair was combed back tidily. He wore a simple Shetland cardigan over an open-neck cotton shirt. So ordinary. Almost homely.

Greg had thought he was beyond any further surprises, but he just stood and gawked until Gabriel bumped into his back, and her curse was sliced off in mid-flow as she caught sight of Armstrong.

He looked both of them over, taking his time. The tip of his tongue moistened his lips. Greg resisted the ridiculous urge to straighten his rumpled dinner jacket.

Mark clattered up the stairs behind them, and hustled them forward. The little living room was beginning to get crowded. Hermione had stretched out in one of the two leather chairs, feigning lethargy. In addition to the man who'd met them outside there was another obvious hardliner hovering around Armstrong, just waiting for Greg to try something.

'Sit him down, Neville,' he said. 'Before he falls.'

The man who'd met them outside the tower stabbed his forefinger at the settee, and Greg collapsed into it gratefully. Gabriel joined him after a second thrust.

His name had given Greg the key, placing the face; astonishing the trivia a mind can hold. Neville Turner: junior Home Office minister in the PSP government, second-in-command of the People's Constables, one of the many shadow figures orbiting Armstrong's periphery.

Armstrong now held up Greg's Trinities card, a prosecuting counsel with a bloodstained, fingerprinted knife.

'You're a Mindstar veteran,' he said. 'What on Earth are you doing consorting with scum like this?'

He was setting the tone, speaking normally, no threats, no gloating dominance charades. The ex-president was concerned only with facts, reality; he didn't possess time to waste on life's inessentials.

'Only a total paranoid would be frightened of ghosts,' Greg said.

The Trinities card was pocketed. 'You mean Philip Evans?' Armstrong asked. 'I admit the potential of that fancy NN core of his alarms me. He was remarkable when he only had a human brain. A giga-conductor with a transcendent Evans masterminding its marketing strategy would be a definite setback for me. He's so depressingly efficient at that sort of thing. A clever man. Pity we have opposing political viewpoints. But that's life.

'However, the conflict between Evans and me goes much deeper than that, as I'm sure you're aware.'

Greg stared at him dumbly.

'Good Lord, he never told you, did he? Think on it, Mr Mandel. You've seen Event Horizon's Prowlers at work, I believe?'

'Yes.' No ultra-hush there, he wasn't giving anything away.

'Military hardware, Mr Mandel. Good-quality American military hardware, as provided by that vicious profiteering little arms merchant, Horace Jepson.'

Greg started. And Leopold Armstrong caught it. 'Didn't you know? Oh yes, Mr Mandel, Jepson is a US government convenience. He sells to their allies, discreetly, mark you, and in return their IRS overlooks Globecast's somewhat irregular tax returns.' He shook his head. 'I don't know what all the fuss about you is. You're not half as good as everyone says. But then Mindstar never did fulfil its promise, did it?'

'You were worried enough, I remember,' Greg said. 'You and your People's Constables. Never had much joy catching us, though, did you?'

Armstrong pursed his lips. 'Quite. Well, now you have the facts, make the connection.'

Greg read the anger in his face, sharp-focused determination, riding him hard. Armstrong was vengeance seeking, said his native intuition, a strong clear message. 'My God,' he said wonderingly. 'Philip Evans blew up Downing Street.'

Gabriel threw Greg a quick startled glance, then twisted sharply to look up at Armstrong.

'Very good, Mr Mandel,' said Leopold Armstrong. 'The electron-compression warhead was brought into the country by one of his Prowlers, smuggled into Downing Street by his security division's hardliners. Kendric here tells me Evans laughed when the warhead exploded, thinks of himself as a more successful version of Guy Fawkes, no doubt, *très romantique*. He obliterated me once, Mr Mandel; just believing I was dead was enough for the country to march in rebellion against the PSP. But now, now that bastard has exploited his money to do it to me again, to do it to all of us. Immortality, Mr Mandel. He has bought himself immortality, with his imperialist power, his obscene personal wealth. Another twenty years I'm good for, and a lot can be done in that time. But what is a pitiful twenty years to Evans now? He has eternity. He will see me dead again, for real this time. And do you know what the real ball-kicker of it is? He won't even care; my actual death will be of supreme indifference to him. Because to him, secure in his present incarnation, we are all less than nothing. That, Mr Mandel, cannot be allowed to pass unchallenged. That is why I risked blowing my cover, all my preparations. Because I am not going to allow him to escape death. Death is universal, making us all equal in the end.'

'How about you, di Girolamo?' Greg asked. 'You believe all

this crap? You've got enough obscene personal wealth to translocate your memories like Philip Evans. You going to die when you don't have to?'

Armstrong put on a pained expression. 'Please, Mr Mandel. Kendric and I are not going to be driven apart by your desperation. Our mutual interests are too strong.'

'I can't figure you,' Greg said to Kendric. 'You knew about the giga-conductor, yet you let Julia buy your family house out of the Event Horizon backing consortium. Why? You've kissed goodbye to a fortune.'

'A deal,' Kendric said thinly. 'In return for informing the President of Philip Evans's NN core I will be given Event Horizon on a plate; not some derisory percentage, all of it.'

'After it's been nationalized,' Armstrong interjected smoothly. 'Then naturally an international financier of Kendric's stature would be a perfect choice as chairman. Regretfully, his appointment would have been difficult to justify if Evans junior had exposed his earlier impropriety, which is why he agreed to sever their financial link. But she won't be in a position to issue such paranoiac ultimatums for much longer, after all, we can hardly allow a teenage girl to run a company so important to the country's economic prosperity, now can we?'

'Julia Evans will be stripped of her wealth and power,' Kendric said. He looked straight at Greg, smiling mechanically, a slim line of flawless white teeth showing. 'You understand, don't you, Mr Mandel? You know how it is between Julia and me. There was a time when it was a fun game, she was an excellent player. But unfortunately she is too young, she does not fully comprehend the rules of this world. If I do not take Event Horizon from her, she will use it to harm me, my family house. What would you do in my place?'

'She understands the rules perfectly,' Greg retorted. 'You just don't like losing. Seventeen years old, and she can outsmart you from dawn till dusk. You shouldn't be worried, Kendric, you should be terrified. But then you are, aren't you.'

Kendric's lips closed. 'It is not I who will feel terror.'

'No?' Greg asked scornfully. 'You even misjudged your new partner here. Armstrong isn't interested in vengeance, he's like you, he's after the giga-conductor. You're just his front man, a cheap puppet.'

'You do have tenacity, don't you, Mr Mandel?' Armstrong said. 'Perhaps that's why Event Horizon hired you. But you're wrong. The money accrued from giga-conductor licence production will be split between us. A valuable source of income to further my aspirations.'

'Aspirations,' said Gabriel. 'What aspirations?'

'Ah yes, Miss Thompson, isn't it?' He affected to notice her for the first time. 'My return to mainstream politics.'

'You can't be serious. You'll never resurrect the PSP.'

'Not the old Party, no. It's a fool who doesn't learn from his mistakes. My new organization will be structured along different lines.'

'Tentimes,' Greg said. 'You've been paying for Tentimes and the rest of Charles Ellis's hotrod team to screw up all those companies.'

'Indeed, and my people have been quick to point out the inevitable failings of the free-market system. There is a large groundswell of resentment building against the New Conservatives and their mismanagement of the economy. One I intend to encourage.'

'Bollocks,' Gabriel snorted. 'No matter how bad things get, nobody's going to vote for hard-left policies again. You don't understand just how much people hated everything you stand for.'

'Miss Thompson, if you could still see into the future you'd know that I'm not aiming for the grand slam this time. You can only ever do that once. I was very unlucky in that events beyond my control conspired to put an end to PSP rule. The energy crisis, the Warming, the Credit Crash. No government could withstand that combination. Take a look around at other countries. How many of the leaders of ten years ago remain in power today? We were the ones who were blamed. People don't like to blame their own greed and exorbitant life styles. They want someone to hold responsible. And government gets it in the neck every time, from outbreaks of food poisoning to hurricanes. Blame the government.'

'From protesters being whipped to death in the street to seed potatoes being dished up on the tables of Party members,' Greg said.

'Those kind of incidents were inevitable to start with. But the abuses were solvable, given time.'

'You had ten years,' Greg said. 'All they ever did was get worse.'

'The people who made up the PSP's local committees were unused to power. If they had been allowed to establish themselves, then we would've seen stability. But of course, Mindstar and that plague of urban predator gangs incited trouble in the cities, goading the Constables.' He flexed his hands in agitation. 'We were . . . misrepresented.'

Gabriel laughed unsteadily. 'What's the matter, Armstrong? Did you think the hard-left had a monopoly on political agitators?'

For a moment Greg thought he would hit her, but the ex-president eventually sighed resentfully. 'This time I have settled for a more slow-burning form of reformation. There are thousands of my appointees still in place throughout the civil service, primed and waiting. The New Conservatives will soon have to order an intervention as the private and denationalized companies begin to falter, bringing them back into the government fold. My people will assume the management duties, with a great deal of success. And I shall direct them, president in all but name and public visibility.'

'We'll fight you,' Greg said levelly. 'We'll fight you with everything we've got. Bows and arrows if that's all that's left, we've done it before. And we beat you before.'

'Yet here I am. This seems to be the month of miraculous comebacks.' He laughed, and grinned round at the faces in the living room. 'I do believe I'm talking to a reactionary. However, I don't intend to spend hours justifying my actions to you, Mr Mandel, nor debating the pros and cons of centrally controlled economies. You were brought here to answer questions. And that is what you will now do.'

Greg thought he must've flinched, certainly he stiffened.

'No, no, we don't go around beating confessions out of people here. There are much simpler methods. But understand one thing, Mandel, you are going to die. Just as soon as you have provided me with every byte I require. How you die will be decided by your behaviour. The old easy way or hard way; you can have a bullet through the head, quick and clean. Alternatively, you can be dumped into the old river bed, alive and kicking.'

'It doesn't make one fuck of a lot of difference in the end, does it?'

Armstrong picked up a cybofax from the coffee table and sat in the last remaining leather chair. 'Think about it,' he said knowingly. 'Dwell on it. You might find your attitude adjusting. Neville, we'll begin now.'

Turner opened a drawer in the rose-teak desk and extracted a spaghetti tangle of nylon straps and optical fibres. 'Take off your shirt,' he told Greg with a doctor's examining-room impartiality.

Greg thought about it. Refusing would be a rather trivial token, the shirt would only be cut or ripped off. Besides, he was thinking of being slung into that bottomless mud. God curse Armstrong. He shrugged out of the jacket and began on the shirt buttons. Flakes of dried blood wedged under his fingernails.

'Good,' Armstrong said. 'Quite an ironic twist for you, Mr Mandel, I imagine. On the receiving end of a lie detector for once.'

Turner velcroed a strap around each of Greg's wrists. They prickled, minute needle-tipped sensors probing into his skin, tasting salinity, heat, conductivity, heart-rate. The St Christopher was flicked to one side and another strap went round his neck, tightening noose-style.

Leopold Armstrong's fingers drummed on his cybofax. 'I have a number of queries. And you'll answer each one honestly. For every lie you make we'll break a bone in Miss Thompson's body. The bigger the lie, the bigger the bone. Understand?' Again, there was no malice, Leopold Armstrong was just telling it the way it was.

'Yeah,' Greg replied, as a tiara band was placed on his head. Turner pressed an infuser against his arm. There was a bee-sting of pain, turning to an ice-spot.

'Relaxant,' Turner said, and began plugging the optical cables into a gear module which was already interfaced with the Olivetti deck. The cube lit with scrawling sine waves. He sat in the swivel chair behind the desk and began typing. Data rolled down an LCD display. 'Name?' he asked.

The correlation went on for what seemed an age to Greg. The relaxant acted like a gentle influx of rosé wine, pleasantly inebriating, amplifying sounds like squeaking leather and rustling clothes, turning the air warm, drying his throat. Of course, he could still concentrate. If he wanted to.

They seemed to have an encyclopedic knowledge of his life stored in the Olivetti. Stuff he could barely remember: secondary school exam results, Army postings, nicknames of barrack mates, neighbours at the time-share estate. Nothing recent, though. Nothing from the last couple of years.

'He's ready,' Turner shouted out eventually.

Armstrong consulted his cybofax. 'One. Does anyone on the mainland suspect I am alive?'

Greg had worked out that this was a crux. To answer or not to answer? Watching Gabriel being systematically snapped apart before him. The noise of all those cracking bones would be deafening. But they were going to die anyway. It would be very noble to confound Armstrong.

Decisions. Decisions. Gabriel was silent. Unhelpful as always.

The relaxant's health-spa glow had seeped through his entire body, levitating him. He was back in the womb again, warm, cosy, and untroubled.

'No,' he said. 'Nobody knows.'

Leopold Armstrong's smile illuminated the whole world.

33

Ade O'Donal had discovered that hard cash had its own special weight. Yeah, like no weight at all. He'd filled two Alitalia flight bags with New Sterling and Euro-francs; thick, hard wads of notes. Kilograms of them, stretching his arms as he walked down the stairs, but he could've carried them for ever. The bags were new, clean, and bright; when people saw them, their exotic foreign logo, they'd know he was for real. One shit-hot guy.

The crappy top stair creaked when he put his foot on it. That was all he needed – Sashy to hear him leaving. He'd waited until late afternoon before scooting, fewer eyes seeing what he was about, and she was still sleeping off an afternoon of *majestic* sex. It'd been one serious way of splitting. He'd been tempted to take her with him. Her compact brown body was the absolute best screw ever, like her brain was loaded with *Kama Sutra* software. But he was travelling light, 'Bat Out of Hell' time, breezing down the open road. A woman would hold him back; worse, Sashy was into family in a big way. Brothers, parents, cousins, hundreds of them. Daft girl spent half the day on the phone. She wouldn't understand, he had to get *lost*, out of here, like he'd never existed. Kick loose from the shit glitching his life right now – Wolf, the two Event Horizon bastards.

He'd spent a couple of days collecting the money from cashpoints after that hard guy and the fat slag had turned up, initially terrified they'd pull the money from his Cayman account because of the blitz. Psychics, fucking psychics! Unhumans. Ade O'Donal still got cold burn in his balls thinking about it. His mind being torn open like a paper bag, thoughts held up to the light and examined. That was heavy-duty shit. Wolf must've gone acid crazy thinking they could get away with a burn against Event Horizon. That company was the biggest scene in England, even *kombinates* pissed themselves about Event Horizon.

Ade O'Donal had plugged himself but good into the circuit after the psychics had left; making *serious* connections, a cruise for any hard-core hotrod. Giga-conductor. New word. The circuit was ringing with it. The biggest deal in the known universe was going down, and Wolf had tried to run a spoiler. Shit. He could've been hurt. Hurt bad. Wasted!

The little patch of red blistered skin on his belly where the Event Horizon hardliner had zapped him with the Mulekick was still sore. A good memory. If he ever thought this was one giant curved syntho trip, that patch would set him straight. Might even be a scar. Girls like scars. Scars were macho.

There was a noise down below in the darkened hall. Footsteps clicking on the tiles.

'Brune? Hey, Brune, that you?'

He'd sent Brune out after lunch to top up the BMW, gas and watts. This was going to be one long flight. Cornwall, maybe. Ade O'Donal hadn't made plans. He'd figured just go with the flow was safest. That way no one could load a tracer on him.

Brune was staying here, Brune with his leg in a tube of quik-set polymer. The guy was out of hardlining for a month anyway. Even the BMW would get axed eventually. Then there'd be just him, the money, some of the memoxes, and the Burrows terminal. That Burrows terminal was going to turn him into the circuit's sexiest hotrod.

After the psychics had left Ade O'Donal had plugged the gate circuits into the Burrows to try and see how the fuck they'd opened it without tripping the alarms. Fifty Richter disaster time. The Burrows had crashed, totally, the only thing left working was the power LED, not even the menu showed. Whatever had been in the gate circuit was hot enough to melt through the hardware core guardian programs Wolf had given him.

That convinced him he had plugged into the biggest under-class operation running. Cancer software that was better than Wolf's! When he settled down he was going to retro that Burrows, no matter what it took. Those bytes were going to earn him mega money, like what Wolf paid was just small change.

He'd go for a total reincarnation, *plastique*, sign on the circuit as a virgin, build a reputation from scratch. A genuine hotrod, not dependent on anyone. Pity about Tentimes, mind, it was a slick kind of handle, told the girls all they needed to know out front.

'Brune?'

There was a figure in the hall, bending over a large crumpled bundle on the tiles. It straightened up as he reached the bottom of the stairs. And something about it was mega-shit wrong. The hospital had shaved Brune's head, coating the back of his skull in dermal membrane. It looked like he was wearing a Jew's skull cap from a distance. Good for a piss-take.

But the guy facing him was albino-white; death-mask face with jet-black lips, a close-cropped Mohican strip of titian hair running from the bridge of his nose over his crown and disap-pearing below the collar of his biker jacket. Ade O'Donal knew the look. Tribal. The guy was from Stoneygate.

Stoneygate wasn't somewhere Ade O'Donal went even in daytime, loaded with freaked-out psychos. Five tribes protecting Leicester's syntho vats, from the police and from each other, that district was wound up but tight.

Ade O'Donal dropped the Alitalia bags, making a dull slap on the hall tiles. 'Brune?' it came out all wavery, like a whimper. And the broken thing on the floor was Brune, a puddle of blood spreading from a jagged rip in the dermal membrane. An ocean of blood, glistening sickly.

'Tentimes?' asked the Stoney.

'Shit, like no way, I ain't never heard of him.'

'Lying, O'Donal, dey squirt me yo' file.'

'Shit, man, I never told those two nothing, not a byte.'

'No crap, Tentimes. No interested.'

Ade O'Donal closed his eyes, didn't want to see the gun, or knife or whatever. Praying it would be quick.

'Job for yo'.'

He risked a peek, ready to slam his eyes shut again. The Stoney was looking at him contemptuously.

'Say what?'

'Job. Burn.'

'That's it?'

'Yay.'

'All you want is like a fucking burn, and you waste Brune for that! You syntho-crashed shit.' Ade O'Donal wanted to smash the Stoney with his fists, pound him into a pulp. His life was exploding into the all-time downer. People out of his nightmares kept coming for him, like every shitty deal in the world was his fault.

There was a tiny click, and a matt-grey ten-centimetre blade appeared a centimetre from Ade O'Donal's eye, diamond tip reflecting tiny slivers of cold blue light. 'Don' gi' me lip, I slice yo'.'

'Sure, OK, no problem, just cool it, man, right?'

'Where yo' terminal?'

The temptation to let the Stoney open the door was near overwhelming. But he was wearing leather gloves, the charge might not be enough to penetrate. Too dangerous. 'Down here,' Ade O'Donal sighed.

The Stoney took in the wine cellar's hardware with a stoic gaze. 'Alien,' he murmured.

Ade O'Donal crumpled into his chair behind the table that held his terminals. 'What's the burn?'

'Wolf say finish Event Horizon, d' core. Suit yo'?'

'How?'

A shrug.

'Shit.'

'Be good. I break cover fo' yo'.'

Cover? What the hell did that mean? No way could this arsehole be Wolf in person. This was getting extreme deep, the kind of deep he wasn't likely to climb out from. 'Hey, listen, how are you gonna know if I take out the core? I mean, you're gonna leave me alone if I pull this off, right?'

'Friends, dey watching.'

'And if it works?'

'Yo' still jiving tomorrow.'

Ade O'Donal nodded slowly, as low as he'd ever been. But the Stoney needed him. If he did the burn there was a chance. Small, though, fucking small. Brune drowning in blood.

There were only two terminals on line, that psychic hardline bastard had screwed the Hitachi and the Akai, the super cancer from the gate had crashed the Burrows; that just left the Event Horizon and the Honeywell, And no way was he going to use the Event Horizon terminal, that name was too much bad karma right now.

Ade O'Donal tapped the Honeywell's power stud, slipping its throat mike round his neck; muttering, typing, eyes locked into the cube. A melt virus got him into Event Horizon's datanet, disguised as a civil engineering contractor's bid for a new flatscreen factory at Stafford. He loaded a memox Wolf had given him for the blitz, studying company procedure. Bids would be processed by the finance division, the lowest three forwarded to the freaky Turing core for a final decision.

He pulled a memox from the shelves, one he'd planned on taking with him. 'This is like the best I've ever written, you know,' he said, a sudden urge to explain, to let the Stoney know he was dealing with a real pro hotrod. 'It scrambles databus management programs. That's the beauty of it, man; once it's in, you can't access the system to flush it out. Total internal communication shutdown. The core will be sliced right out of the datanet, along with anything it's interfaced with.'

'Dat sound sweet.'

'OK.' Ade O'Donal pushed the memox into the Honeywell's slot, hands quivering.

The cube showed the bid's data package wrapping around the virus, geometric tentacles choking a crystalline egg. Ade O'Donal probed the finished Trojan with tracer programs. There was no chink in the covering, nothing that hinted at the black treasure beneath the surface. Smooth. And he had made the quotes for the factory ridiculously low, the bid package would be shunted to the core, no sweat.

Idiotically, pride overrode his depression. This was it, his construct, all his own, a solo hotrod burn. Tentimes had made solo.

O'Donal fed the Trojan an activation code keyed to the core's dump order. It would pass clean through the finance division processors, then once they'd forwarded it to the core the fucker would detonate, digital H-bomb. Wipe-out time.

Index finger tapped: download.

The cube emptied.

'Might take a while,' O'Donal said.

'No matter.'

The diamond-tipped blade clicked softly.

34

Julia had insisted on relieving the nurse at Katerina's bedside in the afternoon, keeping a solitary vigil over her brain-wasted friend. She hated every second of it, knowing she deserved it. Pushing Kats towards Kendric had seemed so clever at the time, an elegant solution. Everybody would wind up with what they wanted, no tears, no heartache.

Greg was right, she'd only thought of the deed, never the consequences. Too shallow and self-obsessed. Still a child. Idiot savant.

Katerina stirred, turning, her sleep troubled. Dr Taylor had given her a trauma suppressor. Short-term amnesiac, the woman had explained, it'll kill the craving for now; but she'd made sure Katerina was infused with tranquillizers throughout the day, only leaving a few periods of brief semi-lucidity for eating and going to the toilet.

Julia had been the one spooning soup into her. Katerina had swallowed automatically, incapable of coherent speech. Compounding the anguish.

Julia had got three of Event Horizon's premier-grade executives working flat out on securing Katerina that Caribbean treatment, trying to buy a place in the detox clinic. They'd been told there was an eight-month waiting list. Julia refused to let that bother her, pulling in the company's favours, bullying the clinic with financial and political pressure. Dr Taylor had warned her that Katerina's cranial blood vessels were saturated with the symbiont; if its grip was ever going to be broken then it would have to be done swiftly.

She'd buy that bloody Caribbean island if necessary. Anything. Anything at all. She just wanted Kats back to her old self. Frivolous, vaguely annoying, and utterly carefree.

The sun had nearly dropped below the horizon, fluorescing a cloud-slashed western sky to a royal gold, fading to black at its zenith. Julia watched it from the bedroom window, seeing the shadows pool in hollows and nooks across Wilholm's grounds, spilling out over the grass. The fountain in the lily pond died down spluttering, its light sensors switching off the pump.

Julia activated a single wall-mounted biolum, then crossed the room and drew the heavy Tudor curtains across both windows. When she'd first left America and the desert she'd been entranced by dawn and dusk in Europe, cool blues and greens gleaming dully under fiery skies, always different. It'd been magical, the expected sadness that she'd miss the desert's beauty never materializing.

Tonight the sight left her totally unmoved. Her emotions seemed to have shut down. The climax would come tonight, she was sure of it. The game had ceased to be a game. And she was responsible, she and Grandpa. Kendric's manoeuvrings and power ploys had been thwarted at every stage. She'd stalemated him all across the board. There was nothing left to him now but the physical. Kendric would have no qualms about that.

Strangely, even Greg had warned her about the danger. Greg the liar. Greg the betrayer. His name was the only one capable of piercing the wrap of numbness around her feelings. She'd believed in him like nobody before. Worshipped from afar, flirted. Opened her soul to him. Confessed the darkest, most shameful secret.

And he'd *lied* to her.

Just like all the rest. Men must look on her as some kind of victim waiting to be abused. Except for Adrian, a bleak inner voice said, Adrian adored her female side. He was immune to her money. So far. But knowing her luck . . .

She still couldn't believe she'd been so mistaken about Greg. He'd said she was beautiful. And she couldn't be fooled by smooth talk any more, not after Kendric.

Then why? Why the lie?

Access BlitzCulmination. So called because it brought all aspects of the case together. The homogenized data packages unfolded within her glacial mind, rotating the bedroom and Katerina one hundred and eighty degrees from her cognizance. Her processor nodes marshalled it into precise channels once more, a construct that incorporated hard facts, assumptions, suspicions.

She ran the logic matrix once more, the fifth time today. It produced a single diamond-hard conviction. No matter how many times she ran it, how much slackness and wishful thinking she incorporated into the matrix channels, the answer was always the same.

Liar. Traitor. Thief. Heartbreaker.

Cancel BlitzCulmination. One thing it never told her was why Greg would do such a thing. She didn't understand human nature well enough to guess. And now she'd probably never know.

Katerina had sunk into an innocent dreamless sleep. Julia pulled the frilly snowdrop-pattern duvet up around her shoulders.

Open Channel to NN Core. Load OtherEyes Limiter#Five.

She felt her grandfather snuggle into her mind, welcoming his touch. The last person on the whole planet she still trusted. And what a sad comment on her life that was.

How are we doing? she asked.

Greg hasnt moved for three hours now. I think Wisbech must be their nesting ground. Clever that. So close, yet so far away. I'm not sure how they got across the Fens basin; too slow for a tilt-fan, possibly a hovercraft.

I trusted him, Grandpa. Really trusted him. Everything he did and said was always right. He made me believe in him. I thought I was safe.

I know you did, Juliet It must hurt. I'm so sorry.

It doesn't hurt. I don't feel anything. I'm not human any more.

Course you are, girl. Don't talk nonsense. You're seeing Adrian again this weekend, aren't you? What you do with him is pretty bloody human. And I approve. He's a nice boy.

If I'm still around by the weekend.

Hey, that's no Evans talking. Wilholm is well protected, and I'm hooked into all the security sensors. Ain't nobody going to sneak up on you, girl.

Suppose it's one of the staff, Walshaw even?

No, Juliet, not Morgan. He's been with me for fifteen years, almost since you were born.

Stake your life on it, huh? She let the irony filter back to him.

That's my girl. Keep shining through. But don't you worry, I'm even watching Morgan. No strain on my capacity.

Julia found herself looking down at the wood-panelled study, initially confused by the unusual perspective, a fly on the ceiling. Walshaw was sitting at the long table databasing with his custom-ized terminal; the bald patch on his crown was larger than she'd realized before. Then the incoming squirt from Event Horizon's datanet bloomed in her mind. Walshaw was reviewing the Cray memories as they were being extracted by the security division programming team. All the memories had been run through search and classification programs as they came out, analysed and indexed. He was running through the categories, accessing every mention of Wolf and Event Horizon, double checking.

He's been doing that for hours, her grandfather said. *Hunting down that clue Greg was talking about. Hardly the act of a turncoat, now is it?*

I suppose. It would be nice to believe in him at least, Julia thought. But this was her life she was gambling with now. And the list of her mistakes when it came to dealing with people was a long one.

Suddenly she was inundated with a rapid-motion tour of Wilholm through the security sensors, visual, infrared, magnetic, electromagnetic, UV laser-radar. Millisecond slices of security division hardliners patrolling the corridors; sentinels prowling the grounds; Tobias in his stables; owls snapped in mid-flight, wings motionless; fieldmice twitching their tiny damp noses in the night air; deserted tracts of landscape, fields and woodland. A kaleidoscope of bright-hued luminous colours, and conflicting geometries.

See, Juliet? All quiet on the western front.

Her heart began to beat faster. *Why is Walshaw bothering with the Crays? We know Kendric has plugged in with the PSP, that the card carriers organized the blitz.*

You and I know, yes, Juliet. But I don't think Morgan has put it together yet.

But it's obvious! she exclaimed.

To you.

Oh, Grandpa! What if Greg hasn't worked it out, either? What if I was wrong about him? He was so tired, I mean totally run down. He's been through hell; and it was Kendric who had him beaten up.

Relax, girl. First thing I thought of.

What then?

If he's innocent, why are the two of them in Wisbech? And why didn't Gabriel warn us about him? She's in it with him.

Oh.

Sorry, Juliet.

The depression enveloped her again, its return total. She could see the world simply now, black and white, no right, no wrong, there was just survival which mattered. Instinctive self-preservation, primaeval, the only complexity lay in method. The acceptance decided her.

When can you hit them? she asked.

Every hundred and eight minutes, starting in seventy-two minutes – mark.

Do it. Her lips synchronized with her thoughts, but no sound emerged.

OK, Juliet. Why don't you take a break? Katerina isn't going any-where.

No, I'll stay here. It wouldn't be right leaving her, not now.

I'll give you a status check nearer the time.

'Love you, Grandee.'

Wipe OtherEyes Limiter#Five. Exit NN Core.

Julia sat down on the barrel-like Copenhagen chair beside the bed, hand automatically sliding down the side of the cushion. Her fingers touched the hard plastic casing, reassuring her. She drew out the weapon. An ash-grey cylinder thirty centimetres long and three wide, a thin grooved handle at one end. It resembled a fat, long-barrelled pistol, weighing about one and a half kilos. The discharge end was solid, with a small circular indentation, gritted with minute carbonized granules. ARMSCOR was printed along the side in black lettering.

She'd stolen it from Greg after he'd brought Kats back to the finance division offices, slipping it off Walshaw's desk and into her bag as soon as the desolating revelation of his betrayal had sunk in. She'd been horribly afraid of him, what he might do.

When she'd got back to Wilholm she'd accessed the manor library's memory core, looking up what she'd got. A stunshot, capable of immobilizing an adult at forty-five metres. Four shots would kill.

The power unit was charged to ninety-five per cent capacity, giving her almost two hundred shots. She'd spent the morning familiarizing herself with it – safety catch, grip, aiming. Kept at it until she was satisfied she could do it by touch alone. It tended to wobble unless she used both hands. The library said there was no recoil.

And nobody knew she'd got it, not even Morgan Walshaw. Her last line of defence. Its solidity and weight injecting a primitive kind of confidence into a badly demoralized psyche. She wished it would be Kendric himself who came. There'd be no inhibition holding her back then. Sending all ninety-five per cent into his jerking, burning body.

But it would be some tekmerc hardliner, anonymous, a fast-moving shadow in the dark. Her one advantage was that he'd have to come to her; a slight advantage, but it might make the difference between life and death. The odds were impossible for the nodes to compute, too many variables, thank the Lord. That sort of foreknowledge was something she could do without.

Julia sat back in the Copenhagen chair, putting the Armscor on her lap, resting her chin on her hands. Looking at Kats she realized she'd even been emptied of envy, her friend's beautiful face meant nothing. In fact when Kats grew older she would've lost far more. You can't lose what you haven't got.

35

The water-fruit field stretched on for ever, a perfect example of perspective, parallel rows of creamy-white globes merging at some grey distance. Eleanor felt around underneath the next globe and cut the thick rope root with her knife. Inky sap puffed out, lost in the reservoir's slow current. She lifted the globe and steered it slowly into the neck of her net bag. There were another twenty water-fruit inside. Almost full. Turning back to the row.

A dolphin snout pushed her hand. The knife missed the root. She looked at her hand, puzzled. Tried again. Two hard bumps on the back of her wrist, almost painful.

Annoyance began to register in her sluggish thoughts. She held up her hand, palm outwards, pushing twice: back off.

It was Rusty. He didn't budge, guarding the water-fruit. Dark shapes slithered effortlessly through the water behind her, churning up a small cloud of silt. When she turned she saw another pair of dolphins had got hold of the net bag, pulling it away.

Angry now, her steady rhythm had been broken. Hanging a metre off the reservoir bed, motionless, trying to outstare a dolphin. How odd.

Now the monotony of harvesting was broken she began to realize just how tired she was, muscles whispering their protest into her cortex – arms, legs, shoulders, back, all laced with fatigue toxins.

Exactly how long had she been doing this? The soft green

light was fading fast overhead, lowering visibility to less than fifty metres. A cold flash of realization pinched her mind. She hadn't quite fallen into the trap of blue lost, but her soul had migrated, fleeing the memories of guilt and pain. Now they rushed back in to her empty brain, unmitigated.

Greg calling, apologetic but firm, ruled by duty. Idiot, she'd answered; trying to disguise a jumble of secret worries and heart-wrenching concern with stiff resolution. He respected toughness. Both refusing to yield.

He'd promised, she'd told him, promised solemnly. But he'd shaken his head, saying it wasn't like that. She'd cried herself to sleep, imagining terrible things happening on the di Girolamo yacht.

How silly it all seemed now. Words spoken, never meant.

Eleanor gave Rusty a submissive thumbs up and headed for the surface, too weary to rush, a few wriggles with her flippers every couple of metres keeping her ascent steady. Rusty orbited her laggardly.

The hireboats had all returned to the fishing lodge at Whit-well, away down the other prong of the reservoir. Even the windsurfers had packed up. The Berrybut estate's bonfire was sending flames shooting into the neutral sky, a spectre-light swarm of sparks lingering above the rectangular clearing in the still air.

Rusty insinuated himself between her legs, and she hugged his dorsal fin gratefully. The ride back to the shore was nothing like the usual turbulent dash. A slow smooth glide. Now why couldn't people be like dolphins – sympathetic, gentle, perennially happy. Magnificent creatures.

The sun had fallen behind a pearl crescent horizon piled high with lacy clouds when Rusty let her off. She stroked his head and bent to kiss him. Rusty would understand. He chittered wildly and sank below the surface, suddenly leaping up again five metres away, twisting in midair and landing with an almighty splash. She laughed, first time all day.

The pebbles on the drying mud cut into her feet as she walked out of the water, her skin like soft crinkled putty after such a long immersion. It'd been midday when she'd begun harvesting. Greg had sworn he'd be back by early morning. Eleanor had waited until lunchtime for him to return, then her tolerance had snapped, and she'd dived into the water, sulky and furious.

Duncan was fire warden this evening. He lived two chalets down from number six. Eleanor stopped to say hello, letting the bonfire's ruddy furnace heat dry her puckered skin, welcoming the warmth permeating through her limbs. Duncan gave her a couple of baked potatoes out of the raw clay oven-tunnel which ran through the heart of the bonfire, eyeing her chest as the flames threw liquid orange ripples across the dull-sparkle nylon of her one-piece costume. She thanked him, straight-faced, and juggled the hot potatoes back to the chalet. Duncan was sweet. And his covert schoolboy glances started her thinking about how she and Greg could spend the evening making up.

The Duo hadn't returned. Eleanor almost dropped the potatoes. Greg had been gone for thirty hours now. No matter how big their row he wouldn't have done that without telling her.

She dumped the mirror lung and the potatoes on the porch, blipping the lock. Inside, and the snug familiarity of the little lounge offered no comfort at all. She activated the Event Horizon terminal, loading Greg's cybofax number.

The delay warned her. Connections never took more than a second. After fifteen seconds the flatscreen printed: THE UNIT YOU HAVE CALLED IS CURRENTLY OUTSIDE EUROCOM'S INTERFACE ZONE.

Now the dark worry she'd held back really began to mount. She didn't even hesitate before loading Gabriel's number.

THE UNIT YOU HAVE CALLED IS CURRENTLY OUTSIDE EUROCOM'S INTER-FACE ZONE.

The heartflutter of panic didn't come from fear, it was not knowing what to do next. Instinct cried out to call the police. But snatching that Katerina girl was incredibly illegal. Eleanor wondered if they'd got caught, flung into prison. She could hardly ask. Then she remembered Gabriel had been with him all the time. Nothing could go wrong with Gabriel there to provide advance warning. A doddle, he'd said, a late, lame attempt to reassure her.

Then why wasn't he back here, her cold mind screamed silently. The ludicrous notion of him running off with Gabriel intruded. Dismissed instantly. She thought for a second, then raced for the bedroom and her cupboard. The Trinities would know – maybe where he was, certainly what to do next.

The card Royan had given her was still in her bag. She showed it to the terminal, praying. The flatscreen remained blank, but she heard scuffling sounds from the speaker.

'Yeah?' The voice was male, flat and uninterested.

'I want to speak to Teddy – Father.'

'No shit?'

'Now!'

Eleanor thought she'd blown it, there was only aching silence. Cursing her brittle nerves.

The screen cleared to show Teddy's face. 'Eleanor, right? What's up, gal?'

She let out a sob of relief.

Teddy's frown grew as she explained. She wondered if she was coming over like a hysterical jilted girl. He had to realize how important this was.

'Greg didn't leave any message for you at all?' Teddy asked when she finished. And he was taking it seriously. Her confidence rose a fraction; she wasn't alone any more.

'None.'

'That ain't right,' Teddy said. 'Greg would always cover himself, standard procedure. And Gabriel's cybofax is dead too?'

'Yes; at least, English Telecom says both of them are outside the satellite footprint.'

Teddy paused for a moment. 'OK, my people left 'em going into the Event Horizon finance division office. I can't believe the company would waste 'em. They knew they could trust Greg, and it ain't that sort've deal anyway. 'Sides, they let my people get clear. Thing that bothers me is Gabriel. She's like invincible, you know?' He started typing on his terminal keyboard, looking at something off camera. Unintelligible voices stuttered in the background. 'OK, I want you to call that Morgan Walshaw guy for me. You'll get shoved around by secretaries and the like, don't take no shit. Insist on speaking to him. Him only. Ask him if he knows where Greg is. Then call me right back; you'll get straight through this time. I'm gonna see what I can find out about Gabriel, if she ever got back.'

'How?'

Teddy's face melted into a fast keen grin. 'I got friends everywhere.'

'Oh.' She felt foolish asking.

'Eleanor, you did good calling me, gal. We'll get him back for you.'

And he was gone before she could thank him.

Eleanor tugged on a silk blouse before she called Event Horizon, respectable from the waist up, twisting damp hair into a pony tail. Morgan Walshaw's number was in the terminal's memory core.

The screen lit with a polite-looking young man in a neat powder-blue business suit.

Eleanor swallowed. 'This is Mandel Investigative Services,' she said. 'I'm returning Mr Walshaw's call on a case we're covering for him.'

He shrugged; friendly, she thought.

'I'm sorry,' he said. 'We can't reach Mr Walshaw at the moment.'

'If you check you'll see our company is cleared for direct access.'

'Hey, I'm not giving you the run-around, not someone as pretty as you. Mr Walshaw really is out of touch.'

'Isn't that unusual?'

'Very. There's some big glitch in our communications net right now, really shot it up. It's headless-chicken chaos around here at the moment.'

'I see.' But she wasn't sure she believed.

'Listen, if it's really urgent why don't I call you back as soon as the glitch has been debugged? We've got Mandel Investigative Services number on file. Who shall I ask for?'

'Eleanor, Eleanor Broady.'

'Pleased to meet you Eleanor, I'm Bernard Murton.'

'That's very kind of you to offer, Bernard. Have you any idea how long it'll take to debug this glitch?'

'Nope, sorry.' He smiled ingratiatingly. She wondered if he'd have enough courage to ask her out for a drink. Struck by how bizarre this all was, being chatted up by a randy assistant while God knows what was happening to Greg. Sliding her mind back on to the problem.

'This data package I've got for Walshaw is very important,' she said. 'I don't suppose you could tell me where he is, I could hand deliver it.'

'Er, sure, no ultra-hush about that. He's with Miss Evans at her home. But you won't be able to get in. It's sealed up tight, something to do with the communication glitch. They don't tell me anything.'

'Thanks, Bernard.' She broke the connection before he could say anything else.

There was a number for Wilholm in the terminal memory, listed as private.

Should've done this to start with, Eleanor thought as the connection was placed. Greg always said go straight to the top for real results.

The terminal's flatscreen dissolved into a tricolour snowstorm, red, green, and yellow specks skipping about. The speaker hissed with static.

Eleanor stared at it uncomprehendingly, then cleared the order, ready to try again.

ERROR, flashed the flatscreen as she punched up the menu.

An icy dread settled on her skin, like a fast autumn-morning frost. Piercing clean into her heart. This was something to do with Greg, she *knew* it was. Greg, Event Horizon, Julia, Gabriel,

Walshaw, Katerina, all bound together in some devil's tangle. Thoroughly spooked, she punched up the menu again.

ERROR.

ERROR.

ERROR.

The flatscreen went dead, not even that absurd will-o'-the-wisp nebula.

Eleanor snatched up the Trinities card and ran out into the twilight. 'Duncan!' People turned to look at her, pale ovals of surprise and concern. 'Duncan!'

He was abruptly standing in front of her, face rapt with a mixture of eagerness and trepidation.

'Your terminal, I have to use your terminal!' she cried.

Duncan seemed startled, her frantic urgency taking a moment to sink in. 'Right-on, sure.'

Eleanor wanted to grab him and shake him as he fidgeted through his cards, eventually finding the right one for his door with a shy apologetic grimace. 'Is it Greg? Is he all right?'

'Yes. No. I'm not sure, that's why I need the terminal.'

The door swung open. 'Here we go.' Duncan had an old Emerson terminal, the keyboard worn, some of the touch tabs completely blank. He tapped the power stud.

Eleanor punched out the phone function with a pulse of anarchic energy, then showed her Trinities card to the key. Duncan's face went white when he saw the bold fist and thorn cross emblem, eyes widening. 'I'll er . . . be outside.'

Teddy's face appeared, leaning forwards, squinting. 'Hell, what's happened with you, gal?'

She told him, barely coherent, words falling over each other in her rush to expel them. Made an effort to calm down.

'Not good,' he scowled. 'Gabriel never made it home either. We wanna find out where they was headed, we gotta talk to Walshaw or that Julia Evans gal.'

'Can't. The security man said Wilholm was sealed up, that I wouldn't be able to get in.'

'And they ain't taking no calls, neither,' Teddy said. 'Hostile to 'em, even. Strange. Something in there they don't want no one to see. Ask me and it's something plugged into whatever the Christ is going down. Gotta be. Lay you down good money on that, gal. You know what?'

'What?'

'Reckon we oughta take a look see.' There was a dense gleam of excitement in his eyes, some of his tension draining away.

'Yes, but – how?'

'Ain't nowhere God can't reach, not if he really wants to. Can you get to Wilholm tonight?'

'Yes.'

'OK, I'll round me up a few troops, meet you outside the main entrance in an hour. How's that grab you?'

'Great.' And she was lumbered with the problem of transport.

'Everything all right?' Duncan called as she ran down the slope to the water.

'Fine.' Lying. Curious eyes tracking her flight.

There were three rowing boats tied up at the Berrybut estate's little wharf, one of them was Greg's. She unwound the painter from its hoop and hopped in. The floating village was three kilometres away, an impossible distance. Why oh why didn't the marine-adepts even have a cybofax between them? Isolation was fine, but not to that extreme.

Eleanor began to row, lifting one of the oars out every ten or so strokes to slap the water three times.

The marine-adepts had a van, an old Bedford pick-up they used to take the water-fruit down to Oakham station. They'd help, and keep silent.

She hadn't gone a hundred metres when the dolphins surfaced around the boat, three of them; agitated, tuning in on her distress. Just in time. The surge of adrenalin that'd got her this far was fading rapidly, arms already leaden.

Eleanor chucked the blouse and dived right into the chilly black water, shockingly aware she'd never been swimming at night before.

The dolphins clustered round, snouts butting her gently. She brought her hands together, making a triangle then pressing her palms together: home fast. Again.

Loud chittering, then one of the sleek grey bodies rose under her. She hung on grimly and they began to slice through the water, curving round Hambleton peninsula towards the floating village.

36

Cold turkey was a bitch. It was convulsive shivering, with hot flushes, cold flushes, dryness burning like vitriol in his gullet. Nothing made sense, light and darkness alternating, noise and silence cartwheeling around each other. Nightmares and nirvana trips entwining, indistinguishable.

It was dark when his fever broke. Greg was sitting uncomfortably on a hard floor, propped up against the wrought-iron railings of the tower's stair. His hands had been pushed through the railings, and cuffed on the other side. He could slide them a metre and a half up or down, his entire range of possible movement. His bladder ached, his mouth tasted as if it'd been rinsed in copper soap. Somewhere along the line his shirt had got lost, that scratchy dinner jacket was tickling his skin.

When he glanced round he saw he was in the tower's first-floor storage room. Biolum light shone up from the basement and down from the lounge. Murmured conversation drifted out of both holes. The smell of cooking was making his stomach growl.

Gabriel was sitting next to him, her arms embracing the railings. She was asleep, her mouth open.

Greg nudged her with his toe. She shook herself awake, blinking at him.

'Christ, Greg. I was worried about you.'

'Yeah, Lord knows what was in that infusion Neville Turner

gave me, bloody sight more than a relaxant, though. How come we're still alive?'

She grimaced and shifted closer. He leant forwards as much as his tethered arms let him. They got their heads within a foot and talked in whispers.

'They're checking out what you told them,' she said. 'From what I can gather, Armstrong has some kind of landline stretching over to Downham Market. He told his apparatchiks to launch another hotrod attack against Philip Evans's NN core. He reckoned that without me there to warn Evans they'd have a good chance of success this time.'

'Figures. What did I tell them?'

Her lips depressed. 'Sorry, Greg. Just about everything. Armstrong was fascinated by how you found Tentimes. Made you give him Royan's life story. That really shook them, the way the Trinities have been killing off ex-People's Constables. They thought the Trinities were an ordinary bunch of street punks. Irritants beneath contempt.'

'Shit. That'll start a bloody war, no messing. The Blackshirts will be screaming for revenge.'

'If Armstrong tells them. He probably doesn't want to draw public attention to PSP remnants right now. Besides, don't write Teddy off so quickly. The Blackshirts would take a hell of a pounding if they ever went into Mucklands Wood.'

Depression welled up. Greg felt useless, and worse, he'd betrayed his friends. A real twenty-four-carat Judas. 'Did I mention Eleanor?'

'Once or twice. But not in connection with anything important. They never showed any interest in her. She'll be all right, Greg.'

One comfort. Bloody small, though.

'Kendric was right pissed off with Julia,' Gabriel said. 'The way she manoeuvred him to clear Katerina from the field so she could nab Adrian for herself. Armstrong had a laugh at that, Kendric out-thought by a randy teenager with a crush. That girl isn't stupid.'

'I told them that?' Greg was disgusted with himself.

'Yes. They questioned you for over two hours. Don't blame yourself, Greg. Interrogations these days are like punching out a data request in a memory core, the answers pop out quick and clean. There's no way anyone can hold out. You should know that.'

'Sure. Thanks.' The only hope left now was Morgan Walshaw, and anything Ellis might've left behind. 'Did I tell them that Walshaw and the Event Horizon security programmers were sifting through the files in Ellis's Crays?'

Gabriel screwed her face up. 'I think so, yes.'

'Did it kick anything loose? I mean were they worried about anything he might find?'

'Not especially.'

'Bugger.' He'd banked everything on Ellis wreaking a silent posthumous vengeance. A folly whose magnitude was now painfully obvious. Even if Ellis had been told exactly who he was working for, he wouldn't have known about this tower hideaway in Wisbech. Need-to-know was an elementary precaution, and Armstrong certainly wouldn't have overlooked anything to do with his personal security. Hindsight must surely be the most useless function of the human brain, torturing yourself over the unalterable past.

Gabriel shifted her knees. 'One item which really got them stirred up was the Merlin,' she said.

'What about it?'

'Armstrong and Kendric weren't the ones who meddled with it.'

'Who did?'

A smile ghosted her lips. 'That's what they wanted to know. They asked you three times if you were sure there had been a rogue shutdown instruction squirted up to it.'

'I bet I was convincing.'

'You were. Armstrong ordered his people to confirm it'd happened; apparently Event Horizon haven't announced the breakdown publicly yet. He said they must make an effort to find out who it was. The enemy of my enemy is my friend, all that crap. Kendric seemed to think it could be one of the rival *kombinates*.'

'Kendric's probably right,' Greg said. 'So when does Armstrong expect the answers to his enquiries?'

'I guess tomorrow morning, there's nothing going on right now. If there are any queries they'll have another session with you. If not it'll be straight into the mud.'

'No doubt with Toby helping me on my way after his own fashion. Where is he now?'

Gabriel inclined her head. 'Kendric's mob are camped out in the basement. Lord and Lady Muck themselves are still upstairs. Maybe Armstrong's got a guest suite.'

'Yeah. That Kendric, I'd never have figured on him being plugged into Armstrong and the PSP.'

'You think someone like him is going to let a little question of ideology stand in his way when he's been offered the kind of profits which giga-conductor licensing is going to rake in?'

'No,' Greg said. 'But I'm wondering if Armstrong might just have let himself in for more than he's realized.'

'In what way?'

'Tell you, this is all down to Kendric trying to snatch the giga-conductor patent from Julia, right? That's apart from his private psychosexual fixation on her, of course. First the memox spoiler, now feeding Armstrong information in return for a partnership when Event Horizon is nationalized. Lucifer's alliance, but which one is Old Nick? My money's on Kendric.'

'Meaning?' Gabriel asked.

'Once Kendric's got the patent in his hands as Event Horizon's chairman I wouldn't like to sell Armstrong any life insurance. Even if his apparatchiks do begin running things again – and I think he's underrating the New Conservative inquisitors there – he can never return to public life. As he's already dead in everyone's mind there will be absolutely no comeback if Kendric has him killed for real. Hell, the bugger of it is, Kendric would even be a hero for doing it.'

'You have a devious nasty mind, Gregory. And I love you for it.'

'If I'm so smart, then why are we here?'

'I didn't say you were perfect.'

'That's the truth, and no messing.'

Gabriel was silent for a minute, contemplative, then, 'I think I've worked out why our glands aren't functioning.'

'The twins.'

'Oh, you know.'

'Process of elimination. I'm quite good at that when it's something paltry. I imagine their glands produce some kind of psi null-zone; I remember something like that being mentioned a couple of times back at the Brigade – never really paid attention. Notice that one stayed with Armstrong while we were snatched. No wonder the other Mindstar vets could never find him after the Second Restoration.'

'So they won't find us now?'

'No. Morgan Walshaw might put it together eventually. But not by tomorrow morning. And even then, there's nothing to lead him to Wisbech.'

Gabriel rested her head on the metal railings, smiling forlornly. 'Pity. I was getting quite used to having a human brain again. I could've lived without the gland. Surprising really. I suppose I associate it with childhood.'

'Armchair psychiatrist,' he teased.

'Greg.'

It was going to be bad news, no espersense required. 'Yeah.'

She took a breath. 'Kendric asked you if we had identified his contact in Event Horizon.'

For a moment he thought the cold-turkey fever had come back to rattle his bruised brain. 'Oh Jesus,' he groaned. 'There was a mole.'

'Yes,' she said feebly. 'We didn't do very good, did we Greg?'

'No. Shit! Who? We checked everybody. Everybody, God damn it!'

'Wish I knew. He must've been the one who fingered us for Kendric's snatch squad. Who knew we were going to the finance office?'

He felt like banging his head against the railing, it certainly wouldn't do any damage, there was nothing inside which bloody worked. No messing. 'Julia, Walshaw, that doctor who sorted Katerina out, Victor Tyo.'

'Victor Tyo? He's a security programmer, isn't he? Convenient. And he knew you were going to visit Ellis. Somebody was bloody quick off the mark there.'

'It can't be Victor.' He dived down through a clutter of memories, trying to bring back the day he boarded the *Alabama Spirit*, interviewing a baby-faced man: eager at the opportunity, anxious at the responsibility. 'Can't be,' he muttered.

'Who then? Even you and I aren't infallible, not the whole time. Take a look around if you don't believe me,'

'I interviewed Victor one on one. Tell you, I might miss peripheral tension, like he's forgotten his girl's birthday card, but that kind of treachery I can spot straight away.'

'Whatever you say.'

He shifted his legs, trying to ease the stiff aching muscles. 'Could we have missed someone?'

'Unlikely.'

'The security headquarters staff,' he said, ticking them off in his mind. 'Both research teams, the manor staff; Christ, I even asked Julia and Walshaw.' He felt an icy spike of fright penetrate his heart. 'Oh Jesus,' he whispered. 'Walshaw.'

'Walshaw?' She was openly scornful.

'No,' he snapped. 'Course not. But Walshaw didn't know Kendric had seduced Julia. Why not?'

'What do you mean? Why should he know?'

'Because Julia has a bodyguard with her twenty-four hours a day, no matter where she goes outside Wilholm. Remember, there was even one in the corridor outside Walshaw's office at the finance centre? That hardline woman. God, what was her name? Rachel. She was at Wilholm too. A bodyguard who reports directly to Walshaw, who should have told Walshaw what happened on the *Mirriam*.'

Gabriel bowed her head. 'A bodyguard: top-rank security, close to every executive decision ever made, knew Julia was going to the finance centre. But a bodyguard isn't part of the security headquarters staff, nor on the manor's staff. Oh Greg, we are a pair of fuck ups, aren't we? She was standing next to Julia the whole time, and we never even bloody saw her.'

'Yeah,' he said. Then gave a start. 'Yeah, the whole time. That's strange.'

'What is?'

'I've only ever seen the one bodyguard: Rachel. Every time I've visited Julia, it's been Rachel on duty. Doesn't that strike you as odd? There's got to be more than one.'

'Did you always let them know you were coming in advance?'

He nodded silently. The death-chill hadn't left his heart. 'Whoever he is, he is still with Julia. Tonight. Now. A hardliner taking orders from Kendric. And Armstrong has already ordered an attack on Philip Evans's NN core.'

Gabriel stared at him with destitute eyes. 'Oh, God.'

He pulled at his cuffs, slowly increasing the strength until his wrists were circles of hot pain. Forearm muscles trembled with the strain. Nothing gave, not the cuff locks, not the iron stair rail. Nothing. 'Shit.' He let go, graze marks livid on his skin. The futility hurt as much as the failure.

'That's it, isn't it?' Gabriel said quietly. 'End of the road. Philip Evans wiped, Julia snuffed by her own bodyguard, and you and I into the mud.'

He couldn't answer. His own death he could handle, even Gabriel's. But Julia. Her whole life had been devoid of any normality, ruined by money, by grudges and power struggles that had been going on before she was born. When he closed his eyes he could see a young oval face with the most trusting expression he'd ever known. Soft eyes regarded him with a belief that bordered on devotion.

He should have fought the drug, should have sacrificed Gabriel's bones. Anything to give Julia a chance at life.

'We had some good times, didn't we, Greg?' Gabriel said vacantly. 'Even in this screwed-up world.'

'Yeah. Good times.' They hadn't outweighed the bad, though. Not even close.

Gabriel's eyes drooped.

Greg leant his shoulder on the railings, as near to comfortable as he'd ever get. Muscles were cramping at the back of his neck. He knew he really ought to have been looking for a way out. Gaoler's keys dangling on a nail, within reach of an improvised hook on the end of his belt. The iron stair railing which was loose. That carelessly discarded loop of monolattice filament in amongst the food crates which he could use to saw through the iron with. Keep dreaming, he told himself.

He did. Waking dreams. Mostly of Eleanor. Now those were good times. They must've been, they hurt.

37

Kats was dreaming. Julia watched her eyelids fluttering, shoulders restless below the duvet, the occasional sighs, half-formed words.

It would probably be Kendric who filled her thoughts. She doubted the amnesia infusion could reach down into the subconscious to root him out. And that was exactly the kind of arcane universe where Kendric would lurk, his home ground.

To this day his phantom still stole into Julia's sleep-loosened mind, a dark oneiromancer calling her back to the velvet shadows of *Mirriam*'s cabin, soft silk sheets, hot hard flesh. That handsome face poised inches above her, smiling as she moaned in erotic delirium. Not even the freshness of Adrian could banish the quondam ecstasy. First loves never die. They just . . . haunt.

She gave Kats a dry smile. Maybe she should go through the detoxification with her, get rid of Kendric that way. Concerned professional doctors prising him out of her mind. Nothing else seemed to work.

OtherEyes Emergency Access Request.

Open Channel to NN Core. Load OtherEyes Limiter#Five. It was a reflexive acknowledgement, her nerves were stretched taut, ready to jump at figments. She sat bolt upright in the chair, grabbing the Armscor.

Juliet. Christ, virus virus, they've Trojaned a virus into me!

Wilholm's banshee klaxon went off outside.

'Grandpa!' she yelled.

Losing my capacity. Some kind of interface scrambler. Bugger, security sensor access went down. The NN core's internal channels are crashing, Juliet. Childhood gone. It's accelerating. I've failed you, girl. My memory patterns are being disconnected. Management routines gone.

'No, Grandpa,' she sobbed. 'You couldn't fail me. Not you.'

You're all that's left, girl Datanet's cut. Unlock me in a century. Trust Walshaw, Juliet. Trust him. My girl. Love you. Take care, Kendric will come for you. Integrity stasis, beat it at its own game. Shutting down. Limbo.

And he was gone. But there was something else intruding in her mind, a smooth, grotesque presence oozing in to corrupt her thoughts. Julia jammed her knuckles in her wide, silently scream-ing mouth. The horror pulled at her memories, prising them out of their neat processor-assigned stacks. She could see them tumbling away from her; stained-glass rosettes, each one a billion-picture mosaic. Her life encapsulated, ruptured, pouring away into some infinite insatiable sink point.

Data Error.

She felt herself falling to the floor, howling in psychosomatic agony, Armscor dropping from deadened fingers. Vision lost in the blinding sparkle of vivid memories flashing by, people, buildings, schoolgames, countryside, mathematical formulae, lists of words.

Memory Node One Index Error.

Her mind was contracting, conscious thoughts slowing as they passed through the processor nodes. The presence was every-where, tainting the entire contents of her cerebrum and memory nodes, eviscerating her own personality and replacing it with its own implacable insentient logic.

She began to claw wildly at her head.

Memory Node Two Interface Error.

The virus, it was in her nodes, Trojaned into her through OtherEyes. She should've realized instantly. Her intellect was crumbling, the supporting experience-based reasoning mentality denuded of references, blocking her ability to think. Only a vestigial essence of bloody-minded stubbornness remained, that fundamental aspect of human ego which the virus was unable to subsume.

Memory Node Three Interface Error.

Fight back, Julia pleaded with herself. Stop it spreading.

Processor Node Two Format Loss.

Disengage Memory Node One, she ordered. The command was terribly slow to formulate.

Her subconscious rose ominously to fill the vacuous gulf left in the virus's wake. Wounded pictures of a world peopled by caricatures of those who walked through her natural universe. It was the alternate she lived in fear of, nightmares fully expressed. Black idolatry, so hard and bright her remaining rationality nearly disintegrated under its impact.

Disengage Memory Node Two.

Floating without weight, seeing herself and Kendric coupling like frenzied rampant beasts. Loving it, hating it. Grandpa watching them, frail, poised ready to die, tears streaming down his cheeks.

Disengage Memory Node Three.

Primate Marcus offering her benediction inside a suffocating bubble of rock. Herself supplicant, putting Event Horizon on the burnished silver collection platter for him. Dropping it, seeing it shatter into splinters of pure data, profit and loss. All important. Grandpa shook his head in dismay and died.

Shut Down Processor Nodes One and Two.

The exorcism. Julia felt the virus withdraw, retreating into the nodes. Then the synaptic interfaces sealed, cutting her free, trapping it in isolation.

There was no physical pain, only loss, all that wondrous knowledge she'd taken for granted had been snatched beyond reach. Her own thoughts and memories, once so ordered, now a tangled seething wreckage.

A sound in her gullet. Struggling to place it. Ah yes. Weeping.

Julia rolled on to her back, drawing breath in shallow gasps. Her dress was cold and damp from sweat.

Vacant watery eyes set in the centre of a golden cloud of hair blinked at her. 'Julie?'

Julia rummaged round for the name. So difficult, surely human brains weren't this inefficient. 'Hi, Kats,' she said weakly.

'I want to go for a pee.'

Laughter and tears got dreadfully muddled in her throat.

'It's not funny,' Katerina said in a wounded tone. 'I'm bursting.'

'Sure thing, Kats. Sorry.' Julia was rather surprised to find her limbs doing what she told them. She managed to clamber to her feet, using the bed for support. The Armscor was lying on the carpet. The sight of it jolted her slowly coalescing thoughts. The klaxon was silent now. She was sure she'd heard it going off. Tried to consult her event timer without thinking, a null request. But it could only have been seconds ago.

Somebody had penetrated Wilholm's defensive cordon. A two-pronged attack, then. Her and Grandpa, and they'd nearly got very lucky.

The door handle rattled. 'Julia? Julia, you in there?'

Kendric. Kendric will come for you.

'Morgan?' she called.

'It's Steven; open up, Julia.' There was a thump followed by a muffled curse.

'Get Morgan,' she told him. *Trust Walshaw, Juliet. Trust him.*

'Julia, open up.' A louder thump, a shoulder hitting the door. She could see it quiver in the frame.

'Morgan, get Morgan here.'

A third blow. She heard the sound of wood splitting.

'Morgan!' Julia grabbed hold of Kats and yanked her off the bed in one almighty burst of strength. Kats squealed and floundered about in the duvet.

'Stay down,' Julia commanded.

She crouched next to Kats, bringing the Armscor up in a smooth arc, thumb flicking off the safety catch. Immensely glad she'd taken the time to learn the weapon.

The door crashed open, frame splintering.

'Morgan!' she screamed.

Pink-white light from the corridor shone into the dimly lit bedroom. A lone figure was silhouetted in the open doorway, Uzi hand laser held ready, stumbling forwards. Definitely male.

Kendric.

The maw of the Uzi swung down towards them, a malignant smile behind it.

Julia jerked her forefinger back on the trigger, holding it down. Bullet-sized pulses of intense blue lightning streamed out of the Armscor, so close together they were almost a continuous flare. They hit the wall around the door, splashing open with a loud crack. Wallpaper ignited in tight balls of garish orange flame. The bedroom was alive with strobing light, huge distorted shadows leapt up across the walls and ceiling.

'Shit!' yelled the silhouette. He was diving to one side, not quite making it.

One of the Armscor's pulses caught his leg as he was still going down. Beautiful. There was an agonized grunt, swiftly choked off. His whole body convulsed, hit by an invisible fist, buffeting him back into the corridor.

Got you, you bastard!

A bright ruby laser beam stabbed out from somewhere down the corridor, striking him on the side of his neck. His body jerked again, keeling over. The laser fired a second time. Blue-white flame flared out of his chest.

Julia sent another barrage of blazing pulses out through the flame-wreathed door. Her retinas were scarred with long purple after-images.

'Julia, for Christ's sake!'

Julia could barely hear the voice above Kats' soprano wailing, but somewhere in her whirling mind the sound connected, that same voice was lodged in tenuous memories. She let go of the trigger, peering along the barrel, bewildered.

'Rachel?'

'Yes, for Christ's sake! Now, will you put the fucking gun down. Please!'

'Where's Morgan!' she cried.

'He's coming, Julia. I promise.'

'I . . .' Julia stared at the Armscor as her wrists drooped, letting it fall on to the bed. And all she could do after that was watch, because anything else was just too much. Her fate was all down to Rachel now. Could everybody in the world be against her?

Rachel appeared in the doorway, her face furious as she stood over the prone smouldering body, Uzi hand-laser held in a professional double-handed grip, pointing straight down. She pumped two more slices of red energy into his head.

Their eyes met. It seemed as though time was stretching out. Then Rachel gave a little sigh of relief. 'It's all over now.'

After that, events became kind of remote, out of focus. All the biolums were activated as the bedroom filled with people. Excited babbling shouts echoed around her. Someone used a fire extinguisher on the burning wall, filling the air with chemicals and soot. Three people held on to poor old Kats, who was having blue-fit hysterics. Morgan Walshaw arrived at a dead run, face ashen.

Julia put out her arms to the security chief, as she used to do for her mother years past remembering; too weak to rise from the bed. He sat beside her as Dr Taylor discharged an infuser tube into Kats' neck, his own arms going round her, squeezing tight, rocking her gently. Cheeks pressed together, his stubble. He held her for a long time, until everything in her mind quietened down, and the world didn't hurt any more.

Trust. And it worked, for the very first time.

*

The shower was revitalizing, washing away the smell of sweat and fear. Julia felt herself come alive again under the sharp spray, hot lime-soaped water thrumming against her shoulders and back. It was a physical punctuation mark, she decided, separating out the past and future. She turned off the soap and let the suddenly icy water rinse her down.

The two would be different, she thought determinedly, as she stepped out on to the bathroom's rich shag carpet.

Rachel was standing right outside the shower cubicle, still holding her Uzi, jaw set. She hadn't been more than two metres away from Julia since she killed Steven.

A real live avenging angel.

After Julia towelled herself down, she chose a plain black cotton vest dress from her wardrobe; it seemed apt somehow, right for a born-again human, one with faith in herself, her pure self, unaugmented.

A big man called Ben was waiting for her in the bedroom when she came out of the bathroom, ruthlessly combing knots from her still-damp hair. She gave him a tight smile and he responded with a brief nod. Polite and respectful, perfect for a personal bodyguard. But then with Morgan choosing them, they all were.

'How are you feeling?' Rachel asked.

'Still a bit dazed. It's fading though. Remembering things isn't so difficult now.' Julia slipped a couple of big butterfly clips into her hair. 'Let's go.'

Her bedroom door was splintered around the lock. All Wilholm's locks had been glitched by the virus. She nearly got the shakes again when she thought about that. If they hadn't been glitched, Steven would have just walked straight in. Luck, or chance. Fate.

Rachel walked beside her, Ben taking up position a couple of paces behind. At least she didn't have to be shown the way to the study, that was too ingrained. But she simply couldn't match a name to the face of one of the manor's anxious-looking domestic staff as they walked past. It was definitely a member of staff, though. That was something.

'Thank you, Rachel,' she said, suddenly shy.

'What for? You did all the work. Even after all you'd been through you held it together just perfect. Most of us would've gone completely to pieces. By rights you ought to sack the lot of us. Some bodyguard I turned out to be.'

'No. Steven wasn't your fault. How could we have known?'

'It's my job to be suspicious. All that sudden calling in sick every time your psychic friend Mandel turned up. I should have known.'

Julia frowned. That couldn't be right. Greg and Steven were both working for Kendric. Weren't they? She requested a logic matrix. 'Oh,' she sighed in disappointment. The loss of the nodes was going to take some getting used to.

'I don't want you to worry any more,' Rachel said. 'No greasy little hardline tekmerc is going to get near you. Not with us here.'

Julia could see Rachel was bottling up a core of hearty excitement, almost as if she relished the prospect of a tekmerc attack. It sent little roots of doubt into Julia's mood, because it made her seem like nothing more than an excuse for the two sides to let fly at one another, they enjoyed it.

'Isn't that right, Ben?' Rachel called over her shoulder.

'God's honest truth, Miss Evans.'

Julia turned at the unexpectedly mellow voice, giving an embarrassed little grin. 'That's just Julia, please.'

He nodded warmly.

Rachel tipped her a wink as she pushed the study door open. The lock had disappeared, leaving a rough semicircle of charred wood. Morgan had been in a *hurry*.

She walked in feeling better than she had any right to. Rachel had never spoken to her like that before. Friendly. Who'd have thought it?

There were about ten people in the study, four of them sitting at the paper-littered table. She could name seven, five in security, two manor staff. The buzz of conversation faded out, all heads turning to look at her. She saw concern and relief register in their faces. They cared about her.

Morgan rose from his seat and she went to his side.

'OK now?' he asked tenderly.

'Yah. Thank you.' She cleared her throat. 'I'd like to thank all of you, actually. I'm really very grateful for your support.' She sat quickly, not meeting eyes. The chair was the one next to Morgan's, she'd always sat at the head of the table before, or opposite him. No more. She sensed Rachel take up position behind her. 'What happened?'

'Ha, you tell me,' Morgan said.

'Grandpa said someone had managed to squirt a Trojan into him.' Julia glanced up at the rustle of sounds, smiling faintly at the curious glances thrown at her. Her finger lined up on the NN core, ultra-hush belonged in the past too. These were her people, they had a right to know. 'His memories are in there, translocated before he died. Still are from what I can gather. He shut himself down to stop the virus spreading. Once we write an antithesis program we can unlock him.' She stopped, pleased with herself, gear terminology had all been node-referenced.

'The NN core's still drawing power,' Morgan said. 'Small but constant.'

'Great. What do we do in the mean time?'

'Stay put, I'm afraid. We don't have a lot of choice.'

'What do you mean?'

'Piers will tell you.'

Julia knew that name. Piers Ryder, one of the security division staff, technical.

He was sitting on the other side of the table from her, none too happy at being the centre of attention, reflected in a slightly strained voice. 'One of the assault methods we anticipated was an attempt to knock out the defence gear around the manor with a virus program as a prelude to hardliner physical penetration. Consequently, the gear is all designed to revert to a fully autonomous mode if such a virus is detected in the security datanet. And that's exactly what has happened. For all its power this virus is easily detectable, in fact you can't fail to notice it. From what I've managed to ascertain it only attacks databus management programs, the 'ware processors themselves are left unscathed. Basically it's a spoiler virus, it can't do any actual damage.'

'Really?'

Piers Ryder shifted at the irony in her drawl, dislodging some of the sheets of hard copy he'd covered in thin wavery handwriting. 'I mean, not long-term damage.'

'So it was aimed at the security gear rather than Grandpa's NN core?' Julia asked.

'That's what I think. There would be no point in directing it at a bioware core; as you've seen, the programs stored inside won't actually suffer any damage. The hotrod who squirted it in must have known that.'

'Which implies that we're going to have visitors sometime soon,' Morgan Walshaw said.

'Then why are we still here?' she asked. 'The finance division offices are just as secure. And they won't know I'm there if we move fast.'

Ryder took an awkward breath. 'Miss Evans, Wilholm's defences will shoot anything larger than a rabbit which moves inside the grounds, apart from the sentinels.'

'Including us?' Julia asked incredulously.

'If anyone were to step outside, then yes.'

'We're perfectly safe,' Morgan Walshaw said. 'Just can't get out, that's all.'

'All!'

'And no one can get in. The attack has failed, Julia.'

'You hope.'

'We're patrolling the manor on the inside. I've got lookouts with photon amps scanning the gardens. If anyone does get past the sentinels and the defence gear they'll be sitting ducks for our hand-lasers.'

'Oh.' Julia tried to spot a flaw in his reasoning, and couldn't, to her immense relief. 'Guess we're going to be all right, then.'

'Good girl. We'll just sit it out in here for the rest of the night.'

Julia realized that there was something Ryder hadn't said. 'How long before your team finishes the antithesis program?' she asked him.

'There's only me here,' Piers Ryder replied. 'I can't do

anything by myself, you need a lightware cruncher to write an antithesis.'

'Haven't they even given you an estimate?'

'We can't talk to anyone outside, Julia,' Morgan said.

'Why not?'

'The virus has contaminated all the communications consoles. Your grandfather's NN core was plugged into every landline, ours and English Telecom's.'

'Well, what about the satellite uplinks?'

'Same problem,' said Piers Ryder. 'Even the dish servos are glitched.'

'So use a cybofax.'

Piers Ryder looked crestfallen, he glanced at Morgan Walshaw for support. The security chief responded with an empty wave.

'One of the security systems protecting the manor is an all-spectrum electromagnetic jammer,' said Piers Ryder. 'We thought a tekmerc penetration squad would have to be equipped with some kind of military-grade communication gear to co-ordinate their assault. A commercial cybofax couldn't possibly break through the jamming blanket. I'm sorry.'

Julia felt a pang of sympathy for Ryder. 'Don't apologize, I had no idea I was so well protected.'

'The security office in Peterborough will know exactly what's happened,' Morgan said smoothly. 'They'll be working on it now.'

'All they need is the antithesis,' Ryder said earnestly. 'Once they've cracked it, they'll load it into the company datanet and send it into our communications consoles through the optical cables, it'll flush the virus in seconds.'

'Right then.' Julia gave them all a bright smile.

Morgan sensed her agitation had ebbed, and relaxed into his chair. He'd already drawn up schedules for the patrols on the back of hard-copy sheets. Even his terminal's dot-matrix printer was glitched.

The security people began marshalling Wilholm's domestic staff into a bedroom near the study. Morgan said he didn't want anyone but the patrols moving through the manor. Julia stayed in the study, where there would always be at least four security hardliners in the room with her.

Tea arrived in an ornate silver pot and she went round silently, pouring for everyone. Morgan smiled fondly as she offered him the biscuits. Ginger nuts, his favourite. Now, she remembered that. Funny what had stuck.

38

The marine-adepts' Bedford van stank of stale water-fruit and pigshit; its thirty-year-old combustion engine wheezed asthmatically from the methane it was burning, a fuel it'd never been designed to run on. Eleanor neither noticed nor cared about its failings, the van moved, and that was all that mattered right now.

Nicole drove, hunched forward over the steering-wheel, staring myopically down the weak beams its headlights threw along the narrow uneven road. There weren't any doors; wind whipped through the cab, frosting Eleanor's legs.

'Should be along here somewhere,' the marine-adept woman said.

'Greg said it looks just like a farm road.'

'Right.' Nicole leaned even further forwards, nose almost touching the cracked windscreen. 'What the hell's this?'

As they turned a corner Eleanor saw about fifteen cars and four methane-fuelled Transit vans parked along both sides of the road, all of them had flashing lights on top, blue and orange in equal numbers. 'Police?' The ever-present fear increased its hold.

'Some of them.'

Nicole slowed. A uniformed bobby was standing in the middle of the road, flagging them down. The headlights of the parked vehicles had been left on, casting pale beams of light along the tall hedgerows, turning the leaves grey. There were a lot of people milling about on the road, less than half were wearing police uniforms, the rest had green nylon windcheater jackets with Event Horizon's logo across the back.

The bobby looked into the cab and smiled. 'Evening ladies, won't keep you a moment. There's a C9 division van backing off the road up ahead.'

'I have to get to Wilholm manor,' Eleanor said. 'I've got an appointment with Julia Evans.'

The bobby looked her slowly up and down. Eleanor had thrown a thick lumberjack shirt over her swimsuit, and there were some borrowed trainers on her feet. His eyes tracked her long bare legs. 'Oh yes, ma'am?'

Nicole didn't turn her head, gripping the wheel tighter.

'Please, I really do.'

'Name?'

'Eleanor Broady.'

The bobby pulled out a slim cybofax and typed quickly. Eleanor's heart sank.

'I don't think you do, Miss Broady,' he said.

'Well, it's really Morgan Walshaw I'm booked to see.'

He began to walk away. 'Drive straight through when the road's clear.'

'Arsehole,' Nicole muttered.

'What is going on here?' Eleanor could see the big van ahead, creeping into a gap between two powerful Vauxhall ground-cruisers with the Event Horizon logo on their sides, there were armed men inside.

'Lotta heavy shit going down.'

They both jumped at the voice. There was a young man standing on the running board next to Nicole, dressed in a black jumpsuit with a rubbery collar which came up to his chin.

Familiar face, unpleasant memory. 'Des, isn't it?' Eleanor asked.

Des grinned wolfishly. 'Kinda memorable, right? Listen, Father's hung out a hundred metres past the last of the pigs. See ya there.' He jumped off.

Nicole grunted and shoved the Bedford into gear and they

growled slowly between the lines of stationary vehicles. Eleanor saw what must've been Wilholm's entrance, a cattle grid which opened into the fields of sugar cane. It was illuminated from below by a harsh orange light, as though something was burning beneath it. Several people were standing watching it, none venturing particularly close.

It was Suzi they saw first, standing in the middle of the road, hands planted firmly on her hips. She was wearing the same kind of jumpsuit as Des, a photon amp across her eyes, and a maroon beret on her head. She waved them on to the grass verge.

Nicole pulled over and switched off the engine and lights. Eleanor looked round to see Suzi marching determinedly down the road towards the ant's nest commotion outside the manor's entrance.

Teddy swarmed into the cab, sitting beside Eleanor. ''Lo there, Nicole, thanks for bringing her.'

'No problem. Good seeing you again Ted.'

Eleanor hadn't known they knew each other. The military mates thing again.

'OK, we've got problems,' Teddy said. 'Royan can't access Wilholm to see what the hell's going down; the manor's 'ware has been burned by a virus. Event Horizon and English Telecom have both physically unplugged it from their networks, it was doing too much damage hooked in. Half of Peterborough's telephones have already been glitched by the fallout.' His thumb jerked back towards the entrance. 'That's why the cavalry's here.'

'Someone's attacked the manor's 'ware again?' Eleanor asked.

'Yeah, third time. Persistent buggers.'

'Why are the police waiting out here?' she asked. 'Why haven't they gone in?'

'Can't,' said Teddy. 'All the manor's defence gear is running loose. They've got to deactivate it first, which ain't gonna happen before morning, some of that stuff is seriously hazardous. And when they do get in the likes of you and I aren't gonna be first on the guest list.'

'But we've got to find out about Greg, it's been hours!' Eleanor felt Nicole's restraining hand on her shoulder, sympathetic, alleviating some of the anguish.

'I know, gal. Looks like we're gonna have to go in ourselves if we want some answers.'

'Hey, Father.' Suzi calling with soft urgency.

Teddy and Eleanor climbed out of the cab.

Suzi had a man in tow, oriental looking with a young face, wearing one of the Event Horizon jackets. 'Man here is Victor Tyo,' Suzi said. 'Met him last night, one of Julia's security people. Captain no less.'

'I know you,' Eleanor said quickly. 'You went up to Zanthus with Greg.'

Victor Tyo seemed puzzled. 'That's right, although can't say I remember you. I'm sure I would do.'

'Greg's my man,' she said simply.

'And we'd like to know what's happened to him,' Suzi said.

'Happened?'

'Yeah,' said Teddy. 'He never got back home after snatching that phyltre junkie from the di Girolamo yacht. Eleanor here is loaded up with grief about that. You know anything about it?'

Victor glanced round at the circle of faces. 'I don't understand. Greg left the finance division offices right ahead of Miss Evans's convoy.'

'When?'

'About half-past four this morning.'

'You saw him leave?'

'Yes, he had Miss Thompson with him in the Duo. He said he'd be back later to help analyse some holomemories we'd acquired.'

'The Crays from Ellis?' Teddy asked.

'How did you know?'

'Always cover yourself, Victor. Someone you trust. And don't sweat yourself, man, I ain't interested in no corporate politics. So Greg never showed today at all, right?'

'Not at the finance offices, no. But the programming team assigned to crack the Crays squirted all the data they pulled out up here to the manor. I thought he must be here.'

'Don't get it,' said Suzi. 'Nothing could happen to Greg, not with that Lady Gee in tow. She's in-fucking-credible, like nothing happens without her seeing it first. Nothing!'

'Then why did this virus get into the manor's gear?' Eleanor said. They all looked at her, faces gusted by random beams of blue and orange light from the vehicles in the distance. 'Gabriel predicted the second hotrod attack against Wilholm, why not the third?'

'Shit,' from Suzi.

'OK, so strike Gabriel,' said Teddy. 'She and Greg have been zapped—' he flinched, glanced at Eleanor, started again. 'Least, we don't know what's happened to 'em; same time Wilholm gets burned again. You like maybe see a connection there, Victor?'

The Security Captain nodded earnestly. 'I'll make absolutely sure that you get to the manor right after we debug the defence gear.'

Teddy snorted. Eleanor was struck by just how menacing he'd become; nothing like the directionless thuggishness of Des, he focused his energy and anger with deadly precision. And she was very glad she wasn't on the receiving end of it. Victor Tyo was wilting under his stare, unable to look away.

'You're not reading me right, man,' Teddy said softly. 'The answers are in that fancy mansion your lady boss lives in, and we want them. Tonight. Now.'

Victor spread his arms helplessly. 'We're calling in all our security programmers, but it's the middle of the night. They'll produce an antithesis, but it's going to take time. There is *nothing* I can do that'll get us in there any sooner.'

'Wrong, man. We're going in now, and you're coming with us.'

'What?'

'Think about it. Security hardliners inside see us coming at them it's gonna be target-practice time. We need you out in front to show them we ain't hostile.'

'You're insane,' Victor Tyo said. 'Do you have any idea what kind of hardware is guarding that manor?'

Teddy grinned and beckoned.

There were five electric Honda bikes behind the hedgerow. Des was waiting with them, along with Roddy and another Trinity called Jules. All of them wearing the same black jumpsuit. Eleanor began to think it must be more than just a uniform.

Teddy flipped open a cybofax, showing it to Victor Tyo. 'See this? List of Wilholm's defence gear. We know what they're loaded with, where it is, line of fire. Got our approach all figured out. We can handle the automatics, all we need now is some way of convincing the security hardliners not to shoot after we've broken through. That's you, man.'

Victor Tyo took the cybofax, holding it gently as he read down the screen, dismay growing on his face. 'Where in Christ's name did you get this from? Every byte here is ultra-hush.'

'Snatched right out of your security division cores,' Teddy said. 'Now you believe we're serious?'

Royan, Eleanor knew. The thought that he was behind them, an intangible general, bolstered her in a way she couldn't define. She actually began to believe there might be hope after all.

*

The Hondas took them across country, heading for the back of the Wilholm estate in a long, flat curve to avoid the police patrols checking the perimeter. Eleanor rode pillion behind Suzi, clinging tenaciously to the wiry Trinities girl, sugar cane beating at her legs and arms. She could see the front wheel-fork's chrome suspension springs hammering up and down as the bike bounced over the compacted furrows of sandy red soil. They were travelling in single file, with Teddy leading; Nicole was his passenger.

There'd never been any question over the marine-adept

woman joining the break-in team, which irked Eleanor, because Teddy hadn't wanted to take her along.

'No offence, gal,' he'd said calmly. 'But you ain't used to this kind of heat.'

'So how many times have you broken into a place like this?' she'd retorted.

'That ain't the point. My troops, they got the discipline, know weapons.'

'I used shot-guns and rifles at my kibbutz. And I'll just follow you after you go in.'

'Shit, OK gal, but Greg'll have my arse if he ever finds out. Guess there's more to you than – well, you check out neat.'

More than tits 'n' ass, Eleanor had filled in silently. But Teddy had stopped objecting after that. Some part of her wished he hadn't.

It was Suzi who'd given Eleanor one of the jumpsuits to put on. 'It's an energy dissipater,' she'd explained intently. 'It can hold out against a hand-laser for a good twelve seconds. But with those Bofors masers they've got up at the manor, you've got maybe three, four seconds to skip out of the beam before burn through.'

Along with Victor and Nicole, Eleanor had stripped off before pulling the heavy garment on, its slippery, spongy lining clinging to her skin. When it had adjusted to her figure there was virtually no restriction of movement. A tight cap held her hair down, and a hood with an integral photon amp came over her face, sealing to the collar.

Once it was on she became appreciably colder, the thermal shunt fibres siphoning out her body heat.

'It's no use against bullets,' Suzy went on. 'Then you can't have everything. 'Sides, Wilholm only has beam weapons. So Son says. Better be fucking right.'

The world as seen through the photon amp was a place of ghostly shadows, shaded blue and grey. Eleanor was gradually growing used to it; depth perception was a little misleading, but as long as she remembered that, there'd be no trouble. Suzi had shown her how to up the magnification, bleed in infrared. There was a throat-mike activated graphic overlay, the jumpsuit's internal gear already loaded with the route Royan had devised into Wilholm. Eleanor ran through an articulation acceptance check, and practised calling up the various data projections.

The Hondas were riding down a slight incline. Teddy's bike was slowing up ahead. Eleanor searched her mind, but there was no fear, only determination. A sense of inevitability.

Teddy pulled up beside a broad fast-flowing stream at the bottom of the slope, sugar cane had given way to thick reedy grass. Suzi braked beside him.

They all gathered together at the water's edge. 'We'll use a diamond formation,' Teddy said in a low steady voice. 'Eleanor and Victor at the centre; you two will carry the Rockwell cannon and its power units, it's heavy, but we're gonna need its firepower to take out the manor's Bofors masers when we get within range. The rest of you are gonna provide us a three-sixty cover. Now you look out for those sentinel panthers, OK? You ain't never been up against 'em before, but I have. They're not simple modifications like police assault dogs, they're gene-tailored. Hazards don't come any bigger, they don't behave like animals, they're smart and sneaky with it. Your AKs can handle 'em, but it's gonna take more than one hit. OK, now remember, we stick to the water. The estate's got lotsa ground traps. They're listed, but in these conditions you're gonna have trouble matching the graphics to the landscape. The stream bed's safe, Jules, you stay out here, see to the receiver.'

'Hey, screw that, Father.'

'It's important, boy. Might all wind up depending on that receiver before tonight's out. Gotta be done properly.'

Jules looked away across the fields, anger showing in the set of his shoulders. Eleanor wondered if he was blaming her.

'Radio communications to the manor are out,' Victor said. 'There's a jammer blocking all frequencies.'

'Yeah I know, a Grumman ECM788,' Teddy said. 'We got us a tactical message laser, nothing gonna interfere with that. Jules'll take the receiver up to the top of the valley; Son says we'll have direct line of sight from there to the manor.'

'Christ,' Victor muttered in an undertone. 'Walshaw's going to kill somebody when this is over.'

'Anything else?' Teddy asked. 'OK. We'll ask the Lord for his blessing.'

The Trinities bowed their heads. Eleanor saw Victor look round in surprise. She lowered her own head.

'Lord, we ask for your guidance and protection in our task ahead. We're going to see if we can help our lost brother and sister, and we believe our cause is right and just. If in your wisdom you could grant us success we will remain thankful for such mercy for the remainder of our mortal life. Amen.'

'Amen,' the Trinities whispered in chorus.

'Amen,' Eleanor added.

'OK. Tool up. Move out.'

The Rockwell was a wound monolattice-filament tube one and a half metres long and twenty centimetres wide. It had a broad leather strap so Eleanor could carry it across her back. She lifted it up and realized just how dependent she was going to be on the Trinities for protection from the sentinels. She was confident she could carry it to the manor, but the weight was going to slow her down.

After she'd settled the cannon into place, Suzi clipped a Braun laser pistol on to her belt. 'Twenty-five shots, or a five-second continuous burn,' Suzi said. 'Don't fret yourself none about getting it wet, it's waterproof.' Five power magazines were added. Eleanor felt like protesting about the extra weight, but held her tongue. Suzi's normally infallible barbed humour had evaporated.

The seven of them splashed into the middle of the stream. Teddy and Suzi paired at the front, Roddy took up station on Eleanor's right-hand side. On her left was Victor, who was carrying a couple of high-density power units for the Rockwell along with the message laser. Nicole was on his left, and Des brought up the rear.

The graphics display had reproduced a perfect profile of the stream's winding course for her; a memory loaded straight from the security core Royan had burnt. It'd been built by the landscape team who had fashioned the manor's grounds; they had made the actual bed from fine, hard-packed sand, then layered it with long strips of worn limestone pebbles. The width was a near constant four metres where she stepped in, with the water coming half-way up her shins. After a minute she managed to find the best rhythm for walking, not quite lifting her sole out of the water. At least they were going in the direction of the flow. Heat was draining out of her feet. Her toes were already numb.

Teddy held his hand up. 'OK, people. Hoods on.'

Eleanor reached back and pulled it over her head. A circle of skin around her eye sockets tingled briefly, The photon amp fed its monochrome image into her retinas, suit graphics confirming the neck seal's integrity. She breathed air through the filters, dry and metallic.

She took it as an offhand compliment that nobody checked to see if she'd fixed her hood properly.

The stream ran through a thick braided cassia hedge ten metres ahead, the dividing line between the sugar-cane fields and a broad tract of undulating meadowland. Eleanor saw a line of posts spaced seven or eight metres apart had risen up in front of the hedge, two metres high and featureless except for a small red light flashing away on top. The earth around them had been torn as they'd pushed their way up out of their recesses.

Her photon amp picked out a band of forest about eight hundred metres past the hedge. She didn't like to think about lugging the Rockwell all that way. And how far was the manor beyond the forest?

THREE HUNDRED METRES, the graphics told her. Oh well.

'Boundary,' Teddy said. His voice was muffled by his hood filters. 'Now is when it starts to hit the fan. OK, Suzi.'

Both of them brought up their AK carbines. There was a bass stutter and the two posts on either side of the stream disintegrated. They switched their aim to the next pair.

In the end they took out eight before Teddy was satisfied. His arm signalled the advance.

Eleanor meshed the infrared into her image, alert for any sign of the sentinels. The function fuzzed the outlines a little, but she saw a couple of pink spots pelting away from the stream. Stoats, invisible before.

The meadowland here offered little or no cover. The grass was knee-high, laced with weeds and keck. Nothing had grazed on it for months.

Two hundred metres past the boundary markers and Teddy stopped them again. He plucked one of the smallest spherical grenades dangling from his waist and twisted the timer. 'Down.'

Eleanor squatted, her backside below the surface of the water. Growing cold. Teddy lobbed the grenade out across the meadow-land. Crouching down. Five seconds later there was a barely audible thud.

Another line of posts rose out of the ground ahead of them. Eleanor could hear grass and soil ripping. This time there were no red lights on top.

Suzi and Teddy took aim with their AKs.

PRESSURE-SENSITIVE PICKET, said the graphics, when she asked. There were another two picket lines between them and the forest. The memory core didn't have any information about what they did if you walked between them. Presumably, if you were talented enough to be on this kind of mission you ought to know.

They yomped on.

The stream's banks were growing perceptibly steeper. Eleanor thought the water was getting deeper too. Her view across the meadowland was shrinking. Thick patches of watercress choked both sides of the stream. Roddy and Nicole had to walk through it, kicking away a tangled wrap of tendrils from their legs every few paces.

Eleanor was glad of the brief rest when they came to the next picket line.

Victor pressed his head up to hers. 'You OK?'

The AKs demolished another set of pillars.

'Fine.'

There was a quick squeeze on her upper arm.

Suzi and Teddy reloaded their carbines, jamming in fresh magazines with hard snaps.

The stream fell on harder rock. It was narrower now, deeper. The water came up to Eleanor's knees. Teddy slowed the pace, edging cautiously round the sharper turns.

'How about a couple of us walk along the side?' Suzi said. The banks had risen until they were level with Eleanor's head. She couldn't see much of the meadowland now. What was visible seemed to be small deep hollows, and ground-hugging bushes. There could've been anything hidden out there. Her breathing was coming faster.

'No,' Teddy said.

Suzi didn't argue. Discipline. Eleanor thought it would've made a lot of sense to have someone who could look out over the meadowland.

They rounded a bend and saw the last line of picket pillars had already emerged from the earth. Five AK carbines came up in reflex. There was a moment's pause.

The sentinel came at them through the air like a guided missile. Eleanor saw it as a pink streak arcing overhead, forelegs at full stretch, an angel of death reaching for Des. All five AKs opened up, filling the air with a guttural roar. Des was falling backwards, still firing. The sentinel's heavy streamlined body juddered in mid-flight, its edges distorting as the slugs chewed it apart. Momentum kept it going. Des hit the water. Eleanor's image was suddenly degraded by a spray of blood painting her hood's photon-amp receptors. The sentinel landed almost on top of Des, already dead.

'Keep watching!' Teddy bellowed as they all began to move towards the carcass.

Des still hadn't surfaced. Eleanor felt vomit about to rise from her belly. Forced herself to hold it down. She'd drown if she puked with the hood on.

'Eleanor, Victor, see to him.' Teddy's words became lost in a strident whistle; already piercing it was rapidly broaching her pain threshold. Eleanor jammed her hands over her ears and floundered towards the dark soggy hump which was the sentinel.

The four pillars nearest the stream had begun to glow violet. Eleanor's photon amp hurriedly faded them down. She felt her bones beginning to shake from the noise.

Victor was at her side, shoving at the bulky sentinel. She helped him, pushing its hindquarters. It began to move with desperate slowness. The sound from the pillars had turned to fire, drilling into her ears. Concentration was becoming impossible. The dead cat rolled over, and Des thrashed to the surface. Victor pulled at his hood, breaking the neck seal. Des was choking, squirting water, and gasping for air.

The hideous sound level had begun to reduce. Eleanor risked a glance round. Teddy and Suzi were blasting away at the brilliant pillars. Nicole and Roddy were poised in a half crouch, AKs held ready, scanning the top of the banks.

Des's desperate coughing subsided. The last violet pillar crumpled. Eleanor found she was trembling violently.

Silence closed about them.

Victor shook Eleanor's arm.

'What?' She couldn't even hear her own voice.

He was jabbing a finger at Des's arm. She saw the jumpsuit fabric was torn above the elbow, slashed by the sentinel's claws. Blood was streaming out of the wound.

The sight snapped Eleanor out of her daze. She made Victor clamp his hand around the wound, reducing the flow of blood. Nicole was carrying the field first-aid kit. She let Eleanor take it from her without ever breaking her vigilance.

Teddy fished the Rockwell and its power units from the water while Eleanor pulled an elasticated sheath up around Des's wound. It ballooned out as she touched the inflation stud, analgesic foam setting in seconds. She helped Des to his feet. Even with the photon amp's peculiar vague shading she could tell his face was chalk white.

414

Teddy handed an AK to Victor and hung one of the power units on Des. He gave the second power unit to Eleanor after she'd lifted the Rockwell again, taking the message laser himself.

'Come on. Outta here.'

Eleanor knew Teddy must've shouted it, but barely heard the sound over the occlusive ringing in her ears. The weight of the weaponry was tormenting her spine. Her mind chucked out stupid irrelevances like cold feet and keeping watch across the meadowland to concentrate on the important: thrusting one foot at a time through the churning water. Her flesh was going through the routine, disjointed from her mind. Solitude's anguish unravelling around her. Alone with people she didn't know, walking to a place she didn't want to go to.

They were fifty metres from the forest when Nicole opened fire, her AK a subliminal rumble. The sentinel was hunkered down behind a bush, a clenched shadow, coiled up waiting to leap. It managed a short jump before the slugs bit into its skull. Crashing down into the watercress.

Teddy never even broke stride.

Eleanor trudged past the sentinel, dimly acknowledging how stately its huge head was, humiliated by cracked bone and ripped flesh. There was no honour in death, and it wasn't even a true enemy.

We malign life, she thought, suborning its grace and majesty to our own purpose, mocking it. Even the reservoir dolphins were a sin, so far from their true home, tame, unable to return. She knew water would never be a refuge for her again, not after tonight.

The stream's banks dipped down as they reached the forest, but the water remained knee-high. Tall acacias and virginiana trees threw boughs right across the stream; black heart leaves interlaced above Eleanor, blocking even the ashen phosphorescence of moonlit clouds. The trunks were knotted columns coiled by ivy and ipomoea vines; grape-cluster flower cascades dangled down, brushing against her head. A thick carpet of fleshy flowers covered the forest floor, tiny star shapes closed against the night, light grey in her image feed. She imagined the air would be thick with their scent if she removed her hood.

The forest had to be a human concoction, a designer ideal of fey woodland wilderness. Eleanor was staggered by how much it must've cost.

'OK,' said Teddy. And she could hear him better this time. 'So far, so good. Now, we've got a couple of lasers overlooking the stream before we reach the lake. Suzi, you trailblaze, clean 'em out. The rest of you keep watching for sentinels. This here is prime ambush country. When you leave the tree cover remember to keep yourselves below the water before you reach the lake; means crawling, but make fucking sure you don't let more than your head show. Those Bofors masers will zap anything over fifty centimetres in diameter. If you do get hit, dive fast, wind up cannibal lunch otherwise.'

'What about the people inside Wilholm?' Victor asked. 'They've got to know we're here after the racket the pickets kicked up.'

Teddy patted the message laser. 'We put this on wide-beam and use morse code to rap with 'em.'

'Morse code!'

'Sure, man. Walshaw's ex-military, isn't he?'

'Yes,' Victor agreed.

'Then he'll know morse. Tell him to take a look at you. Means your hood's gotta come off, though. You be careful.'

'Careful. Christ.'

'OK, let's move,' Teddy barked.

Suzi took the lead, walking down the living wooden tunnel a couple of metres in front of Teddy.

The forest was alive with creatures, picked out by the infrared as quick-moving pink blotches snaking around the trees. Squirrels, Eleanor guessed. More pink spots slipped across the ground, not even disturbing the flowers. It was faintly macabre, seeing the unseen. Distracting.

The stream began to change, big quarried rocks had been used to line the banks, similar to marble. Water was frothing around their rough-hewn edges. It was getting slippery under-foot, Eleanor's soles were sliding over loose oval stones. The water was climbing up over her knees.

Suzi stopped in mid-stride, her jumpsuit glaring an all-over claret, rising swiftly towards vermilion. Eleanor marvelled at the girl's cool as the AK carbine swung round slowly, picking out the laser hidden in the tree. She could never have done that, more like scream and run round in circles. Finally understanding what Teddy meant by discipline, far more than following orders. Curlicues of steam were rising from the stream around Suzi's legs, the water bubbling. The girl had found the laser, taking sight, pulling the carbine's trigger.

A sentinel landed on Roddy's back. Jaw clamped on his neck, hind legs raking his lower back with dagger-like claws.

Eleanor screamed.

Roddy pitched forwards, ridden down by the sentinel. Foaming water fountained up as the two writhed about beside her.

'Behind you!' someone yelled.

Victor began firing his carbine back up the stream.

Teddy was pointing his at Roddy and the sentinel, unable to shoot. The sentinel was tossing the man about as though he was a doll.

Eleanor yanked the Braun from her belt, leaning forwards. Saturated black fur twisted into view below her outstretched hand, she jabbed the laser down until it hit something solid and tugged the trigger. There was a blur of infrared energy, flash of singeing fur.

Hot pain smashed into her belly, ripping. Oblivion was smothering in soft black velvet—

*

'. . . coming outta it.'

'Come on gal, up you get.'

Swirling pearl-grey mists resolved into two figures wearing energy dissipater jumpsuits. Hard lumpy stone pressed into Eleanor's back. Water was gurgling round her feet.

'The sentinel,' she cried.

'Dead,' Teddy answered.

There was absolutely no sensation coming from her abdomen; no cold, warmth, pain. Nothing. That frightened her more than having a nagging pain. She glanced down: a cauliflower oval of analgesic foam was clinging to the front of her jumpsuit. 'Roddy?'

'Giving St Peter a hard time. Come on, gal. Up.'

Strong hands gripped under her shoulders, lifting. She stood, fighting the dizziness which blanked out her vision for a moment.

'Can you carry anything?'

'I – yes, I'll try.' Eleanor was curiously unmoved by Roddy's death. His body had been dragged out of the stream, lying on the rocky bank, limbs bent oddly, head kinked at an impossible angle. They must've infused her with something; and she didn't particularly mind, it was nice having thoughts this peaceful.

Teddy handed her the Rockwell again, Nicole taking the second power unit. Suzi took up position on her flank. When Eleanor looked round she saw Victor limping behind her, a ring of analgesic foam around his left thigh.

One dead, three walking wounded. If it wasn't for the drug she knew she'd have given up right there and then.

Teddy led them on.

The stream continued its inexorable advance up Eleanor's legs. Solid footing was hard to find, the fast current pushing insistently at the back of her knees. A raggedy curtain of pigtail ivy ribbons hung from the gnarled branches above her, long enough to trail in the water, an irritant she was constantly having to sweep aside. There were big boulders in the stream now, creating a turbulent white-water surface. The stone-lined banks were closing in, becoming steeper. She and Des were pressing together, Suzi occasionally bumping into her. The stream was being channelled for some reason.

Teddy made them stop, then walked on alone, struggling to keep his balance. The second laser found him, inflaming his jumpsuit to a lambent crimson. His AK sent a burst of slugs back along the beam. A pyrotechnic shower of sparks erupted from a big acacia tree.

'OK people, last stage. Easy does it.' Teddy waited for the others to reach him, and they began to move off together.

Eleanor heard a low rumbling coming from somewhere ahead. Couldn't quite place the sound, her ears still had a residual ringing from the pickets. The water reached her waist.

'Hey—' Victor began.

Teddy snarled a curse and vanished from view. Eleanor took a step forwards, and found the stream bed falling away. Instinct made her tighten her grip on the Rockwell, she knew she'd never be able to fight the water, she had to let it take her. Her feet were swept from under her, dunking her below the water. She breathed out, expelling air from the filter nozzle until she broke surface. Bobbing around like a piece of driftwood. The stone banks were like cliffs whizzing by. Ivy fronds slapped at her. She shifted the Rockwell round, hugging it to her numb chest. The rumbling was growing steadily louder. Memory placed it: waterfall.

Eleanor twisted desperately, getting her feet out in front, locking her legs straight. Slaloming round the last bend she saw Wilholm manor dead ahead. The building was floodlit, its roof blanked out, hidden in shadow. Biolum lights glared from the windows of the top two storeys, the ground floor was a feature-less slate-grey band. There was a vast expanse of flat exposed lawn surrounding it. Killing ground, she thought. Then she went over the lip.

The waterfall wasn't high, three metres. She seemed to hang in the air, floating down.

MASER ATTACK, shouted scarlet graphics. The photon-amp image dimmed. Thick fog exploded around her.

Eleanor hit the lake hard, her backside taking the impact. The Rockwell knocked the breath out of her. *Don't drop it*, her only thought.

The weight of the weapon and the jumpsuit held her down. Rising with terrible slowness, her lungs bursting. Water had defeated the photon amp, all she could see was a uniform powder-blue mist.

Eleanor surfaced, keeping the water level above her shoulders, bracing herself for the graphic warning again. It remained off. Treading water. Somehow she'd turned round to face the waterfall. A dark figure shot over the lip, arms flapping at the air. The curving torrent of water behind it boiled furiously again as the manor's Bofors masers fired.

'Check in,' a voice called out.

'Teddy? Teddy, I'm here, it's Eleanor.'

'Christ, gal. OK, you still got the Rockwell?'

Eleanor padded her one free hand, cumbersome in the thick garment, turning until she spotted him, a small mound protruding from the lake's gently rippling surface. 'I've got it.'

'Thank you, sweet Jesus.'

'Father. Suzi here.'

'Victor held the power unit.'

'Terrific.'

Eleanor saw Teddy bring the message laser out of the water.

'Shit,' Des's voice, high and panicky. 'Being lasered.'

There was a splash somewhere off to Eleanor's left.

'Nicole, 'nother unit.'

The façade of the manor seemed to flicker, its brightness oscillating. Tiny points of bright-red light twinkled from the second-storey windows.

LASER ATTACK. The photon-amp image went completely white.

Eleanor drew a deep breath and sank below the surface. The photon-amp image reverted to blue with slashes of black. This time she could make slightly more sense of it; three intense dots of brighter blue above her, where the lasers from the manor were striking the surface, bubbles fizzing up around her. She kicked with her feet, moving away.

'—look you bastards,' Teddy was shouting as Eleanor came up. 'Christ,' he ducked below the lake.

White. LASER ATTACK.

The blueness was speckled with red and green, throbbing. Her lungs burnt. Can't do this many more times.

Up again.

Droplets of water came in with the air. Eleanor coughed, swallowing some. It tasted foul.

'They've stopped,' Suzi called out.

'Now what?' Des asked.

'Wait,' said Teddy. 'Eleanor, you and Victor come over to me, slow and easy. I wanna get that Rockwell sorted.'

Eleanor rolled over, letting herself float on her back with the water lapping round her chin. Waving her feet, creeping towards Teddy. Will they think grouping together is hostile?

Eleanor was about five metres short of Teddy when a voice boomed out from the manor. 'Who the hell are you people?' It sounded angry.

Teddy began to flash the laser again. Eleanor stopped moving. Whatever morse code was, it seemed incredibly ponderous.

'You want to come in and talk about Mandel? Who've you got as a guarantee?'

'Do your thing, Victor,' Teddy grunted.

'Right.' He submerged.

Eleanor felt insufferably weary. Just wanted it all to be over. The infusion must be wearing off, she thought.

Victor came up without his hood, hair plastered across his forehead.

'Smile, man.'

'Victor,' the voice blared. 'Hell, it is you. Are these people genuine? We've got them covered if they try and force you. Nod for yes. Shake for no.'

'Jesus wept,' said Teddy. 'Paranoid or what.'

'All right,' said the voice. 'And just how do you reckon on getting across the lawn? We can't shut off the masers, and the ground floor's sealed tight.'

The message laser flashed out a long complicated story.

'No way!' the voice called.

'Screw you, arsehole,' Suzi shouted.

'Throttle down, gal,' said Teddy, and even he sounded tired. The message laser flashed once more.

'All right,' said the voice, 'Listen good. Only Victor may use the cannon. If one of those plasma shots lands anywhere but on a maser you are dead.'

'And up yours, too,' said Teddy. 'OK, let's get the Rockwell together.'

Eleanor started kicking again, her legs like lead. Teddy and Victor were moving forwards, towards the shore.

'Touching ground,' Teddy said. He was five metres short of the lawn.

Eleanor came up beside him, toes prodding the viscous lake bed.

'Let's have it, gal.'

Victor drifted up on the other side. He and Teddy started muttering at each other as they mated the Rockwell's cable to the power unit by touch alone.

With the Rockwell gone, Eleanor thought she'd be able to fly. She weighed nothing at all.

Victor stuck the Rockwell's targeting imager over his right eye, its cable coiling down below the water.

'Ready,' he said.

Eleanor saw that Des, Suzi, and Nicole had swum up level with her. Unidentifiable, blind tumours of crêpe fabric. Behind them, on the shore where the trees bordered the lawn were two swift-moving red blobs. No, her mind cried. Enough, we've had enough. 'Sentinels,' she called out, voice rasping in her throat. 'Sentinels, they're coming.'

Victor fired the first plasma bolt. A solar-bright fireball tearing through the night, overloading Eleanor's photon amp. A near-ultrasonic whine ending in a stentorian thunderclap. One of the manor's chimney stacks exploded.

The sentinels were sprinting for the lake shore. Eleanor watched the two people closest to them churn about, trying to reach their weapons. Steam billowed up around one of them as the frantic motion lifted their shoulders out of the water. Eleanor started to swim breaststroke. Suzi had said the Braun was waterproof, although she had no idea if it would work in the water.

Both sentinels leapt together.

MASER ATTACK. Eleanor duckdived fast.

Surfacing, just in time to hear the second concussion as more of the manor's masonry was vaporized. Three more to go. A locust-swarm of slate fragments tumbled through the air high above Wilholm.

The sentinels were in the water, two whirlpools of surf. Des was screaming. Eleanor headed for the nearest conflagration. Couldn't even remember if she'd recharged the Braun.

MASER ATTACK. Plunging.

A sentinel shrieked in mortal terror, a keening that sliced right through Eleanor. The sound electrified, freezing her limbs. What in God's name could a sentinel possibly fear? She saw it disappear below the surface of the lake, sucked down backwards in a maelstrom of bubbles. Something was floating inertly where it'd vanished, undulating with the swell.

The third plasma bolt speared a small ornate rotunda, its detonation shockwave flinging smoking chunks of stone halfway across the lawn.

Eleanor was looking straight at a sentinel three metres away. Its jaws were open showing a double layer of shark-teeth, huge eyes staring at her. Powerful bands of muscle rippled along its back as it paddled towards her.

Cats can't swim!

Her feet sank into muck up to her ankles and she stood. MASER ATTACK. Counting off the seconds. One. A storm-cloud of steam raged around her. Two. THERMAL INPUT APPROACHING MAXIMUM SHUT CAPACITY. The sentinel was a metre and a half from her when its fur ignited. It yowled in pain, skin crisping, cracking, thick fluid oozing out. Three. Eleanor could feel her skin beginning to blister as a wave of searing heat poured through the jumpsuit insulation. The sentinel gave a convulsive shudder, its

423

back was flayed down to its ribcage, skull exposed, eyes roasted. Blood gushed out of its mouth, splattering on her suit. Four. THERMAL SATURATION ALERT. Dead.

Eleanor collapsed back into the lake, her own body on fire. Somewhere inside her belly she could feel dampness. The sentinel's corpse sank as she floated up.

A plasma bolt flashed overhead. Part of a very distant universe.

Something shot up out of the water near by. 'Got the bastard!' Nicole.

The marine-adept woman swam clumsily over to the floating shape. 'Eleanor, hey, Eleanor, give me a hand with Suzi. Think she's still alive.'

'Go on, gal,' Teddy called. 'Masers are out.'

Eleanor moved sluggishly. Between them they dragged Suzi on to the lawn. The girl's jumpsuit was in tatters, blood soaking the grass. Eleanor knelt beside her, and tugged her hood off, water flooded out. Suzi's tongue protruded.

Victor appeared and bent to breathe air into her. Eleanor was thankful, she certainly didn't have the strength left to resuscitate her.

'Lost the aid kit,' Nicole said dully. Her forearms were lacerated, tatters of skin hung loosely.

'They'll have something for her in the manor,' said Teddy.

Suzi spluttered weakly, liquids gurgling inside her.

There was no sign of Des.

'OK, let's move,' Teddy urged. 'Remember the ground traps.'

Eleanor slowly pulled her own hood off, sobbing softly. Proper colours deluged her eyes. The foam across her abdomen was flaking off, blood mingling with water in her lap.

'Come on, gal,' Teddy said. 'You made it now. Jesus must really love you.' He handed her his AK. 'Safety's off. Cover us if any more sentinels show.'

Rabbits, she'd shot rabbits back at the kibbutz.

Victor hoisted Suzi on to Teddy's back, and the big man set off towards the manor, message laser banging against his side.

They followed in single file as he traced a path across the lawn, Wilholm's floodlights casting long spidery shadows as they wove round the traps.

Flat metal slabs had slid out of the manor's stonework to seal the ground floor's doors and windows. Teddy set Suzi down against the wall and unslung a small pack.

Eleanor and Victor watched the grounds, AKs held ready, as Teddy slapped a thermal-slice tape on the slab of metal covering a window. It was a thick flexible tube which hissed as it adhered to the slab.

'OK, don't look.'

Startlingly bright blue-white light glared out, buzzing and sizzling. Eleanor saw sparks skipping along the paving slabs around her feet. She could feel its warmth on the back of her neck.

'Here it comes.' The light dimmed, and there was a loud resonant clang, smashing glass. A fan of milder biolum light spilled out across the grass.

Eleanor kept looking over the lawn. Her nerves raw-edged. She expected to see a mass charge of sentinels coming at her. They'll never let us get in. Not those devils.

There was grunting and shuffling from behind her. 'Don't touch the edge,' she heard Teddy warning. He was shoving Suzi through the hole. 'Got her? OK, for Christ's sake go easy. You next, Nicole.'

Eleanor began to back towards the window, shivering uncontrollably.

'You make it with that leg, Victor? OK, I'll boost you.' Silence. Eleanor knew she was alone. Sweeping the AK in wild arcs. Nothing moved on the lawn.

'Move it, Eleanor.'

The jagged hole was roughly square, one and a half metres high, its lower rim a metre off the ground. She put a leg through.

'All right, lady, hands where we can see them, and moving real slow.'

The room inside was huge, its floor an intricate mosaic of

olive-green and cream tiles; there were chandeliers hanging on gold chains, pastel frescoes of waterfowl on the walls, Regency furniture, a grand piano. Smoke layered the air, two people were using fire extinguishers on the windowframe, glass crunched under her foot. A small army was pointing Uzi hand-lasers at her.

Standing in the middle of the room was a dignified grey-haired man whose face was stiff with tension and suspicion. Had to be Walshaw.

Suzi was lying on the floor, chest a mass of gore, blood pooling on the shiny tiles. There was a woman kneeling beside her, working frantically. Medical gear modules were scattered round, red and amber LEDs flashing, their needle sensors jabbing through the remnants of the jumpsuit. The woman slapped a bioware mask over Suzi's face, a rubbery sac concertinaed out of it and began palpitating.

Nicole was slumped motionless against a wall. Two of the security people were covering her with Uzis while a third wrapped fluffy aquamarine towels around her shredded arms, blood staining them brown.

Victor was standing, hands on head, eyes red with pain. A grim-faced woman was frisking him with expert thoroughness.

Three security people surrounded Teddy. He was facedown on the floor, spread-eagled, his hood thrown back, an Uzi pressed against the back of his bare neck.

Right at the back of the room Eleanor saw a tall teenage girl with a pretty oval face, and long straight chestnut hair, wearing an expensive black dress. Julia Evans; shouldering her way past a big man and an imposing woman, arm rising to point a rigid accusing forefinger straight at Eleanor.

'SIT!' Julia barked in a voice so commanding that Eleanor's nerves went dead.

She heard a quiet sighing sound at her back, and turned to see a sentinel folding on to its haunches not a metre behind her. It licked its muzzle with a long pink tongue.

'Good girl,' Julia enthused warmly. 'Who's a good girl, then?'

Eleanor's legs gave out.

426

39

'Greg!'

'Huh, yeah?'

Monastic silence had enveloped the tower, the light diffusing into their makeshift prison reduced to the minutest candle glimmer from above. The basement was inky black.

Gabriel's strained face was ghostly pale. 'Greg, we're going to die.'

'Come on, Gabriel. Don't give the bastards the satisfaction.'

'Screw you, Mandel,' she hissed. 'I'm not cracking up. I've got it back again, thank Christ. The future. It's all fuzzy. But I can see it, and it all comes to an end in about forty minutes.'

Greg's cuffs clanged loudly against the rail as her words penetrated. He squirmed round to look at her, trepidation and hope heating his blood. Psi meant crushing Armstrong's mind inside his skull, raping every thought with obscene distortions, drowning him in his own agonizing insanity. Making him love his own death.

Greg hadn't known he could hate someone that much. But he could do it. For Armstrong, he could do it. No messing.

The gland: quavering like a cardiac victim. He waited in a funk of anticipation for the tower to fade from sight, for his thoughts to levitate, liberating him from the confines of his own skull. But there was nothing, only the bitter sense of frustration.

'Are you sure?' he hissed back testily. 'I still can't sense your mind.'

'Sure? Course I'm fucking sure,' Gabriel raged. The *old* Gabriel. Fabulous. But why hadn't his own ability returned?

'Can you see a Tau line which has us escaping?' Greg demanded.

'It's not like that. Not my usual ability. No Tau lines. There's only the one vision. Christ, Greg, the whole tower's just going to blow. Like an atom bomb, or something.'

'A nuke?' he asked incredulously. He was picking up on the rising panic pulling at her thorax. He believed without the espersense. An event so powerful it'd burst through the twins' nullifying blockade. Which meant it was all too real.

There was the weirdest tickle at the back of Greg's throat. He knew if he opened his mouth it would burst out as a giddy laugh.

'I don't know,' Gabriel protested. 'There's no details, just a bloody great bang.'

'Electron compression,' Greg said, half to himself. 'Has to be.' Doubt rotted the upspring of bold conviction. Philip Evans had been given a warhead once. For one specific task. The American government wouldn't hand them out like sweets. And yet . . . the original warhead had been intended for Armstrong. Could Julia or Walshaw have got hold of another one from Horace Jepson? They would have to prove Armstrong was still alive, first. Concrete proof.

'Ellis,' Greg said excitedly. 'Lord bless that skinny little fart. He came through.' But uncertainty still nagged malevolently. Even if Ellis had left details about Armstrong in the Crays, someone had moved bloody fast to mount a strike by tonight. Perhaps it was just a colossal conventional bomb. Julia had Prowlers, maybe she'd got a B5 stashed away somewhere, too. Or a Hades. Or a Tochka. Now that was an interesting way to spend your last half-hour, he mocked himself. See how many tactical weapon systems you can name which could blow you out of existence.

At least anything powerful enough to take out the entire tower promised to be quick. Not for Gabriel, though. She had half an hour of mental torment left. Better than being beaten to a pulp for his heroism, or thrashing about in the mud's embrace.

'This attack must mean Armstrong and Kendric aren't having it all their own way,' he said with a barely suppressed excitement. 'Maybe Julia survived. Yeah. And Walshaw interrogated the mole. They're hitting back, Gabriel.'

Gabriel's breathing was coming in ragged gasps. 'But what do we do?' she whined.

Greg took an iron grip on his nerves. 'Say nothing. At least this way we'll take Armstrong and Kendric with us.'

'Is that all you can think of?'

'Well, what the hell else is there?' Greg snapped back, suddenly furious. Despising his own fear, because it would be so easy to let it win.

'You want to shout a warning?' he asked. 'Is that what you want to do? Is it? Wake them up, tell them what you can see, let them get clear? Silence is all we've got left, Gabriel, our vengeance weapon. This way we get our revenge. It doesn't matter that we don't get to see it, we're dead anyway.'

Gabriel bit her lower lip, trembling. He caught a glimpse of moisture glinting in her eyes as she hugged the railings hard.

40

Eleanor sat on a hard wooden chair in Wilholm's study. Someone had put a bone china breakfast cup of tea in front of her. She hadn't drunk any. The air was warm and stuffy from too many people breathing it. Six Event Horizon security hardliners were standing watching her and Teddy, four on the other side of the table, two behind them.

Stupid. Farcical. But Eleanor hadn't complained. Didn't have the energy. Her belly was cold now, colder than ice.

A harassed Dr Taylor had broken off attending to Suzi long enough to give Eleanor an infusion that'd taken her down to a state where peripheries, like injuries and the manor's fabulous wall-to-wall glitter, didn't register much. Then some kind of bioware dressing had been stuck over the claw wounds, and a salve was sprayed over skin that was red raw where the maser had leaked through the dissipater jumpsuit. Dr Taylor wanted her to lie down for a more elaborate treatment. She refused point-blank.

Eleanor had to know about Greg, persuade the Evans girl and Morgan Walshaw to help find him. Except they didn't seem to be getting anywhere. She was wrapped in a jade towelling-robe, sitting beside Teddy who was also in a robe, one which was too small for him. Julia Evans and Morgan Walshaw sat opposite them. Matched contrasts.

Julia was quiet, sticking to Walshaw wherever he went. Mouse timid. Nothing like the way Greg had described her.

Further up the table a man called Piers Ryder had opened up the squat cylindrical message laser, much to Teddy's impotent fury. Ryder had plugged a cybofax into the laser's hardware with optical cable, looking for bugs on Walshaw's orders.

There was no trust in the study. And after all the horror they'd endured; Eleanor could've wept, except it wouldn't have changed anything.

Teddy and Walshaw were doing all the talking. Arguing, actually. All down to Walshaw's totally unbelievable statement that Greg had gone somewhere with Kendric di Girolamo.

'You think Greg's sold out, you outta your ballsed-up mind,' Teddy said; loud but not shouting, his anger a dangerous undercurrent.

'Even I find it difficult to believe,' Walshaw said. 'But none the less, he did leave with di Girolamo on the *Mirriam*.'

'Going where?'

'Does it matter? The complicity exists.'

'Fucking right it matters. He ain't with that arsehole di Girolamo outta free will. Once we find him my troops gonna snatch him back.'

'You can't,' said Julia. It was the first time she'd spoken.

'Why not, gal?' Teddy asked. He wasn't quite so abusive to her.

'I'm not quite sure of his exact position any more.'

'Way they was headed will do. We'll pick 'em up soon as they put into port.'

Julia consulted Walshaw silently. The security chief shrugged.

'Last time I checked, Greg was in Wisbech,' Julia said.

'Wisbech?' Teddy asked.

'Yah.'

'What, Wisbech in the basin? How the fuck did he get there?'

'I'm not sure. It wasn't fast enough to be a plane, we thought perhaps a hovercraft.'

431

Teddy narrowed his eyes. 'How come you know that? You weren't following him.'

'I gave him my St Christopher. It's got a transmitter in it, a very complex frequency hopper. Event Horizon's Earth Resource satellite platforms are equipped with sensors which can pick up the signal anywhere on the planet. I wear it in case I get kidnapped.'

'And you gave it to Greg? Why, for Christ's sake?'

'I wanted to know what he was doing, where he was. You see, Kendric has done a deal with the PSP and Greg didn't tell me.'

'PSP?' Teddy half rose from the chair. 'You telling me PSP is plugged in on this?'

'Yah,' Julia said.

'Then, gal, you are way, way outta line saying Greg ain't on the level. While rich bitches like you were living it up abroad, that rat-prick Armstrong was screwing us into the ground. Me and my troops, we were fighting his Constables. We fucking died so you could swan back here and make money outta us. Eight years Greg was out on those streets. Hardest there is, and they nearly broke him. But he stood and fought. So don't you ever sit in front of me and tell me he's gone and done a deal with no fucking Armstrong relics. You ain't good enough to shovel up his shit. You hear me!'

Julia shrank back in the seat, her tawny eyes wide. 'I wasn't sure,' she pleaded. 'That's why I gave him the transmitter. Because I didn't understand.'

'Understand what?'

She swallowed hard, looking round the room in desperation. 'Victor. You were there at Ellis's flat. Ellis told you that the Cray which Greg crashed was loaded with millions of personal files. Everyone important in England, that's what he said.'

'Yes,' Victor agreed cautiously.

'See?' Julia asked Teddy.

'See what?'

Julia covered her face in her hands, veiling the sting of misery in her eyes. 'Nobody sees. It's me. Those bloody nodes. I kept looking at it until I had the answer.' Her hands dropped to the table, palms down, fingers wide. 'Who? Who, in this whole wide world is going to compile millions of files on people living in this country?'

'God damn.' The anger fled from Teddy; his chair creaked as it took his full weight again. 'PSP.'

'The amount of data in even one of the Crays was far too much for anyone to snatch from a mainframe, the squirt would last for days. Ellis had to have direct access to the Ministry of Public Order mainframe at some time before the circuit hotrods crashed it and the PSP fell. The one explanation which fits is that he was an ex-apparatchik; and only a high ranker would have an authority code that'd clear duplication copying on that scale. And he was running a team of hackers that are disrupting the English economy. That's the oldest trick in the political book; cause dissatisfaction with the current government, and people always turn to the opposition. It had to mean that Ellis was still actively working for the PSP.'

'OK,' Teddy said. 'So maybe Greg ain't so fast these days, didn't see the connection straight off. Don't mean he's turned.'

'I know that,' Julia shot back. 'I didn't want to believe he'd do that to me, not Greg. I trusted him, like nobody else. That's why I slipped him the St Christopher. To find out what he was doing. Then he went with Kendric, and I had to believe.'

'It's all down to Gabriel Thompson,' Walshaw said. 'Her precognition ability would suggest it is impossible to snatch or even surprise her. Therefore she and Greg went with di Girolamo out of their own choice.'

'Christ, man, I don't know about that. Gabriel is one hotshot gal, but that psi gland messes her about something serious. You've only ever seen her on the up. In Turkey I seen her down, and you just can't get any lower and still be human.' Teddy made a fist and rapped on the table with it. 'OK, listen; you count Gabriel and her precog outta all this, you gotta scene where Greg's in deep shit. Right? Ain't I right?'

Julia turned to Walshaw, face tilted up with hope.

'Yes, all right,' said the security chief. 'Psi was always looked on as a wild card when I was in active service. I just thought they'd improved it since my day. Greg and Gabriel seemed to have it down pat.'

Teddy gave a fast grin. 'Now we are getting somewhere.' He looked at Julia. 'OK, gal, you work your magic spy trick on Greg again, tell us exactly where he is, and we'll squirt the co-ords out to my troops.' He glared at Ryder. 'That's if you ain't screwed my laser. And maybe Event Horizon can loan the Trinities a couple of Prowlers to jump 'em out to wherever Greg is now. I wanna get this settled soon as.'

Julia became fluttery with concern. 'I can't find out where Greg is now. Grandpa was plugged into every piece of gear Wilholm has. It's all glitched by the virus. We have to wait until the company security people outside write an antithesis.'

Teddy's face wound up with pain. 'Jesus. They've had Greg for hours. You got any idea what they could've done to him by now? That bimbo friend of yours wasn't the half of it. They were being nice to her.'

'The situation is hardly Miss Evans's fault,' Walshaw said smartly.

Julia had closed tortured eyes.

'Yeah, OK,' said Teddy. 'So let me use the message laser, plug it into the man's NN core. I got someone who can write an anti-thing in zero time.'

'There is nobody better than our experts,' Walshaw said.

'Bullshit! Son is the best there's ever been. Melted through your security core guardians like butter to get at the manor defence specs, didn't he? We wouldn't have been here if it wasn't for him. How the hell do you think Greg found Tentimes? Who backtracked Ellis for you?'

'You expect me to allow some kind of super hacker to plug directly into Philip Evans's NN core?' Walshaw asked. 'The heart of the entire company? Not a chance. I'm more than willing to do whatever I can to help Greg, once the virus is broken. But that is out.'

'You *owe* us, man. You owe us so bad it's gonna take you a couple of centuries to kick your debt. You are responsible for Greg being where he is now. You hired him, you put him there.'

Eleanor watched Walshaw stare up at the ceiling, brows knotted with furious concentration. Greg's life was being decided inside his skull, she realized. It was obvious that Julia would follow his decision. The girl looked dreadfully unhappy.

'Miss Evans?' Eleanor said. She was distantly bemused by how such an awfully reedy voice as hers had become could attract everyone's rapt attention. They all wanted someone to produce a miracle, blow away their dilemma. She couldn't, of course. 'You don't know me, Miss Evans, but I live with Greg, and I love him. He would never betray you. I suppose you think of him as a hard man, never showing much feeling. He is in a way. I have only ever seen him let emotion overrun common sense on one occasion. That was when he found out what di Giroiamo had done to your friend, Katerina. All he could think about was getting her out. He cared about her, a girl he'd only ever met for a few minutes before. Does that tell you anything about him? I have also met Royan, the hacker Teddy wants to plug into your grandfather's NN core. I was sick to my stomach for a day after I met him, I couldn't eat, couldn't drink. Royan doesn't even have any legs, Miss Evans. He doesn't have any arms. He doesn't even have eyes. To look at him you wouldn't even believe he was a human being. Physically he is a lump of flesh with a digestive system and a brain which is plugged into some gear. The PSP did that to him, their People's Constables. But I've talked with him, had coffee with him, he's one of the most decent, bravest people in the world. He knows what pain really is; he isn't about to harm you or your grandfather.'

Julia might've been carved from stone, staring at Eleanor with fascinated revulsion, unable to look away.

'Right now there are two people lying dead in your grounds,' Eleanor went on. 'The only reason they came to Wilholm was to help Greg. I'm going to wake up screaming every night for the rest of my life remembering that trip. But I'm glad I will, because

I thought coming here meant there would be a chance of getting Greg back. All of us, Miss Evans, we all believe in Greg. Even you did once, I think. He's just an ordinary man, nothing special in the way of the world. But I'd be very grateful if you could do what you can to bring him back to me. Thank you.'

The speech exhausted the last of her strength, she withered back in the chair, spent. Someone gripped her freezing hand in a vice-like hold, which verged on the painful. She knew it must be Teddy.

Julia turned to Ryder. 'Plug it in.'

41

'What are you doing?' Gabriel asked tersely.

Greg had crouched down, squashing his face against the cold banister, trying to bend a wrist double to reach his dinner jacket's breast pocket. 'What I should've done hours ago. Getting us out of here.'

'How?' she squeaked.

'Tell you, it's not going to be easy, all right? At the moment, we're already dead, so a bit of damage now isn't going to make a whole load of difference. Handcuffs are a bureaucrat's fallacy to the condemned. Especially the condemned fitted with cortical nodes.'

'Oh.' Gabriel's eyes widened in comprehension.

'Yeah,' he said, suddenly disquieted. 'Besides, you should've thought of this too; you went to the same tactics courses as me.'

'Tactics courses! Christ, Greg, I was a flaming nurse before Mindstar dragooned me.'

Greg's scrabbling fingertips found the top of the handkerchief sticking out of his breast pocket, and he tugged the square of white silk out into the air. It wasn't as big as he'd have liked, but it would have to do. 'Listen, this is going to look bad, OK? But self-mutilation is a damn sight better than dying. If you've got a different solution, now's the time.'

She shook her head silently. Very pale now.

Greg outlined what he wanted her to do and stretched out to

give her the handkerchief. Her hands were shaking when she took it.

She leant forwards to press her face into a gap between the stair rails and bit into the handkerchief, chewing it into her mouth. Her cheeks bulged out.

'Bite hard,' he instructed.

She ducked her head in acknowledgement.

'OK. Now let's get into position.'

They faced the tower's curving wall, as though they were praying at an altar, Greg thought. He held Gabriel's eyes as she knelt on the floorboards, willing her on. She pulled the cuffs right up to the railing and rested her hands on the ten-centimetre lip of solid oak planking. Her fingers stuck out over the edge, but her knuckles remained on the wood.

Greg went the other way, sliding his arms right up to the banister and standing on his left foot. He pushed his right leg through the gap in the railings above Gabriel's left hand.

'Fist your right hand,' he told her, 'Then disengage all the nerves below the left elbow.'

She looked up at him, her shoulders quivering, dry weeping. The sight nearly broke his determination.

Slowly her right hand clenched into a fist, leaving the left open.

'Can you feel your left hand?' he asked.

She shook her head.

'Are you sure?' He was worried about the stunshot charge they'd both been hit with; if there was any damage to the cortical node there'd be no chance of pulling this off.

She glared at him.

'Look away,' Greg said.

Her head turned.

'Right away,' he said, deliberately harsh. He couldn't risk her flinching.

She jerked her head forcibly aside.

He concentrated on the leg he'd stuck through the railings.

He had to get it perfect first time. If he didn't, he doubted she would ever allow him a second go.

He was wearing sturdy leather shoes. Grubby and scuffed now, but with a hard, flat sole.

Lining the heel up in the funereal glimmer of light.

Greg pushed up with his hands, as though he was trying to lift the banister off the top of the railings. Bunched muscles tightened the jacket fabric across his shoulders. His left foot was pressed hard on to the floor. He could even hear a feeble groan from the oak as it adjusted to the new stress pattern. Praying the strength he'd built filling up the chalet's water tank would be sufficient.

Ready.

He stamped down.

The heel smashed down on to the top of Gabriel's knuckles, *giving*. Bone snapped, a liquid-dulled crack.

She convulsed, slumping forward into the railings, her puling muted by the ball of silk.

Greg tugged his leg back out of the railings, and hooked the back of his calf inside Gabriel's left elbow. Her head twisted round, there was a small tail of cloth sticking out of her mouth. Shock-wide eyes screamed up at him in pure terror. He jerked his leg back savagely.

Her arm moved with sickening slowness. Then suddenly there was no more resistance, and Greg was swinging wildly, left foot slipping, backside coming down fast. The cuffs made an excruciatingly loud racket scraping down the railing. He sat heavily, his coccyx trying to punch its way up into his throat.

But Gabriel was free. She lay face down on the floor, right hand still through the railing, left arm curled limply at her side, its pulped hand brushing her hair. Her whole body was quaking softly. The handkerchief had begun to emerge out of her mouth like some vile glistening imago escaping from its chrysalis.

She rolled over, gulping, a half-choke. A trail of thin vomit ran down her chin. She wore the expression of the torturer's victim, an utter incomprehension of how one person could do this to another. Frightened eyes found her left hand. She drew it up to her face, mesmerized, and began to cry.

'Gabriel?'

She was curling up into a foetal ball, sucking down air in shallow gulps.

'Gabriel, did the cortical node work?'

'Yes.'

'Gabriel, you have to get up.'

A shiver ran down her spine. 'I want to go home,' she whispered through clenched teeth.

'We are going home. Now get up.'

Gabriel rocked back on to her knees, cradling her left hand. Tears streaked her cheeks. 'Oh, Christ, Greg.'

'I know,' he said. 'Now look round and find something you can use as a club.'

'No. No, I can't do that. Don't make me do that. Please, Greg. Please.'

'You can't leave me here.' Greg deliberately let a note of desperation filter into his voice. Bullying her with guilt. There's only about thirty minutes left before the tower blows.'

She clambered to her feet in slow-motion stages, never allowing her arm to leave her side. He could see the film of sweat on her forehead, and felt clammy apprehension rise. The grisly snap of cracking bone seemed to be echoing around the room.

She tottered off behind him, rummaging through the stacks of food crates. He didn't look, keeping still, eyes on the ancient worn brickwork on the other side of the stairs.

'Will this do?' she asked. She couldn't think for herself. Shock numbness had set in.

The length of wood she'd found was a metre long, four or five centimetres wide. Three rusty screws jutted out of the middle. It ought to be heavy enough, he thought.

'It'll do.' With grim horror he realized that after she'd smashed his hand, he'd have to yank it free through the handcuff himself. She could never manage that.

'Gabriel, you must be hard. Swing the club real hard, no messing. Imagine it's Armstrong's hand, or something. Don't do it to me twice. Promise?'

'Right.'

He put his left hand on the ledge of wood, then instructed his cortical node to disengage the nerves of his left arm. From the elbow down he could feel nothing, not even the dead meat coldness of anaesthetic, the buoyant release of morphine. His forearm and hand had ceased to exist.

'OK,' he said, finding out just how much it'd cost Gabriel to say that.

Gabriel pushed the handkerchief into his mouth. It was disgusting. Soggy, tasting of sour acidic stomach juices. Good. Focus on the revulsion. Shutting out the sight of Gabriel steadying herself on the second step. Knuckles whitening as she clenched the makeshift club. Her face mimicking the intense concentration he'd once seen on a golf pro's face as he lined up his putter for an albatross.

Greg heard the swish of air.

Shock was worse than pain in its own way. His brain seemed to expand time, letting him see the full horror of his flesh being triturated, every detail slamming into his mind. The sight flushing away the intention to pull with all his strength. It took the animal fear of impending death to twist his mind back, over-riding reluctance. Greg pulled.

He felt the scream rising inside him as he watched his ruined hand squeezing through a metal circle that was two centimetres too small. It was obscenely malleable, damp cracking sounds marking its progress.

His hand came free, and a lungful of air blasted the handkerchief from his mouth. There was nothing to stop the scream that would vent some of his anguish. He hovered on the brink for one eternal second. Closed his gaping mouth, contracting the throat muscles that would've formed the blissful release of sound.

Gabriel: laughing, crying, whimpering. 'We've done it.' Wiping tears from her face. 'We've fucking done it.'

Greg drank down litres of fresh clean air. His right hand was still on the other side of the railing. He turned it slowly and brought it and the cuff through the gap. His left hand was something from a butcher's stall, crushed, swelling with blood, pussy fluid leaking from the graze where the club had struck.

Greg shared a long glance with Gabriel, a love that wasn't physical, didn't need to be. They were blood siblings, a far stronger bond. 'Time to go,' he said. It broke the spell.

She went to work on the store room's central biolum panel, easing it away from its clips. He started on the Harrods hampers and found a case of three-star brandy.

He clamped the first bottle between his knees, and unscrewed the cap with his right hand. The aroma set up a satanic craving in his maltreated stomach.

After opening five bottles, Greg tiptoed around the room, soaking the kelpboard cases with the liquor. Taking care not to spill any on the floor with its wide cracks.

'The window's behind this lot,' Gabriel whispered, poking a tall stack of cases. 'It'll take an age to shift them.'

'Forget shifting them. Our exit isn't going to be stealthy. You got the biolum?'

'Yeah.' She'd cracked the back open, exposing the activation trigger. A finger-sized pewter cylinder with enough charge to activate the motes' bias. There was also enough charge to spark – two, maybe three times if their luck was in.

He impaled a wad of paper on the screws of Gabriel's club, sloshing brandy over it. She put it on the desk, eagerness animating her features, dulling the pain.

He put his shoulders to the stack of crates, tensing. Nodded.

Two idiot smiles.

A minute blue spark sizzled between the cylinder electrodes and one of the screws. The paper caught at once, a bright yellow tongue of flame that left sharp purple after-images on his retinas.

Gabriel picked up her torch and thrust it against some of the cases he'd doused. Flames bloomed wherever it touched. She carried it round in a triumphal circuit.

The room was becoming dazzlingly bright to Greg's gloaming-acclimatized eyes; but he waited until the fire began to crackle noisily before heaving at the cases. The stack toppled with a crash which seemed deafeningly loud in the small room. Cases burst open, scattering tins of meat with Brazilian labels across the oak floorboards.

Greg jumped on to the two remaining cases below the window, kicking out the glass. It shattered into wicked ice daggers, scything off into the galactic-deep night outside.

'Out,' he yelled, and used his good hand to haul Gabriel up on to the cases. She balanced on the narrow dirt-ingrained windowledge, crouching down for the jump. There were shouts coming from the basement. The fire had really taken hold now. Greg could feel its heat on his face and his right hand.

Gabriel had already gone. And someone was pounding up the stairs. Greg flexed his knees and leapt into the cool damp air.

42

Processor Node One Status: Loading Basic Management Program.

Processor Node One Status: Loading Basic Management Program.

Julia's head jerked up. She hadn't actually been sleeping, just allowing her rattled, abused thoughts some peace.

Processor Node Two Status: Loading Basic Management Program.

'What?' asked Walshaw.

Memory Node One: File Codes Loaded.

The huge black man, Teddy, was giving her that eagle-eyed stare again, as if he was examining her soul. Finding it flawed.

Memory Node Two: File Codes Loaded.

'Lord Jesus.' She clapped her hands in excited delight. 'He's done it. Royan. He's in the 'ware.'

Memory Node Three: File Codes Loaded.

The fabric of the nodes' artificial mentality rose out of nowhere to fortify and enrich her own thoughts. Dictionaries, language and technical lexicons, encyclopedias, logic matrices, all returned to their warm familiar places.

Neural Augmentation On Line.

Walshaw was leaning over his terminal, hands reaching for the keyboard. The cubes were full of crazed graphics, slowly returning to equilibrium.

Hello, Juliet.

'Grandpa!'

Her view of the study was suddenly riddled with cracks, it fragmented and whirled away. She was looking down on Earth from a great height. But the picture was wrong, there were no half-shades, the colours were all primary; an amorphous jigsaw of emerald, crimson, turquoise, and rose-gold oil patterns. It was overlaid by regular grid lines. *False-Colour Thematic Image*, supplied the nodes. There was a town at the centre of the image, one which was curiously blurred around its outskirts.

Wisbech, Julia said, intuitively. There was no sound to hear, no tactile sensation present in this flat universe which had captured her, only the image itself. She could sense her grandfather's presence by her side. They weren't alone.

Juliet, I'd like you to meet a very smart young lad. Goes by the name of Royan.

Pleased to meet you, Miss Juliet. I've never met an heiress before.

Thank you for unlocking my grandpa, Royan.

It was a breeze; whoever wrote the virus was dumb.

It didn't seem that way when I was on the receiving end.

I'm not surprised. You know, you ought to load some proper protection into your nodes. They're terrific pieces of gear, wish I had some. But the guardian bytes you're using leave them wide open.

I used to think I had proper protection.

I could write you some. I wouldn't want anything bad to happen to you, you're a friend of Greg's. And the PSP hates you. That makes you an A-one person in my book.

I'd take him up on that, Juliet, if I were you. Royan and I have been having a long chat. Boy knows what he's talking about.

Long? she asked.

You're operating in 'ware time now, Miss Juliet. Fast fast fast.

Oh. Thanks for the offer, Royan. But I think we'd better do what we can for Greg first.

Yeah, said Philip. *Misjudged him in a big way. Jumping the gun. Never would've done that in the flesh. Reality shouldn't have done it now. But we can make amends soon enough.*

Julia concentrated on the thematic image. Her grandfather was squirting a solid stream of binary pulses up to a company Earth Resources platform through Wilholm's one remaining up-link, a hum in the background of her consciousness.

Greg's moving, look, he said.

A diamond star had appeared on the thematic image. The magnification leapt up. Wisbech's outskirts disappeared. The town was slashed in two by a broad meandering band of deep turquoise. Like a rain-swollen river, Julia thought, even though she knew the whole place was mudlocked. Her grandfather jumped the magnification again. Then again. The star was gleaming a few hundred metres east of the turquoise band. A small dot of crimson on the edge of the turquoise band was turning a brighter scarlet.

Something is warming up down there, Philip said.

I think I can help, said Royan.

A crude transparent map was superimposed on the thematic image.

Ordnance Survey, Royan explained. *The last one before the PSP came to power. Nothing much changed between then and the start of the Warming.*

The map rotated slowly clockwise until the two sets of grid lines meshed, then it swam in and out of focus, matching up the street patterns.

Close as we'll get.

Disused mill, Julia read. The dot had become a fluorescent ruby.

Thermal emission rising sharply, said Philip. *It's on fire. And Greg's moving away, dead slow. Means the boy's on foot, swimming rather, in that gunk.*

Escaping, said Royan.

Could well be. I wonder if Gabriel is with him.

If she's alive, she'll be with him, Royan censured.

Julia sensed the adoration verging on love that Royan had somehow managed to convey into their inanimate medium. His belief was unshakeable. And she knew he was right, Greg didn't desert people to save his own skin.

Grandpa?

I know, Juliet The strike window ends in ninety seconds – mark. Decision time.

Mr Philip told me about that, Miss Juliet. It's a grand idea. He said it was your suggestion.

Certainly was, boy. She's an Evans, through and through. And we don't do anything by halves. No sir.

I wonder who's in that tower, Royan asked.

Someone big, Julia said. *Someone important, important enough to make Kendric visit him, not the other way round. And if you knew Kendric like I do, you'd know how few people in the world would be granted that concession.*

The first instance of sensation invaded their private universe, an electric tingle reminding her of far-off nerves. Julia looked down on the mill, judging it with the dispassion of some Olympian goddess.

Could it really be? Philip asked.

There was never any body, said Royan. *Never any real proof. Not even Mindstar knew.*

We'd have to hurry. The timing is tight, very tight.

No, Julia said, bold with conviction. *The timing is perfect. Synchronized.*

Gabriel? Philip enquired.

I expect so, she said. *Whatever the reason, we cannot ignore this opportunity.*

I agree, said Royan.

That makes it unanimous, then. Access the Ordnance Survey's memory core and download that mill's co-ords, m'boy, accurate as you can get. We've only got the one satellite uplink left after your friends came a-knocking. I would've preferred to keep watching Wisbech, just in case we need to update. But we'll simply have to make do.

You're lucky you've still got that one. Father is efficient.

Julia's awareness shifted as the thematic image faded. She was plugged directly into Wilholm's myriad gear systems, a bright-glowing three-dimensional cobweb of data channels. New strands were coming on line at a phenomenal rate as the antithesis poured through it, purging the virus.

A quick status check showed her that there were only three functional servos out of the eight which steered Wilholm's one remaining satellite dish. Accelerated time stretched for what seemed like aeons as the dish swivelled round on its axis to point at the western horizon. Her grandfather had overridden the servos' safety limiters, allowing them to take a double load. Temperature sensors relayed the heat from overloaded motors straight into her medulla, interpreted as scalding hands.

Sorry, Juliet.

Her pain vanished.

The dish's rotation halted, smaller azimuth servos began tracking it across the sky.

Co-ords ready for loading, Mr Philip. Got them down to half a metre.

Anything within three hundred metres would be enough, Julia said.

Don't brag so, girl, Philip said as he loaded the figures into an OtherEyes personality package. But a sliver of pride escaped from his thoughts.

So, that just leaves the reactivation code. Juliet, your honour.

She allowed herself one moment of supremely self-indulgent satisfaction.

Access AvengingAngel. The long string of binary digits emerged from her nodes to hang between the three of them. Her grandfather integrated it into the OtherEyes personality package. The completed data construct squirted into the dish transmitter, streaming upwards at lightspeed.

This time, you bastard, this time I'll get you.

43

In his mind the theory was perfect. They weren't particularly high up, and the mud around the tower shouldn't have been deep. Of course, there was no way of actually testing it in advance.

Greg hit the thin coating of surface water and kept on going, his momentum only slowing when the water reached his thighs. He let his knees bend, absorbing inertia. Thick viscous goo rose up his shins, embedding them. That was the point where his left hand thumped into the water, finally overloading his beleaguered cortical node. Greg screamed at the lancets of pain its faltering barricade let through. Brilliant starbursts of light danced across his vision.

His feet were resting on something solid. He could see guttering orange light washing across a big clump of reeds about three metres in front of him, marking the perimeter of a low mound of rubble. A gable end was sticking up in the middle of it, inclined at forty-five degrees, supported by a buttress of rafters which resembled some bizarre geometric whale skeleton.

The water had come up to the bottom of his ribcage, leaving his folded legs entirely under the mud. Greg tried to straighten his knees. It took an age before even the faintest tremble of motion began. The mud refused to let go.

Panic churned his gut. He had absolutely nothing to grip, nothing he could use to drag himself out. His legs muscles had to do all the work. And any second now Kendric's crewmen would be storming out of the tower.

'Where are you, Greg?' Gabriel called.

'I'm coming.' Was he rising fractionally faster? The pain from his left hand had been suppressed again, making it easier to concentrate. He could feel the mud sliding down his thighs. 'Get into the reeds. Go on! Move.'

His buttocks left the mud behind, and he stood up. There was water up to the top of his legs, the mud still incarcerated his knees. Greg brought his left foot out of the mud's suction clutch, standing stork-style, then fell forwards, windmilling his arms.

The strain on his right knee was incredible, his bodyweight was trying to bend it in exactly the opposite direction to which it was designed to hinge. He grabbed at the reeds with his right hand, pulling himself along towards the cover of the mound. The mud relinquished its hold on his right leg with extreme reluctance.

A chorus of wild shouting broke out behind him. Mark's voice rose above the others, bawling to bring some lights.

Greg grasped at another clump of reeds. His progress was a combination of swimming, slithering and crawling, all at a snail's pace. He was completely hampered by his desperation to avoid any commotion. Thankfully, the reeds began to get thicker and higher.

He heard a long erratic stutter of muffled thuds from behind him, and guessed at food cans rupturing in the fire.

A quick glance round let him see the tower, a black phallic monolith probing a cloud-smeared night sky. The first floor's broken window was a glaring yellow rectangle, while others glowed with biolum's softer pink-white radiance; sketchy shadows were moving about inside. Several people were dashing about on the grass ring around the tower's base; three were splashing through the shallows, but not venturing far. If they wanted to get across to the reeds they'd have to get down on their bellies and squirm; it was the only way. They didn't have the motivation. A couple of intense torch beams stabbed out, scouring the reeds.

Greg rolled back on to his stomach and began his serpent wriggle again. Thirty seconds later there was hard ground under his elbows. Reeds competing with stiff blades of grass. He was using his knees as well as his elbows now, scuttling towards the gable end, and cover. He knew exactly what Kendric and Armstrong would do next. Flinty pebbles and rapier grass lacerated his skin. Somewhere over to his left another heavy body was burrowing through the vegetation.

An electromagnetic rifle opened up, warbling loudly. Bullets thudded into the mound, pinged against the brickwork, ricocheted off, whining. Greg kept going.

'Get over there.' That was Kendric's unmistakably enraged voice. Murmurs of argument followed.

The white torchlight trimmed the tips of the reeds around Greg. Tiny reddish-brown ovate flowers glowed lambently. Midges formed a silver galaxy overhead. The light passed on. The electromagnetic rifle had fallen silent.

Greg reached the sloping brickwork. Gabriel was ahead of him, panting heavily at the end of a streaky mud trail.

'God, the smell,' she exclaimed.

'What smell?'

'Some people.'

He climbed gingerly to his feet. The island they were on was about twenty metres at its widest. Greg had cherished a half-notion that the mounds would all be connected. But the next one was a good forty metres away. Algae-curdled water sloshed like crude oil between the two. It didn't look as though there was much of it on top of the mud.

'Clothes off,' Greg said, then flinched as the electromagnetic rifle poured another fusillade of bullets into the gable end.

'Do what?' Gabriel asked. She was cradling her left hand again. Her face was haggard, totally lethargic.

'We've got a lot of swimming to do. Clothes are going to drag us under.'

'Swim where?'

'Clear of the tower, remember? Kilometre at least. How long have we got?'

Gabriel closed her eyes. 'About twenty minutes, maybe less.'

'Do we survive?'

'Some of us do, some of us don't.' She sounded completely disinterested.

Greg ducked his head round the side of the bricks, bringing it back fast. 'Bugger!'

'Now what?'

'They've put the fire out. I was hoping it would be a beacon to the ships on the Nene. Somebody might report it.'

That brought a half-hysterical giggle from Gabriel, ending in a gurgling cough. 'Don't you worry, Greg. Lots of people are going to see your tower before tonight's out. You betcha.'

'Oh, yeah.' He felt stupid. 'Let's go.' He started shrugging out of the dinner jacket, clenching his teeth as his left hand dragged through the arm, it'd swollen badly, skin stretched taut, pulling open the grazes. Trousers followed, and the discovery that buckles are tricky one-handed.

More shouting had broken out from the tower. Lots of conflicting orders interwound with Kendric's repeated urgings and Armstrong's controlled barks.

Gabriel gave him a remorseful stare before starting halfheartedly on the buttons of her blouse. Greg peeled his trousers off and helped her pull her blouse gingerly over her inflated left hand.

'Put your shoes back on,' he said.

A third burst of rifle fire lashed the bricks.

They bent double, keeping the bulk of the small pyramid between themselves and the tower as they crept down to the grey slime. The stuff was semiliquid, a thick gelatine that squelched and undulated alarmingly as Greg immersed himself. It closed around him, finding its way into every orifice. But he didn't sink. In fact the worst of it was on the surface. A sixty-centimetre stratum of water had been sandwiched between the spongy mud and lathery algae.

Gabriel groaned as she lowered herself behind him and the cold mire enveloped her.

Greg began to move, a tortuously slow sidestroke, kicking hard with his feet. Big faecal gobs of the pulpy algae clotted his right arm, splattering over his face. He had to stop every four or five strokes and wipe it off. His eyes were stung raw. Gabriel had it easier. He was pathbreaking for her, clearing a ragged channel.

When they reached the second island, Greg began to worry about what kind of chase was being organized back at the tower. He looked over his shoulder and saw that someone had opened the tower's top-floor window, they were raking the torch beam over the first island and the surrounding water. The light wasn't powerful enough to reach him, but he made Gabriel keep below the wavering tops of the thin reeds as the pair of them crossed over to the island's opposite side.

Away to the right, Greg could see the bloated humps of decomposing tree trunks protruding from the algae like surfaced whales. The number, about thirty, implied some sort of park, which ruled out that direction. They needed to move fast now. Build distance before the tower blew. The park would be genuine swamp, impossible to traverse.

A hundred and fifty metres ahead were the first ranks of buildings recognizable as such; detached houses, their walls partially collapsed and roofs concave, but remaining upright. Bridging the gap was a pockmarked landscape of ash-green atolls separated by hoary stretches of slough.

'Any preference direction-wise?' Greg asked.

Gabriel shook her head. 'No. But you were right about getting clear. That explosion is a brute. I hope I can make it.'

She was a state. Loose folds of flab were caked in thick sable mud, her hair was a tangle of ossifying dreadlocks. Every breath was asthmatic, a battle against coagulating catarrh. She twitched like a palsy victim.

'No problem,' he said, wishing to God he meant it.

They waded into the first slough channel.

The fifth island they came to was much larger than the previous four. Iron girders were sticking out among the sedges. There was more grass than reeds on the crest. Soil had begun to accumulate in the crevices between the fragments of stone and cement. Greg cut his calf on something jagged. Cursed.

The island's far shore brought them to within thirty metres of the houses. One more immersion and back on to solid ground. This time it was a long straight ridge parallel to the row of houses. It was cluttered with twisted, drooping chimney stacks, and buckled rafter apexes gnarled with scabby lichens; slate tiles formed a loose flaky shingle beneath their feet, making the going hard.

Just as he reached the summit, Greg heard the sound. A low-volume hum in the background. But rising in pitch and intensity, in menace. A note he was irksomely familiar with.

'Move out, doubletime,' he said. 'The bastards have inflated the hovercraft.'

'No more,' Gabriel said wretchedly.

'One last time. That's all. Then it'll all be over.'

'Yes. Yes, you're right. Only a few minutes left. It's clearing, Greg. So much clearer now.'

Realization struck. He could sense her mind. A pale disconsolate mist of disjointed thoughts, fluttering aimlessly, corrupted with coarse threads of harrowing pain. Gabriel was animated by adrenalin alone, and her endocrine glands were virtually exhausted.

They'd escaped the twins' nullifying effect. Greg let his gland run riot, charging his cerebellum to overload, and screw the risk. Synapses vibrated shrilly under the stress, delusional ripping sounds filtered into his ears, coming from inside his skull, neurone membranes splitting open. His espersense swept out. It was a heady boost. Whole once more.

Two hovercraft were curving away from the tower, each containing three minds, radiant hard-wound balls of mercurial

454

malevolence. Greg recognized Toby riding in one of them, along with a couple of crewmen he couldn't place. Mark and Kendric were paired in the second, along with its pilot. There was no sign of the other minds Greg knew to be out there – Armstrong and Turner, not even Hermione. The tower was an empty shell to his espersense, which meant at least one twin had remained behind. The big question was whether the third hovercraft had been inflated.

A faint haze of small minds glowed around the wavering perimeter of his espersense, occasional twinkles within. Animals of some sort, clinging to a dour existence amid the ruins. Abandoned pets reverted to their true feral nature, rodents scrabbling to stay above the mud, an invasion of reptiles.

He pulled Gabriel roughly down the slope and into the bog which covered the street, ignoring her weepy cries of protest. They didn't have to swim. The syrupy mud drowning the tarmac was only a few centimetres deep, lapping over his feet like slushed snow. It was possible to wade. The raft of algae came up to mid-thigh.

Greg was nearly tempted to hide in one of the houses. None of them had doors or windows left. Pick one at random and cower down. Unless the hovercraft boasted some pretty sophisticated sensors, Kendric and Toby would never find him in time. But the dangerously dilapidated condition of the walls stopped him. If the tower went up with anything like the violence Gabriel claimed the friable houses would collapse on top of them.

They reached a mouldering dune which had once been a leylandii hedge, and squelched over it. Greg saw two white aureoles sliding fluidly across the horizon behind them, winding down through the slough channels. The drone of the hovercraft propellers drifted in and out of audibility. Kendric and Toby were fanning out, their search pattern carrying them further apart. At least it was only two.

He steered Gabriel down the narrow dank gully between two houses. There were animals on the other side of the walls, more than he'd originally thought, scurrying around frantically. The garden at the rear of the house backed on to another garden. Head-high panel fencing marked out the boundary, putrefying laths drooping under their own weight. In one corner was a greenhouse whose panes were pasted with hand-sized valentine leaves. Some abandoned horticultural treasure had thrived in the heat and abundant nutrient-soaked mud, making it look as though the aluminium-framed structure was about to burst apart at the seams.

Caustic fingers of silver-white light probed through a gap between a couple of houses a hundred metres away. The propeller noise was loud, fluctuating in strident piccolo whistles. Greg sensed Toby's churlish mind; the man was spite-laden, yearning to be the one who found the quarry. Instinct chafed at him. He knew Greg was near by. A nature-ordained hunter.

The bulk of the houses blocked off the light as the hovercraft glided down the street. Then the questing fingers reappeared, closer this time, three houses away.

Greg urged Gabriel behind the greenhouse, and waited until the searchlight fluoresced the verdant avocado-green leaves.

The green corona died as the hovercraft moved on, but Greg knew that knot of determination in Toby's mind. He'd order the pilot to take the hovercraft down the gardens once he reached the end of the street.

His espersense tracked Kendric, who was still patrolling the slough channels. They couldn't go back, and the blast would turn the confined gardens into a death-trap of flying masonry.

'Through there.' Greg pointed ahead. The row of houses in front of them was virtually identical to the ones behind, only in slightly better condition. Gabriel moved like an automaton.

Greg kicked at the panel fence, tearing through it like tissue paper. There was a fruit cage on the other side, a box made from galvanized steel poles wrapped in a tattered cobweb of black nylon netting. The sight of it sparked an idea.

He reached up to one of the crossbeams with his right hand and began to tug. The pole was held in place between the uprights by two moulded plastic sockets at each end, both of them fractured and bleached by the decade-long torrent of UV-infested sunlight. One of the sockets crackled at the pressure he applied, then snapped abruptly. Greg yanked the other end of the pole out of its socket with a burst of ebullient strength, tearing the netting as it came free. The pole was three metres long, in good condition; the zinc coating had whitened down the years, but it'd protected the steel from rust.

'What's happening?' Gabriel asked.

'I'm improvising a little present for Toby.' There was no longer any vindictiveness at the prospect, nor even malice. This was an intrinsic fight for survival now, nothing more. His mind had relegated Toby to an obstacle which had to be tackled. Hatred was all the other man's problem.

Greg clamped the pole between his knees and tied on a strip of the ripped nylon mesh. It was a laborious job, he had to use his teeth to grip the end of the strip while his fingers formed the knot. Spears didn't come any more primitive, but the rudimentary tail ought to keep its trajectory stable for a few metres.

They slogged towards a narrow alleyway between the two houses ahead, the disturbingly concave walls had so many bricks missing they looked like two vertical checkerboards. There was an unstable aggregation of brick chunks and sandy earth in the gap, rising half a metre above the algae. Greg had lost his shoes somewhere in the slough channels; his feet were unrecognizable, lumps of gummy tar which ached abominably. If he stood on anything sharp they'd go completely numb as the pain breached the cortical node's threshold. When they reached the small front garden they were knee-deep in the greasy mire again.

The street they found themselves in was virtually intact. Greg could almost believe he'd walked out into a pre-dawn autumn morning of fifteen years ago. Rusted, windowless hulks of petrol-driven cars were parked along the road. Barren trees stood tall, low brick walls were topped by fanciful wrought-iron railings, the lampposts were still vertical. It was a well-ordered slice of middle-class suburbia. Only the algae-matted water shattered the illusion of normality.

A curtain of light streaked out at the far end of the houses a hundred and fifty metres away. Toby's hovercraft had turned down into the gardens. Greg sensed the excitement rising in the man's mind. Toby's native instinct was telling him his prey was near by.

Greg found it uncanny to observe, almost as though his own ability was being turned against him. He and Toby must share the same mental genotype.

'I want you to walk down to the other end of the street,' he told Gabriel.

She didn't reply, standing with shoulders drooping, arms dangling at her side. Her left hand looked appalling, tumescent and inflamed. Mud had dried and cracked on it, as though she was shedding a hardened outer skin, allowing new, blue-tender flesh to break through. He refused the impulse to check his own.

'Listen, Gabriel. You must walk down the street. And when the hovercraft comes, you fall down. OK? That's all. Can you manage that for me?'

A confused frown puckered her forehead. 'Walk?'

'Yes.' Greg pressed his hand on her back, starting her off. 'And when the light shines, you go for cover.'

Gabriel's feet had found a shuffling rhythm. 'Fall down?'

'That's right.'

'Orders,' she mumbled vaguely. 'I won't let you down, Greg. I won't.'

Greg left her doing her apathetic sleep walk, feeling a prize turd for using her as bait; and headed back up the street towards the wide beam of light which kept shooting out, document-ing the hovercraft's progress. Algae foamed around his knees. Slithery mud tried to pull his feet from under him. Sometimes he thought he could feel the hardness of the tarmac.

The light shone out of the gap in front of him. Greg stood still, listening to the drone of the propeller growing louder, echoing back and forth across the street. The light was extinguished. A faint trace of it rippled along the roof of the house.

Toby's hovercraft drew level with him. Light slammed out of the gap, transfixing him like a rabbit in a headlamp.

A scream of ecstatic triumph burst from Toby's mind. Greg's vision was wiped out in a sparkling pink mist as his retinas were overwhelmed by a targeting laser. He lurched forwards. The warbling of electromagnetic rifle fire punctured the night. Bullets stitched a line of small craters in the algae behind him. The propeller drone rose to a crescendo as the pilot fought to turn the hovercraft.

Greg was dumped into the darkness again. The laser impact abated, and he saw a smattering of stars through the shredded gauze of cirrus clouds. He could hear the ripping sounds of the hovercraft riding roughshod over fences.

Greg felt his nerves cooling, heartbeat slowing, tension abating. Going with the flow.

He sensed the hovercraft racing down the gardens, heading back the way it'd come.

A final visual check on Gabriel showed him a forlorn figure bumbling through the mire. His espersense showed her mind was operating with cyborg simplicity, completely absorbed by the mechanics of walking.

He lowered himself into the algae.

The hovercraft had reached the end of the gardens now, rounding the last house in the row. Greg caught a glimpse of its insect eye array of lights sliding into view as he dropped below the surface.

Espersense revealed all he needed, real and hypersense universes entwining smoothly. Toby leaning against the prow, fists clenched, eyes bugging, slipstream plucking at him. The merciless lights finding Gabriel. Her legs buckling, sending her toppling forwards. Toby's howl of revenge consummation.

Greg could hear a throbbing sound transmitted through the filthy water, getting louder.

Toby's mind was a lurid spew-point of animus thoughts zooming towards him.

Greg pressed his feet down hard as the hovercraft rumbled

directly overhead. He broke surface, bringing a cloying cone of algae with him. A blast of desert-air wind escaping from beneath the hovercraft skirt ablated the mucus from his face. He kept rising like a shabby tenth-rate Neptune, galvanized spear in his hand, already drawn back for the throw. Aiming. The pole steady. And *fling*.

It shot through the wide mesh of the protective carbon fibre grille at the rear of the hovercraft, hitting the spinning propeller full on. The trajectory bent then as the tip was chopped by the blade's leading edge, tugging it down and round. That, by itself, wasn't disastrous, the blade edge was designed to handle bird impacts. But the length of the pole meant it was deflected right into the mounting. The propeller's axle-bearing sheared off instantly under the terrible impact stress. And a two-metre-diameter five-hundred-r.p.m. buzz-saw exploded out of the grille to digest the rear of the pneumatic hovercraft.

There was a thunderclap blow-out, and the prow of the hovercraft bucked up into the air, losing rigidity, light beams strafing the sky. Three bodies and pieces of loose equipment were catapulted in a short arc. A tremendous spume of water jetted up as the propeller hit the algae, chewing through. One of the bodies fell into its base. The shredded hovercraft hull flopped back down. The lights went out, and the spume died.

It began to rain gobs of mud and algae, pattering down over a wide area.

One mind had survived, the body which housed it writhing feebly. Another body was face down in the water, Toby. Of the third there was no sign.

Greg waded forward. It was easy going. A vast patch of the street had been stripped of its covering of algae.

Gabriel was floating on her back, half submerged. Greg got his hand under her head and lifted her. She coughed weakly. 'I did it, didn't I, Greg? Just like you wanted.'

'Sure did, and no messing.'

'Did you get 'em?'

'Yeah, they aren't going to hazard anyone again.'

Four lightbeams pinioned him. Kendric's hovercraft was turning down into the street. He froze into place. Too exhausted to run. Besides, he could never have left Gabriel.

The hovercraft approached at a cautious unhurried pace. Greg shielded his eyes against the glare. Kendric was standing in the prow, in front of the Perspex windscreen. The epitome of the great white hunter, electromagnetic rifle cradled in a light grip, one foot on the gunwale.

Greg saw it coming, reading it straight from Gabriel's mind. Genuine telepathy. His mouth gaped, and he pointed high into the western sky.

Kendric's mind registered sublime contempt that Greg would try such a pathetic stunt. Then vacillation set in, precisely because it was so unlikely. He looked round to follow the direction of Greg's accusing finger, just in time to see a frigid saffron dawn expand across the sky above Wisbech.

The light source was directly above them, a cold dazzling star which crawled through the genuine constellations at an infinitesimal pace. Its radiance was throwing shadows as sharp-edged as daylight. Greg could see wisps of flurry cloud gusting high overhead, they must've been kilometres away.

Gabriel began to laugh.

The false star was as intense as noonday sunlight, then brighter. It began to elongate. Brick walls glared scarlet. Dew-mottled algae sparkled like a diamanté ice floe.

Intuition whispered into Greg's brain. He *knew*. The Merlin. Then his far-flung espersense delivered the final shock, a single band of incendiary thought originating from the space-probe's bioware nodes: Philip Evans's unholy vengeance glee as he hurtled inexorably towards Leopold Armstrong.

The Merlin descended at orbital velocity, boring a vacuum-tunnel through the lower atmosphere. A purple-white plasma comet with a rigid incandescent tail of superionized air, stabbing down like some monstrously overpowered strategic defence laser.

Greg flung his arms desperately over his face, trying to save his eyes. There was carmine blood-light, then sable blackness.

461

The blast wave was a white-noise tsunami. It plucked Greg out of the mire and sent him spinning through space. He could see the street's houses disintegrating, slates taking flight, bricks avalanching. The air had become a blizzard of giant splinters and powdery fragments.

He saw the tower. Rather, where the tower had been: a thick column of fusion-hot air fountaining up into the darkening sky. Its flickering vermilion fluorescence was sheathed by ragged braids of ebony soot-clouds. Garish blue-green static webs discharged around its mushrooming crown.

For a liquid, the water was incredibly hard.

44

Greg woke to peace, body and mind. Blissful. He could feel his entire body except for his left hand, and nothing hurt, nothing felt abused. There was just warmth and softness.

Makes a bloody change.

He opened his eyes. Even the light was gentle, pale pearl. Rapid blinking resolved the blurred shapes around him.

He was lying on his back looking up at an ivory-coloured ceiling with inset biolum strips. A young man in a white medical-style coat was removing an electrode hoop from his forehead.

'Welcome back, Mr Mandel,' he said.

That humourless tone, his intent professionalism. He had to belong to Event Horizon.

'There is no need to worry,' the doctor assured Greg. 'You are a patient in Event Horizon's Liezen clinic – that's in Austria.'

'Who's worrying?'

The doctor nodded earnestly. 'Ah, good. Sometimes there is disorientation following a prolonged somnolence induction.'

'What do you call prolonged?'

'Eight days. In addition to your physical injuries you were suffering from advanced cerebral stress due to an overdose of neurohormones. I've loaded a prohibition order into your cortical node preventing any gland secretions. Come back in three months, and I'll wipe the order; or you might consider having the gland itself extracted.' His nose twitched. 'I don't approve of them, personally.'

'Thank you, Doctor.' Julia's cut-crystal voice chopped off any further admonishments. 'That will be all.'

The doctor sighed resignedly, and backed away.

Greg turned his head. He was in a small tidy room with plenty of medical gear modules stacked beside the bed. A picture window looked out over sunny parkland dotted with grazing llamas.

The bed was elevating him smoothly into a sitting position. His arms lay outside the ochre blankets. A chalky-coloured bioware bladder had been inflated around his left hand, trailing scores of fine fibre-optic cables to the gear modules, its nutrient fluid veins pulsing rhythmically. Just as well, he didn't particularly fancy looking at the hand.

Julia was wearing a crinkled navy-blue sundress. The skirt was shorter than her usual, its hem hovering well above her knees. She was watching him with silent diligence.

'The hair's nice,' Greg told her. Tiny corkscrew curls had fluffed it out into a candyfloss cloud. A chain of minute blue flowers formed a delicate tiara above her brow. Given a posy of primroses she would've made a good bridesmaid, he thought.

'Oh, you think so?' A dainty long-fingered hand lifted to pat a few of the more wayward strands. 'Adrian likes it this way.'

'Lucky old Adrian.'

The door closed behind the doctor.

Julia's face fell, giving him a woeful stare. 'I'm so sorry, Greg. Really I am. None of this need have happened. It's all my fault.'

'Don't be silly.'

'But it is.'

Greg listened as she launched into an explanation about the Cray files, her mistrust, the St Christopher. There was no energy in him to power any strong feelings about it, one way or the other, anger or despair. The issue seemed an abstract. It was over, all it could ever be now was an exercise in 'what if'. The whole bloody great cock-up was down to his over-reliance on mystic intuition, treating it as infallible, giving logical thought the big elbow. His own stupid fault.

He let out a long dispirited sigh, and said, 'Forgiven. Besides, you were right, I should've seen Ellis's connection with the PSP. And I missed Steven as well. That's got to make us quits.'

'Really? Did you really mean you forgive me?' She was studying his face, trepidation lurking in her expressive tawny eyes.

Julia wanted absolution, so he smiled and said, 'Yeah, I really do. No messing.' He'd sought it for himself often enough. He could hardly deny her.

She flashed him a hundred-watt grin and sat on the edge of the bed. 'I've been terrified of you waking up all week. You were the last loose end. I've made my peace with everyone else.'

'Everyone?' His thoughts moved slowly. 'Hey, what about Gabriel?'

'She's all right. Everyone is all right now. Treating you all at the clinic was the least I could do.' Her lips came together pensively. 'They took Gabriel's gland out two days ago. She insisted, said it was part of her deal.'

That would take a while to sink in, Greg knew. Gabriel without her gland would be interesting. Maybe she'd even get back into shape, take part in life. Nice idea.

'How did you get us out?' Greg asked.

'Oh, Teddy and Morgan Walshaw jumped a Prowler over to Wisbech about twenty minutes after the blast. I wanted to go.' Her face hardened slightly at the memory. 'They both said no. Only thing those two ever did agree on.'

'Teddy? How do you know Teddy?'

Julia's smile was taunting. 'You've got a bit of catching up to do. I'll let Eleanor explain. I pulled rank to be here when they woke you, but I'd better not stay much longer or she'll be bashing the door down to get at you. She's good at that.' The smile turned devilish. 'I might've known you'd prefer the buxom type. And you're lucky to have her, Greg. We've spent a lot of time talking this last week. I've got to know her quite well. She's a smashing girl.'

'You think I don't know?'

Julia nodded in satisfaction. 'Good. You'll be quite all right to have children, by the way The Merlin's isotopes were left in orbit, there was no radioactive fallout.'

'You did it. You shut it down.'

'Yah. It was all I had, Greg. I told you, I knew it was Kendric who was behind the blitz; somehow, somewhere along the line, he'd be there. I didn't know who to trust. The Merlin was the one global-range weapon which was totally under my direct control, I didn't have to go through anyone, ask anyone's permission. My executive code gave me unlimited access to the Astronautics Institute's memory cores. I pulled the Merlin's command codes, and used them to put it into stasis. I was going to kill Kendric with it. When he was out at sea on the *Mirriam*, where no one else could get hurt. The Merlin can fly twelve million kilometres and find a rock two hundred metres across; dropping it three and half thousand kilometres on to a sixty-metre target is no problem. All I'd need to do was place a satellite call to Kendric, and I'd have *Mirriam*'s position down to a metre, constantly updated. Not that I needed a direct hit; even with its isotopes and ninety per cent of its fuel dumped, the Merlin still masses over a tonne. And, well, you saw how big a kinetic punch it packed travelling at that velocity.'

'Yeah, I saw. What did happen to Kendric? I survived.'

Julia glanced out at the grassland beyond the window, expression neutral. 'They only brought you and Gabriel back. I didn't ask. You can if you want.'

'No. Not necessary.' Not with Teddy in the rescue party. Walshaw too, come to that; maybe especially Walshaw.

Julia bent over and touched her lips to his, a soft dry kiss. 'First time,' she murmured huskily. 'Thank you, Greg.' There was a draught of some expensive Parisian scent, then she was standing up briskly. 'Memento for you.' She hung the St Christopher on the bedpost. 'Don't worry, it doesn't work any more.'

'Pity, I'd feel safer.'

'Must dash, got a lesson with Royan. He's teaching me to write proper hotrod software.'

Greg almost asked. But settled for hearing it from Eleanor instead.

Julia opened the door. Eleanor stood outside, looking grand even in the shapeless white clinic robe she was wearing. There was something not quite right about the way she walked, and the skin on her face seemed to be peeling, except for two patches around her eyes.

The two girls exchanged a glance as they passed. Smiled knowingly.

'All yours,' said Julia.

A QUANTUM MURDER

1

It was the third Thursday in January, and after a fortnight of daily drizzles the first real storm of England's monsoon season was due to arrive sometime in the late afternoon. The necklace of Earth Resource platforms which the Event Horizon corporation maintained in low Earth orbit had observed the storm forming out in the Atlantic west of Portugal for the last two days: the clash of air fronts, the favourable combination of temperature and humidity. Multi-spectrum photon amps tracked the tormented streamers of cloud as they streaked towards England, building in power, in velocity. The satellite channels had started issuing the Meteorological Office warnings on the breakfast 'casts. Right across the country, in urban and rural areas alike, people were hurrying to secure their property and homes, lead animals to shelter, and protect the crops and groves.

Had the Earth Resource platforms focused on the county of Rutland as the dawn rose, any observer would have been drawn to the eastern boundary, where the vast Y-shaped reservoir of Rutland Water was reflecting a splendid coronal shimmer of rose-gold sunlight back up into the sky. The Hambleton peninsula protruded from the reservoir like a surfaced whale, four kilometres long, one wide. Hambleton Wood was sprawled across a third of the southern slope, its oak and ash trees killed off by the torrid year-long heat of the Warming which had replaced the old seasons. The rotting trunks were now besieged by a tangled canopy of creepers and ivy, carrion plants feeding off the mulchy bark of the once sturdy giants they choked. Another, smaller, expired copse lay broken on the northern side, adding to the general impression of decay. But a good half of the remaining farmland had been converted to citrus groves, sprouting a vigorous green patina of life. The peninsula was an ideal location to grow fruit; Rutland Water provided unlimited irrigation water during the parched summer months. Hambleton itself, a hamlet of stone houses with a beautiful little church and one pub, nestled on the western side, the whale's tail, above a narrow spit of land which linked it with the Vale of Catmose. There was a single road running precariously along the peninsular spine; grass and weeds nibbling away at the edges of the tarmac had reduced it to a barely navigable strip.

At quarter-past nine in the morning, Corry Furness turned off the road a kilometre past Hambleton, freewheeling his mountain bike down the sloping track to the Mandel farmhouse, tyres slipping dangerously on the damp moss and loose limestone.

Greg Mandel caught a glimpse of the lad from the corner of his eye, a slash of colour skidding down the last twenty metres of the slope into the farmyard, clutching frantically at the brakes. Greg had been out in the field since half-past seven, planting nearly thirty tall saplings of gene-tailored lime trees in the sodden earth, binding them to two-metre-high stakes which he hoped would given them enough anchorage to withstand the storms. When it was finished the lime grove would cover half a hectare of the ground between the farmhouse and the eastern edge of Hambleton Wood. The planting should have been safely completed a week ago, but the saplings had arrived late from the nursery, and the mechanical digger he was using had developed a hydraulic fault that took him a day to fix. He still had two hundred trees left to put in.

Greg had thought his early start would give him enough time to finish at least fifty before lunch: he was already resigned to carting the rest into the barn until the storm passed. But watching Corry barely miss the side of the barn, then shout urgently at Eleanor who was painting the ground-floor windows, he knew even that small hope had just vanished. Eleanor pointed at him, and Corry ran over the shaggy grass.

Greg switched off the little digger and climbed out of the cab, wellingtons squelching in the mud. He was on the last row, just twenty saplings and stakes left to go. They were all laid out ready. Patchy clouds tumbled across the sky, and the reservoir's far shore gleamed from last night's rain, wisps of mist already rising as the day's heat began to build.

'Sir, sir, Dad sent me, sir,' Corry shouted. The lad was about ten or twelve, his face ruddy from exertion, fright and exhilaration burning in his eyes. 'Please sir, they're going to kill him, sir!' He slithered the last two metres, and Greg caught him.

'Kill who, Corry?'

Corry struggled to gulp down some air. 'Mr Collister, sir. There's everybody up there at his house now. They're saying he used to be a Party Apache.'

'*Apparatchik*,' Greg corrected grimly.

'Yes, sir. He wasn't, was he?'

Greg started walking towards the farm. 'Who knows?'

'I liked Mr Collister,' Corry said insistently.

'Yeah,' Greg said. Roy Collister was a solicitor who worked in Oakham; an unobtrusive, pleasant man. He came into the village pub most nights. Someone who moaned about work and the price of beer and inflation. Greg had shared a pint with him often enough. 'He's a nice man.' And that's always the worst thing about it, Greg thought. Four years after the People's Socialism Party fell, ending ten years of a disastrous near-Marxist style government, people found it hard to forget, let alone forgive the misery and fear they had endured. Hatred was still simmering strongly below the surface of the nation's psyche. As for Collister, Greg had seen it before: the allegations, the pointed finger. One hint, one whispered suspicion, was all it took: the serpent of guilt never rested after that, gnawing at people's minds. Even the informants working for the People's Constables weren't as bad; at least they had to produce some kind of evidence before they got their blood money.

Eleanor was already backing the powerful four-wheel-drive English Motor Company Ranger out of the barn when he reached the yard. It was a grey-painted farm utility vehicle, with a squat boxy body on high, toughened suspension coils; the marque was the first of a new generation, powered by Event Horizon giga-conductor cells instead of the old-fashioned high-density polymer batteries.

She gave him a tight-lipped look which said it all. It took a lot to upset Eleanor.

They had been married just over a year. She had been twenty-one years old the day she walked down the aisle of Hambleton's church, seventeen years younger than him, although that had never been an issue. Her face was heart shaped, liberally splattered with freckles; a petite nose and wide green eyes were framed by a mane of thick red hair which she brushed back from a broad forehead. Physically, she was an all-out assault on his preferences. An adolescence spent on a PSP-subsidized kibbutz where manual labour was emphasized and revered had given her the kind of robust figure a channel starlet would kill for. Eleanor didn't see it quite in those terms, though she had come to accept his unending enthusiasm and compliments with a kind of bemused tolerance. Even now, dressed in a paint-splattered blue boiler suit, she looked tremendous.

Greg climbed into the Ranger's passenger seat, and shut the door. 'I want you to walk back into the village,' he told Corry. 'Will you do that for me?' He didn't want the lad to witness the lynch mob, whatever the outcome was.

'Yes, sir.'

'And don't worry.'

'I won't, sir.'

Eleanor steered the Ranger out of the farmyard and on to the track, moving expertly through the gears as the tyres fought for traction on the treacherous surface.

'Did you know about Collister?' she asked.

'No.' Which was odd. Not even his intuition had given him an inkling. And it should have done. Intuition was one of his two psi faculties which were educed by neurohormones.

It was the English army which had given him a bioware endrocrine gland implant, a sophisticated construct of neuro-secretory cells which consumed his blood and extravasated psi-stimulant neurohormones under the control of a cortical processor.

He had been transferred out of his old parachute regiment when the combined services' assessment test graded him ESP positive and shoved straight into the newly formed Mindstar Brigade, along with five hundred other slightly befuddled recruits. Psi-stimulant neurohormones had been demonstrated the year before by the American DARPA office, and Mindstar was the Ministry of Defence's eager response to the potential of psychics providing the perfect intelligence-gathering corps. An idea the tabloid channels swiftly dubbed 'Mind Wars'. It was a pity nobody paid much attention to the number of qualifiers in the early DARPA press releases.

Based on the assessment test results, Mindstar expected Greg to develop an eldritch sixth sense, a continent-spanning X-ray sight which could locate enemy installations, no matter how well concealed. Instead he became empathic. It was a useful trait for interrogating captured prisoners, but hardly warranted the mil-lion and a half pounds invested in his gland and his training.

He wasn't alone in disappointing the Mindstar brass. The assessment tests only indicated the general area of a recruit's ability; how a brain's actual psychic faculties would develop after a gland was implanted was beyond prediction. The results were extremely mediocre: very few Mindstar recruits produced any-thing like the performance expected. The brigade had been reluctantly disbanded a few months before the PSP took its ideological knife to the defence budget.

Greg's claims that his intuition had also been enhanced by the gland were discounted by the sounder minds of the general staff as typical squaddie superstition. He shrugged and kept quiet: never volunteer for anything. But intuition had saved him and his tactical raider squad on more than one occasion when he saw action in Turkey.

So why hadn't it given him any forewarning about Ray Collister?

'Nobody expects you to be perfect,' Eleanor said quietly.

He nodded shortly. She could plug into his emotions with the same efficiency as his espersense rooted around in other people's minds. 'I'll bet Douglas Kellam is leading the pack,' he said. Douglas Kellam, who fancied himself in the role of local squire, the village's loudest anti-PSP Momus. Now it was safe to speak out.

'From the rear, yes,' she agreed.

He grunted wryly. 'Who would have thought it, you and I rushing to rescue an *apparatchik*?'

'But we are though, aren't we? Instinctively. It's not so much what Collister was, but what Kellam's mob will do. There'll be hell to pay the morning after, there always is.'

'Yeah.'

'But?'

'What if he turns out to be one of the high grades?'

'He won't,' she said firmly. 'You would have known if he was anything important.'

'Now there's confidence.' He hoped to God she was right.

The EMC Ranger lurched out on to the road. Eleanor gunned the accelerator, wheels tearing gashes in the tarmac's thin moss covering. Fans of white spray fountained up as they shot through the long puddles which lay along the ruts.

Greg looked out of the window. On the other side of the reservoir's broad southern prong he could see the Berrybut Spinney time-share estate sitting on the slope directly opposite the farmhouse. It was set in a rectangular clearing above the shoreline, a horseshoe of wooden chalets with a big stone clubhouse and hotel at the apex. The spinney was a mix of dead trunks festooned with creepers and new trees, tanbark oaks,

Californian laurels, Chinese yews, and other varieties imported from tropical and sub-tropical zones as the year-round heat killed off native vegetation. Their shapes and colours were strange in comparison to the glorious old deciduous forests which occupied so many of his childhood memories.

The hurriedly enacted One Home Law had enabled the local council to commandeer the chalets and hotel to provide emergency accommodation for people displaced from low-lying coastal lands by rising seas. He had spent the PSP decade living in one of the chalets, telling people he was a private detective, a perfect cover occupation for someone with his, ability. He even managed to attract a few paying cases to add authenticity. Then a couple of years after the PSP's demise Eleanor came into his life, and at the same time the gigantic Event Horizon company hired him to clear up a security violation problem. The case had turned out to be far more complex and involved than anyone had realized at the start, and the bonuses and favours he and Eleanor were given by its extremely grateful owner, Julia Evans, were enough to retire on – enough for their grandchildren to retire on, come to that. Multi-billionairesses, especially teenage ones, he reflected, had no concept of gracious restraint, certainly not when it came to money.

It left him and Eleanor with the problem of what to do next. Lotus eating was fine, they both agreed, providing it was in the context of a break from real life. They had sunk some (a fraction) of their money into the run-down farmhouse with its neglected fields, and moved in after their honeymoon, both of them eager for the kind of quiet yet busy life the citrus groves would give them.

He could see a pile of ash just below the chalets, a pink glow still visible. The residents lit a bonfire each night, using it to bake food, and as a focal point for company. An undemanding style of life; not quite the archetypical poor but happy existence, but damn close. Geography wasn't all the move across the water entailed.

*

A horse-drawn cart, piled high with bales of hay, was clumping slowly down Hambleton's main street as they drove in. Eleanor swerved round it smoothly, drawing a frightened whinny from the mud-caked shire horse and a shaken fist from the driver. If it wasn't for the glossy black solar panels clipped over the slate roofs and a clump of well-established coconut trees in the churchyard the hamlet could have passed as a rural scene from the nineteen-hundreds. Gardens seemed to merge lazily into the verges. Tall stumps of copper beech and sycamore trees lined the road, festooned in vines which dangled colourful flower clusters; a frost of greenery which brought a semblance of life to the dead trunks. But only from a distance; wind, entropy, and vigorous insects had already pruned away the twigs and smaller branches, leaving frayed ends of pale-grey sun-bleached wood jutting out of the shaggy hide.

Roy Collister's home was one of the smaller cottages a couple of hundred metres from the Finch's Arms. It personified the retirement-cottage dream; gentrified during the end of the last century, yellow-grey stonework pointed up, windows double-glazed, brick chimney-stacks repaired. More recently it had acquired a row of solar panels above the guttering to provide power after the gas and electricity grids were shut down at the start of the PSP years. Three bulky air conditioners had been mounted on the side wall to cope with the stifling air which invariably saturated the interior of pre-Warming buildings. The front garden was given over to vegetable plots, and the fence had disappeared under a long mound of gene-tailored brambles, with clumps of ripe blackberries as large as crab-apples hanging loosely.

Greg was already opening his door as Eleanor drew up outside. He was vaguely aware of pale faces in the windows of the houses opposite, interested and no doubt appalled by what was going on, but not doing anything about it. The English way, Greg reflected. People had learned to keep their heads down during the PSP decade, avoiding attention was a healthy survival trait while the Constables were on the prowl. A habit like that was hard to snuff.

The wooden gate through the dune of brambles was swinging slowly to and fro on its hinges, and two of the ground-floor bay windows had been smashed. When he reached the front door he saw the wood around the lock was splintered; judging by the marks on the paintwork someone had taken a sledgehammer to it. There was the sound of angry voices inside.

Greg walked into the hall and ordered a low-level secretion from his gland. As always, he pictured a lozenge of liver-like flesh nestled tumour-fashion at the heart of his brain, squirting out cold milky liquids into surrounding synapses. In fact, neither gland nor neurohormones looked anything like the mental mirage, but he'd never quite managed to throw off the idiosyncrasy – Mindstar psychologists had told him not to worry, a lot of psychics developed quirks of a much higher order. His perception shifted subtly, making the universe just that fraction lighter, more translucent. Auras seemed to prevail, even in inert matter, their misty planes corresponding to the physical structures around him. Living creatures glowed. A world comprising coloured shadows.

There were twelve people in the lounge, making the small room seem oppressively crowded and stuffy. Greg recognized most of them. Villagers, that same quiet friendly bunch in the pub each night. Frankie Owen, the local professional dole-dependant and fish poacher, leaning on his sledgehammer, resting after a bout of singularly mindless destruction. He had set about the furniture, smashing up the Queen Anne coffee table and oak-veneered secretaire and dresser; the three-metre flatscreen on the wall had a big frost star dead centre. Expressing himself the only way he knew how. Mark Sutton and Andrew Foster, powerful men who worked as labourers in the groves, were sitting on Roy Collister behind the overturned settee. The slightly built solicitor's clothes were torn, his face had been reduced to pulped flesh, cuts weeping blood on to the beige carpet.

Clare Collister was being held by Les Hepburn and Ronnie Kay. Greg hadn't seen much of her since he moved into the farm, she didn't venture out very often; an ordinarily prim thirty-five-year-old, with rusty brown hair and a long face. She had obviously been struggling hard, one eye was bruised, swelling badly, her blouse was torn, revealing her left breast. Les Hepburn had a vicious grip on the back of her head, knuckles white with the strain of forcing her to watch her husband being beaten.

And of course, Douglas Kellam, chief cheerleader, standing in the tight circle of onlookers, a forty-five-year-old with a round face, slender moustache and fading brown hair; dressed in blue trousers and white shirt, thin green tie. Smart and respectable even now, although his face was flushed from the kind of exhilaration Greg was wearily familiar with: the thrill of the illicit. Douglas was the descendant of the original Victorian toff, a master of duplicity. Perfectly suited to attending a charity dinner then going on to a pit-bull fight, watching Globecast's Euroblue channel at night, condemning it by day.

The jeering and shouting cut off dead as Greg stepped into the lounge. Andrew Sutton froze with a fist cocked in midair, his knuckles wet with Collister's blood, looking up at Greg, suddenly pathetic with guilt.

With his espersense expanded, the group's emotions impinged directly into Greg's synapses, a clamour of blood-lust and anger and secret guilt. They were feeding off each other, building up a collective nerve for the finale. It would end with a shot-gun blast, the cottage set on fire, consuming bodies and direct evidence. And the police would turn a blind eye; overstretched, undermanned, and still trying to regain public trust, to shake off the association with the People's Constables. They couldn't afford to be seen taking sides with PSP relics.

'What the fuck do you think you're doing?' Greg asked, and there was no need to force a tired tone into his voice, it came all too easily.

'The bastard's Party, Greg,' someone called.

'No messing? Have you seen his card? Was it signed by

President Armstrong himself?' He was aware of Eleanor coming to stand behind him. Her presence sparked off a ripple of severe agitation in the minds around him.

'He's guilty, Greg. The Inquisitors said he was an *apparatchik* over in Market Harborough.'

'Ah . . .' he said. The Inquisitors (actually, the Inappropriate Appointee Investigation Bureau) had been set up by the New Conservative government to purge PSP appointees from Civil Service posts, where it was feared they would deliberately misuse their positions to stir up trouble in their own interest. Identifying them had turned out to be an almost impossible task, a lot of records had been lost or destroyed when the PSP fell. Nearly all the old Party's premier grades had been routed out, they were notorious enough in their own areas for the Inquisitor teams not to need official datawork; but the small fry, the invisible Party hacks who did the committees' groundwork, they were hard to pin down. A lot of suspect names had been leaking from the Inquisitors' office lately. Rough justice eradicated the tricky problem of no verifiable evidence.

'An official charge has been brought against him, has it?' Greg asked.

'No,' Douglas Kellam said. 'But we've heard. Bytes that came straight from the top.' His voice changed to a slicker, more appealing tone. In his mind there was still the hope that he could win through, a refusal to admit defeat. And nervousness that was beginning to churn up through his subconscious, like all of them, all disquieted by Greg and the infamous gland.

Sometimes, Greg reflected, an unending diet of tabloid crap could be useful. He smiled humourlessly. 'Sure they did. Your cousin's friend's sister, was it?'

'Come on, Greg. He's Red trash, for Christ's sake. You don't want him around Hambleton. You of all people.'

'Me of all people?'

Kellam squirmed, searching round for support, finding none. 'Christ, Greg, yes! What you are, what you did. You know, the Trinities.'

'Oh. That.' No one in Hambleton had actually mentioned it out loud before. They all knew he had been a member of the Trinities, Peterborough's urban predator gang, fighting the People's Constables out on the city's sweltering streets; the stories, fragmented and distorted, had followed him over the water from the Berrybut estate. But the New Conservatives, as a legitimate democratically elected government, could not officially sanction the massive campaign of hardline violence which had helped rout the PSP. So Greg's involvement had earned him a kind of silent reverence, a wink and a nudge, the only gratitude he was ever shown. As if what he had done wasn't quite seemly.

'Yeah, me of all people,' he said deliberately, looking round the troubled faces. 'I would have known if Roy was Party. Wouldn't I?'

They began to shuffle round, desperately avoiding his eye. The high-voltage mob tension shorting out.

'Well, is he?' Kellam asked urgently.

Greg moved forwards. Collister was groaning softly on the floor, fresh blood oozing out of the gashes which Foster's heavy rings had torn. Foster and Sutton exchanged one edgy glance, and hurriedly scrambled to their feet.

'Do you really want to know?' Greg asked.

'What if he is?' Kellam said.

'Then you can call the police and the Inquisitors, and I will testify in court what I can see in his mind.'

Kellam gave a mental flinch, stains of guilt blossoming among his thought currents. Panic at Greg's almost casual reminder that he could prise his way into minds triggering a cascade of associated memories.

'Yes, sure thing, Greg, that's fine by me.'

There was a fast round of mumbled agreement.

Greg pursed his lips thoughtfully, and squatted down beside Roy Collister. He focused his espersense on the solicitor's mind. The thoughts were leaden with pain, sharp stings of superficial cuts, heavier dull aches of bruised, probably cracked, ribs, nausea like a hot rock in his belly, warmth of urine between his legs, the terror and its twin, the knowledge that he would do anything say anything to make them stop, a bitter tang of utter humiliation. His mind was weeping quietly to itself. There was little rationality left, the beating had emptied him of all but animal instinct.

'Can you hear me, Roy?' Greg asked clearly.

Saliva and blood burped out from between battered lips. Greg located a small flare of understanding amid the wretched thoughts.

'They say you were an *apparatchik*, Roy. Are they right?'

He hissed something incomprehensible.

'What did he say?' Mark Sutton asked.

Greg held up a hand, silencing him. 'What were you doing in the PSP decade? Don't try and speak, just picture it. I'll see.' Which wasn't true, not at all. But only Eleanor knew that.

He counted to thirty, trying to recall the various conversations he and Roy had had in the Finch's Arms, and rose to his feet. The lynch mob stood with bowed heads, as sheepish as school-boys caught smoking. Even if he said Collister was guilty, there would be no vigilante violence now. The anger and nerve had been torn out of them, sucked into the black vacuum of shame. Which was all he had set out to do.

'Roy wasn't an *apparatchik*,' Greg said. 'He used to work in a legal office, handling defence cases. Did you hear that? Defence work. Roy was supporting the poor sods that the People's Constables brought into court on trumped-up charges. That's how he was tied in to the government by your bollock-brained Inquisitors, his name is on the Market Harborough legal affairs committee pay-slip package. The Treasury paid him for provid-ing his counselling services.'

The silence which followed was broken by Clare Collister's anguished wail. She ran over to her husband, sinking to her knees, shoulders quaking. Her fingers dabbed at his ruined face, slowly, disbelievingly, tracing the damage; she started to sob un-controllably.

Douglas Kellam had paled. 'We didn't know.'

Greg increased the level of his gland secretion, and thought of a griffin's claw, rigged with powerful stringy muscles and tendons, talons black and savagely sharp. Eidolonics took a lot out of him, he had learnt that back in his Mindstar days: his mind wasn't wired for it, which meant he had to push to make it work. On top of that, he hated domination stunts. But for Kellam he'd overlook scruples this once. He visualized the talon tips closing around Kellam's balls. 'Goodbye,' he said, it was a dismissal order. Black needles touched the delicate scrotum.

Kellam's eyes widened in silent fright. He turned and virtually ran for the door. The others filed out after him, one or two bobbing their heads nervously at Eleanor.

'Oh sweet Jesus, look what they've done to him,' Clare groaned. Her hands were covered in blood. She looked up at Greg and Eleanor, tears sticky on her cheeks. 'They're animals. Animals!'

Greg fished round in his overall pockets for his cybofax. He pulled the rectangular palm-sized 'ware block out, and flipped it open. 'Phone function,' he ordered, then told Clare: 'I'll call for an ambulance. Some of those ribs are badly damaged. Tell the doctors to check for internal haemorrhaging.'

She wiped some of her tears with the back of a hand, leaving a tiny red streak above her right eye. 'I want them locked up,' she said, fighting for breath. 'All of them. Locked up for a thousand years.'

Greg sighed. 'No, they didn't do anything wrong.'

Eleanor flashed him a startled glance. Then understanding dawned, she looked back down at Clare.

'Nothing wrong!' Clare howled.

'I only said Roy was innocent,' Greg said quietly.

She stared at him in horror.

'When the ambulance comes, you will leave with it. Pack a bag, some clothes, anything really valuable. And don't come back, not for anything. If I ever see you again, I will tell Douglas and his friends exactly whose mind is rotten with guilt.'

'I never hurt anybody,' she said. 'I was in Food Allocation.'

Greg put his arm round Eleanor, urging her out of the lounge.

The sound of Clare Collister's miserable weeping followed him all the way down the hall.

*

Eleanor kissed him lightly when they reached the EMC Ranger. There was no sign of the lynch mob. Nor the watching faces, Greg noted. The only sound was the bird-song, humidity gave the air an almost viscid quality.

'Are you all right?' she asked. Her lips were pressed together in concern.

His head had begun to ache with the neurohormone hangover which was the legacy of using the gland. He blinked against the sunlight glaring round the shredded clouds, combing his hand back through sweaty hair. 'Yeah, I'll live.'

'That bloody Collister woman.'

'Tell you, she's probably right. Food Allocation was a little different from the Constables and the Public Order Ministry.'

'They took away enough of the kibbutz's crops,' Eleanor said sharply. 'Fair and even distribution, like hell.'

'Hey, wildcat.' He patted her rump.

'Behave, Gregory.' She skipped away and climbed up into the Ranger, but her smile had returned.

Greg slumped into the passenger seat, and remembered to pull his safety belt across. 'I suppose I ought to sniff around the rest of the village,' he said reluctantly. 'Make sure there aren't any premier-grade *apparatchiks* lurking around in dark corners.'

'That is one of the things we came here to get away from.' She swung the EMC Ranger round the triangular junction outside the church, and headed back the way they came. 'You and I, we've done our bit for this country.'

'So now we leave it to the Inquisitors?'

Eleanor grunted in disgust.

They met Corry Furness on the edge of the village. Eleanor stopped the Ranger and lowered her window to tell him it was all right to use his bike again.

'Mr Collister wasn't one of them, was he?' Corry asked.

15

'No,' Greg said.

Corry's face lit with a smile. 'I told you.' He pedalled off down the avenue of dead trees with their lacework of vines and harlequin flowers.

Greg watched him in the mud-splattered wing mirror, envying the lad's world view. Everything black and white, truth or lie. So simple.

Eleanor drove towards the farm at half the speed she'd used on the way in, suspension rocking them lightly as the wheels juddered over the skewed surface. The clouds on the southern horizon were starting to thicken.

'You'll have to give me a hand to get the lime saplings into the barn when we get back,' Greg said. He was watching the way the loose vine tendrils at the top of the trees were stirring. 'I'll never get them planted before the storm now.'

'Sure. I've nearly got the undercoat finished on all the first-floor windows.'

'That's something. It's going to be Monday before I'm through with the saplings. After this downpour it'll be too wet to get into the field for the next couple of days, and then we'll have to spend Sunday clearing up, no doubt.'

'Better make that Tuesday. We've got Julia's roll-out ceremony on Monday,' Eleanor said. 'That'll cheer you up.'

'Oh, bugger. I'd forgotten.'

'Don't be so grumpy. There are thousands of people who would kill for an invitation.'

'Couldn't we just sort of skip the ceremony?'

'Fine by me, if you want to explain our absence to Julia,' she said slyly.

Greg thought about it. Julia Evans didn't have many genuine friends. He was rather pleased to be counted amongst them, despite the disadvantages.

Julia had inherited Event Horizon from her grandfather, Philip Evans, a company larger even than a kombinate, manufacturing everything from domestic music decks to orbital microgee-factory modules. Two years ago she had been a very lonely seventeen-year-old girl; wealth and a drug-addict father had left her terribly isolated. Greg had got to know her quite well during the security violation case. Well enough for her to be chief bridesmaid at his wedding. Julia, of course, had been thrilled at the notion of adding a little touch of normality to her lofty plutocrat existence. The mistake of asking her had only become apparent when he and Eleanor had left for their honeymoon.

Every tabloid gossipcast in the world had broadcast the pictures. Greg Mandel: a man important enough to have the richest girl in the world as his bridesmaid. More millionaires than he knew existed wanted to be friends with the newly weds; buy them drinks, buy them meals, buy them houses, have them as non-executive directors.

Julia had also developed a mild crush on him for a while. A hard-line ex-urban predator and gland psychic, the classic romantic mysterious stranger. Of course, he had done the decent thing and ignored it. Hell of a thing, decency.

Greg found he was grinning wanly. 'I don't want to try explaining to Julia.'

2

Nicholas Beswick looked out of his mullioned window, watching a near solid front of thick woolly clouds slide over the secluded Chater valley. It was mid-afternoon, and the storm was arriving more or less on time. The warm rain began to fall, a heavy grey nebula constricting oppressively around the ancient Abbey.

His room faced west, giving him a good view out over the long gentle slope of grassy parkland which made up that side of the valley. But the brow was no longer visible, in fact he was hard pressed to see the road slicing through the park outside the front of the building, beyond the deep U-shaped loop of the drive. Mist was struggling to rise up from the grass, only to be torn apart by the deluge of hoary water.

There would be no swimming in the fish lakes this evening, he realized ruefully, no opportunity of seeing Isabel in her swimsuit. The daily swim had become an iron-cast habit for the six students; Launde Abbey didn't have any outdoor sport pitches or indoor games courts, so they clung to whatever activity they could make for themselves with a grim tenacity. The lack of facilities had never bothered him. He had been at the Abbey since October, and he still found it hard to believe he had been admitted. Launde Abbey was looked upon as a kind of semi-mythical grail by every university physics student in England: the chance to study under Dr Edward Kitchener.

Kitchener was regarded by most of his peers as the Newton of the age, a double Nobel Laureate for his work in cosmology and solid-state physics; his now-classic molecular interaction equations had defined a whole range of new crystals and semiconductors which could be produced in orbiting microgee factories. The royalty payments from the latter work had made him independently wealthy before he reached forty, which also kicked up the embers of envy among his colleagues whose work tended more to the intellectual. Nor did it help that he was slightly unconventional in the way he approached his subject matter; at his level of theorizing, physics verged on philosophy. He considered he had a perfect right to intrude on the country of the mind, to develop new aspects of thought processes. It had led to some fierce disagreements with the psychology establishment, and he didn't always confine his arguments to the pages of respected journals – critics were often subjected to an open tirade of abuse and scorn at scientific conferences. Then twenty-two years ago, after nearly twenty years of ill-tempered confrontation with his fellow theorists, he had, with characteristic abruptness, resigned from his position at Cambridge and retreated to Launde Abbey to pursue his theories without carping interference from lesser minds, his brilliance and loud vocal intolerance of the dry, crusty world endemic to academia creating a media legend of Bohemian eccentricity in the process.

When psi-stimulant neurohormones were developed, seventeen years ago, he awarded them an unqualified welcome, saying they gave the human mind direct access to the cosmos at large, presenting physicists with the opportunity to perceive first-hand the particles and waveforms they had only ever seen on paper and in projection cubes. Even after it became clear that neurohormones couldn't produce anything like the initial over-optimistic results predicted, he never lost his conviction. Psi, he contended, was the greatest event in physics since relativity, exposing hitherto unquantifiable phenomena. Simply defining the mechanism of psi in conventional terms was enough to fascinate him, a rationale which would tie up nature and supernature, something beyond even the elusive Grand Unification theory.

This tenuous goal was one to which more and more of his time was devoted. But every year he invited three degree students into his home for an intensive two-year session of lectures, research and intellectual meditation.

And childish tantrums, Nicholas had discovered, at first to his embarrassed surprise, and then with secret amusement. Even the most brilliant of men had character flaws.

Launde Abbey wasn't just about profound reasoning and scaling new heights of metaphysics. The human dynamics of six young people cooped up with an increasingly crotchety sixty-seven-year-old was weird. Fun, but weird.

Nicholas could now see a tributary network of steely rivulets coalescing on the grassland, trickling across the road and running down the slope into the first of the three little lakes to the north. The rain was incredibly heavy, and Globecast's news channel said it would last for six or seven hours. The River Chater at the bottom of the valley would flood again; it was probably up to the rickety little bridge already.

There was some sort of vehicle crawling along the road, heading down towards the river. He frowned and peered forward, nose touching the chilly glass. It was a rugged four-wheel-drive Suzuki jeep. Probably the farmer who leased the park's grazing rights checking to make sure he'd rounded up all the sheep and llamas.

Lightning burst across the valley, ragged sheets of plasma ripping the gloom apart. It revealed the small powder-blue composite geodesic dome sitting like some baroque technological sentry on the brow of the valley. Nicholas could see a couple of the hexagonal panels were missing. The gravity wave detector which it housed was now long abandoned. In the height of summer sheep used the dome for shade.

Another bout of lightning erupted overhead, vivid blue-white forks lashing down, giving him the impression that the sky itself was fracturing. One of the flashes was bright enough to dazzle him and he jerked back from the window, fists rubbing the blotchy purple after-images from his eyes.

Thunder rattled the glass. The farmer's vehicle had gone. Humidity was steaming up the windows.

Nicholas abandoned the monsoon with a reluctance rooted in a perennial child-awe of the elements. He turned on the conditioner to cope with the rampant humidity, punched up some Bil Yi Somanzer from his music deck, then retreated back to his desk. His room was on the top floor of the Abbey, a large L-shape, with old but expensive furniture. It had a small private bathroom at one end. The bed was a large circular affair, easily big enough for two, which often made him think of Isabel on sleepless nights. There was an array of large globular cacti in red clay pots on a copper-topped table below the window: he was mildly worried that he wasn't watering them properly, there had been no sign of the flowers Kitchener told him to watch out for.

He hadn't brought much to the room himself, a couple of big rock band holoprints, his music deck, reproduction star-charts, some reference books (paper ones); his clothes didn't take up half of the drawer space in the solid oak chest, and the wardrobe was almost empty. He had been too nervous back when he arrived to bring much in the way of personal possessions, unsure what liberties Kitchener would tolerate – after all, the Abbey was nothing like student digs. Of course, now he knew the old boy didn't care what the students did in their rooms, or at least claimed he didn't.

Bil Yi's *Angel High* thumped out of the speakers, drowning the sound of the storm in howling guitar riffs. Nicholas activated his desk-top terminal; it was a beautiful piece of gear, a top-of-the-range Hitachi model with twin studio-quality holographic projection cubes. He used the keyboard to access the CNES mission control memory core in Toulouse and requested the latest batch of results from the *Antomine 12* astronomy satellite platform. A map of gamma ray sources began to fill one of the cubes, and he called up his frequency analysis program. It was a marvellous sensation, being able to punch a data request into any public-access memory core on the planet without having to worry about departmental budgets. Back at the university, a

21

request like this one would need to be referred almost back up to the dean. Kitchener's data costs must be phenomenal, but all his students had to pay for were their own clothes and incidentals.

His subroutines jumped into the second cube, and he started to integrate them. Kitchener might or might not ask how his gravity-lens research project was progressing at supper but he wanted to be ready with some kind of report. The old boy simply didn't tolerate fools at all, let alone gladly. That fact alone did wonders for Nicholas's self-esteem. He knew he was bright, his effortless formal first at Cambridge proved that: but the downside was the trouble he had trying to fit in to the university's social scene; he had always preferred his studies to the politics and culture-vulturing of his fellow students. Bookish eremitism was all right at university, you could get lost in the crowd and nobody would notice, but it wasn't possible at Launde. Yet Kitchener had agreed after a mere ten-minute interview, during which Nicholas had mumbled virtually every answer to the old boy's questions.

'We can sort you out here,' Kitchener had said wryly, and winked, 'there's more than one type of education to be had at Launde.'

Nicholas had experienced the unsettling notion that Kitchener had perceived the sense of destitute isolation which had clung to him for as long as he could remember.

After he got in to Launde Abbey, money ceased to be a problem for the first time in his life. His parents had always been proud of his university scholarship, but they hadn't been able to contribute much to his grant; they were smallholders, barely able to feed themselves and his sister. He went to Cambridge a month after the People's Socialism Party fell; the country was in complete turmoil, jobs and money were scarce. He scraped through the first year working as a fast-food cook grilling krillburgers in the furnace heat of a cramped McDonald's kitchen for six nights a week. It wasn't until halfway through his second year that the economy stabilized, and the New Conservative government began to prioritize the education department. But after he graduated and then received that golden invitation, sponsorship for the two-year sojourn had been ridiculously easy to find. Eight medium-sized companies and three giant kombinates had made him an offer. In the end he settled for accepting the money of Randon, a French-based 'ware and energy systems manufacturer, mainly because it was coupled with the promise of a guaranteed research position afterwards.

All of Launde's graduates tended to enjoy a privileged position later in life; Kitchener did seem to have a knack for spotting genuine potential: they formed one of the most élitist old-boy networks in the world. It was all part of the price of spending two years isolated in the middle of nowhere. Nicholas didn't mind that at all; after his appalling first year at Cambridge, he thought it was quite a bargain.

*

Supper at Launde Abbey was held at half-past seven prompt each night. Everybody attended, no matter how engrossed they were with their work. It was one of Kitchener's house rules. He didn't lay down many, but God help the student who broke one of them.

Nicholas had a quick shower then put on a clean pale-blue T-shirt before he left his room at quarter-past seven. It was dark outside, the wind soughing plaintively as it slithered around the chimney-stacks.

Uri Pabari and Liz Foxton were coming out of Uri's room, a couple of doors down from Nicholas's. They were talking in low, heated voices as they emerged into the corridor, some sort of argument. Both of them looked belligerent, faces hard and unyielding.

An awkward grin flickered over Nicholas's lips. He hated it when people argued in the Abbey; cramped together as they were, everyone else always seemed to get dragged in. It was doubly excruciating when the argument was a personal one. And he had enough experience to recognize a personal argument between Liz and Uri. It didn't happen often, but when it did . . .

They caught sight of him, and the sibilant words stopped. There was a moment's hesitation during which they held some invisible negotiation, then Uri's arm was round her shoulder and they walked towards him. He waited, trying to hide his trepidation. They were both older than him; Uri was twenty-four, Liz twenty-two, in their final year at Launde.

Out of all the students at Launde, Nicholas felt closest to Liz. She wasn't quite as stilted as him when it came to other people, but she was one of the quietest, always giving the impression of thoughtful reserve. She was half a head shorter than him, with a pleasant round face, hazel eyes, and shoulder-length raven hair. Tonight she wore a simple fuchsia one-piece dress, its skirt coming just below her knees, something indefinably American about its cut.

By contrast, Uri was perpetually easygoing. The ex-Israeli had a dark complexion and a thick mass of curly jet-black hair that reached his shoulders. His build was stocky, yet he was the same one-metre-eighty height as Nicholas, a combination which made his varsity rugby team welcome him to their ranks with open arms. Recently he had piled a couple of kilos on around his waist, which Liz had started to nag him about during meals. He was in jeans and a bright-green rugby shirt.

'Missed your swim?' Liz asked as the three of them walked down the stairs.

Nicholas nodded. 'Yes, but I managed to catch up on some of my datawork.'

'No formal graduation exams, no last month sweat and panic . . . That's the thing about this place.' She grinned, mimicking Kitchener's waspy tone. 'You know whether or not your mind can work, it's not up to me to tell you.'

The Abbey's rooms were divided into two distinct groups: the formal ones, which had been maintained in a reasonable degree of the original style despite the privation of the PSP decade which followed the physical and economic chaos of the Warming; and the rest, which were turned over to Kitchener's lifelong pursuit of quantifying the entire universe: the two laboratories, a compact heavily cybernated engineering shop, the computer centre, Kitchener's study, a small lecture theatre, and a library with hundreds of paper books. The dining room was definitely one of the former; its gold-brown wooden panelling had been immaculately preserved, and the Jacobean fireplace never failed to impress Nicholas. It had been furnished with a long Edwardian mahogany table, polished to a gleam; the fragile-looking chairs around it were upholstered with dull rouge leather, covered with a web of ochre cracks. Nicholas was always terrified he would split one of the antique masterpieces when he sat on it. Above the table, two biolum chandeliers emitted a bright, slightly pink, light.

Cecil Cameron was lounging in one of the chairs, the last of the second-year students. A rangy twenty-four-year-old with frizzy blond hair, cut short. He was using his kinaware left hand to open a bottle of white Sussex wine, chrome-black metalloceramic nails shining dully every time he twisted the corkscrew. The hand's leathery skin had a silver sheen, which Cecil said he had chosen in preference to flesh-tone. 'Why bother going through life being boring? If you're enhanced, then flaunt it.' He claimed he'd lost his forearm in an anti-PSP riot. True or not, and Nicholas wasn't entirely convinced, Cecil exploited his hand and the interest it earned him quite shamelessly to his own advantage.

Kinaware was still rare (and expensive) enough to draw attention wherever he went. Not that the six students got out much: a weekly trip to the Old Plough in Braunston, the nearest village; an occasional foray into Oakham. Cecil was forever bitching about the confines of the Abbey, and worked a little too hard on projecting his boisterous image. But Nicholas had to admit he was a first-rate solid-state physicist.

'Don't look so eager, proles,' Cecil drawled. 'The storm means Mrs Mayberry isn't here. Our lord and master sent her home after lunch. So it's cook it yourself night tonight.'

Nicholas and Uri let out a groan.

'So why aren't you cooking it?' Liz asked.

Cecil flashed her a smile. 'I always find the female of the species is so much better at that kind of thing.'

'Pighead!'

'Go on, admit it, did you really want to taste my cooking? Besides, I looked in a minute ago, little Isabel is coping just fine.'

'Isabel's cooking supper?' Nicholas asked. He hoped it had come out sounding like an innocent enquiry.

Cecil's smile broadened. 'Yes. All by herself. Say, Nick, why don't you go and see if she wants a hand, or anything else?'

Nicholas could hear what sounded like a chuckle coming from Uri. He refused to turn and find out for sure. 'Yes, all right,' he said.

Liz was giggling by the time he reached the door into the kitchen. Well, let them, he thought; he didn't mind the steady joshing the others gave him now, it was all part of a day at Launde Abbey. Funny what you could get used to if it went on long enough.

Isabel Spalvas had arrived at the same time as him, a mathematician from Cardiff University. At first he didn't even have the nerve to meet her eyes when they were talking – not that they talked much, he could never think of anything to say. But mortification at his own pathetic shyness eventually bullied him out of his shell. They were going to be under the same roof for two years, if nothing else he could talk to her as if she was just one of the boys, it was often the simplest approach. That way at least they'd be friends, then maybe, just maybe . . .

The kitchen had a long matt-black cast-iron range running along one whitewashed plaster wall, with a set of copper pots and even an antique bedwarmer, hanging above it. A wicker basket stood at the end, piled high with logs, but for once the fire was out. The big square wooden table in the middle of the room was covered in dishes and trays; there was a mound of wet lettuce leaves drying out in a colander next to a collection of sliced tomatoes, cucumbers, radishes, and chives.

Isabel was busy carving a joint of ham. She was the same age as Nicholas, twenty-one, about a head smaller, with sandy-blonde hair that was arranged in a mass of tiny curls just brushing her shoulders. The way she was bent over the table meant the strands obscured her face, but he could visualize her features perfectly, at any time. Almost invisible lashes framed enchantingly clear ice-blue eyes, pale freckles decorated the top half of her cheeks, the lips were narrow. Nicholas was fascinated by the dainty features, how expressive they could be: fearsomely intent when she was listening to Kitchener, beaming sunlight smiles when she was happy, when the students got together for their evening meetings in one of the rooms. She laughed most at Cecil's jokes, of course, and Rosette's acid gossip; Nicholas never had been able to master the art of perfectly timed one-liners, or even rugby club style stories.

He paused for a second, content just to look at her, for once without all the others nudging and pointing. She was wearing tight, faded jeans, and a sleeveless white blouse, with Mrs Mayberry's brown apron tied round her waist. One day he'd have the courage to come out and say what he felt to her face, say that she was gorgeous, say that she made the whole world worth living in. And after that he'd lean forwards for a kiss. One day.

'Hello, Isabel,' he blurted. Damn, that had come out too loud and gushy.

She glanced up from the joint. 'Hi, Nick. It's going to be salad tonight, I'm afraid.'

'You haven't done all this yourself, have you? You should have said, I would have helped. I did some cooking when I was at Cambridge. I got quite good at it.'

'It's all right, Mrs Mayberry prepared most of it after lunch. You didn't think she'd trust us with it, did you? I'm just finishing off. Do you think this'll be enough?' She wagged the knife at the plate of meat she had cut.

'Yes, fine. If they want any more, Cecil can cut it.'

'Hmm, that'll be the day.'

'Is there anything I can do?'

'Take the trays through, would you.'

'Right.' He grabbed the one nearest to him, piled high with plates and dishes.

'Not that one!'

Nicholas put it down with a guilty lurch. The plates threatened to keel over. Isabel put her hand out hurriedly to stop them.

'Those are the plates from lunch, Nick,' she said with a tinge of reproach.

'Sorry.' How stupid, he raged silently. He knew the heat he could feel on his face was a crimson blush.

'Try this one,' she said in a gentler voice.

He picked up the one she indicated, and turned for the door, feeling totally worthless.

'Nick. Thank you for offering to help. None of the others did.'

She was giving him a soft smile, and there was something in her expression which said she understood.

'That's OK, any time.'

Nicholas and Uri were setting the places when Edward Kitchener and Rosette Harding-Clarke came in at twenty-nine minutes past seven. He saw the old boy was in his usual clothes, baggy white trousers, white cotton shirt, cream-yellow jacket with a blue silk handkerchief tucked into his breast pocket, and a tiny red bow tie, which always made Nicholas think a butterfly had landed on his collar. There was still an air of the tiger left in Kitchener, age was not a gift he accepted gracefully. He was reasonably slim, carrying himself with undiminished vigour; his face was a long one, with skin stretched thinly around his jaw, scratchy with stubble; a crew-cut of silver hair looked almost like a cap.

Rosette Harding-Clarke walked beside him, taller by ten centimetres, an athletic-looking twenty-three-year-old, with soft auburn hair, styled so that long wavy strands licked her back well below her shoulder-blades. Her presence alone intimidated Nicholas. She had arrived along with him and Isabel, with a degree in quantum mechanics from Oxford, but her aristocratic background gave her a self-confidence which he found daunting. He had suffered too many casual put-downs from her social clique at Cambridge not to flinch each time that steel-edged Knightsbridge voice sliced through the air. She was wearing dark-grey tweedy trousers and a scarlet waistcoat with shiny brass buttons, the top two undone. And nothing underneath, Nicholas soon realized. He prayed he wasn't blushing again, but Rosette could be overpoweringly sexy when she wanted to be.

Kitchener and Rosette were arm in arm. Like lovers, Nicholas thought, which he privately suspected was true. It wasn't only Kitchener's attitude towards his fellow physicists which caused conflict in his earlier years. Tabloid channel 'casts were always sniping with rumours of him and female students. And how Kitchener had lapped that up, relishing his media-appointed role as the notorious roué! There had even been a statement, shortly after he bought Launde Abbey, that he was only going to invite female students to become his tyros, providing himself with a harem of muses. He never had, of course, it was always a fifty-fifty split, but which member of the general public made the effort to discover that? The legend remained solidly intact.

'Anybody been watching the newscasts?' Kitchener asked after he sat in the carver's chair at the head of the table.

'I've been correlating the gamma ray data from *Antomine 12*, Nicholas said.

'Well done, lad. Glad somebody's doing something in this slackers' paradise. Now what about that little problem I set you on magnetosphere induction generators, hey, have you solved that yet?'

'No, sorry, the gravity lens idea was fascinating, and nobody else has been tabulating the data the way I am,' Nicholas offered by way of compensation. He ducked his head, unsure how it would be received. The topics for research were always set by Kitchener, but sometimes the old boy displayed a complete lack of interest in the answers. You could never work out what he was going to press you on, which could get disconcerting. That aside, Nicholas reckoned he'd learnt more about the methodology of analysing problems in the three months he'd been at Launde Abbey than in his three years at university. Kitchener did have the most extraordinary insights at times.

'Bloody typical,' Kitchener groused. 'How many times do I have to tell you delinquents, the abstract is all very well, but it makes piddle-all difference to the human condition. There's no bloody point in me teaching you to think properly, if you can't use those thoughts of yours to some benefit. The way this clapped-out world is limping along, a clean source of fresh energy would be like manna from heaven right now. A wealthier world will be better able to support eggheads chasing metaphantoms. It's to your own advantage. God, take me, unless I'd come up with those molecular interaction equations—'

'You could never have bought Launde,' Uri and Cecil chorused, laughing.

'Little buggers!' Kitchener grunted. He glanced down at the plate Isabel put in front of him, and started to poke around distrustfully with a fork. 'And don't giggle, lad,' he said without looking up, 'only bloody women giggle.'

Nicholas clamped his mouth shut, and concentrated on his plate. From the corner of his eye he could see Isabel laughing silently.

'I was watching the newscasts this afternoon,' Kitchener said. 'It looks like the Scottish PSP is about to fall.'

'It's always on the verge of collapse,' Cecil protested loudly. 'They said it wouldn't last six months after our lot got kicked out.'

'Yes, but Zurich has cut off their credit now.'

'About time,' Liz muttered.

Nicholas knew she had lost her mother when the PSP was in power in England. She always blamed the People's Constables, but thankfully never went into details. His own memories of President Armstrong's brutish regime were more or less limited to the constant struggle to survive on too little food. The PSP never had much authority in rural areas, they had had enough trouble maintaining control in the urban districts.

'I hope they don't want to link up with us again,' Cecil said.

'Why ever not?' Rosette asked. 'I think it would be nice being the United Kingdom again, although having the Irish back would be pushing the point.'

'We can't afford it,' Cecil said. 'Christ, we're only just getting back on our own feet.'

'A bigger country means greater security in the long run, darling.'

'You might as well try Eurofederalism again.'

'We'll have to help them,' Isabel said. 'They're desperately short of food.'

'Let them grow their own,' Cecil said. 'They're not short of land, and they've got all those fishing rights.'

'How can you say that? There are children suffering.'

'I think Isabel's right,' Nicholas said boldly. 'Some sort of aid's in order, even if we can't afford a Marshall plan.'

'Now that will make a nice little complication for the New Conservatives during the election,' Kitchener said gleefully. 'Trapped whichever way they turn. Serves 'em right. Always good fun watching politicians squirming.'

Conversation meandered, as it always did, from politics to art, from music to England's current surge of industrial redevelopment, from channel-star gossip (which Kitchener always pretended not to follow) to the latest crop of scientific papers. Cecil walked round the table, pouring the wine for everyone.

Isabel mentioned the increasing number of people using bioware processor implants, the fact that the New Conservatives had finally legalized them in England, and Kitchener declared: 'Sheer folly.'

'I thought you would have approved,' she said. 'You're always on about enhancing cerebral capacity.'

'Rubbish, girl, having processors in your head doesn't make you any brighter. Intellect is half instinct. Always has been. I haven't got one, and I've managed pretty well.'

'But you might have achieved more with one,' Uri said.

'That's the kind of bloody stupid comment I'd expect from you. Totally devoid of logic. Wishful thinking is sloppy thinking.'

Uri gave Kitchener a cool stare. 'You have few qualms about using other enhancements to get results.'

Nicholas didn't like the tone, it was far too polite. He shifted about in the chair, bleakly waiting for the explosion. No one was eating, Cecil had stopped filling Rosette's glass.

But Kitchener's voice was surprisingly mild when he answered. 'I'll use whatever I need to expand my perception, thank you, lad. I've been a consenting adult since before you were shitting in your nappies. Being able to discern the whole universe is the key to understanding it. If neurohormones help me in that, then that makes them no different to a particle accelerator, or any other form of research tool, in my book.'

'Neat answer. Pity you don't stick to neurohormones, pity you have to expand your consciousness with shit.'

'Nothing I take affects my intellect. Only a fool would think otherwise. Expanded consciousness is total crap, there's no such thing, only recreational intoxication, it's a diversion, stepping outside your problems for a few hours.'

'Well, it's certainly helped you overcome a few problems, hasn't it?' Uri's face was blank civility.

'I always thought bioware nodes would be terrifically useful if you want to access data quickly,' Rosette said brightly.

Cecil's hand came down on Uri's shoulder, squeezing softly. He started pouring some wine into Uri's glass.

Kitchener turned to Rosette. 'Use a bloody terminal, girl, don't be so damn lazy. That's all implants are, convenience laziness. It's precisely the kind of attitude which got us into our present state. People never listen to common sense. We shouted about the greenhouse gases till we were blue in the face. Bloody hopeless. They just went on burning petrol and coal.'

'What kind of car did you use?' Liz asked slyly.

'There weren't any electric cars then. I had to use petrol.'

'Or a bicycle,' Rosette said.

'A horse,' Nicholas suggested.

'A rickshaw,' Isabel giggled.

'Perhaps you could even have walked,' Cecil chipped in.

'Leave off, you little buggers,' Kitchener grunted. 'No bloody respect. Cecil, at least fill my glass, lad, it's wine not perfume, you don't spray it on.'

Nicholas managed to catch Isabel's eye, and he smiled. 'The salad's lovely.'

'Thank you,' she said.

Rosette held her cut-crystal wineglass up to the light, turning it slowly. Fragments of refracted light drifted across her face, stipples of gold and violet. 'You never compliment Mrs Mayberry when she cooks supper, why is that, Nicky, darling?'

'You never complimented Mrs Mayberry or Isabel,' he answered. 'I was just being polite, it was considered important where I was brought up.'

Rosette wrinkled her nose up at him, and sipped some wine.

'Well done, lad,' Kitchener called out. 'You stick up for yourself, don't let the little vixen get on top of you.'

Nicholas and Isabel exchanged a furtive grin. He was elated, actually answering back to Rosette, and having Isabel approve.

Rosette gave Kitchener a roguish glance. 'You've never complained before,' she murmured in a husky tone.

Kitchener laughed wickedly. 'What's for dessert, Isabel?' he asked.

*

The storm began to abate after midnight. Nicholas was back in his room watching a vermiform pattern of sparkling blue stars dance through his terminal's cube like a demented will-o'-the-wisp. The program was trying to detect the distinctive interference pattern caused by large dark-mass concentrations; if there was one directly between the emission point and Earth (a remote chance, but possible), the gamma rays should bend around it. Kitchener was always interested in the kind of localized spatial distortions such objects generated. His program was using up a good third of the Abbey's lightware cruncher capacity. The kind of interference he was looking for was incredibly hard to identify.

He had thought about making a start on the magnetosphere induction problem, but the dark mass project was *much* more interesting. It was worth enduring another of Kitchener's tongue-lashings to be able to see the results as they came in from orbit. Dark-mass detection was well down the priority list of CNES's in-house astronomers, it was exciting to think he might actually be ahead of them, up there at the cutting edge. Nicholas Beswick, science pioneer.

He had been in Uri's room for most of the evening after supper, along with Liz and Isabel. It had been a good evening, he reflected; they'd chatted, and the flatscreen had been tuned to Globecast's twenty-four-hour news channel with the sound muted. And it really did look like the Scottish PSP was going to be overthrown at last. There was rioting in Glasgow and Edinburgh and the assembly building had been firebombed, the flames soaring impressively into the night despite the heavy rain. They had watched the text streamers running along the bottom of the flatscreen and talked, drinking another bottle of Sussex wine. The others never seemed to mind that he didn't say as much as them, he was under no pressure to venture an opinion on everything.

They had packed up around midnight, or at least, he and Isabel had left Uri and Liz alone.

He shut Uri's door, thinking that for once he might find the nerve to ask Isabel into his room.

She stood on the gloomy landing glancing at him expectantly.

'It was a nice evening, thanks,' he said. Pathetic.

Her lips pressed together. It was her solemn expression, the one that made her look half-tragic.

'Yes, I enjoyed it,' she said. 'Let's hope there's a new government in Scotland tomorrow. Liz will be over the moon.'

'Yes.' Now, he thought, now say it. 'Goodnight,' he said meekly.

'Goodnight, Nick.'

And she'd walked off to her room.

Surely if a girl liked a boy she was supposed to show it: some small word or deed of encouragement? But she hadn't actually discouraged him. He clung to that. If it hadn't been for the fact he could never keep his mouth shut Nicholas might have asked Cecil for advice. Cecil never had any trouble chatting up girls when they visited the Old Plough.

The clouds above the valley were disintegrating, pale beams of moonlight probed down through the tattered gaps. Nicholas looked up from the cube, watching them shiver across the undulating parkland. After the uniform darkness of the storm they seemed preternaturally bright. Trees and bushes imprinted on his retinas, ragged platinum silhouettes which vanished almost as soon as they were revealed.

A face looked back at him through the glass. It was a woman, probably not much older than him; her features were slightly indistinct, misted somehow, but she was certainly attractive, with thick red hair combed back from her forehead.

All he did was gawk for a second, his thoughts shocked into stasis, a gelid fingertip stroking his spine. Then he realized her spectral image must be a reflection. She was standing behind him! He yelped in panic, and jerked round in the chair, a thousand-volt current replacing his normal nervous impulses.

There was nobody there.

He twisted back to stare at the window. There was no face.

Slowly, his shoulders were trembling faintly, he let out a long sigh. Idiot! He must have been dozing, dreaming. The clock on the bedside cabinet read quarter-past one.

Too late, Nicholas, he told himself wanly. Besides, since when did beautiful women ever come stealing into your bedroom in the middle of the night?

He cancelled the gamma ray search program. That was when he heard somebody talking on the landing outside, two people, voices murmuring softly. The chilly breath of static washed down his back again; but he was wide awake now. He frowned, concentrating, filtering out the intermittent patter of residual rain on the window. He knew one of them was Isabel, by now he could have plucked her voice out of hell's bedlam.

Curiosity warred with dread, he wanted to know what she was doing, he was terrified of making a fool out of himself. But if he didn't go to the door quickly, the chance to do either would be lost. In the end it was the thought of having to live with not knowing, spending days wondering while his over-active imagination summoned up grotesque scenarios, which propelled him up out of the chair.

He turned the brass door handle, already trying to think of an excuse. I was just going to fetch something from the library, my toilet's blocked . . . Feeble.

There was only a single biolum globe illuminating the landing, its weak pink-white lambency disfiguring the familiar corridors and twisting the proportions of the stark wooden chairs outside each door. Long serpentine shadows dappled the walls, veiling the vague figures depicted in the dusty hanging tapestries behind a crepuscular fog.

The two girls had their backs to him, walking with a measured companionable pace towards the stairs. They stopped as soon as the bright fan of light from his room splashed out into the landing, and slowly turned towards him. Rosette was wrapped in a jade-green silk kimono, embellished with fantastical topaz griffins. She was obviously riding some kind of high, he'd seen enough of that at Cambridge to tell; black sun pupils, dawdling movements. Probably Naiad, a sophisticated derivative of street-syntho, guaranteed no bad trips, no cold turkey. The vat in the lab downstairs was elaborate enough to produce it.

Isabel was still in her jeans, held up by a braided leather belt she'd fastened with a big loop tucked back into her waistband. She had taken off her blouse, leaving just a plain black bra to cup her high, exquisitely shaped breasts.

Nicholas stared at her with lightheaded dismay, the kind of sensation he got whenever his father butchered spring lambs. The scene and all it implied was too macabre, too lascivious to take in. In the gloom behind the girls he could see the red-headed woman again, all of her this time. She was tall and broad shouldered, wearing some kind of jacket with a long skirt. He blinked, dizziness forcing him to grip the door to stop himself falling. His skin was ice cold, needled with hot beads of sweat. He thought he was about to be sick. The world buckled alarmingly, sight and sound dissolving under a suffocating wave of heat. He was hallucinating, he was sure of it, the only explanation, trapped in a terrifying loop of nightmare. When his vision shimmered back into focus the phantom woman had gone. But Isabel and Rosette were still solidly, undeniably present.

A corner of Rosette's mouth lifted in a lazy chaffing smile, as if she was glad he'd interrupted them. 'Adults only, Nicky, darling,' she said in a throaty voice. 'Sorry.'

He looked at Isabel, a long, anguished appeal that this wasn't happening. All she did was give a minute shrug, a gesture of almost total indifference. It was a blow which hit him harder than the first shock of discovery.

He stared in abject misery as they continued silently down the landing, Rosette's feet unseen inside the kimono, giving the impression she was gliding above the carpet. Isabel had her shoulders square, lean bands of muscle shifting pliantly below the flawless skin of her tapering back.

They walked all the way past the stairs, along to the north wing, swallowed up in the gloaming. Then orange light shone out of the door Rosette opened. Kitchener's suite of rooms.

She didn't even glance back to see if he was watching before she closed the door behind them.

Why? He couldn't understand it. She wasn't on drugs. She wasn't suffering from delusions. She was always so levelheaded. Not like him, having fantasy women and the agony of sexual treachery running loose in his brain, twisting his mind up until he could barely think.

Nicholas clawed at his sheets, petrified the red-headed woman would materialize again, hoping in some perverse way that she would. Nothing made sense any more.

Why? Was it a price the female students had to pay for admission? But he would have heard, the ones that refused would have run screaming to the tabloid channels.

The moon had set now, leaving cold starlight to kiss the valley. He could hear lost gusts of wind swirling round the eaves, gurgles of water from the overflowing lakes.

Why? She didn't have to do it. Not with Kitchener. Not with Rosette. So she must want to. Why? Why? *Why?*

*

Nicholas snapped awake, his head rising off the pillow in a reflex jolt. What had woken him? He was still in his T-shirt and jeans, waist button undone. The duvet was a crumpled mess below him.

It was like every nerve fibre was shooting distilled trepidation into his brain. He knew it was going to be bad, very bad.

The scream assaulted his ears. Female. Powerful and utterly wretched. Dragging on and on, enough to leave a throat raw and withered.

He rolled off the bed fast. There was just enough pre-dawn light leaking through the window to see by. The scream stopped as he reached the door, then started up again as he pulled it open.

He looked about wildly. Orange light was shining down at the far end of the north wing. He could see Rosette kneeling brokenly in the doorway to Kitchener's suite, clinging desperately to the wooden frame.

Getting to her was a confused blur. His feet pounding. The other doors opening. Pale anxious faces. That unending, spine-grating scream.

Tears were streaming down Rosette's face. She was shaking violently.

He rushed past her and saw the bedroom for the first time. The curtains were still shut and tinted biolum globes shone from the middle of bulbous paper-moon shades that hung from the ceiling. The furniture was supremely tasteful, a dark antique dresser, matching wardrobe, Chinese carpet, full-length mirror, a porcelain-topped table below the window, brass ornaments on the mantelpiece, monk chest. The centrepiece was a large four-poster bed with an amber canopy.

Edward Kitchener was lying on the snow-white silk sheets, at the middle of a deep scarlet bloodstain spreading to the edge of the mattress. He felt the intolerable pressure of his own scream building in his chest.

Kitchener's head was intact, showing an almost serene peace-fulness. But the body . . . Ripped. Torn. Squashed. The ribcage had been clawed open, pulped organs spread across the bed.

Nicholas's scream burst out of his mouth. The roaring in his ears meant he couldn't even hear it. He was vaguely aware of the other students crowding in behind him.

His leg muscles pitched him on to the floor, and he vomited helplessly on to Kitchener's superb Chinese carpet.

3

The nineteen-fifties vintage Rolls-Royce Silver Shadow glided along at eighty kilometres an hour, its white-walled tyres soaking up all the punishment the gritty ruts of the decrepit M11 could inflict without a hint of exertion. Julia Evans adored the old car; it was the absolute last word in style and its rugged old-fashioned engineering was easily equal to the strengthened suspension and broad silicone rubber tyres of any modern car. Apart from a closed loop recombiner cell which allowed it to continue burning petrol without leaking fumes into the atmosphere, and the installation of various security systems, it hadn't needed any modifications to cope with England's decaying road network.

Outside the darkened glass she could see the rug of grass, weeds, and lush emerald moss which had swamped the hard shoulder; even the crash barriers along the central reservation had been swallowed up by bindweed, snow-white trumpet-shaped flowers pushing out from between the cloak of broad leaves. The original tarmac surface was still in use, scored by deep tyre-ruts along each carriageway; this afternoon it was solid because of the weekend's cooling rains, but for nine months of the year the sun reduced the roads to swaths of mushy black treacle.

The New Conservative government agreed in principle that nationwide road refurbishment should be given priority, coating the millions of kilometres of tarmac with a layer of tough thermo-cured cellulose, but they were hanging back until giga-conductor-powered vehicles became widespread before starting.

The Rolls approached junction ten, and the lead car in their four-strong police escort switched on its blue strobe lights. There seemed to be a lot of people lining the slip road.

'Who are they?' Julia asked.

Rachel Griffith, one of her two permanent bodyguards, was sitting in the jump seat opposite. A twenty-five-year-old security division hard-liner, wearing a smart blue two-piece suit. She turned round, scanning the road ahead. Her lean face flashed Julia a quick reassuring smile. 'Just some protesters,' she said. 'You and the Prime Minister at the same event is a publicity opportunity they can't ignore.'

Julia nodded. Rachel had been with her for five years, tough, smart, and loyal. She liked to think of her as a friend as well. If Rachel wasn't worried, there was nothing to be worried about.

'This is as near to the Institute as they can get,' said Morgan Walshaw, Event Horizon's security chief, from the second jump seat. Even sitting, he couldn't appear relaxed, spine stiff, shoulders squared, wearing an immaculate charcoal-grey suit. He fitted her conception of a crusty old retired Home Counties general perfectly. Except Morgan was far shrewder than any general. Thank God.

He was sixty-two years old, silver-grey hair clipped down to a centimetre from his skull, the thick, tanned skin of his face heavily crossed with narrow lines, hard-set light-blue eyes which always made her feel incredibly guilty whenever he stared at her. Everything she did eventually filtered back to him: nights out with her girl friends in Peterborough's clubs, holiday adventures, party antics, boys. Morgan had been with the company for years, protecting her grandfather, and now her, a job he performed with superb efficiency and complete devotion. His approval was always tremendously important to her, mainly because he would never make a gratuitous compliment. She had to *earn* it, something that never happened with most of the people in her life. And words of praise had indeed been awarded, albeit grudgingly, with more frequency in recent years. She often caught herself wishing he was her real father. The knowledge that he would be retiring in a few years was something she always tried to bury right at the back of her mind; it was a horrifying thought.

Access RollSpeech, Julia told her bioware processor node silently. Colourless words flowed from one of the three memory nodes buried at the back of her skull, forming a ghostly script behind her eyes. She reviewed it for what must have been the tenth time since breakfast. Event Horizon's PR department had written it for her, but she'd made a few alterations. It had sounded terribly stilted before. She couldn't forget it, of course, not with the nodes reinforcing her memory, but they couldn't help her out if she stumbled over pronunciation.

The roll out was going to be the technological event of the year; she couldn't afford to make a mistake. There were going to be too many people, too many channel cameras. It felt as though a squadron of butterflies were performing dynamic aerobatic routines in her stomach.

The four-thousand-pound Sabareni suit she had chosen to wear for the ceremony was sheer silk, a bright coral pink. The tailored jacket had a broad collar and large white buttons, its skirt was straight, hem five centimetres above her knees. Sabareni was one of her favourite designers, the suit made her feel wonderfully elegant. She had decided against ostentatious jewellery, settling for her usual gold St Christopher, and a Cartier diamond brooch. Her maid had straightened her chestnut hair so that it fell down her back almost to her hips; it was a lot of trouble to condition, but after growing it for a decade, she was damned if she was going to have it cut now. Besides, a lot of girls were copying the 'Julia' hair style. She had a media profile which rock stars and channel celebrities could only fantasize about.

Exit RollSpeech. If she didn't know it now she never would.

She could hear the faint shouts of the protesters through the thick glass. 'They look too well-fed to be dole dependants,' she observed as the Rolls left the motorway, cruising past a big green and gold sign which read:

DUXFORD
Event Horizon Astronautics Institute

A rank of police, wearing bulky navy-blue riot uniforms, stood along the side of the slip road, arms linked, forming a human barricade to keep the protesters back from the little convoy. The protesters Julia could see seemed to be in their early twenties, dressed in T-shirts and jeans, most of them male. They were clean, healthy. Probably students.

'Most of them come from colleges at Cambridge,' Morgan said.

Julia awarded herself a mental point.

'Rent-a-mob fodder,' he continued. 'They were bussed out here this morning by a couple of radical groups, Human Frontier and the Christian Luddites, they actually get paid attendance money. Nobody would come otherwise.'

Access Company Security File: Christian Luddites, Radical Group. She had never heard of them before, the name conjured up all sorts of amusing images. Their file squirted into her mind, illusive datastacks she could run or hold on a whim, not quite sight, not quite sound. Raw neural information. The Christian Luddites claimed to be a back-to-the-earth movement, rejecting technology in all forms except for medical purposes. Security said there were possible links with ex-*apparatchiks*, as yet unproven. They had fifteen chapters, spread around the major cities, a couple more in Europe. A detailed membership list had been compiled. She scanned the hierarchy, most of whom were involved in other small intense activist groups. Today's radicals were a nepotistic incestuous lot, she thought.

Cancel File.

'It must cost a lot of money to mount protests if you're paying attendance fees,' she said. 'Where did it all come from originally?'

'We're looking in to it,' Morgan said.

43

'Shouldn't be allowed,' said Patrick Browning, who was sitting next to her. 'They're just gaining publicity at your expense.' He gave her his positive smile, the one that said he would champion her against the whole world if need be.

Patrick was twenty-one, with golden blond hair coming down to his collar, a very handsome angular face, deep hazel eyes that held just a hint of wickedness, and a body which any Greek god would envy. His family were wealthy, a typical European finance dynasty, with interests in shipping, construction, and medium-scale engineering, operating through anonymous Zurich and Austrian offices. So money wasn't quite so much an issue as it had been with previous boyfriends. He had just earned a business administration degree at Oxford, which gave him a nice air of self-confidence; coming on top of his debonair mannerisms and beautifully realized sense of fun, it made him virtually irresistible.

Five weeks ago she had been at a party when she overheard his previous girlfriend, Angela Molloy, boasting that he had the rutting stamina of a bull in springtime. Throughout the following fortnight it seemed as though Patrick couldn't go to a party or club without bumping into Julia. It was uncanny, one might almost suspect fate was pushing them together. After he realized how many mutual interests they had, asking her for a date was only logical.

And Angela had been quite right.

'They have a perfect right to be there,' Julia said neutrally. 'This county paid the most appalling price so that individuals had the right to express opinions again, however extreme or unwelcome. Only PSP *apparatchiks* try to oppress people for saying what they think.' She met Rachel's eye levelly, reading the meticulously contained amusement in the hardliner's composed expression.

Patrick paled slightly at the rebuke, for an instant looking like a five-year-old who had just had his chocolate bar confiscated. 'Yes,' he said carefully. 'But I don't like it when it's you they're expressing about.'

Julia nodded fractionally. There were substantial dividends to be collected by keeping boys on their toes, unsure precisely where they stood. That way they always knew exactly who was in charge.

She leant over Patrick to get a closer look at the placards being waved. It wasn't strictly necessary, the protesters were on both sides of the slip road, but the angle would give Patrick a good view down her cleavage. She held back on a smile when she caught his eyes straying down to her neckline. Mr Suave was no different to any of the others, Mr Hormones in masquerade. Easy meat.

She read some of the placards, the usual obscenities and crude caricatures printed in yellow and pink fluorocolours, then started to giggle.

'What is it?' Morgan asked. He was peering out of the window.

'That one.' She pointed.

A red-haired youth in a blue sweatshirt held up a kelpboard placard which said:

> *Julia already owns the Earth,*
> *don't let her have the stars as well.*

Company security guards in immaculate grey-blue uniforms saluted sharply as they passed through the first of the Astronautics Institute's ten gates. The police escort peeled away, leaving the Rolls to drive on to Building One alone. The circular structure was made up from an outer ring of offices, laboratories, design bureaux, computer centres, cybernetic integration bays, and test facilities; five storeys high, eight hundred metres in diameter, presenting a polished cliff-face of green-silver glass to the outside world. A jet-black dome of solar collector panels roofed a central space hardware assembly hall.

In the distance she could see Building Two, a twin of One, as yet unoccupied; contractors were busy dismantling the scaffolding. A week late, they were going to pay a hefty penalty clause for that. Architectural data constructs of Building Three were already well advanced, big enough to put One and Two inside then rattle them around.

Julia always got a kick out of the Institute; its sheer size, sprawled over the old Imperial War Museum site and now beginning to creep out towards Thriplow, was a spectacular statement of intent. Event Horizon was staking out its claim on the future for everyone to see, rekindling the old High Frontier dream. There was something fundamentally exciting about commanding such a grandiose venture.

Philip Evans, her grandfather, had started to build the Institute a month after the PSP fell. He believed passionately that space industry would be the catalyst in reinvigorating the country's post-Warming economy. His aim was to develop a centre of excellence where every discipline of space industry could be cultivated and refined, ensuring the company had complete technological independence.

Microgee material processing had already established itself as a hugely profitable enterprise. The number of low Earth orbit factory modules churning out 'ware chips, crystals, exotic compounds, and super-strength monolattice filament had grown steadily even during the worst of the global recession which followed the Warming. But the raw materials the factories needed had to be lifted from Earth, battling against gravity throughout the whole ascent. Philip Evans's vision had the giga-conductor revolution reducing launch costs to a fraction of the chemically powered boosters', increasing profits by orders of magnitude. After that, he predicated, the exploitation of extraterrestrial resources would become economically feasible, and he was determined that as the solar system opened up England would be the trail-blazer, with Event Horizon at the forefront. Julia had inherited that faith along with the material reality.

She had continued to pour money and resources into the Institute and its ambitious programmes in the two years since he died, despite all the pressure and criticisms from the company's financial backing consortium. Now the first phase of her plan was coming to fruition, after Heaven alone knew how many minor setbacks and delays.

Today was the day she would shut those whining know-nothings up for good. She wanted to sing and shout for the sheer joy of it. If nothing else, Patrick was in for the night of his life tonight.

Building One's vast car park was full to capacity with company minibuses and rank after rank of scooters – private cars were still a rarity. The Rolls drove past it, and out on to the concrete desert on the other side of the building. Two long temporary seating stands had been erected on the apron, covered from possible showers by red and white striped canvas awnings; they formed a broad avenue, leading away from Building One's huge multi-segment sliding doors. There were seven thousand invited guests waiting for her: Institute personnel and their families, premier-grade executives from most of the kombinates, channel celebrities, politicians, the Prime Minister, Prince Harry, even a few friends.

A press stand had been built at the far end of the avenue. Every place was taken, which gave her a final heart-flutter of nerves. She had secretly hoped the reporters would all still be up in Scotland after the momentous weekend.

Over a hundred cameras swivelled round as the Rolls drew up beside the VIP podium at the side of Building One's doors. Julia took a breath as the Institute's general manager scuttled forwards to open the door, then climbed out with a professional smile in place.

*

Julia was thankful that the usual January heat was tempered by scrappy clouds and a full breeze. If it was up to her there wouldn't even be a ceremony, but politics dictated otherwise, and the workforce needed some kind of recognition for their efforts. So she sat patiently while the bunting flapped noisily overhead and overdressed women kept a surreptitious hand on wide hats.

The Prime Minister, David Marchant, made the first speech; he was a dignified fifty-two-year-old in a blue-grey suit, the embodiment of calm competence. He praised Philip Evans and Julia for their foresight and optimism, then moved on to the workforce and complimented their professionalism, followed up by a couple of political points against the three main parliamentary opposition groups. Julia found herself envying his delivery; he avoided rhetoric and theatrical emphasis, the words just flowed. When it was her turn she accessed the speech and let her words glide straight from the node to her vocal cords, promising that her commitment to funding the space programme remained unchanged, giving a brief outline of projects that would be initiated over the next three years – the larger low Earth orbit dormitory station, expanded science programme, constructing a manned asteroid-survey craft – and managed to get in a joke about one of the engineering apprentices who had been strung up from a hoist by his mates a couple of months ago. She had been on an inspection tour of Building One at the time. It brought an appreciative cheer from the section of the stands where the workers and their families were sitting.

She handed over to Prince Harry for the actual roll out. He got more applause than she had. But then royalty always did. Since the Second Restoration people saw them as a continuity jump-lead to the past; they were a symbol of good times, when there was no Warming and no PSP. Now they were back, and life was picking up again.

Building One's doors slid open ponderously when Prince Harry pressed the button on the pedestal, somewhat predictably a band struck up the 'Zarathustra' theme, and the *Clarke*-class spaceplane emerged into the afternoon sunlight, escorted by a troupe of engineers in spotless white overalls. It had a swept delta planform with a fifty-metre span, sixty metres long; the metalloceramic hull was an all-over frost-white, except for the scarlet Dragonflight escutcheons on the fin. Two streamlined cylindrical nacelles blended seamlessly with the underbelly, air-scoop ramps closed; reaction-control thruster clusters on the nose and around the wedge-shaped clamshell doors at the rear were masked by protective covers, *remove before flight* tags dangling.

Julia clapped along with everyone else, impressed despite herself. The spaceplane was giga-conductor powered, the first of its kind, capable of lifting fifty tonnes into orbit without burning a single hydrocarbon molecule to injure the diseased atmosphere any further. Event Horizon already had orders for two hundred and twenty-seven, with options on another three hundred.

It was an icon to the new age which the giga-conductor was ushering in. The power-storage system was the ideal cheap, easy to manufacture Green solution to the energy problems of the post-Warming world, where hostility to petrol and coal was a tangible, occasionally fatal, aspect of life. And Event Horizon held the worldwide patent; every kombinate, company, and state factory on the planet paid her for the privilege of manufacturing it. The royalty revenue was already over two billion Eurofrancs a year, and it had only been available for twenty-three months. Every nation was racing to restructure their transport systems around it.

She had seen artists' impressions of the commercial hyper-sonic jets which kombinate aerospace divisions were developing, long arrow-finned needles that looked like scaled-up missiles, cutting the transit time between continents to less than an hour. Car companies, those which had survived, were eager to bring out new vehicles, retooling factories which had lain idle for nearly fifteen years. Scooter sales were already booming.

Julia walked down the VIP podium's steps, accompanying the Prime Minister and Prince Harry, lesser dignitaries trailing after them. She kept a beautifully straight face as she showed them round the spaceplane, pointing out features of interest; for once grateful for the steely discipline she had learnt at her Swiss boarding school. But it was hard – this is the air scoop, these are the wheels.

They posed under the flattened bullet nose as the press gathered for a video bite opportunity.

'I would just like to say how immensely proud I am to be here today,' David Marchant told the gaggle of reporters and channel crews. A forest of arms thrust AV recorders towards him. 'This spaceplane is a quite tremendous achievement by the Event Horizon company. A clear sign that our social market policies are the right ones to put England back on its feet again. And my New Conservative government wishes to demonstrate its firm commitment to the space industry by awarding Dragonflight the contract to dispose of eleven thousand tonnes of radioactive waste. This waste is made up of the cores and ancillary equipment of redundant nuclear reactors, currently being stored at great public expense around the country. And we hope that ultimately all the old reactors in this country will be broken up and disposed of in a similar fashion.'

His aide stepped forward and handed him a sheaf of paper. He smiled and passed it to Julia. The contract's datawork had been completed a week ago, but they had both decided to give it a high profile. The roll out was a golden opportunity. With the elections due in two months it would be a valuable campaign issue for the New Conservatives, supporting industry without direct PSP-style subsidies, and showing a practical commitment to the environment.

'Thank you very much, Prime Minister,' she said as the reporters shouted questions. 'I'll just give you a brief clarification of what the contract entails. Firstly Event Horizon will be vitrifying the waste into ten-tonne blocks in our Sunderland plant. Dragonflight will then lift them into orbit, where they will be assembled into clusters of five and attached to a solid rocket booster which will launch them into the Sun. This way we shall be getting rid of the waste once and for all. Something I'm sure we all have cause to celebrate.'

'How much is the contract worth, Julia?' someone shouted. Too loud to pretend she hadn't heard.

'As it says quite clearly in your information kit, operating costs for the *Clarke*-class spaceplane work out at four hundred pounds New Sterling per tonne lifted into low Earth orbit. If you know anyone who can offer a cheaper price, I'm sure the Prime Minister would be interested to hear from them.' She took a pace back and turned sharp right as soon as she finished speaking, gesturing to Prince Harry and David Marchant towards Building One. A posse of aides and management staff instinctively clustered round, isolating her. Nobody else got a chance to shout any more questions.

Access GeneralBusiness. She loaded a note to postpone the announcement about the new cyber factories for a couple of weeks. There were eighteen of them, due to be built under stage twelve of Event Horizon's expansion programme, ranging from a precision machinery shop to a large-scale composite structures plant, employing nearly thirty-five thousand people when they were complete.

Exit GeneralBusiness. It would never do for people to draw any unwarranted connections between the waste disposal contract and the siting of all eighteen factories in marginal constituencies.

*

The VIP reception was held in Building One, a spacious rectangular lounge on the second floor. Chairs had been pushed back against one wall, leaving room for the caterers to set up their table opposite. The seafood buffet was proving popular with the guests. Waiters circulated with glasses of Moët champagne on silver trays. A loud purr of conversation was drowning out the pianist.

Julia stood by the window wall sipping some of the champagne, watching the crowd of spectators traipsing round the spaceplane below. It was mainly family groups, parents leading eager children, stopping to take pictures under the nose. Five different channel news teams were recording their reporters using the spaceplane as a backdrop.

Patrick left the buffet table and came over. 'You should eat something,' he said around a mouthful of shrimp and lettuce.

'I didn't think you liked fat girls,' she retorted.

'I don't.' There was a gleam in his eye she knew well enough. 'How long have we got to stay here?'

'Another hour, at least. Be patient. It could be rewarding.'

'Could be?'

'Yah,' she drawled.

'All right.' He gave her a hungry look.

She grinned back. It would have been exciting to sneak off into one of the disused offices upstairs. But there were security cameras everywhere, and experience had taught her that Rachel would never let her get out of the lounge alone.

'I suppose I'd better do my eager hostess act,' she said in resignation. Most of the people in the lounge were so much older than her, which meant she'd have to stick with small talk, or business. So boring. She had seen Katerina and Antonia and Laura milling about earlier, along with their boys. But they would all be chatting to the channel celebs. She didn't fancy that either; the silver-screen magic tarnished rapidly in real life, she found. Greg and Eleanor were over on the other side of the lounge, talking to Morgan Walshaw and Gabriel Thompson, the woman he lived with. Greg looked uncomfortable and serious, but then he hated having to wear a suit and tie. She started towards them, at least she could tease Greg.

'Miss Evans.'

The urgency in the voice surprised her. It clashed with the day's mood. She turned.

It was Dr Ranasfari. Julia sighed inwardly, very careful not to show any disappointment. She couldn't even make small talk with Dr Ranasfari. The tall, wiry physicist was forty-five years old, neatly turned out, as always, in a light-grey suit, white shirt, and a pink tie that matched her own suit's colour. His dark face looked strained, brown eyes blinking incessantly, glossed back raven hair shone a spectral blue under the lounge's bright biolum panels.

Dr Ranasfari was another of those people Julia always felt she had to impress. Though she doubted many people could impress Ranasfari. He was the genius in charge of the research team which had produced the giga-conductor for Event Horizon. It had taken him ten years; but her grandfather had never doubted he could do it.

'The man's dedicated,' Philip Evans had told her once. 'Bloody boring, mind, Juliet, but dedicated. That's what makes him special. He'll spend his life on a project if needs be. We're lucky to have him.'

After the giga-conductor was unveiled to the world, and the need for total security was abolished, she had built Ranasfari a laboratory complex in Cambridge, and gave him a budget of twenty million pounds New Sterling a year to spend on whatever projects he wanted. He was currently working on a direct thermocouple, a solid-state fibre which would convert thermal energy straight into electricity, eliminating any need for conventional turbines and generators. The potential applications for geothermal power extraction alone were colossal. If he asked for fifty million a year she would grant it.

'No drink, Cormac?' she asked lightly. He never actually objected to her using his first name, although she was always Miss Evans to him. 'You really ought to have one glass at least, this is as much your day as it is mine.'

His lips twisted nervously, showing a flash of snow-white teeth. 'Thank you, no. Miss Evans, I really must speak with you.'

She had never seen him so agitated before. Her humour spiralled down. 'Of course.' She signalled to Rachel.

*

Julia supposed she ought to be grateful Ranasfari had come directly to her, it was a silent acknowledgement of her authority. There were dozens of premier-grade executives who supervised Event Horizon's innumerable divisions, but ultimately they all answered to her. The company wasn't just hers in name, she took sole responsibility for its management, to the amazement and increasing fascination of the world at large. Responsibility, but not the burden of organization, that was shared, quietly, unobtrusively.

The Neural Network bioware core was the final gamble of a dying billionaire, a bid for immortality of the mind. It had to be a billionaire, nobody else could afford the cost. Philip Evans had spliced his sequencing RNA into the bioware, replicating his own neuronic structure. When the NN core had grown to its full size his memories had been squirted out of his dying brain and into their new titanium-cased protein circuitry.

And it had worked. His memories operated in a perfect duplicate of his neural pathways, providing a continuation of personality. Julia had never heard the NN core utter a single out-of-character remark. It was Grandpa.

He had plugged himself into Event Horizon's datanet, orchestrating the company's expansion with an efficiency far in excess of any ordinary managerial system. Seventy years of experience, knowledge, and business guile put into practice by a mind with more spare processing capacity than a light-ware number cruncher. No detail was too small to escape his scrutiny, every operational aspect could be overseen with one hundred per cent attention. With him to guide her faltering steps it was no surprise that Event Horizon had flourished the way it had. Poor old Patrick with his dusty academic degree could never hope to match her when it came to business tactics. In tandem with her grandfather she made more commercial and financial decisions in a day than he would make in the next ten years working for his family organization.

And at the end of the day she could confide in Grandpa totally. He always understood. The invisible friend of childhood imagination, upgraded for the rigours of adult life, infallible, and virtually omnipotent. It was wonderfully reassuring.

The empty office Julia and Ranasfari wound up commandeering overlooked Building One's giant central assembly hall. Even today, with half of the hall's staff attending the roll out ceremony, there was a lot of activity on the floor. Integration bays around the inner wall were brightly lit, showing white-coated technicians manoeuvring large sections of machinery into place, or crowded round terminal display cubes. Little flat-top cyber trucks followed colour-coded guidance strips along alleyways formed by bungalow-sized blocks of equipment. The spaceplane production line dominated the centre of the hall. The way the craft in various stages of construction were pressed nose to tail along its length was reminiscent of some biological growth process, Julia thought, a cyber-queen's birth passage, straight out of one of those big-budget channel horror shows. At the far end were skeletal outlines, triangles of naked ribs and spars which caged spherical tanks and contoured systems modules coated in crinkled gold foil. As the spaceplanes progressed down the line, sections of the metalloceramic hull had been fitted, the wheel bogies added, engines installed. Three almost complete craft were parked in the test bays right in front of the doors, people walking over their wings, big ribbed hoses and power cables plugged into open inspection hatches, polythene taped over various vents and inlets.

Julia sat in the swivel chair behind the desk, a black imitation-wood affair with an Olivetti terminal linked into a complicated CAD drafting board. The office belonged to a middle-manager in the microgee module power systems bureau. Rachel checked it out, then closed the door behind her, standing sentry duty. Dr Ranasfari sank into the cheap thickly padded chair in front of the desk.

'What is it, Cormac?' Julia asked.

He gave another nervous grimace. 'Perhaps I should have gone to Mr Walshaw, but I really feel this must be taken up at the highest level. And the Prime Minister is here, he will listen to you.'

Julia moved from studious interest to outright fascination. Ranasfari never showed the slightest concern for anything outside his work.

Open Channel To NN Core.

Hello, Juliet, what's the problem? I thought you'd be enjoying yourself today, Philip Evans said soundlessly into her mind.

55

It's Ranasfari, she told him. *I'd like you to listen in on this. I might want your opinion.*

'That sounds very drastic, Cormac,' she said out loud. 'But you know I'll help in whatever way I can.'

He nodded, squeezing the knuckles of his left hand. 'Thank you. It concerns Dr Edward Kitchener. You know I used to be one of his students?'

'I didn't know that, no. But I've heard of Edward Kitchener.' Even as she said it she remembered: Kitchener's gruesome murder had dominated the newscasts three days ago, even managing to nudge Scotland off the premier bulletins on Friday night. She couldn't remember seeing much else about it since, although there had been an update this morning, some poor detective in the hot seat, unable to satisfy the incessant questions that reporters were flinging at him.

Grandpa, have they caught the killer yet?

No.

Ah. I think I see where we're leading.

'His death was a tragedy,' she said hurriedly.

'Yes. And the culprit still has not been brought to justice. That is what I want Miss Evans, justice. Kitchener was a brilliant man. Brilliant. He had flaws, weaknesses, we all do. But his genius is undeniable. Simple dignity demands that his murderer is caught. I'm not asking for vengeance. I do not want the return of the death penalty. Nor do I want this barbarian quietly eliminated. But I do want him caught and tried, Miss Evans. Please. The police ... they've had three days. I'm sure they're doing their best, but after all Oakham is just a provincial station. You must impress the Prime Minister, and through him the Home Secretary, on the absolute urgency of this case.'

Tricky one, Juliet. According to finance division records, we were paying Dr Edward Kitchener for research work.

What? I don't remember that.

It was a contract issued by Ranasfari.

Bloody hell.

Damn right, girl. You start pushing Marchant for action now, and people will accuse you of meddling in police affairs. There's enough allegations about you and Event Horizon having undue influence over the New Conservatives as it is.

'What project was Dr Kitchener working on for us?' she asked Ranasfari.

He stopped playing with his hands. 'I didn't think it was worth bringing to your attention,' he said evasively.

She decided to go all out on the friendship routine. 'Cormac, you know you have my full confidence. That's why your budget doesn't have to be cleared through the finance division first, I don't want you having to justify yourself to accountants. I genuinely do appreciate the value of pure research.'

Seductress! Mental laughter echoed faintly.

'Well, thank you.' Ranasfari ducked his head. 'I asked Edward to look into wormholes for me. It corresponds with his field of interest. He was quite intrigued by the prospect. We discussed a fee, but he was more interested in the specialist programs our software division could provide for his light-ware processor than actual money. He agreed to take the contract, and I would channel his software requests through my laboratory. The money was just a token.'

Access General Encyclopedia. Query: Wormholes, Category Physics.

A neat little précis emerged from the processor.

'When you say wormholes, you mean the instantaneous connections through space-time, I take it?' she asked.

'Yes. Wormholes are quite permissible under Einsteinian relativity.'

'I know it's off the point, but what exactly is your interest in these wormholes?'

'I thought, Miss Evans,' he said stiffly, 'I thought that there might be a possible application in interstellar transit.'

'A stardrive?' she said in a surprised whisper.

He nodded, thoroughly miserable.

'Faster than light travel?'

Another brief nod.

'Bloody hell,' said Julia. She summoned up a logic matrix

from the processor node, feeding in the relevant bytes. The combination of irrational brain and coldly precise nodes gave her an ability to dissect problems from oblique angles, fusing intuition and syllogism in a way no pure computer could match. Data packages flowed and merged through the mental construct, budding into ideas. Most she rejected, the remainder opened up interesting options.

'Who else would know that Kitchener was working for us?' she asked.

'Secrecy was not something I would wish to impose on Edward. But he was not naturally communicative, certainly not to the media. His students would know, of course, probably several high-level theoretical cosmologists. He maintained contacts throughout the physics community, in fact academia in general. The free exchange of ideas is vital in such a field.'

She ignored the defensive tone.

How about it, Grandpa? Could Event Horizon be tied in?

You mean, was he killed to prevent us from obtaining a stardrive?

Yes.

It's a probability, Juliet, you know it is. But I can't see anyone getting so worked up about it that they'd butcher the old boy, not for something that hypothetical. Besides, if it is possible to build an FTL stardrive, then ultimately it will be built. Kitchener might have been a wild card, but plodders have their place too. I expect Ranasfari could crack it if he put enough time in.

Lord, I hope he doesn't. I rather wanted that direct thermocouple.

What are you going to do, Juliet?

Well, we can't ignore Kitchener's murder now. If there is someone that paranoid about Event Horizon walking round loose, then I want them behind bars pronto.

Attagirl.

She put her elbows on the desk, and pressed her palms together. 'I will have Morgan Walshaw contact the Home Office directly,' she said. 'I think I can see how we can get this terrible crime solved quickly.'

'How?' Ranasfari asked.

'The Home Office can authorize local police stations to hire specialist advisers when the circumstances warrant it.'

'What sort of specialist?'

She smiled. 'I was thinking a psychic might be appropriate.'

4

Greg stood behind the moss-covered stone wall of his farm-yard and watched a swarm of bilious clouds buffet the southern sky, blocking out the clean gold and orange colours of the low morning sun. Fast, cool gusts of air chased random wave-patterns in the shaggy grass around the lime saplings, twitching the slate-grey water of the reservoir into small peaks.

In the long thistle-mottled field running between the groves and Hambleton Wood he could see the rabbits venturing out of their huge warrens hidden below the dead trees. Small tawny mounds sloping through the nettle clumps and spindly mildewed forget-me-nots which flourished around the rank of perished hawthorn bushes marking the boundary of the wood. There must have been over eighty of them. He and Eleanor went out on regular shoots two nights each week, infrared laser hunting-rifles picking off fifty at a time. It never seemed to make the slightest difference to their numbers the next morning.

The hot climate had expanded their breeding season to ten months of the year, and the impenetrable tangle of lush under-growth in the wood meant he couldn't reach their warrens to cull them properly. A Forestry Commission logging team was sched-uled to fell the dead trunks in a couple of years, replanting with Chinese pines, otherwise he would probably have torched the wood at the height of summer, and to hell with the owner. The rest of the peninsula's citrus farmers certainly wouldn't object.

Rabbits were a countrywide problem; despite the massive shooting and trapping campaigns which had turned them into a cheap staple meat, they were making serious inroads into England's food crops. The Ministry of Agriculture was holding discussions with the Farmers' Union about releasing a new virulent strain of myxomatosis. It was a nasty virus, but Greg couldn't see an alternative.

He shrugged his black leather jacket over a dark-blue short sleeve cotton sports shirt. His olive-green trousers had a tropical weave, which should keep him from sweating. He would have preferred shorts, but that was pushing it. At least he could wear comfortable suede ankle boots today, the Armani suit and shiny black leather shoes Eleanor had made him put on for the roll out ceremony had been a torture. Too stiff, too hot. It reminded him of the dress uniforms he had had to wear for regimental dinners. But at least they had been introduced to Prince Harry at the VIP reception, which made up for a lot. Then Julia waylaid him with her oh-so-reasonable favour.

He shook his head at the memory. He was irritated, more by the fact that she had automatically assumed he would help the police than being dragged back into that kind of work, but he couldn't honestly say there was any real anger. In any case, the idea of a killer as psychotic as Kitchener's stalking the district wasn't a particularly welcome one. Just so long as this wasn't going to set a precedent. The citrus groves were his life now, and hopefully children before too long.

Eleanor came out of the front door and blipped the lock. She was wearing a navy-blue waiter-cut jacket over an embroidered Indian cotton blouse, deep purple culottes. Her gaze ran over the windows she had been painting before the weekend; the frames were coated in a dull-pink undercoat, waiting for the white gloss finish. She crinkled her nose up.

'Maybe I should stay,' she said, sounding unconvinced.

'Not a chance, if I have to go, so do you. I've still got those limes to plant. And our neighbouring army of killer bunnies is waiting for a chance to eat the ones I did put in, look.'

She glared at the mounds of brown fur bopping about through the undergrowth. 'Perhaps we ought to torch the wood after all.'

He opened the EMC Ranger's door, and climbed in behind the wheel. 'It's too near Hambleton, and it's not the real solution anyway.'

'I suppose.' She sat in the passenger seat. 'I hate the idea of myxomatosis.'

He drove up the slope, and into the village. The broken windows on the Collisters' cottage had already been boarded up with clean sheets of plywood and a heavy padlock held the front door shut. Someone had picked all the ripe brambles from the hedge.

Eleanor gave it a sombre look as they went past, but didn't say anything.

The EMC Ranger's fat, deep-tread tyres made short work of the slushy vegetation matting the peninsular link road. Monday night's rains had left the flat fields beside the road looking like rice paddies. They were planted with gene-tailored barley, a design which utilized the increased level of atmospheric carbon dioxide to produce high yields. Long lines of verdant green shoots as thick as his thumb were poking up through silver pools of water; flocks of gulls waded up and down the ranks, pecking up the bounty of worms which had risen to the surface.

When they reached the roundabout on the Oakham bypass, Greg steered straight round and headed down the A606. The fields of gene-tailored barley gave way to cacao plantations for the last kilometre into town. Over the last few years Oakham had gradually been encircled by the bushes, and more ground was being prepared, expanding the plantations outward like a vigorous mushroom ring. They were a valuable addition to the town's economy. The price of the seed was rising all the time as processed food factories came back on stream, bringing chocolate back into the shops; and the gene-tailored variety flowered twice a year. Their cultivation also soaked up a fair fraction of the unemployed refugees who had been billeted on the town when the Lincolnshire Fens were flooded by the rising sea.

The expanse of small amber flowers was just starting to bloom, but Greg ignored it. In his mind he was still running through yesterday afternoon's conversation with Julia.

'It'll just be half a day's work for you,' she'd said. 'It's *really* important to me. Please, Greg.'

All he could see was a pretty young oval face and big tawny eyes looking up at him entreatingly. That kind of sly appeal, the not quite innocent adolescent adoration, was really below the belt. Typical Julia. The number of boys with broken hearts left in her wake could populate a small city.

'I'm a psychic,' he said out loud.

Eleanor turned and gave him an expectant glance. 'Yes?'

'So how come I can never win an argument with Julia?'

'Because you want to lose. You know the way she feels about you.'

'Why didn't you object? This Kitchener thing, it's exactly why we moved out to the farm, to get away from it.'

She flashed him a dry, knowing smile. 'I didn't object because you were interested. Julia was right when she said you could clear it up in an afternoon. And once she mentioned it, you were hooked. Admit it.'

'Yeah,' he said. Immensely grateful that she understood, once again. Though right at the back of his mind was a tiny smack of disquiet, a subliminal certainty that something didn't quite gel. His intuition playing up again, although he hadn't used his gland since leaving the Collisters' cottage. It had started as soon as Julia mentioned Kitchener's murder at Launde Abbey. And the more he tried to resolve it, find the reason, the more elusive it became. It would come eventually, of course, and then he'd kick himself for missing the obvious.

*

Inside Oakham, the road surface improved noticeably; thistles and twitch grass still burrowed up through the tarmac near the kerbs, but the streets were open to two-way traffic. Scooters and bicycles clogged the middle of the town, forcing Greg to reduce speed; horse and cart rigs queued up patiently behind pre-Warming juggernauts. The big lorries had been converted to burning methane, true dinosaurs now, paintwork scarred and fading, drive mechanisms cannibalized from a dozen different wrecks.

The ramshackle stalls which used to run the length of the High Street during the PSP years had recently been evicted, and the tarmac sealed over with thermo-stabilized cellulose. Greg used to enjoy the souk-like atmosphere of the town centre, but the economic upswing was steadily squeezing street traders and spivs out of national life. Die-hard stallholders had moved back to the market square, but it wasn't the same. Shops were in vogue again. Almost two-thirds had re-opened, and he could see another three being refurbished; although they mainly sold consumer products and clothes, the market retained its hold over supplying fresh food. He wondered sourly how long it would take for the supermarket chains to re-establish themselves. Back to sanitized mass-produced packets of tasteless pap. A sure sign of prosperity.

The way the country was right now was just about perfect, he reckoned. Emerging from the nightmare past, and looking forward to a future rich with promises – most of them made by Julia.

They turned off the High Street and drove down Church Street, past Cutts Close, the central park. It was bounded by earth ramparts, and terribly overgrown; dead oak trees lying where they had fallen, waist-high grass choking the ancient swings. The affluence of the High Street didn't extend far.

A cluster of thirty-odd sleek white and silver trailers and caravans was drawn up in the middle of Cutts Close, looking like some kind of futuristic gypsy convoy. Greg saw the corporate logos of channel newscast companies splashed on them, a thicket of tripod-mounted satellite uplink dishes pointing up into the southern sky.

His fingers tightened around the steering-wheel in reflex

64

dismay. Of course! How stupid, he should have realized. A groan escaped from his lips.

'What is it?' Eleanor asked.

'Them!' He nodded ahead.

The police station was sited just past the bottom of the park, backing on to what had once been the famous public school's playing fields. The rugby pitches and cricket squares had long since been dug up to provide allotments for the Fens refugees displaced by the rising seas; over two hundred families had been crammed into the school buildings by the PSP Residential Allocation bureau. It was only a temporary accommodation, they were promised. Now, twelve years on, they were still waiting for proper housing.

The main part of the station was a broad two-storey building built out of drab rusty-coloured brick, roofed by steel-grey tiles. A single-storey wing jutted out of the front, almost like an afterthought, long, narrow windows facing the road. It dated from the tail-end of the last century, and despite the architect's use of curves and split levels to reduce its starkness it had a fortress-like appearance. The image wasn't helped by the relics of the People's Constables' tenure. Metal grilles had been fitted over the long ground-floor windows, black security camera globes hung from the eaves, and the entrance to the rear car park was guarded by a high fence of thin monolattice slice-wire with skull and crossbones warning signs on each post. The brickwork facing the street was covered in ghostly remnants of paint-bomb impacts and fluorospray graffiti; an ineffectual solvent wash had left several anti-PSP slogans visible. Tapering soot scars, like frozen black flames, showed where the molotovs had hit.

The rioters and celebrants who had laid siege to the station the day the PSP fell had now been replaced by the media army.

'Good God,' Eleanor murmured when they reached the end of Church Street.

Greg guessed there must have been over two hundred of them; and it was like an army, rank denoted by the uniform:

reporters in smooth suits, broadcast crews in T-shirts and shorts, production staff in designer casuals. The majority had taken over the broad pavement opposite the station, although some camera operators had staked out positions on the park's earth embankment giving them a good view of the station. Several fast-food caravans had set up shop in front of the Catholic church a hundred metres further down the road. They were doing a good trade with production PAs.

Greg sounded the horn as he indicated to turn into the station. A knot of twelve people were just standing in the middle of the road, channel logos on their jackets.

'Well, I suppose the local pubs will be happy,' Eleanor said.

There was a lone bobby standing outside the gate in the slice-wire fence. He was about twenty-five, wearing dress whites, shorts, and half-sleeve shirt, with a peaked cap, and looking very fed up.

'Oh, bugger,' Greg muttered as he lowered the window. The rear-view mirror showed him the reporters converging *en masse* on the EMC Ranger.

'Yes, sir?' the bobby asked.

'I'm here to see Detective Inspector Langley,' Greg said. He held up his general ident card, pressing his thumb on the activation patch.

The bobby pulled out his police-issue cybofax, and the two exchanged polarized photons in a blink of dim ruby light. Reporters were clustering round the bobby, jostling to see what was going on. Two camera operators had shoved their lenses up against Eleanor's window.

'Go straight in, sir,' the bobby said after his cybofax had confirmed Greg's identity. He blipped the gate lock. It started to swing open.

The action triggered off a barrage of questions from the reporters.

'Who are you, mate?'

'What have you come here for?'

'Are you a relative of Kitchener?'

'Smile for us, luv!'

Greg toed the accelerator as soon as the gate started to open, nudging the EMC Ranger towards the gap in short jerks. The bobby was trying to shove the crush of reporters to one side.

Greg switched to a broad Lincolnshire accent, and bellowed out of the open window: 'I'm here to see about me bleedin' sheep, ain't I? Some bastard's been pinching 'em right out o' the field. What's it got to do with you buggers? Get out the bleeding way!'

The EMC Ranger must have added authenticity, a mud-caked farm vehicle, even though it was new and expensive. A chorus of groans went up. The reporters gave each other annoyed shrugs, and gave up.

The gate closed behind them.

Eleanor was smiling broadly. 'Very good. I give it less than twenty minutes before they discover you are the Greg Mandel who had Julia Evans as a bridesmaid at his wedding.'

'I expect you're right.'

There were five police vehicles parked in the yard, four old EMC electric hatchbacks, powered by high-density polymer batteries, and a rust-spotted Black Maria with ten-year-old number plates. Greg parked the EMC Ranger next to a line of scooters.

There was a woman officer waiting for them. She introduced herself as Detective Sergeant Amanda Paterson, a pleasant-faced thirty-year-old with mouse-brown hair, wearing a white blouse and fawn skirt. She shook hands with a surprisingly strong grip, but her manner was fairly reserved.

'I'll take you to see Inspector Langley,' she told them briskly. 'He's heading the inquiry.'

'Are you working on the case?' Greg asked.

'Yes, sir.' There was no elaboration. She opened the door, and ushered them into the station. The air inside was cool and stale, there were no fans or conditioners to circulate it. Biolum strips screwed on to the ceiling cast a weary light along the corridor. The original electric tubes had been left in place, their pearl glass covers grey with dust.

It was all very basic, Greg thought, as she led them to the central stairwell. The grey-green ribbed carpet was badly worn, walls were scarred with rubber shoe marks above the skirting-board, cream-coloured paint had darkened, doors were scuffed and scratched and didn't even have 'ware locks.

The police didn't enjoy much public confidence right now, he knew. But starving them of money and resources was hardly going to help their morale and efficiency, certainly not at a time when the New Conservatives were trying to claim the credit for resurrecting an honest and impartial judicial system.

They passed a mess room, and three uniformed constables glanced out. Their faces hardened as soon as they saw Greg and he began to wonder just what sort of stories were orbiting the station.

The CID office was on the second floor. Amanda Paterson knocked once on the door, and walked in. Greg followed her into the noise of shrilling phones and murmuring voices. There were six imitation-wood desks inside, three of them occupied by men, detectives in shirt sleeves typing away at their terminal keyboards, one with an old-fashioned phone handset jammed between his shoulder and jaw. They all stared at Greg and Eleanor. Metal filing cabinets were lined up along the wall next to the door, kelpboard boxes piled on top. A big flatscreen covered the rear wall, displaying a large-scale map, with half of Oakham showing as a red and brown crescent along the right-hand side. The air was warm despite two of the windows being open; a single conditioner thrummed loudly.

Detective Inspector Vernon Langley was in his late forties. He was almost a head smaller than Greg, and his dark hair had nearly vanished, leaving a shiny brown pate. He was sitting behind a desk at the head of the room, jacket draped over the back of his chair, mauve tie loosened, buttons on his white shirt straining slightly, looking about seven kilos overweight.

The desk was littered in printouts, folders, thumb-sized cylindrical memox crystals, and sheets of handwritten notes. Langley was typing on an English Electric terminal. The model was a decade out of date, and pretty inferior even when it was new. English Electric had been a nationalized conglomerate formed by the PSP, a shotgun marriage between a dozen disparate 'ware companies. Only government offices used to buy their equipment, everyone else went to black-market spivs for up-to-date foreign gear.

He stood up to greet them, wincing slightly, one hand rubbing the stiffness from his back as he rose. He had obviously been working close to his limit on the Kitchener case: his face was lined, there was a five o'clock shadow on his chin. Greg felt exhausted just looking at him.

'I wasn't informed that there would be two of you,' he said as he shook hands with Eleanor.

'I act as Greg's assistant,' Eleanor said levelly. 'I am also his wife.'

Vernon Langley nodded reluctantly as he sat back down again. 'All right, I'm certainly not going to make an issue of it. Find yourself a seat, please.'

Greg drew up a couple of plain wooden chairs. At a second nod from Vernon, Amanda Paterson left them to go and sit at a desk next to the other three detectives. The four of them put their heads together, talking in low tones.

Greg was tempted to use his gland there and then, but he guessed the only emotion in the room would be resentment. They had all been working hard on an important case, under an immense, and very public, burden to produce quick results, now some civilian glamour-merchant had been brought in over their heads because of political pressure. He knew the feeling of frustration well enough, army brass had worked according to no known principles of logic.

'The Home Office called me at home this morning,' Langley said. 'Apparently you have been drafted in to act as my special adviser on this case. Officially, that is. Unofficially, it was made fucking clear you are now in charge. Would you mind telling me why that is, Mandel?' The lack of any inflection was far more telling than any bitterness or anger.

'I am ex-Mindstar,' Greg said deferentially. 'My gland gives me an empathic ability, I know when people are lying. Somebody once described me as a truthfinder.'

'A truthfinder? Is that so? I've heard you spent a lot of time in Peterborough after Mindstar was demobbed.'

'Yeah.'

'They say you killed fifty People's Constables.'

'Oh, no.'

Langley's eyes narrowed in suspicion.

Greg couldn't resist it. 'More like eighty.'

The detective grunted. 'Had a lot of experience solving murders, have you, Mandel?'

'No. None at all.'

'Twenty-three years I've been in the force now. I even stuck it out in the PSP years.' He waved a hand airily as Eleanor shifted uncomfortably. 'Oh, don't worry, Mrs Mandel, the Inquisitors cleared me of any complicity with the Party. That's why I was posted here from Grantham, a lot of Oakham's officers failed that particular test. Not politically sound, you see. Well, not as far as this government is concerned.'

'I wonder if Edward Kitchener cares what political colour the investigating officers are,' Eleanor said.

Langley gave her a long look, then sighed in defeat. 'You're quite right, of course, Mrs Mandel. Please excuse me. I have spent the last four days and nights trying to find this maniac. And for all my efforts, I have got exactly nowhere. So tempers in this office are likely to be a little frayed this morning. I apologize in advance for any sharp answers you may receive. Nothing personal.'

'I didn't know the Home Office had told you I was in charge,' Greg said. 'As far as I'm concerned, it's still your investigation. I really am just a specialist.'

'Sure, thanks,' said Langley.

Greg decided to press on. It was obvious there wouldn't be the usual small talk, the getting-to-know-you session. He'd just have to do what he could. 'The press reports said Kitchener was butchered, is that true?'

'Yes. If I didn't know better I'd say it was a ritualistic killing. Satan worship, a pagan sacrifice, something like that. It was utter barbarism. His chest was split open, lungs spread out on either side of his head. We have holograms if you want an *in situ* review.'

'Not at the moment,' Greg said. 'Why would anybody go to that much trouble?'

Langley gestured emptily. 'Who knows? I meet some evil bastards in this job. But Kitchener's murderer is beyond me, that kind of mind is in a class of its own. Nobody knows what makes someone like that tick. To be honest, it frightens me, the fact that they can walk around pretending to be human for ninety-nine per cent of the time. I suppose you can spot one straight off?'

'Maybe,' Greg said. 'If I knew what to look for.'

'Whoever he is, he's not entirely original. It was a copy-cat method.'

'Copy cat?'

'This spreading the lungs gimmick; Liam Bursken used to do it.'

Greg frowned, the name was familiar.

'He was a serial killer, wasn't he?' Eleanor said.

'That's right, he roamed Newark picking people at random off the streets then butchering them. The press called him the Viking. He murdered eleven victims in five months. But that was six years ago. Now he really was psychopathic, a total loon. Newark was like a city under siege until he was caught. People refused to go out after dusk. There were vigilante groups patrolling the streets, fighting with People's Constables. Nasty business.'

'Where is he now?' Greg asked.

'HMP Stocken Hall, the Clinical Detention Centre where they keep the really dangerous cases. Locked away in the maximum security wing for the rest of time.'

'That's close,' Greg murmured. He conjured up a mental map of the area. Stocken Hall was only about fifteen kilometres from Launde Abbey as the crow flies.

'Give me some credit. I did check, Mandel. Bursken was there four nights ago. They won't even take him out of the Centre if he gets ill; the doctors have to visit him.'

'There is no such thing as coincidence.' Greg smiled apologetically. 'OK. It wasn't Bursken. You say you haven't got a suspect yet? Surely you must have some idea.'

'None at all.' The detective slumped further back into his chair. 'Embarrassing for us, really. Considering there are only six possible culprits. A neat solution, somebody we could charge quickly, would have been the best thing that could have happened to this station. Not the town's favourite sons, we are.' He flicked a finger at Amanda Paterson. 'And daughters, of course. As it is, I can't even go outside to that pack of jackals and say I hope to make an arrest in the near future.'

'Who are the six possibles?'

'Kitchener's students. And a bigger bunch of wallies you've never seen; bright kids, but they're plugged into some other universe the whole time. Typical student types, naïve and fashionably rebellious. They were the only ones in Launde Abbey at the time. The Abbey's security system memory showed no one else sneaked in, and it's all top-grade gear. But I'm not just relying on that as evidence. It was a nasty storm the night Kitchener was murdered, remember?'

'Yeah,' Greg said. He remembered the day of Roy Collister's lynch mob.

Langley climbed to his feet, and went over to the big flatscreen on the rear wall. 'Jon Nevin will show you what I mean. He's been checking out all the possible access routes to the Abbey.'

One of the other detectives stood up; in his late twenties, thinning black hair shaved close, a narrow face with a long nose that had been broken at some time. He made an effort to rein back on his hostility as Greg and Eleanor trailed after Langley.

The map was centred on Launde Park, an irregular patch

coloured a phosphorescent pink. A tall column of seven-digit numbers had been superimposed alongside. From the scale, Greg judged the park had an area of about a square kilometre; he hadn't quite realized how remote it was, situated half-way up the side of the Chater valley. A lone road bisecting the valley was its only link with the outside world.

Nevin tapped a finger on the little black rectangle which represented the Abbey. His face registered total uninterest. If he'd still been in the army, Greg would have called it dumb insolence.

'Because of its isolated position we don't believe anyone could have got to Launde Abbey at any time after six o'clock last Thursday afternoon,' Nevin recited in a dull tone.

'What time was Kitchener killed?' Greg asked.

'Approximately four-thirty on Friday morning,' Langley said. 'Give or take fifteen minutes. Certainly not before four.'

'The storm arrived at Launde Abbey at about five p.m. on Thursday,' Nevin said. His hand traced northwards along the road outside the Abbey. 'We estimate the bridge over the River Chater was submerged by six, completely unpassable. The rainfall was very heavy around here, fifteen centimetres according to the meteorological office at RAF Cottesmore. Basically, that bridge is just a couple of big concrete-pipe sections with earth and stone shovelled on top; it's a very minor road, even by the last century's standards.

'That just leaves us the route to the south. The road goes up over the brow of the valley, and into Loddington; but there is a fork just outside Loddington which leads away to Belton. So in order to get on to the road to Launde you have to go through either Loddington or Belton.'

Greg studied the villages; they were tiny, smaller than Hambleton. Long columns of code numbers were strung out beside them. He could see where Nevin was leading. They were small insular farming communities, and anything out of the ordinary – strangers, unknown vehicles – would become a talking-point for weeks. He pointed to the thin roads that led to Launde Park. 'What sort of condition are these roads in?' he asked.

'The map is deceptive,' Nevin admitted. He swept his hand over the web of yellow lines covering the land to the west of Oakham; it was a bleak stretch of countryside, furrowed with twisting valleys and steeply rounded hills. A few lonely farmhouses were dotted about, snug in the lee of depressions. 'All these minor roads are down to farm tracks in most places. Some stretches are completely overgrown, you have to be a local to know where to drive.'

'And you're saying nobody went through Loddington or Belton after six o'clock on Thursday?' Eleanor asked.

'That's right, there wasn't even any local traffic,' Jon Nevin said. 'Everybody was battened down before the storm began. We did a house-to-house enquiry in both Loddington and Belton.' He pointed at the columns of numbers. 'These are our file codes for the statements; you can review them if you want, we interviewed everybody. You see, the streets in both villages are very narrow, and if any vehicle had gone through the residents would have known.'

Eleanor shrugged acceptance, and gave him a warm smile. The detective couldn't maintain his air of indifference under those circumstances. Greg pretended not to notice.

Langley went and sat behind the nearest desk, hooking an arm over the back of the chair. 'In any case, the important thing is, we know for a fact that nobody came out of the valley between six o'clock Thursday evening and six o'clock Friday morning. The murderer was there when we arrived.'

'How do you figure that?' Greg asked.

'The Chater bridge was still under water until midday Friday. That just leaves the south road again. If you were coming out of the valley, you had to use it.

'The students called us from the Abbey at five-forty on Friday morning. It was Jon here and a couple of uniforms who responded. They took a car down to the Abbey just after six.'

'We were the first to use that road after the storm finished,' Nevin said, 'and we had a lot of trouble. It was covered in fresh mud from the rains, and it was absolutely pristine. No tyre tracks. I was very careful to check. And you couldn't cut across country, not with the ground in that state, it was saturated; even your EMC Ranger would sink in up to the hubcaps. The only people in that valley when Kitchener was killed were his students.'

Greg checked the map again, and decided they were probably right about the roads. He thought about how he would go about killing Kitchener. There had been enough similar missions in Turkey. Covert penetrations, tracking down enemy officers, eliminating them without fuss, stealing away afterwards, leaving the Legion troops unnerved by their blatant vulnerability. An old man confined in a verified location would be an easy target.

'What about aircraft?' he asked.

Langley let out a soft snort. 'I checked with the CAA and the RAF. There was nothing flying around the Chater valley early Friday morning, nor Thursday evening for that matter.'

'Can we shift this focus to show the rest of the Chater valley?' Greg asked.

'Yes,' Langley said. He waved permission to Nevin. The detective started to tap out instructions on a desk terminal. After a minute the map blinked out altogether, and he cursed. Amanda Paterson joined him at the terminal.

'This is how it goes here,' Langley said, half to himself. 'I don't suppose your Home Office contact considered allocating us a decent equipment budget as well?'

'I doubt it.'

He curled up a corner of his mouth in resignation.

The map reappeared, flickering for a moment, then steadied and slowly traversed east to west until Launde Park touched the left-hand edge of the flatscreen.

'Is that all right?' Paterson asked.

'Yeah, thanks,' Greg said. He tracked the River Chater out of Launde Park towards the east. It was almost a straight course. Further down from Launde, the floor of the valley was crossed by a few minor roads, but essentially it was empty until he reached Ketton, twenty kilometres away. 'If it was me,' Greg said,

75

his eyes still on the map, 'I would use a military microlight to fly in. You could launch anywhere west of Ketton, and cruise up the river, keeping your altitude below the top of the valley to avoid radar.'

The detectives glanced about uncertainly.

'A microlight?' Langley said. His mind tone betrayed a strong scepticism.

'No messing. The Westland ghost wing was the best ever made, by my reckoning anyway. They had a high reliability, a minute radar return, and they manoeuvred like a dream. Nobody could hear it from the ground once you were above a hundred metres; and you glided down to a landing.' His fingernail made a light *click* as he touched the screen above Launde Park. 'The gradient of the slopes around the Abbey would be ideal for an unpowered launch afterwards.'

They were all staring at him, humour and contempt leached away.

'The winds,' Eleanor said matter-of-factly into the silence.

'Yeah. They could be a problem, certainly right after that storm. We'd have to check with RAF Cottesmore, see what speeds they were around here.'

'This is somewhat fanciful, isn't it?' Langley asked mildly.

'Somebody killed him, and you say it wasn't any of the people who were there.'

'We haven't proved any of them did it,' Nevin countered. 'But we're still interviewing them.'

'Even if someone did fly in like you say,' Paterson said, 'they still had to get past the Abbey's security system.'

'If a hardline tekmerc had been contracted to snuff Kitchener, he would go in loaded with enough 'ware to burn through the security system without leaving a trace.'

'A tekmerc?' Langley asked. Disbelief was thick in his voice.

'Yeah. I take it you have drawn up a list of people who disliked Kitchener? From what I remember, he was a prickly character.'

'There are a few academics who have clashed with him

publicly,' Nevin said cautiously. 'But I don't think a grudge over different physics theories would extend to this. Everyone acknowledged he was a genius, they made allowances for his behaviour.'

Greg looked round at the stony faces circling him. He had entertained the notion, absurdly guileless now, he realized, that he would be welcomed by a team who would be delighted to have his psi faculty at their disposal. He wasn't expecting to be taken out for beers and a meal afterwards, but at least that way he could have approached the case with some enthusiasm. All Langley's dispirited squad could offer was a long uphill yomp.

'Did any of you know that Kitchener was working on a research project for Event Horizon?' he asked.

The reaction was more or less what he expected; flashes of disgust, quickly hidden, tight faces, hard eyes. Langley dropped his head into his hands, fingertips massaging his temple.

'Oh shit,' he said thickly. 'Greg and Eleanor Mandel, who had Julia Evans as their bridesmaid. How stupid of me. She had you sent here. And there I was thinking that it was just the Home Office panicking for a quick arrest.'

'Did you know about the contract?' Eleanor asked waspishly. Her face had reddened under her tan.

'No, we didn't,' Langley replied, equally truculent.

Greg touched her shoulder, trying to reassure her. She flashed him a grateful smile. 'Well, I suggest that corporate rivalry is now a motive for you to consider,' he said. 'Does that make any of the students a likely candidate?'

'No, of course not.' Langley was struggling to come to terms with Event Horizon's involvement. Greg guessed he was trying to work how this would affect his career prospects. Maybe a quiet word when the rest of the CID wasn't looking on would help smooth the way. It certainly couldn't make the situation any worse.

'Does Event Horizon have any idea who might have murdered Kitchener? Which rival would benefit from having him snuffed by a tekmerc?' Langley asked.

'No. No idea.'

'They don't know? Or they don't want us to know?' Paterson asked.

'That'll do,' Langley said quickly.

She gave Greg and Eleanor a sullen glare, then turned and went back to her desk.

'What sort of research was Kitchener doing for Event Horizon?' Jon Nevin asked.

'Something to do with spatial interstices,' Greg said. Julia hadn't managed to explain much about it to him. He didn't think she entirely understood it herself.

'What are they?'

'I'm not entirely sure. Small black holes from what I gather. It all goes a long way over my head.'

'Are they worth much?' Langley asked.

'They might be eventually. Apparently you can use them to travel to other stars.'

This time the silence stretched out painfully. The detectives clearly didn't know what to make of the idea.

Join the club, Greg thought.

'All right, Mandel,' Langley said. 'What is it you wish to *advise* me to do now? Because I'm buggered if I know where to go from here.'

Greg paused, attempting to put his thoughts in some kind of logical sequence. Most of the training he'd received in preparation for Mindstar had been data correlation exercises. 'Firstly, I want to visit Launde Abbey, have a look round. Then I want to interview the students. Where are they?'

'We're still holding them.'

'After four days?'

'Their lawyers advised them to co-operate. For the moment, anyway. It wouldn't look good if they start throwing their legal rights around too much. But we had to agree that six days is the maximum limit, after that we'll either have to apply to a magistrate for them to be taken into police custody or let them go.'

'OK. I want to see their statements before I meet them. And the forensic and pathology reports as well, please.'

'All right, we'll assign you an authority code so you can access the files on this case. And I'll take you out to Launde myself.'

5

Three more uniformed bobbies had been drafted in to help keep the channel crews back from the police station gate. Ribbons of sweat stained the spines of their white shirts as they shouted and pushed at the incursive horde. Eleanor drove out into the road, and turned hard right, heading down towards the railway station. The way to do it, she discovered, was imagine the road to be empty, and just *go*. Reporters and camera operators nipped out of the way sharpish.

She had been right about them tracking down Greg's personal data profile, though.

'Mr Mandel, is it true you're helping the police with the Kitchener murder?'

'You don't farm sheep, Greg, what are you here for?'

'Did Julia Evans send you?'

'Is it true you used to serve in Mindstar?'

'Eleanor, where are you going?'

'Come on, Greg, say something.'

'Can we have a statement?'

She passed the last of them level with the fast-food caravans, and pressed her foot down. The hectic shouts faded away. A smell of fried onions and spicy meat blew into the EMC Ranger through the dashboard vents.

'Christ,' she murmured. When she lived on the kibbutz she had often accompanied her father and the other men when they took the hounds out hunting. She had seen what happened to foxes, wild cats, and even other dogs when the hounds ran them down. They would keep on worrying the bloody carcass until there was nothing left but shreds. The press, she reflected sagely, had an identical behaviour pattern. For the first time she began to feel sorry for Langley, having to conduct his inquiry with them braying relentlessly on his heels.

If she had known about them as well as the way the police would treat her and Greg, she might well have played the part of shrewish wife and told him no. Too late now.

A quick check in the rear-view mirror showed her the police Panda car carrying Vernon Langley and Jon Nevin was following them. Langley had assigned Amanda Paterson to accompany her and Greg in the EMC Ranger. Eleanor wasn't quite sure who was supposed to be chastised by the arrangement. Amanda was sitting in the rear of the big car, hands folded across her lap, a sullen expression on her face as she watched the detached houses of Station Road whizz past.

So defensive, Eleanor thought, as if the Kitchener inquiry was some shabby secret she was guarding. And now the barbarians were hammering on the gate, demanding access.

'You OK?' Greg asked.

'Sure.'

He held her gaze for a moment. 'How about you, Amanda?' he asked.

Startled, the woman looked up. 'Yes, fine, thank you.'

'Have they been like that the whole time?' Eleanor asked her.

'Yes.' She paused. 'It hasn't helped when we went round the villages collecting statements. They often got the residents' stories before we did.' Her mouth tightened. 'They shouldn't have done that.'

Eleanor drove over the level crossing and took the Braunston road. The clouds were darkening overhead, a uniform neutral veil. It would rain soon, she knew, a thunderstorm. Weather sense was something everybody cultivated these days.

Greg inclined his head fractionally towards her, then flipped open his cybofax and started to run through the statements he'd loaded into the memory. Grey-green data trundled down the small LCD screen, rearranging itself each time he muttered an instruction.

Devious man, she thought, holding back a smile. Among his other qualities. She could read him so easily, something she'd been able to do right from the start; and vice versa, of course, him with his gland. Greg always said she had psychic traits, although he didn't want her to take the psi-assessment tests. Not putting his foot down, they didn't have that kind of relationship, but heavily opposed to her having a gland. He was more protective about it than anything else, wanting to spare her the ordeal. Several Mindstar veterans had proved incapable of making the psychological adjustment necessary to cope with their expanded psi ability.

There were so few people who saw that aspect of Greg: his concern, the oh so human failings. Gland prejudice was too strong, an undiluted paranoia virus; nobody saw past the warlock power, they were dazzled by it.

Countless times she had watched people flinch when they were introduced to him, and she could never decide quite why. Perhaps it was all the time he'd spent in the army and the Trinities. He had the air of someone terribly intimate with violence; not an obvious bruiser type, like those idiots Andrew Foster and Frankie Owen, more like the calm reserve martial arts experts possessed.

The first time they met, the day she ran away from the kibbutz, her father had come looking for her. He backed down so fast when Greg intervened; it was the first time she had *ever* seen her father give way over anything. He always had God's righteousness on his side, so he claimed. More like incurable peasant obstinacy, she thought, the cantankerous old Bible-thumper. The whole of her life until then, or so it seemed, had been filled with his impassioned skeletal face craning out of the pulpit in the wooden chapel, broken purple capillaries on his rough cheeks showing up tobacco-brown in the pale light which filtered through the turquoise-glass window behind the altar. That face would harangue and cajole even in her dreams, promising God's justice would pursue her always.

But all it had taken was a few quiet-spoken resolute words from Greg and he had retreated, walking out of her life for good. Him, the kibbutz's spiritual leader, abandoning his only daughter to one of Satan's technological corruptions.

She had moved in to Greg's chalet that night. The two of them had been together ever since. The other residents at the Berrybut time-share estate warned her that Greg could be moody, but it never manifested with her. She could sense when he was down, when he needed sympathy, when he needed to be left alone. Those long anarchistic years in the Trinities, the cheapness of life on Peterborough's streets, were bound to affect him. He needed time to recover, that was all. Couldn't people see that?

She always felt sorry for couples who were unable to plug into each other's basic emotions. They didn't know what they were missing; she'd never trusted anyone quite like she did Greg. That and the sex, of course.

'Kitchener was fairly rich, wasn't he?' she asked Amanda.

'Yes. He had several patents bringing in royalties. His molecular interaction equations all had commercial applications, crystals and 'ware chips, that kind of thing. It was mostly kombinates who took out licences, they paid him a couple of million New Sterling a year.'

Eleanor let out an impressed whistle. 'Who stands to inherit?'

Amanda's features were briefly illuminated with a recalcitrant grin when she realized how smoothly they had breached her guard. 'We examined that angle. No one person benefits. Kitchener had no immediate family, the closest are a couple of younger cousins, twice removed. He left a million New Sterling to their children; there are seven of them, so split between them it doesn't come to that much. The money goes into a trust fund anyway, and they're limited to how much can be withdrawn each year. But the bulk of the estate goes to Cambridge University. It will be used for science scholarships to enable underprivileged students to go to the university; and funding two of the physics faculties, with the proviso that it's only to be spent on laboratory equipment. He didn't want the dons to feather their nests with it.'

'What about Launde Abbey, who gets that?'

'The university. It's to be a holiday retreat for the most promising physics students. He wanted them to have somewhere they could go to escape the pressure of exams and college life, and just sit and think. It's all in his will.'

'That doesn't sound like the Edward Kitchener we hear about,' Eleanor observed.

'That was his public image,' Amanda said. 'Once you've talked to the students, you'll find out that it really was mostly image. They all worshipped him.'

The EMC Ranger started up the hill which led out of town. A new housing estate was under construction on both sides of the road, the first in Oakham for fifteen years. The houses had a pre-Warming Mediterranean look, thick white-painted walls to keep out the heat, silvered windows, solar-cell panel roofs made to look like red clay tiles, broad overhanging eaves. And garages, she noted, the architects must share a confidence about the future.

She had been relieved when the council passed the planning application. Considering all they'd been through when they lost their homes, and the cramped conditions of the school campus, the Fens refugees deserved somewhere for themselves. After the economy started to pick up, she had worried that they would develop into a permanent underclass, resentful and resented. A lot of them had actually been employed to build the houses, but despite that and the cacao plantations the numbers of unemployed in the Oakham district was still too large. The town urgently needed more factories to bring jobs into the area. The transport network wasn't up to supporting commuters yet, allowing people to work in the cities like they used to. She often wondered if she should ask Julia to establish an Event Horizon division in the industrial estate. Would that be an abuse of privilege? Julia could be overbearingly generous to her friends. And there were a lot of towns which needed jobs just as badly as Oakham. Of course, if the Event Horizon factory had to be built anyway, why not use what influence she had? At the moment she was just waiting to see if the council development officers could do what they were paid to, and attract industrial investment. If they hadn't interested a kombinate after another six months or so, she probably would have a word.

A favour for a favour, she thought, because God knows this Kitchener case is tougher than either of us expected. Julia would have to site a whole cyber precinct next to the town to be quits.

She took the west road out of Braunston. It was a long straight stretch up to the recently replanted Cheseldyne Spinney. The turning down to Launde Park was five hundred metres past the end of the tanbark oak saplings. There was a row of yellow police cones blocking it off, tyre-deflation spikes jutting out of their bases like chrome-plated rhino horns. One of Oakham's Panda cars, with two uniformed constables inside, was on duty in front of them. Eleanor counted ten reporters camped opposite, their cars parked on the thistle-tangled verge.

As soon as the EMC Ranger stopped by the Panda car, the reporters were up and running. Cybofaxes, switched to AV record, were pressed against the glass like rectangular slate-grey leeches.

Amanda pulled out her police-issue cybofax and used its secure link to talk to the bobbies in the Panda car.

Eleanor saw one of them nod his head languidly, then they both climbed out and walked towards the cones.

'Are you taking over the case from the police, Mr Mandel?'

'Is it true the Prime Minister appointed you to the investigation?'

'Are you Julia Evans's lover, Greg?'

Eleanor refused to snap the retort which had formed so temptingly in her mind. Instead she forced a contemptuous smile, thinking how good it would feel to stuff that tabloid channel reporter's cybofax where the sun didn't shine.

The bobbies finished clearing away the cones and waved Eleanor on. They could have cleared them away before we arrived, she thought; perhaps it's part of the needling, making us run the press gauntlet.

The Chater valley was a lush all-over green, the steep walls bulging in and out to form irregular glens and hummocks. Dead hawthorn hedges acted as trellises for ivy-leaf pelargoniums, heavy with hemispherical clusters of cerise-pink flowers. The fields were all given over to grazing land, although there was no sign of any animals; the permanent grass cover helped to prevent soil erosion in the monsoon season. As they moved over the brow on the northern side she began to appreciate how secluded the valley was, there had been no clue of its existence from the road out of Braunston.

They started to go down a slope with a vicious incline. The road was reduced to two strips of tarmac just wide enough for the EMC Ranger's tyres, speedwells forming a spongy strip between them, tiny blue and white flowers closed against the darkening sky. Trickles of water were running out of the verges, filling the tarmac ruts. Eleanor slowed down to a crawl.

'Mr Mandel,' Amanda said. There was such a sheepish tone to her voice Eleanor actually risked glancing from the road to check her in the mirror.

Greg looked back over his shoulder. 'What is it?'

'There was something else we didn't release to the press,' Amanda said. 'Kitchener had a lightware number cruncher at the Abbey, he used it for numerical simulation work. Its memory core was wiped. I didn't think about it until you mentioned Event Horizon's involvement. Whatever Kitchener was working on, it's lost for good now.'

'No messing?' Greg said. He sounded almost cheerful.

'We weren't sure if the 'ware had been knocked out by the storm or something. We didn't really connect the two events. But if you take commercial sabotage as a motive for the murder, then it was probably deliberate.'

'Do you know when the core was wiped?' Greg asked. 'Before Kitchener was murdered? After? During?'

'No. I've no idea.'

'What did the students say?'

'I don't know. I can't remember if they were asked.'

Greg thought for a moment, then started defining a search program that would run through the statements stored in his cybofax. Eleanor heard Amanda doing the same thing. That was when they reached a really steep part of the road, just above the Chater itself. She put the EMC Ranger into bottom gear, and kept her foot on the brake pedal. The water channelled by the ruts was running a couple of centimetres deep around the tyres.

'Are you sure about the bridge?' she asked Amanda.

'It should be passable by now. There was only a five-centimetre fall last night.'

'You mean you don't know?' There was a bend at the foot of the slope. Eleanor nudged the EMC Ranger round it, dreading what she'd see. Turning round here would be difficult. Right at the bottom of the valley the river had worn a cramped narrow gully in the earth. The scarp had been scoured of grass and weeds by the recent monsoon floods, leaving a pockmarked face of raw red-brown earth. Ahead of the EMC Ranger the road had miraculously reappeared in full, grass, moss, nettles, and speedwells swept away by the water.

The Panda car was holding back, she caught a glimpse of it on top of the final slope.

Waiting for us to find out what the river is like, she thought, bastards.

'We're waterproof, remember,' Greg said. He winked.

She grinned savagely, and urged the EMC Ranger along the last ten metres to the bridge. The Chater was a turbulent slash of fast-flowing brown water, boiling over the bridge. Eleanor used the white handrail as a guide as she gingerly steered over it. Water churned around the wheels. She estimated it was about fifteen centimetres deep, not even up to the axle.

Once they were over the river, the road turned right. Greg pulled at his lower lip, looking back thoughtfully. The smaller Panda car was edging out over the bridge, water up to the base of its doors.

'Tell you, Jon Nevin was right; nothing would have got over that on Thursday night and Friday morning,' Greg said.

There was a lake ahead of them, a rectangle fifty metres long, draining into the Chater through a crumbling concrete channel. A small earth bank rose up behind it, sprouting dead horse-chestnut trees which were leaning at precarious angles.

They started to climb up the slope, a dreary expanse of scrimpy, slightly yellowed grass. The road surface on this side of the Chater was even worse than the northern side. Past the end of the first lake, and ten metres higher, was a second, a triangular shape, a hundred metres along each side. It was being fed by a waterfall at the head. A decrepit wooden fence slimed with yellow-green lichen ran around it.

'Stop here,' Greg said.

Eleanor pulled up level with the end of the lake. She guessed there was another above them.

Greg opened the door and got out, standing in front of the bonnet, staring at the lake. His eyes had that distant look, the gland neurohormones unplugging him from the physical universe. *A world sculpted from shadows*, he'd said once, when he tried to describe the way neurohormones altered his perception, *similar to a photon amp image, everything dusty and grainy. But translucent; you could see right through the planet if you had enough strength. The shadows are analogous to the fabric of the real world – houses, machinery, furniture, the ground, people. But not always. There are . . . differences. Additions. Memories of objects, phantasms I suppose.*

And I can perceive minds too. Separate from the body. Minds glow, like nebulas with a supergiant star hidden at the core.

The remoteness faded from his face. He gave the lake a last look, fingers stroking his chin, a faintly puzzled expression pulling at his features.

'What did you see?' she asked as he got back into the passenger seat. His intuition was almost as strong as his empathy. When they first looked round the farmhouse on the Hambleton peninsula he had suddenly grabbed hold of her as she walked into one of the small upstairs bedrooms. He couldn't give a reason, just that she shouldn't go in. When they gave it a thorough examination they found that a whole section of the floorboards in front of the door was riddled with woodworm. If she had just marched in she would have fallen straight through.

'Not sure,' Greg said.

The Panda car was lumbering up the road behind them. Eleanor started off towards the third lake. The first tiny spots of drizzle began to graze the windscreen.

'A microlight landing spot?' she asked.

'No.'

Amanda was giving them a slightly bemused look from the back seat.

The third lake was a slightly larger version of the second. She could see the ruins of a small brick building situated halfway up the earth bank on the far side. She thought it might be an ancient ice-house. A flock of Canada geese were grazing round the thick tufts of reedy grass which flourished around the shore.

'I'm sure I remember reading something else about Launde Abbey,' Greg said. 'Or maybe it was on a channel newscast.'

'I can't remember anything,' Eleanor said.

'It was a few years ago. I think. Seven or eight, maybe more.' He didn't sound very convinced. 'What about you, Amanda? Have there been any other incidents up here?'

'No, not that I can recall.'

'What sort of incident?' Eleanor asked.

He gave her an abashed grin. 'Can't remember. Definitely something newsworthy, though.'

'And it's connected to the Kitchener murder?' she asked.

'Lord knows. I doubt it, not that long ago.'

Launde Abbey was another hundred and fifty metres past the third lake, set in a broad curving basin that seemed to have been chiselled into the side of the valley. A wooden fence marked the boundary of the parkland. The EMC Ranger rattled over a cattle grid, and the grass magically reverted to a shaggy verdant green. Large black tree stumps were scattered about, each one accompanied by a new sapling – kauri pines, giant chinquapins, torreyas – healthy replacements that relished the heat, turning the park back to its original rural splendour. Tarmac reappeared under the tyres. Eleanor turned off the road which disappeared over the brow of the basin, and drove down the loop of drive to the Abbey.

She was somewhat disappointed with what she saw. She'd been expecting some great medieval monastery, all turrets and flying buttresses: reality was a three-storey Elizabethan manor house, built from ochre stone, with a broad frontage and projecting wings. The roof of grey-blue slate was broken by five gables, a row of solar panels capping the apex. There were two sets of chimney-stacks, one on each wing; three cream-white globes were perched amid the southern wing's stacks, weather coverings for the satellite dishes. Climbing roses scrambled over the stonework around the porch, scarlet and yellow blooms drooping from the weight of water they had absorbed, petals mouldering.

It backed on to a copse of high straggly pines, most of which had survived the Warming, their depleted ranks supplemented by some new banyan trees.

Two unmarked white vans and a Panda car were parked outside, belonging to the police crime scene team that had been combing the Abbey for clues since Friday. Eleanor drew up behind them. It was raining steadily and they made a dash for the porch.

A constable was waiting just inside, he saw Amanda and waved them all through. The interior was vaguely shabby, putting Eleanor in mind of a grand family fallen on hard times. The elegance still existed, in the furnishings, and decor – the staircase looked exquisite – but it had been almost neglected. Clean, but not polished.

Vernon Langley and Jon Nevin came in, shaking the rain from their jackets.

Langley took a breath. 'I forgot to mention it before, Mandel,' he said. 'But the Abbey's lightware memory core has been wiped.'

'So Amanda told me,' Greg said drily.

Eleanor kept her grin to herself. One to the good guys.

'I see.' He straightened his jacket. 'Well, we've set up shop in the dining room, if you'd like to come through.'

*

There was very little of the dining room table left visible. At one end the forensic team had set out their equipment, a couple of Philips laptop terminals and various boxy 'ware modules which Eleanor guessed were analysers of some kind, although one looked remarkably like a microwave oven. The rest of the table, about three-quarters, was covered in sealed polythene sample bags. She could see clothes, shoes, books, hologram cubes, a lot of kitchen knives, glasses, memox crystals, small porcelain dishes, candlesticks, even an old wind-up type clock. Some of them looked completely empty. Dust, or hair, she thought.

She was still puzzling over why they'd want to seal up a potted cactus when Vernon Langley introduced Nicolette Hutchins and Denzil Osborne, a pair of forensic investigators who had stayed on to continue the *in situ* examination. They had been drafted in from Leicestershire, part of a ten-strong team which the Home Office had ordered to the Abbey. Both of them were wearing standard blue police one-piece overalls. Nicolette Hutchins was in her forties, a small woman, with a narrow, slightly worn face, her dark hair wrapped in a tight bun. She glanced up from one of the modules she was engrossed with, and held out her hands. 'Excuse me for not shaking.' She was wearing surgeon's gloves.

Denzil Osborne had the kind of build Eleanor associated with ex-professional sportsmen, muscle bulk which was starting to round out and sag. He must have been in his late fifties, with a flat, craggy face, and receding blond hair tied into a neat pony-tail. He had a near permanent smile, showing off three gold teeth, a flashy anachronism.

He shook Greg's hand warmly. Then his smile broadened even wider when he took Eleanor's.

'And I'm *very* pleased to meet you.'

The play-acting made her grin. His genuine welcome was a refreshing change from the rest of the investigating team.

'So, you were in the Mindstar Brigade, were you?' Denzil asked Greg.

'Yeah.'

'I was in Turkey, Royal Engineers; worked with a Mindstar Lieutenant called Roger Hales.'

Greg smiled. 'Springer!'

'That's right.'

'We called him Springer because it didn't matter what kind of booby trap the Legion left behind, Roger could always spot it and trip it,' Greg explained to Eleanor. 'He had one of the best bloody short-range perceptive faculties in the outfit.'

'Saved my arse enough times,' Denzil said. 'Those mullahs were getting plenty tricky towards the end of that campaign.'

'No messing,' Greg said.

'I was chuffed when I heard they were bringing you in. Our Nicolette here doesn't believe what you blokes can do.'

'I do believe,' she said, not looking up from the analyser module. 'I just get bored with hearing about it day in day out. You'd think Turkey lasted for a decade the number of stories you tell.'

'Well, don't worry, Greg won't bore you today,' Denzil said. 'Far from it. Today is the day when this investigation gets moving again. Right, Greg?'

'Do my best.'

'You need something to fixate on?'

'No. I need data.'

Denzil's eyebrows went up appreciatively. 'Intuitionist?'

'Yeah.'

'OK, what do you want to start with?'

'The security system,' Eleanor said.

'No problems with that,' Denzil answered. 'It's all top-grade gear. Fully functional.'

'Could an intruder melt through it, and then back out again, without leaving a trace?' Greg asked.

'Hell, no, it's built by Event Horizon; a customized job. Low-light photon amps, windows wired, internal-motion sensors, IR, plus UV laserscan. Unless your identity and three-dimensional image is loaded in the memory core you couldn't move a millimetre inside the building without the alarm screaming for help. And it's got a secure independent uplink to Event Horizon's private communication satellite network as well as the English Telecom West Europe geosync platform. Why? You think somebody got in here?'

'Possibly,' said Greg. He explained his theory about the microlight, then went on to the contract Kitchener had been given with Event Horizon.

When he had finished even Nicolette Hutchins had abandoned her analyser module to listen. 'That adds some unusual angles to our problem,' she said with morbid interest. 'Nobody was thinking along those lines when we arrived, we all thought it was a murder not an assassination. And it's too late to look for signs of a microlight landing now. There have been three heavyish rainfalls since Thursday night's storm. They would have washed the valley clean.'

'Ever the optimist,' Denzil retorted.

She shrugged, and returned to her LCD display.

'Hell, Greg, I don't know about a tekmerc penetration,' Denzil said. 'If it happened that way, then the software they used against the security core must have been premier grade. I wouldn't even know how to start writing it.'

Eleanor exchanged a knowing glance with Greg. 'Let me have what details you have on the system,' she said. 'We know someone who can tell us if it's possible to burn in.'

Vernon Langley would clearly have liked to ask who. But she just gave him her best enigmatic smile as Denzil typed an access request on his Philips laptop.

'Here we are,' he said. 'Complete schematics, right down to individual 'ware chips, plus the layout.'

Eleanor held up her cybofax and let him squirt the data package over.

'I think the murder scene next,' Greg said.

*

Eleanor didn't know about Greg, but she was picking up bad vibes from the minute they walked in to Kitchener's bedroom. Apart from the furniture and Chinese carpet, it had been stripped clean: there were no ornaments or clothes; the occupier's stamp of personality had been voided. There were some funny patches on the carpet close to the door, as though someone had spilt a weak bleach on it, discolouring the weave, adhesive tags with printed bar codes labelled each one. More tags were stuck over the table and the dresser; the tall free-standing mirror was completely swathed in polythene.

The curtains had been taken down. Rain was beating on the window, unnaturally loud to her ears. And it was warm. She saw the air conditioner had been dismantled, its components scattered over a thick polythene sheet in one corner.

'We wanted the dust filter,' Denzil said absently. 'Surprising what they accumulate.'

Langley and Nevin had followed her in. Amanda had stayed with Nicolette in the dining room. 'I've seen it enough times,' she'd muttered tightly.

Eleanor looked at the four-poster bed and grimaced. The sheets had been removed. There was a big dark brown stain on the mattress. Three holographic projectors had been rigged up around the bed, chrome silver posts two metres high, with a crystal bulb on top. Optical cable snaked over the floor between them.

The player was lying on the carpet at the foot of the bed. Denzil picked it up, and gave her an anxious glance. There was no sign of his smile. 'Standard speech, but it really isn't pretty.'

'I'll manage,' she said.

'All right. But if you're going to vomit, do it out in the corridor, please. We've cleaned enough of it off this carpet already.'

She realized he wasn't joking.

An egg-shaped patch of air above the bed sparkled, then the haze spread out silently; runnels dripped down the sides of the mattress on to the floor, serpents twisting up the carved posts. Edward Kitchener materialized on white silk sheets.

The remains of Edward Kitchener.

Eleanor grunted in shock, and jammed her eyes shut. She took a couple of breaths. Come on girl, you see far worse on any schlock horror channel show.

But that wasn't real.

The second time it wasn't quite so bad. She was incredulous rather than revolted. What sort of person could calmly do this to another? And it had to be a deliberate, planned action; there was no frenzied hacking, it had been performed with clinical precision. A necromantic operation. Hadn't the Victorian police suspected that Jack the Ripper was some kind of medical student?

She glanced round. Greg had wrinkled his face up in extreme distaste, forcing himself to study the hologram in detail. Jon Nevin was looking at the floor, the window, the dresser, anywhere but the bed.

'Yeah, OK,' Greg said. 'That's enough.'

The faint aural glow cast by the projection faded from the walls. When she looked back at the bed, Kitchener had gone. Air hissed out through her teeth, muscles loosening. Edward Kitchener had looked like such a chirpy old man, a sort of idealized grandfather. A gruff tongue, and a loving nature.

'How was he actually killed?' Greg asked.

'We think he was smothered by a pillow,' Vernon said. 'One of them had traces of saliva in a pattern consistent with it being held over his head.'

'So what did all the damage?'

'Pathology says a heavy knife,' said Denzil. 'Straight blade, thirty to forty centimetres long.'

'One of the kitchen knives?'

'We don't know. There are drawers full of them downstairs, some of them are virtually antiques. We catalogued eighteen, and none of those had any traces of blood. But the housekeeper can't say for sure if one is missing. And then there's all the lab equipment, plus the engineering shop, plenty of cutting implements in those two. Blimey, you could make a knife in the engineering shop then grind it up afterwards. Who knows?'

Greg led them all back out into the corridor. 'Did the murderer leave any traces?'

'The only hair and skin particles we have found anywhere in the bedroom belong to either Kitchener, the students, or the housekeeper and her two helpers.'

'What about when the murderer left?' Greg asked. 'Do you know the route they took? There must have been some of Kitchener's blood or body fluid smeared somewhere.'

'No, there wasn't,' Denzil said, vaguely despondent. 'We've spent the whole of the last two days in this corridor going over the walls and carpet with a photon amp plugged into a lightware number cruncher running a spectrographic analysis program – had to get a special Home Office budget allocation for that. This carpet we're standing on has blotches of wine, gin, whisky, cleaning detergent, hair, dandruff, skin flakes, shoe rubber, shoe plastic, a lot of cotton thread from jeans. You name it. But no blood, no fluid, not from Kitchener. Whoever it was, they took a great deal of care not to leave any traces.'

'Was Liam Bursken that fastidious?' Greg asked Vernon.

'I'm not sure,' the detective said. 'I can check.'

'Please,' Greg said.

He loaded a note into his cybofax.

'What does that matter?' Nevin asked.

'It helps with elimination. I want to know if someone that deranged would bother with being careful. A tekmerc would at least make an effort not to leave any marks.'

'We do think the murderer wore an apron while he murdered Kitchener,' Denzil said. 'One of the housekeeper's was burnt in the kitchen stove on Friday morning. The students had a salad on Thursday night. So the stove was lit purposely, it was still warm when we arrived. But there are only a few ash flakes left. We know there was blood on the apron, but the residue is so small we couldn't even tell you if it was human blood. It could have come from beef, or rabbit, or sheep.'

'The point being, why go to all the trouble of lighting a fire to destroy an apron, if it wasn't the one used in the murder,' Vernon said. 'You and I know it was the one the murderer used. But in court, all it could be is supposition. Any halfway decent brief would tear that argument apart.'

'If it was a tekmerc, why bother at all?' Eleanor asked. 'Why spend all that time fiddling about lighting a fire, when they could simply have taken the apron with them? In fact why use one in the first place?'

'Good point,' said Greg. He seemed troubled.

'Well?' Vernon asked.

'Haven't got a clue.'

'Sorry,' Eleanor said.

They shared a smile.

Greg looked at the carpet in the corridor, scratching the back of his neck. 'So we do know that the murderer didn't leave by Kitchener's bedroom window,' he said. 'They went straight down to the kitchen, burnt the apron, then left.'

'If he or she left,' Vernon said.

'If it was one of the students, then they would have to make very certain no traces of Kitchener left the bedroom, or they would be incriminated,' Jon Nevin said. There was a touch of malicious enjoyment in his tone. 'That would fit this cleanliness obsession, the need to avoid contamination.'

'Contamination.' Greg mulled the word over. 'Yeah. You gave the students a head to toe scan, I take it?'

'As soon as they were back in Oakham station,' Vernon said. 'Three of them had touched Kitchener, of course, but only in the presence of the others.'

'Figures,' said Greg. 'Which three?'

'Harding-Clarke, Beswick, and Cameron. But it was only a few stains on their fingertips, entirely consistent with brushing against the body and the sheets.'

'OK,' Greg said. 'I'd like to see the lightware cruncher that's been wiped. Is there anything else our murderer tampered with?'

'Yes,' Denzil said. 'Some of the laboratory equipment. We found it this morning.'

*

The computer centre was at the rear of the Abbey, a small windowless room with a bronze-coloured metal door. It slid open as soon as Denzil showed his police identity card to the lock. Biolum rings came on automatically. Walls and ceiling were all white tiles; the floor had a slick cream-coloured plastic matting. A waist-high desk bench ran all the way round the walls, broken only by the door. There were three elaborate Hitachi terminals sitting on top of it, along with racks of large memox datastore crystals and five reader modules.

The Bendix lightware number cruncher was in the centre of the room, a steel-blue globe one metre in diameter, sitting on a pedestal at chest height.

'Completely wiped,' Denzil said. He crossed to one of the terminals and touched the power stud. The flatscreen lit with the words: DATA LOAD ERROR. Above the keyboard, a few weak green sparks wriggled through the cube. 'Kitchener used to store everything in here, all his files, the students' work. He didn't need to make a copy; the holographic memory is supposed to be failsafe. Even without power, the bytes would remain stable until the actual crystal structure began to break down – five, ten thousand years. Probably longer. Who knows?'

Eleanor looked round the room. There was one conditioning grille set high on a wall; the air was clean but dead. She couldn't see a blemish anywhere, the tiles and floor were spotless, as were the terminals.

'Could the storm have knocked it out?' she asked.

Denzil gave her a surprised look. 'Absolutely not. This room is perfectly insulated; and even if the solar panels were struck by lightning there is a triplicated surge-protection system. Besides, a voltage surge wouldn't cause this.'

'So what would?' Greg asked.

'There are two things. One, a very sophisticated virus. An internecine, one that wipes itself after it's erased all the files, because there's no trace of it now. Second, someone who knew the core management codes could have ordered a wipe.'

'Who knew the codes?'

'I don't know,' Vernon said apologetically.

'All right, we'll ask the students when I interview them. What about access to this room, who is allowed in?'

'Kitchener and the students,' said Denzil. 'But there are terminals dotted all over the Abbey. You could use any of them to load a virus, or order a wipe.'

'What about someone outside plugging in?'

'You can only plug into the lightware cruncher through one of the terminals in the Abbey,' Denzil said. 'But all the terminals are plugged into English Telecom's datanet. So you have to be inside the Abbey to establish a datalink between the Bendix and an external 'ware system.'

'And to get inside the Abbey you have to be cleared by the security system,' Greg murmured. 'Neat.' He turned to Vernon Langley. 'English Telecom should be able to provide you with an itemized log for the datanet. Check through it and see if there were any unexplained datalinks established on Thursday night or Friday morning.'

'If it was a tekmerc operation, it was the best,' Denzil said soberly. 'The very best.'

*

The laboratory was virtually a caricature, Eleanor thought. Either that, or set designers on channel science fiction shows did more research than she had ever given them credit for. But it was a chemistry lab, not a physics one.

The room was spacious, with a high ceiling, and the usual

ornate mullioned windows, which helped to give it the *Franken-stein* feel. Tall glass-fronted cabinets were lined up along the walls. Three long wooden benches were spaced down the centre of the room. Each of them had a vast array of glassware on top, immensely complicated crystalline intestines of some adventure-some beast, plastic hardware units clamped around tubes and flasks, a spaghetti tangle of wiring and optical cable winding through it all. Small Ericsson terminals, augmented with custom-ized control modules, were regulating each of the set-ups.

Denzil led them to the middle bench. 'Take a look at this.' He was indicating one section of the glassware, spiral tubing and retorts surrounding what reminded Eleanor of an incubator. 'We found it yesterday when we started classifying the equipment.' He shot a wily look at Vernon Langley. 'Recognize it?'

The detective shook his head.

'It's a syntho vat. High-quality stuff, too. Well above what you find on the street; this formula is similar to Naiad.'

'Were the students on it?' Greg asked.

'Three of them were using it on Thursday night,' Vernon said. 'We took blood samples as soon as they came into the station. Harding-Clarke, Spalvas, and Cameron. But the count was low, they're not addicts.' He sighed. 'Students experiencing life, it's a thrill for them, a little taste of adventure. I imagine bright sparks of that age could get bored very easily with this place.'

Eleanor thought he pronounced *students* with well-emphasized contempt.

'And the other three?' Greg prompted.

'Clean as newborns,' Jon Nevin said. 'Of course, all six of them had been drinking. They had wine at their evening meal, and then some more in their rooms later on.'

'But not enough to unhinge them?'

'No.'

'Kitchener was taking the syntho as well,' Vernon said. 'It was in the pathology report. Expanding his mind, no doubt. Some such nonsense. He was always on about that, his New Thought ideology.'

Greg exhaled loudly. 'At his age. Christ.'

'And he encouraged the students,' Jon Nevin said disapprovingly.

'Yeah.'

'And this,' Denzil said theatrically. 'Is something we found this morning.' He rapped at another chunk of the glassware on the third bench. It had more hardware units than the rest. 'You ought to know what this is, Greg, there's a smaller version in your head.'

'Neurohormone synthesizer.'

'Well done. Themed neurohormones, to be precise. Makes your blanket educement look old fashioned.'

'Kitchener was using neurohormones?' Greg asked in surprise. 'Psi stimulants?'

'Yes,' said Vernon. 'Quite heavily, as far as we can determine. It's all in the pathology report.'

'What sort of psi themes?' Eleanor asked.

'Ah, can't be as helpful there as I'd like,' Denzil said. 'There is a low-temperature storage vault full of themed ESP-educer ampoules. But those are a standard commercial type from ICI; he was a regular customer, apparently. However, there's also a small batch of unmarked ampoules which I'll send off for analysis, although we may have problems with identifying it, especially if it's something experimental. We don't have a large database on the stuff. As far as I know this is the first time it's ever cropped up in a police investigation.'

'We may be able to help you there,' Greg said. 'I'll find out if Event Horizon has any information on neurohormones.'

'Fine.'

'Do you know what he was using the ESP theme neurohormone for?'

'Apparently it was part of his research, according to the students,' Vernon said. 'He wanted to perceive electrons and protons directly.'

'Get a meeting with Ranasfari set up,' Greg told Eleanor. 'I want to know if there's any connection between these

101

neurohormones and the research work Kitchener was doing for Event Horizon.'

'Right.' She flipped open her cybofax.

'You will inform us, won't you?' Vernon said.

'Yeah,' Greg growled back.

He tried not to flinch at the stab of animosity. Eleanor diplomatically busied herself with the cybofax file. That good old Mindstar reputation again.

Greg ran a forefinger along a module on the top of the neurohormone synthesizer. 'Is this the stuff in the unmarked ampoules?'

'No idea,' Denzil replied. 'It would be the obvious conclusion, but the control 'ware has been wiped clean just like the Bendix. There's no record of the formula they were producing.' He pointed at the dark grey plastic casing of the hardware modules which were integrated into the refining structure. 'These units contained endocrine bioware. Very complex, very delicate. They are dead now.'

'How?'

'Somebody poisoned them. They infused a dose of syntho into the cells. It was all quite deliberate.'

'The murder was tied in with his work,' Greg said quietly.

'If this was his work, then yes.'

6

The silver-white Dornier executive tilt-fan dropped through the cloud layer above the imposing condominiums and exclusive shopping arcades of Peterborough's New Eastfield district and banked to starboard, heading out over the Fens basin. Julia ordered her nodes to cancel the company's last quarter financial summaries which they were displaying behind her eyes. They would be landing soon.

Another bloody ceremony. Wheel me on, point me at the cameras, and wheel me off again. Might as well use a cyborg.

But it was important, a crux in company development, so she had to go.

When isn't it important, vital?

She was sitting on a white leather settee in the lounge at the rear of the little plane. Alone for once. Her staff were in the forward cabin. She imagined them swapping gossip, laughing; it would have been easy to go forward and join them, or invite them back. They weren't that inhibited around her. But it didn't fit her mood.

Being alone was becoming a precious commodity these days.

It might have been her mood, the broodiness which came from anticipating the meeting later in the day, which had prompted her rather drastic image overhaul this morning. She had dressed up in full Goth costume, improvising with a three-thousand-pound velvet Deveraux skirt, a scarlet one, sweeping round her ankles, then black suede boots from Paris, five gold Aztec pendants hanging on thin leather straps round her neck, and a black web-like jacket from Toska's. Her maid had darkened her hair and given it a tangled arrangement. They had argued about make up; eye wings of black mascara on her complexion would have been criminal, so in the end they settled for some strategic highlighting. She was quite pleased with the effect; it was far less stuffy, and lots more fun, than yesterday's outfit at the spaceplane roll out. It would certainly make people take notice.

She looked out of the window. All she could see ahead was mud; dun-brown supersaturated peat tinged with an elusive grey-green hue from the algae blooms. It came right up to the city's eastern boundary, slopping around the ruins of the Newark district, long regular silt dunes freckled with bricks and fractured timbers marked the outline of drowned streets. Newark had lacked that crucial extra metre when the tide of sludge came oozing and gurgling across the Fens.

Two parallel green lines stabbed out from the southern end of the city, the Nene's new course, stretching into the gloomy heat haze which occluded the eastern horizon. It had been dredged deep enough to allow cargo ships to sail right into the heart of the city where a nourishing deep-water port had been built. The banks were gene-tailored coral, covered with thick reeds, intended to prevent the mud from dribbling back in, although two dredgers were on permanent duty sailing up and down the channel, scooping out the sludge which did build up, and flinging it back over the banks.

The Nene would have to be widened soon, she knew, the volume of traffic it could carry was approaching its limit. Just like everything else in Peterborough these days. The city's own success was turning against it, stalling further development.

Ninety per cent of the Fens refugees had retreated to Peterborough, establishing a vast shanty town along the high ground of the western perimeter. They'd found dry, high land, and a working civil administration; it was enough, they were through with running, they sat there and refused to budge.

The PSP was faced with a nightmare of relief work at the worst possible time, when every resource in the country was being deployed against the ecological destruction and economic collapse. The refugees needed work and housing. The Treasury certainly couldn't fund the kind of massive schemes necessary, so the Party was forced into making an exception to its ideological golden rule of repudiating any form of foreign investment, the bogeyman of economic imperialism.

Peterborough was declared a special economic zone, and huge concessions granted to any investors, planning regulations became virtually nonexistent. Money began to pour in, and new housing estates rose up to replace the shacks of plastic and corrugated iron. They served as dormitory villages for the fast-growing industrial estates occupied by kombinate subdivisions and the supply companies which sprang up to provide them with specialist services. Their products were exported, duty free, all over the globe, helping to pay off the loans for the housing. A self-contained micro-economy, free from the decay and chaos rampant throughout the rest of the country. Peterborough was unique in the PSP decade, prospering while every other English city declined. After the PSP fell Philip Evans selected it as his headquarters when he moved Event Horizon back to England. With its plethora of modern industries to supply the company's cyber-factories with components it was an ideal location.

But now, four years later, Event Horizon was suffering from space restrictions inside the city boundaries. New cyber-factories were being parcelled out around the rest of the country, easing the load. But they were subsidiaries, non-critical; what Julia wanted was a nucleus, a focal point for administration, research, finance, security, and the strategically important giga-conductor manufacture. The data age notwithstanding, distance brought control problems, exacerbated by England's shoddy transport links. It all added up to reductions in efficiency that even her grandfather's NN core couldn't compensate for. They needed the major installations in one area, under their collective thumb.

She sighed lightly, shifting in her seat. Management problems were like a fission reaction, each one triggering a dozen more. And if they weren't dealt with swiftly and correctly, they would soon multiply beyond her ability to solve.

Still, at least she'd circumvented the expansion problem. For a price.

The communication console bleeped for attention. The call was tagged as personal, Eleanor's code. Julia leaned over the leather settee's arm rest, pecked the keyboard to let it through, and Eleanor's face appeared on the bulkhead flat-screen. She was sitting at some kind of table, scratched wooden surface piled with printouts. Her forehead was damp with perspiration, she looked irked.

'That bad?' Julia said quickly. Get in fast, and be disarming. Eleanor was more big sister than a friend, she could tell her anything without ever having to worry about it being splashed by the tabloid channels. But at the same time she could be a trifle formidable. And not just physically; Eleanor was only three years older, but her adversarial background had given her self-determination in abundance.

'No messing,' Eleanor said.

'Where are you?'

'Oakham police station. We've just arrived back from taking a look round Launde Abbey.' Eleanor shivered. 'God, I hope we catch the killer soon.'

'Did Greg find anything out there?'

'Several ambiguities.'

'So it wasn't one of the students?'

'Can't say for sure; he's interviewing them now. We should know in an hour or so. But assuming none of them did it, I have some requests.'

'Sure, shoot.'

'First we want to talk to Ranasfari about these wormhole

theories he had Kitchener working on. Tomorrow afternoon, we're both busy in the morning.'

Julia loaded a memo into her node's general business file. 'He'll be at Wilholm waiting for you.'

'Fine. Second, I take it Event Horizon has a biochemical research division?'

'Yes, of course.'

'Anyone there conversant with neurohormones?'

Access Biochemical Division Files, Research Facility Departments: Current Projects and Specializations. The list slipped through her mind, a cool jejune stream of bytes.

'Yes,' she said. 'We have two projects running. After Greg's last case for us, Morgan decided it would be a good idea to introduce psychics into the security division. I thought it best that we weren't dependent on external sources.'

'Good. There were some ampoules of themed neurohormones at Launde. I want them analysed. The police forensic lab is good, but this is somewhat out of their league. No doubt that is going to bruise some pride . . .' Stress lines appeared at the corners of Eleanor's mouth as she tightened her jaw muscles. Julia remained prudently silent. 'Well, the hell with them,' Eleanor said. 'We need to know what the theme is as soon as possible, please.'

'Weren't they labelled?'

'No. The endocrine bioware which produced them was deliberately killed, and its control 'ware was wiped. There are no records. It was one of Kitchener's private projects. But it's obviously an important one for the murderer to single it out like this. Nothing else in the lab was touched.'

'I see. No problem. I'll have a courier at Oakham within the hour.'

'Which brings us to the final point,' Eleanor said with a baleful relish that had Julia squirming. 'Greg and I have just become media megastars again. Julia, there are hundreds of bloody reporters here! They've already connected us with you, God knows what conspiracy theories they'll be producing by the evening bulletins.'

Julia closed her eyes, and let out a groan. 'Oh, dear Lord.' She should have foreseen it. Hindsight was so bloody wonderful.

'A bit of intervention on your part wouldn't hurt,' Eleanor said. 'We're not circus performers, you know.'

'I'm sorry. I didn't know about the reporters. I'll do whatever I can, I promise.'

Eleanor gave her a quizzical look. 'All right. But for God's sake, no strong-arm tactics, don't make it any worse.'

'I won't,' she said meekly.

'Sure. See you tomorrow.'

'Yah, unless one of the students did it,' Julia said.

'Don't hold your breath. Bye, Julia.'

'Bye.'

Eleanor's image blanked out.

'Bugger!' Julia yelped. Why could nothing ever be *simple*?

*

A pre-Warming map superimposed over the quagmire would have told Julia the Dornier was descending over Prior's Fen, six kilometres due east of Peterborough. Below the extended under-carriage bogies thick concrete groyne walls were holding back the mud from a hexagonal patch of land three hundred metres in diameter. Five large Hawker Siddeley cargo hovercraft were docked to raft-like floating quays outside; and a couple of saucer-shaped McDonnell Douglas helistats were drifting high overhead, their big rotors spinning idly as they waited for the ceremony to finish so they could start unloading.

I wonder how much it's costing to keep them up there, she thought. The nodes would tell her, but somehow she didn't want to know. Everything to do with PR seemed such a folly. Yet all the experts swore by it, the God of good publicity, of customer relations, being and being seen to be a good corporate citizen.

Fan nacelles on the Dornier's canards and wings rotated to the vertical, and the plane touched down on one of the floating quays. There was only Rachel Griffith, Ben Taylor, her second bodyguard, and Caroline Rothman, her PA, in the cabin forward of the lounge. For once Morgan had stayed in his office. It must mean he trusts me, she thought, or more likely Rachel.

She wished Patrick was there as she stepped out of the plane and into the most appalling humidity. Just someone who could hold her hand, in both senses; she always hated the way the crowds stared at her during these events. But Patrick was busy in Peterborough, helping to establish an office for his family company.

Steeling herself against the incursive eyes, she smiled as her boots reached the rough metal grid of the floating quay. She put on a very foppish wide-brimmed hat of black suede, grateful for the scant relief it offered from the sun. There was a strong whiff of sulphur coming off the quagmire, mingling with brine.

Stephen Marano, the project engineer, trotted up to greet her. He was in his mid-forties, stuffed into a light-grey suit which didn't really fit. He was a perfect choice to boss the labour crews, but completely out of his depth talking to her. His smile flickered on and off, words got tangled in his throat, he seemed taken aback by her Goth get-up.

She wanted to tell him not to say anything, ease his suffering a bit, but he would only interpret that as a rebuke, so she let him struggle on and introduce her to the fifteen-strong management team of architects and site engineers. A long exercise in tedium and discomfort.

Three channel camera crews followed the procedure from a distance. She recognized one of the teams from the Globe-cast logo on their jackets.

After the introductions they all trooped down a long ramp to the foot of the excavation. Julia realized they were actually below the level of the mud outside. Yellow JCB diggers were parked on the black peat, crews standing around them. They whistled and cheered as she went past. She didn't actually hear any jeers, but there were plenty of wolf-whistles. Stephen Marano winced at each of them.

It was wet underfoot; mercifully her skirt hem hovered five centimetres above the ground, but her boots received a liberal splattering. The site had been crisscrossed by drainage trenches, their pumps whirring noisily in the background.

They stopped by a wood-lined square hole close to the sheer groyne wall. A big cement mixer lorry stood beside it, its rumbling dying away as the operator pressed a button on its side.

One of the managers handed her a microphone.

Access FootingSpeech.

She cleared her throat, the sound echoing loudly round the groyne walls. The camera crews focused on her. Rachel and Ben stood unobtrusively on either side, heads moving slowly back and forth as they scanned the assembled crew.

'I don't suppose you want a long speech,' Julia said, suddenly very self-conscious about her finishing-school accent. 'And you're not going to get one, not while you're on my time.' She saw smiles appearing under the coloured hard hats. 'I would simply like to say that although the company space programme draws most of the media attention, you people slogging through the mud out here are just as important. Space isn't the only direction the future lies in. Out here we have got a vast wasteland which everyone despises and resents, while back on shore there are too many people living too close together. This tower which we are starting today is going to lead the way in alleviating some of the pressure on population density, as well as the demands which industry is placing on the green belt. Land is becoming a very precious resource, and I am extremely proud that Event Horizon is setting this example that expansion is possible without coming into conflict with the environment. In the scramble to rebuild our economy, we must never forget the reasons for the Warming. We cannot afford to ignore the painful lessons of the past if we are to prevent the repetition of our grotesque mistakes in the future.'

Exit FootingSpeech.

She handed the microphone back as the management group applauded loudly.

'This way, Miss Evans,' Stephen Marano said. He gestured to the cement mixer.

The operator was a stocky man in a yellow T-shirt, grubby jeans, and an orange hard hat. He grinned broadly and pointed to the small control panel on the back of the lorry. It had five chrome-ringed buttons running down the centre. The green button had a new sticker above it which said: PRESS ME.

'Even I can't make a mess of that,' Julia told him. Lord, what a dumb thing to say.

'No, miss.' He bobbed about, delighted at being the centre of attention.

Julia pressed the button.

The mixer started up again, concrete sliding down the chute into the footings.

It looks like elephant crap, she thought.

The management team started clapping again.

She clamped down on a laugh which threatened to escape. Didn't they realize how stupid they looked?

But of course they did. They were less worried about appearing foolish than they were about annoying her.

She sobered sadly, and offered Stephen Marano her hand to shake. 'I didn't appreciate what the conditions were like out here before today, Stephen. You really have done a terrific job getting this phase completed, and on time too. Thank you.'

He nodded in gratitude. 'Thanks, Miss Evans. It's been tough, but they're a good bunch of lads. It should be easier next time, now we know what we're doing.'

She guessed that was about as subtle as he would get. It made a nice change, sometimes she was ten minutes into a conversation with a kombinate director or a bank finance officer before she realized everything said was a veiled question. Business talk was conducted in its own special code of ambiguities.

They started to walk back towards the ramp.

'The next two times,' she told him. 'I want to bring a couple of complete cyber-precincts out here next, and link them to the city with a train line. Of course, we'll have to build a service tributary from the Nene as well.'

He gave her a genuine grin. 'I wish you'd been around before the Warming, Miss Evans. A few more people with your kind of vision and we'd never have wound up in this damn great mess.'

'Thank you, Stephen.'

Access GeneralBusiness: Review Stephen Marano, Civil Engineer. Invite To Next Middle Management Dinner Evening.

As they reached the base of the ramp a group of about ten workers moved towards her. Rachel and Ben closed in smoothly. Nothing provocative, but *there*, ready.

Julia gave the group an expectant look as they stopped short. One of them was nudged forwards by his mates. He looked about seventeen, not quite needing to shave every day, wearing the regulation jeans and T-shirt, shaggy dark hair sticking out below his scuffed light-blue hard hat. He was clutching a bouquet of red roses with a blue ribbon done up in a bow. She suspected he'd been chosen for his age, there couldn't have been many younger than him working out here. And he clearly wanted to be anywhere right now but standing in front of her.

'M-M-Miss Evans?' he stammered.

She gave him a gentle encouraging smile.

'Er, I, that is, all of us. Well, we really appreciate what you do, like. Investing so much in England, and everything. And giving us all jobs as well, 'cos we wouldn't be any use in no office or a cyber factory. So, like, we got you these.' The bouquet was jerked up nervously. 'Sorry it's only flowers, like, but you've got everything . . .' He trailed off in embarrassment.

Julia accepted the bouquet as though she was taking a baby from him. She prayed the cameras weren't recording this, for the boy's sake.

'What's your name?' she asked.

'Lewis, Miss. Lewis Walker.'

'Did they bully you into this, Lewis?'

'Yeah. Well, no. I wanted to anyway, like.'

She deliberately took her time sniffing the roses. The humidity stifled most of the scent. 'What a lovely smell.' She put one hand on her hat, and leant forwards before the boy could dodge away, brushing her lips against his cheek. 'Thank you, Lewis.'

A rowdy cheer went up from the onlookers. Lewis blushed crimson, eyes shining.

*

The Dornier lifted from the floating quay, cabin deck tilting up at a ten-degree angle as it climbed, nose lining up on Peterborough.

Julia thought about the incident with Lewis as the hexagonal site dropped away below the fuselage. It couldn't possibly have been one of the 'spontaneous' demonstrations the PR division was forever dreaming up. They would have plumped for something far more elaborate. The sheer crudity had made it incredibly touching.

She had given the bouquet to Caroline Rothman as soon as they were back in the tilt-fan. 'Put them in water. And I want them on the dining room table this evening.' Pride of place.

She couldn't get rid of the image of Lewis Walker, being joshed and having his back slapped by his mates as he returned to them. As she was returning to the Dornier; her world.

That poor, poor boy, there was something utterly irresistible about someone looking so lost. And his T-shirt had been tight enough to show a hard flat belly. Real muscle, not Patrick's designer gym tone.

She allowed herself exactly one lewd grin.

It couldn't happen, not with Lewis Walker, but fantasies existed to be enjoyed.

Funny how different they were; yet only a couple of years apart. Him stammering, elated and terrified at being thrust into the limelight; her simply breezing through every public appearance on automatic, bored and resentful.

She could monitor him from afar to make sure he did all right, a modern day fairy godmother, pushing opportunities his way. Event Horizon ran dozens of scholarship schemes for workers who wanted to advance themselves. And she was on the board of two charities promoting further education.

Of course, he wouldn't dare refuse if a place was offered. Nobody in the company ever did refuse her gifts. She saw the site management team clapping conscientiously – obediently. But would he be happy plucked from what he was doing now and shoved into night schools and polytechnic training courses?

Should I interfere?

That's what it boiled down to.

No. The only possible answer. Not unasked. Not in individual lives. People had to be responsible for themselves.

She activated the phone, and placed a call to Horace Jepson. Uncle Horace, though he wasn't really, just a friend of her grandpa's, and now hers. A solid rock of support when she took over Event Horizon. He was the chairman of Globecast, the largest satellite channel company in the world.

His ruddy face appeared on the bulkhead flatscreen. He was in his early sixties, but *plastique* had reversed entropy, and returned him to his late forties. A rather chubby late forties, she thought disapprovingly.

'Julia! How's my favourite billionairess?'

'Soldiering on, Uncle Horace.'

'You don't look like you're suffering. You look gorgeous. Damn, but you grew up pretty. I wish I was twenty years younger.'

She put on her most innocent expression, and batted her eyelashes for him. 'Uncle Horace, why ever do you want to go back down to being sixty again?'

'Julia!' He looked crestfallen.

'Have you been skipping your diet again?' she asked sternly.

'Terrific. I don't hear a word for three weeks, and she phones me up to nag.'

'You have. Well, stop it. You know what your doctor said. You should get out of the office and down to the executive gym.'

'Sure thing, Julia. I'll start tomorrow.'

She sucked on her lower lip, a bashfulness that wasn't entirely artificial. 'Uncle Horace.'

'Oh, my God. How much is this going to cost?'

'Nothing. Um, I need a sort of favour.'

'You owe me fifteen.'

'Can we go for sixteen?'

He rolled his eyes dramatically. 'You don't want to meet another actor, do you? Some of my guests still ain't talking to me after that party.'

There was a warm tingling in her cheeks at the memory. She was sure she hadn't been as tipsy as everyone said. 'No, Uncle Horace,' she said firmly. 'Definitely no more actors. Do you remember Greg and Eleanor Mandel?'

'Sure, who could forget Eleanor? Greg seemed like a nice guy, on the level. Psychic, right?'

'Yes. I've asked him to assist the police working on the Edward Kitchener murder case.'

He frowned, fleshy wrinkles deepening around his eyes. 'You're involved with that?'

'Event Horizon had a research contract with Kitchener. Right now I'm praying that isn't the reason behind his death. Greg will find out for me.'

'I see.'

'But the press are giving him a hard time.'

'Now come on, Julia.'

'I don't want them to stop reporting the case,' she said hurriedly. 'If they could just lay off badgering Greg. He didn't want to take the case in the first place. And you know he doesn't play the political game, he's too honest. The last thing he needs is the press jumping all over him just for doing his job.'

Horace Jepson sighed resignedly. 'All right, Julia. I'll tell the editors to go easy.'

'Uncle Horace, you're an angel.'

'And I'd like you to come to a programme launch party next month.' He started typing on a keyboard out of the camera's

115

field of view. '*Dreamland Nights*, it's called, a ten-part fantasy drama. It's gonna be big, Julia. This summer's ratings winner.'

'I'll be there. Promise.'

'Cliff is gonna be organizing it,' he said hopefully.

Her contented expression never wavered. She was proud of that self-control. 'That'll be nice. I haven't seen him for ages.' Clifford Jepson was Horace's son from the first of his four marriages. Julia couldn't stand the sight of him, he had his father's drive without any of his father's charm. It made him come over as brattishly domineering. The trouble was, Uncle Horace had them down as the perfect match, with himself as Cupid.

'OK, Julia, my staff will squirt the details to your office.'

'Fine. I'll look forward to it. And thank you again, Uncle Horace.'

He signed off smiling happily.

Julia pursed her lips in antipathy. She'd solved Eleanor's grouse; but there was no way she could get out of that bloody launch party now.

7

The interviews were the one part of the case Greg had been dreading. The word association game, watching the way minds reacted to key phrases, was chained too tightly to his army days. It intimated funereal dug-out bunkers, sweating defiant prisoners in torn bloody fatigues, the smell of gun oil and vomit, the high-voltage emotions of hatred and terror, perceptible even to non-psychics. The seemingly limitless brutality which men were capable of.

Even the interview room at Oakham police station was a party to the anamnesis; sombre fawn-coloured walls, a leaden grey desk, acutely curved plastic chairs, scuffed black door. A rectangular conditioning grille emitted an annoying buzzing sound just on the threshold of audibility. Steely light shining through a high window was complemented by a harsh glow from two biolum panels set in the old fluorescent tube recesses in the ceiling. A wide-angle camera was mounted on the wall above the desk, optical cable running down to a twin-crystal AV recording deck.

Greg sat on one side of the desk, Langley and Nevin flanking him. He took out his cybofax and summoned up the list of questions he wanted to ask, then placed it on the desk.

Rosette Harding-Clarke came in, accompanied by her lawyer, Matthew Slater. Since the New Conservatives had been elected, anyone being interviewed by the police was entitled to legal advice, irrespective of whether they were being charged or not. The measure was intended to allay public mistrust of the dodgy practices which the People's Constables had included in police procedure.

There were three lawyers, out of Oakham's pool of five, representing the six students. They had objected when he said he wanted to interview the students.

'You aren't an official investigating officer,' Lisa Collier, a matronly fifty-five-year-old, had told him pompously. 'You have no authority to conduct an interview, certainly not with co-operating witnesses, which is all the students are at this point. And I'm not having my clients subjected to a psychic privacy invasion. They have a right to silence so they don't incriminate themselves.'

Greg had simply turned to Vernon Langley. 'Arrange for a magistrate's hearing this afternoon. Charge all six students with suspected manslaughter.' He gave Lisa Collier a thin smile. 'As a specialist assigned to the investigation I am entitled to sit in on any subsequent questioning of legally detained suspects. And any evidence acquired psychically during those interviews is admissible in court.'

The three lawyers had gone into a huddle, and decided not to call his bluff.

Matthew Slater slotted a matt-black memox crystal into the recording deck, and sat down beside Rosette. She was wearing a black singlet of some glossy fabric, a cropped black jacket with thin white curlicues embroidered on the shoulders, and a short black leather skirt. Her auburn hair was folded in a neat pleat.

She gave Greg a fleeting glance of acknowledgement, completely ignoring the detectives behind him. The whole act informed them that she wasn't going to be intimidated.

He had to admit she was an impressive girl physically. Nor was there any hint of weakness in her emotional make up.

Langley pushed a memox crystal in the recorder's free slot, and touched the power stud. 'Interview with Rosette Harding-

Clarke,' he said formally. 'Conducted by CID advisory specialist Greg Mandel in the presence of officers Langley and Nevin.'

Matthew Slater leaned forwards. 'For the record, Miss Harding-Clarke's participation in this interview is entirely voluntary. She is here because of her wish to help apprehend the killer of Edward Kitchener. And therefore she reserves the right to refuse to answer any question which is not directly applicable to this topic.'

Rosette Harding-Clarke stared straight at Greg, and gave him a lopsided knowing smile. 'Silence wouldn't do me any good, would it?' she said. 'Not with you. You could strip anything you wanted from me.'

He ordered a low-level secretion from his gland. Her amusement began to impinge on his perception, it bordered on contempt. Rosette looked down on everybody from her own private Olympus.

'The reaction of your mind to questions cannot be disguised,' he said.

'I can run, but I can't hide.'

'Yeah. Something like that.'

'If you begin to ask Miss Harding-Clarke irrelevant questions then we shall be forced to terminate the interview,' Matthew Slater warned.

'No, I won't,' she said. 'I'm glad you are here. This case is obviously well beyond the ability of these bumbling Mr Plods. And I want the bastard caught. Too bad we haven't got the death penalty any more. So ask away. Did I do it? No. You can confirm that, can't you?' Her eyebrows arched challengingly.

'Unfortunately it's not that simple. I need to know what happened that night at Launde, build up a complete picture, so I have several questions.'

'Yes, all right, get on with it then.'

'Did you make any external calls that day, or establish a datalink to an outside 'ware system?'

'I made a few phone calls, sure. Just friends. I'd go bananas if the only people I had to talk to were the other students. And I was doing some work that morning, Edward had me trying to produce a more accurate figure for the age of the universe. I plugged into the Oxford University astronomy department mainframe for reference data.'

'Now, that Friday morning, you were the first to find the body. Is that right?'

'Yes.'

'What time was that?'

'God. It's in the statement, I must have told these oafs a hundred times.'

'What time?'

'God, all right. About half-past five on Friday morning, give or take five minutes.'

'And you didn't see anyone else in the corridor when you went to Kitchener's room?'

'No.'

Greg tightened the focus of his espersense. 'How about a presence you weren't sure about? A shadow? A noise? Something you didn't want to mention to the police because you couldn't prove it, or you thought it would sound stupid.'

'No. Nothing. Nobody.'

'Where were you before you discovered the body?'

'In my room.'

'Was anybody with you?'

'No.'

'Half-past five is a funny time to be visiting Kitchener. Was there a reason?'

She rubbed an index finger along the bottom of her nose. 'So I would be there when he woke up. Edward didn't like to be alone.'

'Nicholas Beswick said you went into Kitchener's room at quarter-past one that morning. Is that true?'

'Poor old Nicky. Yes, it's true. You want to know something else? I was having sex with Edward, I had been for three months.

120

And to save you the trouble of working it out, he was forty-four years older than me.'

'You had sex with him at quarter-past one?'

'Yes.'

'When did you leave?'

'Isabel and I packed in about half-past two. Edward was nearly asleep by then anyway.'

'Why not stay?'

'Edward snores. Silly, isn't it? But I'm a light sleeper, as well as being a virtual insomniac. I only need two or three hours' sleep each night. So out I creep after he's nodded off, then I get my head down for a while, and I'm back snuggled up beside him when he wakes. He probably knew, but . . .'

'So everybody would know that you left him alone for a few hours each night?'

'Every peeping Tom, yes.'

'Which of the other students knew about you and Kitchener?'

'I would say all of them. Even Nicky, though he would never dare talk about it outright.'

'So it was common knowledge?'

'Yes.'

'What about the housekeeper and her staff?'

'Oh, yes, Mrs Mayberry knew. You can't keep secrets from the person who collects your sheets.'

'Did you wash after you left Kitchener?'

Rosette sat up straighter. 'Pardon me?'

'Did you wash, take a shower, bathe?'

'Yes. I had a shower afterwards. I always do.'

'How long had Isabel Spalvas been having an affair with Kitchener?'

Rosette gave him a derisive grin, and started to laugh. 'I'm sorry. The way you said it. "An affair". Like some Victorian aunt. Rutland really is the back of beyond, isn't it? Are you married until death do us part, Mr Mandel? Or may I call you Greg? Eleanor seems like quite a spectacular girl, physique-wise,

121

that is. I saw the two of you on the channel newscasts at lunch-time.'

'I'm happily married, thank you.'

'And Julia Evans, no less, was at the ceremony. Your brides-maid.'

'Is that a problem for you?'

'No, an observation.'

'Careful, your lawyer might stop this line of questioning.'

Matthew Slater shot Greg a look of undiluted malice. Rosette burst out laughing again.

'Oh, yes,' she said. 'I can see why they sent for you. Nobody gets off the hook when you're on their case, do they, Greg?'

'No. Now, Isabel Spalvas?'

'She wasn't having an affair, or whatever else you want to call it, with Edward.'

'You said she was in his room for sex.'

'She was there for pleasure, for interest, for self-exploration. I'm not saying they didn't have sex. They did. She also took some syntho. Perhaps it made it easier for her.'

'Made what easier?'

'Sex with Edward. Oh, he was still reasonably capable. But he was sixty-seven, after all. You couldn't ignore it; not, lie back and think of England. She found it difficult with me as well, to start with.'

'You and Isabel made love?'

'I'm not sure about love, Greg, darling. But sex, yes. Edward enjoyed watching. She enjoyed it too, eventually, when the syntho was really boosting her. Am I turning you on, Greg?'

'No.'

'Really? You surprise me. The first time I made this statement, all the boys in the office found an excuse to listen in.' She cocked her head at Nevin. 'Didn't you, Jonnie darling?'

Greg caught his mind clogging with fierce embarrassment.

'Was there any pressure placed on female students to sleep with Kitchener?' he asked.

'Not if you mean blackmail. Come to bed with me or I kick

you out of the Abbey. Edward doesn't need to, he is ... intriguing. Girl students are almost a double bluff. You understand? He tells the world he does. He tells us he wouldn't dream of it. And there he is, one of the geniuses of the age, complete with wicked reputation. Always there, day in, day out. He had this mockery for convention. He was so very clever at ridiculing any stricture society placed on his life. He makes you examine and challenge your own beliefs. That's why Isabel had joined us, she was probing her own limits, finding out where they lie. You can do that with Edward there to guide you. He made us feel safe, we trusted him. He'd never let us hurt ourselves, not with drugs or sex, or radical politics come to that. He knew what we were capable of, and showed us how to achieve it, intellectually, emotionally, physically. Launde was an incredible experience, spiritual more than anything else.' She shook her head softly, re-emerging from the vortex of reminiscence.

Greg could perceive how sincere she was when she talked about Kitchener. Fondness for the old guru acted as a subtle reinforcement for the philosophies he had spun out. He was suddenly very curious about Edward Kitchener. How much of this professional dissident ideology had he believed in, all or none?

'How long had Isabel been taking part in these sessions with you and Kitchener?'

'Sessions! You have no soul, Greg, darling, no poetry. About a fortnight, I think. As soon as we came back from the New Year break.'

'Did Nicholas Beswick know that Isabel was becoming involved with Kitchener?'

Rosette pursed her lips, contrite for once. Her thought currents were subdued. 'Oh, dear little Nicky. No, he didn't know a thing about us until that night. Caught us sneaking down the corridor to Edward, he did. Such a shame. He is quite infatuated with Isabel, did you know that? Now that is authentic love, Romeo and Juliet revisited. Teasing him was such fun, it's so dreadfully easy. Nicky lacks that cosmopolitan touch necessary to survive adult life, he's just a country boy at heart. He makes me seem terribly jaded and old by comparison. Edward was delighted with him, of course.'

'Why, "of course"?'

'Because people like Nicky are the reason he founded Launde in the first place. Nicky is very intelligent, he's far smarter than I am. And if the four of you in this room were to add up your IQs, the figure would be less than half of mine. That gives you some idea of what he's like. But he's flawed; emotionally retarded, if you like. Edward called it perpetual adolescence. Whatever, Nicky has this terrible trouble relating to other people. And that is what Launde is for, to cure us of our adolescence, realign our thought patterns into sensible maturity. Edward plays the tyrant king to great effect, and the students bond together for mutual protection. You can't do anything else, survival depends on it. And for all its crudity, the technique works. Even with Nicky, although it was pretty slow going in his case, but there was definitely some progress. When he arrived, Nicky would sooner starve than ask someone to pass him a knife and fork. Then the evening before Edward was killed, Nicky actually answered me back at supper. Me! Edward didn't stop talking about it for the rest of the evening, he was simply over the moon. Then I went and ballsed it up by getting caught when I went and fetched Isabel out to play. Naughty me.'

'So Nicholas Beswick would have been on an emotional roller-coaster that night?'

Rosette's eyes narrowed. 'Oh no you don't, Greg, darling. You're not pinning that perverted atrocity on Nicky. He wouldn't do that. Besides I was there when he came into the room and saw what had been done to Edward. He was in hysterics, worse than me. Go away and harass someone else, Greg. Not Nicky.'

'And how about you? Were you at all jealous that Kitchener was becoming involved with Isabel?'

'My, my,' she cooed. 'And I thought I was a prime bitch. No, Greg, darling. I wasn't jealous. But I am disappointed. In you, darling. I thought you would be able to see why not. You should do. If you're any good, that is. Or is Mindstar like a rock star's codpiece, pumped up with hot air?'

It was the tone which keyed him in. Greg concentrated on the shimmering thought currents in front of him, congealed with hauteur, and smug complacency. Something was helping her to recover from the anguish of Kitchener's death, the shock scars of the psyche were healing too rapidly. When he went deeper, he found her cherishing a brittle triumph. Intuition kicked in. He refocused his espersense, moving it down through her body, feeling the grainy texture of warm cells, a fast surge of blood through veins like velvet pipes, obtuse chemical reactions flared and died all around, nerves flashed like lightning conductors. He left her brain behind, slipping past her throat, neck, breasts, chest, further down.

'Oh, shit,' he said. 'You're pregnant.' The embryo hung in the centre of black and scarlet shadows, a delicate white porcelain sculpture, beautiful, tiny, and tragically fragile.

'What?' Langley jerked upright.

'This interview is now over!' Slater cried.

Rosette slapped her hand against the desk as the detective and the lawyer started to shout at each other. 'Not yet!' she yelled. 'We haven't finished yet.'

Slater bent over her urgently, plucking at the arm of her black jacket. 'Miss Harding-Clarke, I must insist you do not continue.'

'No.' She waved him away. 'You are afraid the child gives me a motive. That I can contest Edward's will on behalf of the baby. That's right, isn't it?'

Slater glanced round at the detectives, his lips pressed together. 'That is a likely argument for the prosecution, yes.'

'My family is richer than Edward. Money is irrelevant to me.'

'Please!' he implored her.

'Are we still being recorded?' she asked.

'Yes,' Nevin said.

Greg sat perfectly still. He could guess what was coming next. Like she said, she had an IQ well above average.

'Excellent. Now I've been sitting patiently in this squalid filthy little room, and opened my soul to one of the most experienced and highly trained psychics in the country. I haven't held anything back, and I've answered every question put to me. Now, Greg darling, would you please tell everyone here whether I've been telling the truth.'

'You have,' he said, awash with the sense of inevitability.

'Did I kill Edward?'

'No.'

'Thank you!' She stood up. A grinning Slater rose behind her.

'Rosette?' Greg said.

She turned, exasperation on her face. 'Now what?'

He pointed casually at the camera. 'For the record, could you tell us which of the other students at Launde you slept with, please?'

Her fists clenched and unclenched, long red nails leaving white imprints on the flesh of her palms. 'Cecil,' she said woodenly, 'that's all.'

'Thank you, Rosette. No more questions.'

*

'You used to be Rosette's lover,' Greg said.

Cecil Cameron inclined his head reluctantly. 'Yes. When she first came to Launde, last October. Talk about impact; we started screwing the day after she arrived.'

'How long did it last for?'

'About a month.'

'Why did it end?'

He shrugged expansively. 'You've met Rosette. How long could you put up with her for?'

Greg heard Vernon chuckling softly behind him. Lisa Collier, who was acting as Cecil's adviser, tapped on his arm, giving him a disapproving frown. 'No opinions,' she murmured.

'I didn't even get on with her to start with,' Greg said. 'You obviously did.'

'For a while. I mean, don't get me wrong. Rosette and me are still good mates. But she's difficult to please. She thrives on variety, everything has to be fresh for her. Her tolerance threshold is non-existent. We burnt out. I knew it would right from the beginning. It was good while it lasted, mind. I mean, let's face it, she can take her pick.'

'Did she pick Kitchener?'

'No. That was mutual attraction.'

'What were you doing on Thursday night after supper?'

'Working on a project of Kitchener's; I was studying theoretical perturbations in electron orbits.'

'Were you interfacing with the Abbey's Bendix lightware cruncher?'

'Yes. Why, you think I can do that kind of thing in my head?'

'What time did you stop using the Bendix?'

'About eleven o'clock.'

'Could you be more precise, please?'

'Five past, ten past, something like that.'

'Was it functioning normally when you were interfacing with it?'

'Yes.'

'Did you use the English Telecom datalink to access any 'ware cores outside the Abbey that night?'

'No.'

'Did you use the datanet for anything that night?'

'No.'

'What did you do after you stopped work?'

'Rosette came in, that's why I stopped. We had a drink and a talk. The other four were in Uri's room. She doesn't get on terribly well with Liz, and Nick isn't exactly enthralling conversation at the best of times.'

'Do you like him?'

'Who, Nick? Yeah, I don't mind him. He's a bit shy, but he's a sodding genius when it comes to physics. We all knew that.'

'How long was Rosette with you?'

127

'Until after midnight – quarter-past, half-past maybe. She went off to see Kitchener then.' He pulled an indignant face. 'What a waste. Old man like that. Her choice, mind.'

'What about the other three students, how did you get on with them?'

'Fine. Uri and Liz had been involved for a year. Uri's great, one of the lads. Liz too, come to that.'

'And what about Isabel?' Greg watched the conflicting emotional surges corrupt Cecil's thought currents, the twinges of guilt coupled with an almost paternal urge of protectiveness. Cecil was being pulled apart by indecision.

'Nice girl. Bit disorientated by Abbey life, but she was coping.'

'Did you sleep with her?'

'Hey! I said we were friends.'

'Your relationship is something more than an ordinary friendship, though.'

Cecil looked round at Lisa Collier for guidance.

'It's a legitimate question,' she said sourly.

'You can tell that from my mind?' Cecil asked apprehensively.

'Yeah.'

'OK. Well, I meant what I said, mind. We weren't screwing each other. Wish we had been, she's got a terrific body. I asked her often enough, but she wasn't keen. She said that it couldn't last, not with me leaving at the end of the year, so it would be pointless, she'd only wind up getting hurt. I might have managed to change her mind in the end. Still ... I was happy enough playing big brother to her. There weren't many others she could turn to. I mean all that New Age crap Kitchener spouted about liberating your mind. Christ. The longest chat-up routine ever written. He said anything that would get them into bed with him, and they did as well, two by two. Isabel was confused by it. So we talked, that's all. Nick would have burst into tears if she'd told him what she was up to with Kitchener. As for Liz and Uri, hell, it's a miracle if they get out of bed for a meal! And Rosette, well she was with Kitchener.'

'Did Isabel come and talk with you that night?'

'No.'

'You were taking syntho. Why was that?'

Cecil drummed his kinaware fingers on the desk, black nails producing a tiny click on the smooth surface. 'Because it was available. I never took much.'

'You infused some that night.' Greg found himself staring at the silver-hued hand. Powerful enough to make the butchery easy?

'Yes.'

'When?'

'Rosette brought some in. I was bored. I'd been in the Abbey all day. We didn't even get out for a swim.'

'A swim?'

'Yes, we usually went for a dip in the top lake in the afternoon. Mornings as well, if it was fine. We're all reasonable swimmers, even Nick.'

Greg hesitated, that ambiguous notion returned at the mention of the lake. What was it about those three lakes? He hadn't been able to explain, not even to Eleanor. It was more than intuition, there was memory involved as well. Something had happened at Launde, quite a while ago. For the life of him he couldn't think what. It was bloody annoying.

'Was there ever anything unusual about those lakes?' he asked.

'No, not as far as I know.' Cecil gave Lisa Collier another mistrustful glance. She maintained her cantankerous expression, eyes not leaving Greg.

'OK.' Greg gave up. He touched a key on his cybofax, bringing up another page of questions. 'Did you ever take any syntho with Isabel?'

'Once or twice, yes. She was always timid about narcotics. Her background is very middle class.'

'Could anybody help themselves to Kitchener's stash?'

'It wasn't kept under lock and key. I always asked him, or Rosette. He would have known if someone had been taking it. The only thing he was concerned about was that we didn't OD.'

'Tell me what happened when the body was discovered.'

'Christ. The screams woke me up. That was Rosette. By the time I got into the corridor Nick and Uri had already got there. I . . . went in to Kitchener's bedroom . . . Wish to God I hadn't. That was one sick fucker who did that, Mr Mandel. I mean seriously fucked.'

'I know.'

'Yes. Well. Nick was puking his guts up. Uri was in shock, he just stood there, like he wasn't seeing it. What do they call it? Thousand-metre stare. I think Rosette had fainted by then. Passed out, swooned, something. She'd stopped screaming, anyway. I got in one look and tried to stop Liz and Isabel from going in.'

'When did they arrive?'

'Right after me.'

'Both together?'

'God, I don't know. Yes, more or less.'

'Did you see any movement in the corridor before you got to Kitchener?'

'The murderer, you mean? No. If I had, I would have killed him.'

Lisa Collier gave a censorious cough.

Cecil looked round at her. 'I would have killed him,' he repeated firmly.

'When did you wash that night?' Greg asked.

'When did I wash?'

'Yeah.'

'About eleven o'clock. I had a shower. My conditioner couldn't cope with the storm. My room was like a sauna. I couldn't open the window, not with the rain we had that night.'

'OK, thanks, Cecil.'

'That's it?'

'Yeah.'

'Aren't you going to ask me if I did it? I thought that's why they brought you here.'

'There's no need, not a direct question. It wasn't you.'

*

Greg stood up and flexed his arms while they waited for Uri Pabari, shrugging off the stiffness which came from sitting in a chair designed for Martians. The air in the interview room was growing stuffy.

'Vernon, do you remember anything else ever happening at Launde?' he asked. He just couldn't ignore the presage – if that's what it was.

'Such as?'

'I don't know. Something important enough to be news-worthy, or gossipworthy.' Where did I hear it? Or did I see it? Bugger.

'Kitchener was in the news once or twice each year with his lectures,' Langley said reasonably. 'Universities and societies used to invite him to make addresses. He was famous, after all.'

'No, not Kitchener, not something he said. An event. Or an incident.' He was annoyed at the amount of petulance creeping into his voice.

'Kitchener and a girl student?' Nevin suggested. 'I mean, he's had two out of the three staying with him this year. Maybe one of them objected.'

'Could be,' Greg said. But he knew it wasn't.

They both looked at him expectantly.

'Buggered if I can remember. Can you run a check through your files for me?'

'Yes.' Langley loaded a note into his cybofax. He had been laying off the dudgeon since Greg started the interviews. More impressed, or unnerved, by his espersense than he was willing to admit. Even Nevin had stopped looking for flaws in everything he said, the opportunities to underline the obvious.

Progress. Of sorts.

*

Edwin Lancaster was representing Uri Pabari. The first of the three defence counsellors who actually looked like a lawyer, to Greg's mind. A sixty-year-old in a suit and silk waistcoat, pressed white shirt, small neat bow tie. He sat behind Uri, stiffly attentive. Instead of using a cybofax, a paper notebook was balanced on his leg, the tip of his gold-plated Parker biro flicking constantly, producing a minute shorthand.

Uri gave Greg a curious stare as he settled into the chair, not nearly as apprehensive as Cecil.

The student had a powerful build. Greg called up the police data profile on the flatscreen. Uri had played rugby for his university, he was also a karate second dan.

'You were the third into Kitchener's bedroom, is that right?' Greg asked.

'Yes. I got there on Nick's heels.'

'And prior to that you were with Liz Foxton all evening?'

'Yes.'

Greg caught the tension budding in Uri's mind. 'Pleasant evening, was it?'

Uri tried to smile. 'God, that gland of yours is quite something, isn't it?'

'So what happened?'

'We had a row. Early on, before supper. Stupid really.'

'What was it about?'

'Kitchener. His syntho habit. Except Liz didn't think it was a habit. She said . . . Well, she kind of drinks up that dogma of his. Everything he says is right because he's the one that says it. Me, I'm a bit more sceptical.' He grinned reflectively. 'Kitchener taught me that. And that evening, things got said that shouldn't have been, you know how it is.'

'Do you and Liz quarrel often?'

'No. That's what makes it worse when we do. And Liz was already wound up tight over Scotland. She can get a bit political at times, she had a rough ride in the PSP decade.'

'Didn't we all,' Greg murmured under his breath. 'Is that why there was a scene at supper between you and Kitchener?'

Uri laughed. 'There's a scene at every meal. God, he was an obstinate old sod.'

'And afterwards? You made up, you and Liz?'

'Yes. We're in love.' He looked at Greg, trying to gauge the reaction he was getting. 'Hopefully we'll get engaged. I was going to do it during the summer, I thought it would be a nice way to leave Launde.'

'OK, back to Thursday. What happened after supper?'

'Nick and Isabel came up to my room, and we sat around talking and watching the newscasts. They left around midnight.'

'When did you wash?'

Uri's forehead formed narrow creases as he frowned. 'Just before we went to bed. Liz and I had a shower. It was hot that night.'

'What time did you go to bed?'

'About half twelve.'

Greg couldn't help a small smile. 'And what time did you go to sleep?'

'Just after one. Liz was still watching the newscasts, though. I don't know what time she fell asleep. But we were both awake at three again.'

'Who woke who?'

'Dunno. It just happened, you know.'

'Was your flatscreen still showing the newscasts?'

'Er, yeah, I think so. Couldn't swear to it in court. Wasn't paying much attention, see?'

'Were you aware that Rosette was having an affair with Kitchener?'

Uri gave a mental flinch at Rosette's name. He wasn't afraid of her, Greg decided, more like demoralized.

'Yes,' Uri said. 'It was bound to happen, those two.'

'Oh?'

'Two of a kind. Intellectually, you know. Didn't give a stuff for convention.'

'And did you know about Isabel?'

Uri scratched his stubble. 'The old nocturnal visiting? Yes. Shame that. I blame Rosette more than Kitchener.'

'Why is that?'

'She'd enjoy seducing Isabel. It would be a challenge to her.'

'You liked Kitchener, didn't you?'

'He was bloody amazing. I don't just mean his work. When I came to Launde I was almost as bad as Nick, all meek and tongue-tied. It's trite, but he really was like a father to me. He brings people out of themselves. God, the stories he told us! That reputation of his was one hundred per cent earned. He was wicked, disgraceful, terrible. And absolutely beautiful. Totally unique. The only thing I disagreed about was the syntho, but it didn't seem to affect his serious thinking. And he's still pushing at frontiers even now—' The lively smile on Uri's face died a tormented death. 'Was pushing . . .' he whispered.

'Did you notice anything out of the ordinary about the Abbey that night?'

'Like what?'

'A visitor.'

'No – God, I would have told the police if I had!'

'Yeah. There was no trace of syntho in your blood when the police took a sample.'

'Well, there wouldn't be,' Uri said cautiously.

'Have you ever taken it at Launde?'

Edwin Lancaster's gold biro halted, its tip poised a couple of millimetres in the air. 'You are asking my client to incriminate himself,' he said. 'I'm sorry, but that wasn't part of the basis for this interview.'

'We are not interested in bringing charges against anybody concerning past narcotic infusion,' Langley promised. 'Providing it is external to this case.'

'As a police officer, you have a duty to investigate illegal narcotics abuse.'

'We know the source of syntho at Launde. Kitchener's vat is in police custody, it cannot be used to supply anyone in future. And we have no desire to prosecute past victims.'

'Your client has infused syntho at some time,' Greg said.

'Hey!' Uri protested.

'I simply wish to know how familiar you are with the narcotics availability at Launde, that's all,' Greg said. 'It's going to help me a lot.'

'OK. All right,' Uri held up his hands in placation. 'No big deal. Yes, I tried it. Once, OK? One time. Like I told you, it's not my scene. I don't like that kind of loss of control, not in myself or other people. Infusing it just confirmed my view. It's stupid, self-destructive.'

'You know where it was grown?'

'Yes. The vat in the lab. Everybody knew that.'

'Thank you. Did you use the Bendix that night?'

'No.'

'Do you know its management program codes?'

'No, not offhand, but they're all stored in the operations file. We all have access to that. Kitchener trusted us not to do anything stupid; we're all 'ware literate.'

'What about the datanet; did you use it on Thursday, plug into a 'ware system outside the Abbey?'

'No.'

*

Liz Foxton, Greg decided, was the kind of girl who was always open to other people's problems. To say that she was motherly would be unfair, she had a steely reserve, a no-nonsense practicality, but in addition there was a definite aura of reassurance about her. Even he felt less disquieted about this interview.

'I've been told you don't get on well with Rosette Harding-Clarke; is that true?' he asked.

'I don't dislike her,' Liz said defensively. 'There is no percentage in grudges, not when you have to spend a whole year cooped up in the same house together. I understand her perfectly; I'm just unhappy with her, that's all.'

'Why?'

'She made a pass at Uri. More than one, actually. He turned her down each time.'

'I see. What time did you get to sleep last Thursday night?'

'About two o'clock. I was watching the Globecast news channel. I was so happy about Scotland. Now this.'

'I understand you were, um, active at three o'clock Friday morning. Did you hear or see anything unusual at that time?'

'No. There was just us.'

'Was the flatscreen showing the newscasts at that time?'

'Yes. I'd fallen asleep watching it.'

'What about after three o'clock, did it stay on?'

'Yes. I watched it for a while. I don't know how long for, I dozed off again.'

'And you were woken by Rosette's screams?'

'Yes,' she said in a tiny voice.

'Then you went straight to Kitchener's bedroom?'

'Yes.'

'Was Uri in the bedroom when you woke up?'

'Yes! He was out of the door before me, but only by a few seconds.'

'Do you remember if you arrived at Kitchener's bedroom before or after Isabel Spalvas?'

'Before, I think. She was standing behind me. She caught me. My legs went, you see.' Her eyes filled with liquid. She blinked furiously, dabbing at them with a handkerchief.

'I understand,' said Greg. 'Just a couple more questions.' He gave Lancaster an admonitory look. 'Did you ever take syntho at the Abbey?'

She sniffed. 'Yes, a few times. Three, I think. That was last year, about a month after I arrived. Just to try it. Edward was there to make sure I'd be all right. But that was the last time, Uri has a real bug about it.'

'And you argued about it?'

'Yes. So silly.' She gave him a fast plaintive grimace. 'You remember the old song? The best part of breaking up, is making up. That's us.'

'Right. So you must have known that syntho was being cooked up at the Abbey, that there was a vat in the lab?'

'Yes.'

'Were you using the Bendix on Thursday?'

'No, I should have been, but Scotland seemed so much more important. I was watching the newscasts for most of the day.'

'So you didn't use the datanet either, then?'

'No.'

'Did you ever sleep with Edward Kitchener?'

He perceived the answer in her mind, in amidst all the turmoil of guilt, adoration, remorse, and grief. She took a long time to speak. The answer in her earlier statements to the police had been a resolute no.

'I did once,' she said. 'When I first went to Launde. I was lonely. He was kind, sympathetic.'

'Was that one of the times when you infused syntho?'

'Yes,' she whispered.

'Does Uri know?'

'No.' Her head was bowed. 'You won't tell him, will you?'

'These interviews are strictly confidential,' Greg said. 'There's no need for him to know.'

She rose slowly from her chair, gratefully accepting the hand Lancaster offered. 'Do you know who it was?' she asked.

'Not yet, no.'

*

Isabel Spalvas looked as tired as Greg felt. She was wearing jeans and a baggy mauve sweatshirt, her light fuzzy hair tied back in a pony-tail. Her face had wonderfully dainty features. She would have been very attractive under ordinary circumstances, he guessed, but today her skin was sallow, almost grey, there were red rings round her eyes from crying, slim lips were turned down mournfully. She moved listlessly when she came in, sitting down, showing no real interest in the proceedings. Matthew Slater sat behind her, looking appropriately concerned.

Greg could sense just how grave her depression was, a bleak distress interwound with every thought. Out of all the students so far, she was easily the most affected by the murder. He would go so far as to say traumatized.

'I understand you were seeing Edward Kitchener,' Greg said delicately after Langley had started the AV recording.

She nodded apathetically.

'You were with him that night?'

Another nod.

'What time did you go to him?'

'Quarter-past one.'

'Until when?'

'Half-past two.'

'So you left Uri's room about midnight, and stayed in your own room until Rosette arrived, is that right?'

'Yes.'

'What time did she arrive?'

'Half-past twelve, I think. She'd been in Cecil's room. We talked for a while, then we got changed ready for Edward. Rosette is quite fun when she's relaxed, when she's not trying to prove something. Don't get the wrong impression about her, most of that attitude is put on. She can't help it.'

'When you left Kitchener's room, did you see anyone else in the Abbey?'

'No.'

'Did you hear anything strange?'

'No.'

'What about lights; shining under someone's door, or down-stairs, outside even?'

'No. Oh, there was a bit of light in Uri's room. Bluish. I think the flatscreen might have been on. We were watching it in there earlier.'

'You were taking syntho that night. Had it worn off by then?'

'Not quite, I was just starting to come down. I don't—' She took a breath, then looked resolutely at the floor. 'I don't like being in there after the boost has gone.'

'In Kitchener's bedroom?'

'Yes.'

'Why not?'

'I get cold. Not physically cold, but it's hard to face them afterwards. We get so high together, you see; when it comes to sex, Edward and Rosette have lifetimes more experience than me, they made me feel completely free with them. The way a child trusts an adult. His bedroom contained our own private universe, we were safe inside, nothing mattered apart from ourselves and what we wanted. But then when it was over the illusion vanished so quickly. And this shabby old world with all its inbuilt guilt comes flooding back in.' She tugged at a strand of hair, twisting it nervously round and round her index finger. 'You must think I'm horrible.'

'I'm not a judge, Isabel. Your sex life is entirely your own. But I'd like to know why you started going, please?'

'Rosette started – well it was just hints at first. Joking. Then . . . I don't know. Somehow it wasn't a joke any more. And then I went home for Christmas. There was nothing wrong with that, my family. Except it was sort of pale, lacking substance; I was going through the motions. The Abbey, Edward, we were learning so much there, learning how to think, how to question. It was so much more real. Colour, that's what Launde had. I was glad to get back. I wanted more of it, more of the adventure. They offered me that.'

'Cecil said you were unhappy.'

'Not really. It's peculiar, what I was doing, so far outside my norm. Edward called it walking the boundaries of the mind. I had trouble adapting to the affair at first; when I was with Edward and Rosette it didn't matter at all, it was just outside, afterwards, when it seemed wrong, or stupid, or both. I was going to them more frequently, and staying longer too. But that wasn't the answer, not shutting myself away with them. Talking about it to someone who understood helped me. Cecil was the only one I could really go to. Cecil is worldly wise, or so he claims. He sympathized in a funny sort of way, and he didn't criticize. That meant a lot to me.'

'Did you know Rosette was pregnant?'

Isabel's head came up, her blue eyes full of melancholy. There was no resentment in her mind, which was what he actually wanted to know. No grudge. He didn't think a gentle soul like Isabel *could* hold a grudge.

'Yes,' Isabel said. 'She never said. But I knew. I'm glad in a way, certainly now. It means there will be something of Edward left. I almost wish it was me.'

'How about Kitchener, what sort of mood was he in that night?'

'Edward? Happy. Rosette and me ... I ... It was good that night.'

'No, apart from that. His general mood that night, over the last few days. Was he preoccupied at all? Worried about something? Agitated?'

'No.' She gave him a brave little smile. 'You don't know Edward or you wouldn't even have asked. He pretended to be this awful old monster. But it was all a sham. Oh, he'd shout at us if we were blatantly stupid. And politicians infuriated him. Apart from that, he didn't have any worries. That was part of the attraction, I've never met anyone so carefree. He'd done so much in his lifetime, won so many battles. I don't think anything could upset him any more.'

'I have to ask this, Isabel: how do you feel about Nicholas Beswick?'

'Oh, God!' She buried her face in her hands. 'Why did he have to come out and see us? He's so sweet. I didn't want to hurt him. Really. Why did any of this happen? What did we do?'

Slater patted her gently, but she shrugged him off. He shot a silent appeal at Greg.

Greg waited until she finished screwing tears from her eyes with damp knuckles.

'Were you the last to reach Kitchener's bedroom after Rosette discovered the body?' he asked, feeling a prize turd for pressing the anguished girl.

'Yes. I think so. They were all ahead of me. I don't remember much. I'm sorry.'

'No matter. Before then, after Nicholas had found you and

Rosette together in the corridor, did you tell Kitchener he had seen you?'

'No. God, I couldn't. I didn't know what to do about that. Even Rosette was upset. Edward had a real soft spot for Nick, he had such high hopes for him. Nick has a very high IQ, and he wants to learn, I mean really wants. The whole universe is a glorious puzzle to Nick. That's the only time he ever comes out of his shell; when we're talking about the everyday things like the channels or politics he sits quietly in the corner; but say anything about Grand Unification or quantum mechanics and you can't shut him up. He's lovely like that, so animated. I'm rambling, sorry.'

'Did you and Rosette discuss what to do about Nicholas seeing you?'

'Not much. It was a sort of mutual silence. I made up my mind to go and see Nick in the morning. Really I was. I would have tried to explain. He was about the one person I would have given Edward up for. I looked after I left Edward, but Nick's light was out. And anyway, it wouldn't have been right, not going in straight afterwards. That would have seemed like Edward had total priority on me. But then . . .'

'Nicholas Beswick's light was off at two-thirty? You're sure of that?'

'Yes.'

'When did you wash that night?'

'I had a shower before I started getting our supper ready, then I had another after I left Edward.'

'Were you using the Bendix at all on Thursday?'

'Yes, most of the afternoon.'

'Did you access any external 'ware systems?'

'No.'

The last question slid from his cybofax's little screen. He couldn't think of any more. Isabel already looked like he'd physically wrung the answers from her.

It was raining outside again, big warm drops beating incessantly on the high window.

'OK,' he told Vernon. 'Let's have Nicholas Beswick in.'

8

It was raining over Peterborough again. Sheet lightning sizzled through the covering of low cloud, highlighting the new tower blocks which stood on the high ground to the west; austere monoliths looking down on the organic clutter of the smaller buildings in the city's original districts.

Julia hated flying in thunderstorms. Her Dornier tilt-fan might have every safety system in existence built in, but it seemed so insignificant compared to the power outside.

Another flash burst over the city. Glossy roof-top solar panels bounced some of the light back up at her, leaving tiny purple dazzle spots on her retinas. She had seen the Event Horizon headquarters building dead ahead, a seventeen-storey cube of glass, steel, and composite panels. There was nothing elegant about it, thrown up in twenty-six frantic months so that it could accommodate the droves of head office data shufflers necessary to manage a company of Event Horizon's size, as well as Morgan's security staff. A monument to haste and functionalism. Its replacement out at Prior's Fen would be far more aesthetic; the architects had come up with a white and gold cylinder which, with its panoply of pillars and arches, resembled the Leaning Tower of Pisa. Only straight this time, of course. Event Horizon didn't build crooked.

She poured herself a chilled mineral water from the bar, and switched the bulkhead flatscreen on, flicking through the channels until she came to the Northwest Europe Broadcast Company. Jakki Coleman was on, a middle-aged woman with iron-cast gold-blonde hair, wearing a stylish mint-green satin jacket. She was sitting behind a Florentine desk in the luxurious study of some mansion.

Julia grinned gamely as she sprawled back on the white-leather settee, propping her feet up on the chair opposite. Jakki Coleman was the queen of the gossipcasts; rock stars, channel celebrities, aristocrats, sports personalities, politicians, she shafted them all.

'Pauline Harrington, the devoutly Catholic songstress, seems to have mislaid her religious scruples,' Jakki said, her French accent rich and purring. 'At least for this weekend. For whom should I see but the delightful Pauline, who is at number five with "My Real Man" in this week's white soul chart, with none other than Keran Bennion, number one driver for the Porsche team.'

The image cut to a picture of Pauline and Keran walking through the grounds of a country hotel, somewhere where the sun was shining. They were hand in hand, oblivious of the fountains playing in stone-lined ponds around them, in the background bushes blazed with big tangerine blooms. The recording had obviously been made with a telephoto lens, outlines were slightly fuzzy.

'Perhaps Keran's wife sent him for singing lessons,' Jakki suggested smugly. 'The three days they spent together should certainly have got his voice in trim.'

A swarthy young male in a purple and black Versace suit walked into the office and put a sheet of paper in front of Jakki. She read it and 'Ohooed' delightedly. 'Well, fancy that,' she said.

The item was about a Swiss minister and her toyboy. After that was one about a music biz payola racket.

Julia took a sip of the mineral water, then noticed her boots. They were crusted with mud from the tower site. She tried rubbing at them with a tissue as Jakki stage whispered that certain pointed questions were being asked about a countess's new-born son, apparently the count was absent the night of the conception.

Julia chortled to herself. It was the set she moved in which featured in the 'cast, Europe's financial, political, and glamour élite; snobbish, pretentious, corrupt, yet forever projecting the image of angels. And she had to deal with them on that level, the great pretence, all part of the grand game. So it was a joy to watch Jakki spotlighting their failings, taking a machete to their egos; a kind of second-hand revenge for all the false courtesies she had to extend, the interminable flatteries.

'The *big* event in England yesterday was the Event Horizon spaceplane roll out,' Jakki said. 'Simply anybody who is anybody was there, including little *moi*.'

Julia held her breath. Surely Jakki wasn't going to lampoon the Prince's haircut? Not again?

'And I can tell you several self-proclaimed *celebrities* were left outside explaining rather tiresomely that their invitations had been squirted to their holiday houses by mistake,' Jakki gushed maliciously. 'But leaving behind the nonentities, we enter the *interesting* zone. Appropriately for an event so large, and *très* prestigious, it boasted the greatest laugh of the day.' Oh, dear Lord, it was going to be the Prince: 'Mega, mega-wealthy Julia Evans has spent a rumoured three and a quarter billion pounds New Sterling on developing the sleek machine intended to spearhead England's economic reconstruction.'

Julia scowled. Where had Jakki got that estimate from? It was alarmingly close to the real one. Not another leak in the finance division, please!

The flatscreen image switched to the roll out ceremony, showing her escorting the Prince and the Prime Minister around the spaceplane.

'Unfortunately,' Jakki continued, 'these daunting design costs must have left poor dear Julia's cupboard quite bare. Because, as you can see, her otherwise enviably slim figure was clad in what looks to me like a big Valentine's Day chocolate-box wrapper.'

*

The Dornier landed on the raised pad at the centre of the headquarters building's roof. Caroline Rothman held a broad golfing umbrella over Julia as they made their way to the stairwell door. Rachel and Ben marched alongside. Nobody was looking at her. It could have been coincidence. But then they had all been incredibly busy when she came out of the tilt fan's rear lounge as well.

Be honest, girl, she told herself, stomping out of the lounge. That *bitchsluthussy*!

Sean Francis, her management division assistant, was waiting for her inside the building. She actually quite liked Sean, although he annoyed a lot of people with his perfectionist efficiency. She had appointed him to her personal staff soon after inheriting the company.

He was thirty-four, a tall dark-haired man with a degree in engineering administration who had joined Event Horizon right after graduation. It said a lot for his capability that he had risen so far so fast. Greg had checked him out for her once; his loyalty was beyond reproach.

He was wearing the same conservative style of suit as every other data shuffler in the building. Sometimes she wondered what would happen if she let it be known she preferred employees to wear tank-tops and Bermuda shorts. Knowing the way people jumped around her, they probably would all turn up in them.

Might be worth doing.

'Did you have a nice flight, ma'am?' Sean asked pleasantly.

Julia put her hands on her hips. 'Sean, it's pissing down with rain, and the bloody plane nearly got skewered by lightning bolts. What do you think?'

His jaw opened, then closed. 'Yes, ma'am,' he said humbly. 'Sorry.'

She caught a tiny flickering motion from the corner of her eye, and thought Caroline was making a hand signal. But when she turned her PA was rolling up the umbrella, a guileless expression in place.

It's a conspiracy.

She took a grip on her nerves. I am not affected by what that senile whore Jakki Coleman said. I'm not.

'My fault, Sean.' She gave him one of her heartbreaker smiles. 'Those thunderbolts are frightening when you're so close to them.'

'That's all right, ma'am. I'm scared of them, too.'

*

The conference room was on the corner of the headquarters building; two walls were made from reinforced glass with a brown tint, giving a view over the rain-dulled streets of Westwood. It was decorated in the kind of forced grandeur which was endemic among corporate designers the world over: deep-piled sapphire-blue carpet, two Picassos and a Van Gogh hanging between big aluminium-framed prints of the Fens before the Warming, huge oval oak table, thickly padded black-leather chairs, pot plants taller than people. Everything was shameless ostentation.

Julia was all too aware that her boots were leaving muddy footprints as she walked to her chair at the head of the table. There were several startled glances among the delegates when they saw her Goth clothes. Damp hair hanging in flaccid strings didn't help.

Eight of her own staff were sitting along one side, premier executives from each of the company's divisions. Lined up against them were Valyn Szajowski, Argon Hulmes, Sir Michael Torrance, Karl Hildebrandt, and Sok Yem, the representatives from Event Horizon's financial backing consortium. There were over a hundred and fifty banks and finance houses in the consortium, making it one of the largest in the world. In the first two years after the fall of the PSP they had extended seventy per cent of the money which Philip Evans had needed to re-establish the company in England. Event Horizon under his guidance had proved to be an ultra-solid investment; even though there had been some nervousness about his enthusiasm for the company's space programme, he had never missed a payment. With the global economy at that time still extremely shaky, membership of the consortium was highly prized, and jealously guarded.

But then two years ago, after Julia inherited the company lock, stock, and barrel, the once eagerly proffered loans became suddenly hard to obtain and those that were available had inordinately high interest rates. The conservative financial establishment had zero faith in teenage girls as corporate owner-directors. They wanted more say in the way Event Horizon was run, a position on the management board, possibly even the directorship. Just until she was older, they explained, until she understood the mechanism of corporate management – say in about twenty years. Their reluctant but firm insistence had turned into the biggest tactical error in modern financial history. Respected financecast commentators were already calling it the Great Loan Shark Massacre.

Armed with the giga-conductor royalties, and (unknown to the consortium) her grandfather's NN core, she stuck up a grand two-fingered salute, and carried on expanding the company at an even faster rate. Existing loan repayments came in ahead of schedule, with corresponding loss of interest payments, and fewer loans were applied for. The consortium's income began to fall off while Event Horizon's cash flow and profits grew; their golden egg was tarnishing rapidly.

Sean pulled her chair out, and she sat down, glowering at the artificial smiles directed towards her. Sean and Caroline sat on either side.

Open Channel To NN Core.

Well hello there, Miss Grumpy Guts. And what's today's temper tantrum all about?

I am not in a temper, Grandpa.

Ha! I'm plugged in to the conference room's security cameras. If looks could kill, my girl, you'd be in a room of corpses.

Did you see . . . Never mind. No. Did you see Jakki Coleman's 'cast this morning?

Bloody hell, girl, I haven't got time for crap like that, not even with my capacity.

She was on about what I wore yesterday. I had three fittings for that outfit, you know. Three.

Really.

Sabareni is one of the best haute couture houses in Europe. It's not like I'm going to Oxfam.

That's a great relief to hear.

Seven thousand pounds it cost.

I wouldn't want you stinting, Julia.

Don't be so bloody sarcastic. Seven thousand pounds! Well I can't possibly wear it again. Not now.

Juliet, could we possibly start the meeting, please.

Yah, all right. I bet they all saw the 'cast. Seven thousand pounds!

Oh, Gawd . . . The silent voice carried a definite air of pique.

The management team and consortium representatives sat down, their earlier *bonhomie* fractured by her black mood.

Good. They might cut short the usual smarmy attempts to ingratiate themselves.

The terminal flatscreen recessed into the table in front of her lit up with the meeting's agenda.

'I am happy to report that, as I'm sure you all saw yesterday, the *Clarke* spaceplane project is on schedule,' Julia said. 'First flight is due in a month, first orbital test flight should take place ten weeks later. Assuming no catastrophic design flaw, deliveries will start in a year.'

'That's excellent news, Julia,' Argon Hulmes said. 'Your Duxford team is to be congratulated.'

'Thank you,' she replied equably.

The consortium representatives had all been changed over the last two years until not one of the original members remained.

This new batch were all younger, a not very subtle attempt to make her feel more comfortable. Although even now the banks still couldn't quite bring themselves to appoint anyone under thirty-eight; Sok Yem from the Hong Kong Oceanic Bank was the youngest at thirty-nine. Rumour said that Argon Hulmes's superiors had ordered him to have *plastique* before he got his seat, bringing his appearance down from forty-three to thirtyish.

Thirty and then something, Julia thought. He was always trying to talk to her about groups and albums and raves; his Christmas present had been a bootleg AV recording of a Bil Yi Somanzer concert. She imagined him dutifully plugging into the MTV channel each evening, updating himself on current releases, who's hot and who's flopped. A fine occupation for a middle-aged banker.

'We will break even on three hundred spaceplanes,' she said. 'That should come in about three years' time. My space-line, Dragonflight, has just placed firm orders for another fifteen, and options on thirty-five, to cope with the nuclear waste disposal contract we were awarded yesterday. We are expecting additional disposal contracts from five or six more European governments to be signed over the next few months, and of course national aerospace lines will want to get in on the act.'

Sean Francis took his cue flawlessly. 'Nuclear waste disposal has enabled us to upgrade our estimates on space-related industry turnover by forty-five per cent over the next four years,' he said. 'It is a completely untapped revenue source. Should it be exploited fully, its potential is staggering. No government on the planet will be able to refuse its electorate a safe and final solution to disposing of radioactive material. And there are currently forty-three redundant nuclear power stations in Europe alone, with a further seventeen scheduled to be decommissioned over the next decade.'

'Such a pity the consortium didn't consider my Sunderland vitrification plant a worthwhile investment,' Julia said. 'You could have shared in the profits. The margin is considerable, given that I now have a virtual monopoly on the technology.'

Sir Michael leaned forward earnestly. 'We would be very happy to fund any expansion to the vitrification plant, Julia. Now that the requirement has been proved, and very ably proved if I might say so. The nuclear waste disposal contract is a marvellous development, we're all very pleased.'

No, Juliet, absolutely not, cut them out of the vitrification. Squeeze the bastards.

She gave Sir Michael a smile which withered his sudden display of enthusiasm. 'The vitrification plant was a five hundred million pound risk,' she said in her lecturer's voice. 'And having taken that risk all by myself, I intend to benefit all by myself. The profits generated by this new venture will be more than sufficient to fund its own expansion. Thank you.'

'Julia, I think we are all agreed that your handling of the company is impeccable,' Sir Michael said. 'And in view of this we would like to offer to set up a floating credit arrangement of three billion New Sterling which you can call upon at any time to fund new ventures. This way we could avoid the delays and queries inherent with having to process loan requests through the consortium's standing review committee.'

The other representatives murmured their approval, all of them watching her, willing her to accept.

We've got 'em, Juliet. They don't offer anyone a blank cheque unless they're under a lot of pressure. Now, remember what we agreed, girl?

Hit them with the wind-up scenario. Then the Prior's Fen scheme. That's my girl.

She tented her fingers, and gave them an apologetic look. 'Oh dear, how embarrassing. I believe my finance director has a summary he wanted to present. Alex, if you would, please.'

Alex Barnes stood up, a fifty-three-year-old Afro-Caribbean with a receding cap of grizzled hair. His suit with velvet lapels did at least lift him above the level of corporate clone. He began to recite a stream of accounts; figures, dates, and percentages merging together in a wearisome drone of statistics.

The representatives were looking very itchy by the time he finished.

'What it means,' Julia said sweetly, 'is that the loans which the consortium has so far extended to Event Horizon will be repaid in seven years. After that, the company will be totally self-financing. Now, as the company's expansion plans have already been finalized for that period, with the exception of Prior's Fen, I really can see no reason to extend my period of indebtedness. Certainly not at the level of your floating credit proposal, which I have to say is disappointingly paltry given Event Horizon's size.'

There was a moment of silence as the representatives exchanged a comprehensive catalogue of facial expressions. Interestingly, only Argon Hulmes allowed any ire to show. So much for solidarity amongst fellow youth-culture subscribers.

Some clandestine and invisible voting system elected Sir Michael as their spokesman. 'Exactly what were you proposing to do out at Prior's Fen?' he enquired in a chary tone.

*

Karl Hildebrandt remained behind after the meeting. The request for a talk – 'Not business, I assure you' – from the wily old German was intriguing enough for Julia to humour him.

Sean remained seated at her side, while Caroline helped shepherd the others from the room. Eventually there were only the three of them left at the table, plus Rachel sitting quietly on a chair by the window.

Diessenburg Mercantile, the Zurich bank which Karl represented, was one of the larger members of the consortium, accounting for six per cent of the investment total. Karl himself was in his late forties, and putting on weight almost as fast as Uncle Horace; a fold of pink flesh was overlapping his collar (she could count about four chins), his blond hair was veering into silver. His suit came from Paris, a narrow lapel helping to de-emphasize his barrel chest; steel-rimmed glasses were worn for effect, bestowing an air of dependability.

She approved of him for the one reason that he didn't try to pretend, like Argon Hulmes.

'I know it has been said before, Julia,' he said. 'But you are quite a remarkable young girl.' There was hardly any German accent. Perhaps one of the reasons he'd been selected as a representative.

'Thank you, Karl. You're not going to come on to me like Argon, are you?'

He laughed softly, and closed up his cybofax, slipping it into his inside jacket pocket. 'Certainly not. But to squeeze a fixed interest twelve billion pound investment loan out of banks and finance houses is an achievement beyond some kombinates.'

'Prior's Fen is a viable project. No risk.'

'The cyber-precincts, maybe. But to make us pay for a rail link before we can invest in them. That's cruel, Julia.'

'You get your interest payments, I get my cyber-precincts. Point to a victim, Karl.'

'None, of course. That is why you triumph all the time.'

'So you think the review committee will approve the loan?'

'Yes,' he said simply.

'I thought this wasn't going to be business.'

'I apologize. But everything has its roots in politics.'

She couldn't ever remember seeing Karl in such an ambivalent mood before. It was as if he wanted to talk about some important topic, but didn't quite know how to broach the subject. A parent explaining sex to a giggly teenager. 'You want to talk about politics? I wasn't old enough to vote at the election even if I had been in the country. I will in the next, though.'

'You certainly play politics like a master, Julia. That's why I was not surprised when you were given the nuclear waste disposal contract. Admiring, but not surprised.'

'Thank you, it took some arranging, but I'd like to think I am flexible when it comes to co-operating with the English Ministry of Industry.'

'Yes. However, there are questions being asked in some

quarters about the closeness of Event Horizon and the Ministry. It might almost be referred to as a partnership.'

'I have never offered cash to an MP,' she said. 'And I never will.'

'No. But the relationship, imaginary though it is, can be seized upon by opposition parties. The Big Lie, Julia; say something loud enough for long enough, and people will begin to believe. Ultimately that will affect Event Horizon; artificial constraints will be placed on you. Your bids will be refused simply because they are yours; politicians publicly demonstrating that they are not showing any favouritism. And that cannot be allowed.' He smiled crookedly. 'It's bad for profits, if nothing else. Bad for us.'

Julia began to wonder which 'us' he was talking about. 'I will just have to shout louder. And I can shout, very loud indeed.'

'An official denial is like an Oscar to a rumour.'

'Are we going to sit here all afternoon and quote *bons mots* at each other, Karl?'

'I would hope not.'

'Well, what would you like to see me do?'

'Some circumspection wouldn't hurt, Julia. I know you are reasonably adroit, that's why I find your latest action somewhat puzzling.'

She sneaked a questioning look to Sean. But he just shrugged minutely.

'What action?'

'Imposing that Mindstar veteran, Greg Mandel, on the Kitchener inquiry. It was terribly public, Julia. You were his bridesmaid. Really! It leaves you wide open to the rabble-rousers and conspiracy theorists.'

She regarded him thoughtfully. 'How did you know about Greg?'

'It was all over the channel newscasts.'

'Oh.' Even so, it was odd that he should know so quickly. She had spent most of the morning swotting up on datawork for the meeting, and that was with nodes augmenting her brain. Did he really have each news item concerning Event Horizon brought to his attention? Then she remembered Jakki bitch Coleman. It hadn't been every minute, after all. 'I take your point, Karl. Actually, I've already started damage limitation.'

'Mandel has been taken off the case?'

'No, I need to know who killed Kitchener. But you won't be hearing about the link between Greg and myself any more, not on the channels.'

'Ah. I'm glad to hear it.'

9

Nicholas wasn't really interested in his surroundings any more, so the pokey interview room didn't lodge in his mind until Greg Mandel looked at him. Looked inside him, more like, right through his skull into his brain.

The lawyer, Lisa Collier, had explained about the psychic being assigned to the investigation. She had seemed very irate about it, going on about how his rights were being violated, procedural irregularities, hearsay being taken as evidence. Nicholas didn't mind a psychic being appointed; anything, anything at all which would bring the killer a step nearer to justice was totally justified. That was simple logic, obvious. Why couldn't the Collier woman see that?

He had been staying in one of the cells at Oakham police station since Friday, although the door was always left unlocked. 'You aren't being held on remand,' the police kept explaining. 'You're just here to help us.' He nodded at their anxious faces, and answered every question the detectives asked. They seemed surprised that his answers were so consistent. As if he could forget anything that had happened on that night.

It was the last night of his life. Nothing had happened to him since. There was only the mechanics of the body, eating, going to the toilet, sleeping. That was all he had done since then, slept and answered questions. He was allowed to mix with the other students, but they never expected him to say anything anyway.

They had moaned about the accommodation, about not being allowed out, the food, the bathroom.

The one person he wanted to talk to, Isabel, was further away from him now than she had ever been at Launde. She would sit in one corner of the rest room they had been assigned, her legs tucked up against her chest, peering vacantly out of the window; and he would sit in the corner opposite, just gazing at her. He was too afraid even to say good morning, because if they did talk he would have to hear about her and Kitchener and Rosette. What happened in that bedroom, how many times it happened. Even why it had happened. He couldn't possibly stand that.

Kitchener had been the architect of his mind. For the first time in his life he had really begun to think straight. Kitchener, with his own love of knowledge, had been the one who nurtured his talent, who made him realize his ability was nothing to be ashamed of, wasn't freakish like people said. Kitchener was the one who encouraged him to join in the Abbey's camaraderie.

Kitchener had taken Isabel from him.

Kitchener was dead.

The world, which had been so close to becoming accessible, had eluded him once again. Which was why he said he didn't mind the psychic asking questions; after all, Kitchener had used neurohormones. They couldn't be bad.

Except, now he was faced with the prospect of actually going through with the interview, it didn't seem quite so easy.

There was a very unforgiving quality about Greg Mandel as he sat patiently behind the desk, some weary tolerance which even Nicholas, with all his social inadequacy, could recognize. The man had the appearance of having been everywhere, witnessed every human state. Excuses would not work, not on him. Yet at the same time, he could see how receptive Greg was. It was confusing, the two almost contrasting aspects of character existing side by side.

Nicholas dropped into the chair, not in the least reassured by the formality of the proceedings as Vernon Langley and Lisa

Collier made their stiff lead-in statements for the AV recorder. There was something unnaturally creepy about someone rooting round in his mind; for a start there were so many pathetic secrets about himself, all those hundreds of failings and disasters littering his life.

'I can't plug into your memories,' Greg said in a palliative tone. 'So you can stop worrying about the time you pinched your little brother's chocolate bar.'

'I haven't got a brother,' Nicholas blurted. 'Only a sister. And I've never stolen anything from her.'

'There you are then, I can't tell.'

'Oh, right.' He felt such a fool. 'How did you know I was worried about you reading my memories?'

'Because everybody does that when they meet me. Vernon and Jon here are worried about the cash they lifted from the station's Christmas party box, Mrs Collier is extremely worried about her dark past. But the only thing I can sense inside a brain is the emotional content. So the sooner you relax and all that worry vanishes, the sooner I can ask the questions, and the sooner you can be out of here. OK?'

Nicholas nodded vigorously, secretly cheered by the way Lisa Collier's disapprobation had darkened still further at the gibe. 'Yes. Of course. I do want to help.'

'Yeah, I can see that. You really liked Kitchener, didn't you?'

Lisa Collier had warned him never to lie to the psychic; no matter how painful any admission, he would see it, and it would be entered against him. 'I did. I do. But . . .'

'Isabel,' Greg said sympathetically.

'I didn't know about her and Kitchener. Not before that night.'

'What time did you see her and Rosette going into Kitchener's room?'

'About a quarter past one.'

'And then what did you do?'

'Went to bed.'

'Did you sleep?'

'Suppose so. I was thinking a lot at first. But I was asleep when I heard Rosette screaming.'

'Before you went to sleep, did you hear anything?'

'No!' Nicholas said hotly.

'I meant, Nicholas, anybody walking about in the Abbey?'

He knew he would be blushing again. Why couldn't he ever understand what people meant straight off? Why did they always have to use baby talk to get through to him? 'Oh. Sorry. No, nobody was moving round.'

'So you didn't hear Isabel and Rosette leaving Kitchener's room?'

'No.'

'What were you doing in the time between leaving Uri's room and seeing Rosette and Isabel?'

'Running the *Antomine 12* data through a detection program. I was looking for dark-mass concentrations.'

'Dark mass?' Greg sounded privately amused.

'Yes. In space. Kitchener was interested in them. He thought they might act as wormhole termini. You see, if you move a wormhole in a specific fashion it may be possible to generate a CTC directly. A non-paradoxical temporal loop would ...' Nicholas forced himself to stop, chastened. He'd done it again. There was that dreadfully familiar expression of polite incomprehension on Greg's face. 'Sorry,' he mumbled.

'Don't be ashamed of a gift, Nicholas.'

He looked up, startled. But Greg was serious.

'I go on, sometimes,' he said limply. 'I don't realize. Cosmology is *interesting*, Mr Mandel.'

'I know what it's like. My wife tells me I talk about Turkey too much.'

'Turkey?'

'The war.'

It took a moment before Nicholas remembered the Jihad Legion. He had been eight or nine at the time the Islamic forces had invaded Turkey, so it was classed alongside all the other terrible incidents which childhood jumbled together. 'Oh, yes.'

'About the detection program,' Greg prompted. 'Were you running it on the Abbey's Bendix?'

'Yes.'

'Until when?'

'When I saw Isabel and Rosette, quarter-past one. I couldn't work after that.'

'Did you use the English Telecom datanet that night?'

'Yes.'

'Why?'

'I had to, the *Antomine* data comes direct from its mission control in Toulouse. There's no other way of accessing it.'

'So you only used the one datalink?'

'Yes.'

'OK.' Greg typed something into his cybofax. 'Did you know Rosette was mildly insomniac?'

Funny question. He couldn't think why Greg should want to know. 'No. But she was never tired at the end of an evening, when we were in a room, or if we went to the Old Plough. And she was usually first up. So I suppose, thinking about it, I knew she didn't sleep much.'

'Have you ever taken syntho, Nicholas?'

'No,' he said, because it was true, so he could say it without any guilt showing. But he dropped his gaze in shame. There was an achingly long moment of silence.

When he risked looking up, Greg was giving him a calculating stare. All his doubts about the psychic searching freely through his memories returned in a flood.

'Let's see,' Greg said. 'You took another kind of narcotic?'

'No,' Nicholas said miserably.

'Somebody offered you syntho?'

'Yes.'

'Rosette?'

'Yes.'

'And you refused?'

'Yes. I know Kitchener says there's nothing wrong with it. But I didn't want to.'

'I can see the incident has a lot of connotations for you, what else happened?'

Nicholas decided the best thing to do was just say it fast. Greg might move on to another subject. He stared unblinkingly at his Nike trainers. The lace on the left foot was fraying. 'She wanted me to go to bed with her.'

'When was this?'

'November the third.'

'Did you?'

'No! She thought . . . She thought it was funny.'

'Yeah; I can imagine, I've been introduced to Rosette. So you knew syntho was available at the Abbey?'

'Yes.'

'Did you know where the vat was?'

'In the chemistry lab.'

'You were the first person to arrive at the bedroom after Rosette screamed, is that right?'

'Yes.'

'Did you see anybody else in the Abbey, apart from the other students?'

'No. Well . . .' Nicholas tugged at the front of his sweatshirt. It seemed to be constricting around him; his skin was very warm. Both detectives were studying him keenly. This was all going to sound so incredibly stupid, they really would think he was backward now. 'There was a girl,' he said reluctantly.

Greg's eyes had closed, his face crinkled with the effort of concentration. 'Go on.'

'It was earlier. When I saw Isabel and Rosette. She was a ghost.'

Nevin let out an exasperated groan, leaning back in his chair. 'For Christ's sake!'

Greg held up a hand, clicking his fingers irritably to silence him. 'You said: girl. How old?'

'About my age. She was tall, very pretty, red hair.'

'How do you know she was a ghost?'

'Because I saw her outside first. Then she was in the corridor behind Isabel and Rosette.'

'You mean she was out in the park?'

'No. Right outside my window. I thought it was a reflection in the glass at first.'

'Your room is on the second floor, isn't it?'

'Yes. That's why she couldn't be real. I think I imagined her. I was very tired.'

'Have you ever seen the combat leathers which army squaddies wear?' Greg asked. 'They are a bit like biker suits, only not so restrictive, matt-black, broad equipment belts, and there's normally a skull helmet as well.'

'Yes, I think I know what you mean.'

'Was this girl wearing anything like that?'

'Oh, no. She had a jacket on, that was quite dark, but it was just an ordinary one; I think she was wearing a long skirt, too.'

Greg opened his eyes, and reached up to scratch the back of his neck. 'Interesting,' he said guardedly.

Nicholas studiously avoided eye contact with the two detectives.

'Hardly relevant, Mandel,' Langley said.

Greg ignored him. 'Have you ever seen her before?' he asked Nicholas.

'No.'

'What about other ghosts, or visions?'

He hung his head. 'No.'

'What time did you get up that morning, Nicholas?'

'Half-past seven.'

'OK. It probably was just fatigue.' He sounded satisfied. 'A lot of squaddies used to suffer from it in Turkey; amazing what they thought they saw after two or three days without sleep. There; told you I talked too much about my old campaigns.'

Nicholas smiled tentatively, it didn't seem as though he was mocking.

Greg yawned and squinted at his cybofax. 'When was the last time you washed?'

'Lunchtime, just after the lawyers finished briefing us about you conducting our interviews.'

Nevin's face split into a huge grin.

'No, Nicholas.' Greg was labouring against a similar grin. 'I meant last Thursday. When was the last time you washed prior to the murder?'

Blood heated his cheeks and ears. 'Just after seven o'clock. Before I went down to supper.'

Nevin frowned and pulled out his cybofax. He muttered an order into it, and scanned the screen.

Greg had turned to watch him.

'Must have been later than that,' he said in a low tone.

Langley took the cybofax and looked at the data on display.

Greg joined them, the three of them put their heads together, talking quietly.

Nicholas squirmed unhappily. He wasn't sure what he'd done wrong this time. At least Greg hadn't accused him of lying.

'What sort of wash?' Nevin asked.

'A shower. We've all got showers.'

He pointed at the cybofax screen. 'There, see? The back of his hands are as clean as his legs.'

'Yeah, but the particle accumulation on both is quite well established,' Greg said.

'That doesn't mean . . .'

Nicholas stopped listening. He remembered the body scan they gave him when he arrived at the station. It was in a white composite cubicle, similar to a shower. A sensor, like a brown bulb the size of his fist, had telescoped down from the ceiling on the end of a waldo arm, and slowly spiralled round his naked body. He had imagined it sniffing like a dog. Then there had been the blood tests, the urine sample; his clothes taken away for examination, finger- and palm-prints recorded.

'Did you wash later on?' Greg asked. 'After supper?'

'Yes. My hands, a few times. I went to the toilet; and we were eating peanuts in Uri's room, they leave your hands sticky.'

'The time is wrong,' Nevin insisted.

'It's not tremendously reliable,' Langley said grudgingly. 'We can't contest anything with those results.'

'What is it?' Nicholas asked, pleased that he had found the courage from somewhere.

'The amount of dirt you were carrying on Friday morning is rather low, that's all,' Greg said. He closed his eyes. 'Tell me again, what time did you have a shower?'

'After seven, about quarter-past. We have to be down for supper at half-past, you see.'

'And you didn't have another shower later?'

'No.'

'He's telling the truth.'

'Is there a point of contention?' Lisa Collier asked.

Greg and Langley both looked at Jon Nevin. The detective gave the cybofax screen one last scan, then snapped the unit shut. 'No.'

10

Maybe it was the rain, a relentless heavy downpour, which had cleared the reporters from the pavement outside the police station, or maybe the prospect of incurring Julia's wrath had put the fear of God into them. Whatever the reason, when Greg drove out of the station gates late on Tuesday afternoon, there was only a handful of camera operators in plastic cagoules left to watch him go.

'Thank heavens for that,' Eleanor muttered beside him. 'I thought they'd put down roots.'

He turned up Church Street, and flicked on the headlights. The sun hadn't quite set, but the solid clouds had smothered Oakham in a grey penumbra. Raindrops emitted a wan yellow twinkle as they slashed through the beams.

'Yeah,' he agreed. 'You had a word with Julia, then?'

'Absolutely. You know, it's still hard to associate the girl we know with this demon-machinator billionairess all the channels carp on about. I mean, the Prime Minister couldn't call off reporters like this. They'd all race up to the top of the nearest hill and start screaming about oppression and press freedom.'

'No messing. But then Marchant doesn't own the launch facilities which boost the broadcast satellite platforms into geo-sync orbit.'

'There is that.'

Greg glanced over at Cutts Close; lights were shining in all the caravans, dark figures shuffled across the grass. They hadn't actually retreated then, just regrouped ready for tomorrow.

He nudged the EMC Ranger up to thirty-five kilometres an hour. The rain had driven most of the traffic off the roads, leaving a few cyclists pedalling home, faces screwed up against the spray. His neurohormone hangover was ebbing, it wasn't as if he had to strain for the interviews. The Launde students had been co-operative, a welcome change from the hideously antagonistic mullahs in Turkey.

'What did Julia say about analysing the themed neurohormones?' he asked.

'No problem, we should have the answer some time tomorrow. The courier came and picked the ampoules up while you were doing the interviews.' Eleanor gazed blankly at the deserted stalls in the market square. It was the empty expression she used whenever she was more irritated than she wanted to admit. 'I had to threaten to call the Home Office for clearance before he authorized their release.'

'Who, Denzil?'

'No, one of the detectives in the CID office.'

'Oh. Tell you, I think Vernon is softening, and Jon Nevin isn't far behind.'

'Great.' The tone was biting.

'Nothing pleasant in life ever comes cheap.'

She let her head loll back on the support cushioning. 'No. As you always tell me. So how did you get on with the students? Are they all innocent?'

He grinned at the double meaning. 'I'm pretty certain none of them killed Kitchener. Although God knows enough of them had the motive. He's actually slept with all of the girls.'

Eleanor gave him a sideways look. 'All of them?'

'Yeah. Sixty-seven years old; now that's the way I'd like to go.'

'Humm.' Her lips pouted disapprovingly. 'Which of the students had a motive?'

'Isabel Spalvas. She wasn't actually sleeping with Kitchener

165

against her will, but it's bloody close. Nicholas Beswick. I feel kind of sorry for him. Nice kid, but a bit naïve, head in the clouds type; you know, bright and stupid at the same time. He's head over heels in love with Isabel, although I doubt he's even kissed her yet, they're certainly not lovers. Finding her with Kitchener that night was a monumental shock, but he adored the old man too. Uri Pabari might have had a motive if he'd known Liz Foxton had slept with Kitchener.'

'But he didn't know?'

'I didn't ask him; I'll have to check.' Greg sagged mentally at the prospect. 'And if he didn't know, he will after that kind of leading question. Bugger.'

'I thought you said none of the students did it. What's the point of asking Uri about that?'

'Psi isn't an exact science. I can't get up in court and give absolutes, you know that, and I'm bloody sure the lawyers do. All I can ever say is that I haven't perceived them giving me false answers. But suppose somebody had an overwhelming motive to kill Kitchener, they might just be able to conceal their guilt from me, because they don't feel any. Certainly not if I ask them directly. So I creep up on the fact, by checking the peripheries. They can't lie about everything and get away with it, I'll catch them eventually.'

'OK, so are there any other students who have a plausible motive?'

He kept his eyes firmly on the road. 'One. It's a possible money motive. That belongs to our Miss Rosette Harding-Clarke. Although if anyone at Launde Abbey was due to be murdered, I would have put money on it being her.'

Eleanor perked up. 'This sounds interesting, especially with the way you're trying to crush the steering-wheel.'

'Yeah, well maybe I'm imagining it's her neck. Jesus, Eleanor, you've got to meet her to disbelieve her. Tell you, how she survived life this long with that attitude of hers is a bloody mystery to me. I felt like giving her a damn good smack, but she'd probably only enjoy it.' He tried to halt that line of thought.

No personal involvement; the first law. Although how anybody could view Rosette dispassionately was beyond him.

'But I thought Rosette Harding-Clarke was the rich one,' Eleanor said.

'Yeah, so she claims. She is also the pregnant one.'

'Pregnant?'

He smiled at the surprise in her voice. 'That's right. And the kid is Kitchener's, or at least she claims it is. And she believes it too, which makes me inclined to believe her. So the first thing I want you to check out tomorrow morning is whether Rosette really is as rich as she says she is. A lot of these so-called aristocrats are worse off than people drawing the dole. And we'll need a legal opinion as well, will the kid stand to inherit anything even though it's not mentioned in the will? Rosette says she won't contest it, but I would have thought the executors have some sort of obligation to provide for the child.'

'Right.' Eleanor pulled her cybofax out, and loaded the order into it.

*

After living in a two-room chalet for over a decade, the interior of the farmhouse always seemed vast. Furniture rattled around, nothing was ever conveniently near to hand.

The builders had renovated most of it before they moved in, fixing up the roof tiles, replacing the rotten floorboards, stripping out the damp plaster, installing new plumbing and air conditioning, rewiring. They were lucky to get the work done at all. England's industrial regeneration meant the building trade was in the middle of a boom; old factories were being restored, new ones constructed, housing estates were springing up across the country. There was very little spare capacity right now, certainly not for refurbishment jobs in out-of-the-way villages. But Julia's name ensured they were given top priority with the firm they hired, although even her clout didn't extend all the way down into the shady levels of subcontracting. There were still three rooms waiting to be plastered, and the conservatory was a stack of cut and primed wood sitting on the lawn, ready to be screwed together.

Eleanor had already suggested that he could put it up. As if the groves didn't occupy all his time.

But the farmhouse had definitely acquired that indefinable sense of being home, the animal refuge against a howling world. Returning to it caused a tangible wash of relief. He had half expected some reporters to be standing at the entrance to the drive.

The interior had been decorated by a London firm, their designer working in tandem with Eleanor, to give an early twentieth-century theme; the country house of Victorian nobility. Everything was light and somehow rustic, curtains and carpets in pastel shades, the furniture in delicately stained pine. Neoteric domestic systems were all built in to reproduction units. The only modern setting was the gym, filled with black and silver chromed equipment.

When they arrived back from the police station, Greg slumped down on a settee in the lounge and pointed the remote at the long mock-painting of an eighteenth-century harvest scene which disguised the inert flatscreen. The picture shivered away into a game show where contestants were hanging upside down from the studio ceiling on long bungee cords; they were bouncing in and out of large barrels filled with water, trying to bob apples with their teeth.

He stared at it incredulously for a minute, then shook his head in weary dismay. Mr Domesticity, back home after a hard day at the office, with the wife bustling round in the kitchen.

Except, as usual, his mind was full with little scraps of information from the case, all of them swirling round in a chaotic vortex, stirred by the witching fingers of inquisitiveness and intuition in the hope they would settle into some kind of recognizable pattern. His army mates had called him obsessive. Maybe it could be deemed a character flaw, but he could never let go of a problem. He had almost forgotten how involved he could become in a case. The worrying thing was, it felt good. On the chase again. That bastard who had chopped up Kitchener *needed* to be put away.

Eleanor came in with a couple of lagers in tall Scandinavian glasses. She took one look at the game show and switched the flatscreen off. Merry peasants and bales of hay snoozing under a sky of golden cloud reappeared.

'You weren't watching it,' she said when he protested. 'You were thinking about Kitchener.'

He snagged one of the lagers. 'Yeah.'

'You said Rosette was a real bitch,' Eleanor said as she sat down on the settee, wriggling her shoulders until she was nestled up snugly against him. 'Do you really think she would kill the father of her own baby just for money?'

'No. Now you put it like that, I don't. Tell you though, the one thing those students did have in common was the way they idolized Kitchener. That came through loud and clear; a couple of them actually called him a second father. Instinct says it isn't any of them. But . . . it's funny. There are a lot of things which don't add up, certainly not if it was a tekmerc snuff operation.' He put his arm round her, enjoying the warm weight pressing into his side.

'The apron,' she said. 'Now that is really strange.'

'That's right. Like you said, why bother with it at all? I can't believe our hypothetical tekmerc used it simply to incriminate the students. First off, we actually can't implicate one of them with it. If they were going to plant evidence why not the knife, some bloodstains?'

'Too obvious.'

'Maybe. But the apron isn't obvious enough. And why spend precious time starting a fire? I know covert penetration operations, Christ I've been on enough in my time, the cardinal rule is get *out* once you've finished, don't loiter.'

'Whoever it was, they must have been there a while, though. First they had to wait until Kitchener was alone, then the Bendix was burnt, as well as the neurohormone bioware. It all adds up to a lot of time spent in the Abbey.'

'Which gives them an even stronger reason to leave straight after the murder,' he countered. 'Every extra minute in the Abbey is one more minute when they could be discovered. And why use syntho to kill the bioware in the first place?'

'Because it's there, saves carrying a poison in with them.'

'Exactly, but how did they know that? It must have been someone totally familiar with the lab set-up, and even then they couldn't have known for sure that there was any syntho available that particular night. Suppose Kitchener and good old Rosette had been infusing heavily? A tekmerc would have brought a poison, or more likely used a maser. Whatever the method, it would never have been left to chance.'

'There are all sorts of other chemicals in the lab, as well as the acids, and the heaters,' she said. 'There was bound to be something which could kill the bioware. Pure chance they used the syntho.'

'Yeah. Could be.' But the junked up thought fragments refused to quieten down, he kept seeing flashes of Launde Park, the Abbey, those bloody lakes, Denzil's data-rich tour, the students' broken shocked faces. None of them connected in any way.

He took a gulp of the lager; it was cold enough to numb the back of his throat. 'But that still doesn't explain the time they were in the Abbey before the murder,' he said.

Eleanor gave a tiny groan.

'Sorry,' he said quickly. 'We can drop it for the night.'

'And put up with moody silences while you're thinking about it. No thanks. But next time Julia can definitely go find someone else. This is Mandel Investigations' last case, Gregory.'

He flashed her a smile, squeezing her tighter. 'No messing.'

'So what about the time?' She sipped at her own lager.

'Why wait until Rosette and Isabel left Kitchener? A tekmerc wouldn't care about snuffing them as well, in fact it would even be beneficial from the mission's point of view. Two less people to spot him leaving, raise the alarm.'

'But they were a complication, Greg. Killing three people in

170

one room would be risky. Certainly one of them would manage to shout.'

'Maybe. But it would mean he had to wait somewhere inside the Abbey for hours. No tekmerc would do that, the exposure risk is too great. And in any case, it implies he knew Rosette would leave Kitchener alone for a while.'

'Everyone knew she was an insomniac.'

'Her friends, yes. But how would anyone else know?'

'Good question.' She leant forward and rescued her cybofax from the coffee table. 'There's a couple of other points. Amanda Paterson and I spent the afternoon chasing up English Telecom.' She started reading the data on the cybofax screen. 'The only datalinks from the Abbey on Thursday were the three we've accounted for: Nicholas and CNES, Rosette and Oxford University, and Kitchener himself, he was plugged into Caltech, over in America. On top of that there were twenty-one phone calls made from cybofaxes; two of them were Mrs Mayberry's, the housekeeper, one of her helpers made another, then Rosette made nine, Cecil made a couple, so did Liz, Nicholas and Isabel both made one each, the other three were all Kitchener's. Amanda and another detective are calling the numbers and confirming the calls were vocal. We thought someone could have plugged a cybofax into one of the Abbey's terminals, the bit rate would be substantially lower, but you could still use it to squirt a virus into the Bendix.'

'Yeah, assuming it was done on Thursday. There's nothing to prevent you from loading the virus a month ago, and putting it on a time-delay activation.'

She gave him a disappointed look. 'We had to start somewhere.'

'Yeah, sure. Sorry. But nobody's going to remember a phone call from a month or half a year ago.'

'I know, but what else can we do?'

'Nothing, it was only ever a very long shot, closing off options. I can't see anyone wanting to wipe the Bendix until after Kitchener was dead, not if the object was to destroy his work. To wipe it when he was alive would be counterproductive, he would be able to recreate his equations or whatever, and you'd alert him to the security problem. And if it was loaded a month ago, how did they know the timing, or when the students would stop accessing it. No, I'm sure it must have been done from within the Abbey after he was killed, that's the only scenario that makes sense.'

'You're probably right. Anyway, while Amanda was running down the phone calls, I checked with RAF Cottesmore about the weather conditions on Thursday. There were winds up to a hundred kilometres an hour locally that night, some gusts reached a hundred and twenty. Here is their squirt.'

'Bugger.' He put down the lager and looked at the meteorological data which the cybofax was displaying. The purple and blue cloudforms of the weather radar image were superimposed over a map of Rutland; pressure and wind velocity/direction captions flashed across it.

'Can you fly a microlight in that?' Eleanor asked.

'Not a chance. Even high level would be risky; low level with the microbursts you'd get in the Chater valley, impossible.'

She rubbed his arm. 'Couldn't they just hike in and out?'

'It's four kilometres to Launde from the A47 by the straightest possible route, eight there and back. The trip there would be in the middle of a hurricane, with a diversion round Loddington to be sure they weren't sighted, and carrying enough gear to melt through the security system. You wouldn't catch me trying to do it.'

'But it could be done?' she persisted.

'Theoretically, yeah, an inertial guido would place you within a couple of centimetres. But that terrain, well, you saw it.'

'Yes.' She gave him back the glass of lager, and curled her legs up, resting her head on his shoulder.

He felt the kiss on the bottom of his jaw, then she was rubbing her cheek against his. Up and down, slowly. 'You're all tensed up,' she murmured in his ear. 'You won't solve anything like that.'

For a moment he thought of pulling away. But only for a moment. Besides, she was right, he wouldn't settle it tonight.

*

The bedroom overlooked the reservoir's southern prong, a long dark stretch of water with its wavelets and gently writhing curlicues of mist. Walls and furniture were silky white; vases, picture frames, curtains, sheets, and the bedposts were all coloured in shades of blue; the oaken floorboards smoothed down and waxed until they resembled a ballroom floor.

None of that really mattered, not the surroundings, just the bed, with Eleanor. Clad in black silk and lace, naked, provocative, sensual, demanding, submissive, thick red hair foaming down over her shoulders. She possessed a myriad sexual traits, combinations ever-changing, making each time different, unique.

The only light came from the bonfire on the opposite shore, a distant orange glimmer, barely enough to show him her outline. He undid the bows and buttons of her nightdress, licking at the flesh which was exposed tasting the salt tang of damp skin, the heat of arousal.

Embraced by the warmth and folds of shadow he had learned to cast off reticence, taking his lead from her. Eleanor didn't care, wasn't ashamed. Maybe rampancy was a gift of youth, or just part of her nature. So he was free to lose himself in the feast of sensuality, the feel of her body. Long powerful legs wrapped round him, big breasts weighed down his hands. He sucked on an erect nipple, caressed her belly. A tiny neurohormone secretion showed him her body's reactions, which action brought the greatest rapture. The material world faded to dream silhouettes, revealing Eleanor's nerve strands alive with neon-blue light, her naked excitement. He slid inside her, a drawn-out penetration accompanied by her fervid groan, and joined her at the centre of that blazing animal euphoria.

*

But afterwards intuition, or possibly plain confusion, played hell inside his skull and he couldn't let go of the case. He lay back on the crumpled sheeting, hands behind his head, staring up at the shivers of firelight on the ceiling. Snapshots of Launde, the students, Kitchener, police reports, they all chased across his consciousness in endless procession, sharp-edged and insistent.

'So much for my prowess,' Eleanor grumbled softly.

'I thought you were asleep.'

'No.'

'Sorry.'

'This really has got you bothered, hasn't it?' She sounded more concerned than annoyed. 'You were never so intense about a case before, at least not since I've known you.'

He rolled on to his side, his face centimetres from hers. Warm breath gusted over his cheeks. 'Tell you, what I don't understand, what's really got me beaten, is why bother?'

'What do you mean?'

'What is the point of murdering an old man in such a grotesque fashion? Even if one of the students had murdered Kitchener, it wouldn't be like that. You've read the statements, what happened when they found him. They were having fits. And I don't blame them, that hologram was bad enough. I'm bloody sure I couldn't do it, not like that. A maser beam through the brain, quick and clean, yes. But who could do that to someone else? Like Cecil Cameron said, it was one sick fucker.'

'Sick enough for you to perceive with your espersense?'

'I would have thought so. That's one of the reasons I want to visit Liam Bursken tomorrow, so I know what mental character-istics to look out for.'

'Urgh.' She shivered slightly. 'You're welcome to him. Even in the kibbutz we heard about him.'

'Yeah, he was notorious enough. But he was mad. He didn't have a reason for killing. Somebody had a reason for killing Kitchener. And a lot of preparation went into it. But I just don't understand why the tekmerc used that method. It can't be an attempt to throw us off the scent, because even the police were convinced it wasn't one of the students. And that was before my interviews backed up their alibis. So why bother? Why not just send a sniper into Launde Park on a clear night? It doesn't make any sense!'

Her forefinger traced a line from the corner of his eye to his mouth. He sucked the tip gently.

'Like you said; this tekmerc is good,' Eleanor said. 'The snuff was done this way for a purpose. We don't have all the facts yet, that's why it seems so weird.'

'Yeah. Paradox alley, and no messing.' He frowned, trying to remember some scrap of conversation; word association was involved. 'Hey, do you know what CTCs are?'

'Aren't they the things which helped to screw up the ozone?'

'I don't think that's what he meant.'

Eleanor's finger had reached his chin, she tickled his stubble. 'Who?'

'Nicholas Beswick.'

'The wimpy one?'

'He's not wimpy, just very innocent. You'd probably like him. Trigger your maternal instinct.'

She made a fist and rapped on his sternum. 'Chauvinist!'

'Parental instinct, then. I went easy on him; anything else would have seemed like bullying. It was like coaxing answers out of a ten-year-old.'

'But you were hard enough to be sure it wasn't him.'

'Oh yeah, no room for ambiguity . . . except, the sensor data was questionable.'

'In what way?'

'He said he had a shower about quarter-past seven Thursday evening. And the police gave him a scan at nine o'clock the next morning. He was still quite clean. His body ought to have picked up more dirt than it did in that period.'

'How reliable is that kind of scan?'

'It's not the scan, that's perfect; if the body has any contaminants, the sensor will detect them. Vernon told me afterwards they could never take the dirt accumulation record into court, because no one could say how much dirt he would have picked up in that time, not with any degree of certainty. There are far too many variables; where he was, how active he was, how dirty his sheets are, even if his clothes picked up a static charge. They are all contributory factors. But as a general rule of thumb, it should have been more.'

'Did he lie about the time of the shower?'

'No.'

'So he didn't wash off the bloodstains?'

'No. Actually, he was one of the students who did touch Kitchener. But Cecil Cameron confirms that, it's in his statement. So that's not in question.'

'Humm.' She placed her hand palm down on his chest and began to stroke him, moving in an expanding circle. 'What does your intuition say?'

He leant closer and kissed the end of her nose. 'Nothing. Not a bloody thing. You were right. We need more information.'

'In the morning.'

He slipped his hands round her hips, squeezing the taut curve of her buttocks. 'No messing.'

11

The next morning began with a break in the rainclouds. Only a few immobile strips of cirrus were left crouched over the eastern horizon, fluoresced a pale saffron by the rising sun. According to the channel weathercasts, the next stormfront would arrive by teatime.

The A47 into Peterborough was even more snarled up than usual. Scooters were in the majority, the city's morning shifts on their way to work, riding up to four abreast in the spaces between juggernauts, vans, and company buses. They were used to the traffic, Eleanor wasn't. By the time she reached the section of road which ran alongside the Ferry Meadows estuary she was shouting at the three riders keeping station two metres ahead of their bonnet. The glittery red and blue metallic helmets with their black visors remained unmoved by her diatribe, easily anticipating the surges of the methane-powered van in front of them, braking smoothly. In comparison she seemed to be hopping forwards like a kangaroo. A steady stream of cyclists zipped by on the inside. Infuriating.

Thirteen years ago the raised land to the north of the estuary had been a mix of open countryside and pleasant woodland. Twelve years ago it had been swamped by a slum zone of shanty housing the like of which Europeans had only ever seen in 'casts from the Third World. Now it was a solid cliff of whitewashed apartment blocks, long balconies dribbling fronds of colourful vegetation from clay pots, washing hanging on lines between support arches. Solar-cell roofs glinted brightly in the morning sun.

Below the concrete embankment the tide was going out, leaving long stains of milk-chocolate mud visible above the sluggish water. A line of artificial stone islands was strung out across the two-kilometre width of the estuary, the eddy turbine barrage, creating vast, slow-moving whirlpools in each gap.

The first time she had ever come to Peterborough – the first time she had ever been to any city – she had accompanied Greg along the same route, visiting the same person. Even two years on, the difference was pronounced. More traffic, more people, more urgency, less tolerance. It was all due to Julia. Event Horizon's arrival had tweaked the city's dynamic economy into overdrive. After ten years of copious growth and financial exuberance Peterborough still hadn't lost its Frontiersville verve. Everybody was on overtime, chasing impossible directives. And they seemed to thrive on the compulsive *achiever* atmosphere.

My God, is this what regeneration is bringing us back to? Traffic jams and yuppies?

At least none of the vehicles was burning petrol. Not even Julia could take that short cut. Energy generation and supply was becoming a problem again, countrywide. Worldwide, from what the 'casts said. Solar cells simply couldn't meet industrial demands, coal was out of the question. Hydro dams were one possibility for England, given the increased rainfall, but the country's chronic land shortage all but ruled them out. Tidal barrages were a viable option, but they were big, their construction time could be anything up to a decade. England needed the electricity *now*. Peterborough had its eddy turbines in addition to its quota from the beleaguered National Commerce Grid, but even that fell well below the level demanded by Event Horizon, the kombinates, and the plethora of smaller light-engineering companies nesting in the suburbs.

Eleanor couldn't think how Julia intended to power the tower and cyber-precincts she was beginning out at Prior's Fen.

It couldn't be fusion; the JET5 reactor at Cullham had passed the break-even point a year ago, but commercial applications were still seven or eight years away, and looked like being at least as expensive as fission. Perhaps Julia was planning to ship it in using old oil tankers converted to carry giga-conductor cells. They could be charged up in equatorial ports; the power would be there if she spread a few hundred square kilometres of solar cells over the new deserts in Africa and Asia. Her Prior's Fen project was certainly pitched at that sort of macro-scale.

The channel breakfast newscasts had devoted a lot of time to reports of Julia pouring the first footings of her new headquarters building. Eleanor and Greg had watched it in bed, eating toast and sipping tea, enjoying the quiet period of togetherness. Because she damn well knew it would be the only one they'd get today.

The traffic began to quicken, her three helmeted outriders opening some distance. She drove past the entrance to the Milton park estate. Normally she used it as a short cut into Bretton, but at this time of day she would have to fight her way through the traffic in the Park Farm industrial precinct. Quicker to stick to the trunk road.

A comet's tail of red brake lights flared up ahead.

*

Bretton was a hive of construction activity. Neglected through the PSP decade as the vivacious new developments flourished in what had once been the green belt, it was now back in demand with property developers despite its strategically disadvantaged position sitting between Mucklands Wood and Walton. Housing and industrial units tussled for space in old parklands, streets were parking yards for the lorries of various building contractors.

Eleanor parked behind a low-loader carrying a pair of factory-new dumper carts. The first thing she missed were the children. Bretton used to be swarming with them.

Rounded up and carted off to school, most likely. And a good thing too. There was so much catching up to do. The one thing she always regretted was not having a formal education; all the kibbutz had given her was the basic reading, writing, arithmetic, and databasing lessons, then they put her straight into animal husbandry courses. She had enjoyed them at the time, because it meant that for three nights a week she went into Oakham to the sixth-form college. Two hours just sitting down and not having to work. Heaven.

The adult courses, or at least getting out of the kibbutz and seeing there were alternative ways to live, had planted the seeds of rebellion which ultimately resulted in meeting Greg that night two years ago. She knew all she needed to run the groves with Greg, although she still toyed with the idea of going back and picking up some more qualifications. One of those warm misty daydreams which helped life slip down a little easier, a *what if* which was slightly more than idle fantasy.

Now, of course, education for children was a New Conservative priority, and a real one, not just a manifesto declaration. One of the reasons for the current bout of inflation was the amount of money the Treasury had to print to pay for repairing schools and providing them with up-to-date equipment. So Julia always said. But then it was Julia who was so insistent that total education be implemented as soon as possible.

Only because she needs computer literates to work in her cyber-factories. And what Julia wanted, Marchant granted, so went the opposition chant. *And why am I being so cynical this morning?*

'You were dead ten paces ago,' a gravelly female voice said in her ear.

Eleanor turned. It was Suzi.

The Trinities girl only came up to the base of Eleanor's neck; she was slim to the point of androgyny, with spiked purple hair and a bony face. She wore a pair of tight black jeans, and a brown singlet under a new leather biker jacket which had the Trinities symbol stamped on the right breast – a fist closed round a thorn cross, drops of blood falling. Her age was impossible to pin down, though Greg said she was in her mid-twenties. In a girlie summer frock she could have passed for fifteen.

She was grinning up at Eleanor.

'I saw you skulking about as soon as I got out of the Ranger,' Eleanor said, making it as condescending as possible. 'I just didn't want to hurt your ego, that's all.'

'Bollocks!'

Eleanor laughed, and scrupulously refrained from ruffling Suzi's hair. For all her butch swagger, Suzi could get very touchy about her lack of centimetres.

She had met the Trinities girl back when Greg took his first Event Horizon case. It was her first, and please God last, experience of hardlining. Both of them had been hurt during the mission, although Suzi had suffered by far the worst injuries.

Eleanor still wasn't quite sure if they were friends; Suzi had a very frugal social behaviour pattern. *Relationship* wasn't a word or concept which featured heavily in an urban predator's mental lexicon. But there was certainly a degree of respect, which was a big step; non-urban-predators were universally regarded with complete contempt.

'What have you come for?' Suzi asked as they walked up the slope towards the Mucklands Wood estate.

'I need to have a rap with Royan.'

'Yeah?'

Eleanor grinned at the blatant curiosity. 'Greg's working on a case again.'

'No shit. I thought you weren't going to let him do that again.'

'I wasn't. But Julia asked him to.'

Suzi chuckled delightedly. 'Christ, that girl bypasses their brains and plugs directly into their balls. What's she got that I haven't?'

'Ten trillion pounds and a medieval virgin princess's hairstyle.'

They laughed together.

As they approached the housing estate Suzi drew a large Luger maser pistol from a shoulder holster, carrying it quite openly.

Mucklands Wood always reminded Eleanor of old Soviet-style cities in the last century. It was a cultural and architectural throwback to prudent realism: low-cost council housing, the PSP's contribution to the refugee crisis, a magnet for the underclass who couldn't hope to get into one of the overseas-funded projects. Rich with the nutrients that bred resentment, the starkness and dejection of lives condemned to the dole.

Fifteen identical tower-blocks, twenty storeys high, sheer concrete walls hidden beneath a scale of cheap, low-efficiency solar panels. Crushed limestone covered the ground around them, sticky with a tar of mud; weeds and nettles grew in defiant clumps, the only vegetation. A few small single-storey workshops had been built by the council, earmarked for PSP skill-training projects. But they were all empty shells, burnt out, breeze-block walls already alarmingly concave; another couple of years would see entropy and vandalism reduce them to rubble.

Eleanor always hated coming to Mucklands. It infected aspirations and dignity like a cancer. You could never rise out of Mucklands, you could only fight. The Trinities exploited that ruthlessly.

She caught glimpses of people lurking among the workshops, walking between the towers. All urban predator types, leather jeans, camouflage jackets, and AK carbines. Even though she had a Trinities card, she always called in advance, waited until there was someone to escort her in.

'Do the kids here go to school?' she asked Suzi.

'Yeah. Father makes sure they do. It's a pain, some of 'em make good scouts. Who's gonna suspect a nine-year-old?'

'You'll cope.'

Suzi gave her a glum look. 'I know what you're thinking. Get 'em out, fill 'em with smarts, break the poverty cycle.'

'That's right.'

'Brilliant. Then who's going to carry on the fight?'

The fight against their nemesis the Blackshirts was everything for the Trinities, the reason for their existence. Black-shirts were the remnants of the People's Constables with whom they had fought a running war for nearly a decade along Peterborough's cluttered frantic streets. And the two were still fighting as if nothing had changed, as if the PSP was still in power. There were too many dead, too many old scores to settle.

'You can't fight for ever,' Eleanor said, knowing it was a waste of time. Trinities lived for combat, lived for death. It was sequenced into their genes now, unbreakable.

'Try me,' Suzi growled dangerously.

*

Two guards stood outside the tower's door, saluting sharply as Suzi walked through. Eleanor didn't even feel a reflex laugh coming on, it was too sad. The inside of the tower was kept meticulously clean, a sharp contrast to the external atrophy.

Suzi knocked once on the door of the old warden's flat and went straight in. The far end of the room was lined with dilapidated metal desks supporting a range of communication gear; six Trinities, all girls, were operating the systems. Seven flatscreens were fixed to the wall above them, showing images fed from cameras which had to be perched on the top of the towers. Five of them displayed a panoramic view of Mucklands Wood, scanning slowly; while the remaining two were zoomed in on Walton, two kilometres away on the other side of the A15, a dense conurbation of rooftops and chimneys, interspaced with the tapering tops of evergreen pines. The quagmire of the Fens basin was just visible in the background, a grubby brown plain vanishing into the distorted haze line which occluded the horizon.

Walton was to the Blackshirts what Mucklands was to the Trinities: headquarters, barracks, recruiting ground, armoury, police and public no-go zone. Both areas were resented by the rest of the city. Even the reserve of gratitude people felt for the Trinities, in their role as focal point for local opposition to the PSP, had withered to nothing over the last four years.

Peterborough's residents wanted the guerrilla war stopped, wanted to be rid of the urban predators, wanted to get on with their lives without the constant threat of violence and anarchy hovering in the background. The city council was already talking of implementing a clampdown, maybe even sending in the army to flush Mucklands and Walton clean of undesirables.

Eleanor knew it would never end that way. You couldn't drive the Trinities and Blackshirts any further underground. Long before any clean-out operation finished the bureaucracy-stultified preparation phase the two of them would have it out, head to head, straight on, putting everything they'd got into one final hardline strike.

The communication gear operatives were emitting a constant murmur as they talked into their throat mikes, occasionally switching the flatscreens to different cameras. It looked like a very professional operation.

The instigator of it all sat at a desk behind the operators, command position. Teddy La Croix, an ex-English army sergeant whom the Trinities had named Father, swivelled round in his chair and grinned broadly. He seemed to get bigger each time she met him, easily two metres tall, with at least two-thirds of his bodyweight made up from muscle, probably more, she couldn't imagine anything as soft and vulnerable as human organs being a part of Teddy's make up. Biolum light glinted dully on the dark ebony skin of his bald scalp. He was dressed in his usual combat fatigues, cleaned and ironed as though they had only been out of the laundry for an hour.

Boa constrictor arms circled round her, and he gave her a hug, kissing her cheek. 'Goddamn, gal, you finally did it, you left him and ran away to me.'

'Stop it,' she giggled and slapped at his shoulder. 'I'm legally hitched to him till death do us part, you were at the wedding. So behave yourself.'

He gave a theatrical sigh and put her down. 'You're looking good, Eleanor.'

'Thanks.'

They stood and looked at each other for a long moment. Teddy was one of Greg's oldest friends; they had both served together back in Turkey. She had been secretly thrilled at gaining Teddy's trust; approval like that came hard, but it brought her orbit just that fraction closer to Greg's.

'What's that?' She pointed to his left hand. It was covered in a thin flexible foam of blue dermal seal.

'Bit of extra-parliamentary action couple o' days back. Nothing bad.'

Eleanor heard Suzi's soft snort. She could guess just how fierce it had been.

'Oh, Teddy.'

He rolled his eyes. 'Yeah, yeah, I know. I'll be careful.'

'That'll be the day.'

He put his arm round her shoulder, and walked to the back of the room, away from the communications operators. 'Tell me something. You're here to see Royan, right?'

'Yes.'

'Special visit, coming by yourself. This some sort o' deal Greg's working on?' He sat on the edge of a wooden table covered in maps and thick folders, resting his buttocks on the edge. The legs let out little creaks of stress.

'Yes.'

Teddy's expression turned serious, forbidding. 'He's outta that, gal. He's got the farm, he's got you. You got a job now, you gotta keep him out. He's made it, clean free. Outta all this shit.'

She put a hand on his forearm. 'No hardlining, Teddy. I wouldn't let him do that again, you know I wouldn't. This is just a case for Julia. It's puzzling, and it's ever so slightly bloody weird, but it's nothing physical. OK?'

Teddy worried at his front teeth with a fingernail. 'Julia?' The tone was indecisive.

'Yes. She needs his espersense.'

'There's other psychics. This themed shit they's shovelling out these days.'

'Name one as good as Greg.'

'Yeah,' he growled. 'Well, you tell that rich bitch from me, it's her ass if anything happens to Greg.' His eyebrows lifted in emphasis. 'Or you.'

She stood on tiptoes and planted a kiss on his forehead. 'You're gorgeous.'

'Jesus, shit.'

Was he actually blushing?

'What is this fucking case, anyway? Gotta be heavy duty shit for her to ask in the first place. Last time we rapped, she's as hot as me for Greg to quit.'

'Edward Kitchener. She needs to know who killed him.'

'The physics guy? Why?'

'He was working on something for her.' She put her hands up in surrender. 'Don't ask me what. I don't understand a word of it.'

'Yeah, well, I can see why you need to rap with Son. Crap like that, right up his alley. Now don't you go tie up all his capacity, we need him too, more'n ever right now.'

Her lips turned down. 'Teddy . . .'

'No choice, gal.' He waved at the two screens covering Walton. 'Fucking Party's crawling like ants down there. Someone gotta stomp on 'em. Don't see no police doing it. Or this new fucking wonder government we got lumbered with. You ask Julia, you don't believe me. Three o' her factories hit by thermal bombs this month, not five klicks from here.'

She nodded weakly. Trinities and Blackshirts; it was all a far more deadly version of the *apparatchiks* and Inquisitors game, a game with no rules, nor time limit, nor physical boundary. She knew from bitter experience that it wasn't something which could be solved by police, the due process of law; Greg's last Event Horizon case had shown her that. In that respect the world terrified her, there was too much subterranean activity, too much hidden from public view. Dark circuitry wiring subliminal power shifts. Ignorance could be a blissful thing, almost enviable.

He patted her gently. 'Don't you fret so, gal. You ain't got the face for it. Now then, been too long, you gotta stop by more often.'

'You know where the farm is, Teddy. I'd like you to come and see it some time. Stay over for a few nights. You know how much Greg would love that.'

'Turtle out of its shell, gal.' He glanced about the room, taking his time, as if he hadn't seen it for a while, checking to see that everything was in its proper place. ''Sides, won't be here much longer.' His voice dropped to a doleful whisper. 'Not long now. I can feel it coming, gal, like summer heat. Ain't nobody got no respect for the Trinities no more. Time was, you could walk down any street in this town, and you'd get treated like a superhero. Well, that time's over now. But we know what we gotta do 'fore we go. Bibles in hand, AKs primed, yes sir. We ain't gonna turn tail now. Gonna *finish* what we started. Gonna finish those Card Carrying sons of bitches, gonna finish them but good.'

*

'I'll give this a miss,' Suzi said when the lift opened on the tower's top floor.

'There's nothing that ultra-hush about it,' Eleanor protested.

'Nah, 'sall right. I'll be downstairs when you want out.' She pressed the button for the ground floor, forcing Eleanor to hop out. The lift doors slid shut, cutting off Suzi's wave and wolfish grin; and any chance to argue.

Eleanor thought she knew the real reason. Julia's Austrian clinic had been good, repairing all the physical damage both of them had suffered. But the memories of its infliction were hard to suppress. Royan could act as an all too potent reminder.

The corridor was narrow, windowless. A long ceiling-mounted biolum strip, with an emission decaying into the green edge of the spectrum, lit her way. She stopped outside 206, and knocked.

Qoi opened the door, a fifteen-year-old Oriental girl in a blue

187

silk robe. She bowed deeply. 'Pleasure to see you again, Miss Eleanor.' Her voice was high-pitched and scratchy.

Eleanor followed her into the tiny hall, as always slightly uncomfortable at Royan's combination nurse and guardian angel. The door to the lounge slid open, and Qoi ushered her through, doll-like face smiling politely.

The air was hot, saturated with a smell of vegetation that was almost fungal, a dozen braids of flower perfume clotted together. Long plant troughs were laid out on the floor, hosting a fabulous collection of flowers, vivid primary colours shining under the glare of the ceiling's Solaris spots. Little wheeled robots roamed among them; they looked as if they had been cobbled together out of a dozen different cybertoy kits by someone working from a very distant memory of a cartoon-channel mechanoid. Forks, copper watering roses, and secateurs protruded with no sense of rationale.

One wall was completely obscured by the glass bricks of ancient television screens, removed from their cases and bolted into a grid of metal struts. They were all switched on, showing a multitude of channel 'casts and data sheets. A broad workbench was piled high with gear modules, parts of gear modules, individual components, circuit boards, pieces of mechanical junk; two big waldo arms stood silent sentry duty at each end.

A camera on an aluminium tripod followed her cautious steps round the troughs. It acted as Royan's eyes, fibre-optic cable plugged into the black modem balls in his eye sockets. He was sitting on a metallic green nineteen-fifties dentist's chair in the centre of the room. Sitting wasn't quite the right word: propped up, wedged in by cushions. Royan had no legs or arms; plastic cups covered the end of each stump, axon splices, trailing more fibre-optic cables to banks of 'ware cabinets next to the bench. His torso was covered by a white T-shirt spotted with food stains down the front.

Greg had told her Royan was a victim of the People's Constables, a street riot years ago. He'd been there the night it happened, although he never went into details. Despite his youth and agility Royan just hadn't been fast enough to escape the bullwhips of the Constables as they charged the protesters. He had been badly burnt, too, in the cascade of molotovs which followed.

Every time she came, she thought she'd be immune to the sight of him, exposure building up a protective crust around her emotions. Every time he affected her just as badly as the first. Coldness flickered through her, dendritic frost fingers twisting up her stomach.

The images and datasheets on the old television tubes vanished, replaced by metre-high green letters which moved right to left across the wall, delineation frequently interrupted by the individual screen rims.

HI, ELEANOR, YOU LOOK LOVELY LOVELY LOVELY TODAY.

'Hello, flatterer. What have you been up to then?' She spoke fairly loud, trying not to make it obvious; slow clear words always made her think of the way people addressed the retarded. Royan was anything but. His audio nerves were about the only genuine sensory input he retained, everything else was electronic, enhanced by the modules he had gradually cocooned himself in. Gear had become his interest, his obsession, his speciality. His comprehension of 'ware systems was probably equivalent to a degree, Greg reckoned, maybe even better. His hands-on experience was total, he had to learn simply to survive, and he had nothing else to do but learn, sit passively and absorb the bytes flowing through the country's datanets, day after day after day. And once he had mastered his art, he returned to the fray with a vengeance, fuelled by a cold malevolent hatred whose compulsive power only Greg could fully perceive. He became Son to the other Trinities, their digital oracle, a passive presence backing up each campaign with the smartest intelligence data, tracing Blackshirt positions and strength through every memory core in the city and beyond, exposing them wherever they were hiding.

BEEN OUT DANCING, SURFBOARDING, CYCLING. THE USUAL.

'I brought you these,' she said, and pulled the envelope of seeds out of her jeans pocket. 'They're orchids, *Ludisia discolor*, they've got red leaves and a white flower. I think you'll like them.'

His lips parted to reveal a few bucked yellow teeth. THANKS THANKS THANKS.

Qoi stepped forwards and took the envelope, bowing slightly.

Greg always brought bits and pieces of gear for him, but she preferred cuttings or seeds. He went to a lot of trouble nurturing his little garden, there wasn't an unhealthy plant anywhere.

After Qoi disappeared into the kitchen Eleanor ducked round a hanging basket of pink begonias, and sat herself in a plain oak admiral's chair.

COFFEE???

'Please.' It was part of the visit ritual.

One of the robots trundled over, a pot of coffee resting on its flat top. She poured herself a cup. It tasted perfect.

YOU LOOK TIRED.

'I've been working.' More disapproval slipped into her tone than she intended.

ON THE FARM?

'No. Mandel Investigations got hauled out on a case.'

JULIA JULIA JULIA. HAS TO BE. GREG WOULDN'T DO IT FOR ANYONE ELSE.

'You've been peeping.'

NO. I KNOW YOU ALL TOO WELL. MY FRIENDS. I WATCHED JULIA ON THE CHANNELS THIS MORNING. A BILLIONAIRESS POURING CONCRETE, FUNNY FUNNY FUNNY. I WATCH HER EVERY DAY, YOU KNOW. SHE'S NEVER OFF.

'I know. She could make another fortune if she charged the newscast programmes an appearance fee.'

SHE'S PRETTY PRETTY PRETTY. JUST LIKE YOU. LUCKY LUCKY LUCKY ME. TWO PRETTIEST GIRLS IN THE COUNTRY ARE MY FRIENDS.

She took another sip, surprised to find herself relaxing. 'Aren't you going to ask me why I'm here?' she asked slyly.

I KNOW WHY. HE WANTS SOMETHING, SO HE SENT YOU. HE KNOWS I'M A SUCKER SUCKER SUCKER FOR A BEAUTIFUL GIRL. I AM TOO.

'We had to split up, actually. There's a lot of ground to cover today.'

WHAT'S THE CASE?

'The Kitchener murder.' She started giving him a review of the data they'd amassed. As far as she could tell he was listening attentively, certainly the vaguely eerie lettering faded from the screens, a sure sign of contemplation. The session wasn't turning out as emotionally arduous as she had been expecting. The trick was to block out the rest of his life, the daily horror of eating, crapping, peeing, the pain spasms which convulsed him every few hours. Pretend everything stopped when she wasn't there, that all he did was meet visitors who brought him gossip and problems he could gain a measure of satisfaction from solving. It was weak of her to think like that, craven, but it was the only way she could get through. The suffering he went through was a tragedy on an epic scale.

IF IT WASN'T THE STUDENTS, AND IT WASN'T A TEKMERC SNUFF DEAL, THEN WHO WHO WHO DUNNNNNIT?

'Good question. I didn't say a tekmerc definitely wasn't involved; but they certainly didn't drive in, and they didn't fly in either. Of course, we're not ruling out the possibility that someone yomped in, but Greg says he doesn't think it's likely.'

IF HE SAYS IT DIDN'T HAPPEN, IT DIDN'T DIDN'T DIDN'T.

'He says he's not sure.'

Royan's rucked smile appeared again. WHAT DO YOU THINK???

'I think it would have been absolutely impossible for anyone to walk in and out of the Chater valley that evening. It was bad enough driving our EMC Ranger in yesterday. Launde Abbey is very isolated.'

I BELIEVE YOU. WHAT DO YOU WANT ME TO DO?

She put down the empty coffee-cup and held up her cybofax. 'I've brought the schematics for the Abbey's security system. I need to know if it is possible for someone to burn through, enter the Abbey, and then get out again afterwards without raising the alarm. The police forensic team say it was completely undisturbed.'

One of the 'ware modules on the top of the bench let out a small bleep. When she turned, blue and green LEDs were winking on the front of the scuffed grey plastic casing.

SQUIRT THE BYTES OVER. NO NO NO PROBLEM FOR ME.

She pointed the cybofax at the module and keyed a squirt.

GOT IT. I'LL START LOOKING FOR A WAY THROUGH. SHOULD HAVE AN ANSWER BY THIS AFTERNOON.

'Fine.' Eleanor slipped the cybofax into her back pocket. 'Can you also find out if any hotrod was contracted to supply this hypothetical burn virus?'

I'LL ASK. MIGHT NOT GET A HUNDRED %%%%%% ACCURATE ANSWER. IF IT WAS DONE, THE WRITER WON'T BE ADVERTISING.

'Have you heard of anyone asking for a virus like this?'

NO NO NO. CROSS HEART.

'OK, final point; Greg thinks it would be useful to know what sort of rumours are floating about. Ask around the circuit, find out what people think Kitchener was working on for Julia, whether they even knew he was working for Julia; and also, did Kitchener owe money to anyone?'

HE WAS A MILLIONAIRE MULTI MULTI MULTI.

'He was a regular syntho user, and so were some of the students. He had his own vat at Launde, but the basic compounds still cost money. So it probably wouldn't be banks we're talking about.'

GOTCHA. KITCHENER USED SYNTHO?

'Yes.'

MAN LIKE THAT. WOW WOW WOW.

She gave him a sad smile. 'Yes, a man like that. Funny old world, isn't it. You wouldn't think he'd need it, a brain like his.'

MAYBE BECAUSE HE HAD A BRAIN LIKE THAT. NOBODY ON THIS PLANET WAS HIS EQUAL. MAYBE HE WAS LONELY LONELY LONELY.

'Oh, no, not Kitchener, not lonely. One of the girl students is having his child.'

There was no answer for a moment, the last LONELY remained splashed across the three right-hand screens. Then the word evaporated like morning dew. She heard the lens on the camera whirring softly, zooming in on her face.

HE WAS OLD.

'Sixty-seven, I think.'

ALL THAT TIME. SO MANY YEARS.

'He accomplished an awful lot,' she said, uncertain where Royan was leading. Not true, at the back of her mind she knew exactly. She just didn't want to acknowledge it.

DO YOU LIKE ME, ELEANOR?

That grin didn't have to be forced. 'I keep coming back, don't I?'

YES YES YES. THANK YOU.

She stood up, straightening the creases out of her sweatshirt. 'Now don't spend all your time working on the Abbey's security system. Teddy says he needs you for Trinities work.'

BUGGER HIM . . . PARDON MY FRENCH. I DECIDE MY OWN PRIORITIES. ME ME ME.

'You'll get me into trouble.'

NEVER. SAY HI TO GREG. TELL HIM HE HAD BETTER SHOW UP HIMSELF NEXT TIME.

'I will.'

AND YOU. COME BACK. SEE ME.

'Yes.' She gave him a last glance, non-human, shamed by the fact that she could never in a million years show so much bravery. There was no point in even asking him to come out to the farm. It could be done, physically, with stretchers and vans and plenty of advanced planning. But his inheritance tied him to Mucklands far tighter than the web of fibre-optic cables ever did. Him and Teddy, neither of them would leave; there was no point, they were Mucklands, it went with them wherever they were.

Qoi popped up out of the kitchen without being summoned, and showed her to the door.

12

'As always, the sylphlike Julia Evans remains resolutely wedded to her fallal dress sense,' Jakki Coleman said. She was at her Mediterranean villa, lounging on a sunbed at the side of a kidney-shaped pool. On the far side was a white stone balustrade, guarding the steep drop down to a muzzy blue sea. Tall palm trees were growing out of stone barrels, fronds stirring in a gentle breeze.

'Considering the perennial obsession which the Gothic cult has for the afterworld, this particular selection of garments worn for the Prior's Fen footings ceremony is highly appropriate. Because, let's face it, our poor dear Julia looks as if she's been exhumed after a few weeks residing in a grave.'

'BITCH!' Julia shrieked.

Her tea cup hit the flatscreen in the centre, smashing into crescent fragments; it was the first object her searching hand could find, a big yellow and blue breakfast cup from the bedside tray. Sugary dregs began to trickle down the flat-screen, smearing the dark-haired young man who climbed out of the pool and began towelling himself off.

Patrick raised his head from the mounds of pillows which had accumulated on his side of the bed, blinking sleep from his eyes. 'What?' he grunted blearily.

'Oh go back to sleep.' Julia fired the remote at the flat-screen, imagining it was a laser pistol, beam scorching a hole through

Jakki Coleman's head, her *middle-aged* head, and the shiny blue swimsuit showed her thighs were getting flabby too. She folded her arms below her breasts and glared at the blank rectangle.

Her bedroom was decorated in a soothing montage of pink and white tones, extremely feminine, with exquisite lacy frills on all the furniture, subdued lighting, a huge four-poster bed with a Romany canopy, ankle-deep pile carpet. It was the third redesign in four years; each time she edged closer to her ideal, the romantic French-château image she secretly treasured.

And what would Jakki Coleman have to say about it? Bitch!

'You're upset about something,' Patrick said.

'Oh, ten out of ten, give it a banana.'

'Was it me?'

'No,' she said tightly.

'Ah, right.' He subsided back into the pillows.

Well that ruined the morning mood, Julia thought, there would be no sex now.

She pointed the remote at the windows. The thick imperial-purple velour curtains swept aside to show her the balcony. Wistaria vines, gene-tailored against the heat of the new seasons, were wrapped round the wrought iron railings, producing a solid wall of delicate mauve flower clusters. Wilholm's rear lawns formed a splendid backdrop with their English country house formality, she could just see the long trout lake at the bottom, its fairytale waterfall tinged brown from the silt washed down the stream by the heavy rains.

Not even the garden's naturalistic perfection could break her ire. Bugger Jakki Coleman anyway. Who cared what she said?

Although that wasn't the half of it. She still felt guilty about asking Greg to look into the Kitchener murder. And the murder itself was a complication she could do without. Right now Morgan's security division was stretched pretty thinly defending the company from conventional threats – industrial sabotage, industrial espionage, crooked accountants, hotrod hackers infiltrating the datanet. Why would anybody feel strongly about something as weirdly abstract as superphysics wormholes? Surely it couldn't be an anti-Evans gesture? Not slaughtering a defence-less old man? She couldn't believe anyone was that sick and warped; besides, there had been no announcement. If any oper-ational PSP remnants had killed Kitchener they would have been crowing about it all across the media by now.

At least there hadn't been much mention of Greg on the news-casts she had caught before flicking over to the Coleman trollop. Some jerky pictures taken from a shoulder-mounted camera, the operator running after the EMC Ranger as it drove out of the police station, Eleanor's tight-lipped anger, Greg impassive as always.

Patrick touched her shoulder. 'You're very tense.' His fingers slid down her arm to the elbow, then stroked her breast, circling the nipple.

She tilted her head back and sighed through clenched teeth. 'No, Patrick.'

His tongue nuzzled her ear, stubble scratching her collar bone. 'I can massage all that tension away. You know I can.'

It was very very tempting. There wasn't a chime in her head Patrick couldn't ring whenever he chose. But for all that ecstasy, he was a mechanical lover. She had begun to suspect a great deal of his excitement came from the way he controlled her body, almost a voyeur of his own performance.

'No,' she said abruptly, and shoved her feet out of the bed. 'Sorry, I've got a busy morning.' She picked up her négligé from the floor where he'd thrown it last night and went into the bathroom.

*

She sat on the side of the circular marble bath and dropped her head in her hands, staring glumly at the swan mosaic on the wall opposite. There were just so many issues clamouring insistently for her attention right now; the petty, the important, and the personal.

She made an effort to blank them out, as if her whole mind was one giant processor node she could shut down when she wanted. It didn't work; Patrick was easy to ignore, a feat which raised its own slightly disquieting question, but she found herself returning to yesterday's strange conversation with Karl Hildebrandt. Greg was always telling her to trust her native instinct; it's a variant on precognition, he explained, not quite rational, but ninety per cent reliable. And right now her instincts said that conversation was desperately wrong.

The bad PR she had been picking up from leftish organizations and pressure groups had been more or less constant for two years, ever since the giga-conductor was announced to the public. In that context Greg and the Kitchener case was just one more incident. Nothing special. The way she was siting factories in marginal constituencies was far more blatant, provocative.

The PR angle was a blind, then, it had to be. Karl had wanted Greg off the case, plain and simple. From what she had heard about the strange circumstances out at the Abbey, Oakham's CID would be very unlikely to find the murderer without Greg and Event Horizon's resources behind them. How would Karl benefit from that?

Wrong tack, she realized; Karl was the bank's mouthpiece, the perfect corporate cyborg. How would Diessenburg Mercantile benefit from allowing Kitchener's murderer to go free?

Open Channel To NN Core.

Morning, Juliet.

A wan smile crept on to her face. Good old Grandpa, he was so indefatigable.

Morning, Grandpa. Anything important happen last night?

Someone tried to break in to our Leicester music deck factory warehouse; it was a local gang, they'd even brought a lorry with them to cart away their loot. Security suspects someone on the inside was feeding them information on the shipments. There was an attempt to snatch data out of the genetics research division memory core, we think they were after the land-coral splices. The guardian programs prevented any data loss, and security are working with English Telecom to see if they can backtrack the hackers. Hopeless, of course. The pound closed three cents up on the dollar, and the FTcast index was up eight points. Market confidence is high after the spaceplane roll out. There was a lot of data traffic between our backing consortium partners right into the wee small hours. Got 'em on the run, we have, Juliet.

Did you break any of their squirts?

No, they're using a high-order encryption code. It could be done, but it would tie up a lot of processing capacity. Not cost-effective. They'll agree to Prior's Fen.

Hope so.

Everything all right, Juliet?

Yes. No.

Executive material if ever I saw it. So bloody decisive you are, my girl.

What do you think of Patrick, Grandpa?

Handsome, rich, cultured, quite clever, well mannered. Picked yourself a good one again, Juliet.

There was a shade too much emphasis on *again* for her mind. She glanced up at the mirror above the basin. And boy oh boy did she look melancholy. Her hair was a complete mess as well. Patrick did so enjoy seeing it tossed about. His husky voice in the dark, encouraging her, whispering how wild she was. It never seemed to matter in bed, excitement overriding everything.

Yah, she replied. *So how come they never last?*

I said good, I never said flawless.

Do you think he's going to start asking me for shipping contracts?

No. Even if his family shipping line needed 'em, he wouldn't ask. And they don't need 'em, I've had our commercial intelligence division keeping an eye open.

My very own guardian angel. You're wonderful, Grandpa.

You'll find him one day, Juliet. I'll be a great-grandfather yet.

Don't hold your breath, not the way I'm going.

I watched that Coleman woman this morning.

I don't want to talk about it! She reached for a comb and began to pull it through the knots. The face in the mirror was scowling petulantly.

I don't like you being ridiculed like that, Juliet. Let me tell you, my girl, it would never have happened in my day. People should have more bloody respect. You ought to blacklist that channel, no adverts, and pass the word round everyone Event Horizon does business with. That frigid Coleman cow would soon get the message.

It was the second time temptation had been put in front of her that morning. She considered it, something like envy colouring every thought. *No, Grandpa. If I started using my power like that, where would it end?*

Use it or lose it, girl. I've told you before.

That is misuse, as you well know. I get into enough trouble using it where it's beneficial.

Ah, Juliet, a little bit of self-indulgence occasionally never hurt.

Don't you worry about me, Grandpa. I'll get that Jakki Coleman, you'll see.

My girl.

She put the comb down, the worst of the knots out. It would be safe to ask her maid Adelia to wash and set it now. Adelia always got mighty prickly if she was faced with a big untangling job every morning.

I've been thinking about Karl Hildebrandt, she said.

Oh, yeah? I don't think he'd be a suitable replacement for Patrick.

Behave! I meant his wanting me to take Greg off the Kitchener case. There's something very funny about that.

Well . . . it was a very high-profile appointment, Juliet. Bloody marvellous it is, girl, the first time in four years the company hasn't had an ulterior motive in twisting Marchant's arm, and everyone starts banging on about undue influence. We just can't win.

Karl is a front for Diessenburg Mercantile, Grandpa, first, last, and always, even in these circumstances. He was too quick off the mark, and too insistent asking to see me just to be offering sociable advice. He was ordered to do it.

Conceded, it is a bit odd. Do you think it's important?

Yes. Why would Diessenburg Mercantile have any interest in a ghoulish murder in the middle of the English countryside?

Beats me, girl.

Well, find out.

Oh, yes, bloody abracadabra. Here you are.

Don't get stroppy, Grandpa. It's simple. Run down a list of Diessen-burg Mercantile's other investments for me, and see if any of them comes into conflict with the work Kitchener was doing.

What, a stardrive!?

She went to the basin, and ran the cold tap, splashing some of the water on her face. It did sound pretty unlikely now she had spelt it out. *Yes, I know it sounds totally wonky, Grandpa. But there has to be a reason.*

I suppose so, girl. You've got to remember all this nonsense about actually building flying saucers sounds pretty bloody impossible to a relic like me. Listen, when I was a lad the Daleks were the wildest piece of imagination ever to hit England. I was terrified of them. One time when the Doctor was caught in some caves by . . .

Yah. If you could get that data correlated in time for the conference this afternoon I'd be grateful.

Bloody hell, Juliet, you've got a heart of ice. Black ice.

I wonder who I inherited that from?

All right, I'll get on to it.

Thanks, Grandpa. I really am jolly busy this morning. I've got a video bite opportunity with the national swimming squad; then there's the Nottingham councillors' delegation, and the meeting for the Home Counties region managerial report.

You should complain to the union steward, they're working you too hard.

If I ever get the chance, I'll tell him.

Cancel Channel To NN Core.

She called Adelia on the housephone and asked her to be ready in half an hour. There was just time for a quick bath, wash off last night's tussle.

Hot water gushed out of the wide tap nozzle, kicking up clouds of steam. She stood in the middle of the bath as it twisted round her, reviewing what clothes to wear for meeting the swimming team. Event Horizon sponsored the England squad, so it was mainly a PR event, but she took a genuine interest in the team's performance. Swimming had been her sport at school.

She sat down when the water reached her knees, and switched on the spa. Water jets and bubbles pummelled her skin, easing the tension out of her muscles.

It was no good, she couldn't think what to wear.

Access Dictionary File. Define: Fallal.

Fallal, the memory node reported. *Gaudy or vulgar, in reference to jewellery, or clothing, or ornament, etc.*

Bitch!

13

The original buildings of HMP Stocken Hall were still virtually intact, a regimented complex of stolid cell blocks squatting behind the five-metre perimeter fence topped with razor wire. Solar panels had been added to the south-facing walls, although they only came up to the bottom of the second-storey windows, leaving a band of ginger brickwork free. The tall concrete-segment chimney of the old utility building was swathed in dark ivy, abandoned now, the machinery it served rusted beyond repair. Solar water-heaters had been set up on the flat roofs, like giant silver flowers with long tubular midnight-black stamens.

Greg could see work parties tending the vegetable plots inside the fence, men in grey one-piece uniforms lethargically scratching at the waterlogged soil with rakes and hoes. Prisons were officially responsible for producing fifty per cent of their own foodstuff, though the actual figure was often much higher. Grow it, or go hungry. A concept which the PSP had introduced, and the New Conservatives saw no need to alter. Dismay at the idea of prisoners sitting unproductively in their cells for twenty-two hours a day was something both sides of the political divide shared, especially when Treasury funds were scarce.

He drove past the first set of large gates in the fence. The land around was rumpled with low rolling hillocks and gentle dells, meadows, and beanfields cluttered with the spindly grey sentries of dead trees which marked the line of old hedgerows. A couple of largish woods to the north had that verdant shine which betrayed the new vine species establishing themselves on the bones of the past.

Stocken Hall itself straddled a rise east of the A1 just north of Stretton village, a fifteen-minute drive from Hambleton. He had taken the Jaguar; the car had been a present from Julia two Christmases ago. It was a powerful streamlined vehicle which looked as if it had been milled from a single block of olive-green metal. He always felt incredibly self-conscious driving it, and Eleanor was no better, which was why it stayed in the barn eleven months of the year. But he had to admit in this instance the image of professional respectability it fostered was probably going to be useful.

The second gate was the one he wanted; two red and white pole barriers, with metal one-way flaps in the concrete. There was a big steel-blue sign outside which read:

HMP Stocken Hall
Clinical Detention Centre

He stopped in front of the barrier, lowering the window to show his card to the white sensor pillar at the side of the road.

'Entry authorization confirmed, Mr Mandel,' the pillar's construct voice said. 'Please park in slot seven. Thank you.' The barrier in front of him lifted.

If anything, Stocken's new annexe was even drabber than its older counterparts. The building was a three-storey hexagon, fifty metres to a side, with a broad central well; a metal skeleton overlaid with gunmetal-grey composite panels, three rings of silvered glass spaced equidistantly up its frontage. Modular, factory-built, easy to assemble, cheap, and twice as strong as the traditional brick and cement structures.

He hadn't been expecting such a sophisticated set-up; like most government ministries the Home Office, and therefore its subsidiary the prison service, was currently cash starved. And even in pre-Warming times, improving prison conditions had never rated highly in MPs' priority lists. Constituents didn't appreciate their tax money being spent on giving criminals a cushy number.

As he drove round to the car park outside the Centre's main entrance he saw another prison party at work in the dead forest at the back of the perimeter fence. Trunks were being felled, then trimmed before they were hauled off to a sawmill set up under a green canvas awning. It was hard work, rain had turned the ground to a quagmire, but even so he was surprised the inmates were allowed chain saws. Stocken was a category A prison.

He hurried over the band of granite chips which encircled the building, discomfort trickling into his veins, as tangible as a gland secretion. Too many of his mates from the Trinities had wound up being sent to places like Stocken in the PSP years, and not all of them had survived transit.

There was another sensor pillar outside the big glass entrance doors. Greg showed his card again. The reception hall had a semicircular desk on one side and a row of plastic chairs lined up opposite. Walls and ceiling were all composite, powder-blue in colour; the linoleum was a marble swirl of grey and cream. Biolum panels were set along the walls, below tracks of boxy service conduits. The place had the same kind of utilitarian layout as a warship interior.

That military image was reinforced by the two guards sitting behind the desk; they both wore crisp blue uniforms with peaked caps. One of them took Greg's proffered card and showed it to a terminal. An ID badge burped out of a slot.

'Please wear it on your lapel at all times, sir,' he said as he handed it over along with the card.

He was fixing the badge on when one of the doors at the far end of the reception hall opened. The woman who came through was in her late thirties, dark hair cut short without much attempt at styling. Her face had pale skin, slender winged eyebrows, a long nose, and strong lips. She wore a white coat of some shiny material, there was no hint of what clothes might be worn underneath. Her shoes were sensible black leather with a small buckle, flat heels. A cybofax was gripped in her left hand.

'Mr Mandel?' She stuck out her hand.

'Greg, please.'

'I'm Stephanie Rowe, Dr MacLennan's assistant. I'll take you to him.'

The corridors were windowless, running through the centre of the building. They passed several warders, all in the neat navy-blue uniforms, and always walking in pairs or larger groups. On two occasions they were escorting prisoners. The men had shaven heads, wearing loose-fitting yellow overalls, white plastic neural-jammer collars clamped firmly around their necks.

Greg frowned at the retreating back of the second prisoner. 'Are all the prisoners fitted with neural jammers?'

'Yes, all the ones in the Centre. We house some of the country's most ruthless criminals here. I don't mean the gang lords or syntho barons. These are the violence and sex orientated offenders, killers, rapists, and child molesters.'

'Right. Do many of them try and escape?'

'No. There were only two attempts in the last twelve months. The collar's incapacitation ability is demonstrated to each inmate as they arrive. Besides, most of them are resigned when they arrive here, depressed, withdrawn. The kind of crimes they commit mean even their families have rejected them. They were loners on the outside, there is nowhere they can go, no organiz-ation which will hide and take care of them. It's our experience that a high percentage of them actually wanted to be caught.'

'And do you think you can cure them?'

'The term we use now is behavioural reorientation. And yes, we've had some success. There's a lot of work still to be done, naturally.'

'What about public acceptance?'

She grimaced in defeat. 'Yes, we anticipate a major problem in that area. It would be politically difficult releasing them back into the community after the treatment is complete.'

'Was Liam Bursken one of the two who tried to escape?' Greg asked.

'No.'

'Has he ever tried?'

'Again, no. He's kept in solitary the whole time. Even by our standards, he's considered extremely dangerous. We cannot allow him to mix with the other inmates. It would cause too much trouble. Most of them would want to attack him simply for the kudos it would bring them.'

'No honour amongst thieves any more, eh?'

'These aren't thieves, Greg. They are very sick people.'

'Are you a doctor?'

'A psychiatrist, yes.'

They climbed a staircase to the second floor. Greg mulled over what she had said. A professional liberal, he decided, she had too much faith in people. Maybe too much faith in her profession as well if she believed therapy could effect complete cures. It couldn't, papering over the cracks was the best anyone could ever hope for, he knew. But then the gland did give him an advantage, allowing him to glimpse the true workings of the mind.

'So why do you want to work here?' he asked as they started off down another corridor.

She gave him a brief grin. 'I didn't know I was the one you wanted to question.'

'You don't have to answer.'

'I don't mind. I'm here because this is the cutting edge of behavioural research, Greg. And the money is good.'

'I've never heard anyone say that about civil service pay before.'

'I don't work for the government. The Centre was built by the Berkeley company, they run it under licence from the Home Office. And they also fund the behavioural reorientation research project, which is my field.'

'That explains a lot. I didn't think the Home Office had the kind of resources to pay for a place like this.'

Stephanie shrugged noncommittally, and opened the door into the director's suite. There was a secretary in the outer office, busy with a terminal. She glanced up, and keyed an intercom.

'Go straight through,' she said.

The office was at odds with the rest of the Centre. Wall units, desk, and conference table were all customized blackwood, ancient maps and several diplomas hung on the wall, louvre blinds stretched across the picture window, blocking the view. It was definitely a senior management enclave, its occupier claiming every perk and entitlement allowed for in the corporate rule book.

Dr James MacLennan rose from behind his desk to greet Greg, a reassuring smile and a solid handshake. He was thirty-seven, shorter than Greg, with thick dark hair, heavily tanned with compact features. His Brazilian suit was a shiny grey-green.

'For the record, and before we say anything else, I'd like to state quite categorically that Liam Bursken did not slip out for a night, it simply isn't possible,' MacLennan said.

His mannerisms were all a trifle too gushy and effusive for Greg to draw any confidence the way he was intended to. He guessed that Berkeley's directors were none too happy at suggestions that psychopaths like Bursken could come and go as they pleased. The method of Kitchener's murder hadn't been lost on the press.

'From what I've seen so far, I'd say the Centre looks pretty secure,' Greg said.

'Good, excellent.' MacLennan gestured at a long settee.

Greg settled back into the bouncy cushioning. 'I will have to ask Bursken himself.'

'I understand completely. Stephanie will arrange your interview. Make as many checks as you like. I like to think our record is flawless.'

'Thank you, I'm sure it is.'

Stephanie leant over the desk and muttered into the intercom, then came and sat at the table next to the settee.

'Right, so how can we help?' MacLennan crossed his legs, and gave Greg his undivided attention.

'As you probably saw in the newscasts, I'm a gland psychic appointed to the Kitchener inquiry by the Home Office.'

MacLennan rolled his eyes and grunted. 'God, the press. Don't tell me about the press. I've had the lot of them clamouring on the door to interview Bursken, harassing the staff when they come off duty. You see them on the channel 'casts, these packs which follow politicians and royalty around, but I just never appreciated what it was like to be on the receiving end. And that kind of microscopic attention is precisely what we didn't want, Stocken is supposed to be a low-key operation.'

'Suppose you fill me in on some background. What exactly is this behavioural reorientation work you're doing here?'

'You know what kind of inmates we hold here?'

'Yeah. That's why I'm so interested in meeting Liam Bursken. I saw the holograms of Kitchener *in situ*. Tell you, it was plain butchery. I've seen atrocities in battle, and not just committed by the other side. But the kind of mind which perpetrated that was way outside my experience. I want to know what it looks like.'

MacLennan nodded sympathetically. 'Well, the motivation behind their crimes are basically psychological, in all cases deep-rooted. None of the serial killers sell drugs, or steal, or commit fraud, any of the normal range of criminal activities. That sort of everyday crime is mostly a result of sociological conditioning; broadly speaking, solvable if they were given better housing, improved education, a good job, stable home environment, etc. – it's a process for social workers and parole officers – whereas the Centre's inmates probably had those advantages before they came in. They do tend to have reasonable IQs, steady jobs, sometimes even families.'

'Do any of them have exceptional IQs?' Greg asked.

MacLennan flicked an enquiring glance at Stephanie Rowe. 'Not that I'm aware of,' he said. 'Why do you ask?'

'Kitchener's students are all very bright people.'

'Ah, I see, yes.'

'No one here has anything above average intelligence,' Stephanie announced; she was studying her cybofax. 'Certainly we have no geniuses resident. Do you want me to request past case histories?'

'No, that's all right,' Greg said.

'What we are trying to do at Stocken,' MacLennan said, 'is alter their psychological profiles, eradicate that part of their nature which extracts gratification from performing these barbaric acts.'

'Brainwashing?'

'Absolutely not.'

'It sounds like it.'

MacLennan gave him a narrow smile. 'What you refer to as brainwashing is simply conditioned response. An example: strap your subject in a chair and show him a picture of an object, say a particular brand of whisky. Each time the whisky appears you give him an electric shock. Repeated enough times the subject will become averse to that brand. I have grossly over simplified, of course. But that is the principle, installing a visually triggered compulsion. What you are doing in such cases is ingraining a new response to replace the one already in place. But it can only produce results on the most simplistic level. You cannot turn criminals into law-abiding citizens by aversion therapy, because criminality is their nature, derived subconsciously, not a single yes/no choice. And what we are dealing with in Stocken's inmates is a behaviour pattern often formed in childhood. It has to be erased and then replaced.'

'How?'

'Have you heard of educational laser paradigms?'

'No,' Greg said drily.

'It's an idea which goes back several decades. It was the subject of my doctoral thesis. I started off in high-density data-handling techniques, but got sidetracked. Educational paradigms were so much more interesting. They are the biological equivalent of computer programs. You can literally load subject matter into the human brain as though you were squirting bytes into a memory core. Once perfected, there will be no need for schools or universities. You will be given all the knowledge you require in a single burst of light, sending the information through the optic nerve to imprint directly on the brain.' MacLennan shrugged affably. 'That's the theory, anyway. We are still a long way off achieving those kind of results.'

'It sounds impressive,' Greg said. 'And you can use it to install new behaviour patterns as well?'

'Behaviour is rooted in memory, Mr Mandel. Conditioning again. You fall into a pool when you are a young child, nearly drowning; and in adult life you are wary of water, a poor swimmer, nor do you have any enthusiasm to improve. It is these countless cumulative small events and incidents in your formative years which decide the composition of your psyche. You are a soldier, I believe, Mr Mandel?'

'Was a soldier. I'm retired now.'

'You volunteered for the army?'

'Yeah.'

'And were you any good as a soldier?'

Greg shifted his weight on the settee's amorphous cushioning, conscious of Stephanie's stare. 'I was mentioned in dispatches once or twice.'

'And yet thousands, hundreds of thousands, of men your age were totally unsuitable for the military life you excelled in. Physically no different, but mentally, in outlook, your exact opposite. The respective attitudes both determined in the period between your fourth and sixteenth birthdays. We are what we are because of that time, the child being the father of the man. And that is the time we must alter in order to eradicate real-time psychoses. My aim is to substitute false paradigmatic memories for real recollections, thus effecting a radical change of temperament.'

'Have you had any success?'

'Limited, but most promising given we have only been here two years. We have already succeeded in assembling some highly realistic synthetic memories. There is one, a walk through a forest.' He closed his eyes and the eagerness and tension which had built up as he spoke drained out of his face, leaving him strangely peaceful. Almost the same expression as a synthohead, Greg thought.

'I can see the trees,' MacLennan said, his voice reduced to a placid lilt. 'They are large, tall as well as broad, in full leaf, oaks and elms. This is pre-Warming, midsummer, with sunbeams breaking through the overhead branches. I can see a squirrel, a red one; he's racing up an oak, round and round the trunk. I'm standing below watching him, touching the bark. It's rough, crinkled, dusted with a powdery green algae. The grass is ankle-high, dewy, wetting my shoes. There are foxgloves everywhere, and weasel-snout; I can smell honeysuckle.'

'Lasers can imprint a smell?' Greg asked sceptically.

'The memory of a smell,' Stephanie said pedantically. 'We adapted the paradigm from a high-definition virtual reality simulation, then added tactile and olfactory senses, as well as emotional responses.'

'Emotional responses?'

'Yes. Interpretation is a strong part of memory. If you see a particularly beautiful flower in the forest, you feel good about it; tread in a dog turd on the path, and you're disgusted.'

Greg thought about it. He couldn't fault the logic, it was just that the whole concept seemed somewhat fanciful. But someone on the Berkeley board obviously had enough faith to invest in it. Quite heavily, judging by the facilities the Centre offered.

'Have you received this memory as well?' he asked her.

'Yes. It's very realistic. It feels like I was actually *in* that forest. James forgot to mention the birdsong. The thrushes are warbling the whole time.'

Greg turned back to MacLennan, who was watching him levelly.

'How does this help to cure axe murderers?' Greg asked.

'Imagine when you were young if you took that same walk through a tranquil forest for half an hour instead of having to endure your drunken father beating you. If you had that walk, or played football, every evening he came home drunk; if you

211

could remember your mother giving him a kiss instead of crying and screaming for mercy, I think you'd find your outlook on life would be very different.'

'Yeah, and is it going to be possible?'

'I believe so. Once we have solved the problem of how to erase, or at the very least weaken, old memories. This is the area of research which requires the most effort in order for the project to succeed. Neurology and psychology to date have concentrated on memory recovery, helping amnesic victims, developing hypnotic recall techniques for vital witnesses, even preserving memories in the face of encroaching senility. The only comparable work in the opposing direction is with drugs which induce a form of transient amnesia, like scopolamine. These are no use to us, as they only prevent memories from being retained while the drug is in effect. What we need is something which will go into a subject's mind and hunt down the original poisonous memories.'

'Sounds like a job for a psychic,' Greg said.

'It's an option we've considered. In fact it was one reason I was particularly delighted when I was informed you would be coming today. I wanted to quiz you on the parameters of psi. The Home Office said you were one of the best ESP-orientated psychics to emerge from the Mindstar project. Are you able to interpret individual memories?'

'No. Sorry, I'm strictly an empath.'

'I see.' He clasped his hands together and rested his chin on the knuckles. 'Do you know of any psychic who can do that?'

'There were a couple in Mindstar who had the kind of ability you're talking about. They used to be able to lift faces and locations out of a suspect's thoughts.' He almost said prisoner, but with Stephanie leaning forward in her seat, hanging on to every word, that would never do. He wanted her wholehearted co-operation. 'I don't think they could perform anything like the deep-ranging exploration you require.'

'That's a pity,' MacLennan said. 'I might apply for a licence to practise with a themed neurohormone if one could be developed along those lines.'

'Are you completely stonewalled without psychic analysis?'

'No. There are several avenues we can pursue. Paradigms could be structured to wipe selected memories. A sort of anti-memory, if you like. The major trouble is again one of identification. We need to know a memory in order to wipe it – the nature of it, the section of the brain where it is stored.'

'A real-time brain scan might just tell us,' Stephanie said. 'If the subject recounts a particularly traumatic incident it may be possible to locate the specific neurons which house it. The erasure paradigm could then be targeted directly at them. Magic photons, we call it, after the magic bullet; like cancer treatments which kill tumour cells without harming the ordinary cells around it.'

'You would need some very sophisticated sensors to scan a brain that accurately,' Greg pointed out. 'Not to mention processing capacity. Part of my psi-assessment tests involved a SQUID scan, but there was no way you could get the focus fine enough to resolve individual neuron cells.'

'Berkeley has allocated us considerable resources,' MacLennan said. His chirpy everything-under-control smile had returned. 'We have one SQUID brain scanner already installed here at the Centre. Although, admittedly, its resolution does fall some way short of the requirement Stephanie envisages for the magic photons concept to function. But it is a modest first step. And several medical equipment companies are working on models which offer a higher resolution. I have high hopes for the project.'

'This paradigm research is an expensive venture,' Greg said. 'The Board must have a lot of faith in you.'

'They do. I didn't promise them instant results and success. They fully understand that it is a medium-term project, commercial viability will not be realized for at least another seven to ten years. But they agreed to back it because of the potential. You

213

see, if paradigm-based treatment does work, it will revolutionize the entire penal system. We would have to rebuild our institutions from the ground up. The only people who will actually require detention are petty criminals, everyone else will be reformed in medical facilities.'

'Yeah, I see.' He showed Stephanie a sardonic grin. 'I still say you'll have trouble convincing people to let them out again.'

She shrugged.

'Have you actually tried implanting any of these alternative memories in an inmate?' he asked.

'Indeed we have,' MacLennan said. 'Nothing dramatic. It's early days yet. We are in the process of acquiring baseline data on how well the paradigms are absorbed.' He might have been talking about lab rats for all the emotion in his tone. 'The older the subject, the more difficult it becomes, naturally.'

'What about Liam Bursken? Has he been given any synthetic memories?'

'No. He was unwilling to co-operate. At the moment it remains a purely voluntary programme, although we do reward participants with extra privileges.'

'So essentially he is the same person now as he was when he arrived.'

'Yes.'

'Great.' Greg stood up. 'I'd like to see him. He should be able to offer me a few insights.'

'As you wish,' MacLennan said. 'Stephanie will take you down.'

'Do you have records of the correspondence he's received?' Greg asked.

MacLennan glanced enquiringly at Stephanie.

'Yes,' she said. 'It's not much, mostly death threats.'

'I'd like copies, please.'

'I'll assemble a data package,' MacLennan said. 'It'll be ready for you when you leave.'

'Thanks.' There was always the possibility someone had

admired Bursken enough to copy the murder technique. Pretty tenuous, though.

'How has Bursken reacted to the Kitchener murder?' Greg asked Stephanie when they had left MacLennan's office.

'He's shown a lot of interest,' she said. 'He believes it is a vindication of his own crimes.'

'Oh?'

'According to Bursken, he is one of God's chosen agents of vengeance in a sinful world. Therefore someone murdering in the same way is proof that God is now instructing them. Therefore, God was instructing him in the first place. QED.'

'What's he like? I mean, what sort of formative years did he have that could push him into that?'

She hesitated as they walked into the stairwell, her companionability glitched momentarily. Greg was actually allowed to see worry and even confusion.

'The honest truth, Greg, is I haven't got a clue. We did some research into his background, for all the good it did us. He had a perfectly ordinary childhood. There was some bullying at school, nothing excessive. We could find no evidence of any sexual or mental abuse, no deprivation. Yet even by the standards of this Centre's inmates, he is completely insane. There is no rational explanation for why he went haywire. We have studied him, naturally; his brain function shows no abnormality, there are no chemical imbalances. Currently we're trying to determine the actual trigger mechanism of his psychosis, whether there is a single cause to send him off on his killing sprees. MacLennan thought that if we could just gain one insight into how Bursken functions we might eventually be able to understand his mentality. That's why he's prepared to devote time and money on such a hopeless case. By studying the real deviants, we gain more knowledge of the ordinary. But the results have been very patchy, and completely inconclusive. I doubt we ever will understand. I simply thank God that Bursken is a rogue, very rare.'

'You mean, even your laser paradigm couldn't cure him?'

'I shouldn't think so. You see, as far as we can tell, there is no evil memory sequence to replace, no trauma to eradicate. Maybe he did hear voices, who knows?'

*

The Centre's interview room was slightly more hospitable than the one at Oakham police station. Greg imagined it had been patterned from a conference room at a two-star hotel, cheap but well meaning. The table was a cream-coloured oval with five comfortable sandy-red chairs around it, almost like a dining room arrangement; certainly the confrontational element was absent. It was on the ground floor and a picture window ran the length of one wall, looking out on the patio garden which filled the building's central well. Conifers and heathers were growing in raised brick borders, tended by a working party of inmates under the watchful eyes of warders; there were several wooden park benches with inmates sitting and reading, or just soaking up the unexpected bonus of sunlight. They all had a blue stripe on their uniform sleeve.

Two guards brought Liam Bursken in. He wasn't a particularly tall man, five or six centimetres shorter than Greg, but powerfully built, with broad sloping shoulders; his shaved skull had a slightly bluish sheen from the stubble, giving the impression of a long gaunt face. The neural jammer collar was tight enough to pinch his skin, Greg could see it was rubbing red around the edges. Sober, almost mournful, emerald eyes found Greg, and regarded him intently. There was a red stripe on his yellow uniform sleeve.

He sat down slowly, his joints moving with the kind of stiffness Greg associated with the elderly. The guards remained standing behind him, one with his hand in his pocket. Fingering the collar activator, Greg guessed.

He ordered a secretion from his gland. The four minds in the room slithered across his expanding perception boundary, their thought currents forming a constellation of surreal moire-patterns. Both guards were nervous, while Stephanie Rowe by contrast displayed a cool detached interest. Liam Bursken's thoughts were more enigmatic. Greg had been expecting the ragged fractures of dysfunction, like a junkie who simply cannot rationalize, but instead there was only calmness, a conviction of supreme righteousness. Bursken's self-assurance touched on megalomania. And there was no sense of humour. None. Bursken had been robbed of that most basic human trait. It was what unnerved people about him, Greg realized, they could all sense it at a subconscious level. He wondered if he should tell Stephanie, help her understand the man.

He put his cybofax on the table, and keyed in the file of questions he'd prepared. 'My name is Greg Mandel.'

'Psychic,' Liam Bursken said. 'Ex of the Mindstar Brigade. Adviser to Oakham CID in the murder of Edward Kitchener. Strongly suspected to have been appointed at the insistence of Julia Evans.'

'Yeah, that's right. Though you can't believe everything you see on the channels. So, Liam, Stephanie here tells me you've been following the Kitchener case with some interest.'

'Yes.'

Greg realized Bursken was neither being deliberately rude, nor trying to irritate him. Facts, that was all the man was concerned with. There would be no garrulous ingratiation here, none of the usual rapport. Stephanie had been right, Bursken was utterly insane; Greg wasn't entirely sure he could be labelled human.

'I would like to ask you some questions, do you mind?'

'Any objection would be irrelevant. You would simply take your answers.'

'Then I'll ask them, shall I?'

There was no response. Greg began to wonder if he could spot a lie in a mind as eerily distorted as the one facing him.

'How old are you, Liam?'

'Forty-two.'

'Where did you live while you carried out your murders?'

'Newark.'

'How many people did you kill?'

217

'Eleven.'

Greg let out a tiny breath of relief. Liam Bursken wasn't attempting to evade, giving his answers direct. That meant he would be able to spot any attempts to scramble round for fictitious answers. Even a total mental freak couldn't escape the good old Mandel thumbscrews. He wasn't sure whether to be pleased or not. To comprehend insanity did you have to be a little insane yourself? But then who in his right mind would have a gland implanted in the first place?

He noticed the wave of hatred washing through Bursken's mind, and clamped down on his errant smile.

'Where were you when Edward Kitchener was killed, Liam?'

'Here.'

True.

'Have you ever been out of Stocken?'

'No.'

'Have you ever tried to get out?'

'No.'

'Do you want to get out?'

Bursken demurred for a moment. Then: 'I would like to leave.'

'Do you think you deserve to leave?'

'Yes.'

'Do you think you have done anything wrong?'

'I have done as I was bidden, no more.'

'God told you to kill?'

'I was the instrument chosen by our Lord.'

'To eliminate sin?'

'Yes.'

'What sin did Sarah Inglis commit?' The personal profile his cybofax displayed said Sarah was eleven years old, snatched on her way home from school.

'Let he who has not sinned cast the first stone.'

'She was a schoolgirl.' It was unprofessional, he knew, but for once didn't care. Anything which could hurt Bursken, from inducing pangs of conscience to a knee in the balls, couldn't be all bad.

'Our Lord cannot be held accountable.'

'Yeah, right. What do you know about Edward Kitchener?'

'Physicist. Double Nobel laureate. Lived at Launde Abbey. Advances many controversial theories. Adulterer. Degenerate. Blasphemer.'

'Why blasphemer?'

'Physicists seek to define the universe, to eliminate uncertainty and with it spirituality. They seek to banish God. They say there is no room for God in their theories. That is the devil speaking.'

'So that would qualify Kitchener as a legitimate victim for the justice you dispense?'

'Yes.'

'If you had been allowed out of Stocken would you have killed him?'

'I would have redeemed him with the sacrifice of life. He would have been blessed, and thanked me as he knelt at our Lord's feet.'

'Would this redemption involve mutilating him?'

'I would leave behind a sign for the Angels of the Lord to help with his ascension into heaven.'

'What sign?'

'Given him the shape of an angel.'

'It's the lungs,' Stephanie said. 'If you look down directly on the body, the lungs spread out on either side represent wings, like an angel. Liam did it to all his victims. The Vikings used to do something similar when they came over pillaging.'

'I'm sure they did,' Greg muttered. He keyed up the next series of questions on the cybofax.

'OK, you know Kitchener lives at Launde Abbey, and you know there is a kitchen there. Would you take your own knife?'

'The Lord always provides.'

'Does he provide from Launde's kitchen, or does he provide beforehand?'

'Beforehand,' Bursken whispered thickly.

Stephanie leant over to him, an apologetic smile on her lips. 'What are you getting at?' she asked in a low voice.

'Assembling a profile of the mind involved. Whoever did it has to have something in common with Bursken here. It wasn't an ordinary tekmerc, even they would baulk at performing that atrocity. It must be someone whose normal emotional responses have been eradicated, like Bursken. What I want to know is how rationally can they function under these circumstances. If they were following a plan, could they stick to it? Sheer revulsion would cause most ordinary minds to crack under the stress, mistakes could be made. So far this investigation hasn't uncovered a single one.'

'I see.' She flopped back in her chair again.

'Which would be more important to the Lord,' Greg asked: 'redeeming Kitchener, or destroying the computer records of all his blasphemous work?'

'You mock me, Mandel. You speak of the Lord, yet you carry no reverence in your heart. You speak of blasphemy, and you revel in its execution.'

'Which would you prefer to do, kill Kitchener, or erase his work?'

'A computer is a tool, it can be used or misused. In itself it is unimportant.'

'Secondary then, but knocking it out would be a good idea, you would try and do it?'

'Yes.'

'Were you ever nervous when you murdered those people in Newark?'

Bursken's throat muscles tightened, his thought currents spasmed heavily, thrashing about like wrestling snakes. Loathing predominated.

Greg allowed a smile to play on his lips. 'You were, weren't you? You were frightened, trembling like a leaf.'

'Of being discovered,' Bursken spat. 'Of being stopped.'

'Did you take precautions? Did you clean up afterwards.'

'The Lord is no fool.'

'You followed his instructions?'

'Yes.'

'To the letter? Right afterwards, I mean the minute after you had spread those lungs, you would start cleaning up?'

'Yes.'

'No hesitation? No gloating?'

'None.'

'During, what about during? Did you take care then?'

'Yes.'

'It was hard work, bloody work, and there was always the danger someone might stumble in on you. The fear. You're seriously telling me your concentration never wavered?'

'Never,' Bursken said gleefully. 'The Lord cleansed me of mortal weaknesses for my task. My thoughts remained pure.'

'Every single time?'

'Every single time!'

'The police found some skin under Oliver Powell's fingernails. Your skin. You missed that, didn't you?'

'They lied. There was no skin. Powell was struck from behind. He cried out but once before I silenced him. A plea. In his heart he knew his sin, he did not attempt to thwart the Lord's justice.'

Greg could read it from his mind, the supreme pride in what he had done. The glowing sense of accomplishment, a kind Greg had encountered before in sports tournament winners, someone receiving favourable exam results. Healthy dignity. 'Jesus!' Stupefaction pushed Greg back in his chair. Staring in bewilderment at the creature opposite, it had flesh and blood and bone, but that wasn't enough to make it human, nowhere near. 'He's not fucking real.'

Stephanie exchanged an embarrassed glance with one of the guards and made a cutting motion across her throat.

'Was there anything else, Greg?' she asked.

Greg shut down his gland secretion. Defeated, soiled and shamed by having been privy to Bursken's thoughts. 'No. Absolutely nothing.'

The lunatic sneered contemptuously as the guards led him away.

14

Julia's Rolls-Royce passed under a broad stone arch, watched by a pair of silent moss-laden griffins perched on either side. The wrought-iron gates swung shut as the car sped down the long gravel drive.

Even with the new year's punishing weather, Wilholm's grounds were maintained in pristine condition. Formally arranged flowerbeds alternated with cherry trees along the side of the drive. Broad lawns dotted with dumpy cycads rolled away to a border of glossy shrubs; behind them a thick rank of Brazilian rosewoods completed the shield against prying eyes. The Nene was a couple of kilometres away to the south-east. In the summer she could look out of the manor's second-storey windows and watch the little sailing boats cruising up and down the river, dreaming of the freedom they possessed. But this time of year always saw the valley floor flooded by the monsoon rains, the boats safe on dry land. The water was deeper each year as more and more soil was washed away by the powerful current. Further down, between the A1 and the tail end of the Ferry Meadows estuary, it became a permanent salt marsh, fetid and inutile.

But the secluded Wilholm estate remained a passive refuge, protected from environmental ravages by a wall of her money, changeless apart from the spectacular cycle of flowers which varied from month to month. Philip Evans had bought it as soon as he returned to England, paying off the communal farmers who had occupied it under the PSP's auspices. Landscape teams had laboured for months, returning it to its former splendour. Actually, it was probably a lot better than it used to be, she suspected, especially after she saw how much it had cost. Grandpa hadn't cared, he wanted elegance, and by God that's what he got.

It was worthwhile, though. Wilholm was easy on the eye, time flowed just that fraction slower across its trim lawns and through the sumptuous interior. The fact that she never, but never, used it for business of any kind helped strengthen the sensation of relief she always experienced when she crossed that invisible, and ultra-secure, threshold. Wilholm was for parties and lovers and friends. Today counted as friends, the Kitchener case was too intriguing to be classed as work.

She pursed her lips in self-chastisement; calling the murder intriguing in front of Cormac Ranasfari would never do.

Royan Access Request.

Expedite, she told the nodes.

Hi, Snowy.

She grinned broadly. On the jump seat opposite, Rachel gave her an expectant look then went back to the view across the lawn. A black-furred gene-tailored sentinel panther was just visible loping along the grass in front of the shrubs.

Royan was the only person to call her that. It was her middle name, Snowflower, bestowed by the American desert cult with which she had spent her childhood. She never used it, but there was no unit of data on the planet Royan couldn't access.

Hello to you, she answered. Talking to Royan was always a real opiate. He had taught her all sorts of programming tricks. Thanks to him she could write better hotrod software than half of England's professional hackers. She wasn't sure what he got in return, probably just the satisfaction of having someone outside his concrete eyrie who would listen. That and the fact she was the Julia Evans. Whatever, they had been firm friends ever since Greg's first Event Horizon case. He was another of those rare people who was honest with her.

Eleanor has been to see me.

I don't know. All these girlfriends.

I like Eleanor.

All you men like Eleanor.

Jealous jealous jealous. Is what you are.

Certainly am, all I've got is money.

How is Patrick?

Fine, I suppose.

Oh, Snowy, you haven't finished with him already? You only met him five weeks ago.

Don't you start, I get quite enough of that from Grandpa and Morgan and Greg.

They care. I care, Snowy. It's nice to have people who care.

Yah.

I saw you on the channels this morning.

Did you now?

Yes yes yes. Would you like me to put out a snuff contract on Jakki Coleman?

I would truly love you to put out a snuff contract on that bitch.

Really?

The only trouble is, everyone would know I was behind it. Lord, I hope nothing does happen to her! I never thought of that before. The way conspiracy theories are flying round at the moment . . .

Guilty guilty guilty. Chuckle. Serves you right.

Yes. Well, you would spring me from jail, wouldn't you?

For a price.

Thanks a bunch, some friend you are.

Seriously, I could glitch her 'cast something chronic. How about superimposing a blue AV recording? Give the porno starlet her face.

Julia had to rub her hand over her mouth to stifle the laugh. Rachel didn't look this time, she had probably guessed what was going on.

Don't tempt me! Julia implored. *I'll get that Coleman slag, one day. You see if I don't. It won't be public, but she'll know and I'll know. And that's what truly counts.*

Let me know if you need a hand.

224

Yes, I will. Thanks.

I've been going through the Launde Abbey security 'ware for Greg and Eleanor.

Yes, and . . .?

You were really looking out for Kitchener, weren't you?

Not me, I didn't even know a thing about him until two days ago. Apparently Cormac Ranasfari insisted on upgrading the security at the Abbey. He's always been concerned that Kitchener didn't have adequate protection, and this was a perfect opportunity to insist.

Oh. Well, that security system your people installed is top grade. The guardian bytes are hot hot hot stuff.

You can't melt through?

Didn't say that. I could. And possibly another five or six people in the country could. But it's tough.

Oh, so that takes the tekmerc penetration mission out of the possible, and into the improbable.

Looks like it.

Thanks for telling me. Do you want to sit in on the conference?

Yes yes yes.

*

Wilholm itself was a splendid eighteenth-century manor house. A broad grey stone façade with pink and yellow roses clotting the sturdy trelliswork on either side of the overhanging portico. The long windows were fitted with silvered glass against the heat. Julia saw a hundred tiny reflections of herself climbing out of the Rolls. Lucas, her butler, was walking down the steps to greet her.

There were a couple of other cars parked outside. Morgan's caramel-coloured Rover and a cobalt-blue Ford which she guessed was Ranasfari's.

'A pleasant morning, ma'am?' Lucas asked. He was in his mid-sixties, wearing a tailcoat with bright brass buttons, wonderfully dignified. The PSP had kept him on the dole for ten years, saying personal service was a humiliating anachronism, and they'd find him proper employment. The day after Philip Evans bought Wilholm he had cycled out from Peterborough and asked for a job. The manor functioned so smoothly under his supervision; and he'd never attended corporate management-training courses.

· She handed him her raincoat and boater. 'Let's say, I covered a lot of ground.'

He inclined his head. 'Yes, ma'am. Mr and Mrs Mandel have just passed the gatehouse, they will be here shortly.'

'Great. Show them up to the study as soon as they arrive.' She raced up the steps and through the big double doors. Most of her major friends together, working on a problem, and including her. It looked like being a great afternoon.

The study was on the first floor. Julia took her deep-purple blazer off as she went up the curving staircase. She was still undoing her slim bow tie as she barged into the study. Morgan Walshaw and Cormac Ranasfari were waiting, along with Gabriel Thompson.

Gabriel was the only person Julia knew who was ageing in reverse. The woman was another ex-Mindstar officer Greg had introduced her to. Her gland had been taken out two years ago, the precognition faculty it educed having brought too many psychological problems. Seeing into the future, Gabriel lived in perpetual fear of watching her own death drawing steadily closer. After leaving the army she had gone to seed, badly.

Now, with the gland out, she was taking care of her appearance again; she watched her diet, kept up her health, and was beginning to expand her interests. After starting out as a dowdy spinster who looked about fifty-five, she had worked her way down to become a pleasant-faced forty-five-year-old, with a pretty brisk attitude to life. Although Julia had detected some brittleness on more than one occasion.

Officially Gabriel was acting as adviser to Event Horizon's security division while Morgan set up a team of psychics – Greg had refused the assignment point-blank. The two of them had moved into the same house eighteen months ago.

'Hello, Gabriel,' Julia said brightly. She gave Morgan a quick peck on the cheek as she carried on down the long oak table which filled the centre of the study. 'Thank you for coming, Cormac.'

Cormac had half risen from his own armchair; he ducked his head before reseating himself.

Julia plopped down in the hard chair at the head of the table, and activated the terminal in front of her. 'I asked Royan to attend, is that all right?' she asked Morgan. He didn't strictly approve of Royan.

'Certainly.'

Her fingers pecked at the terminal's keyboard, loading the familiar code. Above the stone fireplace, the flatscreen she used for videoconferencing flickered dimly.

PLUGGED IN, it printed in bold orange letters.

Royan always refused to use a vocal synthesizer; the closest he came was the silent speech when her nodes were interfaced with the 'ware stacks in his room. Eleanor had described him to her once. Ever since, Julia had experienced a subtle guilt at her relief that she would never actually have to meet him. Although a bleak presence always seemed to float on the periphery of their electronic link, as if he was struggling to project himself through at her.

You're paranoid, girl, she told herself.

Another code and Grandpa was there, plugged into the study's systems. She talked banalities with the three of them as the first raindrops of the afternoon began to speckle the lead-framed windows. Sluggish grey clouds lumbered over the Nene valley, making the oak-panelled study seem funereal. Wall-mounted biolum globes came on, giant luminous pearls on curving tubular brass arms.

Lucas's unmistakable soft knock sounded on the door. He ushered Greg and Eleanor in.

Julia listened to their résumé of the case, trying to conceal a shudder when Greg ran through his interview with Liam Bursken.

She could see he was still wound up about it, and it took a lot to affect Greg. Whenever she glanced at Cormac, he had the same politely attentive expression in place.

Can't fool me, Cormac, she thought, not any more. His aloofness was a defence against the craziness and stupidity of the world, as much as his physical retreat into his laboratory complex. But now the world had pierced clean through and bitten him.

With some surprise, she realized she was actually feeling sorry for him.

After Eleanor finished talking Julia asked Greg to squirt all the police files stored in his cybofax into the NN core. 'Grandpa can run correlation exercises for us,' she said.

'That's right, bloody skivvy I am,' Philip muttered. 'Nice to know why I was invited.'

Greg smiled thinly and aimed his cybofax at her terminal. Eleanor added the bytes she'd built up.

'So it's definitely not one of the students,' Gabriel said thoughtfully.

'Yes, I'm sure they didn't kill Kitchener,' said Greg. 'Although how my opinion would stand up in court, I'm not so certain about. But the physical evidence does tend to corroborate my interviews. Besides, none of them had a mind anything like Bursken's.'

'Your opinion is good enough for me,' Morgan said.

'Even your new friend Rosette Harding-Clarke is in the clear,' Eleanor flashed Greg a spartan grin. 'Her family is very rich, and according to Julia's legal office the child wouldn't get a penny out of Kitchener's estate. If the Harding-Clarkes were poor, Rosette might have been able to apply for a maintenance order against the estate. However, the question doesn't arise.'

'Then it must have been a tekmerc snuff,' Morgan said.

YOUR SECURITY GEAR PROTECTING LAUNDE ABBEY WAS THE BEST. NO ONE ON THE CIRCUIT HAS HEARD OF ANYBODY WANTING TO BUY THE KIND OF PROGRAMS WHICH COULD BURN THROUGH.

Morgan turned his head to look at the flatscreen. 'How reliable are your sources?'

VERY VERY VERY.

'Somebody got in.'

'I still maintain it would be difficult for anyone to get in and out of the Chater valley that night,' Greg said.

'Then who did do it?' Walshaw asked; his voice had risen a notch.

Gabriel caught his eye, a silent rebuke.

'Logically, it was a tekmerc snuff,' Greg said unhappily. 'Nobody else would have the know-how and operational expertise to get in and out without leaving a trace. That's what I find incredible. There wasn't a single trace, not one.' He shook his head.

'We're missing method and motive at the moment,' Eleanor said.

MOTIVE I HAVE PLENTY OF.

'What?' Julia asked.

ACCORDING TO THE CIRCUIT, KITCHENER WAS WORKING ON A BORON PROTON REACTOR FOR YOU.

'Edward was doing no such thing,' Cormac objected.

Philip chortled, the sound reverberating out of hidden speakers, directionless. 'Ah, but it fits, m'boy. Doesn't it? Kitchener's speciality was atomic and molecular interaction. A successful boron proton reaction would be almost as worthwhile as giga-conductor. Look at it from an economic point of view, a successful boron proton fusion produces energized helium, that's all, no pollutants, no radioactive emission. It's a bloody marvel, or it would be if we could build one. Kitchener is just the kind of man to iron out the bugs involved in getting a smooth fusion process going.'

'It would be a logical assumption,' Morgan said grudgingly. 'If someone was aware Kitchener was contracted to Event Horizon, was receiving money from us, they could well think it was for energy research. Especially if they knew it was coming from Cormac's office, the inventor of the giga-conductor.'

Eleanor rapped a knuckle lightly on the table, and tilted her head to look at Julia. 'How are you going to power Prior's Fen?'

It took a second for her thoughts to jump between subjects. 'I'm considering two options. The first is an Ocean Thermal generator system, with floating platforms anchored out in the Atlantic, and bringing the electricity ashore with superconductor cables. Second is to drill a couple of hundred deep bore holes across the Fens basin, then insert direct thermocouple cables down them, siphon energy right out of the mantle. The tower and the projected cyber precincts certainly can't be powered from existing mainland sources, the capacity simply doesn't exist. Costwise, direct coupling has the edge, naturally since there are no moving parts to maintain once the holes have been sunk. In engineering terms, ocean thermal is a more mature technology. So at the moment I'm just waiting to see if Cormac makes any significant progress on direct thermocoupling in the next ten months. We don't have to make the actual selection until the end of the year.'

'I'd like it to be earlier,' Philip muttered.

'Behave, Grandpa.' She found the camera lens above the flatscreen, and gave it a stern look.

'So it would make a lot of sense for you to be working on third, fourth, even fifth alternatives,' Eleanor mused.

'Yes, absolutely. But we're not.'

'What other embryonic technologies could supply the rise in industrial demand?' Greg asked. 'And more importantly, who is working on them?'

'Grandpa?'

'Easy enough, m'girl. There are really only five viable candidates. Jetstream turbines, when you tether large vacuum bubbles twelve kilometres up and fit them out with giant rotor blades. The wind velocities up there are pretty impressive. Next, you've got cold fusion.'

Cormac grunted disparagingly. But when Julia looked at him, he just moued and went back to gazing out of the window.

'Well they might crack it,' Philip said grumpily. 'I'm just listing options.'

'Go on, Grandpa.'

'Microfusion reactors, which is a sort of advanced version of cold fusion, using molecular-scale compression techniques to fuse extremely small clusters of deuterium atoms in a gizmo the size of a processor chip. Something that small does away with the heat sink problems you get in tokamaks, but you'd need to group a lot of reactors together to produce a decent output. Ocean current turbines. But there's a question mark over which currents. Gulf Stream, Mozambique current, the Kuro Shio, East Australian current, Cape Horn current; they're all possibles, but they're all remote from Europe. Then there's solar satellites. Cheap and practical, especially now we've got the *Clarke* space-plane. But there isn't a government in the world that'll grant a licence to site a receiver array. Too many environmental – or rather environmentalist – problems when it comes to beaming energy through the atmosphere.'

'Who is researching them?' Greg asked.

'Apart from the powersats, just about every kombinate, plus dozens of universities under government contract. The whole world needs an energy source which won't add to the Green-house effect.'

Julia clasped her hands together, mind devouring the problem eagerly. She didn't even need to bring the nodes on line. 'Grandpa, are there any research teams working on boron proton fusion?'

'Yes, several.'

'OK, compile a list of the twenty-five most promising research and design teams for boron proton reactors, and each of the other projects you mentioned, then cross-reference them with Diessenburg Mercantile.'

'Gotcha, girl.'

'Isn't that one of our banks?' Morgan asked.

'Yes.' She told them about the conversation with Karl Hilde-brandt.

'Interesting,' Greg said. 'I wish I'd been there.'

'Got one, Juliet,' Philip said. He sounded slightly apprehensive, which was unusual. 'The Randon company. They have a loan package of eight hundred and fifty million Eurofrancs with Diessenburg Mercantile, two hundred million New Sterling. Two-thirds of it was spent constructing a laboratory complex outside Reims, which is dedicated to investigating microfusion techniques.'

'Has to be,' Morgan said quietly.

'Randon also sponsor Nicholas Beswick,' Philip said flatly.

Greg sat up straight, staring at the terminal at the head of the table.

'No such thing as coincidence,' Gabriel said. It came out almost as a challenge.

Greg glanced at her fleetingly. 'No,' he said firmly.

'Oh, come on, Greg. Psi isn't perfect.'

'Tell you, if it had been any one of the others, I would have said, maybe. But Beswick, no chance.'

'If you say so,' she looked away, uninterested.

'This is all based on very spurious assumptions,' Cormac said.

'Yeah, maybe,' Greg said. He sounded troubled. 'Royan, this rumour about Kitchener working on boron proton fusion, did it exist before he was snuffed?'

YES YES YES. HEAVY DUTY SPECULATION AS SOON AS EVENT HORIZON PAYMENTS WERE MADE TO HIS BANK ACCOUNT.

'For Christ's sake,' Morgan said tightly.

SORRY, BUT PEOPLE LIKE KITCHENER ARE ALWAYS BEING SCANNED BY HOTRODS. HIS WORK IS INTERESTING, NOT TO MENTION COMMERCIAL.

'But nobody knew for certain what he was doing, right?' Greg persisted.

RIGHT. THE LIGHTWARE CRUNCHER AT LAUNDE WASN'T PLUGGED INTO ANY DATANETS. KITCHENER PROBABLY DIDN'T WANT TO RISK HAVING DATA-SNATCHES RUN AGAINST HIM. SMART MAN. THAT'S WHY THERE WAS THE INTEREST IN HIM.

The lines on Greg's face deepened, he looked down at the table, lost in contemplation. Eleanor gave him a concerned glance.

Julia found the level of almost unconscious devotion between them was utterly enchanting. Chiding herself for peeking.

'It couldn't be Nicholas Beswick,' Eleanor said, 'because he knew Kitchener *wasn't* working on boron proton fusion for Event Horizon. So he wouldn't have wiped the Bendix, would he?'

Greg let out a relieved sounding sigh, and smiled at her. 'I think I'll put a bonus in your wage packet.'

She grinned back.

'Exactly what was Kitchener working on for you?' Gabriel asked.

'Wormhole physics.' Cormac started to explain.

Julia was moderately surprised Morgan hadn't told Gabriel about the research contract. He must take need-to-know far more seriously than she'd ever imagined. She didn't know whether to be amused at the notion or not.

'A stardrive!' Gabriel said incredulously when Ranasfari finished. She looked at Julia for confirmation.

'Yes, 'fraid so.' Schooldays discipline rescued her once again. But Gabriel's expression did look so funny, probably the same as hers when Cormac had first confronted her about having the murder solved.

'Royan,' Greg said slowly. 'Was there *any* hint of that on the circuit?'

NO NO NO. NO! WOW. A STARDRIVE, ULTRA EXCLAMATION MARK. HOW FAR HAD HE GOT?

'There was no prospect of him ever developing a stardrive mechanism,' Cormac Ranasfari said, distaste at the idea showing on his compact face. 'Edward was simply working on the physics which could open the opportunity for theoretical instantaneous transit.'

'Did this research involve neurohormones at all?' Greg asked.

'Most certainly. Edward was attempting to formulate a themed neurohormone which would enable him to investigate the possibility of CTCs existing. He and I considered that to be the most promising route to verification.'

'CTCs?' Greg clicked his fingers. 'Nicholas Beswick mentioned them. What is one?'

Cormac maintained a blankly impassive expression. Julia knew he was disappointed, having to explain concepts which were so *obvious*.

'A Closed Timelike Curve is a loop through space-time.'

'No messing?' Greg appeared so innocently interested.

'It has been postulated that they exist on a sub-microscopic scale, foaming space-time; approximately ten to the minus power thirty-five metres wide and stretching back ten to the minus power forty-two seconds. Theoretically you could use one to travel into the past.'

'What about creating a paradox?' Gabriel asked, there was bright interest in her eyes. 'Killing your own grandfather?'

'If you killed him ten to the minus forty-two of a second ago instead of right here in the present, how would you know?' Morgan asked mildly. 'I don't think you'd notice a vast difference.'

She waved him down irritably, concentrating on Cormac.

'Yes, the classic question,' Cormac said politely. 'Travelling back to kill your grandfather before your father was born, thus creating a paradox. If your grandfather was killed how could you have been born to travel back to kill him? This is a null question, because quantum cosmology allows for multiple parallel universes, an infinite stack of space-times with identical physical parameters except each one has a different history – Hitler triumphant, J. F. Kennedy never killed, the PSP remaining in power. If CTCs do exist, the multiple histories will interconnect, effectively integrating the parallel universes into a unified family and facilitating travel between them. In this instance quantum mechanics permits the establishment of as many connected universes as there are variant outcomes of the time traveller's actions. So you *can* travel back in time to kill your grandfather, because in another universe, the one you travelled from, your grandfather will remain alive to conceive your father.'

'Yes.' Gabriel sucked her cheeks in. 'Whenever I looked into the future, I saw multiple probabilities; the further into the future the more probabilities there were, and the wilder they became.'

'Wilder?' Julia asked, fascinated.

'Improbable. Mammoths roaming round in Siberia, the Greenhouse effect suddenly reversing, obscure politicians becoming statesmen, weird religions taking hold. I never looked too far,' she added contritely.

Because death haunted those extremes, Julia completed privately.

'Had you looked back in time, you would have seen that same multiplication of alternatives,' Cormac said. 'That is what Edward hoped to see.'

'What?' Gabriel asked sharply.

'To look in the past.'

'You said Kitchener was developing a neurohormone to perceive CTCs, not look into the past,' Greg said.

Cormac's smile was wintry. 'But don't you see, that's the same thing. Edward theorized that CTCs are the basis of psychic ability.'

Greg and Gabriel exchanged a glance bordering on pained anxiety. 'What made him think that?' Greg asked.

'These microscopic holes through space-time are too small for physical objects to pass through, so he suggested that they facilitate the exchange of pure data. Your mind, Mr Mandel, is quite literally connected with billions, trillions, of other minds; a vast repository of visual images, smells, tastes, and memories. This so-called psychic trait in certain humans is no more than a superior interpretation ability, you can make sense of our cosmological heritage, filter out the scream of the white noise jumble, pick over the bones.'

'If that's true, then how could I reach as far as I can? You said these CTCs are microscopic.'

'Indeed, but there are so many of them. If you go down one of these wormholes, back in time for that fraction of a second, move an infinitesimal distance, you will be able to find another

CTC at its terminus, perhaps several, and that connection will allow you to extend another increment further outward. You understand? It is like a chain, appallingly convoluted, which accounts for the limits in range you experience, but a clear link none the less, stretching across infinity, and up and down eternity.'

'But I could see into the future,' Gabriel said. 'How could these CTCs produce that effect? You said they go back in time.'

'They do. But the *now* we are in is the past of the futures you perceived.'

'Yes,' said Gabriel, though she sounded unconvinced.

'However, by itself looking into the future isn't sufficient to prove the existence of CTCs. Psychic is such a prejudicial term, you see, people have always laid claim to the power of foresight. But if CTCs exist, then the past should be available on an equal basis. Edward hoped that by producing a neurohormone capable of opening up the past in the way that precognition opens up the future he would make a case for microscopic CTCs which would be irrefutable. There could be very few alternative explanations.'

'Julia?' Greg's voice was dead, devoid of all inflection. Everyone looked at him. 'What was the result of the analysis on those ampoules Eleanor gave you?'

She had some trouble forming the words, her throat had dried up as soon as she started thinking about the implications. 'The laboratory said it was a themed neurohormone, sharing some characteristics with the standard precognition formula. But it's not a type they were familiar with.'

'Edward succeeded in formulating a retrospection neurohormone?' Cormac asked with a feverish note of hope.

'Looks that way, doesn't it.' Greg was staring at Gabriel. Julia saw she had gone quite white, her hands were trembling slightly.

'No,' Morgan said. He didn't use a loud voice, but the authority he conveyed was final. He took hold of Gabriel's hand. 'You're not infusing it.'

'Who else can?' she answered. 'My temporal ability is a proven one.'

'You are proposing to use it?' Cormac asked, he blinked owlishly at Gabriel. 'Why? We don't even know if it works, all Edward's records were erased.'

Julia cursed under her breath. It was a perpetual mystery to her how someone as smart as Cormac could be so oblivious to the problems of life itself. 'If it enables us to look into the past, we can use it to see who killed Kitchener,' she told him, using the strained tone reserved for making company divisional managers wish they'd never been born.

Cormac opened his mouth to speak, then glanced at Gabriel, blushing furiously. 'I . . . I'm sorry. I wasn't thinking. This whole series of events has been extremely stressful . . .' He trailed off.

'I'll infuse it,' Eleanor said.

'No bloody chance!' Greg snapped.

'Why not? These themed neurohormones are designed to amplify single psi traits. Anyone with even a faintly psionic ability should be able to infuse one. And you always say I'm sensitive.'

Greg's face darkened. 'That's hardly a qualified objective opinion.'

'What have we got to lose? If it doesn't work, there's no disaster, we simply carry on the investigation as before. If it does work, we find out who the murderer is.'

It was quite peculiar; Julia was watching Greg garner himself for a tirade, desperately trying to think of some way she could defuse the situation before it degenerated into a vicious personal row. She knew from past experience just how forceful Greg could get when he was really upset. And Eleanor was just as bad. Both of them complete stubborn-heads. But something happened, because Greg suddenly gave Eleanor a perplexed, almost awe-struck, stare, and sat back limply in his seat, his anger visibly draining away.

'What is it?' Eleanor asked. She was frowning at his behaviour.

'Nothing.'

Which Julia didn't believe for a second.

'You mean you don't object?' Eleanor said, suspicion charging her voice.

He gave her a lame grin. 'No.'

'Oh.'

Julia looked at Morgan for guidance, but all he could manage was a confused grimace. She couldn't think what had made Greg change his mind so abruptly. The mood swing had struck him so swiftly she was tempted to call it a revelation.

'If Gabriel's precognition is any example, we'll need to do this at Launde Abbey itself,' Greg said. 'You'll have a job trying to focus on the temporal displacement of a location outside your immediate area. Right, Gabriel?'

'Right.'

'OK, two points. Well, three, actually. I'll use my empathic ability to monitor your attempt, or at least try to. I want you fitted with a somnolence inducer; that way if anything does go wrong I'll sense it and simply send you off to sleep until the neurohormone wears off.'

'Good idea,' Eleanor said. She seemed relieved Greg was taking it seriously.

'Gabriel, I'd like you there as an adviser. You too, Doctor, if it's no trouble.'

'I will be happy to attend,' Cormac Ranasfari said stiffly.

'Finally, we can't really exclude Vernon Langley or his team, I suggest we don't try. But I want him to bring Nicholas Beswick with him.'

'Why?' Julia asked.

'You'll see tomorrow. Or at least, I think you will.'

15

An agitated fleece of cloud was stretched over the Chater valley the next morning, an easterly wind scattering meagre curtains of drizzle across the slopes of Launde Park. The water flowing over the bridge was down to a couple of centimetres when the EMC Ranger splashed over it. Greg drove up past the series of lakes, hopeful that this time he might remember. Disappointed once more.

Maybe Vernon would have pulled something out of the police records by now.

Eleanor sat in the passenger seat, gazing out at the desultory stone-grey drizzle. She had been silent for most of the journey, his espersense revealing the pensive timbre of her thoughts, although she was careful to keep a neutral expression on her face.

He turned off down the loop of drive towards the Abbey.

'You know exactly what I'm thinking,' he said. 'Which means there's no point in my saying it. So I'll say it anyway. I didn't really want you to do this, and if you want to pull out I won't stop you.'

She leant over and gave him the briefest of kisses. 'So why the dramatic about-face yesterday?'

'Because . . . Well, you'll see in a minute.'

'Sounds intriguing. Is it going to make me change my mind?'

'No. Quite the opposite, actually.'

She gave him another of her penetrating stares, then turned back to the window.

One thing, he was going to be bloody glad when this was over, and no messing. When the snap of intuition had hit him in Julia's study yesterday it was tough not to simply say it out loud. Then this morning he had lain on the bed with belly muscles cold and hard in anticipation as he watched her getting dressed.

She had gone through the big chest of drawers taking out a couple of blouses along with her underwear; then she'd started rummaging around the racks in the wardrobe. Two skirts were removed, and she went through the usual procedure of comparing them in the thin light coming through the window. He'd never noticed before how long it all seemed to take. In the end she had slipped into a lime-green blouse and a full-length cotton flower-print skirt, with a walnut-coloured fleece-lined sweat jacket that came down over her hips.

'Good enough for you?' she had asked tartly when she zipped the front of the jacket up.

'Sure.' He hadn't realized how obvious his stare had been.

The two white vans belonging to the forensic team were parked in their usual places outside the Abbey, three police cars from Oakham and a blue Ford which had brought Gabriel and Ranasfari, were drawn up alongside. They were the last to arrive, as he'd intended.

Eleanor pulled her jacket hood up and allowed him to take her arm as they walked to the front door. The roses along the Abbey's façade looked very scraggly now, sodden and beginning to rot. A uniformed bobby standing in the porch gave a quick salute as they hurried in out of the damp.

There were a lot of people milling around in the hall, the familiar figures of the CID team; Gabriel and Ranasfari standing together along with Ranasfari's bodyguard. The physicist was in earnest conversation with Denzil Osborne. A couple of uniformed bobbies made up the complement.

Greg spotted Nicholas Beswick standing at the foot of the stairs, hands shoved into the pockets of his jeans, his elbows sticking out at awkward angles, avoiding eye contact, trying to go unnoticed amid the hubbub of small-talk. The affection he felt at the sight of the boy was spontaneous; he wanted to go over and put a hand on his shoulder, reassure him everything was going to be all right: there was something oddly appealing about someone so timid.

He watched Nicholas very closely as Eleanor greeted the others in the hall. The boy turned round to see what was going on, full of reluctance. Then he caught sight of Eleanor. His brooding expression twisted into shock then outright fright. Both hands lurched upwards, almost as though he was warding off a punch. 'You!' It came out as a mangled yell. He took an instinctive pace backwards, and tripped on the bottom step, sitting down jarringly.

Everyone in the hall froze, staring at him. Colour began to rush into his cheeks.

Greg went over and offered him a sympathetic arm. 'She was your ghost wasn't she?' he asked gently.

Nicholas struggled to his feet, still staring thunderstruck at Eleanor. 'Yes, but look, she's real now. She's alive.'

'No messing. Allow me to introduce you; this is Eleanor, my wife.'

Nicholas gave him a wild trapped look. 'Wife?'

'Let me explain,' he said kindly.

'About time,' Eleanor grumbled in his ear.

*

'You knew all along,' Eleanor said, she was hovering between anger and bemusement. Undecided.

'I guessed all along,' Greg temporized. And Lord preserve us if she decides on anger.

They were sitting on the circular bed in Nicholas's room. All the furniture was still in place, but swathed in plastic sheeting, embargoed by the forensic team, although there had been no need for the wholesale dismantling exercise which had occurred in Kitchener's room.

Nicholas had claimed the chair behind the desk, the translucent plastic rustling at each tiny movement. He had shrugged off his reticence as Greg explained his hunch about the ghost and the retrospection neurohormone. Asking questions, making observations. Almost behaving like a regular person.

Ranasfari was sitting on the window-seat in a virtual trance state. One hand stroked the stonework absently. Greg wondered what ghosts Launde had conjured up for him.

Gabriel had listened to him explain with a smile blinking on and off. She had assumed that knowing air of elder sister tolerance he remembered so well.

Vernon, Amanda, and Denzil were grouped together in mutual confusion, attentive but saying little, swapping moody, baffled glances.

'You are saying this looking-back notion has already worked?' Amanda asked.

'No,' Greg said. 'Just that the retrospection neurohormone will work. I had some reservations at first, you see.'

Eleanor's hand squeezed his leg playfully. 'You wait till I get you home, Gregory.'

'But ... Oh, I don't know.' Amanda's arms flapped in expressive dismay. 'You really think this drug is going to let you look back and see who murdered Kitchener?'

'She has pervaded the correct tau co-ordinates,' Nicholas said. 'I saw her. Dressed exactly as she is now.'

Amanda's eyebrows shot up.

Probably never heard him speak unless he's been spoken to before, Greg thought.

'So what would happen if Eleanor doesn't take the neurohormone?' Gabriel asked. Her whole attitude was pure wickedness. 'We know it works, so why don't we give it to someone else? Vernon here, he's a likely lad, and it is his investigation.'

'Behave,' Greg said. The others wouldn't be able to tell how

242

serious she was. Gabriel took some getting used to. He'd known her for close on sixteen years, through the good times and the bad, and he wasn't sure he really understood her. Made for interesting company, though.

'Perfectly legitimate question.' She affected injured innocence. 'Nicholas says he saw her, so what would happen if she doesn't go?'

'You and your paradoxes,' Eleanor muttered.

'Nothing would happen,' Ranasfari said. 'As I explained yesterday, quantum mechanics eradicates any inconsistency. The ghost which Nicholas witnessed originates from a universe in which Eleanor will infuse the neurohormone. There are others in which she does not.'

'Another me,' Eleanor said wonderingly.

'This version does me fine,' Greg said. But there was an image in his mind he couldn't shake free; a million Eleanors saying yes and infusing the neurohormone, another million pandering to Gabriel's whim, and refusing. Universes torn asunder. And never the twain shall meet.

Eleanor smiled at him, hand gripping tighter.

'Well what's it going to be, then?' he asked.

'Oh, I'll infuse it, of course.' She looked at Nicholas, her smile turning impish. 'I'm sorry I'm going to startle you last Thursday night.'

'That's all right.' His eyes shone adoringly.

Greg had the uncomfortable thought that Eleanor and Nicholas were actually both the same age. Only chronologically though, an evil voice said inside his mind.

*

Eleanor lay down on the bed and let Denzil fit the somnolence induction loop round her head. A pearl-white tiara with a coil of cable connecting it to a slim oblong box of blue plastic. It reminded Greg of the neural-jammer collars at Stocken. The technology was the same.

'You should be able to reach down the landing into

243

Kitchener's bedroom without any trouble,' Gabriel said. 'I could tell what was going to happen to a general area about a kilometre across. Or if I fixated on a person, I could track him three or four days into the future even if he went to Australia.'

'She used to fixate on a lot of men,' Greg told the room at large. Nicholas started to giggle.

'Bugger you, Mandel.'

'I'll be happy if I can just manage to find the Abbey last Thursday,' Eleanor said.

'You did,' Nicholas said. 'Or you do, I don't know which.'

'Shall we just get on with it,' Eleanor said.

Greg could feel the nerves building in her belly. 'OK.' He sat beside her, plumping up a pillow, then took her hand. Her grip was strong, in search of reassurance, of a rock of stability.

Denzil handed him the somnolence induction box. There were three buttons and a small liquid-crystal display on the front. A column of black numbers changed occasionally below a row of symbols he didn't recognize.

'I've preset it,' Denzil said. 'Press this button and she should be under in five seconds.'

'Right.' He rested his forefinger lightly over the button. Hoping to God he wouldn't have to use it.

Gabriel held up an infuser tube. 'You want me to do this?'

'Please,' said Eleanor.

Gabriel bent over her, face sober and professional, and pressed the tube to her neck, just over the carotid.

'Keep your eyes closed,' Gabriel instructed. 'You'll be seeing enough visions without trying to untangle optical images as well.'

Eleanor's eyes closed and she clamped her jaw shut, facial muscles hard as stone. Greg ordered a secretion – gland thudding away like a second heartbeat – and joined her in the country of the mind.

*

Eyes closed, blockading the sleet of photons into the brain's reception centre, a tide of starless night engulfed him. Eleanor's mind rose silently into the void, a gas-giant as seen from one of its innermost moons. Vast and heavy. Thought currents swirled, individual strands showing pink, white, and ochre-red, like meandering stormbands, curling round each other to produce complex interlocking vortices. Stains of trepidation bled up out of the deeper psyche, dissolving into the surface thoughts, quickening the rhythm.

Relax, he told her.

The mind's superficies quaked in surprise, sending out distortion ripples.

Greg?

Yeah. Why, who did you think?

Just remember this is all new to me.

I haven't experienced this sort of affinity many times, myself.

Oh. Greg? I think I can see the bedroom. My eyes are still shut, aren't they?

He snatched a fast look. *Yeah, they're shut.* He let his own mind relax into passivity, a pure receiver. That eerie phosphorescent cloudscape lost cohesion, filming over with watery streaks of alien colour. When he studied them closer they resolved into walls, furniture, people, himself. He was still sitting on the side of the bed. Gabriel was stuck in a ridiculous posture; mouth open, hands captured in mid-gesture.

You are smiling, Eleanor said.

I've just seen me as you see me. It's interesting.

The room is all still, like a hologram.

Yeah. Now, what I want you to do, very slowly, is hunt round for a watch, and just imagine yourself sliding towards it. Got that?

No problem.

The perception focus shifted, they curved out and upwards, an eagle in flight, heading for Gabriel's wrist. Her watch was a plain silver band with dry scarlet numbers flush with the surface, as if they were floating on a lake of mercury.

Nine forty-seven, Greg read. *About eight minutes ago. OK, now can you see anything around the fringes of the room?*

Like what?

245

A lack of definition, something like the blurred multiple you get right at the edge of a mirror.

No. Nothing like that.

OK. Pull back from the room, the opposite of when you zoomed in on the watch.

Ah, yes.

The image flowed, rushing past so fast he thought he could feel the wind of its passage. Yet the walls, the furniture, the fittings, they all stayed in the same place. Darkness fell, siphoning out every shade of colour. In the night sky outside the window, stars traced sparkling arcs across the heavens, flickering in and out of existence as blankets of cloud churned past at supersonic speed.

Very good, he told her drily, *but can you stop?*

The vertiginous motion slowed. Halted. It was dusk, a paltry smattering of rain leaking from bleak clouds. The room was deserted, its frost of plastic sheets glimmering a dirty indigo.

Bloody hell, said Eleanor. There was a dazed quality to her thoughts, almost like giddiness. *I did it, Greg. The past!*

Yeah. Yesterday evening, I think. How are you standing up?

OK. There's this feeling of pressure. Inside, you know? Like I'm pushing against something.

If it ever gets to be an effort, then stop. Right away, Eleanor. Don't try and tough it out.

OK.

Any sign of alternatives yet?

God, no, Greg. This is bad enough.

Just asking. Now let's go back to the night of the murder. One week, Thursday night, midnight, or as close as we can get.

All right.

The room surged around him again.

They stopped a few times, watching Denzil or Nicolette come in and run hand-held sensors over the furniture and carpet. Sometimes they would bag an item up and take it out.

Last Friday was a blur of activity, with as many as seven or eight people crowding in at once, whizzing around. The sheets of plastic crumpled up, shrinking, vanishing, leaving the chairs and tables exposed again.

Night closed in.

Here we go, Eleanor said.

He could sense the tension, and the effort, in her mind, thoughts stretched as taut as an athlete's sinew.

Nicholas Beswick was sitting at the desk, absorbed with the dense sapphire graphics slithering through his terminal's cube. Erratic moonbeams were raking the parkland outside.

You were right about Nicholas, Eleanor said, *he does need looking after, doesn't he?*

Yeah. I like him.

Me too.

This ought to be about the time when Rosette and Isabel traipse off to see Kitchener. Move in to the bedside cabinet, we'll have a look at the clock.

The perception point drifted downwards until it was level with Nicholas's head. Surprise scrawled across his face, eyes widening.

He can see me!

Greg could sense her own startled thoughts as Nicholas opened his mouth to emit what must have been a gasp. There was no sound. Perturbed, Eleanor started to pull away, the image slowing. Graphics in the cube moved with increasing sluggishness until they finally froze.

This is what we came for, he reminded her.

Sorry.

She had moved directly above Nicholas when animation returned to the scene. Nicholas jerked round frantically in his chair, searching about. After a moment the tension seemed to evaporate from him, he rubbed his hands over his eyes and typed a code into the terminal. Then he stiffened, his head turning slowly until he was looking at the door.

This is it, Greg said. *I want you to try and follow Rosette and Isabel down to Kitchener's bedroom, OK?*

Do my best.

Nicholas had walked over to the door. Greg watched him gathering up the courage to turn the handle.

As soon as the door opened, Eleanor glided through it, staying near the ceiling and looking down. Rosette was wearing a green silk kimono. Isabel was just in her bra and jeans; her raw sexuality was devastating.

Rosette said a few words to Nicholas, then both girls left him behind as they walked down the gloomy corridor. Greg didn't like the stricken expression on Nicholas's face, not one bit. The boy was far too young to have his heart broken so cruelly. But then, when is a good age?

That poor boy, Eleanor said.

No messing.

The two girls exchanged furtive whispers as they headed for Kitchener's room. Both of them looked guilty.

Hope you choke on it, Greg wished them silently.

Kitchener was wearing white cotton pyjamas. He greeted both girls with an effusive smile. The old man gestured a lot, Greg saw, arms constantly on the move. Rosette and Isabel were both kissed exuberantly. Some of their chirpiness had returned.

The first thing Rosette did was go over to a bedside cabinet and take out an infuser tube. It was gold plated, the size of her middle finger. She applied it expertly to Isabel's neck.

Wants to get her cloudsailing before she says anything about Nicholas to Kitchener, Greg thought.

Isabel wriggled sinuously out of her tight jeans as Kitchener sat himself down in a big armchair beside the bed. His eyes never left her, Isabel moved into Rosette's embrace where her hair was stroked, cheeks caressed. More than anything it looked like she was being soothed, calmed like a skittish animal.

Tell me, Gregory, exactly how much of this do you envisage watching?

He sensed she wanted to make a joke of it, but the mental tone fell terribly short. In a body a long way away anticipation was building like a static charge along his spine. He had said he couldn't envisage what kind of man would commit such barbarism, now he was going to be shown the atrocity in its entirety.

A naked Isabel stood at the side of the bed, facing Kitchener, her head tipped back slightly, eyelids fluttering, hands rubbing insistently up and down the outside curve of her hips. The old man's eyes traced over her figure as he sipped a glass of port. Rosette began to kiss her throat with provocative tenderness, tongue licking at the curves and hollows of flesh. She descended along the cleft between Isabel's conical breasts, on to the flat expanse of belly, hungry now, her hands clasping the smaller girl's buttocks. Isabel's mouth parted to sigh, her eyes and soul shining by the light of syntho's icy fire.

Take us ahead to when they leave, Greg said.

Isabel lay back on the sheets, spreading her limbs wide, torso flexing sensually. Rosette dropped her robe and climbed on to the bed, slowly lowering herself on to Isabel.

Eleanor's focal shift accelerated the two squirming figures into hazy smears. The third figure rose from the chair and joined them. In combination the trio had that same rarefied blur as a dragonfly wing.

The girls left at twenty-seven minutes to three. They were leaning against each other, Rosette with her arm thrown protectively around Isabel. The smaller girl was drowsy, a lifeless smile of satisfaction on her lips. Kitchener snoozed on the bed, white hair askew.

How are you coping? Greg asked.

That feeling of being squeezed, it's much tighter now.

OK, let's shift forward a little then.

The door opened at eighteen minutes past four. Nicholas Beswick walked in.

'Greg!' The voice encompassed anguish and dread, finishing with a tiny whimper.

He heard it, actually heard it, the force breaking through the neurohormone's isolation.

No no no, her mind cried.

Stay with it. Keep centred, Eleanor, you must keep your mind centred here.

But Greg!

I know. It might not be him. Just a few minutes more, that's all, please.

He'd said it, but he didn't believe it.

Nicholas was wearing a brown apron, naked underneath except for a pair of underpants. His right hand gripped a thirty-centimetre-long carving knife.

Through a clammy chill of disbelief, Greg watched the boy walk over to the bed. He put the knife down on the cabinet, and picked up one of the pillows. Kitchener stirred briefly. Nicholas lowered the pillow on to the old man's face.

Greg, oh Greg, stop him.

I can't, darling. I can't.

Kitchener woke at the very end, scrawny limbs thrashing about. Nicholas's teeth were bared in a feral smile, biceps standing proud as he kept the pillow in place. The feeble scrabbling stopped after less than half a minute. Nicholas didn't lift the pillow for another ninety seconds. After that, he put it back with the others at the head of the bed, smoothing out the wrinkles with the edge of his hand.

He looked down at Kitchener, head bowed almost reverently, then crossed himself. It took him two minutes to methodically unbutton and remove the old man's pyjamas, folding them neatly and placing them on the armchair. When he was finished, he straddled the corpse across its hips. The tip of the knife was brought to rest just above the belly button, dullness of the well-worn metal contrasting against the now etiolate skin.

Nicholas leant forward, pressing down with all his weight. The knife penetrated smoothly, almost up to the handle, and he began to move it forwards, up the chest, in a rough sawing motion.

16

It was truly a cell now. The door remained locked, even when Nicholas knocked on it. Meals, interviews, and his lawyer; that was all it opened for. And the trip to the magistrates' court.

The police had taken him there on Friday morning, twenty-four hours after Eleanor Mandel had tossed about on the bed in his room at the Abbey, opening her eyes to reveal abject revulsion, and rolling over to throw up on the glossy polythene sheet covering the carpet. It was the look she had given him which wounded him the most, the absolute horror, as if his very presence could contaminate her soul. And she'd been so nice to him before, so friendly, not seeming to notice his embarrassment at the shock her appearance had triggered. Girls didn't normally treat him like that; he was either nonexistent or an object of pity, sometimes of scorn. He was secretly a little bit in love with Eleanor; she seemed so forthright, able to cope with life. She was also staggeringly pretty, even though thinking that was disloyal to Isabel.

The words had come stammering out of her mouth as she gagged, Greg hugging her shoulders, protective and concerned. 'He did it. Jesus, he didn't even blink.' She sucked down some air, wiping a sticky thread of vomit from her lips. 'What are you?'

That was when her mad eyes found him, their stare an almost tangible force, tightening round his throat.

Something shivered inside him then, enervating his legs. The cold terrible certainty that she must mean him. She was accusing him!

'Who?' It was spoken by half the people in the room. He may even have joined in. He couldn't remember.

But she said nothing. Just glared, her ragged breathing the only sound. Then Greg's stare was added to hers, calm and hateful, and Nicholas felt his face reddening even as the clamour of bewilderment inside his skull made him blurt: 'What? What? What have I done?'

'He did it,' Greg told the detectives. His voice had gone husky, saddened more than anything.

Langley had looked at Nicholas, then Greg, then back again. 'Him?' he asked incredulously. 'Beswick?'

'For Christ's sake put some handcuffs on him,' Eleanor rasped. 'If you'd only seen what he did . . .'

Greg's arm tightened round her. She had started to tremble.

'But you interviewed him,' Vernon Langley said. 'You cleared him.'

'I told you when we started. I'd never seen that kind of mind before, didn't know what to look for. Well, now I do. He's completely cracked, won't even admit it to himself. Jesus, he was fucking inhuman back there.'

'No,' Nicholas said. But nobody appeared to have heard him. 'No. I didn't. I didn't do that.'

'Are you sure?' Langley asked Greg reluctantly.

'Yeah. It was him.'

'No,' Nicholas said. 'No.'

Amanda Paterson and Jon Nevin had somehow moved to stand on either side of his chair. He glanced up at them, face pleading. 'I didn't.'

'Is there any proof; solid proof, I mean?' Langley asked. 'Can we test the clothes he was wearing?'

'I can do you one better than that,' Greg said. 'I can show you where he left the knife.'

'I didn't do it!' Why wouldn't anyone *listen*?

'It's downstairs, in the kitchen,' Greg said.

'We checked the kitchen,' Amanda retorted indignantly.

'Not all of it.'

'You two' – Langley signalled his colleagues – 'bring him with us, and keep an eye on him. I don't want any sudden sprints across the park.'

'I'll stay up here,' Eleanor said shakily.

'Me too,' Gabriel said.

'OK,' Greg said. He patted Eleanor's shoulder. 'I'll be back straight away.'

She nodded weakly, hunching in on herself as though she was freezing.

Nicholas felt Jon Nevin's hand on his forearm. He didn't protest. His strangely leaden limbs needed all the help they could get to rise out of the chair. Gabriel had gone to sit beside Eleanor, the two of them with their heads together, murmuring quietly.

In the kitchen, Greg walked straight over to the iron range. 'It's in here,' he pointed to the copper bedwarmer hanging on the wall. 'He hid it when he was burning the apron.'

'Don't touch it,' Denzil said. He and Nicolette cleared the kitchen table, covering it with a broad sheet of polythene. They put on thin yellow gloves and gingerly took the bed-warmer off its hook. The three detectives crowded round as Denzil opened it; Nicholas couldn't see.

Langley turned round, his face struggling against an expression of loathing. 'Nicholas Beswick, I am arresting you on suspicion of the murder of one Edward Kitchener.'

'No!'

There was a long knife in the bedwarmer, its blade snapped off at the base so that it could be wedged in the tarnished copper basin. The handle was rolling loose in the bottom. Both were stained black from dried blood.

'You do not have to say anything at this time, but anything you do say will be taken down and may be used as evidence against you in a court of law.'

His hands were jerked behind him. Rings of cold metal constricting his wrists. The *snick* of the locks.

'I didn't do it.'

They were deaf, immune to any words he said. They also detested him. He had never known that before. People so rarely paid him any attention at all. In the first few days after the murder, the Oakham police had treated him with a slightly puzzled indulgence, as if he was some kind of foreign animal that they didn't know how to feed properly.

But after Nevin brought him back from the Abbey it had been different. The word had gone out in advance. Off-duty officers had stood in doorways as he was marched through the station corridors to his cell. He'd cringed from the way they regarded him, the naked revulsion, expecting to be set upon and beaten. There had been no violence. The cuffs had been tight, though, his hands swelling and swelling until he thought they would burst. They had left them on for ages, long after his fingers had gone numb, dragging out the booking procedure.

He had caught one glimpse of Isabel, just as he was being put into the cell. Nevin was finally taking off his cuffs in the corridor outside when she emerged from the cell she'd been sleeping in. He cried out her name, and she turned. That was when he saw her face was like all the others.

'I didn't do it.'

Her head tipped to one side, faintly nonplussed, at one remove from the world, like the times he'd seen her performing a difficult equation. There was virtually no sign of recognition.

'*Please*, Isabel. I didn't.'

Her bottom lip turned down, as if it was all of no consequence, trivia. She was still utterly beautiful.

A shove between his shoulder blades sent him stumbling into the cell as blood and feeling shot violently back into his hands. The door slammed shut, lock whirring.

He had thought the night was bad, alone with near-suicidal confusion, the memories of the allegations. Eleanor's desolated face, the knife with its awful scale of black flakes. Nobody would talk to him, the sergeant who brought his evening meal simply slammed the moulded tray down on the table, mute.

Somehow, somewhere, there had been a terrible mistake. He had waited and waited for them to find out where they had gone wrong, to come back and set him free. He didn't want an apology, he just wanted to be allowed to go.

Gnats and small ochre moths emerged from the dead conditioning grille, fluttering silently round the biolum panel. The light stayed on all night. Nicholas huddled into a corner of the cell below the high window, drawing his knees up against his chest, a blanket round his shoulders, waiting, waiting—

*

Friday morning was worse, thrusting him from the extreme of his solitude into the bedlam of the media madhouse.

Oakham magistrates' court sat in the castle hall. It was a short drive around the park from the police station. Nicholas spent the whole time in the car with a blanket over his head.

He felt the car judder to a halt. The door was opened. Shouts were flung at him.

'Did you do it?'

'What was your motive, Nick?'

'Were you on drugs?'

He tried to screw himself into the car seat. A hand like steel clamped on to his arm, pulling him out.

'Come on son, this way, keep looking at your feet, there's no step.'

The questions merged into a single protracted yowl. He could see tarmac below his trainers, then pale yellow stone. The light changed. He was inside.

The blanket was pulled off.

He was in a short passage with whitewashed walls, narrow and cramped. Lisa Collier was standing in front of him, the two of them at the centre of a jostling circle of police.

'I didn't do it,' he told the lawyer frantically. 'Please, Mrs Collier. You have to believe me.'

255

She ran a hand back through her hair, giving him a flustered glance. 'Nicholas, we'll get all that sorted out later. Do you know why you're here?'

'Where are we?'

She groaned, shooting Langley an evil stare. 'Christ. All right, now, this is the magistrates' court, Nicholas. They've convened a special sitting. The police want you remanded in their custody for seventy-two hours so they can question you. You haven't officially been charged with anything yet, all right? There is no basis for me opposing the application. Do you understand?'

'I didn't do it.'

'Nicholas! Pay attention. We're not entering pleas today. They'll just remand you in custody and take you back to the station. There will be a lawyer present at every interview. Now do you want me to continue as your lawyer?'

'Yes, yes please.'

'All right, now look, we're going right in. You won't have to say anything, just confirm your name when the clerk of the court asks. Got that?'

'Yes. My name.'

'Fine. Now look, there's no way I could have the press excluded, so it's a bit of a circus in there. But they're not allowed to take pictures in an English court, thank God. Do your best just to ignore them.' She looked him up and down, then rounded on Langley. 'There's no bloody excuse for him turning up in this state. It amounts to intimidation in my book.'

Langley tweaked his tie. He was wearing a neat grey suit. 'Sorry, we were a bit rushed for time back there. Won't happen again.'

'You're damn right it won't,' she said in disgust.

The ancient hall was so bizarre that Nicholas was convinced he'd fallen into some *Alice in Wonderland* nightmare. There were six thick stone pillars supporting a high vaulted ceiling; each whitewashed wall was covered in horseshoes of all sizes, ranging from the genuine article up to elaborate gilded arches a metre and a half high. Most of them had crowns on top, all were inscribed with the names of the nobles, dignitaries, and royalty who had presented them to the county.

The court itself only took up the front half of the hall, an enclosure of tacky wooden pew benches painted a light grey, a defendant's box at the back. Behind that was an open space about twenty metres square.

When he walked out of a small door in the front wall, handcuffed to Jon Nevin, he nearly faltered. There were about a hundred reporters packed on to the rear floorspace. Every one of them was staring at him.

He was led to the box facing the magistrates' bench, ever conscious of those greedy eyes boring into the back of his neck. The proceedings were short, formularized. He remembered to acknowledge the clerk, then all he had to do was listen to the police lawyer read his request from a cybofax. Flowery legal language, grotesquely arcane. Why did the world stick to these rituals?

His lawyer was on her feet, saying something. Nicholas could hear the shuffling feet behind him, smothered coughs, gentle persistent clicking of fingers on cybofax keys. He could feel the curiosity they radiated, a silent demand to know, as though they had more right than the police and the lawyers.

'Granted,' said the chief magistrate, a middle-aged woman from the same stout mould as Lisa Collier.

The officials on the pew benches were standing up, talking together in low tones.

'Come on,' Nevin said.

Nicholas got to his feet, and halted. The reporters held still, collectively silent, expectant. Nevin was tugging insistently at his arm, equally uncomfortable at being in the limelight.

'I didn't do it,' Nicholas said. They would listen, at least. Nobody else did. 'I didn't.'

There was no answer.

He was frogmarched out by Nevin and two uniformed constables.

The ignominious blanket, the car ride. He could hear rain pounding on the streets.

The cell. Confinement, keeping the monster behind bars, protecting the public from his savagery. Old men could sleep safer in their beds now. This time the walls were closer together, the ceiling lower. At night they closed around his body, embedding him in cold black marble.

*

Rosette was a natural channel star, the graceful curves of her face bewitching the camera, promoting her regality, betraying no sign of her contumacy. She was standing on the pavement outside Oakham police station, beside a long modern navy-blue Aston Martin driven by a chauffeur. The front passenger door was open and she held herself poised to enter, doing the reporters a big favour by indulging them. The sunlight caught her fair hair to perfection as it fell on the shoulders of her leaf-green jacket.

'The baby is due in seven months,' she said. 'I expect to have it in a London clinic. But it will definitely be born in England, Edward would have wanted that. He was a great nationalist.'

The baby was news to Nicholas. He accepted the fact numbly. There ought to have been some tiny part of him which was glad, but he couldn't find it. Was that the kind of cyborg mind which enabled people to butcher their murder victims? But if he was so insensitive, why had he fallen in love with Isabel? It was most puzzling, his mind.

'How long had you and Kitchener been having an affair?' a reporter asked.

'I think I fell in love with Edward when I was eight years old. I remember seeing him on a channel science 'cast. He was so impassioned about his subject, and yet he always allowed his sense of humour to shine through. He was so much more alive than any other person. It was after that I concentrated on science subjects at school. He remained in my thoughts, an unsung mentor, an inspiration. Being invited to study at Launde Abbey was a lifetime ambition.'

'He was a lot older than you, did that pose any difficulty, some tension?'

'His mind was fresher than anybody's on this planet.'

'Do you know what he was working on when he was killed?'

'A stardrive, darling. A faster than light stardrive. Edward was going to give us the galaxy. He believed in human destiny, you see. It was to be his gift to all the peoples of the world, so none of us would ever be restricted and oppressed again. We could spread our wings and truly blossom amid the splendour of the night.'

'It wasn't a stardrive,' Nicholas said to the cell's flatscreen. Typical Rosette to go for theatrical effect.

'A working stardrive?' Even the reporter was sceptical.

'Oh, yes. He was studying the loopholes allowed for in General Relativity. With his genius and Event Horizon's money, I genuinely believe a starship could have been built. Now, though, who knows.' Her face was haunted by poignancy. 'I have a dream that one day our child will take up the banner of his father's work, and bring us that liberation Edward sought. Perhaps it is only an exiguous hope, but I believe, after all this, that it is a hope to which I am entitled.'

'How do you feel about the murder?'

'Grief, nothing but unending black grief. The other students have all been tremendously kind and supportive; we've cried together, and we've laughed about the good times Edward gave us. You see, darling, he would have scolded us terribly if we hadn't laughed. It's the way he was. So alive, a celebration of life.'

'And what about Nicholas Beswick?'

Rosette came right out of the flatscreen to stand in the cell beside him. A tall, glorious Venus; a goddess wronged and brutally vengeful. 'I hope he is raped by every demon in hell.'

Nicholas turned over, shuddering, and buried his head under the blanket.

*

He must have fallen asleep, because Lisa Collier was shaking him, her face anxious. 'Are you all right?'

He blinked against the pink-white light of the biolum panel directly overhead. 'Yes. Fine, thank you.'

'Good. I brought you some clothes.' She dropped his maroon shoulder bag on the floor by his cot. 'Vernon Langley is going to start the interviews this afternoon. At least you can turn up looking respectable on the AV recording.'

'Oh.' Nicholas's mood damped down.

She shifted her skirt about and sat at the foot of the cot. 'Now then, Nicholas, the idea of a police interview is to keep recapping the same ground until you start becoming inconsistent. That can only happen if you don't tell the truth in the first place. Which brings us to the murder, and what happened that night.'

'I didn't do it.'

'Nicholas, please; just hear me out. If you choose to tell the police you are guilty, we can enter a plea of temporarily diminished responsibility. Kitchener was a tetchy old man, inflicting verbal abuse for several months, you'd just found out your girlfriend was sleeping with him. You certainly had enough cause to lash out, a judge would probably be sympathetic with that, although I have to say the actual nature of the crime would probably eradicate any possibility of a light sentence.'

Nicholas took a deep breath. 'Mrs Collier, why will nobody listen to me? I didn't do it.'

Her watery eyes were placid. The sort of gaze his mother used to rebuke him with when he was small. 'Nicholas, there is a vast amount of evidence amassed against you, there is both motive and opportunity. And, Nicholas, your fingerprints were all over the knife. On top of that we have the evidence from the Mandels. I might be able to nullify their testimony, or at least blunt it slightly, the courts are still pretty hazy on interpreting psychic visions. But at the moment it adds up to a very convincing case in the prosecution's favour. I have to tell you, the way it stands the jury is going to find you guilty.'

He sat perfectly still, turning the novel concept over in his mind. They, Mrs Collier, the police, the reporters, Rosette, all truly genuinely believed him guilty. Against all logic and reason, he was going to have to accept that.

'Rational discrimination,' Kitchener had said once, 'that's the dividing line between savagery and civilization. We've thought ourselves up to where we are today, out of the caves and into the skyscrapers. Bodies never have mattered a toss, you are your mind.'

So if you're smart, Nicholas told himself, think your way out of this, prove your innocence. Images of that night cluttered his vision again. He'd seen the girls, he'd cried on the bed, he'd heard the screaming. And that was it, the total. There was nothing new, no key out of the logic box. If he could just show he had been in his room sleeping, force them to accept that. But how?

'Will you still be my lawyer if I plead not guilty?' he asked cautiously.

The cybofax she held in her lap bobbed up and down as her hands twitched unconsciously. 'Yes, Nicholas,' she said slowly. 'I'll still be your lawyer.'

'Thank you. I want to plead not guilty.'

'Nicholas, I will still be your lawyer if you admit you did it. A lot of people say they are innocent because they are too ashamed even to acknowledge their crime to their lawyer. It works against them in the long run.'

'I understand. I didn't kill Edward Kitchener.'

'Right.' She unfolded the cybofax and touched the power stud. 'Nothing like an uphill struggle.'

It was the first frivolous thing he'd ever heard her say. He almost asked if she believed him, but fright that she might say no held him back. 'I suppose I need an alibi,' he said.

Her right eyebrow arched. 'Yes. Have you got one you didn't want to mention before? We know Uri and Liz were together in his room all night. Were you with one of the other girls, secretly, Isabel or Rosette? You said Rosette did make a pass once.'

'No.'

'Now, don't get me wrong, I have to ask. Cecil Cameron?'

The Nicholas of yesterday wouldn't have understood the question. Today he thought it was simply a logical thing to ask. 'No.'

'How about a channel programme, were you watching one?'

'No.'

'The other students, is there a likely candidate who would frame you?'

'No. Look, I know it's not much, but Greg Mandel said I didn't do it. At least, that's what he thought after he interviewed me. Doesn't that count for something?'

'Hmm.' She paused, her expression distant. 'I can probably use any vacillation of opinion on his part to call his psychic ability into question. But that really isn't anything like good enough to get you off. It's the knife, you see. Have you any idea how your fingerprints did get on that knife?'

'No.' And now he thought about it, really thought, the fingerprints were impossible to explain away. The murderer creeping in to his room and wrapping his hand round the handle as he slept? Unlikely, he didn't sleep that deep. Drugged? But the police had taken a blood sample.

The first stirring of panic began to creep over his body, like immersion in a cold lake. Suppose he couldn't prove it? Suppose a jury did find him guilty?

There was a state he could sometimes reach, one where the external world became a fable, irrelevant, leaving his mind free to concentrate on problems. Like yoga, he always imagined, except yoga was for contemplating spiritually. He dealt with hard facts, that was all he knew.

'I didn't do it,' he said. 'Therefore somebody else did. That somebody also framed me. And they framed me in a spectacularly clever fashion. They even have me doubting. So in order to prove my innocence, we have to find them.'

He knew Lisa Collier thought he was crazy. Mood changes, from retarded child to punctilious cyborg. Who wouldn't think it of him? It didn't matter, because she could never get him out, not by herself. But she was a lawyer, she had to abide by the rules.

'Yes, Nicholas,' she said. 'But how are you going to find him?'

'I'm not. I'm not good enough, I admit that. We need a professional detective.'

'Who?'

'The best.' It was so simple; sneaky, perhaps even underhand, but practical. And the last thing he could afford right now was scruples. At the back of his mind the manes of Edward Kitchener nodded approvingly. He relished the endorsement. Nicholas Beswick finally twigging human emotions, what made people tick. How about that? 'And I know how to get him.' He gave Lisa Collier a rapturous grin, and pointed at her cybofax. 'Am I allowed a phone call?'

17

There was a crescent of dun-coloured fur partially obscured by the tall spires of grass on the edge of the orange grove. The picture dominated Greg's optical nerves, fed to him by his Heckler and Koch hunting rifle's targeting imager. A fan of nearly invisible pink laser light swept across his vision from left to right, producing minute sparkles when it touched the dew-drops clinging to the grass. A grid of red neon materialized in its wake. The discrimination program cut in, analysing the shape behind the tussock from the tenuous laser return, and the grid began to fold, shrink-wrapping around the rabbit. Cartoon-blue target circles materialized, and Greg shifted the rifle slightly, his finger on the trigger.

The infra-red laser pulse drilled the rabbit straight through its cranium. A tiny wisp of blue smoke curled up from the five-millimetre circle of singed fur. It rolled over without any fuss.

I hope it fucking hurt, you fur-clad locust bastard.

Eleanor hadn't slept much for the last few nights. Snuggled up in his arms, quiet face shaded by sporadic glints of moonlight. She wouldn't voice her fear, so he kept his peace, and let her hold him for the reassurance she needed.

Even he, hardened by Turkey and the inevitable propensity towards murderous fury by some squaddies, had found Nicholas Beswick's profanity difficult to exorcize.

A rabbit was squatting on its haunches at the base of an

orange sapling, wet nose sniffing the air, whiskers vibrating eagerly. Thanks to the target imager's enhancement its melancholic liquid eye was thirty centimetres across. The laser speared the shitty little vermin straight through its pupil.

How his espersense could miss such an abominable maelstrom of insanity in the boy's unruly thoughts was impossible to comprehend. He *knew* minds, from the sad and pathetic to the most dangerous brooding psychotic. He could tell, instantly. Engaging Liam Bursken's mind had been a horrendous feat – there had not, could never be, any common ground with such a demented personality. But Nicholas Beswick, he was so appealing, with his timidity and rashness, a humorous reminder of Greg's own adolescent shortcomings, an amplification of all the angst and fervour so wonderfully endemic to that age group.

I *liked* him.

To be so wrong, so blind, was to invite a fundamental disbelief in his entire empathic ability. But there had been nothing, no hint.

Two rabbits were frolicking together, a big old buck and a frisky doe. He took the buck first, then cooked the doe's brain as she quivered in confused distress.

Fifteen down, a thousand lucky charms to go.

Ranasfari had been badly upset. Shocked that a fellow Launde acolyte could do such a thing to his old mentor. Hiding his grief behind a flimsy gruffness, saying he was perturbed that there had been no alternates in the past. It didn't fit the theories. Gabriel had taken him home, for once subdued and sympathetic herself.

The alternative universe notion was something Greg had clung to for a brief hopeful moment. Suppose Eleanor, untutored, on her first neurohormone infusion, had wandered sideways into one of those timelines where Hitler's grandchildren governed the world from a gleaming Berlin metropolis, where their Nicholas Beswick was certifiably deranged. That would give him the out he needed, that would mean he could carry on liking the boy.

But, as always, there was the knife. Here, in real time, real history. And so many peripheral details, the timing of the shower, Isabel, a possible complicity with the Randon company, the implausibility of a tekmerc penetration mission.

Only his ineptitude had failed to spot the psychopath. And intuition. It couldn't be him, not that boy.

He slammed the rifle over to rapid fire, and sent a barrage of laser pulses streaking into the long grass. Rabbits toppled over, small flashes of orange flame mushroomed from the dead under-growth. The entire warren began to flee, bounding through the grass. Half the ground seemed to be on the move.

Fucking vegan rodents.

'Greg.'

It was Eleanor's voice.

He plucked the target imager's monocle from his face, a ring of skin around his eye tingling as it peeled free. He had been leaning against the wooden bar fence around the grove for some support. Now he saw it had left smears of damp algae across the front of his jeans and black sweatshirt. He made a half-hearted attempt to brush it off, holding the rifle in one hand.

There were three people with Eleanor, walking towards him from the farmyard. A middle-aged couple and a young girl. The woman had a heavily drawn face, sun ripened and lined; her curly brown hair flecked with lighter strands, not yet grey, but on the verge. Her ankle-length dress was a dun brown, a decade-old Sunday best, smart but fading slightly, the hem and neck fraying. Her husband – they were so obviously married – was as tall as Greg, but leaner, arms and legs sinuous, large labourer's hands mottled with blue veins. He was in a suit, trousers with a multitude of iron creases down the front, never quite managing to fold down the same line, his grey shirt open at the neck, showing a V of tanned skin. The colour of his thinning sandy red hair was unpleasantly familiar. Greg felt his churlish anger at the rabbits grounding out, opening up a dark void inside.

Eleanor gave him a soulful look, her hands gripped in front of her, fingers knotting in agitation. 'Greg, this is Derek and

Maria Beswick.' She gave the girl a hesitant smile. 'And it's Emma, isn't it?'

The girl nodded shyly, her eyes wide, staring at Greg's hunting rifle in trepidation. She was about thirteen, holding her mother's hand. Not a pretty girl, nor destined ever to be one, Greg thought, her cheeks were too plump, a bulge of cellulite already building up under her weak chin. Her blouse and skirt looked handmade, a green and blue print, with a generous cut.

Back when Mindstar was starting up, the specialists and generals had talked of educing a teleport faculty in some recruits. Flipping around the world, from country to country, over oceans, in zero time; just think of a location and *zip* you were there. Like all the rest of Mindstar's brochure promises it had come to nothing. Which was a great pity, because right now Greg wanted to be anywhere else on the planet – a dungeon in Teheran, an African republic police cell.

'We've come about our boy, Mr Mandel,' Derek said. There was a lot of strain in his voice. Derek Beswick was a proud man, not used to entreating strangers.

'I'm sorry,' Greg said miserably. 'It's all out of our hands now.' Shit, and he'd called Nicholas a wimp.

'He didn't do it, Mr Mandel,' Maria said. 'Not my son. Not those terrible things the channels are saying. I don't care how upset he was over a girl. Nicholas would not do something so awful.'

Greg wanted to shout: I saw him, I watched him do it! But he couldn't do it, not to a woman like Maria Beswick.

'I don't understand the things Nicholas talks about, Mr Mandel,' Derek said. 'The physics and the cosmic phenomena things in deep space. He tries to tell us when he comes home, but it goes over our heads. We're sheep farmers, that's all. But I was so proud of that boy, my boy, when he got to university, a scholarship ... He was going to better himself. He wouldn't have to get up at five every morning, like me. He could make something of his life. And when he left home it was about the worst year anyone could go to university, with all the troubles and everything. But he struggled through. Then he got asked to go to Launde. Blimey, even I'd heard of Dr Kitchener. Nicholas worshipped that old man. He didn't kill him.'

'There is a lot of evidence.'

'Nicholas told us you were a detective,' Maria said. 'That you were the best detective in England. He said that at the start you didn't think he did it. Is that right?'

'It . . .' It's not that simple! 'Yeah.'

The Beswicks exchanged a pathetically hopeful glance.

'Please, Mr Mandel,' Derek said. 'We can see you've got the farm to tend and everything, and we're not nearly as important as Julia Evans, but could you just keep investigating the case for us? Just one more day would help, something might turn up, something that might exonerate him. Jail would kill Nicholas as sure as a death penalty. He's a gentle boy.'

Your gentle son stuck a knife into the belly of a sixty-seven-year-old man and ripped him in two.

'We'll look into it for you,' Eleanor said. Greg gaped at her.

'Do you mean that?' Emma asked, she was looking up at Eleanor, chubby face filled with apprehension. 'Really mean it?'

'Yes, I mean it. There are one or two ambiguities which need clarifying in any case.'

Derek and Maria consulted each other silently.

'Anything,' Derek said. 'Anything you can turn up would help. That lawyer woman, Collier, she seems to think Nicholas is guilty.'

'It's been a good year for us so far,' Maria said. 'Really, very good. There are a lot of our ewes pregnant, the lambs should fetch a good price in the spring. So, could we possibly pay you in instalments, please?'

Greg just wanted to curl up and die. 'There's no fee,' he managed to say.

Maria's face stiffened. 'We're not asking for charity, Mr Mandel.'

'It isn't charity,' Eleanor said quickly. 'We can't accept a fee, not legally. You see, we're still on the Home Office payroll for the Kitchener case, and we remain on it until the trial is complete. How we run the investigation is entirely at our discretion, that's in the contract we signed.'

Maria looked as though she was about to protest, but Derek took her hand, squeezing a warning.

'Where are you staying?' Eleanor asked.

'I have to get home,' Derek said. 'With the sheep, and all. But Maria's got a room in a bed and breakfast house in Northgate Street, not far from the police station.'

'OK, we'll be in touch.'

*

'What did you go and tell them that for? I can't believe you said that!'

'Calm down,' Eleanor said.

'Calm down? That boy is a psychopathic killer, and you tell his parents we're going to get him off?'

'You don't think that.'

'Don't think what?'

'That he did it,' she said patiently.

'I saw him fucking do it! And so did you!'

'That's not what I said, Gregory. I said you don't think he did it.'

'I . . .' He covered his face with his hands, massaging his temple. She was right. Eleanor was always bloody right, especially when it came to what went on in his mind. Bloody unfair, that was.

He gave her a reproachful smile. 'How do you do that?'

'I had a good teacher.'

'What ambiguities were you talking about?'

'The fact that your espersense didn't catch the guilt.'

'Psi isn't perfect,' he said automatically.

Eleanor just looked at him.

'Yeah, all right. I couldn't miss something that obvious. But we saw him do it, though.'

'We, or rather I, had a vision that he did it. That's all.'

'A vision that was backed up by finding the knife, complete with fingerprints.'

'If Nicholas was framed, then of course physical evidence would be planted to corroborate the vision.'

'So how did you come to have the vision if it wasn't what actually happened?'

'I don't know. Another type of psychic who can make the images seem real? A fantasyscape artist? You tell me. You're the expert.'

'I never heard of any psi ability remotely like that back in Mindstar, not even rumours. The nearest would be eidolonics, but no eidopath could work up an image like that.'

'You hadn't heard of a retrospection neurohormone until last Wednesday.'

'No, Eleanor. I just don't believe it. It's too complicated. The killer tried to obliterate all trace of the retrospection neuro-hormone, remember? He never intended for anyone to use it. So there was no way he would have some psychic on permanent standby in case we infused it to see what happened that night. Besides, I would have sensed another psychic operating at Launde, and don't forget Nicholas saw you. That's the real clincher. He actually confirms you went back there to witness the murder. And every event we observed that night matches the statements which the students gave.'

'Everything except the murder.'

'If everything else was kosher, why should the murder be any different?'

'So you do think Nicholas killed Kitchener?'

Greg thought about it, all the doubts and internal tension that had been twisting him up for the last few days. His intuition was the root, strong enough to keep goading against all logic; like a rash developing in his synapses, an itch you just couldn't scratch. Superstition, people called it. So what it boiled down to was did he believe in his ability? In himself? 'Oh, *shit*.' He took a breath.

'No, I don't think Nicholas did it. I know he didn't. But how the actual murderer pulled that stunt with him and the knife . . .'

'Come on, Gregory, never mind the details; start thinking. Assume you are right and Nicholas is innocent, what do we do next?'

'Prove he was framed. Find the real killer.'

'See? Simple.'

'Thank you. Do you have any equally impressive suggestions how we go about it?'

She gave him a pensive look, tapping a forefinger on her teeth. 'The first thing to do is find out if someone else had a motive to kill Kitchener. Once we know who, we can start to work out how they pulled it off. What does your intuition say?'

'Good question.'

He ordered a small neurohormone secretion, and reached inwards, down into that pool of silent solitude at the core of his own mind, rooting round for convictions. The only time his intuition had tweaked him during the case was when he saw the three little fish lakes at Launde. Which he had then gone on to conveniently forget about once Eleanor had infused the retrospection neurohormone. The lakes, they were the reason he doubted Nicholas's guilt.

But why?

Greg switched the flatscreen in the lounge to phone function as he relaxed back into the settee. He flicked through the notes stored in his cybofax until he found the number for Stocken Hall, and squirted it at the flatscreen's 'ware. A secretary answered and tried to fob him off when he asked for James MacLennan, so he did his conjuring trick with his cover-all Home Office authority again.

'You're getting to be a real bully with that,' Eleanor observed. She was sitting in a chair opposite the settee, out of the flatscreen camera's pick-up field.

'Yeah; feels pretty good, too.' He spread his arms out along the back of the settee with a gratuitous sigh.

She gave him a derisory sneer in return.

Stocken Hall's director appeared on the flatscreen, sitting behind his desk, wearing a smart blue suit. The picture window's blinds were closed, as before.

'Mr Mandel, I believe congratulations are in order.' A warm regular smile displayed perfect teeth.

'The police have a suspect in custody, yeah.'

'Excellent news. Perhaps the media will now leave us all alone.'

'Don't bet your life on it.'

'No. Quite. How may I help you? My secretary said you were calling on urgent Home Office business.'

'Tell you, I need some information on the way the human brain works, specifically in your field: memories. That suspect, Nicholas Beswick, he actually managed to fool me. Now he's the very first person ever to have done that. As you can imagine, that makes me a little nervous.'

'Indeed. By fooling you, do you mean your empathic sense?'

'Yeah. He said he didn't do it and I believed him. You see, there was no evasion, no duplicity. Any mention of that murder should have triggered his memory of the event, and with it all the usual associated feelings of guilt and remorse. But I didn't sense a single suggestion of iniquity or deception. His mind appeared utterly normal, nothing at all like that cracked monster Liam Bursken.'

'I see. It does seem somewhat strange.'

'What I wanted to know was: is it possible he could deliberately make himself forget? I mean, even subconsciously; just wipe the murder from his brain? Beswick is still claiming he hasn't done it, even though the evidence is pretty conclusive. I remembered you mentioned some kind of drug which would cause forgetfulness.'

MacLennan's smile downgraded to serious concern. 'Scopolamine. Yes. It's a common enough substance, extracted from plants. Normally it's employed as a mild sedative, and for travel sickness. And it has been used for ritual purposes for several

272

centuries. But large doses can be used to induce what amounts to a trance state. There have been many cases of scopolamine intoxication identified, especially in Latin America. It was quite a problem with criminal gangs around the turn of the century. If you mix it with a tranquillizer it can be used to render someone completely docile. And it can be administered with a simple spray. Under its influence people would hand over their valuables, even empty their bank accounts from cash dispensers, and then have no recollection of ever doing so. It went out of fashion when the cashless society became firmly established, of course. Money transfers can be traced too easily these days.'

'Jesus.' The idea was unnerving, muggers armed with aerosols instead of knives, and you knew nothing about it until hours later when you returned to reality in a daze. He didn't like that at all – maybe it had happened to him already, how could he tell? – but then drugs always left him cold. 'Could Beswick have taken scopolamine to forget the murder?'

'Oh, no. It doesn't work that way. Besides, I'm sure the police would have found traces of it in his blood.'

'Yeah. But would they have checked for it?' 'I'll ask.' He loaded a note in his cybofax. 'Is there any other method you can think of?'

MacLennan gazed inwardly for a moment. 'As I told you, memory is perhaps the least explored facet of the human brain. However, there are two types of natural amnesia which I would offer as applicable in this case.'

'Two?'

'Indeed. A condition called transient global amnesia allows its victims to perform their usual jobs and maintain their standard behaviour pattern. But at the end of the day they cannot remember any event which occurred. An example: you could hold a long and intricate conversation with them, to which they would respond entirely within character; yet if you asked them about it the next day they would have no recollection of ever having talked to you.'

'Is there any way of telling if someone suffers from it?'

273

'The person concerned will often realize for themselves, especially if the condition is acute. It's not very common, but a doctor would certainly be able to recognize the symptoms from what the patient was describing.'

'Right, thank you.' Greg made another series of notes on his cybofax. 'What is the second condition?'

'Trauma erasure, which is even rarer; but there have been recorded and verified instances where it has occurred.'

'Such as?'

'A certain type of event, often violent or terrifying. Something literally so horrible that the mind simply rejects it. A particularly bloody road accident, for instance. People have witnessed them, and then failed even to remember they were present when questioned afterwards. Police often have to deal with mugging victims who cannot remember what their attacker looked like even though they were in close proximity for several minutes. But it would have to be an extraordinarily potent event to trigger such a radical neural mechanism.'

'An event like a grisly murder?'

'Yes, indeed. If Beswick acted in a fit of rage, he may not have been able to accept what he had done once that rage wore off. Under those circumstances trauma erasure may have been enacted. I offer no guarantees, of course, I am merely generalizing.'

'I understand. If Beswick is suffering from one of these types of amnesia, would a psychiatrist be able to coax the memory out?'

'I don't know. It depends how deeply it is buried. You say it is beyond even subconscious recall?'

'Yes.'

'Hypnosis may give us access. But from what you've said I wouldn't hold out much hope. In any case, it would definitely be a long-term project. There would be a lot of counselling required first, he would have to want to recover the memories.'

'I see. Well, thank you for your time.'

'Not at all.'

'We're not exactly helping our cause, are we?' Eleanor said after MacLennan's mechanical smile vanished from the flat-screen.

'Not a lot, no. But at least we know it is theoretically possible for Beswick to forget he murdered Kitchener. It explains why my interview with him was such a dud.'

'It might help rebuild your confidence in your psi ability, but it's also a terrific bonus for the prosecution,' she said indignantly.

'Hey, you were the one that told his parents we'd continue the investigation.'

'Yes, I know.' She folded her arms like a rebuked child, giving the carpet a moody stare.

He squirted another number at the flatscreen. Amanda Paterson answered, and once more the Home Office authorization was deployed like a blunt weapon.

'I know what I'd tell you to do with it,' Eleanor murmured airily, her gaze switching to the ceiling.

The flatscreen showed a slightly out of focus view of the Oakham CID office, a couple of detectives working at their desks, the situation screen on the back wall still displaying a map of the town and surrounding countryside. Vernon Langley's face slid across the picture as he sat down facing the camera. 'I was interviewing Nicholas Beswick,' the detective admonished.

'How's it going?' Greg asked.

'Would you believe the little cretin still says he didn't do it? We've even shown him the report on the knife, confirming the fingerprints on the handle are his. He claims he was framed. Christ, and they all said he was the smartest of the bunch. Makes me wonder what the thick one must be like.'

'Yeah, it's a real poser, isn't it?' Greg had felt like this once before, demob happy. When it didn't matter what he said to the brass, they couldn't do a thing about it. This time it was the sheer audacity of going up against ridiculous odds, confounding authority, which was producing an anarchistic glee.

'What did you want?' Vernon asked suspiciously.

'Several things. Firstly, I'm chasing you up over the search program. You haven't squirted over the results yet.'

'What search program?'

'For previous incidents at Launde Abbey.'

'But the investigation is over.'

Eleanor's hands traced an imaginary bulge over her belly, she grinned broadly.

'It ain't over till the fat lady sings,' Greg said cheerfully.

'Hell, Greg, we're busy.'

'Did you run the search program?'

'I think so. Hang on.' Vernon started typing on a terminal keyboard, his face resentful.

Like old times, Greg thought.

'We ran it; there is no record of any previous police call-out to Launde Abbey. Satisfied?'

Greg closed his eyes, considering options. 'How far back do those records go?'

'Four years. The station 'ware was infected with a virus when the PSP fell, the memories were wiped. A lot of stations had the same problem, they were all plugged into the Ministry of Public Order mainframe when the circuit hotrods crashed it. The fallout was pretty severe, they did a lot of damage. And of course the People's Constables weren't exactly sticklers for procedure. There was very little in the way of back-up memories. One of the reasons the New Conservatives formed the Inquisitors is because so many records from that time were lost.'

'And you were transferred to Oakham after the PSP fell, weren't you?'

'Yes.'

'OK, I want you to go around everyone who was stationed at Oakham during the PSP decade, and ask them if they remember anything about Launde Abbey.'

'I see,' Vernon said in a voice which was excessively polite.

'Good. I shall be coming into town to interview Beswick again this afternoon. You can tell me what you found then.' He referred to his cybofax. 'There is also Beswick's blood sample.'

'What about it?'

'All my file says is that it doesn't contain any syntho. There are no tabulated results.'

'So?'

'Did you run any other drug tests?'

Vernon started his laborious typing again. 'There were some traces of alcohol, that's all.'

'Call the lab, I want to know if they checked for anything else, and if so what they found. And even if they did check, I want a full-spectrum analysis run again on both the urine and blood samples today. Tell them to look for scopolamine.'

'Scopolamine?'

'Yeah.'

'Anything else?' The irony hung poised like a scalpel.

'I need to look at Beswick's medical records. If you could have them ready for when I come in, please.'

'Is this official, Greg?'

'Very.'

'In connection with the Kitchener murder?'

'What else?'

'All right, I'll phone the lab.' The image blanked out.

'The first thing he's going to do is phone the Home Office,' Eleanor said. 'Find out if you're still authorized to shove him around like that.'

'Yeah,' Greg mumbled. He patted the settee, and she came over.

'Second thoughts?' she asked. She sat with her legs up on the armrest cushions, back resting against his shoulder.

'Not just yet.' He put his arm around her. 'You do realize we are basing all this on my one tenuous belief that there was some incident in Launde's past. If it does turn out nothing happened, then all we've achieved is to bury Nicholas even further.'

'You really can't remember what it was?'

'No. I'm even starting to question if I did remember anything. It seems so fragile. Maybe it's me who's suffering from transient global amnesia.'

'Not you, my love.'

'Thanks.' He tapped out a number on the cybofax, and squirted it at the flatscreen.

'Who are you calling now?'

'Julia. I want to make sure my Home Office authorization isn't withdrawn. And then she can request a search through all the national and international commercial news libraries for me, going back say fifteen years just to be on the safe side. See if we can find out what happened at Launde that way.'

Eleanor giggled. 'A search through fifteen years' worth of every library's news files?'

'No messing. She ain't broke.'

'She will be after that.'

18

Julia knew she shouldn't be feeling so exultant, it wasn't gracious, but to hell with that for one long sweet moment. Things were coming together just dandy. Maybe people were right when they called her a manipulator.

She was sitting at the head of the table in Wilholm's study. It was a wonderfully sunny Monday outside. For once the windows were wide open, letting her hear the sound of querulous bird-song, a muggy breeze stirring the loose ends of her hair. She wore a sleeveless champagne cotton blouse and a short aqua-marine skirt, dangling her leather sandals right on the end of her toes.

There were twelve memox AV crystals lying on the glossy tabletop around her terminal, recordings of Jakki Coleman's show going back six months. Event Horizon's media research office had compiled them for her.

Caroline Rothman had delivered them that morning when she brought the usual stack of legal papers which required a signature. She hadn't said anything as she put them down on the table, but she must have known what they contained. Julia guessed the entire headquarters building was chittering with delight over Jakki Coleman's audacity, waiting for the inevitable counterstroke. This time they were going to be disappointed. It was too personal for threats of sanctions and financial blackmail screamed down the phone to the channel editor. This time she was going to be adult and subtle. But in the end there was going to be just as much blood spilt, and it wasn't going to be hers. What better way to start the week?

Glowing with a strong amber hue in the middle of her terminal's cube was Jakki Coleman's bank statement. She could thank Royan for that, his patient tutoring had enabled her to worm her way round Lloyds-Tashoko's guardian programs last night, splitting their memory cores wide open. Of course, it wasn't every hacker who had exclusive access to top-grade Event Horizon lightware crunchers to assist in decrypting financial security algorithms. To each their own . . .

She hadn't emptied the account, though, that was far too easy. Besides Lloyds-Tashoko would know it was a hotrod burn as soon as Jakki complained, the money would be refunded, another point added way down the decimals on everyone's insurance premium. All she wanted was to look.

The figures burned with cold brilliance. The high-flying finances of a channel superstar laid bare.

Except we're not quite *so* valuable to the channel after all, are we, Jakki darling? Not if that's all they're paying you.

Beside each transaction was the creditor's code. A standard finance directory search would take care of that. Julia set it up, and watched identities wink into existence alongside the columns. She knew some of them, big-name companies, department stores, travel agencies, hotels; the rest, the unknowns, she plugged into another search program.

It was interesting to see what was there, and even more interesting to see what wasn't. Jakki Coleman didn't buy any clothes, not one single item in the last three years.

Julia clapped her hands in delight, and slotted the first memox AV into the player deck beside her terminal. Jakki Coleman, six months younger, but looking just as antique, smiled out of the flatscreen above the fireplace. She was wearing a black two-piece suit with a bold mauve and green jungle-print blouse.

'For that fuller figure,' Julia said to the flatscreen. She studied the style intently – the suit was either a Perain or a Halishan –

and loaded a note into a node file, coded JakkiDeath. She moved on to the next show.

The last show the media office had recorded was the previous Friday's. There was Jakki in a black and white classical suit with an oversize side-tie. And herself, in her purple blazer, and her long white skirt, and her straw boater, with her hair pleated into a long rope, walking along a line of fit young men in dark red swimming trunks, the team coach introducing her to each of them in turn. And afterwards, sitting at the side of the pool while the squad went through their training routine for her.

'Dear Julia seems to have regressed to her school uniform today,' Jakki said. 'Now I remember why I was so eager to get out of mine after finishing lessons every afternoon.'

'To get on your back and earn some money?' Julia asked the image sweetly. She flicked the AV player deck off, and studied the results of JakkiDeath as they floated through her mind. She hadn't been able to identify all the makes, of course, but approximately one-third of all the clothes Jakki wore on her show were by Esquiline. A lot of them even had the trim little gold intersecting ellipses emblem showing, a lapel pin, or the buttons.

Product placement. Jakki's agent had done a deal with Esquiline.

She pulled a summary of the company from Event Horizon's commercial intelligence division's memory core. Esquiline was a relatively new style house, aiming to follow in the footsteps of Gucci, Armani, and Chanel; with shops in every major English city – two in Peterborough – and just starting to expand on to the Continent.

Julia got Caroline to place a call to Lavinia Mayer, Esquiline's managing director, for her. My office calling your office was snooty enough to grab attention, and then there was the added weight of her name as well.

Lavinia Mayer was in her forties, wearing a lime-green jacket over a ruff-collar snow-white blouse. Her blonde hair was cut stylishly short. The office behind her was vaguely reminiscent of art deco, white and blue marble walls, building-block furniture. Impersonal, Julia thought.

'Miss Evans, I'm very honoured to have you call us.'

Julia decided on the idiot rich girl routine, wishing she had some bubble gum to chew just to complete the picture. 'Yah, well, I hope this isn't an inconvenient time.'

'No, not at all.'

'Oh, good, you see one of my friends was wearing this truly super dress the other day, and they said it was one of yours. So I was thinking, you're a style house, do you by any chance supply whole wardrobes?'

Lavinia Mayer wasn't the complete airhead her image suggested, there was no overt eagerness; oversell was always a tactical error. She did become very still, though. 'We can certainly co-ordinate a client's appearance for them, yes.'

'Ah, great. Well I'll tell you what I want. You'll probably think it's really silly, someone in my position, but I've been so busy this winter I really haven't had much chance to plan ahead for spring.'

'That's perfectly understandable. I watched the roll out of your spaceplane myself. It's an inspirational machine. The amount of effort you must have put in is awesome.'

'Yah, it is, not that I ever get any thanks. Everyone thinks it's the designers and engineers who do all the work.'

'How preposterous.'

'Yah, well anyway, the thing is, I've got about eighty or ninety engagements coming up in the next four months or so, and I need something to wear for all of them. It would be such a relief to dump the load off on to someone else, preferably a professional. I have so little free time, you see, this way I might just scrabble a little more. It would mean a lot to me.'

The corners of Lavinia Mayer's mouth elevated a fraction, the smile a talented undertaker would give a corpse. 'Eighty or ninety?'

'Yah. Problem?'

'No.' Her voice was very faint.

'Oh, I'm so glad.' She pushed a twang of excitement into her voice. 'Would Esquiline take me on as a client, then?'

'I will attend to you personally, Miss Evans.'

'Oh, please, Julia to my friends.'

She listened to Lavinia Mayer babble on about organizing a select Esquiline team to cater for her, when would it be convenient for them to call, what sort of engagements, did she have a particular look in mind? After a couple of minutes she palmed her off on to Caroline to finalize details and sat back in the chair, rolling one of the memox AVs in her hands.

It would be interesting to see just how smart Lavinia Mayer was. The woman would never have clawed her way up to managing director without having some intelligence. An exclusive contract to clothe Julia Evans ought to be a prize worth killing for; the channel exposure time alone would cost millions if it had to be bought, then there were the socialite wannabes who would slavishly follow her.

If Jakki Coleman hadn't been dumped or brought to heel inside of two days, Lavinia Mayer was going to have her dream of world domination torn to shreds right under her pointy overpowdered nose. To be rejected publicly – and it would be very public indeed – by Julia Evans would kill their fledgeling reputation stone dead.

Jakki would probably try and go somewhere else; after all, she couldn't afford to buy the *haute couture* her assumed lifestyle required. Julia would follow her, setting up checkmate after checkmate right across the board.

There was a subdued knock on the study door. Lucas came in. 'Your guest has arrived, ma'am.'

A warm buzz invaded her belly. 'I'll be right down.' Yes, this was one day where things were truly going right.

*

Robin Harvey's hands traced an intrigued line down the side of her ribcage before coming to rest lightly on her hips. 'Try and hold your back straighter as your fingers touch the water,' he instructed. 'And stand so that you're balancing more off your heels.'

'Like this?' Julia leant back into him. Right out on the threshold of sensitivity she could detect a minute tremor in his fingertips.

'Not quite that much.' He let go abruptly.

Julia dived into the water, breaking the surface cleanly.

Her pool was a large oval affair at the rear of the house, equipped with high boards and a convoluted slide. There was a plentiful supply of colourful beach balls and lilos, a wave machine. The surrounding patio had a bar and barbecue area. It was all designed with fun in mind.

She surfaced and pushed her hair back. Robin Harvey smiled down at her.

She had noticed him on Wednesday in the England swimming squad line-up, a strong broad face, wiry blond hair, on edge at the prospect of meeting her. His powerful build, youthfulness – he was eighteen, a year younger than her – and that touch of awkward modesty made for an engaging combination. He was so much more natural than Patrick.

She had made a point of chatting to him during the training session. His stroke was the butterfly, and he enjoyed diving, though he claimed he wasn't up to a professional standard.

'Oh, gosh, I've always wanted to do that,' she said guilelessly. 'It looks so thrilling on the sportscasts, like ballet in the air. I don't suppose you could teach me some of the easier ones, could you?' She let a tone of hopefulness creep into her voice at the end. The lonely precious princess not allowed a moment's enjoyment.

Turning down such a plaintive request from the team's sponsor wasn't a serious option.

'That was very good,' Robin said as she climbed up the stairs. 'You're a fast learner.'

I was the Berne under-fifteen schools amateur diving champion. 'That's because I have such a good teacher.'

His grin was a genuine one. Julia liked it. She was going to enjoy Robin, she decided. At least with swimmers she had the perfect excuse to get ninety per cent of their clothes off right away. That remaining ten per cent ought to provide her with a great deal of fun.

She skipped off the top step and breathed in deeply. Robin's gaze slithered helplessly down to the swell of her breasts under the slippery-wet scarlet fabric of her backless one-piece costume. Bikinis always gave too much away, she thought; the male imagination was such a powerful weapon, you just had to know how to turn it against its owner.

'I'd like to try a back flip,' she said.

'Uh, sure.'

*

After they finished swimming, she showed him round the big conservatory that jutted out from the end of Wilholm's east wing. The glass annexe had undergone a complete role reversal from its original function. Tinted glass now turned away a lot of the harsh sun's power, conditioner units whirred constantly, maintaining the air at a cool two degrees celsius. The team contracted to renovate the manor had sunk thermal shields into the earth around the outside, preventing any inward heat seepage. It was a segment cut out of time, immune to the warm years flowing past on the other side of the condensation-lined glass, home to a few rare examples of England's aboriginal foliage.

She led him along a flagstone path between two borders. Young deciduous trees grew out of the rich black soil on either side, their highest branches scratching the sloping glass roof. Streaky traces of hoar frost lingered around their roots.

Both of them were in thick polo neck sweaters, although Julia still felt the cold pinching her fingers. She rubbed her arms, shaping her mouth into an O and blowing steadily. Her breath formed a thin white ribbon in the air.

Robin stared at it, fascinated. Then he started blowing.

'Polar bear breath,' she said, and smiled at him. He looked gorgeous with his face all lit up in delight.

'I've never seen that before,' he said.

'You must remember some winters, surely?'

'No. They finished a couple of years before I was born. My parents told me about them, though. How about you?'

'I grew up in Arizona. But I saw some snow when I was at school in Switzerland. We took a bus trip up into the Alps one day.'

'Lumps of ice falling out of the sky.' He shook his head in bemusement. 'Weird.'

'It's not solid, and it's fun to play in.'

'I'll take your word for it.' He tapped one of the trees. 'What's this one?'

'A laburnum. It has a lovely yellow flower at the start of summer, they hang in cascades. The seeds are poisonous, though.'

'Why do you keep this place going? It must cost a fortune.'

'I can't get into fine art; it always seems ridiculous paying so much money for a square metre of turgid canvas. And of course that whole scene is riddled with the most pretentious oafs on the planet. I'll take my beauty neat, thank you.' She pointed at a clump of snowdrops which were pushing up around a cherry tree. 'What artist could ever come close to that?'

The conservatory always affected her this way, inducing a bout of melancholia. It was the timelessness of the trees, especially the oaks and ash, they were all so much more stately than the current usurpers. They made her cares seem lighter, somehow. She was afraid she might be showing too much of her real self to Robin.

He was gazing at her again, quite unabashed this time, thick hair almost occluding his eyes. 'You're nothing . . .' His arms jerked out from his sides, inarticulate bafflement. 'You're not what I expected, Julia.'

'What did you expect?' she teased.

'I dunno. You come over all mechanical on the 'casts, like everything you do is choreographed by experts, every move, every word. Absolute perfection.'

286

'Whereas in the flesh I'm a sadly blemished disappointment.'

'No!' He bent down and picked one of the snowdrops. 'You should get rid of your PR team, let everyone see you as you are, without pretending. Show people how much you care about the small things in life. That'd stop all those critics dead in their tracks.' He broke off and gave the flower a doleful look. 'I don't suppose it'll happen like that.'

''Fraid not. Nothing is ever that easy.'

He tucked the snowdrop behind her ear, looking pleased with himself.

When she kissed him he was eager enough, but he didn't seem to know what was expected. Her mouth was open to him for a long time before his tongue ventured in.

She was struck with the thrilling thought that he'd never had a girl before. After all, it took a lot of training and devotion to reach his level of performance, a dedication which cost him every spare minute.

Her arms stayed round him as he gave her a delighted boyish grin. He had exactly seven days left to court her, then she'd have him. And this time she would be in charge in bed, so it would be a considerable improvement on the way it was with Patrick.

They rubbed noses Maori-style, then kissed again. This time he wasn't nearly so reticent.

The conservatory door was opened with a suspiciously loud rattle.

'Julia?' Caroline Rothman called.

Robin disentangled himself, looking extraordinarily guilty as Caroline walked round the end of the border.

'Sorry, Julia,' Caroline said. 'Phone call.'

She wanted to stomp her foot in frustration. 'Who?' Whoever, they were already dead.

'Greg. He said it was urgent.'

*

She sat down at the head of the study table, and jabbed a forefinger down on the phone button. The call was scrambled, she noticed, coming through the company's own secure satellite link. Greg and Eleanor materialized on the flatscreen. They were on the settee in their lounge, Eleanor at right angles to Greg, leaning against him, his arm round her. Perfectly content with each other.

The sight simply deepened Julia's scowl. She never shared such a homely scene with any of her boys. Not that she wanted to be stuck in all evening being boring, she told herself swiftly.

'This had better be truly astonishingly important,' she told the two of them loftily. 'I'm very busy.'

They looked at each other, pulled a face, and looked back at the camera. 'Doing what?'

They were so in tune, she thought despairingly, it wasn't fair. 'Financial reviews,' she said with a straight face.

'Sure,' Eleanor crooned.

'What did you want?'

'Couple of things,' Greg said. 'Firstly, I want my Home Office authority reconfirmed.'

'What? Why?'

He gave an awkward grimace, which made her take notice. Something which could faze Greg was always going to be interesting.

'There are some aspects of the Kitchener case which I need to review, and what I don't need is a whole load of flak from Oakham CID right now.'

'What aspects? Nicholas Beswick did it.'

'It would appear so.'

'You saw him. Both of you. You went back in time and saw him!'

'Yeah. Well. Tell you, my intuition is playing up about this.'

'Oh.' Greg placed a great deal of weight on his intuition. A foresight equal to everyone else's hindsight, he always said. She wasn't about to question that. Greg didn't act on idle whims. But— 'Just a minute, there was the knife as well.'

'Yeah. That's what makes this all so embarrassing.'

'Julia, we had Beswick's parents come to see us this morning,' Eleanor said.

'Oh dear Lord, that must have been awful.'

'No messing,' Greg said. 'Look, Julia, just humour me.'

She listened to him explaining his hunch about an earlier incident at Launde, and MacLennan's idea that some form of amnesia might be responsible for shielding any guilt in Nicholas Beswick's mind.

Julia requested a logic matrix from her nodes, her mind condensing what she was hearing into discrete data packages, loading them in. The matrix parameters were easy to define: assign all the case information to the two suppositions, that Beswick had committed the crime and forgotten it, and that some previous incident was involved. See what fits, what supports either notion.

'If it turns out there isn't anything to this incident of mine, then it was probably amnesia all along,' Greg concluded glumly. 'Which brings us to the second point. I'd like you to run a search program through every national and international news library to see if you can find a reference to Launde Abbey at any time during the last fifteen years.'

'Oh, is that all?' Which was letting him off lightly, she could just imagine what Grandpa would say.

'Julia Evans, you yanked both of us into this investigation,' Eleanor said. 'We only did it for you. Just because it isn't working out all neat and tidy doesn't mean you're allowed to back out. You started it, you damn well see it through to the end.'

Why was it all suddenly her fault? She wished she'd never heard of bloody Dr Edward Kitchener. 'I wasn't backing out,' she muttered.

Eleanor nudged Greg. 'You ought to ask Ranasfari if he can remember anything happening at Launde.'

'Good idea,' he said.

'Cormac was there over twenty years ago,' Julia said.

'Yeah, but he kept in touch with Kitchener.'

'Not through the PSP decade. He was working on the giga-conductor in our Austrian laboratory. Grandpa didn't want him mixing with the opposition. He was quite agreeable to the security regimen. You know what he's like, no personal or private life.'

'Yeah, but I'll ask him anyway.'

'Sure.' The matrix run ended. Its results waited for her, not seen, simply present in the null-space which was the axon inter-face. There was no solution in connection with a possible past incident, insufficient data. But the matrix had thrown up one query, though, an anomaly. 'Greg, this idea that Beswick murdered Kitchener because he was so enraged about the old man seducing Isabel Spalvas, and then blanked it out later, how does Karl Hildebrandt and the Randon company connection fit in?'

Greg and Eleanor exchanged another glance, puzzled this time.

'No idea,' he said.

'We don't know for certain that Diessenburg Mercantile was involved,' Eleanor said. 'It might have been a coincidence.'

When Greg opened his mouth she laid a finger across his lips. 'Coincidences do happen occasionally, you know.'

'Yeah,' he said unhappily.

'No,' Julia said with conviction. 'You don't know Karl like I do. He was anxious to talk with me, all to give me that one piece of advice: take you off the case. It was most deliberate.'

'Does he have any financial or corporate interests outside the Diessenburg Mercantile bank?' Greg asked.

'No.' She caught herself and pouted, it had been a reflex answer, she'd been scolded about that enough times by her teachers. 'That is, I don't know. He's never mentioned any.'

'Now I really wish I'd been there,' Greg said. 'Can you arrange a meeting, some kind of party?'

'I suppose I could invite some people round for dinner,' she sighed. 'But it's very short notice, he might suspect something, especially if you start quizzing him.'

'Tough.'

'I'll get on to it,' Julia said. 'Greg, do you really think there's a chance Beswick didn't do it?'

'There's something wrong, Julia, that's all I know.'

'Good enough for me,' she said lightly.

He winked.

She stared at the blank flatscreen for a long moment after the call ended. If nothing else, Eleanor had been right. She had dragged them into it, she had to see it through. Money and power always came with the price tag of obligation.

She pressed the intercom button. 'Caroline, cancel everything for this afternoon. We've got work to do.'

19

For once the afternoon remained sunny. Eleanor could actually hear the Jaguar's conditioner humming away as it battled the humidity. Greg had taken the EMC Ranger to scoot down to Oakham police station, claiming the Jaguar would only antagonize the detectives further. Good excuse, she acknowledged a little enviously.

She actually enjoyed driving the big car: it really was disgracefully decadent, but like Greg she always managed to feel guilty about it. There were still too many people on the breadline right now. She thought England in the nineteen-twenties must have been similar, when the barrier between the aristocracy and the workers was cast in iron, and guarded by money.

A thriving giga-conductor based economy should break down the polarization, like the internal combustion engine before it. Funny how the cycle of achievement and decay was almost exactly a century long. Though she doubted it would happen again. Surely this time we learnt enough from our mistakes?

The A606 into Stamford was one of the better roads, but when she reached the town and turned off down Roman Bank, a street that ran down the slope towards the Welland, she heard the familiar bass grumble as the Jag's broad tyres fought the mushy potholes. This part of the town was strictly residential, two-storey houses with large gardens. Thick ebony stumps of horse-chestnuts jutted up from the unkempt verge, wearing skirts of cheese-orange fungi. New acmopyle trees had been planted to replace them, already four or five metres high, silver-grey leaves casting long back shadows.

At the foot of the slope she turned left, heading towards the town centre.

Rutland Terrace was a solid row of three-storey houses, two hundred metres long; perched strategically halfway up the side of the Welland valley to give the occupants an unencumbered view out across the storm-swollen river and the southern slope beyond. Tiny individual first-floor balconies sported overhanging canvas sun-canopies, striped in primary colours, providing a meagre dapple of shade for the recumbent residents taking advantage of the weather.

She parked in front of Morgan Walshaw's house, halfway down the row. Despite a sleeveless dress chosen for its airiness, she started perspiring as soon as she climbed out of the car. The river's humidity lay over the town, pressing down like a leaden rainbow.

The small front garden could have been laid out by a geometrician, bushes and bedding plants standing rigidly to attention. A clematis had been trained up the front wall, producing a curtain of mauve dinner-plate flowers, broken only by the arched doorway and ground-floor window.

The black front door was opened by a security hard-liner. Eleanor had encountered them at Wilholm often enough now to recognize the type. A young man in a light suit, attentive eyes, not a gram of spare flesh.

He showed her up to the first-floor lounge. The air inside the house was still and relaxing, a coolness which came from the thickness of the old stone walls rather than modern conditioners.

Gabriel came in from the balcony to greet her, wearing a simple silky blue and white top and skirt. Eleanor could never quite bring herself to accept the woman was the same age as Greg. Even after all the counselling, the diets, and the fitness routines of the last two years, Gabriel remained stubbornly middle-aged. And prickly with it.

'What brings you to town?' Gabriel asked.

'Couldn't it just be to see you?'

'This trip isn't, no. And you ought to know better than trying to fool a psychic by now, even an ex like me.'

They walked out on to the balcony and sat on the deckchairs Gabriel had set out. The fringe of the green and yellow awning flapped quietly overhead.

'I'm here because of the Kitchener inquiry,' Eleanor said bluntly.

Gabriel's mask of politeness fell. 'Bugger, now what?'

'Greg's intuition.' She told Gabriel about the Beswicks' visit that morning.

Gabriel folded her arms across her chest, slipping down the curve of the chair's nylon. 'If it was just the boy's parents protesting about how sweet and harmless he is I'd be inclined to forget the whole thing, and bugger how excruciating it is. But Greg getting all worked up, that's different. There's a lot of people walking around today who would have been left behind in Turkey if it hadn't been for that cranky intuition of his.' She opened one eye fully, and gave Eleanor a bleary look. 'Mindstar brass actually put an order in writing that he wasn't to use his intuition when he was assembling mission strategies. It wasn't a recognized psi faculty.' The eye closed again, but her smile remained. 'Dickheads!'

'Greg's sure this incident he remembers is tied in to Beswick and the murder somehow. Do you remember anything happening out at Launde Abbey in the PSP years? I can't, but then we were kept carefully closeted away from the real world in the kibbutz.'

'No, nothing. I was too busy trying to shut life out back then, remember?' She took a long sip from a glass of orange, staring out across the valley. Gabriel never touched alcohol these days, not even to be sociable.

'I also wanted to ask you about the past,' Eleanor said. 'I only saw one. There were none of these multiples which Ranasfari talked about.'

'Ha! I wouldn't go around putting too much store in crap artists like Ranasfari and Kitchener if I were you. They don't know half as much about the universe as they make out they do.'

'You don't believe in the microscopic wormholes, then?'

'I'm not qualified to give an opinion on the physics involved. But I think they're both wrong to try and provide rational explanations for psychic powers.'

'You used to see multiple universes.'

'No, I used to see decreasing probabilities. Tau lines, we call them; right out in the far future there were millions of them, wild and outrageous; then you start to come closer to the present, and they begin to merge, probabilities become more likely, taming down. The closer you come to the present, the more likely they get, and the fewer. Then you reach the now, and there's only one tau line left, it's not probability any more, it has become certainty. That's why I'm not surprised you only saw one past, because there is only one now.'

'Alternative futures, but no alternative past,' Eleanor said, tasting the idea.

'The future isn't a place, don't make that mistake,' Gabriel said sternly. 'It's a concept. I've steered people away from hazards often enough to know. The future is a speculative nebula, the past is solid and irrefutable. Taken from the psychic viewpoint, anyway,' she finished glumly.

'Then we really are in trouble, because Greg and I definitely saw Nicholas Beswick do it. I'd been hoping that I had somehow slipped sideways and seen an alternative past. That way, we would only have to explain away the knife. And it could have been a plant, a very sophisticated frame-up, those students do have high IQs after all.'

'Even if it had been an alternative past you saw, how could you explain finding the knife where you did unless Beswick put it there?'

'Because another student used the retrospective neurohormone and saw where the alternative Beswick put it. Does that make any sense?'

'Not much. If alternative pasts existed, why would you always see just that one?'

Eleanor let out a long breath. 'Haven't got a clue.'

'Now do you see why they stopped fitting people with glands?' Gabriel asked evilly. She poured some more orange juice out of a jug, filling a second glass and handing it to Eleanor.

'Yes. Thanks.' Ice cubes bobbed about as she took a gulp. 'I'm going down to the local newspaper office. It's the one which is most likely to have a record of anything happening at Launde Abbey. So we thought it would be best to give our search request the old personal touch just to make sure it's done properly. Do you want to come?'

Gabriel swirled the juice and slush round the bottom of her glass, staring at it morosely. 'Yes. Morgan won't be home for hours.'

Eleanor got to her feet and stood with her hands resting on the wrought-iron railings. The Welland was a vast light-brown torrent obliterating the floor of the gentle valley, almost five hundred metres wide. Cobweb ribbons of dirty foam swirling across the surface showed her how fast the current was flowing. It couldn't even be said to have burst its banks; there were no banks, not any more. The floodwater had swept them away years ago, as it had Stamford's ancient stone bridge and all of the town's riverside buildings. During the summer, the Welland died down to a slim silver contrail; and the mudflats on either side turned as hard as steel. The kids used it as the world's greatest skateboard park.

'You get on well with Morgan, don't you?' There had been a time when she thought Gabriel wanted Greg. It was only after she met Teddy that she realized all the ex-military people shared a strange kind of bond, almost a brotherhood.

'We fit well,' Gabriel said. 'He's hopeless around the house, of course, so I'm needed here as well as in my advisory capacity to Event Horizon's security division.'

Which was as close as Gabriel would ever come to voicing real feelings. 'I'm glad.'

'How about you and Greg? When are we going to see some little Mandels?'

'The farmhouse is more or less in order, and we've got all the groves planted now. It'll mean a long summer with nothing much to do.'

'Greg did all right with you, better than most of us anyway.'

Eleanor turned. Gabriel was staring moodily into the bottom of her glass.

'Thank you.'

Gabriel grunted and swallowed the last of her drink.

*

The hardliner insisted on walking into town with them. His name was Joey Foulkes, and Gabriel treated him as if he were a small anxious puppy. He accepted it affably enough, grinning at Eleanor when Gabriel's back was turned.

The *Stamford and Rutland Mercury* office was a five-minute walk from the house, situated in one of the older sections of the town, Sheepmarket Square, a small cobbled square just above the river. The offices must back on to the concrete reinforced flood embankment, Eleanor realized; on one side of the building a narrow road ran right down a slope into the surging water. A fragile looking red plastic fence had been thrown along the top, with a couple of council warning signs pinned to it. Four kids had ignored them to stand a metre above the river, chucking bottles and rocks into the water.

The building was made from pale ochre stone, like all the others in the heart of the town. The frontage was newer, a wall of copper-tinted glass showing misty outlines of an open-plan reception area behind. None of the furniture had been changed for years, and sunlight had bleached and cracked the wood varnish; the peacock-blue carpet was threadbare.

Eleanor got an *I know you* look from the girl behind the desk. Her name alone was enough to get them shown directly into the deputy editor's office.

Barry Simms was in his early forties, an obvious full-time data shuffler. Flesh was building up on his neck and cheeks, ginger hair had been arranged in an elaborate, but doomed, attempt to disguise its own thinness. He had a quiet almost weary voice as he introduced himself.

Eleanor put that down to ingrained resignation. At his age, if he hadn't already made it out of a provincial news office, he wasn't likely to now.

'It's not about our coverage, is it?' he asked Eleanor. 'I mean you have to expect some interest if your husband is appointed to head the investigation over the heads of the local police.'

'Detective Langley is, and remains, the investigating officer, Greg was never put in over him.'

'Makes good copy though,' Gabriel said smartly.

'There is the media ombudsman if you wish to complain,' Simms said reproachfully. 'I am obliged to provide you with his address. But I hardly think we were intrusive, certainly not after the pressure we were put under. Both our bank and the satellite company that handles our datatext transmission called us up to complain about unethical behaviour. They said we shouldn't hound you. I don't like having editorial policy dictated to me like that, Mrs Mandel.'

'I think you and I are getting off on the wrong foot,' Eleanor said.

'Guilty conscience,' Gabriel muttered.

Eleanor gave her a hard stare. She rolled her eyes in defeat and folded her arms.

'I don't wish to complain,' Eleanor said. 'I would like the *Mercury*'s assistance in a peripheral matter.'

Simms perked up. 'Is this official?'

'I'm a private citizen.'

'So I can report what you say? Without any hassle?'

'I'll do you a deal, Mr Simms. You help me, and if it turns out to have any bearing on the Kitchener case, I will brief you ahead of any police statement. Interested?'

He stared at her for a moment; reporter's desire to know

warring against having restrictions imposed. 'All right,' he said. 'I thought it was all finished anyway. Nicholas Beswick did it.'

'It looks pretty certain, yes.'

'So what do you want from me?'

'A search through the newspaper's files. I want to know if there have been any other newsworthy incidents at Launde Abbey, specifically in the period between four and fifteen years ago.'

Simms looked thoroughly disgruntled. 'Typical of my luck. Mrs Mandel, if you had come in here asking for anything else we could have obliged. But that is out. Sorry.'

'Your files can't be that confidential,' she said. 'I only want to see what was previously reported.'

'It's not a problem with confidentiality. You don't understand. I want to help, but . . .' He waved a hand at the Marconi terminal on his desk. 'We no longer have that data in our memory core.'

'That seems very odd.'

'Not really, just unfortunate. Look, we were an actual newspaper until 2005, black ink on real paper, then we switched to broadcasting on the local datatext channel, same as all the other regional newspapers. We leave features running for forty-eight hours, but the news items are updated every three hours if need be. It's a good system, any cybofax can receive it. We can turn over a lot of data, cover anything from stories like Edward Kitchener's murder to the results of village flower shows, and never have to worry about capacity the way they did with paper. Any conceivable piece of information which local people would be interested in is available. Naturally, with that volume of data, everything was stored in a lightware memory.' His jaw tightened. 'Then some bastard hotrod went and crashed it all when the PSP fell. They actually went and left a message which said it had been done because we were part of the Party's propaganda effort. Jesus, if they knew what we went through to get stuff past the PSP's editorial approval officer. We might not have been out there physically fighting the People's Constables, Mrs Mandel, but we did our bit. It's not bloody fair! Who the hell are they to sit in judgement?'

'So there's no local record of the PSP years at all?' Eleanor asked.

'No. We've got a complete microfiche library of newspaper issues from 2005 dating back to about 1750, some copies go back even further than that, would you believe. And we now have a triplicated lightware memory of the last four years. But there's a thirty-five year gap between the two, and no way on earth of plugging it. It's bloody disgusting. That's our local history they killed.'

Eleanor consulted Gabriel, who was frowning thoughtfully. 'I only knew about the hotrods crashing the Ministry of Public Order mainframe,' she said.

'How about you, Mr Simms?' Eleanor asked. 'You covered the area in that time. Do you remember anything happening out at Launde Abbey?'

'I was in Birmingham when the PSP rule started. I didn't come back here until seven years ago. But no, I can't remember anything. Kitchener himself got the occasional mention, of course. Some of the scientific papers he published were contested by other scientists. Frankly, there were more important issues at the time. We didn't give him a lot of coverage. What type of incident were you looking for?'

'I don't know.' She rose to leave. 'By the way, our deal stands.'

'Thanks.'

'So as a final favour, could you tell me if there is anywhere else we could go that might have records of that period?'

'It pains me to say it, but you might try our rivals, the *Rutland Times*, or the *Melton Times*, possibly even the *Leicester Mercury*.'

20

Jon Nevin showed his card to the lock, and the bolts clicked back.

'Thanks,' Greg said as he walked into the cell. There was no response.

Back to square one, he thought. He pretended he wasn't bothered by the detective's attitude.

Nicholas Beswick was sitting cross-legged in the middle of his cot. He opened his eyes as Greg came in, but made no attempt to move.

The boy had undergone a profound change in the last three days, there was no sign of the angst-burdened student Greg had interviewed at the start of the inquiry. He ordered a secretion from his gland, and examined the smooth cadence of Nicholas's thought currents. Again there was virtually no trace of the old jittery mind.

Maybe it was a good thing, that earlier Nicholas would have been crucified under cross-examination by a professional prosecutor. But Greg couldn't help thinking that if the boy had changed so drastically once . . .

'I don't know who is the most unpopular at this station right now,' he said, 'you or me.'

Nicholas favoured him with a sly smile, a welcome from one conspirator to another. 'It's me. You only irritate them. I disgust them.'

'Yeah. What you did this morning was a bit over the top, wasn't it? Sending your sister as well as your parents. You upset Eleanor, you know.'

'Exactly how many qualms should a condemned man own? I need you, very badly. There is nothing I wouldn't do to reach you.'

'Jesus.'

'I know what you're thinking. He's changed so much, attitude-wise. If he's done it once, could he do it twice? That's right, isn't it?'

Greg grinned, and pulled the single wooden chair into the middle of the cell, straddling it saloon style, with his elbows resting on its back. 'You really have got a brain in that head of yours, haven't you?'

'Not good enough to think me out of here.'

'That's a fact, and no messing.'

'But you're going to work on the case again, aren't you? Mum said you were. She came back at lunchtime, her and Emma. I didn't know my parents were going to bring Emma with them. She's a lovely girl, we get on really well. Can you think how they're going to treat her at school after this? God!'

Just for a moment the old Nicholas peeped through, insecure and desperate.

'Yeah. I'm still on the case. There are a couple of ambiguities that are bothering me. But, Nicholas, if I clear them up and you still look guilty, an army of weeping relatives isn't going to bring me back.'

'I understand. I'm grateful, really. You're the only hope I've got. Lisa Collier is just going through the motions.'

'OK. Tell you, the way it is, Vernon Langley and the prosecutor are going to nail you with that knife we found. Everything else is circumstantial, and I'm sure Lisa Collier will do her utmost to crush any testimony Eleanor and I provide for the prosecution. But that knife . . . I'm still not entirely convinced you didn't do it. I saw you.'

Nicholas brightened. 'I had one idea: a *doppelgänger*, a tek-merc who underwent a total *plastique* reworking to look like me. If one of the others had seen him walking about in that guise they wouldn't have thought anything of it. And I never used to say much, so they wouldn't expect him to talk to them. Just blush and walk on, that's what I normally did.'

'Yeah, plausible. Except Eleanor and I watched you go back to your room after you hid the knife and burnt the apron.'

'Oh.'

'I want to ask you some more questions. Do you want to get Lisa Collier to sit in?'

'No. I don't think I can dig myself any deeper in, can I?'

'There is that. OK, first: did Kitchener ever mention an incident that happened a few years ago?'

'What incident?'

'That's my problem. I remember seeing some news item about Launde maybe ten or so years back, but I can't remember what it was.'

'No, nothing comes to mind. Kitchener always had so many complaints about the past, people he knew, politicians he'd argued with, the other professors back at Cambridge, that kind of thing. His entire life was one giant collection of incidents, really.'

'Yeah, I suppose it was. Well keep thinking about it; if anything does spring to mind get Lisa Collier to contact me at once. OK?'

'Yes.'

'Right, now you're sponsored by the Randon company, aren't you?'

'Yes, they pay me an allowance, more like a salary actually, eight thousand New Sterling a year for the whole time I'm at Launde. Can you believe that much money? I sent two thousand back to Mum and Dad; they really struggled to help when I was at Cambridge, and I don't spend much at the Abbey, you see. Then there's a fund for any equipment I need for projects.

Within reason, of course. But I never used any of that, most of my research was data simulations, the Abbey's lightware cruncher was enough.'

'Did Randon ever ask you what Kitchener was working on?'

'No.'

'So they didn't know about the wormhole research he was performing for Event Horizon?'

'No.'

'What about anyone else? You obviously knew about it.'

'Not very much, just that he was looking into it. Wormholes would plug very neatly into his cosmos theory.'

'What is that?'

'He called it the Godslayer.'

'The what?'

'Well, religion killer. Kitchener was hoping to put together a structural theory that went beyond Grand Unification. It would explain every phenomenon in the universe from psi to gravity. He said he could use it to prove that there was no such thing as God, that the universe was completely natural, and therefore explainable. Provided you had the maths to understand it.'

Greg tried to imagine what Goldfinch, the Trinities' fundamentalist preacher, would make of that, and failed. It would have been interesting to watch a meeting between the priest and the physicist, though – from a distance. 'Kitchener genuinely didn't care about other people's sensibilities, did he?'

'Yes, he did,' Nicholas said, a shade defensively. 'You never met him, he was kind to me, really encouraging. But he hated religion. He said we'd all be better off without it, that it caused too much trouble, and too many wars. He said people called him the Newton of the age, but he'd rather be the Galileo.'

'And you didn't mind all this talk?' He observed the boy's thought currents boil with surprise.

'No. Why should I?'

'I take it that means you're not religious.'

'Never really thought about it. Mum and Dad sometimes go

to the Harvest Festival service, if they're not too busy. And I can remember going to the Christmas carol service a couple of times when I was young. But that's it.'

'What about the other students? Did any of them consider this Godslayer concept to be sacrilegious?'

'Nobody ever said anything, no.'

'OK. Was Kitchener working on any kind of energy generating system; like microfusion, or proton boron fusion, something new, something radical?'

Nicholas screwed his face up. 'Nothing like that. He gave me a magnetosphere induction problem to solve, though.'

'What's that?'

'Well, it's hardly new, but if you place a length of wire in orbit, its motion as it moves through the Earth's magnetosphere will generate an electric current. It's a simple induction principle, like a generator.'

'How big a current?'

'That depends on the size of the cable, obviously.'

'Yeah, right.' Maybe the boy wasn't so different after all. 'What I need to know, Nicholas, is are you talking about something that can power an AV player, or a city?'

'Oh. A city, definitely, or maybe a medium-sized town. Kitchener was very insistent about that. He said that we had to learn to concentrate on the practical applications of physics, abstract theory was all very well but it doesn't pay the bills. He was right, of course, he was always right. He called it his ninety-ten law. He let us study abstract theories for ninety per cent of the time, but we had to spend at least ten per cent of each week working on practical ideas. He used to set us two projects simultaneously, one of each.'

'How far had you got with this magnetosphere project?'

'I hadn't done much work on it at all, I was spending most of my time on the dark-mass project. But I did confirm its basic validity. I designed a cobweb array, about two hundred and fifty kilometres across. The beauty of that is, if you give it a slight spin it will retain its shape without any additional structural material, you only need the cables themselves. I was going to work on strength of materials limits next. But . . .'

'I thought beaming power down from space was ecologically unsound.'

Nicholas smiled vacantly. 'I was going to use a superconductor cable, tethered between the Equator and geostationary orbit. That's a perfectly practical solution; the orbital tower is an idea even older than magnetosphere induction. It was originally suggested that you build it with magnetic rails and run lift capsules up and down, that way you'd never need any sort of spaceplane to get into orbit. My version was a lot simpler and cheaper, just a single strand fixed to a station that could receive power beamed to it from the induction webs, a bigger version of the communication platforms that are up there now. The superconductor would have to be held up by a monolattice filament, of course, it couldn't possibly support its own weight. It was Kitchener who suggested it as an alternative method of bringing the power down. He joked about it, he said he'd be as rich as Julia Evans if it was ever built. He gets a royalty from monolattice filament, you see. It's only a fraction of a per cent, but for a cable thirty-six thousand kilometres long, it would be a hell of a lot of money. He was really keen to see how the figures came out.'

'Nicholas, how advanced is this project? I mean, could it actually be built with today's technology?'

'I don't know. It was really just a thought experiment, Kitchener tailored them to match our fields of expertise. The equations were interesting, I had to juggle so many factors, but it did look like it would come out pretty expensive. That's why I was excited about Event Horizon's new spaceplane, the way it's going to bring launch costs down. I was going to include those figures in my analysis.'

'But you never got round to it?'

'No.'

'Was the project stored in the Abbey's Bendix?'

'Yes, but I kept a back-up file in my terminal. It should still be there.'

'Did you ever tell Randon that you were working on this idea?'

'Oh, no, I never discussed it with anybody else apart from the other students.'

'So the company never really showed much interest in what you were doing at Launde?'

'They offered me the sponsorship money and a guaranteed research position, that's all. Kitchener's students have this reputation, you see. It's a bit snobby, but a lot of them have turned out to be real high-achievers.'

'Yeah.' Greg couldn't help thinking about Ranasfari. You couldn't get any further apart than him and Kitchener, the cold aesthetic and the glorious old debauchee. The chemistry must have been there, though; Ranasfari clearly revered his mentor. And Kitchener had spotted the potential, just like he had with Nicholas.

'It was all arranged through an agency in Cambridge,' Nicholas said. 'They specialize in placing graduates. I've never actually met anyone from the company itself. I was looking forward to working in France.'

'Do you speak French?'

'Not very well. I've got one of those teach yourself courses on an audio memox. I'll speak it properly by the time . . . I mean, I would have spoken it properly by the time I finished my second year at Launde. There's only a vocabulary and syntax to memorize, that's not much of a problem for me.'

'Interesting. You have a lot of confidence in your memory, don't you?'

'Yes, my recall is virtually perfect. I wasn't trying to boast,' he added contritely.

'I didn't say you were.'

'Kitchener said I should be proud of it. He said it was better than his.'

'Have you ever had days which you can't remember? Events that are lost to you?'

Nicholas regarded him with a tinge of suspicion. 'You mean like transient global amnesia?'

Greg was suddenly glad his thoughts weren't available for Nicholas to read. But he really should have known better than trying to creep up on a topic with Nicholas, especially anything remotely connected with science. 'Yeah, transient global amnesia; or even trauma erasure.'

'You think that's why your psi faculty didn't spot any guilt, isn't it? That I did murder Kitchener, and I just blanked it out.'

'It's a possibility, Nicholas, and you know it is.'

The swift heat of belligerence faded from the boy. 'Yes,' he said softly. 'But I don't have blackouts. And I've never forgotten a day or an hour in my life.'

'OK.'

'I was telling the truth then, wasn't I?'

'Yes, Nicholas. You've never suffered from memory loss.' He rose to his feet, still as undecided as when he'd walked in. 'I'll let you know what happens.'

'Mr Mandel. Thanks.'

'You're not out of it yet.'

*

The CID office had been deluged with another wave of entropy. There were more folders and memox crystals littering the desks. Crumpled fast-food wrappers bubbled up out of the bin, waxed kelpboard trays with congealed smears of sweet and sour sauce.

The detectives formed their usual closed-ranks knot around one of the desks beside the situation screen. Greg was given some dark speculative looks as he came in. Only Amanda acknow-ledged him with anything approaching a smile. Vernon Langley broke away from the group, another man following him.

'Did he admit anything?' he asked.

'No.'

'Christ, that kid is a smooth one. What about your esp, did you pick up any guilt waves this time?'

'No,' Greg said curtly.

'Shame about that.'

'Yeah.'

Vernon held up his police-issue cybofax. 'I asked the lab to re-run tests on the samples Beswick supplied.'

'And?'

'No trace of scopolamine, or any other drug. The boy's blood chemistry is perfectly balanced.'

'OK, it was just a thought.'

'I asked the lab people about scopolamine. You think Beswick made himself forget the murder?'

'It's one option, because he certainly doesn't remember. There must be a reason. What about his medical records?'

Vernon handed over the cybofax. Greg skipped down the datasheet it was displaying. There wasn't much; the usual child-hood illnesses, chicken pox, mumps; a bad dose of flu when he was five; a sprained ankle at eleven. The last entry was a routine health check when he started university: again perfectly clean. Nicholas Beswick was a healthy, ordinary young man.

'Bugger,' Greg mumbled.

'Anything there throw any light on the problem?' Vernon asked.

'No, not a bloody thing.'

'Didn't think there was.' He beckoned. 'This is Sergeant Keith Willet,' he said as his companion came forward. 'Been at Oak-ham quite a while now.'

Greg shook hands comfortably. The sergeant was wearing white shirtsleeves and shorts, regulation black tie in a tiny knot. He was in his early fifties, with the kind of hardened patience that said he'd just about seen it all. If he'd been in the army he would have been perfect sergeant-major material.

'You were here during the PSP years?' Greg asked.

'Yes, sir,' he said. 'Twenty years' service in Oakham now.'

'You might have been right about Launde,' Vernon told Greg. 'Though I still don't see how this fits in with Kitchener's murder.'

Greg looked at Willet. 'You remembered something about the Abbey?'

'Yes, sir. There was a girl drowned in one of the lakes in Launde Park.'

'Shit, yeah!' *Now* he remembered. It had been on a local datatext channel, quite a few years ago. The report had gone on to say that the police were questioning the Abbey's other residents about the accident. At the time he had assumed it was the start of a PSP campaign against Edward Kitchener. Anything like that had interested him in those days; someone as prominent as Kitchener would have made a tremendous addition to the underground opposition. But nothing had ever come of it.

The detectives had all turned to stare at his exclamation.

Greg ignored them. 'Can you remember her name?' he asked.

'Clarissa Wynne,' Willet said. 'She was one of Dr Kitchener's students.'

The name didn't mean anything. 'When was this?'

'About ten years ago, sir. Can't say exactly.'

'Do you remember anything about the case?'

Willet glanced at Langley. He nodded, albeit with a trace of reluctance. Greg wondered what had been said before he arrived.

'Yes, sir, I'm afraid I do. We were ordered to shut it down, straight away, enter a verdict of accidental death. It came direct from the Ministry of Public Order.'

'Jesus, the PSP wanted it kept quiet? Why?'

'I've no idea, sir.'

'Was it an accidental death?'

Willet took his time answering. Greg sensed the disquiet in his mind, a real conflict raging. It was almost as though he was confessing a sin, relieved and shamed at the same time.

'The detective in charge was unhappy about the order. The girl had been drinking, but he thought it was more than student high-jinks that had gone wrong. But there was nothing he could do, certainly not launch an investigation. London said frog, and we all hopped. That was all we ever did in those days.'

'Who was the detective?'

Willet gazed straight at him. 'Maurice Knebel, sir.'

'Ah,' said Greg. Maurice Knebel was the major reason Oakham's police force had such poor relations with the local community. In the last two years of the PSP decade, when it was obvious to everyone else that the Party was faltering, Maurice Knebel had done his best to maintain their authority in Rutland, sending out the People's Constables at the smallest provocation. He epitomized the petty-minded *apparatchik*, blindly following the Party line, the kind who had inflicted almost as much damage on President Armstrong as the urban predators themselves. He was on the Inquisitor's top fifty wanted list. Notoriety of sorts. Nobody had seen him since the night the PSP fell. He had escaped the station minutes before the mob arrived, high on the deadly scent of freedom and vengeance. Not all the People's Constables had been so lucky.

'I didn't even know he was a genuine detective,' Greg said.

'Yes, sir, started out a regular officer. He didn't go bad until later.'

'How much later?'

'Sir?'

'You said he was upset about being ordered to close the book on the drowned girl. Was he a Party member then?'

'I think so. But he wasn't fanatical back in those days. He saw joining the Party as a way to promotion. It was the last three years, after he was appointed as the station's political officer, that's when the real trouble began.'

'OK, fine, I appreciate your help.'

'Sir.' He left the CID office, visibly relieved.

'Well?' Langley asked.

The detectives were still watching him, waiting for the verdict. The psychic's pronouncement.

'Why on earth would the PSP want to hush up a girl student's death? Kitchener wasn't exactly one of their own.'

'You think Kitchener killed her?' Langley asked.

He thought of that white-haired old man watching Isabel undress. The picture he'd built up from all the students, Ranasfari, the worship they awarded him. A larger than life character, capable of both disgraceful roguishness and unselfish charity. 'No, I don't. Let's have a look at the coroner's report. I suppose it'll be a whitewash, but there may be something in it.'

Langley rubbed awkwardly at his chin. The detectives were all abruptly occupied at their work again.

'Sorry, Greg, we can't do that.'

'I thought my Home Office authorization is still valid.'

'It is,' he said drily. 'But the local coroner's office has the same problem we do. The hotrods crashed their memory core when Armstrong was ousted. There are no records left for the PSP years.'

'They crashed a coroner's office? What the hell for? Coroners weren't anything to do with the PSP.'

'I've no idea. Perhaps they regarded all officialdom as the same.'

That familiar cold electric charge compressed his spine. And the gland was barely active. He almost smiled, despite the worry. 'No, I don't think so.'

'Why not?'

'Intuition.' He turned to the group of detectives. 'Amanda, would you run a check through the Home Office for me? I want to know how many other coroner's offices were burnt by the hotrods when the PSP fell.'

She nodded and sat behind one of the desks, activating its terminal.

'Look, Greg' – Langley was trying for the reasonable approach – 'I really appreciate your help in finding the knife. But Clarissa Wynne's death is hardly relevant.'

'Two deaths in the same community, the first one questionable, the second one bizarre. They're connected, no messing.'

'How? They're ten years apart.'

'If I knew more about Clarissa Wynne I might be able to tell you.'

'I can hardly expand the Kitchener case to cover her death. For a start there isn't a single byte on her remaining. We don't even know what she looked like.'

'Yeah.' He let instinct drive him. Important, the girl's death was important. 'Tell you, we're going to have to rectify that.'

'Not after ten years, we're not. The only person who could have told you anything was Kitchener.'

'Wrong. There's Kitchener, the other five students who were at Launde with her, and Maurice Knebel. And out of all of them, good old Maurice has everything about the case I need to know.'

'Knebel? You can't be serious! For Christ's sake, we don't even know if he's still alive.'

'I'll find out.'

He threw his hands in the air. 'Sure you will. I mean, the Inquisitors have only been looking for four years, and their methods don't exactly go by the book. They wouldn't know what a warrant looked like if it pissed on their boot.'

'Nobody can run from Mindstar, not for ever, not even close.' Greg said it with a deliberate bite of menace, enjoying the way it halted Langley's bumptiousness in midflight.

'Greg?' Amanda waved at him from behind her desk. He could see the cube had filled with datasheets, fuzzy green script with a perceptible Y-axis instability.

'What have you got?'

'There were five other coroner's offices in England which had their records destroyed in the two months either side of the PSP's fall. Two were due to firebomb attacks, the other three were hotrod burns.'

'Where were the ones that got burnt by the hotrods?'

She ran a finger down the cube. 'Gloucester, Canterbury, and Hexham.'

'Well spread around,' he mused.

'What are you saying?' Langley asked.

'That it's convenient; four offices in the whole of the country, and one of them is Oakham's, when we know that a dodgy report was loaded into its memory core.'

'You can't be serious.'

Greg clapped him on the shoulder, drawing a startled look. He knew Langley would never believe in a connection. The man was too good a policeman. Facts, facts, and more facts. That's what he needed.

It's also what you need to get Nicholas off, Greg reminded himself soberly.

'You keep plugging away at Nicholas,' he said. 'I'll need to borrow Sergeant Willet for the rest of the afternoon.'

'All right.' Langley seemed relieved that was all he was being asked for. 'Why do you want him?'

'I told you: to find Maurice Knebel.'

21

The light was already beginning to fade as Eleanor drove out of Oakham along the B668, up the hill towards Burley. An advance guard of dark copper-gold clouds probing out of the north had reached the zenith of the opal sky. She wasn't in much of a mood to appreciate sunsets.

The *Rutland Times* hadn't been able to help. Hotrods had crashed their memory core. They had suffered an even worse data loss than the *Stamford and Rutland Mercury*; all of their past issues had been transferred to the core from earlier microfiche records.

She hadn't known the hotrods were so active when the PSP fell. Royan had let slip a few hints that he had been part of the pack which had crashed the Ministry of Public Order mainframe. But as a general rule the PSP had suffered remarkably little electronic sabotage during its decade in power. Maybe the hotrods had been saving themselves for the final assault. Although she found that hard to credit. They were too independent, preserving their anonymity through the faceless circuit. You could call them through the link they had infiltrated into English Telecom's datanet, but you never knew who you'd got.

The Ministry of Public Order mainframe was an obvious target for them, one final shove to a government which was already toppling. It had happened within an hour of the bomb blast that annihilated Downing Street. People had talked about a link between the hotrod circuit and the urban predators, she thought that was pure tabloid, a subconscious public desire to juggle facts into a unified conspiracy theory. The mainframe burn wouldn't have required much forward planning, the viruses already existed, but newspapers were a different proposition. To be burnt on ideological grounds their output would have to be monitored continually, victims selected. That required organization, commitment. A cabal within a cabal. There had certainly never been any word of that. Perhaps Royan could tell her.

Forewarned by her failure at the *Rutland Times* office, she had returned to the parked Jaguar and simply phoned the *Melton Times*.

'I'm very sorry, madam,' the secretary had told her. 'But our records of that period were erased by hackers.'

'There is no such thing as coincidence,' Gabriel had said quietly, as Eleanor swore at the cybofax.

'What do you mean?'

But Gabriel simply shrugged cryptically.

Then Greg had called, and asked her to drive up to Colin Mellor in Cottesmore, saying, 'I'll meet you up there.'

The Jaguar's wheels scattered a volley of loose chippings into the lush verges as they reached the top of the vale, rattling the big scarlet geraniums which had infiltrated the old hedgerows. Four hundred metres to her right she could see the ruins of Burley House casting a stark jagged outline against the rising velvet penumbra. A few fires were burning in the camp of New Age travellers parked in the embrace of its long curving colonnade wings, pink and blue glow of charcoal cooking grills spilling distorted pools of tangerine light. The travellers had been there for as long as Eleanor could remember, ever since the public petrol supply ran out, the wheels of their antique buses and vans rooting in the earth, tyres perished. Not that the ancient combustion engines would work now anyway.

They had raided the stately home for stones, constructing crude lean-tos against some of the rusting vehicles. A hundred metres from the road, they had tried to build a replica of

Stonehenge. Still were trying, by all accounts, it changed minutely every time she went past. Not getting any bigger, but the configuration altered, as if they were still searching for the ideal pattern of astrological harmony.

Keeps them off the streets, she thought wryly. God alone knows where they were supposed to fit in to the promised land of New Conservative regeneration policies. After fifteen years of doing nothing but picking and eating magic mushrooms their brains must look like lumps of gangrenous sponge.

There was an estate of late twentieth-century brick houses on the edge of Cottesmore, ornamental gardens given over to intensely cultivated vegetable plots.

As they moved into the heart of the picturesque village she leant forwards, peering over the steering-wheel. She'd never been to Colin Mellor's house before.

'Further on,' Gabriel said.

'Right.' She hadn't actually expected Gabriel to come with her to the *Rutland Times* office. Conversation was always so difficult with Gabriel, and this time, with Joey Foulkes tagging along loyally, it was virtually impossible.

The main street had a blanket preservation order slapped on it. All the buildings had stone walls, roofs were either grey slate or Collyweston stone. Half of them used to be thatch, which had to be stripped off when the Warming started and the fire hazard became too great. Three staked goats were grazing on a wide grass verge in front of a row of cottages. Several men were sitting with their pint pots at bench tables outside the Sun, thin rings of foam marking their progress.

'Here we go.' Gabriel pointed to a wooden bar gate in a long ivy-clad wall opposite the pub.

Eleanor indicated and turned off. Greg was standing on the other side of the gate. He grinned and tugged at the bolt.

The house was a big converted barn, L-shaped, with a steep grey slate roof. Dull silver windows reflected the sun falling behind the pub. She drew up next to the EMC Ranger on the fine gravel park outside the front doors. There was a long meadow at the rear; she saw three or four horses at the far end, dark coats merging into the twilight.

A police sergeant she didn't recognize was climbing out of the EMC Ranger, screwing his cap ceremoniously into place.

'We only just got here,' said Greg. He introduced the sergeant as Keith Willet.

The house's iron-bound front door opened. Colin Mellor stood inside, leaning on a wooden walking stick; a seventy-two-year-old with bushy white hair, wearing baggy green corduroy trousers and a mauve cardigan. A huge Alsatian nosed round his legs, staring at the visitors. Eleanor shuddered slightly at the sight of the animal. It was a gene-tailored guard hound; grey-furred, muscles sculpted for speed, supposedly owner-obedient. That was a trait which the geneticists didn't always succeed in splicing together correctly. Greg had told her that when the original military combat hounds were taken into the field some of them had turned on their handlers.

And she'd seen first-hand what the modified beasts could do to people. It had been a gene-tailored sentinel panther which attacked Suzi.

'It's friends, look, Sparky,' Colin said, patting the dog's head. 'They're all friends.' The dog gazed round at them with big cat-iris eyes, and blinked lazily. It looked back up at Colin. Reluctantly, Eleanor thought. She could see Joey Foulkes all tensed up, hand hovering near the give-away bulge under his suit jacket.

'Well, come in,' said Colin. The stick was shaken vigorously for emphasis. 'Sparky's smelt you all now. He likes you.' He backed into the hall, shooing the dog out of the way.

Eleanor found Greg's hand and held him tightly as they went inside.

Colin led them into his lounge. It was on the ground floor, furnished in plain teak, the upholstery a light green; big french windows gave him a view out across the meadow. Biolum globes in smoked-glass pendant shades cast a strong light. There were pictures of battle scenes on every wall; the army from the Napoleonic wars right up to Turkey.

'Before anything else,' Eleanor said to Greg, 'I've got some bad news for you. The *Stamford and Rutland Mercury*, the *Rutland Times*, and the *Melton Times* all had their memory cores crashed by the hotrods. The circuit said they were too sympathetic to the PSP. So there's no record of any incident at Launde Abbey.'

Greg clamped a hand on each forearm, and kissed her warmly. 'The hotrods crashed the coroner's office as well,' he said. The pleased tone confused her momentarily.

Colin eased himself delicately into a manor wing chair. Eleanor hadn't seen him since the wedding last year, and even then she'd only had a few words. She thought he looked a lot frailer.

'Now then, Greg,' Colin said. 'What's all this about?'

Eleanor listened to Greg summarizing the case. Somehow she couldn't draw much comfort from the enigma surrounding Clarissa Wynne's death. Greg's intuition had been right. As usual. But the entire sequence of events was becoming equivocal, shaded in a formless grey murk seeping out of the hinterlands, eroding facts before her eyes. It was sadly depressing.

Greg was in his element, of course. And Gabriel, although to a lesser degree.

Right at the centre of her mind was a tired little girl who wanted to say: 'I saw Nicholas do it. That's an end. Let's leave it.' Why do adults always have to be so bloody noble and resolute?

'Someone has gone to a lot of trouble to erase every trace of Clarissa Wynne,' Greg said. 'Not to mention expense. Hotrods don't come cheap, and they've burnt three newspapers plus a coroner's office; maybe Oakham police station was part of it, maybe not. But the fact remains, every last hard byte on the girl has gone. All we're left with is personal memories. And precious few of them.'

'What about the international news libraries?' Colin asked.

'I checked with Julia,' Greg said. 'They all have files on Kitchener, of course. None of them mention Clarissa Wynne.

It was a local matter, and as far as anyone knew an accidental death. Not important enough. Although Globecast's Pan-Europe news and current affairs office think there might have been some kind of hotrod burn against their memory cores. Several file codes relating to that period were scrambled. But they can't actually find anything missing, so there's no way of proving it.'

'I doubt they could help anyway,' Eleanor said. 'If there had been any suspicion that Kitchener was implicated in that girl's death, it would have been headline news the world over. I'd say the PSP's cover-up worked pretty well.'

'Yeah,' Greg admitted.

'Which is where I come in,' Colin said. There was a cheerful smile on his pale face.

Eleanor had the notion he was terribly grateful to be asked. Eager to show he could still pull his weight, not let the side down. Except it was so painfully obvious his health was decaying rapidly. His heart, she guessed.

'If you could,' Greg said. He flashed her a shamefaced look. 'There's no better tracker.'

'Certainly can,' Colin said proudly. 'The map room's down the corridor.' He pressed both hands against the chair, struggling to rise. Joey Foulkes came forward to help him, but he shook off the young hard-liner with exaggerated self-reliance.

*

The map room was a plain white cube, three metres to a side, windowless. It put Eleanor in mind of Kitchener's computer room. Sparky wasn't allowed in.

The biolum panels came on to show a circular flatscreen mounted on one wall. There was a single 'ware module on the floor in a corner.

Colin gave a voice command to the 'ware, and a map of England appeared on the flatscreen. He stood in front of it, both hands pressed on the bulb of his stick, and looked the outline up and down, nodding in satisfaction. 'It's there, Greg, I can still do it, by God!' His voice was a weak growl.

'That's why I came,' Greg said. 'Nobody else in your class.'

She could detect a tremor in his voice. When she looked his eyes were dark with pain. She fumbled for his hand.

'Talk to me, young Keith,' Colin said.

Willet twitched uncomfortably. 'What about, sir?'

'This dreadful Maurice Knebel chap, of course. I need your mind's image of him to work on.'

'Sir?'

'Tell us about an incident you remember,' Greg said. 'A station cricket match where he got caught out. What did he wear? Bad habits, good habits. What sort of food did he eat? Who were his friends?'

'Yes, sir. Well, there was one suit which he always wore, this would be around the time of the Wynne girl's death I suppose. Brown and grey, check, it was. Used to get some stick about it.'

Eleanor filtered out what the sergeant was saying. It was almost unfair to make someone so stolid and reliable relate trivial tales from the past.

Colin had become preternaturally still. His stare had developed that distance of all gland users, seeing at ninety degrees to the real universe.

The old man had been a major in an English army infantry regiment at the time when the Mindstar Brigade was being formed. He was fifty-five and due for imminent retirement when the blanket service psi-assessment tests gave him the excuse he needed to extend his beloved commission. Mindstar hadn't intended to take anyone his age, but his farsight rating was one of the highest they recorded. Fortunately his ESP faculty had almost developed as it was intended.

Willet was droning on about Maurice Knebel and his fondness for Indian food when Colin leant forwards and deftly pressed his open palm against the flatscreen. The map image shifted instantly, expanding the area around his hand. It was centred on Peterborough, she noticed with a start. The vivid featureless turquoise of the Fens Basin had bitten into a third of the screen.

Willet had stopped talking.

'Keep going,' Colin instructed.

'Sir. Curries were his favourite . . .'

Eleanor could see a lone yellow dot in the basin, just east of Peterborough. Prior's Fen, she realized. Colin must keep the map scrupulously updated. He had spent most of the PSP years in France, charging kombinates a small fortune for his services. 'Too old to join the fight against Armstrong,' he had told her bitterly.

He touched the map again. This time Peterborough jumped up to occupy half of the flatscreen, leaving a ten-kilometre band of countryside visible around the outside.

Willet flashed Greg a despairing glance. Greg gave him a fast gesture: *carry on*.

'The woman he was living with left him when he was appointed station political officer. There was talk of him and one of the *apparatchik* women on the town's PSP committee . . .'

'Here,' Colin said. His forefinger touched the map in a positive jab. A district turned a shade lighter, its scarlet boundary line flashing insistently. He stood right up against the screen, face coated in a backwash of artificial blue and yellow radiance, deepening the folds of flesh. 'That's where he is. I can't get any more precise than that. Not from this distance.'

Eleanor could feel a groan of dismay building in her gullet. She was afraid to let it out in case it sounded too much like a whimper.

'Figures,' Greg said. 'He's PSP, where else would he be perfectly safe right now?'

Colin's forefinger was pointing at Walton.

22

Greg's existence had collapsed to a flimsy universe five metres in diameter. Night-time flying was always bad. But night-time and fog, that was shit awful.

He was hanging in a nylon web harness below a Westland ghost wing, gossamer blade propeller humming efficiently behind him. The photon amp band across his eyes bestowed an alien blue tinge to every surface, the glow of electron orbits in decay. A column of neat chrome-yellow figures shone on the right-hand side of his vision field: time, grid reference, altitude, direction of flight, power levels, airspeed. The guido 'ware placed him eight hundred metres high, two kilometres out from Peter-borough above the Fens basin.

Prior's Fen, and the Event Horizon security division tilt-fan which had ferried him and Teddy out there, was twenty minutes behind, isolated by treacherously fluctuating walls of stone-grey vapour. The loneliness which had insinuated itself into his thoughts in that time was total, tricking his brain into finding shapes among the grey-blue desolation, the grinning spectres of nightmare clamouring in on an unwary mind.

He used to be able to put his feelings on hold for missions, concentrate on details and their application to the immediate. It was the army way, training and discipline could overcome every human frailty given time. But he'd lost it. Leaking slowly out of his psyche during endless sunny days beside the reservoir, smoothed away by Eleanor's kisses.

Now he could feel the unfamiliar and enervating stirrings of panic as the wing membrane murmured to itself in the squally air. His sole link to reality was a slim microwave beam punching up through the cloying seaborne mist to strike Event Horizon's private communication satellite in geosync orbit. Directional, scrambled, ultra-secure.

'You there, Teddy?' The modulated question slicing upwards, hitting the satellite's phased array antenna, splitting like a laser fired at a fractured mirror, bounced straight back down. Two beams: one received at the Event Horizon headquarters building in Westwood, the second targeted on another ephemeral five-metre bubble somewhere in the vast emptiness behind him.

'Where the fuck else?' Teddy's gruffness carried a trace of anxiety which Greg was learning to recognize from his own voice.

'Hey, you remember when we used to get paid for this?'

'Yeah. Nothing fucking changes. Weren't no fun in them days, neither.'

'True. OK, I'm one and a half klicks from the east shore now, starting to descend. Morgan? Any air traffic yet?'

'Negative, Greg,' Morgan said, his voice sounding muffled in Greg's earpiece. 'There's some tilt-fan activity in New Eastfield, but the fog has shut down ninety per cent of the city's usual movements.'

That was one sliver of joy, he didn't have to worry about colliding with low-flying planes. 'Roger. Going down.' He shifted his weight slightly, feeling the angle of the slipstream change. The fog density remained the same. According to Event Horizon's Earth Resource platforms it was a belt ninety kilometres wide, extending westwards almost all the way to Leicester. They had watched it boil up out of the North Sea through most of the afternoon. Perfect cover.

*

The mission had taken a day to set up. Naturally, Julia had wanted to send the police in, all legal and above board. She hadn't quite grasped what they were up against. Someone – some organization? – methodical enough to guard against the remotest chance of a query being raised about the death of a girl ten years in the past. Paranoia or desperation – either way, they had it in massive quantities. And they didn't shy away from positive action to eliminate threats.

Even with the channels working themselves into hysterics over the Scottish reunion question, a police operation on a scale large enough to successfully arrest a single man in Walton would attract wide newscast coverage. The Blackshirts would resist the police incursion, there would be riots, sniper fire, a lot of people hurt. After that, leaks would be inevitable, and Julia's name would be foremost among them.

His way was much quieter, safer. Reducing the risk until it focused on just two people.

He would have been happier if Eleanor had shouted at him, put her foot down, told him he was being macho stupid. At least he would have been able to shout back, or argue, vent a bit of feeling. Instead she had stuck to being silent and sorrowful. Which made it harder. Which put him on edge. Which wasn't good.

Gabriel had been reassuringly scathing, but that had taken on the quality of a ritual, she trusted his intuition almost more than he did. Morgan was frankly sceptical about the whole notion. And Greg had to admit even he was having trouble seeing how Clarissa Wynne's vaguely suspicious drowning could be connected to Kitchener's murder.

With the cocoon of fog acting like a mild form of sensory deprivation his thoughts were free to roam through wilder realms of possibility, fantasy equivalents of Gabriel's tau lines. But even among the more fanciful possibilities he conjured up there really was no getting round that memory of Nicholas walking so calmly into Kitchener's bedroom. Maybe the ambiguity he felt so strongly was focused on the boy's motive? Everyone assumed

Nicholas had murdered Kitchener because he was overwrought over Isabel. But there was the question of the method. Maybe Launde harboured some dark secret instead?

Yeah sure. Ghosts and ghoulies and bumps in the night, he told himself mockingly. Secret monsters would be too easy. Somebody wiped all those cores. Three and a half years before Nicholas Beswick ever set eyes on Launde Abbey.

He gave up, pushing the load into the future and squarely on Maurice Knebel's shoulders. Alarmed at just how much he was coming to depend on the absconded detective to provide him with answers when they finally came face to face.

One thing, there was no going back. There never bloody was; his character flaw.

*

His guido put him seven hundred metres out from the city's easterly shore, height one hundred and fifty metres. Closing fast. Fog split around the leading edge of the wing, re-forming instantly behind the trailing edge. A slick coating of minute droplets was deposited on the leathery membrane, streaming backwards and shaking free in a horizontal rain.

The photon amp was boosted up to its highest resolution. He still couldn't see anything.

'Virtual overlay,' he told the guido 'ware. Translucent green and blue and red petals flipped up into the retinal feed from the photon amp. He looked out across a city built from frozen laserlight.

Morgan's people had built the virtual simulation up from the afternoon's satellite passes. Accurate to ten centimetres, more comprehensive than any memory in the city council's planning office data cores.

A flood of neutral pixels darkened and hardened below him, resolving into a solid black plane. He felt the illusion of space opening up around him again. Tremendously reassuring.

He just prayed that the simulation's alignment was correct.

The shoreline buildings of the Gunthorpe district formed a

flat abrupt wall of dimensionless green dead ahead. It was the only eastern district to expand since the Warming; a quirk of fate had placed it alongside a low triangular promontory jutting a couple of kilometres out into the basin. The fields and pastures which had survived the deluge had been swiftly covered in blocks of flats.

Two hundred metres off the promontory's tip was a patch of spiky indigo waveforms, as though an iceberg had endured the Warming and sought shelter in the basin. It was Eye, a village still in the process of being subsumed by the sluggish currents of the mire, reduced to an erratic formation of mud dunes and crumbling brick walls.

The guido 'ware printed a trajectory graphic for him. A tunnel of slender orange rings snaking away from him, round the north side of the urbanized promontory, and curving down to touch Walton.

Greg swung himself to one side, lining up the ghost wing in the centre of the tunnel. Orange rings flashed past silently.

*

Morgan had wanted to send one of his security division hard-liners along on the penetration mission. Greg turned him down politely, hoping he wouldn't make an issue of it. They were tough and well trained, but there was a world of difference between corporate clashes and all-out combat. He needed some-one he could rely on totally.

Back in Turkey, Greg had been in charge of a tactical raider squad when they were cut off and pinned down in a mountain village by Legion fire. Half of the men had wanted to make a break for it, but Greg made them stay put. Teddy was in charge of the back-up team.

He had spent the next three hours cowering under a dusty sky as bullets thudded into the sandstone walls of dilapidated hovels, and mortar rounds fell all around. Time had stretched out excruciatingly, but he never let go of that tenuous trust in his huge sergeant.

Teddy had eventually turned up in their ageing Belgian Air Force Black Hawk support helicopter, flown by a shaken, terrified pilot. Greg didn't learn until much later how Teddy persuaded the man to fly into the heart of a grade three fire zone. There would have been a court martial, except the pilot refused to testify.

Eleanor's right, I do dwell on Turkey too much.

But he was bloody glad it was Teddy in the second ghost wing.

*

The orange circles took him round the north of Gunthorpe. Here the basin mud had surged along a slight depression between Walton and Werrington, engulfing roads and buildings. It was only a metre deep, but the relentless pressure eroded bricks and concrete, exploiting every crack and crevice. Foundations were eaten away, day by day, year by year, cement pulverized, reinforcement prongs corroded, bricks sucked out. Roofs had collapsed, the abraded walls sagged then fell. Even now the piles of rubble were still being assaulted from below, dragged down by the unstable alluvial substratum, a pressure that wouldn't end until the entire zone was levelled. Weeds and reeds choked the rolling mounds in a mouldy mat of entwined tendrils. The satellite image had shown the whole area crisscrossed by paths worn by adventurous children, glimmers of metal detritus peeking through the limp foliage.

The virtual simulation had shaded it in as a lightly rucked pink desert.

One hundred metres in altitude; and five hundred metres up ahead the tunnel of rings had dipped down at a steep angle, narrowing like a whirlwind to touch the apex of an old factory warehouse.

Greg dimmed the simulation, reducing it to a geometric lithograph. He banked the Westland to starboard, preparing to overfly the warehouse roof. The tunnel twisted into an impossible helix. He throttled back the propeller speed to idle, and glided in.

At last he thought he saw something through the scudding fog. Down below, a pale blur, broken by dark irregular smudges. According to the simulation he ought to be over the factory's yard. Big squares of cracked concrete with abandoned gutted lorries, a scattered cluster of railway van bogies in one corner.

With a bit of imagination the dark smudges below could be rusted cabs.

The simulated green skeletal outline of the warehouse was upon him. If it corresponded with the actual structure the Westland should take him six metres above the roof apex.

Solid surfaces suddenly materialized between the green lines, as if the building had been edged in neon tubes. Greg received a fast impression of breeze blocks smeared in rheumy ribbons of algae, and a corrugated roof, red oxide paint flaking away. He laughed as he twisted the throttle grip, shooting back up into the veil of fog.

'Morgan? Tell your programming team they've got a big drink coming. The guido virtual is perfect. I've just surveyed the landing site.'

'Glad to hear it. Could you see anybody waiting?'

'No. It looks clear. I'm going around.'

He made a leisurely turn, and headed back towards the warehouse. This time he came in lower. The orange tunnel stretched out ahead, perfectly level. It terminated halfway up the slope of the roof.

He saw the corrugated panels again, four seconds before he reached them. Legs running in mid-air. Then the rubber soles of his desert boots slapped down.

Every nerve was raw-edged with tension. If the panels couldn't take his weight he was in deep shit and no messing. The satellite image interpreters swore they would hold.

The noise of his running feet sounded like a drum beat after the graveyard silence of flight. He could feel the panels bending slightly under his heels. The apex was three metres ahead of him. Still the panels held.

He yanked savagely at the throttle grip, reversing the propeller pitch. Tilting the wing back up as he fought to kill his forward momentum. The sudden backward impetus nearly toppled him.

'Shitfire! Tell you, next time we do as Julia says and send in the cavalry.'

'Greg?' Teddy called. 'You down, boy?'

He was crouched a metre short of the apex, balancing the wing precariously. Fog swirled beyond the guttering, cutting off any view of the yard below.

'Yeah. Wait one.'

He killed the virtual simulation overlay then activated the Westland's retraction catch. There was a wet slithering sound as the wing folded. The steering bar hinged up and back. He grappled with the frame, slapping the harness release. The ghost wing finished up as a fat damp cylinder three metres long, which he could just hold under one arm.

He scrambled up to the apex, and walked down to the end. When he peered over he could just make out the base of the wall, lined with tufts of grass and sickly dandelions. There was a monotonous dripping from the broken guttering. The roof would give them ample clearance for a swoop launch after they had completed the mission, a genuine running jump. Of course, they had both been trained to launch from a much lower height, and a shallower slope. But those lessons had been an uncomfortably long time ago now.

'OK, Teddy. The panels are solid, and our take-off run is clear. I'm on the southern end of the roof. Come in when you're ready.'

'Gotcha.'

Greg unslung his pack, and riffled through it, looking for the climbing gear. The propeller noise of Teddy's Westland was just audible as he overflew the warehouse on his guido check pass.

'Hell, Morgan, this 'ware is ultra-cool,' Teddy exclaimed. 'The virtual matches clean down the line.'

'All Event Horizon gear works like that.' Morgan sounded slightly indignant.

'Yeah? Man, I wish we'd had this in Turkey. Would've shown 'em Legion bastards.'

Greg found the vibration knife, a slim black plastic handle with a telescoping blade. He crouched down and pressed it against the breeze block just below the edge of the roof. Grey dust spurted out as the blade drove in, buzzing like an ireful wasp.

'Comin' round,' Teddy said. 'Here we go. Jesus Lord protect your dumb-ass servant.'

Greg shoved an expander crampon into the hole. It clicked solidly, locking into place.

Teddy's feet banged loudly on the roof, an elephant charging across sheet metal.

'Teddy!'

'Jeeze.' Teddy was wheezing; an indistinct figure slouched over the apex. 'Greg, I ain't no fucking bat.'

'Yeah, right.'

'Everything all right?' Morgan asked.

'We're down,' Greg said. He clipped a climbing rope into the crampon's eye, and let the coil fall down the side of the wall. Behind him he could hear Teddy folding his Westland ghost wing.

'Roger,' said Morgan. 'The security team is on alert.'

'We'll shout if we want them,' Greg said. Just knowing the hard-line crash recovery team was waiting, that their tilt-fan could be with him in minutes if he hit any hazards, was a heady boost. Rule one: always sort out your escape route first.

He fed the rope through the krab attached to his belt, then swung himself out over the edge, and abseiled down to the yard.

*

Teddy landed lightly on the rucked concrete and unclipped the rope. He was dressed in matt-black combat leathers, a tiny Trinities emblem on his epaulette, 'ware modules attached to his belt, the slim metallic-silver photon amp band around his eyes, navy blue skull helmet. There was an AK carbine strapped tightly to his chest, an Uzi hand laser in a shoulder holster.

Greg was dressed the same, except he was carrying an Armscor stunshot instead of an AK. He wondered what the pair of them would look like to some poor unsuspecting sod who saw them emerge out of the fog.

He had considered wearing civilian clothes, but decided they were impractical; there was too much gear to carry. Besides which, the fog and the night should provide enough cover. The Blackshirts guarded their territory's boundaries tightly, but inside Walton they could move about with a reasonable degree of freedom. And his espersense would warn them of any random patrols.

'OK, Morgan, we're on the ground,' Greg said. 'Put Colin on, please.'

Colin had insisted on being included, even though he really was too ill for an operation which required sustained gland use. But Greg didn't have it in him to say no, not to that brave, silently pleading face. More bloody guilt.

'I'm here, Greg.' Colin's voice was reedy, anxious and eager.

He imagined them all in Morgan's ops room: Eleanor silently worried, Gabriel staring grimly at the communications console, Morgan keen-eyed and serious, Colin sitting in front of a flatscreen displaying the satellite image of Walton, technical support staff hovering around. The hard-line security team commander secretly hoping to be ordered into the fray.

'Where's our man?' Greg asked.

'He hasn't moved. It must be his house.'

'Right, thanks, Colin.' Greg requested the virtual simulation again. Featureless green toytown houses blinked in, marking the perimeter of the factory yard sixty metres away. He tilted the display to vertical, and reduced it until it was a panoramic model of the whole district. The house where Colin had said Knebel was staying flashed a bright amber. It was seven hundred metres away, due south. A route graphic slid out from their warehouse, an orange serpent bending and twisting down the smaller streets and constricted alleys.

'Let's go,' Greg said. The display reverted to its real-scale superimposition, the route a path of tangerine glass.

'I'll keep you updated,' Colin said.

Greg saw Teddy's face turn towards him, blank band concealing his expression.

'No, Colin, just give us another scan when we're a hundred metres away to confirm he's still there.'

'I can manage, Greg.'

'Yeah, but if he starts to go walkabout you're going to have to track him for us. I don't want you overstressed.'

'Yes. Sorry, I wasn't thinking.'

'OK, call you when we're in place.' He summoned up a secretion from his gland, then set off down the orange line, feet sinking into the placid current of photons up to the ankles.

*

The fog was sparser out on the streets, broken by walls and a light breeze coming off the basin. Visibility had increased to fifteen metres. Greg switched the virtual simulation back to outlines, the photon amp image shaded in the actual walls and roads a smoky grey and blue.

Spook town, and no messing.

There were no streetlights. Public utilities in Walton didn't receive much priority from the city council these days. Chinks of biolum light escaped from some houses, glimmers from shuttered windows. The amp showed them as near-solid blades probing out across the street.

Pro-PSP graffiti was splattered on every wall. They walked down one alley with an elaborate mural of People's Constables and socialist-stereotypical workers sprayed on the fence, bold uplifted faces and stout poses; rotting wood had left vacant jagged gashes, mocking the artist's vision.

Black bags like swollen pumpkins and kelpboard boxes full of rubbish formed a humpbacked tide-line along the pavements.

The corrupt smell of putrefying vegetation was strong in the air, mingling with the brine from the basin. Greg saw rats crawling around the bags, gnawing at soggy titbits. Tiny black glass eyes turned to watch him and Teddy pass, quite unafraid.

They had to sink back into the shadows and gaps between buildings several times as Greg perceived people walking towards them. Walton's residents invariably stuck to the centre of the road, as if they were afraid of the buildings and what they contained. They never once heard or saw any kind of powered transport, though bicycles nearly caught them out a couple of times, rushing up silently from behind.

A street-corner pub produced the biggest obstacle. Bright fans of light shone out of its windows and open door, illuminating a broad section of the road. Men were lounging against its walls, drinking in small groups. Jukebox music reverberated oddly across the street, country rap, hoarse vocals booming against a background of a solitary steel guitar.

Greg halted on the fringe of the light field consulting his virtual simulation. He pointed at the entry of a narrow alley on the other side of the road from the pub, and they edged off the street.

'Recognized some active Blackshirts back there,' Teddy muttered.

'Mark it off for the future,' Greg said.

'Sure.'

One of the reasons Teddy agreed to accompany him was because the opportunity to scout round enemy territory was too great to pass up. Greg knew the detailed satellite images stored in the guido's memory would be handed over to Royan who would integrate them with the Trinities' existing intelligence bytes. Lieutenants would pore over the resulting package, fine-tuning tactics for the final assault. Teddy hadn't said anything, but he knew the fight wasn't far away now.

The alleyway they had skipped down brought them out into a cul-de-sac. One side was a brick wall backing on to some gardens, the other was a row of garages, their metal swing-up doors were either broken open or missing entirely. Walton's perpetual tide of rubbish had swollen to form a rancid mattress underfoot, bags rose like lumpy organic buttresses against the bricks. Rats scampered about everywhere.

Greg's espersense found the cluster of minds, just as he heard the low bubbling laughter up ahead. Something about the minds wasn't quite right, their thought currents wavered giddily, emotions burning fiercely. One of them was emitting a mental keening, gibbering with psychotic distress.

'Shit. Teddy, it's a bunch of synthoheads. And they're juiced up high.'

'Where?'

'Ten metres. One of the garages.' He drew his Armscor stunshot, a simple ash-grey pistol with a solid thirty-centimetre-long barrel. 'I'll take them, cover for any runaways.'

'Gotcha.'

The stunshot was only accurate up to twenty metres. If one of the synthoheads got away, Teddy would have to use the Uzi on them, providing the target laser worked in the fog. Tension clamped down hard; this was supposed to be a stealth infiltration. People being killed just for getting in his way wasn't part of the deal.

It was the third garage from the end of the cul-de-sac, a dim yellow glow spilling out on to the sludge of rubbish. Greg flattened himself against the wall, checked the stunshot, then spun round the corner.

There were five of them. Kids, still in their teens, two girls, three boys. Filthy, greasy jeans, frayed black leather jackets, denim waistcoats with studs, long straggly hair. The garage walls were slick with condensation, junk furniture – broken settees and armchairs – lined up around the walls, and an oil lamp hung from the ceiling.

Greg's photon amp threw the whole scene into starkly etched focus. Two of the kids were screwing on the floor, grunting like pigs. Another two stood on either side, watching, giggling. The fifth was huddled in a corner, arms over his head, weeping quietly.

Greg shot the one closest to him. A girl, about seventeen, her neck freckled with dark infuser marks. The stunshot spat out a bullet-sized pulse of blue-white lightning. It hit her on the side of her ribcage. Her squeal was choked off as she reeled round. There was an impossibly serene smile on her face as she crumpled on to the legs of the rutting couple.

Pulling the trigger was incredibly hard. They weren't innocent, not even close. Just profoundly ignorant, pitiable. He had to keep on reminding himself the stunshot wasn't lethal, though God alone knew what it would do to a metabolism fucked up so badly by syntho.

He turned slightly. Aim and fire, nothing else matters.

The second kid gurgled as the pulse hit him in the stomach, curling up and falling forwards. Aim and fire. The girl on the floor was struggling to get up as her partner collapsed on top of her. Aim and fire.

The boy in the corner was looking straight at Greg, face ecstatic, tears streaming down. 'Thank you, oh thank you.'

Aim and fire.

The kid slumped down again, head bowed.

'Lord, what a waste,' Teddy said. 'Someplace else they could've been real people.'

Greg stepped over the prone bodies and extinguished the oil lamp, letting the night claim its own. 'You can get syntho any-where.'

'Not in Mucklands, you fucking couldn't. I look after my kids. Anyone tries peddling that shit near me an' they end up swinging by the balls. Blackshirts don't even look after their own.'

'You're preaching to the converted. Come on.'

According to the bright yellow co-ordinates the guido was flashing up, he was standing fifty metres from the target house. Its green template glowed lambently, the walls and roof remaining outside the photon amp's resolution.

'Colin, how are we doing?'

'He's still there, Greg.'

'OK, we're closing in now.'

He trotted down the road, watching the house gaining substance. It was a large detached three-storey affair, with bow windows on either side of the front door, built from a pale yellow brick with blue-grey slates. Nothing fancy, virtually a cube. Diamond shapes made from blue bricks set between the first-floor windows were the only visible ornamentation. A tall chimney stack was leaning at a worrying angle, a number of bricks from its top were missing. The chimney pots themselves ended in elaborate crowns, all of them playing host to tussocks of spindly weeds.

A metre-high wall enclosed a broad strip of garden at the front. Greg stopped just outside; it took him a moment to realize there were no solar panels. The house's residents must be right at the bottom of the human pile, and in Walton the bottom was as far down as you could get. All the windows had their curtains drawn; the photon amp revealed vague splinters of light round the edges. There was no gate, its absence marked by rusty metal hinge pins protruding from the wall.

He walked down the algae-slimed path. Dog roses had run wild in the garden, reducing it to a thorny wilderness sprinkled with small pale flowers. A panel with eight bell buttons was set into the wall at the side of the door. Very primitive, there was no camera lens as far as he could see. He took the sensor wand from its slot on his ECM 'ware module, and ran it round the door frame. Apart from the lock system, it was clean.

'We're at the front door now,' Greg said. He was surprised by the 'ware lock, a tiny glass lens flush with the wood. He already had the vibration knife in his hand ready to cope with a mechanical lock.

'I can feel you,' Colin said. 'Yes, you're very close now. He's above you, Greg. Definitely higher up.'

'OK.' He showed his card to the lock, using his little finger to activate it rather than the usual thumbprint. A Royan special was loaded in the card, a crash-wipe virus designed to flush lock circuitry clean. There was a subdued *snick* from the lock. He pushed the door open a crack, and slipped the sensor wand in.

'It's clear,' he told Teddy.

The hall went straight through to the back of the house. He saw a set of stairs halfway along. A candle was burning in a dish on a small table just inside the door. Its flame flickered madly until Teddy closed the door shut behind him. The lock refused to engage.

Greg let his espersense expand. There were four people on the ground floor, none of them showing any awareness that the front door had been opened.

They went up the stairs fast. The first-floor landing had five doors. One was open; he could just make out an ancient iron bath inside. His espersense picked out seven minds, two of them children. Murmurs of music from channel shows were coming through some of the doors.

'Which way, Colin?'

'Walk forward, Greg.'

He took three paces down the worn ochre carpet. Teddy stayed at the top of the stairs, watching the other doors.

'Stop,' Colin said. 'He's on your left.' The strain in his voice was quite clear, even through the satellite link.

'Thanks, Colin. Now you shut your gland down, right now, you hear?'

'Greg, my dear chap, there's no need to shout.'

Greg let his espersense flow through the door. There were two people inside, one male, one female, sitting together. Judging by the relaxed timbre of their minds he guessed they were watching a channel.

The door lock was mechanical, an old Yale. With Teddy standing behind him he shoved the blade clean through the wood just above the keyhole and sliced out a semicircle.

Knebel's room was just as seedy as he had been expecting: damp wallpaper, cheap furniture, laminated chipboard table and sideboard, plain wooden chairs, a settee covered in woolly brown and grey fabric, its cushioning sagging and worn; thin blue carpet. The light was coming from some kind of salvaged lorry headlamp on the table, shining at the ceiling, powered from a cluster of spherical polymer batteries on the floor. An English Electric flatscreen, with shoddy colour contrast, was showing a channel current affairs 'cast.

Greg didn't know the woman, a blowzy thirty-year-old, flat washed-out face, straw hair, wearing a man's green shirt and a short red skirt.

Knebel had grown a pointed beard, but Greg would have recognized him anywhere. The *apparatchik* was wearing jeans and a thick mauve sweater, buckled sandals on bare feet. He had aged perceptibly; he was only forty, almost Greg's contemporary, but the flesh had wasted from his face producing sunken cheeks, deep eyes, thin lips. Mouse-brown hair with a centre parting hung lankly down to his ears.

The two of them were sitting on the settee, facing the flat-screen, heads turning at the clatter of the lock hitting the floor. Greg aimed the stunshot at the woman and fired. It sounded dreadfully loud in the confined space. The pulse caught her on the shoulder. She spasmed, nearly slewing off the settee. Her eyes rolled up as she emitted a strangled cry.

Greg shifted the stunshot fractionally.

Knebel stared at him, his mouth parted, jaw quivering softly. His startled thoughts reflected utter despair. He closed his eyes, screwing up his face wretchedly.

'One sound, and you won't be dead, you will simply wish you were,' Greg said. 'Now turn the flatscreen off.'

Teddy closed the door behind him.

Knebel opened his eyes, showing the frantic disbelief of a condemned man given a reprieve. A shaking hand pawed at the remote.

Greg ignored him, his espersense hovering around the other minds on the first floor. Two of them had heard the commotion.

Curiosity rose, they waited for something else to happen. When nothing did their attention wavered, and they were drawn back into the mundane routine of the evening.

He waited another minute to make sure, then pulled the photon amp band from his eyes.

Knebel managed to crumple without actually moving. 'Oh my God. Greg Mandel, the Thunderchild himself.'

It had been quite some time since Greg had heard anyone use his army callsign. Not since he left the Trinities, in fact. But of course, the PSP had access to all the army's personnel files. 'I'm flattered. I wasn't aware Oakham's Lord Protector had taken an interest in me.'

'You were believed to be an active member of the Trinities, and you live in the Berrybut estate. No close family, no special woman as far as we knew. Very high ESP rating. Plenty of combat experience. I took notice all right.'

'Lived. Lived in Berrybut. I've moved now.'

'Of course,' Knebel said with bitter irony, 'do excuse me, I haven't accessed your file lately. My mistake.'

'If you knew all that, how come you never came hunting for me, you and your Constables?'

Knebel stroked the hair of the unconscious woman, gazing tenderly at her shivering face. 'And if we'd missed? Which was more than likely with that freaky Thompson woman guarding your future. I had enough trouble keeping the ranks in order as it was. You were busy here in Peterborough. The last thing I needed was a fully trained, fully armed Mindstar monster gunning for us when we left the station to go home at night.'

'Figures. You people never did try anything physical unless the odds were ten to one in your favour.'

'Could you spare me this ritual of insults, and just get it over with, please?'

Greg gave him a frigid grin. 'Tell you, Knebel, this is the luckiest day of your entire shitty little life. I'm not here to snuff you.'

Knebel's hand stopped. 'What?'

340

'True. I only want some bytes you've got.'

'An' you gonna give 'em to us, boy,' Teddy growled.

Swellings of terror and hope disrupted the surface thoughts of Knebel's mind. 'Are you serious? Just information?'

'Yeah.'

He licked his upper lip, glancing nervously at Teddy. 'What about afterwards?'

'You join her in dreamland, we leave. And that's a fucking sight more than you deserve.'

'God, you must be loving this, seeing what I've been brought down to.' The eyes darkened with pain. 'Yes, I'll plead with you for my life, I'll tell you anything you want, answer any question, I don't care. Dignity isn't something I have any more, your kind broke that. But you gave me something in return; I've found there's a great deal of peace to be had once every pretension has been stripped out. Did you know that Mandel, can you see it? I don't worry about the ways things are any more, I don't worry about the future. That's all down to you now. Your worries, your power politics. And you've wasted your time coming here, because I don't know anything about the Blackshirts' weapons stocks, they never tell me anything. I'm not a part of that.'

'Not what we're here for.'

'Speak for yourself,' Teddy muttered.

'What then?' Knebel asked.

'Launde Abbey.'

'What?' Knebel blurted loudly. He shrank back when Greg motioned with the stunshot. 'Sorry. Really, I'm sorry. But . . . is that it? You came to ask me about Launde Abbey?'

'Yeah. Now I've come a long way, and gone to a lot of trouble to rap with you. So believe me, you don't want to piss me off. You know I'm empathic, so just answer the questions truthfully.'

'All right. I saw you on the newscast the other night. You were appointed to the Kitchener murder, something to do with Julia Evans.' His eyes lingered on the 'ware modules hanging from Greg's belt.

Greg switched on the communication module's external mike. 'Tell me about Clarissa Wynne.'

'Clarissa? God, that was years and years ago. I'd almost forgotten about her until the other day. That newscast brought a lot of memories back.'

'Ten years ago. What can you remember?'

Knebel closed his eyes, slim eyebrows bunching up. 'Ten? Are you sure? I thought it was eleven.'

'It could have been.'

'Well, what does it say in her file?'

'That is the reason I'm here, Knebel. Someone has erased every byte of Clarissa Wynne from Rutland's memory cores; police, council, local newspapers, you name it, the lot.'

'God.'

'Do you know who?'

'No.'

'Right. You say you thought she died eleven years ago?'

'Yes, I'm sure it was eleven.'

'OK, what orders did you get from the Ministry of Public Order about her death?'

'To wrap it up immediately, make the coroner enter a verdict of accidental death, not to cause any ripples, especially not to antagonize Kitchener and the other students.'

'Why not? Why was the PSP so anxious to hush the girl's death up? What made her so important?'

Knebel gave him a humourless smile. 'Important? Clarissa Wynne wasn't important. God, the Ministry didn't even know her name. She was an embarrassment. You see, eleven years ago, the PSP was applying to the World Bank for a very large loan, billions. You remember that time, Mandel; the seas were reaching their peak, we'd got hundreds of thousands of refugees pouring inland from flooded coastal areas, we didn't have any food, we didn't have any industry, we didn't have any hard currency. It was a fucking great mess. We needed that loan to get the economy started again. And the Americans didn't want to help a bunch of Reds. No matter we were elected—'

Teddy growled dangerously. Greg held up a hand, sensing just how hostile Teddy's mind was.

'OK. All right. I'm sorry,' Knebel said. 'No politics. But look, the point was, the PSP couldn't afford a human rights issue. The Americans would have leapt on it as an excuse to block the loan, destabilize the Party. Kitchener, for all he was bloody obnoxious personally, was internationally renowned, someone whose name people knew all over the world. Can you see the disinformation campaign the Americans would have mounted if I'd started questioning the students and Kitchener thoroughly? Their friend and colleague has been tragically drowned, and all the PSP does is persecute them with inquiries and allegations. It would have been Sakharov all over again. We needed that money, Mandel, people were starting to starve. In England, for God's sake! Pensioners. Children. So I did what I was told, and I kept my mouth shut afterwards. Because it was necessary. And to hell with you and your rich bitch mistress. I don't care how wise after the event you are.'

So much anger, Greg thought, and just from one question. Will we ever heal the rift? 'Morgan? Did you hear all that?'

'Yes, Greg.'

'OK, check the date for that World Bank loan application, please. I'd like some verification.'

'Right.'

Knebel had cocked his head to one side, listening to Greg's side of the conversation intently. He still had his arms around the woman, cradling her. A ribbon of saliva was leaking from the corner of her mouth, eyelids fluttering erratically.

'Now,' Greg said, 'why were you so upset about having to close down the inquiry? I was told Clarissa drowned in the lake after some sort of drinking session. Was it an accident?'

'I'm not sure. At the time I didn't think so. You get an instinct, you know? After you've been on the job long enough you can tell if something's not quite right. And I was a good detective, back then. Before it all . . . I cared,' he said defensively.

'Yeah. Keith Willet told me.'

'Keith?' Knebel brightened for an instant. 'God, is he still at Oakham? How is he?'

'Just get on with it, Knebel.'

'All right.' He shot Teddy another twitchy glance, then cleared his throat. 'I wasn't happy with the circumstances around Clarissa Wynne's death. The students said they found her floating in the lake first thing in the morning, that she must have gone for a swim sometime in the night. Apparently the students always went swimming there.'

'Still do,' Greg said.

'Yes? Well, anyway, on the surface it was pretty clear cut. She'd been drinking, she'd infused some syntho. That was the first time we'd ever come across the stuff at Oakham. She must have got into difficulty in the water. Those lakes aren't particularly deep, but you only need five centimetres to drown in.'

'So what was wrong about it?'

Knebel sighed. 'She hadn't drunk much that evening, a couple of glasses of wine. And the syntho, we couldn't be sure, we didn't know much about it back then, but it looked as though it was infused very close to the time she died. Almost as if she took it and dived straight in. Which I don't believe anybody would do, certainly not a bright girl like that. I was going to have the pathology samples sent to Cambridge for a more detailed examination, then the shut-down order came through.'

'Suicide?' Greg suggested.

'Nope. First thing I thought of. We did get to ask the students and Kitchener a few preliminary questions. Clarissa Wynne was one happy girl. She enjoyed being at Launde. Her parents confirmed there were no family problems. In any case, there was some light bruising on the back of her neck.' He shrugged limply. 'It could have been caused by bumping in to something in the water.'

'Or it could have been caused by someone holding her under,' Greg concluded.

'Yes. If the attacker had put her in a Nelson lock on the side of the lake, the bruising would have been consistent with her head being forced under the surface. Especially if she was conscious. She was young, strong, apparently she was in the woman's hockey team at university, a sports type, she could have put up quite a struggle. The attacker would have had to use a lot of force.'

'Any sign of a struggle?'

'No. The grass around the side of the lake was all beaten down. Like I said, the students used it each day.'

A dire chill slithered through the combat leathers to prickle Greg's skin as he thought about Clarissa Wynne's death. She would have struggled, that night eleven years ago, fighting her attacker under the silent, beautiful stars, without any hope of success or help. Terribly alone as her head was shoved under the cold muddy water. She would feel her body weakening, be conscious of the syntho breaking her mind apart. And all the while the red ache in her lungs grew and grew.

No fucking wonder he'd been drawn to the lake. It was a focal node of horror and anguish.

Did her soul haunt it? Was that what I sensed?

But whatever the source of the misery, it still didn't explain how her death tied in with Nicholas Beswick.

'Who did you suspect?' he asked Knebel.

'God, I never had time to find a possible suspect. That Ministry order came through in less than a day.'

'Well, start thinking about it now, Knebel. What about Kitchener himself? I mean, he was sleeping with his female students the night he died. Sixty-seven years old. Eleven years ago he would have been even more capable sexually.'

'No, I don't think so. He was reasonably fit, but not really what I'd call physically powerful. And if Clarissa was held down, it was done by someone stronger than her.'

'One of the other students, then?'

'Yes, possibly.'

'Was there anyone else staying at the Abbey that night?'

'No. And Clarissa was still alive when the housekeeper and the maid left, we confirmed that.'

'OK, can you remember the names of the other students?'

'I think so. There was five of them. Let's see: Tumber, Donaldson, MacLennan, Spencer—'

'Wait! MacLennan? James MacLennan? Dr James Mac-Lennan?'

'Yes. That was his first name, James. I didn't know he was a doctor.'

'Shitfire,' Greg whispered.

23

Julia could barely see the far side of the rooftop landing pad. The fog was pressing in, turning the circle of close-spaced white lights around the perimeter of the pad into a hazy line of phosphorescence. The edge of the Event Horizon headquarters building was lost completely.

She was wearing a light nylon windcheater jacket over her plain amethyst-coloured stretch jersey dress. It was too warm to zip it up, but the fog was almost thick enough to be called a drizzle. Her hair was already hanging limply, sprinkled with a sugar coating of droplets. Rachel stood at her side, suede jacket buttoned up, collar raised around her neck. The rest of the reception party – Eleanor, Gabriel, and Morgan, plus some security people – were huddled together a couple of metres away.

Eleanor's smile was blinking on and off; the outright relief on her face making Julia feel like an intruder just for looking at her.

Thirty seconds, Juliet. Can you hear it?

Not yet, Grandpa, she answered silently.

She saw Morgan raise a palm-size communication set to his face and listen for a moment. 'They're coming in,' he announced.

Now she heard it, the whine of the turbines, low-frequency hiss of air escaping from the fan nacelles. It grew louder and louder until the dove-grey security division tilt-fan was suddenly *there* above the landing pad. Landing gear unfolding, small red and green wingtip strobes flashing. Its fuselage was coated in water, shining dully.

In the end she simply couldn't stay away. She didn't approve. She had made that quite clear. But ultimately it was her responsibility. Greg was only on the case because she asked him. There was no way she could go out clubbing in New Eastfield while he was risking his neck on her behalf.

Another night lost to duty.

The tilt-fan's broad low-pressure tyres touched down, hydraulic struts pistoning upwards as they absorbed the weight. The forward hatch hinged out and up, airstairs sliding down. The pilot cut the turbines. Micro-cyclones of steam poured out of the nacelles as the fans wound down.

Greg was first out, his black leather combat jacket open to show a white T-shirt, his hair sweaty, clinging to his forehead. He had a stunshot with a shoulder strap riding at his elbow, 'ware modules clipped round his belt, skull helmet thrown back, photon amp band hanging over one shoulder. He looked so . . . dangerous.

She watched Eleanor walk over and embrace him, arms going round his waist, a brief kiss, then resting her head on his shoulder. He hugged her tightly. It was far more eloquent than whoops of joy and backslapping.

How she'd love someone to greet her like that. Not to be, though. Although perhaps Robin . . .

Teddy came down the airstairs, scowling round suspiciously.

'Hello, Teddy,' she said brightly. 'Thank you for going in with Greg. I'm really very grateful.'

He grunted in disgust. 'Goddamn fucking stupid thing to do, you ask me, gal. Still, we're back in one piece.' He patted one of the 'ware modules on his belt. 'An' these guido bytes gonna come in mighty useful sometime soon.'

She smiled warmly. Teddy always used to intimidate the hell out of her, with his size and his menacing authority. Not any more. He was a pushover. 'Oh? Going to impress a lady friend with them?' She batted her eyelids.

'Je-zus wept!'

Then the security crash team started to emerge from the tilt-fan. They were wearing suits similar to Teddy's, all of them in their mid- to late-twenties. They shouted a few boisterous greetings at her, and she grinned back. She knew most of them by their first name; they treated her almost as though they were a rugby squad and she was their mascot.

Morgan always kept one team on standby in case there was ever any attempt to kidnap her. She had watched them training a few times. Lord help any tekmerc who ever went up against them.

'Gabriel?' Greg was looking at her, one arm still around Eleanor. 'Where's Colin?'

'One of my people drove him home,' Morgan said.

'How was he?'

'Not too bad, considering,' Gabriel said. 'He'll need to rest for a week or so. Proper rest. I said I'd pop in tomorrow, make sure. You know what he's like.'

'Yeah.'

'Shall we go in?' Morgan said. 'In light of what we learned from Maurice Knebel, I believe we have quite a bit to discuss.'

'And no messing,' Greg said gloomily.

*

Julia led them into the big executive conference room, her pumps treading soundlessly on the pile carpet. Biolums came on ahead of her, banishing shadows. Grey tongues of fog licked at the windows. Westwood could be in a different universe by now for all she could tell.

The conference room was empty with just the seven of them, no secretaries, no aides. She shrugged out of her windcheater and hung it on the back of her chair before she sat down. Freshets of cool air trickled across her bare arms, carrying away the perspiration.

Grandpa, bring Royan in on this. I imagine we'll need him. Besides, she wanted all her true friends together.

Plugging him in now, Juliet.

Teddy lowered himself gingerly into one of the padded chairs around the table, nodding approvingly. His combat leathers squeaked softly as he put his hands behind his head and sat back. 'Man, now this is the life.'

'Do you want anything to drink?' Julia asked.

'Hey, my kinda gal, you gotta beer?'

'I'll look,' Rachel said. 'Anybody else?' She sauntered over to the mirrored nineteen-twenties drinks cabinet.

Julia opaqued all the windows, cutting off the sight of that austere fog.

ON LINE, her recessed flatscreen printed. HI SNOWY.

'Hi.'

Morgan raised an eyebrow.

'I'm here as well,' Philip's voice announced.

Julia enjoyed the startled look on Teddy's face, the way his eyes darted round. Greg had told her Teddy took his religion very seriously indeed. Grandpa was a little bit too much like reincarnation.

'Everybody's up to date?' Greg asked. 'Julia? Royan?'

'Yah.'

YES YES YES.

'OK,' Greg said. 'We have a new player on the field, James MacLennan.'

'I'm assembling a profile,' Philip said. 'Every byte I can find, public and private files; plus a financial run down. Should be ready in quarter of an hour.'

'So what happened?' Julia asked. 'Did MacLennan let Bursken out for the night?'

'I was thinking about that,' Greg said. 'We're faced with the same problem for Bursken as we were with a tekmerc penetration mission. How did he get in and out of Launde Abbey without leaving any trace?'

'Oh, yes,' she felt silly for asking.

'And in any case, Eleanor and I saw Nicholas do it.'

350

'It could have been an alternative past,' Eleanor said; she sounded doubtful.

'No. If you ask me,' Greg said slowly. 'I think it was Nicholas Beswick who actually physically murdered Kitchener.'

'Oh, Jesus,' Eleanor murmured.

He patted her hand, receiving an exasperated glance.

'Physically, he did it. And that was what threw me the first time. Nicholas Beswick isn't the type. We all know that. He couldn't harm a fly, not ordinarily.'

'Ah!' Gabriel slapped a hand against the table. 'Now I get it, the laser paradigms.'

'Right!' Greg said. 'At some time during that Thursday, Nicholas Beswick was targeted by a laser which loaded a paradigm into his brain. One which ordered him to kill Kitchener. And I think I know what the paradigm was: Liam Bursken's memories, his personality.'

'You told me the Stocken Hall team were constructing artificial memories from scratch,' Julia said. 'Like a perfect virtual reality recording. How could they know what Bursken's memories consist of?'

Greg grinned. 'Philip, you listening?'

'I'm still here, m'boy.'

'Care to tell your granddaughter exactly what you are?'

'Oh,' Julia groaned. 'Of course.'

'I'm not saying MacLennan copied every last thought from Bursken's brain,' Greg said. 'Just the basics would do. That unique psychotic behavioural trait. That's what he was after.'

'If paradigms are that sophisticated, why didn't MacLennan simply load a straightforward kill order into Beswick?' Morgan asked.

'Because they're not that sophisticated, not yet,' Greg said. 'All the Stocken team have so far is a few ersatz sensorium experiences, nothing more. That's why MacLennan needed Bursken, as raw material. I told you Nicholas wasn't the type. If MacLennan had just given him something like an advanced version of a hypnotic order to kill Kitchener he might have refused to do it when the moment actually arrived. Not everybody can kill; we can, you, me, and Teddy, because we've been trained to. In battlefield combat situations it's pure reflex, we don't even think. In counterinsurgency or ambush situations it becomes harder, you have time to think, to moralize; but if you hate your enemy enough it's not much of a problem. That's why company commanders always had such trouble finding genuinely good snipers, it's not just marksmanship, it's a question of temperament. It's a rare person who can kill without any qualms.

'I kept asking myself all through this case, who could do such a thing? Cold-blooded butchery on a sixty-seven-year-old. The only person I knew was Bursken. Out of all Stocken's inmates he is the one who can kill without hesitation or remorse every time; he actually enjoyed it, he believed what he was doing was right.

'I'd say MacLennan recorded Liam Bursken's thoughts from a neuro coupling, and then combined them with an order to kill Kitchener. Then after Nicholas Beswick committed the murder the paradigm wiped itself from his mind, presumably along with his recollection of everything he did under its influence. The Stocken Hall research team has already developed a treatment they call magic photons, which can erase a memory, providing they know exactly what it is. And MacLennan certainly did, he made it.'

'If MacLennan wanted a copy of Liam Bursken's memories, the only way he could obtain them would be through a cortical interface,' Morgan said. 'That means Bursken would have to undergo surgery.'

'Good point,' Greg said. 'It's something we can look for, some solid physical proof. Although if he underwent the surgery at Stocken you can bet your life there will turn out to be a legitimate reason for it. But there's no doubt in my mind.' He turned to Eleanor. 'Remember what Nicholas did right after he smothered Kitchener?'

She drew a breath, thinking back. 'He crossed himself.'

'Right. But Nicholas is virtually an atheist. Bursken, on the other hand, is a religious fruitcake; he believes he kills his victims because God tells him they're sinners. I'm telling you, it was Bursken's mentality in Nicholas's brain. A real live cyborg. I *knew* Nicholas was innocent.' He looked pleased. More like relieved, Julia thought, studying him out of the corner of her eye.

'I know he's innocent, Greg,' she said, hating herself for being such a pragmatist, for puncturing his mood. 'We all do. But you have still got the problem of proving it in a court of law.'

'The prosecution still has the knife,' Gabriel said. 'Pretty strong evidence, especially when you'll be dealing with a jury that's going to be lost after the first ten minutes of specialist technical testimonies.'

'Then we shall have to produce some counter-evidence,' Eleanor said smartly. 'Something that Inspector Langley can't ignore, something that'll mean Nicholas never gets into court. The paradigm itself.' She looked at Julia. They both smiled. 'Royan,' they chorused.

*

Julia followed the burn's progress through her nodes. The others used the time to relax; Teddy trying to chat up Rachel over by the drinks cabinet; Greg, Eleanor, Morgan, and Gabriel all with their heads together, talking in low tones. Eleanor still hadn't let go of Greg, her hand gripping his, fingers entwined.

Royan in hotrod mode was awesome to watch. She had learned a lot about hacking techniques from him; modesty aside, she was good, she knew that. Good enough to crack Jakki Coleman's bank account – and Lloyds-Tashoko's guardian programs were the best corporate money could buy. But she watched Royan's infiltration of Stocken Hall's 'ware with something approaching envy; the speed of the penetration was incredible, and he didn't have lightware crunchers to back him up.

He didn't even bother trying to crack the authorized user entry codes, he went straight for the management routines. A melt virus got him past the first-level guardian programs, opening up the prison's datanet. The structure unfolded in her mind, an origami molecule, individual terminals and 'ware cores linked together by a spiderweb of databases. She had access to menus of low-grade security files stored in the terminals, along with the Hall's day-to-day administration details, and financial datawork. But the cell security and surveillance circuits were blocked, along with a vast series of memories in the cores.

Royan squirted a more complex virus at the second-level guardian programs, the ones governing access to restricted core memories.

Let's see what the medical department has on Bursken, Julia said, studying the menu. *At the least his file should tell us whether or not he's got a cortical interface.*

Nice one, Snowy. It isn't on the restricted list. Here we go.

He pulled a Home Office identification code from the administration officer's terminal, and used it to request a squirt from the records terminal in the medical division.

'This is Bursken's medical file,' she said as the datasheets swarmed down the conference room's flatscreens. 'Grandpa, review it for implants, please.'

The datasheets flashed past, too fast to read. 'Here we go, Juliet.' The deluge of bytes halted. She was looking at some kind of official Home Office package. 'Hell, girl, they really were wetting themselves over Bursken. This confinement order gives the director, that is MacLennan, permission to employ any method he sees fit to restrain Liam Bursken, including chemical suppression, or even remedial surgery such as a lobotomy.'

'And who would ever complain?' Greg mused, not looking up from his flatscreen. 'Even the human rights lawyers wouldn't bother arguing in Bursken's favour. He's beyond the lowest of the low. You could do anything you wanted to him, and no one would give a shit.'

'I don't know about anything, boy,' Philip said. 'But a month ago he was wheeled into surgery and given a cortical interface.' A new datasheet slid into place. 'It was ordered by MacLennan, part of a new mental assessment project. According to this it was supposed to provide data on his psychotic state trigger stimulants. Follow up results are restricted.'

'I knew that . . .' Greg looked puzzled for a moment, then clicked his fingers. 'Of course, it was Stephanie Rowe who filled me in on Bursken, MacLennan just sat there and let her recite facts to me. How stupid of me.'

'You weren't interrogating them,' Eleanor said.

'Thanks,' he said.

Julia's nodes showed her the second-level guardian programs falling as the virus penetrated. Huge stacks of data materialized into the nodes' visualization, dense packages of colourless binary digits extending out to her mind's horizon. A batch of Royan's tracer programs slithered through them.

Bursken's surgical records vanished from the flatscreen in front of her. PROBLEM, it printed.

'What's the matter?' Greg asked.

I THINK I'VE FOUND THE PARADIGM FILE. IT IS LISTED AS BURSKEN'S CORTICAL INTERFACE FOLLOW-UP RESULTS, AND IT HAS A DIRECTOR-ONLY ACCESS CODE.

'So what's the problem?'

THEY WILL KNOW IF I ACCESS IT. A NOTIFICATION PROCEDURE IS HARD-WIRED IN TO THE CORES. ALL SQUIRTS ARE LOGGED AUTOMATICALLY.

'But the cores think we're the Home Office,' Julia said. 'Under that premiss, we're entitled to access their data. Berkeley operates Stocken under government licence.'

IF WE ARE THE HOME OFFICE, HOW COME WE CAN ORDER A SQUIRT FOR A DIRECTOR-ONLY FILE??? MACLENNAN WOULD HAVE TO BEAT THE HOME OFFICE TO AUTHORIZE THE SQUIRT.

'OK, let's look at what we want to achieve,' Greg said. 'What we need is for Inspector Langley to go into Stocken first thing tomorrow morning, armed with a data warrant, and find that paradigm. So we have to be sure it's there before we send him in. Is there any chance this file will crash wipe if you order a squirt?'

NO.

'Then I'd say do it. Morgan?'

'I can't see any objection. Even if you were to interrogate MacLennan, a lawyer might conceivably neutralize your testimony; there are still some legal queries over evidence obtained psychically. As Eleanor said, we need tangible proof. The evidence is piling up against MacLennan, to my mind he's guilty as hell. It has to be the killer paradigm in that file.'

'OK, squirt it over, Royan.'

It came through the link, a large construct, taking half a second to transfer. In her terminal cube it was nothing, a moiré patchwork of randomized data. In her mind—

She opened a secure file in one of her memory nodes and let the construct fill it. Analysis programs sifted through the bytes, trying to identify coherent segments. The patterns they formed were like nothing she had ever seen before; there were analogue visual sequences, interlaced with data pulses that defied decryption. She accessed one at random.

Chiaroscuro images, black and scarlet, bloomed silently around her. She was standing on a rainswept street at night, parallel rows of cheap terrace housing, their walls shimmering as sheets of water sluiced down over the bricks, it was almost as though they were melting. There were no stars above, only empty night. A solitary figure walked down the middle of the road, a man in a sodden greatcoat. Julia felt her heart ignite with exaltation.

She was stalking through woodland, the smooth boles of dead beech trees sliding past, a deep claret in colour. Ribbons of black ivy were clawing their way up the crumbling bark, crisp dry leaves like heart-shaped flakes of ash crunched underfoot. She circled a glade, the procession of boles eclipsing the sight of the two young lovers in its centre. All she caught was fleeting glimpses, their bodies moved in a stop-motion sequence. And they were unmarried, profaning the gift of life with their casual coupling. Their skin was salmon pink, their scattered clothes burgundy and ebony. A knife was heavy in her hand, its blade a glowing coral.

Her mind was alive with whispers, enticing dark promises. God's voice. His strength flooding through her limbs.

A face coalesced before her. An old man, with bright smiling eyes, and wispy hair. Mocking eyes. Black eyes, light wells. The man stared into hell and laughed in joy at what he saw.

The whispers grew bolder, caressing her.

Exit.

The nodes shut off with an almost audible snap.

She took a deep gulp of air, shuddering violently.

'What is it?' Morgan asked sharply.

'I'm all right.' She held up her hands, surprised to find them trembling. 'I was accessing some of the paradigm's visual routines, that's all. Greg's right, it is made up from Bursken's memories.' She stopped, remembering the confused montage. A smell of the street's sweet fresh rain lingered in the executive conference room. And she *detested* the God-violator Edward Kitchener. Feeling a wild primitive joy that he was dead dead dead. 'Dear Lord, he's not human.' She stared at Greg. 'And you looked into his mind all the time you interviewed him?'

'Goes with the job.'

'Yech!'

'So that settles it, then,' Greg said. 'Royan, do you understand the paradigm?'

MOST SECTIONS ARE ANALOGUE BUT THERE IS ONE SEQUENCE WHICH IS A DIGITAL COMPOSITION.

'Is it the instruction to kill Kitchener?'

GREEDY GREEDY GREEDY, IS WHAT YOU ARE! THE DIGITAL SEQUENCE IS STRANGE, I WILL HAVE TO WRITE A DECRYPTION PROGRAM. TELL YOU TOMORROW.

'OK,' Greg said casually, as though he didn't care.

Liar! Julia thought.

Teddy walked back from the drinks cabinet to stand next to Greg, a dumpy German beer bottle in his hand, condensation mottling its silver and ice-blue label. 'Hell, man, all this shit about paradigms turning the Beswick kid into a cyborg, it's kinda screwy, but I'll buy it. But you still ain't told us the *why* of it. How come this MacLennan guy wants to snuff his old teacher? He did all right by Kitchener. Christ, made it to the top in his field. Head of a premier-grade research institution, respected man, big bucks backing him. What's he wanna go and risk all that for?'

'Wrong question,' Gabriel said. She was smiling faintly, head tilted right back on her chair, staring at the ceiling. 'What you ought to ask is why did MacLennan kill Clarissa Wynne? That's the real question. After he murdered her he had to get rid of Kitchener; it was inevitable. He was covering himself to protect that cushy number he's wound up with.'

'The neurohormone!' Julia exclaimed, quietly pleased she could keep up with Gabriel.

WELL DONE, SNOWY.

Morgan flicked an ironic glance at the camera.

Gabriel suddenly leant forward, resting her elbows on the table, fixing Teddy with an intent stare. 'MacLennan must have been worried that once Kitchener perfected the retrospective neurohormone he would look into the past and see him murdering Clarissa. That's why poor old Nicholas Beswick was also ordered to destroy the bioware which produced the neurohormone, and wipe the Abbey's Bendix. To eliminate any possibility of anybody looking back. Lucky he missed those ampoules. I don't suppose MacLennan could think of every contingency.'

'I couldn't have seen that far back,' Eleanor said. 'A week was a hell of an effort. Eleven years would have been utterly impossible.'

'Yes,' Gabriel said. 'I never used to look more than a couple of days into the future when I had my gland. That was partly psychological, admittedly. But ... well, with Kitchener working on it, who knows what might have been accomplished in the end.'

'I think I've found the reason why she was murdered,' Philip said.

'Yeah?' Greg perked up. 'Go on.'

'Ten years ago there was a paper published on the possibilities of laser paradigms applied to education. The first of its kind. It was co-authored by James MacLennan and Clarissa Wynne.'

'Ten years?' Morgan asked. 'We confirmed that World Bank loan was eleven years ago.'

'Published posthumously,' Greg said. 'That's why MacLennan killed her. I'll give you good odds that Clarissa did the real breakthrough work on paradigms while she was at Launde. And MacLennan was sharp enough to realize the possibilities. He was very keen to stress that when I talked to him. Once they are perfected, paradigms will be worth a fortune. He reckoned the entire penal system would have to be rebuilt from the ground up, and not just in this country. I suppose it would be the same for schools and universities as well, paradigms could replace lessons and lectures. And he's leading the project. He'll get all the fame and the glory, not to mention a share of the royalties. And it should have been her in charge of Berkeley's team.'

'Ah!' Julia cried. She grinned at the curious faces. 'Grandpa, that financial profile we assembled on Diessenburg Mercantile should still be in our finance division memory core. Access it, and run a check for me. See how much money Diessenburg Mercantile is loaning the Berkeley company.'

'You all hear that?' Philip's voice boomed. 'Now that is a true Evans. Laser sharp. My granddaughter.'

There were times – like *now* – when she wished the NN core was only loaded with a simple Turing management program.

'Got it,' Philip said. 'The Berkeley company has borrowed eight hundred million Eurofrancs from Diessenburg Mercantile. There are extension options covering another two and a half billion, but they're all subject to some kind of clause. Dunno what, it's classified, board members only.'

'MacLennan succeeding with the laser paradigms?' Morgan suggested.

'Very probable,' Philip agreed.

'Two and a half billion,' Julia said, ruminating out loud. 'That's more than Diessenburg loaned us before Prior's Fen.'

'How much would it cost to build and operate an entire continent's educational and penal services?' Greg asked.

'A lot,' she said. 'And Karl Hildebrandt is on holiday. Unavailable for two months. I asked his office yesterday after you said you wanted to meet him.'

'We can't really blame them,' Morgan said. 'They were just protecting their investment. Natural corporate reflex.'

Julia didn't approve of that attitude at all. 'That doesn't take away the fact that MacLennan is a double murderer, nor that an innocent man is in jail because of him.'

'You'll have a terrible job trying to establish degrees of complicity,' Morgan said. 'I doubt Karl will ever reappear anywhere under English jurisdiction. The Diessenburg Mercantile directors will disclaim any knowledge of the affair. And if the bank does allow any of them to come into our courts to testify, you can be sure they will be genuinely ignorant so that Greg here won't be able to implicate them.'

'Maybe,' Greg said. 'But at least we've got MacLennan nailed.'

'Yes,' Morgan said. 'I'll get on to the Home Office, they'll have MacLennan arrested first thing tomorrow morning.'

'I'd like the Oakham police to handle the actual arrest,' Greg said. 'They need the credit. I'll rap with Langley, explain what actually happened. And we'd better have a premier-grade programmer on hand to serve the data warrant. I'd hate anything to happen to that paradigm now.'

'Right.' Morgan loaded a note into his cybofax.

Greg climbed to his feet, stretching laboriously.

Julia stood and tugged her windcheater jacket from the back of the chair. 'Thanks again for helping, Teddy.'

He took a last swig from his beer bottle, and gave her a shrewd look. 'No problem, gal, does me good to get out and about, keep my hand in. But you leave off Greg once this case is over, hear me? He's a fucking orange farmer now. Nothing else.'

'I hear you, Teddy.' She blew him a kiss.

24

It was midnight when Greg and Eleanor reached the farm. Fog had given way to a steady rain, the darkness was total. Greg could hear the wind rustling the tops of the new saplings on either side of the driveway. The EMC Ranger's tyres splashed through long trickles of water as Eleanor let it roll slowly down the slope.

He ran a hand through his greasy hair. What he wanted was a shower, a drink, and bed. Worst of all, he wanted to go to bed to sleep. Arms and belly muscles were stiff and sore from hanging under the Westland ghost wing.

Surprisingly, given all the aches, plus a persistent post-mission edginess, he still felt easier than he had for a week. He grinned at his weak reflection in the side window. I knew Nicholas didn't do it.

'What's so funny?' Eleanor asked.

'Nothing. Tell you, I'm just glad it's over.'

'Me too.'

'Yeah. Thanks for understanding.'

'Make the most of it. Next time, I'll stomp my foot and say no.'

'Good,' he said, with feeling. 'You'd better go and see Mrs Beswick tomorrow, give her the good news. I expect I'll be having quite a busy day. Christ, and Vernon was upset about the murder being complicated before.'

'He'll survive. Like you said, they'll get a lot of credit for wrapping this up.'

'Yeah.' There's justice. But at least it will make life in Oakham more tolerable for everybody.

Beyond the window's reflection, Maurice Knebel's mirage rippled unsteadily on the edge of reality. Greg knew his last memory of the ex-detective would take a long time to dissipate. Knebel had closed his eyes tightly, teeth clamping down on his lower lip, whimpering softly as Greg aimed the stunshot at him. In the background Teddy had muttered snidely about using the Uzi instead.

Then there was the trip back to the warehouse. Walton's minacious streets crowding in on him, plaguing him with the prospect of running into some kind of hazard now the mission was over – the oldest squaddie fear in the book.

The EMC Ranger's headlight beams tracked across the side of the barn, unnaturally bright under the cloud-blocked sky. They touched the house briefly, a flash of moth-grey stone.

Greg began searching round with his hand, lifting the stunshot from the back seat. He slung it over his shoulder. Bloody good job Langley can't see me now, he thought. He had always been dubious of Greg's real motivations, the underground politics behind his assignment to the case. Seeing him in full combat gear would confirm every black paranoid suspicion about Julia's undue influence.

Eleanor stopped the EMC Ranger in front of the door, and the porch light came on automatically. They both climbed out, shoulders hunched against the rain. Eleanor blipped the lock, pulling her navy-blue jacket tighter across her sweatshirt.

Greg heard the lynch mob first. Footsteps crunching on the wet gravel behind the EMC Ranger. His gland gave a lurch, discharging the neurohormone into his brain. He grunted in shock as the five minds trespassed on his consciousness. They were all identical, possessed with unrelenting berserker arrogance, thought currents devoid of any rationality. A teratoid insanity. Recognition was instantaneous; he had encountered that mind once before: Liam Bursken.

They walked into the splash of light thrown by the porch light, a soft dead smile on their lips – Frankie Owen, Mark Sutton, Les Hepburn, Andrew Foster, and Douglas Kellam.

Eleanor twisted round. 'What—'

Mark Sutton raised a double-barrelled shotgun. Thoughts radiant with cool delight.

Greg's training took over. He fired the stunshot even as he was bringing it to bear. The pulse was dazzlingly bright to his night-acclimatized retinas. It missed Sutton, fizzling voraciously as it sliced through the rain. But it was enough.

Sutton jerked aside, complacency shattered. The shotgun went off, blowing out one of the EMC Ranger's rear windows. A lethal blast of crystalline splinters slammed into the stone wall to Greg's right. He felt stingers of pain jab down his chest where the combat jacket was open. Spots of blood bloomed on his white T-shirt.

He saw the other four men jumping back into the concealing murk of rain and darkness which cloaked the rest of the farmyard, surprise and outrage rampant on their faces. Fury that their victim should dare to fight back, resist the Lord's will. His fumbling fingers found the stunshot's fire selector catch, and flicked it to continuous. A solid stream of glaring blue-white lighting speared out of the barrel as he tugged the trigger, illuminating the entire farmyard. Its end grew ragged over by the barn, flickering spasmodically as the close-packed pulses lost cohesion.

He swung the weapon down and round, not really aiming, simply chasing Sutton as the man scrambled for cover behind the EMC Ranger. The torrent of pulses caught him on the shoulder, spinning him round as if it was a high-pressure water jet. The shotgun went flying off into the night as he whirled around, arms extended.

He let go of the trigger, and Sutton collapsed into a bucking heap. To his left he saw Frankie Owen making a grab for Eleanor, his normally sulky face snarled up in an expression of wrath. A flick knife gleamed as it slid out of his fist. Eleanor was blocking the stunshot's line of fire.

A narrow line of damp air in front of Greg suddenly fluoresced a vivid green. Raindrops scintillated with an uncanny beauty as they fell through it. Laser. He was being shot at! Overstressed nerves jerked him backwards. He nearly lost his footing on the gravel as he dropped below the level of the EMC Ranger. He fought to regain balance. Judging by the angle of the beam, it was coming from the tangerine grove on the other side of the barn.

The beam swept along the farmhouse's stonework, across the door, towards the two figures thrashing about. It was too broad to be a rifle targeting-laser. Wrong colour, anyway.

Realization struck like a spike of ice directly into his spine. The paradigm imprinter. MacLennan himself was out there, trying to zombie Eleanor.

'Down!' he screamed, and launched himself at the wrestling figures just as they broke apart. Eleanor was staggering backwards. Green light stroked her torso. He caught her round the waist in a tackle which sent both of them crashing to the ground. Eleanor yelped in shock and pain as they hit the gravel. Somehow he managed to hold on to the stunshot; 'ware modules jabbed painfully into his side. Up above, the laser slashed furiously from side to side, producing a canopy of lurid green radiation between the EMC Ranger and the house, flecked with twinkling jade raindrops.

Frankie Owen groaned, his thought currents disfigured by supreme agony. Greg glanced up to see him curled up on the gravel just in front of them, hands clutching his groin, nursing crushed testicles. A mushy spurt of vomit sputtered out of his open mouth. His face was corpse white, eyes red and wet.

Eleanor did that to him. Greg felt a crazy edge of glee. My Eleanor.

Out on the brink of his espersense those remaining three

joyless minds were congregating. Scattered thoughts refocusing on him.

'Are you all right?' he hissed.

'My arm's numb. Why did you pull me down?'

'Look up, that's the paradigm imprint laser.'

'Oh, Jesus.'

'Let's see if we can get inside.'

He rolled over and rose to a crouch. Foster, Hepburn, and Kellam were moving apart again, fanning out around the EMC Ranger. It was four metres to the door, the laser painted a sharp green line two-thirds of the way up.

'I'll go first,' he told her. 'Start moving as soon as I reach it.'

'Right.'

He tensed his legs, then he was up and running. Fingers reaching for the brass bulb handle. The polished metal was slick in his palm. Turning slowly. His shoulder thudded into the wood, and he was through, skating on the hall tiles.

Eleanor was racing past him less than a second later. He shoved the door shut with a burst of frantic strength. There was a quiet whine as the lock engaged. He aimed the stunshot at it, and fired. The plastic covering melted with a flash of orange flame, droplets spraying out. The 'ware circuits inside flared briefly, sparks fountained, dying embers skittering over the cold tiles.

Someone outside smacked into the door. He saw it quiver in the frame. There was the sound of a fist hammering on the panels.

'Mandel.' It was Les Hepburn's voice, but toneless, that same clipped precision Bursken used. 'Come out, Mandel. You shall not escape the Lord's justice.'

'Fuck off!' He grabbed Eleanor's hand. 'Come on, they'll be inside in a minute.' There was no light in the hall. He felt round for the photon amp band hooked on his shoulder tab, and slapped it into place. The time display and guido coordinates gleamed brightly. Walls, floor, and furniture shimmered out of nowhere, solidifying into their familiar places. He bled in the infrared. The photon amp's grey and blue world tinted into red, becoming fractionally brighter, losing some definition.

'I'll call the police,' Eleanor said.

'No way,' he said, leading her down to the study. 'People like Keith Willet aren't going to be able to cope with a bunch of Liam Burskens, even if they believed us. In any case it would take them too long to get here.'

'Greg! We need help.' She was battling panic.

'I know!' He switched on the communication 'ware, and pulled his skull helmet into place. 'Emergency.'

'What is it, boy?' Philip Evans asked.

'We've been ambushed at the farm. MacLennan is here with five people he's loaded with Bursken's paradigm. And this time it's me they're after.'

'Shit, boy; you all right?'

'For now. We need help and fast.'

'I'm launching the security crash team now. They'll be there in ten minutes.'

Greg opened the study door. The room was supposed to be his den, but he still hadn't got it sorted out. There was a big desk over by the window, a settee, long planks were leaning against a wall, destined to be shelves when he got round to screwing them together. The floor was cluttered with kelpboard boxes full of his accumulated junk. He could just make out the Berrybut estate through the window, pinprick glints of light from the chalets; the rain must have extinguished the bonfire hours ago, the photon amp's infrared function couldn't even pick up the dying cinders.

'Philip's launching the Event Horizon crash team,' he told Eleanor.

'Right. Why are we in here?'

A dark human silhouette moved across the window, eclipsing the chalets. The head glowed brightly in grades of red, hot blood highlighting the cheeks and nose; eyes were cooler, darker. It contained the familiar thought currents of Liam Bursken.

'Shush.' He gripped her hand tighter. Even with the infrared's ambiguous slant, he could recognize the features of the face pressed to the glass. Brendan Talbot, an engineer who lived in Hambleton.

Christ, how many people had MacLennan loaded the paradigm into?

Greg's free hand closed around the stock of the Heckler and Koch rifle lying on the desk. A real weapon.

Ronnie Kay appeared next to Brendan Talbot, and hurled a brick straight through the study window. Eleanor yelled in fright. A torch shone into the room with the force of a solar flare.

The photon amp filters responded immediately, reducing the glare until it was a manageable corona. Greg could see Talbot, his hand reaching through the jagged hole in the glass, scrabbling round for the catch.

'Face your judgement, Mandel,' Kay shouted. 'Embrace us. We will deliver you from sin.'

Greg levelled the rifle at Talbot. And couldn't pull the trigger. It wasn't Talbot, only his body. Brendan had a wife, a six-year-old daughter.

'Shit!' he roared. In his army days it wouldn't have made any difference. None. See a hostile and snuff them. Nothing else had ever been allowed to interfere with that maxim. It was simple survival. Life was so fucking *easy* in those days. Uncomplicated.

Brendan Talbot's fingers closed around the catch.

Greg yanked the stunshot round, strap cutting into his shoulder. Aim and fire. The pulse hit the glass, and splattered, minute static tendrils writhing across the oblong pane. 'Shit shit shit.' Aim and fire. This time the pulse struck Talbot's hand. There was a muffled grunt, and he was flailing backwards. His wrist caught the spikes of glass around the edge of the hole, skin tearing. There was a confused splash of heat.

The torch beam wavered about as Kay tried to catch him.

'Let's go,' Greg said.

Runnels of Talbot's blood were seeping down the window below the hole, glowing like radioactive sludge.

'What's happening now, boy?' Philip asked anxiously.

'Trouble. Where's the crash team?'

'They're getting into the tilt-fan now.'

'Jesus!'

Eleanor gave him a frightened glance as they charged back into the hall.

'The crash team is just taking off,' he told her. 'Philip, have they got stunshots with them?'

'Sure thing, boy.'

'Tell them to use the stunshots wherever possible, remember these people aren't responsible for what they're doing.'

'I'll tell 'em.'

'Upstairs,' he said to Eleanor. They started to pound up the staircase.

There was an almighty crash of breaking glass from the lounge when they were halfway up.

Knocking the whole window out by the sound of it, Greg thought. He handed Eleanor the stunshot when they reached the landing. At least if she did have to shoot she would never have the guilt of killing a complete innocent. He could always use the rifle to immobilize. If he had time, if the mêlée didn't become too confusing, if he could hang on to his scruples. They ran down the landing to the master bedroom.

'Philip, plug Royan in,' Greg said.

'Right-oh, boy.'

The landing's biolums came on just as they reached the bedroom door, three sets of wall globes shaped like lilies. Greg shot them out with the rifle. They disintegrated with loud popping sounds, showering the landing with radiant flakes that died as they bounced along the carpet.

From a tactical standpoint there was little improvement; biolum light shone up from the hall, casting long delusive shadows over the landing walls. He could hear people moving about below.

They went through into the bedroom. 'Keep watching the stairs,' Greg said. 'Anyone comes up, shoot 'em.'

'Right.' Eleanor knelt down beside the door, peering through the crack.

The photon amp's time numerals and guido co-ordinates blurred then merged into a single wavery band of yellow light. There was a moment's pause, then the display printed: I'M HERE, GREG.

'Great. Listen, I've got about half a dozen people who think they're Liam Bursken coming at me. Now there has got to be some way to flush that paradigm out of them. We know it erases itself after a set time. Access the recording you made and look for the magic photons sequence, see if there's any way we can activate it prematurely.'

GOT YOU. ACCESSING NOW.

'They're here, Greg,' Eleanor called softly. She fired the stunshot, ten or twelve pulses *zinged* along the landing, scorching long burn marks into the wallpaper, blistering the paint on the banister rail.

He was aware of the minds on the stairs. One of them ruptured in a flurry of pain, the thought currents fragmenting into comate insensibility. 'You got one.'

GREG, HAVE YOU GOT A LASER WITH YOU?

'Yeah, a Heckler and Koch hunting rifle.'

TOO POWERFUL. HAS IT GOT A TARGETING IMAGER?

'Yeah.'

GOOD GOOD GOOD. PLUG THE IMAGER INTO YOUR SUIT 'WARE.

'Right.'

'The crash team has left,' Philip said. 'Be with you in eight minutes.'

It was going to be too long, that much was obvious.

Greg tugged the rifle's targeting imager monocle out of its recess, and detached it from the fibre optic cable. The interface was standard – thank Christ. He plugged the cable into a socket on the guido 'ware module. Blue target circles hardened in front of him, angling down towards the carpet, the same line as the rifle barrel was pointing.

'Come out, Mandel,' Ronnie Kay shouted up from the hall, 'or we will burn you out. Fire is always the great purifier. Your wife will die with you then. Come out.'

'Don't you dare,' Eleanor said.

'Royan?'

I'VE DECRYPTED IT. STRANGE. NOT LIKE SOFTWARE. NO SUBROUTINES. EVERYTHING STRUNG TOGETHER, SIMILAR TO PIXEL CODES, MUCH HIGHER BIT RATE THOUGH.

'Have you found the magic photons sequence?'

WORKING ON IT.

Greg went over to the window, standing beside it with his back to the wall, expanding his espersense outwards. There were three minds below. He edged the rifle out past the curtains and activated the imager. The photon amp's picture of the bedroom faded away, replaced by a view of the garden below. Three men were standing on the lawn, waiting patiently. One of them held what looked like a shotgun, the other two were carrying clubs of some kind.

'Come out, Mandel.'

Eleanor fired another barrage of stunshot pulses down the landing.

'We'll burn your flesh to ashes. Your last minutes will be the torment of Hell. Repent.'

THINK I'VE GOT IT.

'Thank Christ for that.'

THERE ARE TWO SEPARATE SEQUENCES, BOTH BECOME ACTIVE AFTER A MEASURED INTERVAL FOLLOWING IMPRINT. TIMED BY HEARTBEATS. CLEVER THAT THE FIRST SEQUENCE CONTAINS THE PARADIGM ITSELF AND THE INSTRUCTION TO KILL KITCHENER, ALONG WITH ADDITIONAL ORDERS TO DESTROY HIS RETROSPECTIVE NEUROHORMONE WORK. IT ACTIVATED ITSELF AFTER APPROXIMATELY NINE HOURS. THE SECOND SEQUENCE IS THE MAGIC PHOTONS, WHICH ACTIVATES TWO HOURS LATER.

Even now, Greg couldn't quite shake off his fascination with the case. Nicholas must have been hit before the storm, before the rising waters of the Chater closed the ramshackle bridge.

'Can you trigger the magic photons sequence?'

YES. I'VE ISOLATED ITS ACTIVATION CODE FROM THE PARADIGM'S TIMER SECTION.

'OK, there are three people we can try it on.'

The target circles vanished as Royan took command of the rifle's 'ware. Greg watched the imager's laser sending a fan of ruby light sweeping across the lawn. The grid emerged in its wake, splitting into three sections, folding around the waiting men.

HERE GOES.

The contoured lines around the central figure began to flash.

NOW.

Greg saw a single strobe-like flicker of pink douse the man's face. His espersense showed him the man's thought currents start to seethe furiously. A loud destitute wailing penetrated the glass.

'What's happening?' Eleanor demanded.

'I'm not sure.' Even as he spoke he sensed the new tide of personality usurping Bursken's resolute thought currents. His empathy was caught by the backlash of petrified bewilderment raging inside the abused brain, feedback sending a quake of dismay shuddering along his own synapses. Then the man was dropping to his knees, curling into a foetal position, mind rushing headlong into welcome oblivion.

'OK, we got him. Zap the other two, Royan.'

Their grid outlines began to flash. The targeting laser fired twice.

'Flames, Mandel,' Ronnie Kay shouted. 'They will consume you. There will be no redemption.'

'Wait,' Greg shouted back. 'I'm coming out.'

'Greg!' Eleanor pleaded.

'Those crazies will torch the place if I don't. We have to clear them out.'

'Let the crash team do it.'

'That bastard MacLennan is still out there. He can load Bursken's mind into them as soon as they land. Then where will we be? They are armed and armoured, Eleanor. At least the lynch mob only have shotguns.'

'Come then, Mandel. Come to us.'

She drew a sharp breath through her teeth. 'God, you be careful, Gregory.'

He knew exactly how much that cost her to say. 'No messing.'

*

They waited in the hall at the foot of the stairs. Five of them, a tight arrowhead, with Ronnie Kay at the front. Two shotguns followed him with mechanical precision. Their mouths were curved up in the same slight, vapid smile.

His espersense flowed round them, along the hall, through the empty rooms. They were the only ones inside. Right at the back of his head was the faint thrumming of pressure, the neuro-hormones stressing his synapses to their limit.

He held the rifle casually at his hip as he descended.

'Take the ones with the shotguns first,' he whispered.

RIGHT.

The grid appeared again, peeling into five segments like cybernetic butterfly wings. Closing fluidly around their ignorant prey.

Ronnie Kay blinked, glancing distrustfully at the rifle. 'Put it down, Mandel.'

READY.

'Now.'

The laser lashed out, spiking each of them in turn. Elapsed time seven-tenths of a second.

They wilted in unison, filling the air with a grotesque catlike puling. Arms and legs were infected with a life of their own, waving and flexing at random.

'Shitfire,' Greg murmured.

DID WE GET THEM?

'Oh yeah. We got 'em.'

Eleanor was running along the landing, stunshot held ready, looking as if she was about to start a war.

'The crash team will be there in five minutes,' Philip said.

Eleanor barged into his side, hugging him tightly. She let out a gulping sob. 'I'm sorry.' She wiped her eyes.

His arm went round her, holding her roughly. He kissed the top of her forehead, damp hair rasping across his lips.

They went down the last few stairs, slowly, every step a great effort.

The front door had been forced open, the lock jemmied off. A draught of clammy air swirled in.

Greg used the rifle barrel to push the lounge door open. Shards of glass were heaped on the floor below the broken window. The curtains flapped feebly.

'It's clear,' Greg said. 'I'll go out here, through the window. MacLennan can see the front door.' Eleanor's fingers clutched at him through the combat leathers. 'I've got to finish this.' And this time there would be no hesitation, no reluctance. MacLennan had come hunting him, broaching the sanctity of his own home. Well, now it would be settled on those terms. One on one, zero rules.

'I know,' Eleanor said.

He crouched down, and scuttled over to the window. 'Royan, kill the imager's camera feed. I don't want to be on the receiving end of that paradigm—' He stopped, intuition acting like a dose of wine, stealing warmly into his brain.

The gloomy image faded out, leaving him alone with the time display and guido co-ordinates. He shoved the rifle through the shattered window.

'Give me the laser return.'

The picture which built up was similar to the virtual simulation he had used to fly into Walton, photonic topology, except it was all red. The rickety fence was ten metres in front of him, saplings standing in long rows behind it, grass resolved as a fuzzy gauze mat.

'OK, Royan, there's one last piece of reprogramming I need.'

*

He poked the rifle round the corner of the house. The laser painted in the EMC Ranger, the barn, and the wall around the farmyard. Mark Sutton was lying where he'd fallen. Frankie Owen was crawling towards the driveway. It was like watching a time-lapse puppet in motion, the picture refreshing itself every second as the laser swept back and forth.

A grid tailored itself into a perfect fit around Frankie Owen.

'I'm here,' Greg called out clearly.

Frankie twisted round. When he was looking straight at Greg, the laser fired the magic photon's activation code at him. There was a muffled gurgling, then he lay still. Greg sensed Bursken's thoughts routed by Frankie's usual dull anger and general life-resentment just before consciousness dwindled.

Not much of an improvement, really.

He pointed the rifle at the tangerine grove, where he thought MacLennan had fired the paradigm laser from.

'Focus shift, one hundred and fifty metres.'

The grove filled his vision field. It lacked the sharp-edged clarity of anything close by, degraded by rain, almost like static interference. These saplings had been planted over a year ago, two and a half metres high, starting to spread out at the top. They were covered with leaves and blossom, which showed up like a layer of coarse ice crystals around the core of twigs and branches.

There was a vehicle parked in the middle of the grove, almost hidden by the saplings. A jeep of some kind.

Perfect for the terrain in the Chater valley, he thought.

LASER ACQUISITION, the photon amp display printed.

'Royan?'

THAT'S YOUR ECM DETECTOR WARNING. MACLENNAN IS FIRING THE PARADIGM IMPRINTER AT YOU. ONE MOMENT.

The image fluttered then reappeared. A bright red dot was flashing ten metres to the left of the jeep.

THAT'S THE EMISSION POINT.

'Right. Give me targeting mode.'

The blue circles sprang up. Greg shifted the rifle until they were centred on the jeep. He pulled the trigger. Five shots into the bonnet, three into the front tyre, another five into the bodywork.

MacLennan stopped firing the paradigm laser.

Greg pumped another ten shots into the rear of the jeep. He heard the unmistakable dull thud of an explosion. The back of the jeep rippled, opening up like a flower, jagged metal petals lunging jerkily for the blank sky.

'Cancel targeting mode.' He started to jog towards the jeep. No way could he run: as it was, he had to try and remember what was immediately ahead at each footfall. The wall between him and the grove seemed to lurch towards him in two-metre increments.

A nimbus had engulfed the jeep, altering in size each time the picture updated, never the same shape twice. Flames, he guessed.

He reached the wall and clambered over, moss squelching below his gloves, ignoring the erratic images as the rifle shifted about, working by touch.

LASER ACQUISITION.

He landed on the spongy grass in the grove, and automatically rolled to one side. Paratroop training. Furious flames from the jeep were making a loud crackling.

'MacLennan?' he bellowed. 'It doesn't work on me, you shit!' He stood up, pointing the rifle ahead.

LASER ACQUISITION.

The red dot was flashing from behind some saplings away to his left, dancing about like a firefly caught in a hurricane. MacLennan was moving away from the jeep. Greg started to jog towards the dot, ducking under the low branches, swerving round the trunks.

'Greg?' It was Philip. 'The crash team will be with you in two minutes.'

'Keep them in the air until I give the all clear.'

'All right, boy, it's your show.'

The laser picked out MacLennan running down a row of saplings, about eighty metres ahead. A clockwork humanoid, legs and arms pumping in a fractured rhythm. Slender grid lines chased after him coiling round his limbs and torso.

DO YOU WANT TARGET MODE???

'Not yet. I have to be sure.'

SURE SURE SURE? WHAT KIND OF BLOODY SURE? HE TRIED TO KILL YOU.

Greg ran out into a tractor lane, four metres wide, the branches arching overhead, not quite meeting. It made the going a lot easier; he risked increasing his pace. 'Sure about Clarissa Wynne.'

MacLennan vaulted over the fence at the bottom of the grove, and sprinted over the field towards Hambleton Wood.

Gotcha, Greg thought. He arrived at the fence, scaling it quickly.

MacLennan reached the boundary of the wood, and charged through the waist-high fringe of undergrowth. He suddenly fell forwards, disappearing from sight below the nettles. Greg heard a distant curse.

The grass underfoot was awkward, tufty and slippery with rain. He had to slow down again, especially as he was cutting down the slope. There was that distinctive sound of brittle wood snapping up ahead as MacLennan thrashed about in the dead hawthorn bushes.

Christ, I hope it is MacLennan after all this! But his intuition was giving him a powerful high, as if he was just going through the motions. The outcome was already decided.

MacLennan's upper torso reappeared amid the bushes. He was flinging himself desperately at the knotted tangle of vines strung between the old trees. It wouldn't do him any good, you needed either a tank or a bulldozer to break into the wood. He jerked round, right arm coming up. Red dot.

LASER ACQUISITION.

Greg slowed to a halt thirty metres from the wood, raising the rifle to his shoulder. 'Give me targeting mode, and expand the magnification.' He ordered his cortical node to increase the neurohormone secretion level.

Blue circles clicked into place. The targeting laser sweep contracted around MacLennan. It was as though he was standing two metres in front of Greg, the warped network of red lines bright enough to give off a faint coronal hue. An oversized pistol was gripped in his right hand, nozzle blazing.

His espersense encountered the mind inside the reticulated head. It was MacLennan.

Greg aimed at the pistol and fired.

MacLennan howled, convulsing, right arm hugged to his chest. His pistol tumbling away. A hot throb of pain lanced into Greg's mind. Behind it came the raw malevolence, the near-frenzied fear, and the abhorrence.

'Hold it,' Greg commanded as MacLennan began to look around his feet for the imprinter, the tendrils of desperation uncoiling in his gibbering mind. He walked forward until he came to the edge of the nettles. 'Why did you come here, MacLennan? Why did you set them on me?'

'Because it was you!' MacLennan bawled. 'You! Mindstar freak. You found the paradigm.'

'How did you know that?'

'You were from the Home Office, you burnt into the memory core. You! It was you. Freak fucker.'

'Oh shit.' The rush of energy which had carried him out of the house and across the grove suddenly bled away. There was no determination left in him. No pride at completing the case, only weariness. He just wanted this over. Finished.

MacLennan started sobbing.

'Shut up!' Greg yelled.

'It hurts me! It hurts. You've burnt my hand in half, you bastard. Get me to a hospital, for Christ's sake.'

Every emotion reached rock bottom. Greg felt dangerously calm. 'It hurts, does it, MacLennan? How did Clarissa Wynne feel do you think? When you pushed her head under the lake. Did she hurt, MacLennan?'

'Clarissa?' It came out like a whinny.

'You killed her. Didn't you? Eleven years ago, you shot her full of syntho and killed her.'

'She was going to claim all the credit!'

'Even now you're lying! It was her work.'

'Wasn't!'

Guilt corrupted every thought in MacLennan's head. And there was nothing left to say.

Greg took a laboured breath. 'Royan, shoot it over.'

The grid snapped off for an instant as the targeting laser stabbed at MacLennan's eyes.

He heard the paradigm as it came surging through the communication link, a near-ultrasonic *wheee* in his earpiece, a blast of photons encapsulating the essence of Liam Bursken, accompanied by a monomaniac hatred for one man.

Poetic justice, or intuitive inspiration; Greg didn't know which, only that it was right. It fitted.

He pulled the photon amp strip from his face, twin circles of skin around his eyesockets pinching as it came free. The real world rushed back in on him, dark and dank, awash with human failings. The clean simplicity of the laser return virtual graphics was almost preferable. Somewhere behind him flames were soaring up into the night from the wreck of the jeep. Rain pattered down, beating the dusky vegetation towards the muddy ground.

MacLennan's prim face was contorted with pain, hair plastered down into a straggly cap. His jaw was working silently, as though he was choking.

'Do you know who you hate, Liam?' Greg asked quietly. 'Do you?'

MacLennan stared back at him with insane eyes, mouth screwing into a joyous smile. 'Yes. Me. It's me. Me!'

'That's right.' He took the vibration knife from his belt, switched it on, and dropped it at MacLennan's feet.

MacLennan snatched it up with his good hand. 'Redemption. He has granted me redemption.' He laughed rhapsodically as he shoved the blade into his stomach. Blood foamed out. He sank to his knees, teeth clenched with effort, cheeks bulging, and pulled the blade up towards his sternum. 'Yes. Oh, yes. My Lord.'

Greg turned and walked away. Back to the farmhouse and Eleanor, where he belonged.

High above the reservoir, the security team's tilt-fan dived out of the clouds, turbines shrieking with urgency.

25

Julia found her hand straying towards Robin's hair. He was sleeping sprawled out on his belly in the middle of the bed, head fallen between two big fluffy pillows, mouth slightly agape. She stroked his hair softly, smoothing down the ruffled tufts. Seen in the lush morning light which was prising its way round the edges of the curtains he was even more handsome than the first time she had caught sight of him at the pool. And he was so terribly sweet. Tender, anxious, and eager all at once – excellent body too. He lacked Patrick's ruthless dynamism, which had made their sex far more sensual. She still wasn't quite sure if she was his first. But she was certainly near the front of the queue. A thought to treasure.

He stirred below her hand, and she held her breath. She didn't want to wake him up just yet. The poor dear must be tired after last night.

She would have a cup of tea, skim through the breakfast 'casts, nip into the toilet, *then* it would be time for him to perform again.

NN Core Access Request.

No peace for the wicked. And last night she had been gloriously wicked.

Open Channel To NN Core.

Morning, Juliet.

Morning, Grandpa. We can't be having a crisis this early.

Not a crisis, no.

Thank heavens for that. What then?

I'm curious about something you did yesterday.

Spying on me again?

No. I was just reviewing some of your data traffic. Double checking. That's what I'm here for, your safety net.

Yah, go on. She had a pretty good idea where this was leading.

You accessed one of our biochemical research labs yesterday. Using your executive code, no less. Mind telling me what for, girl?

No, I don't mind. She leaned over to the bedside cabinet and poured her tea from the silver service.

Juliet!

Oh, you wanted to know right now?

If I still had a body, I'd put you over my bloody knee, m'girl.

Grandpa, behave. Besides, I'm too big and too strong these days. And I don't fight fair, either.

You learnt that from me, Juliet. Now are you going to tell me?

She picked up her cup and saucer, and settled back into the pillows. *Yah, all right I wiped every record of the retrospective neurohormone from our memory cores, the analysis report, molecular structure, conclusions, everything. Then I sent Rachel over there, and she tipped all the remaining ampoules into the toxic waste disposal furnace. Happy now?*

Bloody hell, girl. Why?

The tea was too hot to drink. She blew across the top of her cup as she marshalled her thoughts. *Because I don't want something like that let loose in the world, Grandpa. It's bad enough having people like Gabriel being able to see what I might do in the future, or Greg knowing how badly I've been misbehaving just by looking at me. I don't want someone standing in this room ten years from now taking a simple infusion and being able to see what I did last night.*

Hardly a simple infusion, girl.

Exactly. The Home Office have slapped a restriction order on what really happened at Greg's farm and Launde Abbey. Admittedly their main concern is the way MacLennan abused his paradigm project; if word got out that the New Conservatives had been allowing a company to research what amounts to a mind-control system there would be hell to pay. Certainly it would cost them the next election. Marchant didn't need much prodding to include the neurohormone. And there are now only fifteen people in the world who know a retrospection neurohormone is even possible. With those numbers we might just be able to keep it that way. Even if the news does eventually leak out, it would take an immense research effort to produce it again, if we ever could. Kitchener was a very clever man, not to mention idiosyncratic.

You can't fight progress, Juliet.

A retrospective neurohormone isn't progress, Grandpa. Quite the opposite. And there is already more than enough freely available technology in this world capable of being misapplied by tekmercs and others. Corporations and kombinates are going to have to start becoming responsible again. After all, we do fund ninety per cent of all the significant scientific research these days.

Lord preserve us, a global citizen with a conscience.

Somebody has to be, Grandpa. There is more to Event Horizon than making nifty household 'ware gadgets. Do you really want me to use all that influence for the bad?

Juliet, you are beautiful. I'm so proud of you.

She knew her cheeks would be reddening. Didn't care. Not this morning. *Thank you, Grandpa. I am what I am because I have the best teacher in the world.*

I've said it before, I'll say it again. Seductress!

Yah. And proud of it.

Eat your breakfast in peace, Juliet, I've got plenty of data-work piled up for you later.

Exit NN Core.

She took a sip of tea and fired the remote at the wall-mounted flatscreen, keeping the volume low. It was the East England channel, and she was on again. Yesterday's gala reopening of the Stock Exchange. Another invitation impossible to refuse, half the companies listed were heavily dependent on Event Horizon contracts. The exchange had been operating out of temporary quarters at Canary Wharf ever since the PSP had fallen and trading became legal again. Party activists had razed the old exchange a couple of months after President Armstrong came to power. So a new purpose-built building had risen up out of the old site, one with plenty of spare data processing and communications capacity, ready for the challenge of regeneration.

Very symbolic, she thought caustically.

She watched herself walking down the main hall with the exchange officials, most of them male, and most over fifty. So boring, no conversation outside money. Esquiline had dressed her in a white dinner jacket made from a fabric which played clips of old black and white films over its surface.

Superbly unconventional, and formal at the same time. Going to Esquiline had turned into one of the best decisions she had made for a long time – if for no other reason than Esquiline's fitting team was a fantastic new source of gossip, opening up the underbelly of the social scene. According to them, Lavinia Mayer didn't even need to intervene on her behalf with the Coleman cow. Apparently Jakki Coleman's agent had read her the riot act, effectively neutering her; it turned out he had a major contract with Esquiline to fit out several of his clients. And being thrown off an agent's books for being *difficult* was worse than death in the channel universe. At least if you were dead, cult status repeats boosted your ratings.

Jakki hadn't said a word against her for the last three days.

Julia on the flatscreen cut the ribbon to the trading floor as Charlie Chaplin waddled across her back twirling his cane. All the jobbers cheered her enthusiastically.

Now they had been fun to talk to at the reception afterwards. Most of them were under thirty.

She took another sip of tea as the scene changed back to East England's breakfast studio. The blond twentysomething female presenter in a tight sweater was lounging back on a deep settee.

'That was yesterday's opening ceremony,' she gushed warmly. 'And to review it, I have our fashion correspondent, Leonard Sharr.'

The camera panned back to show the most effeminate man Julia had ever seen sitting at the other end of the settee, dressed in leather jeans and a purple jacket with half-sleeves, topaz handkerchief hanging flamboyantly out of his breast pocket. She bit back on her giggles.

'Leonard, what did you think of Julia's clothes?'

'I found her choice so very, very appropriate. Tatty old design, showing tatty old films, at a tatty old function. It said simply nothing to me, except perhaps: look what a disaster I am, and I'm too rich to care. Really, this simply will not do for someone of her standing. She could be such a pretty little girl if she just made an effort and wore some nice frocks.'

'Arsehole!' Julia completely forgot her cup was still half full. The tea went everywhere.

26

The forensic team had cleared away all their polythene sheets and peeled the bar code tags off the furniture, they'd even returned the cacti to the table below the window, but somehow the room wasn't the same. Nicholas stood at the foot of the circular bed, surveying the place that had been home for a few short months. Coming here originally had been the pinnacle of his life. Now it left him totally unmoved. It wasn't that Launde Abbey was full of bad memories, rather it didn't hold any memories for him at all, good or bad. Even the ghosts had departed – Kitchener, Eleanor . . .

He dropped his maroon shoulder-bag at the foot of the bed, and stared round in some perplexity. His rock band holoprints were missing. What had the forensic team wanted them for anyway?

He began opening drawers, and of course none of his clothes were where they should be. He settled for dumping everything on the bed to be sorted out later. The uniformed policeman who had driven him up to the Abbey wasn't going to hustle him along. Oakham police couldn't extend enough courtesies right now.

There had been a press conference to announce they were releasing him from custody, that he was in no way implicated in the murder of Edward Kitchener. The reporters had clamoured for details; but apart from saying he was glad it was all over, and that he thought the police had done a good job under difficult circumstances, and no he wasn't going to sue for wrongful arrest, he didn't answer any questions. Amanda Paterson and Jon Nevin had stepped in sharpish to deflect any awkward shouted queries. And then amazingly the press had left him alone, no intrusion into his private life, no chasing after his parents or Emma, no big-money offers for exclusives. That was down to Julia Evans, he suspected. He was rather pleased he could work out that such underground pressures were being applied. The old Nicholas would have accepted their lack of interest without thought, never wondering about the fast manoeuvring and horse-trading that must have gone on deep below the surface of public awareness.

He smiled. The old Nicholas, as if he'd emerged from a chrysalis, born again. But it was true enough. The world was exactly the same, only his perception of it had altered. Matured, rather. What did they call it? *Realpolitik*. And his first encounter with that phenomenon had come two days ago, the morning Vernon Langley had let him out of the cell, telling him he was free to go.

Greg Mandel had arrived at the station, looking grieved and tired, and told him what had actually happened. There was a secrecy order to sign and thumbprint, and it had been made very clear he wasn't to speak to anybody about paradigms or retrospective neurohormones ever again. Officially, MacLennan had let Liam Bursken out of Stocken Hall for the night, bringing him to Launde to murder Kitchener.

Bursken was permanently incommunicado, unable to protest his innocence, perhaps not even wanting to – let the sinners believe the Lord could reach out to them through bars of steel. MacLennan was dead. Suicide, Greg said. And looking at his stony, impassive face, even Nicholas's perpetual inquisitiveness had tacitly retreated.

As the price of being vindicated, adopting that particular masquerade was cheap indeed.

He emptied the last drawerful of socks on to the bed. It was raining quite heavily again, thick clouds darkening the morning sky. Roll on April and the start of England's long summer. When he walked over to the window he could just make out the grubby grey strip of road running through the park.

Night-time, when the rain had fallen like a biblical deluge. The jeep crawling down the slope towards the river. The vivid flash he had thought was lightning.

He shuddered and turned away.

The cacti on the copper-topped table hadn't been watered for over a week, the soil in their pots was bone dry. And he never had seen them flower the way Kitchener had told him they would.

He decided to take a couple with him. There had to be something of the old man's that would stay with him, some tangible personal memento. And he doubted he would be welcome to visit Rosette and her baby. Although you never knew. Motherhood might soften her . . .

Nah. No chance.

Grinning, he picked up two of the cacti pots.

Someone knocked quietly on the door.

'Come in.' He put the cacti down again, thinking it would be the uniformed policeman.

It was Isabel.

He stared dumbly at her, completely tongue-tied. The old Nicholas wasn't so distant after all.

She was wearing a lavender-coloured dress, curly hair held back by a broad black velvet band. As lovely as always. It was so painful just seeing her. Everything he ever wanted. Unreachable.

'Hello, Nick.'

'Er, hello. I was just collecting my things.' Nothing had changed, he still couldn't talk to her, say what he wanted. Pathetic!

'Me too. The executors are going to take over the running of the Abbey in a couple of days. Did you know they are going to open it as a sort of ashram for university science students?'

'Yes, I'd heard.' He looked down at his trainers.

'I'm sorry I didn't help you with the police.' She clenched her hands in front of her, fingers twisting. 'We all are actually. It was so unfair on you. I don't know how I could have ever believed you were involved.'

'That's all right.'

'Hardly, Nick.'

He risked a glance. She was looking out of the window, face composed, dispassionate.

'I did do it, you know,' he said. 'It was me.'

'No. Your hands, but not you.'

He considered that. If Isabel, someone so intimately involved with Kitchener, could accept his innocence, then maybe he was blameless after all. 'Isabel?' he began.

She parted her lips in a small knowing smile. 'No, Nick, I didn't love him. That was just a part of Launde, the wonder and the craziness. I was swept along like all the others. I wanted to tell you. I was going to tell you the next morning.'

He hung his head.

'And what about you?' she asked. 'What are you going to do next?'

'Er, I've been offered a research post by Event Horizon, actually. In Ranasfari's team at Cambridge. I think I detect the hand of Greg Mandel behind that. If Event Horizon is prepared to employ me, then I must be innocent. That's what people will think, anyway.'

'Yes. That was nice of him.'

'Greg's all right. Once you get round him having a gland.'

'You've changed, Nick. You're stronger now. That's good.'

Not enough. Not enough. I haven't! 'What are you going to do?'

She smiled secretively. 'I'm going to get my doctorate. At Cambridge, actually; I've been accepted by a college.'

Nicholas turned bright red. He heard Kitchener's delighted mocking laughter echoing out of . . . somewhere, and took a deep breath. 'Isabel, I love you. And, I know I'm not much—'

She kissed him softly, silencing him. His arms went round her. They fitted just fine.

ABOUT THE AUTHOR

PETER F. HAMILTON is the author of numerous novels, including *The Temporal Void, The Dreaming Void, The Evolutionary Void, Judas Unchained, Pandora's Star, Fallen Dragon,* and the acclaimed epic Night's Dawn trilogy (*The Reality Dysfunction, The Neutronium Alchemist,* and *The Naked God*). He lives with his family in England.

DON'T MISS
ANY OF
PETER F. HAMILTON'S
UPCOMING TITLES
FROM DEL REY BOOKS

Send a blank email to
sub_peterhamilton@info.randomhouse.com
to subscribe to the
Peter F. Hamilton email list.

Don't miss Peter F. Hamilton's eBook short story collection

MANHATTAN IN REVERSE

Featuring a brand-new novella starring detective Paula Myo, the genetically engineered police investigator whose single-minded pursuit of justice clashes with a postwar citizenry eager to forget old crimes. This and several other thrilling short stories round out the collection—and showcase Peter F. Hamilton's ability to weave scientific speculation into very human storytelling.

Coming to your eReader in Spring 2012 from Del Rey Books!